DISCIPLE

OF A

DARK GOD

DISCIPLE

OF A

DARK GOD

EDMUND GLASBY

Matador
5 Weir Road
Kibworth Beauchamp
Leicester LE8 0LQ, UK
Tel: (+44) 116 279 2299
Fax: (+44) 116 279 2277
Email: books@troubador.co.uk
Web: www.troubador.co.uk/matador

ISBN 978 1848763 708

British Library Cataloguing in Publication Data.
A catalogue record for this book is available from the British Library.

Typeset in 11pt Sabon MT by Troubador Publishing Ltd, Leicester, UK

Matador is an imprint of Troubador Publishing Ltd

Printed in Great Britain by the MPG Books Group, Bodmin and King's Lynn

For those I love and for those I hate...without whom this book would never have been written.

"It is easy to go down into Hell;
night and day, the gates of dark Death stand wide;
but to climb back again, to retrace one's steps to the upper air -
there's the rub, the task."

The Aeneid, Book VI

CHAPTER ONE

Wyrm's Port cemetery was haunted – not so much by the dead, although their presence was certainly felt, but by the living. It was an eerie place; where clandestine gatherings were held, where necromancers performed their unholy rituals and where grave-robbers plied their trade along with the packs of wild dogs. Over the course of many turbulent centuries it had become huge and sprawling, gradually extending to cover much of the south-eastern district of the city. In many places, the living had built their own defences against the encroachment of the necropolis, erecting great stone walls and timber palisades in order to contain it and those who still existed within. Lengths of spiked fence acted as another stretch of boundary, the rusty railings wicked and forbidding.

A chill drizzle and early morning fog impeded the progress of two figures as they approached the outer edge of the cemetery. Then, with the aid of a stunted tree, the higher limbs of which jutted out over the fence, they climbed over, dropping to the wet mud on the other side.

Getting to his feet, the shorter of the two raised his head and took a deep breath. "Ah! It's good to be back. This used to be ma second home back in the..." Realising that his companion had already set off, obviously not caring for his reminiscences, Creeps shut up and scampered in pursuit.

Everus stalked through the swirling fog, leading the way through the many cracked and crumbled headstones towards the most ancient part of the burial ground. Long clumps of weed choked the narrow pathways and here and there the ground had subsided over the centuries. Over everything lay a pall of rottenness.

Thorny brambles crawled around many of the graves, grasping and tearing at their legs. Tangled masses of dense ivy clambered over a sundered memorial of unidentifiable origin at the extremity of their vision and what looked like a giant yew tree stood, leaning unhealthily over to one side, its roots sucking whatever unholy nourishment it could from the corpse-saturated soil below.

The area of cemetery they were in lay on a downhill stretch of ground, the first of the many ruinous, vine-festooned burial edifices emerging, spectrally, from the darkness. Cracked statues fashioned from sinister gargoylic stone leered at them from the shadows, their faces seemingly frozen in anger at this trespass. Some were twisted and fractured, little more than shattered heaps of half-buried statuary. Others were huge and towering, giant shapes laden with malice; fashioned monstrous idols that stood sentinel over certain of the more lavish tumuli and tombs.

"I trust ye know where ye're goin', Everus. For ye don't want to be goin' into some o' these bad places. Some o' the old boys inside don't like ye wanderin' about uninvited, if ye get ma meanin'." Creeps peered towards the large, broken doors of one particularly evil-looking mausoleum. A pair of luminous green eyes glared back at him from its dark interior. "Aye...best we stay well away."

Paying the sepulchre and its resident no heed, Everus turned and headed off towards his left, the ground becoming rougher. Following the directions he had memorised earlier, he negotiated a treacherous flight of worn steps, his companion close behind him. The going became harder as they descended, the steps tortuous and slippery with lichen.

Like ghouls, they crept down, then, looming before them, they saw the sealed entrance to a great barrow. Flanked by leaning columns, a single stone slab, set with a huge iron ring, blocked the opening to the artificially constructed mound. Atop each column squatted a small, bloated, winged gargoyle, arms and talons spread wide, although probably not in welcome. Moss and weathered carvings covered much of the great stone plug.

"Is this it?" Creeps asked.

"This is the one," Everus confirmed. He approached in order to discern some of the inscriptions, having to peer in the semi-darkness.

Creeps ran his hands over the cold and cracked stone. "Looks all right, although it might be a bit o' a bugger to shift." He moved to one side and, squaring his left shoulder against it, gritted what teeth he had remaining and gave a push.

The stone hardly budged.

"Hmm." Creeps stepped back, rubbing his shoulder. He unslung the heavy pack that he carried, unstrapped it and began to rummage about inside. Taking out a heavy crowbar, he wedged it into the side, where cold stone met dank turf, and heaved once more. Veins bulged on his dirt-covered, moustachioed face. Limbs trembling with exertion, he slowly began to prise the seal open. Worms and beetles, stirred into action by his crude probing, fell about his feet.

Everus watched, mildly interested as his tomb-breaking associate toiled and cursed. Soon he would no doubt have to lend a hand, but for the time being he was quite content to stand and wait. This was, after all, Creeps' profession, his sole area of expertise – if one excluded heavy drinking and pipe-smoking. The sounds of the breaching were becoming louder and with that realisation he turned to examine his immediate surroundings, not wanting some graveyard horror to sneak up on them. There were things best left undisturbed here, of that he had no doubt, and with that thought, he drew out the razor-sharp bastard sword he had sheathed on his back. Transferring the handle from one hand to both, he strained his senses, trying to ignore the grunts and scraping as Creeps worked on the stone door.

It did not take that long for the grave-robber to force the portal wide enough for them to gain access. His face streaked with sweat, he turned around. "Phew. Thought it'd never open."

Suddenly something from within screamed like an exorcised spirit and a dark indigo cloud of freezing vapour blasted forth, engulfing the two where they stood. Within the cloud scowled a conglomeration of warped and tortured faces, their eyes bleeding. Then, even as Creeps yelled and fell to the ground, the wraith emitted a blood-curdling scream and sped off into the pre-dawn light.

"Get up."

"What...were that? A ghost o' some sort?"

Everus did not answer. He merely stared, grim-faced, in the direction the spectral entity had fled.

"Do ye think it's gone?" Creeps asked, getting to his feet.

"How should I know? Come on, time to get that lantern lit."

Returning the crowbar, Creeps reached into his pack and withdrew a battered lantern which had obviously seen a lot of use. From a jacket pocket, he removed a flint and steel and quickly got the lantern lit. He shone it inside, the light making a feeble attempt to chase away the reluctant shadows that clung like tattered drapes to the cist graves beyond.

"And?"

"Looks empty." Holding the lantern out before him, Creeps edged through the gap.

With a final look about him, Everus followed, the squeeze somewhat tighter. Clearly the smaller man had widened the entrance with his own dimensions in mind. Now inside, however, he could discern the crude slabs of stone set in protruding layers and the faint marks of soot where certain small offerings had once been burnt. The corbelled ceiling was low but high enough for him to stand.

A thick stench of death and decay hung in the foul air, catching at the backs of their throats.

Sword held firmly, Everus advanced further into the brick and earthen tomb. At the rear of the chamber, he could see what looked like an opening of some sort and as Creeps drew alongside with the lantern, he could make out the outline of a flight of stairs descending into the deeper gloom. Tentatively, he made towards them.

Creeps sniffed the air. "Smells bad down there. It's bad enough up 'ere but down there. Eugh!"

"Stay close and touch *nothing* unless I say so. Understand?"

Creeps nodded, nervously.

Warily, they headed down into the dead-smelling darkness below.

The stone sarcophagus that lay in the centre of the chamber they entered was covered with the accumulated dust of unknown centuries. Its ornately carved lid was cemented down in the hope that it would provide its occupant with eternal security. A huge swathe of spider web stretched from the ceiling down towards it. At some time in the tomb's history a part of the ceiling had collapsed, for near to where it rested lay a jumble of contorted brickwork and timber frames.

Everus strode over to examine the sarcophagus closely, scrutinising the strange designs worked along both the lid and the flanks. With a tenderness that belied his general demeanour, he ran his right hand across the stone lid, wiping away the dust and rat droppings.

"Is this our one?" asked Creeps, excitedly.

Everus looked at his companion and nodded. Stepping aside, he picked up his sword, which he had temporarily propped against the side of the stone coffin, and turned to watch the shadowy openings that led deeper into the catacomb. Unconcerned, he watched as some many-legged thing, its body black and segmented, scuttled up a nearby wall, before disappearing into a crack in the ceiling.

Squatting down, Creeps began to search for a trap concealed within the outer designs and pictograms incised into the stone surfaces. It was a task for which he was well suited, his years spent at breaking and entering all manner of unwelcoming places coming to the fore. All his life he had been a thief, a grave-robber, and there was hardly a lock or trap in the known empire that his skilled fingers could not open or disarm. It was all just a matter of finding them in the first place. Such was his ability that he had detected one such trap already, carefully sliding an almost imperceptible catch aside in order to negate some unwanted effect. Content now that the sarcophagus posed no further threat, he grinned and stepped back.

With open dislike in his eyes, Everus glared as he moved forwards. "*Well?* Is it safe?"

"Aye. Is now. Just a case o' gettin' it open. Shouldn't be too difficult. I'll just get some o' these bastard webs off first." Creeps began searching in his pack for something, soon pulling out a small torch, which he lit in order to burn the webs. From his pack, he then withdrew a second bag. This he unbuckled, and took from it a battered leather wallet, two small chisels, a hammer and a pitted tin cup. From the wallet, he removed two green, coin-sized tablets which he dropped into the cup. From the pack, he got an earthenware jug. Resting the lot on top of the lid, he pulled a filthy handkerchief from his sleeve and tightened it around his mouth and nose before unstoppering the jug and pouring its contents into the cup.

Instantly, acrid green fumes billowed forth.

Eyes stinging, Everus retreated a few steps. He watched as Creeps fished out a strange pipette-like tool from his sack and began to administer the caustic contents in the cup to the accretions sealing the sarcophagus lid.

After a while, and noting Everus' growing impatience, Creeps lowered his handkerchief. "This'll take a bit."

"How long?"

"Ah, well that depends on the strength o' this 'ere brew, don't it?" Creeps raised the still-smoking vessel to his lips as if intending to take a gulp.

"Why don't you? It could be entertaining to watch you convulse as your innards melt."

"I know it's thirsty work, but I think I'll..."

A sudden sound from one of the three chamber exits prompted Everus to spin round. Sword in both hands, he peered into the darkness that lay just beyond the radius of illumination provided by the lantern, which now rested on the stone coffin. Looking around, all he could see were the remains of the dead; shattered limb bones, cracked ribcages, broken skulls, even a few poorly decorated cremation urns. Rats and spiders nested within the debris which lay strewn about. Yet, despite their scurrying, this was a charnel environment, one in which life, certainly human life, was unwelcome.

"What were that?" hissed Creeps.

"I think we have company."

Gently, Creeps rested the cup and the pipette on the stone lid and drew out the dagger which he often carried but seldom used. Picking away a peel of skin from the back of his right hand which had been scalded by a splash from the acid, he crept almost silently to Everus' side.

A baleful groan from behind caused both of them to turn round.

Shambling into the poor light there came the stinking remains of some long-dead being. Stained linen bandages were wound around much of the zombie but the exposed parts were brownish-green, revealing glimpses of leather-hardened, desiccated skin. Bone amulets and tarnished bracelets had been incorporated into its wrappings. Its head was little more than a half-shattered skull from which tufts of ragged hair sprouted. Lambent red fires burned in the depths of its otherwise empty eye sockets.

Shuffling forward, its tread heavy, it raised a wicked-looking, hooked spear.

Everus ran to attack it. With a flash of reflected light, he swung his sword two-handedly in a lethal arc which struck the ghastly thing in the side. The blade buried itself so deep that he had to yank it hard in order to free it, his opponent's flesh almost as dense as wood. And whereas a normal human would probably have been cleaved in two or at the least mortally wounded, the mummy merely grunted and retreated a step. Its movements were rigid yet sufficient enough for it to pull back in preparation for a jab with its spear.

Sidestepping the vicious thrust, Everus cursed and swung again, bringing his sword down overhead, hacking into his enemy's collarbone and neck. A disgusting brown fluid erupted from the gaping wound as the zombie staggered, stumbling back against the sarcophagus, its weapon falling from its grip.

Long-dead skin tore and stretched, the zombie's all but severed head lolling back and forth. Dark goo poured from the cleft, obscenely soaking its tattered torso.

Everus waited, ready for the attack. He was not known for hesitation but something about this entity sparked a memory of a text he had once read, describing the preserved sons of the crazed necromancer, Vorga'la Thrangu.

"What're ye waitin' for!? *Hit it!*" urged Creeps.

The animated corpse, insanely deciding that its damaged head was impairing its actions, grabbed it with both hands and tore it off. More of the sickly, snot-like goo burst forth as the skull and a long trail of ragged backbone was ripped free. Dashing its grisly body parts to the ground it then leapt at Everus.

A reeking, clawed hand flashed before his face as, stepping back, Everus swung out at the self-mutilated cadaver once more. This time his sword slashed across the thing's abdomen, cutting a messy swathe just above where its navel should be. With the gagging stench of ancient resins and long-digested food, the mummy's preserved stomach and internal organs slopped out onto the ground. And this time Everus' enemy went down, collapsing in its own nauseating puddle. Sword raised, he watched with morbid curiosity as his putrefied, headless victim convulsed and tried to undo his handiwork, scabrous hands feebly re-stuffing. For the briefest of moments he wondered why this horror's innards had not been removed during the mummification process as had been customary.

Suddenly Creeps let out a strangled cry.

Looking round, Everus could see his companion frantically grappling with a second mummy which had raised him off the ground in a bear-hug. Splintering bones underfoot, he ran to the thief's aid. He had covered only a few steps when a third linen-swathed horror, its appearance and stench that of a decomposing leper, screamed out of the shadows. With inhuman strength, it grasped him around the throat and lifted him off the ground before rushing him against a chamber wall, smashing him into a rack of rickety shelving.

Ancient pots, a collection of rusty javelins and two old helmets crashed to the floor in an explosion of dust and bone.

Fighting for breath, and with his sword now in but one hand, Everus chopped down. He struck his gruesome assailant, slicing a gash of dead flesh, his sword embedding itself in the zombie's skull.

Yet still it held on, throttling the life from him, its grip tightening. He kicked at it, battering desperately, his vision darkening even as his sword fell from his hand. Stabs of white light flashed through his brain as he began to lose consciousness, that horrible, decayed skull grinning up at him. His eyes rolled back as his airway was crushed.

"Have a bit o' this, ye bastard!" yelled Creeps, leaping up from behind and splashing the remaining contents from his cup over the gruesome head. The green fluid fizzed and sizzled like bacon in a pan upon contact.

Dashing Everus to the ground, the thing tore at its now bubbling face. Wailing like a tortured child, it staggered back, tripping over a large cremation urn. Both it and the pot crashed to the floor. A nest of black crypt cobras that had laired inside the container along with the ashes slithered off in various directions even as the undead stumbled and crawled away.

Creeps helped Everus to his feet, who, nursing his neck, grudgingly nodded his appreciation. His long dark coat was covered in dust and spider web and blood trickled from a cut on his head. His neck was badly bruised. In some pain, he bent down and retrieved his fallen sword, eyes drawn to an approaching snake. The venomous serpent reared to full height and hissed. It then fell dead in two parts as he advanced with his sword and cut it in half.

"They corpse-things were a couple o' tough old bitches, weren't they?"

"There were three of them. Couple means two," croaked Everus, rubbing his neck.

"They were tough all the same."

Stepping over the dead snake, the stiffness in his neck making his movements laboured, Everus looked around, surveying the carnage that remained after their skirmish. The mummy which he had felled at the beginning had apparently crawled off somewhere, as evidenced by the smeared trail of guts it had left behind. He turned, eyes searching for the body of the one that had been grappling with Creeps. A sudden lance of pain in his neck made him wince in agony.

"Ah, that's nothin'. Ye should try danglin' at the end o' a rope for a bit. That'll clear yer thrapple." Creeps lit his clay pipe and took several puffs. "Then ye'll know what pain is. Aye, ye can feel the hounds bitin' at yer arse then. That's no mistake."

Everus looked about, inattentive to what the thief was saying. "What happened to yours?"

"What, ma arse? I were born wi' it."

Everus fixed Creeps with a cold, humourless stare.

"Oh, ye mean the one that nabbed me? Well, the bloody thing's arm snapped off as we fought. Then I stabbed it in the face wi' ma dagger. That shut the bugger up." Creeps pointed to one of the dark archways. "It legged it down that way."

Content that there was no immediate danger, Everus paced over to the sarcophagus. "All right, let's get this bastard open and get out of here."

Dutifully, Creeps crouched down and began loosening the acid-corroded stone sealing with a chisel. After a short time, he stepped aside and began returning the various tools to his sack.

"Done?"

"Aye, there ye go." The thief finished buckling his pack.

Moving into position, Everus heaved against the heavy-looking lid. With a grating sound, the slab slid forward a little, then a bit more. He stood upright, his face marked with exertion, and pushed again. Beads of sweat formed on his bloody and dust-streaked forehead. Stepping back and flexing his right hand, he checked the length of the lid to see if there was an easier way of opening it. Unable to find another means, he pushed again. This time the lid slid relatively easily.

A noisome stench of fetid air blasted out of the funerary container, causing Everus to gag. With the sarcophagus now half open, he looked down at its contents. The corpse which had been encased within was now little more than a brittle skeleton, its exposed bones sickeningly discoloured. Tattered fragments of a once fine robe still hung to the bones in places and around it, sparkling in the lantern light, were hundreds of small gems.

Hung around the skeleton's neck was an ornate, gold amulet.

"What've we got 'ere then?" inquired Creeps, greedily eyeing the glinting jewellery. A broad smile formed on his unpleasant features, displaying his cracked and yellowing teeth.

Everus made to grab the amulet.

"*Oi! Look out! What's that o'er there!?*"

Everus turned to where the thief pointed, sword at the ready. Staring into the dark corners, heart thumping, he steeled himself in readiness for whatever would appear. Who knew what other nameless threats lurked down here? A disturbing moment passed. "I don't see anything."

"Thought I saw summat," muttered Creeps, leaning over the grave goods and stuffing gems into a pouch. "Maybe it were just a shadow."

Cursing, Everus turned, reached in and snatched the amulet, snapping the bony neck in the process. The displaced skull rolled to one side. Holding the amulet closer to the lantern, he could see that it was circular in shape. Within the circle a triangle had been inset, at the points of which red gems, possibly rubies, had been placed. It felt alien to the touch and certainly colder than it should have been. That there was magic about it he had no doubt. Inexorably, he felt drawn to it, entranced by its weird design. He peered both at and *into* it. Suddenly, he felt as though some part of himself was being torn away, dragged into another state of being.

His vision blurred.

All around he could see destruction. Buildings burned. Bodies burned. The very earth burned. The sky was darker than he had ever known it, for no moon or star dared to illuminate this demonic vision. Fierce, dark shapes ran amok, butchering and howling. And blood...everywhere blood...

"Everus?"

Screaming, Everus tore himself free of the nightmare vision even as it seared his soul. *So this is what he had been sent to get.* Trembling, the phantasmagoria melting before his eyes, he found himself looking into the questioning face of Creeps.

† † †

Collar turned up, hands in pockets, Everus stalked the sombre streets, his mood as dark and depressing as his current environment. Six days had passed since he and Creeps had broken into the tomb of Vorga'la Thrangu and made off with the mysterious amulet as well as a bountiful haul of jewellery and the initial thrill of his success had long worn off. What coin he had received from the sale of the gems had been readily squandered on expensive whores and fine liquor, his tastes of late somewhat decadent.

This region of the city always lowered his mood. It was not surprising, for the buildings were grey and drab, uniform and mostly derelict. They were the homes of the poor and the wretched – those miserable beings whose lives revolved around nothing but their daily, hand-to-mouth, survival. Just how many lowlifes dwelt in these forlorn tenement houses he had no idea, but every time he had been here he had counted himself unlucky if he saw a single soul.

Soon he came to a familiar flight of stone steps which led up to a foul-smelling walkway. With a derisive shake of his head, he started the climb, pausing for a moment to look up at a high lattice window, its glass smeared and unwashed. When he saw nothing of note, he completed his climb, traversed the litter-strewn passage and stopped outside a door.

Heaps of rubbish and empty bottles lay nearby and a stink of stale ale pervaded the malodorous air. A mangy cat meowed before leaping up onto the window ledge next door and slinking through a broken window.

Trying the door handle, Everus was not surprised to find that the door was locked – a wise precaution in this run-down part of the city. For a moment, he considered rapping but then stood back and kicked it open. With a crash, the door smashed off its uppermost hinge, the frame almost knocked clear. Pleased with what he had done, he entered, the hallway beyond, gloomy and uninviting. There was no furniture, nor was there any carpet. Directly in front of him a flight of rickety wooden stairs gave access to the floor above and as he prepared to start the upward climb, a door on the landing opened.

"*What the...!?* What're ye doin' wi' ma door?"

Everus looked up. "I knocked. Obviously you didn't hear."

"Aye...well. I suppose ye'd better come up." Confused and more than a little put out at the act of vandalism, Creeps shook his head in dismay.

Taking the steps two at a time, Everus bounded up. At the top, he entered the small, cell-like room, the door to which Creeps held open. He had been here before and each time on leaving he had vowed to himself never to return. The room reeked from various sources. The primary stink was undoubtedly due to the thief's smoking habit – something which, at least to Everus' mind, bordered on the obscene. The very air was thick from it, visible as a light brown haze which hovered near the ceiling and which stained the walls with its presence. But there were other smells; off-putting whiffs and tangs which emanated from some of the heaps of junk and the blanket-rumpled cot.

Then there was the slightly-steaming bucket which lay by the side of the bed...

"What're ye wantin'? Ye scared the daylights out o' me."
Reaching for his pipe, Creeps lit up.

"Still smoking that shit, I see? This room smells worse than a
leper's arse." Everus forcibly opened the single window in order to
allow some fresher air in. He looked out. In many ways the cityscape
appeared worse from up here, the tumbledown residential blocks
stretching for as far as he could see across the urban vastness. Roiling
dark clouds gathered in the distance. He turned around, his eyes drawn
to the carefully stacked coins on the thief's table. From a quick glance,
he thought there had to be almost a thousand gold there, far too much
for someone to be living in this kind of squalor. "We've another job."

Signs of interest and unease registered on Creeps' dishevelled
face. "Oh? How much this time?"

"Same as last time. Five hundred gold. Four for me…and one for
you."

"What for?"

"The usual," answered Everus with an evil smile. "We've a
rendezvous at The Rusty Gibbet. So I guess the question is, are you
in or not?"

Creeps grinned. "Ye know me. I'm up for it. Besides, I haven't
been there for some time. If I remember right they used to serve…"
He stopped, eyes drawn to a sudden flicker of fur under a nearby
table. "Shhh!"

Following the thief's gaze, Everus watched as a particularly large
and scabby rat scampered close to the skirting board, obviously
attracted to the stinking cheese secured to the nasty-looking,
improvised trap. Gingerly, the rodent approached, before trying to
make off with the bait, but it was far too slow. The trap sprung with
an audible twang, a serrated metal bar snapping down and messily
severing the rodent's head.

"*Yes!*" Creeps clapped his hands. "Got the bastard!" A grim
smile flickered across his face as the headless rat twitched for a
moment before dying. He walked over and held the trap open.
Picking his victim's body up by the tail and pinching the head in his
other hand, he went to the window and tossed the dripping animal
out onto the street below.

"Creeps the Ratkiller," commented Everus, sarcastically.
"Scourge of vermin everywhere."

"Anyhow, when've we to…meet this fella o' yers?" asked Creeps,
wiping his hands on his already unclean trousers.

"We'll go as soon as you're ready. Though don't take too long."

After Creeps had prepared a little mixture of his own and flung on his 'street gear'; a green woollen jumper that looked as though it had been knitted from pig bristles, a dirty leather jacket and a pair of battered and frayed leather shoes, they exited his 'apartment' as he was prone to calling home, and set out down the twisting alleys.

The neighbourhood into which they were headed was even worse than that in which the thief lived. The streets became narrower the deeper they ventured, the rubbish piled higher. Every so often they would catch sight of an unappealing face gawping at them from behind a dirt-smeared window or see some shadowy figure retreat into a doorway. That these streets were dangerous and its denizens lawless they had no doubt – the frequent drunk or corpse lying face down in the gutter ample proof of that.

Outsiders seldom came here. The city watch themselves rarely called, well aware that they were not welcome, especially at night when killings, rapes and robberies were most common. Dogs and other scavengers prowled in the shadows, searching for any scrap worth eating.

"A cheery place," commented Everus, taking in the scenes of dereliction and poverty.

"Aye. Ye'd be best no' to rattle any o' the locals around 'ere. They're a funny breed some o' 'em. Ye get some real raggedy bastards, I tell ye. Aye, some real crazies. There used to be one family o' weirdos lived down by Boglemart Street. Someb'dy told me they were done for eatin' folk. They'd a back room full o' half-eaten stiffs. *Gads!* It'd give ye the boak." Creeps checked that his dagger was still at his belt. Walking about unarmed in such a place was not advisable. "Aye, whatever ye do ye've got to watch yer bollocks around 'ere or someb'dy or summat'll have 'em. What some o' these nutters get up to would scunner yer mince."

One of the 'nutters' – a diseased, tattered form pushing a handcart heaped with junk – briefly came into view at the far end of an alley. After a furtive look about, he disappeared, heading off in another direction, one foot dragging lamely behind the other. A lone, scrawny dog loped out of an open doorway over to their left, stopped for a piss and then scurried off in pursuit of the shambling figure.

A little further down, the street before them widened. Over to their right, away from some boarded-up houses, was a burnt-out tavern. Once a gathering point for the denizens of this area, now it lay desolate and heavily vandalised, its remaining walls and rafters broken and blackened. A row of crows perched on its charred framework, ominously silhouetted against the encroaching dusk.

"Nearly there now. It's just down at the bottom o' the hill." Creeps pointed at an area of slums built on a distant decline, the dilapidated hovels criss-crossed by a maze of back-streets. A soot-filled smog, somewhat darker than the clouds above, hung over the ramshackle houses. "That's where I used to live as a nipper. Beggars' Hill. That's what we called it."

Sloping slightly downhill, the way they were going became cobbled and narrow once more, the crumbling houses on either side leaning like dying men against one another for support. Most were built from coarse brickwork and timber and all looked very old. Some were linked by bridges which arched over the street, forming small, shadow-filled tunnels which had probably witnessed more than their share of muggings.

Rats skulked from open sewer gratings as they entered one such tunnel, their beady pink eyes fixing them, hungrily.

"Did ye know that The Rusty Gibbet's haunted?" asked Creeps, feeling the need to make conversation.

Everus did not respond, his mind elsewhere. It was always the same when he was focused on a mission. Nothing distracted him, especially not nonsense.

"Aye," said Creeps, unaware that his companion was not in the least bit interested. "It's haunted all right. Accordin' to what I've heard some poor bugger was caught one night cheatin' at dice by a previous landlord. He was beat up and tortured down in the ale cellar where he was imprisoned. I've heard tell he was bricked up only to be found years later...his bones anyway. It's said that the man who now owns it fed 'em to his dogs. The cage's still there...ye'll see it. It's outside on show. Anyhow, it's him that now haunts the place."

Emerging from the shadow of one of the 'tunnels', Everus looked up at the sky. It was darkening, the clouds various shades of grey and black. Already it was dusk, the temperature dropping noticeably. A light rain began to fall. He thought he heard the faint rumblings of distant thunder. Determinedly, he walked on, eager to reach his destination before the weather became too bad.

When they got there they saw that the tavern was a three-storey structure. Set back from the street, many of its windows had been either completely bricked-up or else covered with sturdy wooden boards, the owner obviously having had enough of constantly repairing his windows every time a brawl erupted. Like many in this part of the city, when night came, the tavern acted as a sort of magnet, attracting both the unwashed and the unruly.

Outside, hanging from a post, was a large rusty cage, inside which was a contorted skeleton, fleshless hands gripping the bars as though trying to escape.

"*Look!* There's that thing I was tellin' ye about," cried Creeps. He pointed as the macabre tavern sign creaked and spun slowly in the growing wind.

Everus walked up towards the entrance, his ears picking up the sounds of raucous dissipation from inside.

Angry shouts and guffaws of laughter grew louder and a moment later a side door neither had noticed before was flung open and two drunks, arms locked around each other's shoulders, staggered out, belching and mumbling. They reeled a few steps before one collapsed, half-dragging the other with him.

Ignoring them completely, Creeps ran a hand down his unshaven face and went to Everus' side. "I take it ye know who ye're after?"

"No, but I have a description."

"Well, that's a start. Anyway, ye'd best watch what ye do in 'ere. As ye've probably guessed, the regulars aren't all that keen on strangers. They're no' that trustin'. They're also known to spike yer ale...if ye know what I mean," warned Creeps, patting a secret pocket. "Talkin' o' which, ye can get the first drink in. An' remember to look out for that ghost I was tellin' ye about. The last thing ye want is that puttin' the willies up ye whilst ye sup."

"That *would* be an eye-opener," commented Everus, dryly.

Inside The Rusty Gibbet over two dozen patrons were gathered. Many were seated around the bar itself, perched on high chairs, drinking, smoking, snorting dubious powder out of small pots and talking to one another. Others were sat at small tables, playing dice or cards. In one corner, a group of particularly boisterous grubbas – the pejorative name generally given to a demi-human race of short and stocky beings – were gathered, engrossed in a rumbustious game of tabletop-thuggery. Every so often one of them would yelp, a sure sign that they were far too drunk to play the game properly.

The air was polluted with foul language and reeked of ale, smoke, sweat and vomit.

Alert for any trouble, Everus paced over to the bar and ordered a round of drinks for himself and the thief. The barman – a big bald bruiser with glaring eyes – studied him warily, before taking the coins and pouring the drinks. Two tankards of cheap ale were placed on the bar before him and Everus looked unadmiringly at them before picking them up and heading over to the table that Creeps had chosen. He sat down and raised the tankard to his lips, surreptitiously eyeing the various patrons.

Creeps took a sip from his drink, nodded his approval and then took a larger gulp, his short moustache doused in ale froth. He leaned forward across the table. "Ye see him?"

Ignoring the question, Everus maintained his icy stare. He watched intently as one of the grubbas walked by clutching his bleeding hand. From the looks of it he had lost a finger, maybe two.

Draining his tankard and letting out a sly and odorous belch, Creeps stood up, one hand delving into a pocket. "Want another?"

Everus looked incredulously at the thief, before turning his gaze towards his own, almost untouched drink. "Later...maybe." He watched as his companion shrugged his shoulders and nonchalantly slouched his way towards the bar for a refill. Looking around, he noticed a gang of unkempt men playing darts and a handful of ugly folk jigging around a table. One of them seemed to be in the process of undressing. Quickly, he took his gaze away and was about to return to his drink, when a snippet of conversation between the darts players caught his attention.

"*Phwoar!* That Katryna's a fine bit o' cracklin'," proclaimed one of the men, preparing to throw, his eyes not so much on the board as on the buxom serving wench who walked by. "Aye, ye've got a fine set o' wabbs on ye missus! Any chance o' ye lettin' an old soldier bury his head there?"

"Go on! Give us a smile an' flash 'em our way!" laughed another, winning a cheeky giggle from the lass in question.

Katryna!

The name stirred dormant memories deep within Everus. Memories that he usually suppressed, but now they rose, unbidden, to his mind.

† † †

At hearing the voice, he slowly began to stir from his slumber.
"Everus! Everus! Wake up!"

Yawning, he rubbed at his eyes, his vision focusing on the beautiful, barely-dressed, young woman standing at the side of his bed. Tall, curvaceous and brown-haired, she was what his heart desired...though not quite everything.

"You did it, Everus. You did it!"

He now sat up, admiring her various charms, aware of her expensive perfume. As it should be, after all it had cost him a small fortune.

"I knew you would." Reaching out, his girlfriend threw her arms about him and kissed him full on the lips.

Gently pushing her back, he looked deep into her eyes. "What, have I...?"

"I'm so happy."

"Tell me, Kat. Are you...?" Apprehension tinged his voice.

Katryna looked away and laughed. "No, stupid."

"So what are you saying? Are you saying that I've...that I've been accepted?" Excitement surged through his veins, causing his mind to reel for a moment.

"Yes. The letter from The Academy arrived whilst you were sleeping."

Gripping his lover in a passionate embrace, he started smothering her in sensual kisses. His mind swam with the realisation that all his hard studies and his years of work had finally paid off. From this day on, his life would never be the same. He stopped abruptly, much to Katryna's displeasure. "I must get up and tell everyone. There's still much to do."

"What, now?" Smiling coquettishly, Katryna seductively fell back onto the bed.

"Well. I suppose it can wait." With a laugh, he reached for her, undoing her bodice.

† † †

"All right scrubber? How's yer mutha?" came a growled slur followed by the hammering of a gnarled and meaty fist on the table. "She all right?"

Rudely shaken from his happy reverie, Everus looked up to see a debauched and blatantly drunk grubba staring bleary-eyed at him.

"How is she?" The short humanoid's ragged, ginger beard was matted with old puke and his breath reeked of ale. An unsightly, hairy wart sprouted on the end of his flattened nose. His face was heavily scarred and what teeth he had on show were black and rotten.

"Dead," answered Everus, coldly. Staring at the swaying drunk, he appraised the broad-bladed axe which hung from the straining belt around the grubba's beer-bellied waist.

"I *said*...how *is* yer mutha?" Mouth dribbling, the grubba leaned closer, farting as he did so. The stench was foul, almost eye-watering. One could have been forgiven for thinking he had a dead rat festering in his bowels. Harrumphing, he slumped against the table before unsteadily regaining his feet. "She still bangin' like a...?"

In a fluid movement, Everus stood up, unsheathed his sword from his back and with a powerful, two-handed overhead swing cleaved the grubba's bearded head in two.

Blood arced towards the raftered ceiling as the sword split the skull asunder. The two halves of the head fell way, revealing the cloven brain and other gory cranial components. A patron sitting nearby screamed as he was showered in a torrent of blood.

"Why don't you ask her?" Everus asked the bloody corpse, still stood upright.

Then, with a thud, both legs buckled and the stocky body collapsed to the floor.

"*Piss on ma mother's grave!* Look at this mess!" cried someone who had the misfortune of passing by at that moment.

"*Eugh!* What's this in ma drink!?" complained another, tongue protruding as he fished out something red and slippery from his ale.

Everus grinned. Then, sword in hand and largely ignoring the shocked drinkers, he headed towards the bar.

Faces turned away, the darts players wisely choosing to become absorbed in their game. Those thronged around the bar muttered to one another and quickly dispersed leaving the sweating barkeeper to stare, open-mouthed, as the implacable killer neared. For a moment, it was clear he was having trouble over deciding what to do next, whether to confront him over his audacious slaying or not. However, common sense prevailed and obviously deciding that discretion was perhaps the better part of valour, he presented Everus with a nervous grin and poured him a drink.

"Thanks." Taking the tankard, Everus walked over to where Creeps sat at the far end of the bar. He settled down to watch the other customers, only half-listening to the thief's ramblings and trying to ignore the background hubbub of the lively but disgusting patrons. This was the kind of place he loathed – not so much the tavern but the people in it. As he watched them, his already judgemental thoughts grew darker. Remembering his killing of the grubba, he thought: *why stop at one?* To distract himself from the pleasurable visions of mass slaughter, he finished his drink and stepped outside for some fresh air. He stood for a while, examining the skeleton in the cage, wondering to himself if Creeps' tale had any merit. Had this unfortunate been bricked up alive or was it merely a purloined corpse, set here to give a worthless tavern a bit of character?

A heavy rain began to fall.

Everus remained outside for a moment longer, relishing the cold and the wet before going back inside. He found Creeps talking to an equally sordid-looking individual. Immediately, he recognised Matt Weaselnest, a grave-robbing lowlife and friend of the thief's.

Weaselnest rose from his chair as Everus approached. Greasy, unwashed hair hung down well beyond his shoulders and one eye stared vacantly. His clothing was shabby and torn, his face; scabby and worn. "Ye all right?" He held out a scrawny hand in a gesture of friendship. He stank of freshly opened graves.

Gripping the offered hand, Everus crushed it, listening with satisfaction as some of the bones cracked. He then let go. The less physical contact he had with this wretch the better.

Stifling a curse, Weaselnest grimaced and squeezed his damaged hand under his opposing armpit. Pain was clearly imprinted on his long, almost horse-like, face.

"Weaselnest. It's been a long time...although perhaps not long enough," said Everus, delighting somewhat in the other man's discomfort. "Still shagging stiffs?"

"Eh? Well...aye. Ye could say that." Grinning madly, Weaselnest nodded. The look of someone who had not fully understood the question, and for that matter was not fully there, on his face.

Disgusted, Everus shook his head. Creeps' habits were bad enough but this character's were deplorable. If only half of what he had heard mentioned about him were true, then surely here was someone who should have been put down at birth; preferably with a big shovel.

"Matt were just tellin' me how he's heard o' some place o'er on Beggars' Hill. Seems someone's left their loot for us to pick up," said Creeps, clearly trying to reduce the tension.

"Aye. Lots o' loot to be had." Nodding enthusiastically, Weaselnest reached for his drink which rested on the bar.

"Not interested," stated Everus, flatly.

"*Eh!?* But this is a good one. Or so I've heard," pressed Weaselnest.

"Come on, Everus. We can at least think about it," protested Creeps. "Let's just find out what..."

"We do what *I* decide," Everus interrupted, stabbing a thumb at his chest in order to emphasise the point. "So, Weaselnest...get stuffed or I'll kill you."

With a pathetic look at Creeps, Weaselnest, realising the threat he was under, pulled up his hood and slouched away.

"Worthless bastard." Everus watched him go. He drained his drink and called for another. The ale, when it arrived, was weak and bitter tasting, certainly not on a par with the fine wines and spirits to which he was more accustomed. Nonetheless, it was still drink and right now, anything which distracted him from Creeps' ugly face and pointless talk, had to be worthy of some merit. Why he continued to put up with the disreputable thief and his associated scum was something he had asked himself many times over the last few years and as yet there was no clear answer. It was certainly not the former's charismatic pull. Looking across, he watched as Creeps withdrew what looked like a ball of dung from a pouch and crammed it into his pipe.

Outside, thunder boomed ominously.

"We should at least see what Matt's got on offer," said Creeps, lighting up. "There's no harm in findin' out."

Everus stared into his tankard, swirling its contents, lost for a moment as his mind tried to reawaken memories of the woman he had once loved.

"Ye know, he's always been quite clued up about these things. Could be there's a bit o' gold to be had."

Ignoring the thief, Everus took a drink.

"Anyhow, I've heard they're closin' early tonight." Creeps looked about at the few remaining drinkers, most of whom were getting ready to leave. "No sign o' yer man? Maybe the weather's kept him away. I mean, let's face it, ye'd have to be nutty to come out on a night like this." He had no sooner finished talking when an almighty crack of thunder exploded directly overhead. He looked to the ceiling as though half-expecting it to come crashing down in sheets of flaming timber.

"I'm going," said Everus. Finishing his ale, he put his empty tankard on the bar.

"Eh? What about yer man? What if he turns up?"

"He won't." A knowing, evil smile flickered briefly on Everus' handsome face.

"Oh, what makes ye so sure?"

"Because I've already killed him." Everus nodded, indicating to where a serving wench scrubbed at the bloodstains on the floor, the grubba's body having been taken out a backdoor by the barkeeper and a lackey.

"*Him?* The grubba? I thought he'd just pissed ye off."

"An added bonus."

"But...but what about ma poison? I've gone to all the bother o' makin' one o' ma brews for ye to use an' ye've just cut his bloody head in two!"

Everus smiled, the action no more than a curl of his mouth. Then, checking that his sword was securely fastened and with no further talk, he left The Rusty Gibbet and strode off into the stormy darkness.

CHAPTER TWO

Everus stood in the secret, underground temple, looking with some interest at the various murals which depicted several different guises of Xethorn – the god of murder and revenge. Even though the lighting was poor, he could see that the work of art was of outstanding quality, the painting covering the entire north wall of the chamber from floor to ceiling. Stepping closer, he then walked to one side, suitably impressed by the dynamic manner in which many of the scenes had been worked. It was an aesthetically and religiously fascinating piece and one that he had always felt drawn to, almost as though it had some meaning for him alone. The vibrant colours had faded slightly with the passage of centuries but he could still discern the violent passion with which the artist had produced this homage to his lord. The scholar he had once been appreciated the painter's skill. The murderer he had become understood the burning desire for the kill.

One section of the ancient mural portrayed the dark god as a large, black hound, eyes red and fiery, jaws wide, attacking a settlement of cowering people. In another scene, a monstrous indigo octopus grappled and constricted numerous hapless underwater beings. In one corner, the god was shown sitting astride a flaming dragon, swooping down from the nightmare skies to spread death and destruction on those below.

The sound of footsteps echoed across the black marble floor.

Everus turned, a slight wave of unease rippling through his veins as he watched high priest Dae'morogin advance towards him, his shadow unnaturally long. He wore a sable robe, the hood pulled over his head, menacingly casting much of his deathly pale face in darkness.

"Ah, my friend. I am pleased to see you once more."

The man's manner was polite, precise and chilling, but that was of small concern to Everus for he had little use for warmth these days. Bending one knee, he gently kissed the high priest's corpse-cold hand.

"Rise."

Everus got to his feet.

"The grubba is dead, I hear. You've done well."

"It was easy."

Dae'morogin nodded, his face devoid of emotion. "With him out of the way our next step should be...*easier.*" Staring up towards the huge mural, eyes narrowing, he muttered a hushed prayer before turning. "Come. Let us walk a little. There are things I would have you see."

At the high priest's side, Everus followed as he was led back the way he had entered the great hall, heading for the gloomy cloisters at one end. He had been here many times over the past decade or so, and believed he was familiar with the many, labyrinthine passageways and chambers, and yet, without his guide, he would have soon found himself hopelessly lost. There were dark galleries which led to deeper dungeons wherein unspeakably bizarre and unholy rites associated with his malign god were performed. In the sprawling torture chambers, he got to witness, first hand, the cruelty exacted on those misguided fools who had crossed the Lord of Murder and His followers.

"How long have you been one of us, Everus?" Dae'morogin asked as they continued their tour around the subterranean temple.

"Over ten years."

"And...tell me, what's the most important lesson you've learned in that time?"

Everus hesitated, framing a suitable response. "Murder is a permanent solution to a temporary problem. Xethorn makes those who murder strong, and in so doing, He helps us to destroy our enemies."

"Anything else?" Dae'morogin asked, nodding to a passing cowled acolyte.

"Our only law is our allegiance to our god. All other laws are but lies which keep us from fulfilling our true potential."

"And what of vengeance?" asked the high priest with a knowing glance.

"Return your suffering a thousandfold," answered Everus, sharply.

"Only a thousand?" Dae'morogin thought for a moment.

"Perhaps one could do better than that. But tell me, what if the target of your retribution happened to be someone, let us say, of importance...a member of The Watchful Eye for instance. And one knew that any crime against them could well prove hazardous?"

Everus hesitated a second time, unsure of the direction this conversation was taking. "Surely, one would care not. For is it not better to meet Xethorn having done His work, rather than cower in a corner afraid of impotent laws? Murder and mayhem prepare the soul for the struggle of that which is to be."

The sound of echoing screams were becoming fainter as they arrived at a stout wooden door which led to Dae'morogin's private office.

The high priest opened the door and stepped inside, permitting Everus to follow. Lowering his hood, he was completely bald underneath. The tired flesh of his face was pulled tightly over his skull so that it appeared waxen. By contrast, his eyes were almost completely black, no doubt a reaction to having spent much of his life away from the upper world. Sitting down in a grand chair at a large desk which was littered with books and papers, he drew out a slender iron key from a pocket in his robe and used it to open a drawer. He paused for a moment, lost in his thoughts, before reaching in and pulling out a bag of coins.

Everus waited in the unsettling silence.

Dae'morogin looked up, the vaguest of smiles tautly creasing his face. It was clearly something he rarely did. "You've learnt much. I oft bemoan the fact that you've never contemplated a full initiation. Your insights...would be most welcome. But perhaps your services to our god are better carried out in your own, unique way." He slid the pouch across the desk.

Everus reached for the money. "You'll inform me when I'm needed?"

"Yes. Return at the darkening of the third moon. For now, however, enjoy your earnings."

† † †

A short time later, after Everus had left, Dae'morogin entered his private subterranean shrine. On the high priest's head, was settled a crimson peaked crown and he had changed into a red silk robe embroidered with sinuous designs, his Xethornite cowl of no use here.

A colony of huge, black bats hung from the cavern ceiling high above.

A stink of foul-smelling incense filled the dank air.

Torches guttered.

His fingers closed around a large, heavy tome, the high priest walked to the middle of the cavern. The grimoire felt wet and sticky. Quickly, as though he were loathe to hold it for too long, he raised it with both hands and laid it on a stone pulpit.

Bats twittered briefly and spread their wings.

Dae'morogin opened the tome at a bookmarked page. On it, written in a language that only a few could read, were many names. He ran a long finger down the yellowing page, coming to the last name listed.

Grumff.

Dipping a raven-feathered quill pen into a small pot of ink, Dae'morogin stared at the name, his eyes narrowing. Pen poised, he pondered briefly over just how hard this one had been to trace. His assassins and spies had worked hard, by day and more commonly by night, trying to ascertain his whereabouts. It was always the same with the lowlifes.

Regardless, the deed was done.

With a silent prayer, he crossed the name out.

For a moment nothing happened.

Then, somehow, the book started to wail, the sound not unlike that produced by the banshees Dae'morogin's predecessor, Dae'dicus, had once kept imprisoned deep within the temple vaults. Horribly, the pages began to rustle, bloody symbols seeping up from the cursed paper like a sick haemorrhage. Slowly at first, the names appeared but they soon came thick and fast, the pages now turning of their own accord.

Dae'morogin watched, transfixed with morbid fascination as the sorcerous process went on until well over a hundred names had been scribed within. The sanguinary recording then came to an end, stopping at the name of Everus' next intended victim.

✝ ✝ ✝

Maliciously, Everus considered kicking Creeps' door in once more, noting the fact that the thief had obviously had it recently repaired. He changed his mind and gave it a loud rap.

There was no answer.

Everus knocked louder, his actions this time greeted by the opening of the upper storey window.

Creeps' head popped out and he looked down, questioningly. "*What?*"

"Get down here and open the door, you drunken bastard. Either that or I'll kick it in a second time."

"All right. Hang on."

Everus waited, tracking the sound of footsteps coming down the stairs.

Bolts were drawn back and the door opened. Creeps, dressed in the same clothes he had worn to The Rusty Gibbet the night before, yawned as he stood aside to allow Everus in. With a furtive look about as though to ensure no one was watching, he closed the door, clicking the new bolts back into place.

Upstairs, in the dingy room, Everus slung a bag of coins onto the table. "Your money." Wincing, he noticed a pile of what looked like cold vomit on the floor.

Following Everus' gaze, Creeps shrugged. "Aye...well. I was goin' to clean it up." He reached for the pouch. A sudden, nauseating reek of drink on his breath and a bad taste in his gullet pushed sick up his throat. With revulsion, he shook his head, forcing himself to swallow.

Grimacing, Everus watched, confused and more than a little disgusted by the thief's behaviour. "What is it?"

The thief stuck his tongue out and shivered. "I've got a bloody shit taste in ma mouth. Tastes like someb'dy's crapped in it." He hawked up a mouthful of catarrh and swallowed before reaching into his trousers and giving his scrotum a quick scratch. Picking up a cup from a shelf, he then went to the open window and took a deep breath. Coughing and spluttering, he dipped the cup into a length of metal guttering just below the window and brought the gathered dirty rainwater to his quivering lips. He drank, twice spitting out some contaminant or other. After returning the cup, he went and sat on the edge of his bed, belching uncomfortably as he did so.

"The height of elegance," Everus commented. "The very pinnacle of social grace."

"Eh?" Snorting like a pig with a bad case of the pox, Creeps looked up from lighting his pipe, certain that a good smoke would remedy matters.

"Never mind. I'm here to tell you that I've had a rethink about last night. I've decided to see what that obnoxious git has to offer."

"Come again?"

"Weaselnest."

"Ah, I knew ye'd see sense. So...ye're interested in what old Matt's got in store. Well, after ye'd left, he told me a bit more about it. Seems that there's a deserted house o'er in Beggars' Hill. It was supposed to have been a safe house for a group o' local rogues but they were all killed by a rival gang. Anyhow, their loot was hidden and forgotten about."

"And it's still there? He knows where it is?"

"Seems to...an', let's face it, if anybody would, he would." Creeps coughed, massaged his head and emitted a low groan. "*Oooh!* Ma brain hurts. I think I must've had a bit too much last night." In an attempt to take his mind off the discomfort, he grabbed the pouch and tipped out the coins. Such was his skill in counting money it did not take him long to tally it up. He raised his face, his look puzzled.

"What?"

"I'm five short." That fact alone hurt more than the headache.

"Expenses."

"*What?*" Creeps' face contorted with discomfort. As though his hangover were not bad enough, he was now beginning to feel the onset of severe toothache. His entire upper jaw on the right hand side felt as though it had been repeatedly kicked and, with his probing tongue, he could tell that several of his remaining back teeth were ready to come out.

"Well, there were the drinks and let's see...why yes, I gave the barkeeper a little something to keep our activities from being bandied around too much. The less the authorities know about this the better. It all adds up, you know."

"Aye, but surely that didn't come to five gold?" Disgruntled, Creeps scrunched a fist into his cheek, the pain now bordering on the intolerable. His normally pale face reddened as he bit down on the stem of the pipe.

"Thankfully, I'm not a smoker, but I didn't think the idea was to eat the pipe."

"It's ma teeth. They're bloody killin' me."

"Painful, is it?" asked Everus with a cruel smile.

Suddenly, Creeps leapt to his feet and began stomping around his

27

small room, his pain-induced madness increasing as his hangover wore off and the toothache kicked in. In his agony, he began cursing and pulling at his hair. There then followed an audible crack as he bit through the stem of his pipe. Spitting out clay chips and tooth fragments, he rushed over to a small wooden cabinet and flung the door wide. Inside were stored many of the thieving tools he used on his criminal forays and, casting aside a box filled with sundry lock-picks and oiled drills, he pulled out a pair of rusty, yet serviceable, hand-held wire cutters. Grinning, he raised them to his face.

† † †

Later that evening, Everus, Creeps and Weaselnest sat around a crude table at the latter's scuzzy abode. Although the room itself was somewhat larger than Creeps', there was a far greater assortment of junk left lying about, cluttering the place up. Empty glass bottles and discarded packets of food were strewn haphazardly over the stained and threadbare rug. The strong stench of stale body odour came from a pile of filthy overalls which hung from a hook behind the door. In one corner, on a shelf at chest height, a large, flea-infested rat stared hungrily from a metal cage.

Against one wall leant Weaselnest's pride and joy – his shovel.

A lantern on the table illuminated a sketchy street map which was currently the focus of attention for the three men. Only Everus sat on a proper chair. Creeps sat on the edge of Weaselnest's bed, whilst their host was perched on an old, empty barrel, which still reeked of ale – a cheap, but relatively effective means of masking the graveyard smell which emanated from elsewhere.

"This is where that loot I was tellin' ye about's stashed." Weaselnest reached over and pointed to the place in question. "Ye see this street 'ere? Well the house's just at the back o' it."

"What do you know about this building?" asked Everus.

"I've heard that it used to belong to the Longshadow Brothers. They then got into a fight wi' some out-o'-towners who tried to muscle in on their patch. Anyhow, it then fell into the hands o' some fella from the East Side who went nuts or summat. I've heard he may've done a bunk wi' some tart from down Ghavin's Keep way or summat like that." Weaselnest took a gulp from his bottle of cheap ale. "But he didn't know about the Longshadows' loot."

"And no one else knows about it? I find that strange."

"Could be that he did go nuts. Could be that he's still there...haunts it, like." With a dirty thumbnail, Weaselnest scraped absently at the poorly-made label on his bottle. "Maybe that's why nob'dy goes there."

"You said this would be easy. Ghosts have a tendency to despise the living."

"Yeh, it'll be easy. Don't worry about that. Money fer nothin'. We sneak in. Get odds an' sods. Get out. Piss easy."

"How much are we talking about here?" asked Everus. "Will it be worth my time?"

Creeps mumbled something neither understood, his crude efforts at dentistry severely inhibiting his speech. With the use of his wire cutters, he had extracted two back molars, a job which, although unpleasant, had surprisingly taken away the toothache he had experienced earlier.

Weaselnest nodded with mad enthusiasm. "Oh aye. Lots o' gold to be had." He pointed to the map once more. "If we were to come from o'er on this side we can get into these backstreets. But the best thing would be if we were all to meet at this place." Shifting his finger across the rumpled sheet, he stopped at a site marked with a large arrow drawn in red ink.

Everus rose from his chair so as to better study the map. Something had caught his attention; a minor, anomalous feature which warranted further investigation. The map was old, though certainly not ancient, and he had wondered on first seeing it how something like this could fall into the hands of a waster like Weaselnest. Peering closer, he could see what appeared to be the faint indentations of neat handwriting on the map. Almost certain that its owner could neither read nor write, he raised the map to the lantern in order to discern the palimpsest, eyes widening as a name became readable.

"Eh? Does...does anybody want...?" His voice trembling, Weaselnest got to his feet and headed for his squalid pantry. "I'll get some more ale, shall I? Got some biscuits somewhere."

Ignoring the grave-robber's nervous actions, Everus returned the map to the table and turned to Creeps. "I think we should see what this place has to offer."

✝ ✝ ✝

The forbidding tenement houses of Beggars' Hill loomed dark and menacing before them, the approaching street on which they stood, dead and eerily quiet. This area of the city was especially run-down, many of its buildings reduced to mere skeletons fit only for the dead and the dying. It was a stinking, threatening environment, home to all manner of reprobate; shadowy, lawless scavengers who existed on the fringes of more civilised society.

There had been at least two attempts in living memory by the imperial authorities to clamp down on the area and return the rule of law. On both occasions dozens of militia men had been lost and now it had become a ghetto into which few ventured and fewer came out.

Clouds of ill-smelling fumes generated from years of industrial and domestic decay polluted the sky above, smothering what sunlight there was.

Everus was not taking any chances. He had donned a suit of black, burnished, plate mail armour for this venture, well aware of the risks involved. It made travelling awkward, the mail bulky and impeding, but he was glad of its protection. The helmet he wore was of his own creation – a visored covering surmounted on its flanks with curled ram-like horns and a hinged face-plate. His long, black cloak rippled in the growing wind. Grim-faced, he stared about him as though defying anyone to attack.

By contrast, Creeps seemed nervous. The fact that Everus was wearing his armour, something he rarely did, for he was well aware of his own prowess with a blade, was certainly cause for concern. He himself owned nothing more protective than the shabby leather jacket he now wore. He looked at the dagger sheathed at his belt, then at the large sword in Everus' hand. Apparently size did matter.

Heading up the hill, Everus made a few practice cuts with his blade, deftly slicing the air and sending a clear signal to any who might be watching. "Tell me a little more about Weaselnest."

"Eh? What like?"

"How you got to know him, that kind of thing." There was a blatant mock politeness in Everus' voice.

"Well, me an' him used to work on the boneyards together. An' no' just the big cemetery but some o' the little ones as well. There were a time when we were the best in the business. Aye, it were like gettin' turnips out o' a field back in them days. We spent a time workin' for 'Mad King Billy', supplyin' him wi' corpses an' things which he used to pretend were long lost friends an' family an' what not. He'd have 'em all sat up around his house. Then there were 'One-Eyed Isaac' who once tried to scare the shit out o' Matt by gettin' his brother to bury him alive so that he could spring out at him when the coffin lid was removed. Hah! We'd all gone for a drink an' he were stone cold dead by the time we got to him. Mad bugger." Creeps seemed to be enjoying reliving the past. "Aye, I could tell ye some tales. I remember the night Matt dug up his old man, just so as he could have a piss on the silly old fart. Now there *were* a character, Matt's dad. Ye think Matt's ugly? Well his old man had a face like a dog's arse. I remember how he used to have this bloody talkin' crow which would..."

"You realise that I have to kill him?" Everus said, casually, staring at the street ahead, cutting through the thief's reminiscences.

"*What!?*"

"Yes. It would appear that your conniving friend has been collaborating with someone I haven't seen in quite some time."

"Hang on, wait." Raising his hands, Creeps tried to get Everus to stop but had no success. "What's this all about? Ye didn't say anythin' about killin'."

"*Didn't I?* I must've forgotten." Everus lowered his visor, his piercing green eyes staring from beyond his helmet. "You see there was a name on that map."

"*A name?* Whose name?"

"The name of the man we're going to see."

Creeps thought about things for a moment. "Are we walkin' into a trap, 'ere?"

"You could put it that way, yes," answered Everus, calmly.

† † †

With a powerful kick, Everus booted the door to the ramshackle house wide open. With a cry, he charged inside, surprising the four armoured men sitting around a table eating from cheap ration packs. His sword danced, beheading one of the ruffians, who had his back to him, before he even had a chance to move.

Screaming, another man staggered to his feet, his torso cut wide in two criss-crossing red gashes.

"Well, well. What have we here?" Everus advanced, hacking down the wounded man who was sent spinning to the floor, landing in a scarlet splash as he reached for his sword.

Shouts erupted as the remaining two sprang back, scrambling for their weapons. Rushing from either side of the table, both charged forward with their axes.

Nimbly dodging one attack, Everus cracked an elbow into his other attacker's bearded face.

Teeth shattered as the man reeled back, blood pouring from his smashed mouth.

Eyeing Everus warily, the other axe-wielder stood his ground. Then, leaping to avoid one of Everus' swings, he rushed forward and chopped down, sparks flying as his heavy blade rang against steel breastplate.

Slightly stunned, Everus pulled back a couple of steps. His armour had protected him well, absorbing most of the damage, but it still hurt. Getting hit by an axe usually did. Bringing his sword down in an overhead swing, he hoped to chop his foe in two, but the man had other plans. Darting behind, he rained down two successive hacks into Everus' right shoulder, striking a chink in his armour.

Blood spattered Everus' face and he half-collapsed, falling back towards the door. Pain lanced through his body as one leg buckled. His blood-smeared sword slipped from his grip and clattered to the floor. Somehow, he managed to stay upright, well aware that if he should go down he could well be finished. No quarter would be asked for and none probably given. Gritting his teeth, he stumbled out into the street.

"*Die, ye bastard!*" Snarling, the bruiser leapt in pursuit and hurled his axe.

Everus braced himself for the blow. With a clang, the axe sparked off his helmet, the impact powerful enough to send him spinning. Seeing double, he watched as the man before him drew out a sword and came towards him; twin images filled with hate.

Creeps saw only one and one was all he needed. With a cry, he thrust his dagger into the man's back. Glazed and unbelieving eyes turned to meet him even as he knifed him a second time. Puking blood, the man died in the thief's cradling arms. The thief then let the body slide to the floor and went to assist Everus, for it was clear he had been hurt.

"Say yer prayers, dog-meat." The bearded man stood in the doorway, a loaded crossbow levelled at Everus. Fingers tightened around the trigger.

"*Wait!*" ordered a voice from inside.

The man with the crossbow stepped out into the street, weapon trained on Everus as two more men exited the house. One of them was Weaselnest, his eyes darting suspiciously. The other, clearly the one who had issued the command, was dressed in a suit of well-kept chain mail. His right hand grasped a large battleaxe. In his left hand, he carried a circular, metal shield. A shock of white hair and a neatly-trimmed beard framed his rugged, tanned face.

With piercing blue eyes the man looked Everus dead in the eye. "*Dragonbanner!*" The words were snarled with clear derision.

Nervously, Creeps looked at Everus and then at Weaselnest, who now stood by the stranger's side, Everus' sword in his hands.

"Don't tell me you've forgotten who I am?" inquired the chain mail clad man.

"Of course not," Everus answered, blood trickling from his cut shoulder. "You're the one who was married to that trollop..."

"*Bastard!*"

Like a hammer striking an anvil, a gauntleted fist battered Everus' helmet. Knocked back, he felt the coppery taste of warm blood filling his mouth.

"You don't know how many times I've killed you in my dreams. And now...thanks to good Mister Weaselnest here, I have you just where I want you."

Everus wiped blood from his busted lips. "As always the coward. Scared to face me one on one. Isn't that right, Otha?"

"Three years I've been hunting you down. Three long years. You took from me everything I held dear. Killing my wife and family. And now...now I expect you want leniency? *Did you show that to them!?*" With a smack, Otha cracked Everus with the haft of his battleaxe, knocking him to the ground. He stepped back, watching with some satisfaction as his enemy painfully got to his feet. "Give the bastard his sword! Let's see who's the coward this day."

"Ye sure about this?" Weaselnest asked, apprehensively. "He's pretty handy wi' it."

"*I said, give him his sword.*"

Weaselnest threw the sword towards Everus and it landed with a clang on the cobbles before him.

It was at that moment that Creeps chose to make a break for it.

"Let the tramp go," cried Otha, as the man with the crossbow prepared to shoot. With a curse, he stepped forward and swung at Everus as he bent to retrieve his sword.

Parrying the attack, Everus fell back. Ducking away from another blow that would almost certainly have taken his head off had it hit, he then launched a swing of his own. Sparks leapt as his sword clashed against Otha's shield.

Deflecting another attack, Otha swung out, his heavy weapon grinding along the edge of Everus' sword. With a gleeful laugh, he launched a surprise strike with his shield, slamming Everus and knocking him to one knee. A follow up kick then sent him sprawling, the ram-horned helmet flying from his head.

Armour bloodied, Everus started to get to his feet. He was hurt badly and he knew it.

Breathing heavily, Otha stood his ground. "Like I thought. Only good at fighting women and kids."

"Come on then! What are you waiting for?" Mustering his strength and fighting back the pain, Everus stood up. Blood covered much of his face and his dark hair was matted with it.

"Do ye want me to shoot the bastard?" cried the man with the crossbow.

"*No! He's mine!*" With a cry of rage, Otha renewed his offensive, hacking and swinging with the anger-tempered training of one of the military elite. The combat zigzagged across the street as he relentlessly attacked, constantly forcing Everus back.

Curious faces appeared at doors and windows all around. There was nothing quite like good old fashioned bloodshed to draw the crowds.

Parrying an attack, Everus staggered back against a door which gave way under his plate-mailed weight. Crashing through into someone's living area, he withdrew up a flight of narrow wooden stairs, Otha storming through in pursuit.

Voices screamed from nearby rooms.

The sound of running footsteps echoed overhead.

Unable to effectively swing their weapons on the narrow staircase, both savagely hacked their way further up, the floor and walls taking the brunt of the punishment. Half-way up, Otha lost his footing and crashed back down, landing with a thump at the bottom.

At the top, Everus backed onto a landing of sorts. Rank-smelling corridors led further into the communal housing complex in many directions and from behind an open door an ugly woman's face peered out.

"Oi! In 'ere."

Dragging a wounded leg, Everus limped over. He needed somewhere to rest and get his breath back. Maybe if he could lie low for a moment he might be able to catch his enemy unawares. With a backward glance towards the stairs, he entered the room and pulled the door, leaving a crack through which he could see.

"Ye in trouble, mister?" croaked the crone.

"Shut up!"

"Ye can get out this window if ye..."

"I *said* shut up!" Everus could hear Otha's heavy tread as he climbed the stairs. Hardly breathing, he watched as the man reached the landing and started searching. To his dismay, he noticed the trail of blood on the floor which led to where he hid.

Otha approached.

"*Die!*" Everus flung the door wide and rushed out, hate burning in his green eyes. Throwing all his power into a mighty swing, he caught Otha off guard, knocking the shield out of his hand and cutting him deeply.

Otha cried out and retreated back, stumbling into another room, almost tripping over a terrified cat as it darted past.

Pressing the advantage, Everus forced Otha back. The room into which they went was small and empty, its wooden floor boards damp and rotting. They creaked ominously as the two fought.

Narrowly dodging one of Everus' swings, Otha chopped down, striking Everus a cutting blow on his right arm.

Everus' sword skidded from his grip. Disarmed, he had no alternative but to leap at Otha, his hands locking around his opponent's neck.

Both men crashed to the floor. There then followed a loud cracking as the timber boards splintered and gave way under the combined weight of the two bloody battlers. For the briefest of moments both were locked in an embrace as they plummeted to the storey below.

With a smash that sent dust into the air they hit the floor.

Plaster drizzled from the gaping ceiling as Everus, whose fall had been cushioned somewhat by landing on Otha, rolled to one side. Coughing, the wind knocked from him, he painfully got to his feet.

Otha lay on his back, dark blood dribbling from the corners of his mouth. He had landed particularly awkwardly, the fact that Everus had landed on him compounding the damage. It felt as though numerous bones had been broken but right now that was the least of his troubles. Feebly, he tried to reach for his battleaxe which lay nearby.

Everus stood on Otha's wrist, crunching it with his heel. "I wonder if you know how long I've been looking for you? Three years, maybe more."

Otha groaned and flapped like a stranded fish, glistening in his scuffed chain mail.

"Your wife destroyed everything that I had, everything that I was. Now, I expect you want *me*...to show you mercy?" Everus had to fight to get the words out, such was the pain. His right leg felt as though it was about to give way and the ache from his shoulder was agonising. Nonetheless, there were things that had to be said before he killed this man.

"Murdering...bastard. Get...it...over...with." Struggling to speak, Otha started to cough, blood spattering his face and armour.

Reaching down, Everus picked up the battleaxe. "You should be made to suffer first." With some effort, he raised the sharp-bladed weapon.

"I hope...one day...to see your...black heart...rot."

"You're too late for that." With a wet thud, Everus hacked down and severed Otha's right leg, just below the knee.

Otha screamed, his whole body going into a tortured convulsion.

Everus was about to hack again, this time perhaps lopping off an arm, when the pain he was feeling began to really bite. The battleaxe became heavy and red lights flashed before his eyes as blood loss began to take effect. Stumbling backwards, he fell through an open doorway, the calls and shouts of Otha's crossbow-armed friend growing louder. Aware that he was in no condition to confront another and that he had to escape, he dug deep into his reserves and started to crawl along a stinking passage, his body weakening all the time. Soon, he could go no further. With some relief, his mind darkened as he slipped into unconsciousness.

† † †

He sat in the small room, listening intently as the robed lecturer began an account of the fall of the ancient kingdom of Toth-Zhamma. From a crumbling book, the old scholar, dressed in a charcoal-grey robe, began to copy an almost indecipherable text onto the blackboard with a piece of chalk. Once complete, he began to point out some of the symbols, indicating their linguistic and historical significance. In a wavering voice, he went on, highlighting other aspects of the language before discussing the primitive background which set the foundations for the incipient kingdom.

The class went on for most of the day. At one stage the lecturer brought out some odd-looking stone artefacts, placing them with due care on the central table where the students could handle them.

When the class had finished and the lecturer had shuffled away, he gathered his books and copious notes together and headed for the small but comprehensive library which was annexed to the Ancient History department of The Academy, determined to conduct further research of his own. Entering, he sniffed deeply, relishing the smell of musty tomes and parchments. This was his favourite place, the tranquil setting of his surroundings a blissful panacea to his otherwise hectic scholastic life.

The knowledge gathered in a place like this was immeasurable and yet, more often than not, the library was empty. That suited him fine. He would spend day after day inside its book-lined confines, reading as much about the distant past as was humanly possible, his own understanding of ancient events growing with each book he studied. He had attained a high level of ability and possessed an unrivalled grasp of his subject, a feat which had been recognised by all of his tutors. In many of his small classes, it was he who could answer the questions posed whilst his peers stared dumbfounded into space. On numerous occasions he had even corrected his tutors.

Yet such a level of study came with a price.

For he displayed little to no interest in his fellow students, holding their ignorance in disdain. Many, he knew, were there simply because their rich parents had bought them their place, their own aptitude and zeal for the subject far inferior to his. He cursed them or ignored them, knowing that he had sacrificed much of his adolescence to be where he now was.

Buried in his tomes, his astute mind absorbed facts like a sponge. Dates and place names he could recall from memory instantaneously. The history of far off kingdoms and empires became his world, individuals who had died hundreds, if not

thousands, of years ago of greater importance to him than the living. He would become a high scholar, an expert in his field. It was his calling. His destiny. All that he had truly longed for...
A cold shadow fell about him, but when he looked up there was no one there. Then, as if from a great distance, he thought he heard a voice, faint and indistinct. A trickle of insidious laughter echoed from somewhere nearby, so real that he now sat up, peering into the deep shadows.

✝ ✝ ✝

"Everus! *Everus!*"

The dream, if that was what it was, was shaken from him. There was a voice, its sound familiar yet strangely uncomforting. He began to stir, the memories fading from his mind.

"Come on. Speak to me."

"What? Where...where am I? What happened?"

"Ye've got blood seepin' out o' ye! That bastard must've givin' ye a hearty beltin'."

His vision beginning to right itself, Everus looked up to see Creeps standing over him. Groggily, he began to take in his surroundings. He was lying propped in an open doorway in a filthy backstreet. Slowly the memory of the fight with Otha began to return. He remembered cutting off the bastard's leg and then crawling on his hands and knees through a tortuous warren of litter-strewn corridors before finally emerging into the open air. His recollection of anything much after dropping the battleaxe was hazy.

"Did ye get him?" Creeps asked, eagerly.

"*Who?* Otha?"

"Aye, that bastard. Well, did ye kill him?"

"No."

"*No?* But I thought the whole point was to spring his trap so as ye could..."

"Death would be too clean for the likes of him. It'll hurt him more knowing that I've survived his trap. That I've bettered him. Besides, he won't get far." Everus winced, both in pain and at the missed opportunity at finishing off one of the many he hated. He had to hope that maybe the bastard would bleed to death.

"Ye're a fool. Ye should've finished him when ye'd the chance."

"Whatever. Are you going to give me a hand or what?"

"Can ye stand?" Creeps asked, pipe in mouth.

By way of an answer, Everus painfully hauled himself to his feet.

"Right. Let's get out o' 'ere. Ye don't want to be around 'ere when it gets dark. That's when the real loonies come out."

CHAPTER THREE

Wyrm's Port played host to several markets; some permanent features, others little more than a disorderly collection of stalls and barrows. By far the largest and most exotic was the Buyer's Bazaar, a sprawling, bustling entrepôt located at the entrance to the North Gate Harbour. Close to the waterfront, it was a heaving place, where merchant ships from all around the empire shipped their weird and wonderful cargoes. These ranged from the mundane and the practical to the truly incredible – on one occasion, a specially chartered vessel from Ullerby, a port town across The Dark Sea, had delivered an entire temple for the inauguration of one of the early emperors.

Almost anything was up for sale and if it was not in stock then, if it was in demand, it soon would be. Trade restrictions were slack, almost to the point of being non-existent; the authorities keen to maintain the peace by giving the populace a free reign in commerce. And there certainly was an appetite for trade. Many of the wealthier citizens embraced such commercial diversity, realising its potential for enhancing their lives with foreign luxury and frequently illegal goods, or for simply lining their own pockets.

However, others, especially those who were forced to live nearby, came to resent the market, for it was invariably noisy and filled with the stink of the unfamiliar. Additionally, as a place where money constantly changed hands, it attracted thieves like...

"*Flies around shit!* Look at 'em! Actin' like they own the place," Creeps muttered darkly as he looked towards a gaggle of dark-skinned merchants from Uttapia who haggled and jostled around a stall selling various incenses. He had no fondness for foreigners, especially ones who let their camels and other pack animals crap all over the place. Besides, their prices were far too high, their merchandise frequently shoddy.

Lost in his own thoughts, Everus headed towards another stall, the various items of exotica on display catching his eye.

One of the vendors had obviously misinterpreted Creeps staring at them as a sign of interest. Dressed in a colourful yellow and turquoise gown and with a matching headdress, he sauntered over, a strange-looking box in his hands.

For a moment the thief considered turning away and melting back into the crowds. He changed his mind, intrigued as to what the foreigner had to offer. It might be a free sample of pipeweed for all he knew.

"Greetings, good friend." With a pearly grin, the merchant bowed, his words heavily accented. It was obvious the imperial language was hard for him.

"Hurry it up. I haven't got all day."

"Pure ebony. Nice, yes?" Still grinning, the man held the box before him, stroking it as though it were a prized cat. "Eight hundred gold."

"Ye're takin' the piss?"

"Seven fifty."

"I don't want it. Now go away."

"I know. I give for six hundred. Good price." The merchant opened the box to reveal its red velvet lining, presenting it to the thief to handle.

Creeps appraised the box anew. It certainly did look expensive and it was of a high standard of craftsmanship, unlike some of the other rubbish the Uttapians normally foisted on others. It felt nice as well. "What is it? Is it magic?"

"Oh yes! Very magic."

"What's it do?"

"Djinn box. Great spirit inside." Furtively, the seller looked around as though half-expecting something unearthly to come tearing through the crowds towards him.

"An' ye've just let it out? Ye daft bugger." Creeps laughed derisively.

"No, my friend." The colourful man shook his head. "Magic word needed to free djinn."

"An' what's the word?"

The Uttapian chortled. "I cannot say. Djinn will be free if I tell."

Puzzled, Creeps stared for a moment at the box before turning to the merchant. He shook his head and handed it back. "No. Changed ma mind. Ye keep it."

"Please. Five hundred. You give and it's yours." Almost pleading now, the merchant's eyes widened to resemble fried eggs.

"No. Go away!" Creeps looked over his shoulder to try and see

41

where Everus had disappeared to.

The Uttapian reached into a pocket and drew out a small, carved, ivory rhinoceros. "Four hundred and I give this too."

"Bugger off!" Agitated, Creeps pushed the man aside, still unable to locate his companion. People clamoured all around as he battled his way through the crowds, heading in the direction he thought Everus had taken. On many occasions he saw the opportunity for a little pick-pocketing but he resisted the temptation, rarely stooping to such petty larceny. Breaking free of the throng, he came to an open square where a troupe of acrobatic fire-eaters, dressed in red leather leotards, were entertaining the buyers as well as clearly trying to draw attention to a covered wagon from which various smoking potions were on sale.

Over to one side, another group of spectators clapped and cheered.

Creeps headed over, curious to see what was going on. Jostling to the front, and drawing more than a few protests, he could see a small, sunken arena. A clearly ill-treated bear, about his size and covered in brown fur was being poked and stabbed by three loin-clothed grubbas armed with wooden spears, a look of annoyance on its grizzled face.

"Ah...my friend."

A hand clamped down on his right shoulder and Creeps turned. Surprised to see the persistent merchant, he shook himself from the man's hold.

"Two hundred."

"Listen pal. Get that box out o' ma face afore I stuff it someplace even a djinn wouldn't get out o'! Now piss off!"

"But..."

Pushing the man aside, Creeps fought his way through the crowd and across the market square. It was only then that he saw the tall and imposing figure of Everus standing by one of the stalls up ahead. Quickly, he rushed over.

"There you are!"

Creeps brushed his jacket down. "Aye, now what?"

Everus took his gaze from the thief and stared intently at a rotund man who was selling home-grown vegetables, imported bananas from Umm-Dabba and a variety of worthless knick-knacks. "We wait."

† † †

"A little more testing, this next one," said Dae'morogin, reaching into a strange-looking cabinet and removing a battered scrollcase. He turned round and took his seat before opening the scrollcase and unrolling a tattered sheet of parchment. He examined it briefly, checking to make sure it was what he thought it was before rolling it back into its tube. "Now, I'm right in assuming that you've never been outside the city, am I not?"

"I've been outside once. Many years ago," answered Everus, flatly. "I accompanied my father on a trip to Trade Peak when I was young."

Dae'morogin nodded. "Then you'll need this. It's a map showing the south road from here to Ghavin's Keep. Although the road is easy to follow, I think it wise that you take it." He paused just as he was about to hand the tube over, his eyes narrowing. "Did our merchant friend *suffer?*"

"Alas no. I had to make it quick. There were many witnesses." Less than a day had passed since the cold-blooded slaying of the street vendor. In Everus' mind, the murder, the way he had just casually walked up behind the grocer and cut him down, seemed to dominate all his other thoughts. The act had replayed itself all afternoon; slashing the man, the merchant stumbling onto his stall, slashing again and again and again. Blood spraying. People screaming. Creeps shouting, distracting the summoned militia men.

Dae'morogin presented Everus with a reassuring smile. "Not to worry. What matters is that the deed is done." He noted his assassin's distant look. "Everus!"

"Yes?"

"Are you all right, my friend?"

"Yes. I...think so."

"Are you sure?" asked the high priest with some measure of concern. "Are you fully healed after your encounter with your Watchful Eye friend?"

Everus nodded.

"Very well then. As I was saying, this next one is a little more challenging. However, I'm sure that you'll find it more in line with your abilities."

"Who is it this time?"

"Tobias," answered Dae'morogin, spitting out the name as though it befouled his mouth. "Sacrosanct Tobias. He's one of

Utterance's Twelve, so getting close to him may prove problematic, but I've heard that there will be a religious procession through Ghavin's Keep in a few days' time. However you choose to do it, I need him dead before the blooding of the first moon, so you should leave as soon as you're ready."

✝ ✝ ✝

Everus paced over to the great South Gate, eyes focused on the small detachment of armed soldiers who sat outside a stone guardhouse. With the thief at his side, he walked right up to the gate itself, studying the huge portcullis and the thick wooden doors beyond. It was a formidable work of defence, no doubt about it, and one that had seen some recent repair, judging from the various patch-ups visible.

Two of the guards came over, clearly intrigued as to what they were up to.

"Raise the gate," said Everus, turning to face them.

"Ye what?" asked one of them, gripping his halberd a little tighter. The fact that Everus carried his sword on his back and looked more than a little dangerous was somewhat intimidating.

"I said, raise the gate. We need to get out."

"Why? On who's orders, citizen?" inquired the second guard.

"On my orders."

"An' who're ye?"

"That's not your concern. Just open the gate."

"*Max! Shaun!* What's goin' on 'ere?" barked a third guard, emerging from the barracks. Dressed in chain mail and proudly displaying the imperial city's insignia – a rearing black wyrm on a pale blue background – on his surcoat, he walked over. There were few in the Wyrm's Port militia whom one could consider intelligent, and those who had been assigned gate duty were generally the thickest to don the livery of the imperial army. He was no exception. "These guys aren't stirrin' up any shit are they? I can't be doin' wi' that at this time o' day."

"Seems these two fellas want us to raise the gate," replied the guard called Shaun.

"Do they now?" The sergeant sauntered right up to Everus, the sway in his walk and the reek on his breath a sure sign that he had been drinking. "What're ye wantin' outside, pal? There's nothin' out there." He belched, wafting the fouled air aside with one hand. "Nothin' but…"

"Myself and my companion have some business that requires immediate attention," Everus interrupted, impassively.

"An' just where are ye an' yer pal headed?" the sergeant slurred.

"South. Towards Ghavin's Keep."

The man nodded. "I see. Wyrm's Port not good enough for ye?" He looked up, sobering slightly as a more thoughtful look crossed his face. "Can't say as I blame ye though. This city's a shit-hole. Ye take it from me." Unsteadily, he stumbled back a step.

"So, will you raise the gate?"

"Don't see why not. Ye realise that our laws don't extend outside though? Ye'll be on yer own on the other side o' those doors." The sergeant shifted his buttocks in order to release a squeaky-sounding fart. "Then there's just the matter o' a small donation to our drinkin' fund. Just a small one. A little summat for the good old guards o' the South Gate." He turned round and drunkenly saluted the two other guards. One laughed and returned the salute.

"But of course." Everus reached into a pouch. "How much? Ten gold?"

"Oh, ye're a pal." The sergeant took the money, his face lighting up. After counting the coins in the palm of his hand, he thumbed to the others to get the gate open. "Come on! Shift yer arses! These men want out."

Everus stepped to one side, waiting as the guards set about raising the portcullis and then opening the doors. It was a noisy affair and he could not help but notice, with perverse amusement, the somewhat guilty look on the sergeant's face as he nervously waited for the doors to open. It was obvious he did not want one of his superiors to turn up and find out about his actions. Questions would be asked, and whilst drinking was acceptable, taking bribes could lead to an instant demotion.

"All right," said the sergeant when the doors were opened. "Off ye go. Be quick about it."

Staring with wide eyes, Everus took in the sheer vastness of the panorama before him. He had been beyond the city gates only once before and he had been young at the time, unable to fully appreciate the stark contrast between the myriad shades of the landscape and the urbanised greyness of the city.

Together they set off, the sense of wonder on Creeps' face in many ways mirroring that of Everus.

The city doors slammed closed behind them, the portcullis clanging with the finality of a guillotine blade.

Creeps turned upon hearing the sound. For a moment, he stared at the doors before turning to Everus. "Do ye think they'll let us back in...ye know, when we come back?"

"Me, yes. You...well, I wouldn't count on it. Come on, let's get going." Plunging his hands into the pockets of the long, dark grey coat he wore, Everus turned his back on the city that was his home and marched off. Under his coat, he wore a suit of studded leather armour, his legs covered by a pair of dark trousers. Around his neck, a long, black, woollen scarf was wound, its ends fluttering like the pennants on the battlements high above. His calf-length boots crunched the dead leaves and loose gravel that covered the road.

The morning was crisp and bright, yet a biting wind swept across the barren plain which lay to the south of Wyrm's Port.

Every so often Everus would turn and look back at the walled city which now dominated much of the northern horizon, the coast line of The Dark Sea just beyond. To the east, he could see the low, grey foothills of The Deadmoor Clumps, the nearest of which had to be a good twelve leagues distant. Both to the west and to the south, the terrain retained its uniform flatness, broken in but a few places by some lone hillock or patch of trees. Like a river of stone, the road wound across the plain before them.

After hiking to the top of a small wooded rise, Everus called a halt so that he could consult the map for, although it was pretty clear which direction to follow, he had no desire to wander off the track.

"We lost already?" Creeps asked, rubbing his hands and taking in the view.

"Do you want to lead?" snapped Everus.

"*Me?* No, I don't want to. I'm more at home in streets an' alleys."

"Have you in fact ever been outside the city?"

"No' as such," said Creeps, evasively.

"Then shut up and let me lead." From their raised vantage point, Everus looked out, intrigued to notice the transformation of the landscape as patches of light and dark, created from the clouds' shadows, danced over it. Looking skywards, back the way they had come, he watched as a phalanx of very large birds soared off into the distance.

"It's gettin' a bit chilly."

"It'll get colder. Come on."

They followed the road as it wound its way down, the trees now thinning out. With the low sun directly behind them they walked on, each aware of the incongruity of their long shadows. Whereas Everus' shadow seemed grim and forceful, accentuated as it was by the long trailing scarf and the protruding hilt of his sword above his left shoulder, Creeps' shadow appeared hunched and distinctly disreputable.

As Everus walked, he began to notice that, perhaps due to some strange trick of the light, Creeps' shadow appeared slightly darker than his own.

✝ ✝ ✝

The two travellers had been going for almost half a day when the road they were following started to become noticeably muddier. The sun retreated behind a wall of clouds which had blown over from the north and the chill wind had picked up in strength, carrying with it the faint tang of the sea, now several leagues behind them.

They followed the road into a small forest.

Stunted trees grew on either side, their lofty branches warped and leafless. In many places some had fallen; bloated fungi clinging to hollow trunks in which wildlife lurked and rummaged. A dense bed of leaves and fallen twigs obscured parts of the road.

As they progressed, an eerie hush seemed to fall about them.

The wind dropped.

There was a thorny twig in one of Creeps' shoes and the discomfort it was causing meant that he just had to stop and get it out. He had hoped to walk on, to at least get clear of this creepy copse, but it was becoming unbearable. Besides, he reckoned he could probably run faster if it was removed. Resting his foot on a rotting tree stump, its rings faded with age, he unlaced his shoe, picked the twig free and was about to slip it back on when a sudden hiss from above brought him to a standstill. After a moment of intense listening, he speedily laced his shoe and ran to catch up with Everus.

Everus turned on hearing the approaching thief.

"Do ye get rats out 'ere?" Wildly staring in the growing gloom, Creeps looked about, his dagger already drawn.

"So, you've seen them, too?"

"Aye. Saw one o' the little buggers scamper up a tree back there."

"And what if I told you that they're not rats?" Everus asked, keeping up his steady pace, his eyes staring fixedly ahead.

"No' rats? What're they then?"

"Death squirrels."

"Are they dangerous?"

Creeps' question was answered as they turned a bend in the road. Less than a stone's throw from where they stood a pack of ravenous, night-black squirrels feasted on the remains of some lone wanderer, probably a peddler, his wares, like his insides, now lying scattered about him. Twenty or so of the cat-sized rodents tore long strands of flesh and clothing from the unfortunate, occasionally breaking off to fight for the bloody morsels amongst themselves. Then, as one, the creatures looked up and stared at the two men with their malevolent, red eyes.

Everus unsheathed his sword.

"Can we no' go round 'em?" whispered Creeps.

"It'd do no good. They know we're here."

Screeching, four of the squirrels broke off from the badly chewed corpse and scampered towards them. Everus moved to meet them, kicking one high into the air and slashing another in half. Of the remaining two, one scurried up his body and narrowly missed biting his face whilst the other bounded past and went for Creeps.

Everus pulled the squirrel off him by its dung-stiffened tail. The rodent repeatedly tried to bite his hand as he swung it around before whirling it into the undergrowth.

Like a dark tide, the main swarm rushed towards him, blood and gore dribbling from their chisel-edged incisors.

With a cry to his dark god, Everus waded into the chittering horde, slashing and hacking with abandon. Small black bodies were sent flying only to be replaced by more, their numbers bolstered by a cascade of squirrels from above. Dodging and twisting, he dispatched many that sought to climb up his legs and body. Numerous others on the ground bit at his boots, ripping and scratching their way to the flesh beneath. Dirty fur flashed before his face.

"*Bugger this!* Let's get out o' 'ere!" cried Creeps as three more leapt at him. He let out a loud scream as part of his right ear was torn free and greedily gobbled. "I'm bein' eaten alive!"

Grinding a squirrel's head into the muddy ground with the heel of his boot, Everus turned briefly to see the thief hold one of them aloft before gutting it with his dagger. Nearly slipping, he fought to disentangle himself from three others which had dropped from the branches overhead.

All around the darkening wood there was movement. Shadows darted up trees, bounding along overhanging boughs. What seemed like hundreds of small red eyes hungrily watched and waited in the bushes and tree tops. Many small shapes darted along the ground.

"*Creeps!* Your torches!" cried Everus, tearing a large rodent free and pounding it twice against the trunk of a tree before dropping its lifeless body. "Get a bloody torch lit!" Crashing through the undergrowth, he sprinted towards the thief, two squirrels clinging to his back. His body wept blood from over a dozen small bites but his coat and armour had saved him from any serious injury. Leaping agilely over a fallen log, he shook off his two attackers.

"*Everus! Help me!*" cried Creeps, blood flowing down the side of his face. "I've got one in ma crackers! It's snappin' at ma bollocks!" He fell backwards over a loose branch and went down, crashing and spinning through a dense growth of ferns. Cursing, he scrambled to his feet using his heavy pack to bludgeon anything that came near.

Slashing savagely, Everus leapt towards the thief, booting another squirrel and breaking its neck. "*Get a torch lit!*" Looking up, he saw a fresh host of the rat-like creatures edging towards them, their beady eyes filled with bloodlust. With a cry, he ran towards them, hoping to give his companion enough time to follow his order, knowing that only fire would keep these bastards at bay.

Blood-crazed beyond normal animal aggression, the dark shapes came leaping towards them, screeching as they came.

Hacking and chopping, Everus stood his ground, blood now leaking from two nasty bites on his left arm and a claw mark on his throat. Still he rained down the attacks…and still the vermin came. By the time the thief had lit a torch, nigh on thirty black furry bodies lay scattered around Everus. Most were dead. Some still twitched. Several others clung to him or else darted madly around his legs, nipping and scratching.

"*Go on! Away wi' ye!*" Creeps dived at the undulating dark mass, flailing his blazing torch from side to side.

The squirrels withdrew from the brandished flame, leaping for the tree cover.

Everus had clamped one to the ground by standing on its tail. He looked down at the squirming creature before mercilessly driving his sword through its body. He turned to Creeps, the skewered thing still writhing on his sword. "Fancy one for supper?"

"Ye what?"

"Never mind." With a flick of his blade, Everus catapulted the squirrel into the darkness. "By the way, you've got a load of squirrel shit on your back...and in your hair."

Cursing, Creeps brushed himself down.

More things were rustling in the bushes, things which sounded a good deal larger than the vicious animals they had just encountered. It was high time to get out of here and both knew it.

The copse before them seemed to be reaching its end, the final line of trees standing stark and wind-blown against the dark horizon. Marching quickly, both now carrying flaming torches, they reached the outer edge of trees and started down a decline. They marched on, keen to put as much distance between themselves and the death squirrel-infested wood as possible before the failing daylight forced them to halt.

Everus chose to camp that night in a small hollow to the side of the road and as Creeps busied himself making a campfire, he rummaged about in the thief's pack, removing crumpled articles of clothing. Pulling out a packet of coiled linen, he began to tear bandage strips from it. From an inner coat pocket, he took out a small vial of clear liquid which he had obtained from high priest Dae'morogin. Dabbing the liquid onto the linen, he then started to apply the bandage strips to the numerous small bites and grazes he had received.

"What's that?" asked Creeps, looking over from the unlit bundle of firewood.

"It's for the bites. I'd use some if I were you."

"Aye, right ye are. Don't want to get the pox now do we? I'll just get the fire goin' an' I'll be right wi' ye."

Everus continued dabbing at his wounds, wrapping a bandage around his right hand.

Creeps sat down, having lit the fire. "Were they bastards poisonous?"

"Not as far as I know. But who knows what diseases they could carry? The Dark Rot, perhaps?"

"*The Dark Rot?* What's that?"

"Very nasty. Within a couple of days you'd be reduced to nothing more than a blackened husk. For you, that may be an improvement."

Emitting a belch, Creeps walked over to where Everus sat. "I suppose ye'd better give me some o' that stuff." When he had received it, he began to treat his bites. His right ear and most of his right arm had been badly gnawed and he winced as the liquid stung his wounds.

Looking towards the night sky, Everus searched in vain for any stars. Two of the world's moons shone full and yellow from behind wispy clouds, the third still shrouded in darkness. There were only a few days left to complete his task, Ghavin's Keep still many leagues away.

"*Shit on me!*" Creeps had unrolled one of the food parcels they had brought with them. "*Bastards!* Everus, they're away wi' half our grub!"

Everus gave a disgruntled sigh and walked over to inspect the damage. Of the four food parcels they had brought with them only one seemed untouched. The three others had been ransacked and all that remained had been bitten and soiled.

"*Bleedin' little bastards!*" Creeps shouted, shaking a scrawny fist at the sky, his face livid.

"Let's divide what remains for tonight. Tomorrow we'll have to go without and if all goes well we should reach Ghavin's Keep the day after." Everus sat down on the ground and started to portion out the contents from the untouched packet. He was halfway through sorting what was salvageable from the other packs when Creeps let out another anguished cry.

"*Bastards!*"

"What now?"

"They've nicked ma bloody pipe!"

Well, that was a bonus, an evening without shit-stinking smoke. Despite the pain from the bites, Everus laughed before biting into a small chicken leg.

† † †

Everus awoke to the noise of Creeps rattling a fork in a tin cup close to his face.

"Wakey, wakey."

"Shut up, or I'll kill you."

Ignoring Everus' frosty salutation, Creeps started to pack up all of their camping gear. He squatted down in order to start fastening his pack. "Come on, up ye get. The sooner we get to this place the sooner I can get ma smoke."

Scrambling to his feet, Everus yawned and took in their immediate surroundings. It had been almost pitch dark when he had chosen this site and now, as he looked about, he saw just how open it really was, the road no more than a dozen paces away. They had been fortuitous in the extreme not to have been woken by something unsavoury during the night.

"Looks like it might be a nice day," said Creeps, hoisting the pack onto his back. "Cold though."

Everus stretched, a mild ache in his right shoulder. "Did you sleep?"

"Did I buggery. Kept hearin' things movin' about. Thought it might've been them scabby what-do-ye-call-'ems."

"Death squirrels."

"Bastard things. I'll come wi' ma traps next time an' kill 'em all. I'll set fire to their trees. That'll teach 'em for takin' ma ear." Deeply motivated by his need for a smoke, the thief was eager to get going and jiggled impatiently while Everus prepared to leave.

Everus absently brushed a coating of frost from his coat and tightened his scarf around his mouth. Checking he had all his belongings, especially the map, he strode off along the road.

The landscape around them retained its bleak uniformity, the moorland before them grey and largely featureless. In places along the road grew twisted, bramble-like vegetation, its thorns cruel and sharp. Within some of the denser patches, they saw clusters of bones, the remains of small mammals which had either ventured, or had perhaps been snatched, therein. The way in which some of the spiky growths shook and rustled as either of them neared led Everus to believe the latter.

As the day wore on, Everus was once more intrigued by the strange appearance of his companion's shadow. He was now convinced that Creeps' shadow was, albeit almost imperceptibly, darker than that of his own. He toyed with the idea of asking the thief about it, deciding in the end to keep the discovery to himself.

Contrary to what Everus had said the previous day, they did manage to find time to take a short stop and to finish off the remnants of their remaining food parcel. It had passed mid-day and following the pattern of the day before, the weather looked as though it was on the turn once more. Grey clouds, undoubtedly laden with rain or possibly snow, scudded from the north, the wind gusting heavily across the exposed barrens.

Creeps returned from taking a shit, crumbs of dry leaf, glued to his filthy underpants, making walking uncomfortable. "Everus! There's folk comin' along the road."

"What!?" Standing up, Everus corked his water bottle. "Where?"

"Ye see 'em?" Creeps pointed towards the far horizon at a barely visible line of movement about a league away.

"Hmm. They're probably merchants out of Ghavin's Keep... heading towards Wyrm's Port."

"What do ye think? Do ye think we should try an' avoid 'em?" Eyes fixed on the distant line of people, the thief ran a dirty hand through his scruffy hair.

"No. I don't see why we should." Everus set out, his face set in a grim scowl. If they wanted trouble, he was only too happy to provide it.

Soon after, both travellers could see a column of at least a hundred individuals wending their way towards them along the road. Several drab wagons were also visible as well as at least six outriders.

"I'll do the talking, if any is needed," Everus said.

Creeps nodded in agreement.

As both groups neared, one of the riders broke away from the caravan and rode towards them, dust billowing under the horse's hooves. The rider, a stern-faced yet youthful woman drew her horse to a halt not far from them. She was dressed in a suit of studded leather armour and had a short, recurve bow on her back as well as a quiver filled with arrows. In her right hand she carried a spear.

Everus' eyes narrowed.

"Hail travellers! My name is Caerwen," the young woman announced. Her brown hair was long and braided. Her eyes were cold and blue. "I'm lead bodyguard of this group of pilgrims from Ghavin's Keep, headed for Araan's Pillar. What's your purpose?"

"Just road weary travellers bound for Ghavin's Keep," replied Everus.

"I see. Is there any way in which we may aid you? For you both appear injured." Caerwen stared openly at the visible bandages on both men, her gaze flinching slightly as it passed over the thief. "What can I offer?"

Everus would not have refused the offer of sharing a hot tub with her. Stroking his unshaven chin, he sized her up, liking what he saw, from the long sweep of her thighs to the full curves of her breasts. A darkness then crept into his mind and he remembered what he had been sent to do. "How far is it to Ghavin's Keep? We had hoped to reach it before nightfall."

"The city is a good six, maybe seven leagues from here."

"Then I guess we should get going." Taking his gaze from her, Everus turned his stare to the wilderness before him.

"Before we part company," Caerwen began. "I should warn you that we sighted a couple of bagh'arulks away to the south. They thought better about tackling our group, but two wayfarers...?"

"We'll look out for them."

Caerwen gave a curt nod and backed her horse up a little. "Then I wish you good fortune and hope that you reach the city safely." She started to ride back to the approaching column.

"*Missus!*" cried Creeps. "Do any o' yer folk puff?"

The rider brought the horse round to face them, confusion visible on her face. "*What?*"

"Ye know," said Creeps, hopefully. "Do any o' yer pilgrim chappies have a spare pipe? I'll pay for it."

Caerwen laughed. "I'd doubt it. They're ascetics. Most of them hardly eat."

"Eh? Hardly eat? Well...what about yersel' missus? Do ye like a wee sly puff now an' then?" Creeps took a step forward, puffing on a pretend pipe. "Ye look like the kind."

Everus gave the thief a push, causing him to stumble and trip over, landing with a curse on the muddy road. Apologetically, he turned to the woman. "Never mind him."

With an offended snort, Caerwen turned and rode off.

Throwing a dark look at Everus, the thief got to his feet.

Together they marched on, aware of the strange stares that were thrown their way as the first of the ox-drawn wagons passed. Many of the travellers were dressed in pale white robes and wore small talismans and symbols promoting their various faiths. Parents were accompanied by their children and their pets. What looked like all of their household goods were flung on the wagons, making it look more like an exodus than a pilgrimage. They looked a cold and sombre lot. Apart from a dark-haired, mischievously grinning boy of about five years who was perched at the back of the last wagon to pass by, there was not a single smiling face amongst them.

The kid gave Everus an unnerving wave.

It was only after they had gone their separate ways that Everus cursed himself for not asking for some rations. It was getting cold and there was now no food left, not even crumbs. Looking about, he wondered for a moment how effective they would be at foraging from the landscape. He certainly had no skill in hunting, or for that matter any knowledge of what plants were edible, and he doubted his companion had either. Now, if it had been scavenging through alleys...

"Where'd that bint say them folk were goin'?"

"Araan's Pillar."

"What's that?"

"It's a mysterious obelisk that was built during the second reign of Wyrmius," Everus answered. He stopped in order to tie a boot lace. "Two thousand, four hundred and forty-six years ago. If one goes by the current imperial calendar."

"Some time back, that." Creeps paused, waiting for Everus to complete his lacing. "Whereabouts is it?" Although he did not sound particularly interested, he seemed to have reached the conclusion that conversation eased the journey.

"From here, I would say it's some fifteen leagues to the west. Though, having never been, I've no idea what state it's now in."

"An' what about them...things, she was on about?"

"The bagh'arulks?"

"Aye. What're they?"

"Large, primitive carnivores. Man-like, though much bigger. Savages. Think of *your* worst neighbour, then double his size."

"*Scary.* Ma worst neighbour that is. There's a man at the end o' ma street who runs about the back alleys naked. He's been known to howl out o' his window an' I'm sure he eats folk. I'm sure o' it. I mean, it's all right crappin' out yer window, but howlin'? That's no' human. Neither's eatin' folk, I suppose. It's true though."

"I can believe it."

"Anyhow, these...*things* sound like the kind o' thing I don't want to run into out 'ere in the middle o' nowhere."

"Nor I," Everus replied. "I think that if we put on some speed we can yet reach Ghavin's Keep this night. So shut up and walk."

The two men trudged on through the cold wilderness as all around, darkness slowly began to envelop them. Everus wrapped his scarf around his mouth and shoved his hands deep into the pockets of his long coat, nestling them there like hibernating creatures.

As the night wore on the snow began to fall more heavily, the road now illuminated by the two bright and icy moons.

"I'm freezin'," Creeps muttered, flexing his fingers and puffing out a trail of wispy breath. "I'm colder than a lawyer's codpiece an' I feel as though ma bones have turned to stone."

Everus nodded with feigned sympathy. "Keep walking."

Head down, Creeps trudged on, each step now painful.

The going was becoming hard for them both, neither used to walking great distances, their lives spent within a city where every destination was relatively close. How far they had already walked this day neither knew, the long and lonely leagues dragging lugubriously.

✝ ✝ ✝

It was not until well past midnight that they saw, up ahead, the torch-lit entrance to Ghavin's Keep.

Everus let out a pained cry of relief. He ached from head to foot and his hair was sodden with snow. Beside him, Creeps was near collapse. The straps from the pack he had been carrying had bitten into the tender flesh around his shoulders and for the past league or so he had done nothing but moan about how he had lost all feeling in his fingers and toes.

As the two staggered through the ankle-deep snow they saw shadows moving in the great archway beyond a portcullis.

"Open up and let us in!" shouted Everus.

Three obviously surprised gate guards answered his call and came to the gate.

"You must let us in. We're weary pilgrims."

"Ye look more like bandits to me," sneered one of the guards, a crossbow in his hands. "An' we don't like bandits prowlin' around our city."

"What happened to ye?" inquired another, his tone more placatory.

"We're the only survivors of the pilgrimage to Araan's Pillar. We were attacked by bagh'arulks on the road some eight leagues north."

"The pilgrims have been attacked!?" responded one of the guards with alarm.

"Yes. We ran and ran through the night. My friend will surely die if I don't get him to a temple healer." Everus gestured towards the limp and exhausted thief.

Through eyes that he could barely keep open, Creeps looked up and did not have to pretend to be close to death. He slumped. His legs felt dead and leaden and it seemed as though each finger had become like ice, ready to snap off at the gentlest touch.

"Quick! Raise the gate!" shouted one of the guards.

When the portcullis was half raised, Everus and Creeps ducked under it and stumbled into the city, footsore and frozen.

CHAPTER FOUR

Buckling on his armour, Everus cast a disapproving look at his surroundings, thankful at least to have had a fairly decent night's sleep. The inn room was not large, containing just a low bunk against one wall, a chair and a small chest of drawers, making it appear almost cell-like. Even the only window had a grille of metal bars set into it, through which came the late morning coolness and the sounds of the city outside. The carpet was torn and stained, and he could not help but feel that something bad had happened in this room some time ago. Probably a murder, if the stains were what he thought they were. He heard the sound of footsteps in the corridor outside, someone approaching his door.

There came a knock.

"Ye in?"

Everus paced over and unlocked the door. "What is it?"

"Summat I think ye'd best know." Scratching his head, Creeps edged his way inside. He had not bothered to get undressed when he had gone to sleep and as a result his clothes were heavily crumpled and smelled. He yawned and rubbed his bleary eyes.

"Well? Get on with it."

"That religious thing ye were on about, ye know, the procession or whatever it is...accordin' to the barman, it's been brought forward to today."

"*Today?*"

"Aye...seems as though there's been some kind o' blunder wi' their dates or summat."

"*Shit!* That's all we need." With an increased sense of urgency, Everus removed his sword from where it hung over the back of the chair and strapped it on his back. "Did he say anything else?"

"No' much. Just that there's goin' to be a lot o' people there. Seems that these priestly nutters attract quite a crowd. They've been known to give out free food an' things like that, so I'd imagine all the beggars an' the like'll be there." The thief grinned. "So..."

"So...what you're saying is, I should throw on an old cloak, cover myself in dung and stumble out into the path of the procession? Then, I'd have to get close enough to Tobias, fight my way through a cohort of temple guards, kill him and battle my way back through the crowd. Sounds easy, doesn't it?"

"Aye. That's the way to go about it. I could help ye get done up. Ye'd make the best beggar in the city. Nob'dy'd see through the disguise."

"You talk some shit, don't you?" Raising his eyes to the ceiling, Everus thought through the different options available to them. The fact that the procession had been brought forward to today meant that there was no real time to prepare, not that he had ever had any clear plan of how to execute this particular assassination. A direct assault on the cathedral where Tobias worked was not a feasible option for it was as secure as the imperial palaces, or so he had heard. For the same reason, a break-in was not viable either or, at the very least, it would be fraught with danger. His thoughts turned to the possibility of having Creeps create some kind of diversion whilst he singled out Tobias. Yet even that was highly risky. After a few moments, he went and sat on his bunk, ruminating.

† † †

People lined the street on either side, faces smiling in anticipation of the forthcoming procession. Most of the snow had now thawed, patches of slush and dripping icicles the only signs of yesterday's freeze. It was still cold though. The relatively good weather and the fact that this was a public holiday for all but essential workers in Ghavin's Keep, contributed to the exceptionally high turnout. The crowds pulsed like a single, raucous creature as the forerunners of the parade whipped them into a state of near-frenzy by cavorting, shouting and throwing food, brightly coloured pamphlets and streamers into the air. The crowd cried out, those able to read intoning the prayers which had been distributed. Others just made any noise which sounded good.

Suddenly a great cheer went up.

Around the corner, the first section of the religious congregation came into view. Flanked on either side by a retinue of temple spearmen, acolytes garbed in robes of various hues of ochre and rattling tambourines walked down the middle of the street, never raising their gaze from the cobbles. Some fifty passed before another part of the parade appeared, this one comprising of solemn, bald-headed monks dressed in purple cassocks. Each held aloft a standard from which a flag fluttered; the trefoil symbol of the three-headed creator god, known collectively as The High Three, emblazoned thereon.

In direct contrast to those who had gone before, a trio of painted drummers, dressed in wild animal skins, then sprang into sight. They beat their drums in a chaotic fashion, pausing every now and then to emit a screeching howl that was answered by many of the spectators.

"What a group o' nummies," commented Creeps to Everus as they watched the proceedings from their third storey vantage point in an abandoned house. "They'll be bringin' out the flatulents next."

His face largely concealed by his wrapped scarf, Everus gave Creeps a confused stare.

"Ye know, those nummies who whip 'emselves raw."

"You mean flagellants," Everus corrected.

"That's what I said."

After the drummers had done their bit, a group of twenty or so attractive women came into view. Each was dressed in a diaphanous gown of shimmering gold silk and each carried a small brass cage in which a peculiar blue bird with bright orange plumage was held. Behind them, standing upright in a golden chariot drawn by two large, hawk-headed, lion-like creatures, came high priest Utterance IV, resplendent in the trappings of the sacerdotal elite.

To either side of the great chariot walked a dozen other priests in turquoise robes. One of their number was Sacrosanct Tobias, his jet black hair and boyish features clearly singling him out.

"Blessed are the meek...for they make easy targets," whispered Everus, squinting down the line of the crossbow that he held tightly in his hands and tracking Utterance's every move. Despite the fact that the high priest was not his intended target, he gloried in the surge of power he now felt, realising that with one squeeze of the trigger he could plunge the entire region into chaos. Sanctimonious piece of filth, he thought.

Creeps laid a black cloth with five crossbow bolts on a stand close by, their tips glistening with the viscous toxin with which he had skilfully coated them.

Everus watched as Utterance began waving to the crowds, blessing them in a liturgical language most had probably never heard before.

The twelve clerics in the turquoise robes held their hands aloft, swirling clouds of magic, changing the very air into bread and fruit, which they then set about distributing to the clamouring populace. The temple men-at-arms did their best to keep the crowd in check.

"Come on you bastard," Everus muttered to himself, annoyed as Tobias temporarily disappeared behind a member of the crowd. A bead of sweat dripped into his eye, momentarily blinding him. He cursed to himself and wiped the sweat away. Realising that he had to act quickly or else the chance would be lost, he aimed and squeezed the trigger. The bolt whistled down and sparked off the cobbles as he instinctively pulled back from the window. He grabbed a second bolt, carefully avoiding the poisoned tip and reloaded.

"Ye missed?"

With baited breath, Everus peered out of the window. He was surprised and relieved to see that the procession went on, the clerics and the soldiers oblivious to his assassination attempt. His target had moved further away though.

"Ye'd better be quick," hissed Creeps, peering out.

"Got you this time." Everus took aim and shot.

With a twang, the bolt sprang from the crossbow and zipped down. It thudded into the leg of one of the men in the crowd who had suddenly made a move towards Tobias. With a cry of pain, he fell to the ground, the child he had hoisted on his shoulders rolling to the cobbles directly towards the wheels of Utterance's chariot.

The two creatures reared up.

Shouts and screams erupted as panic broke out. People began to fight to get away, many unsure as to what had happened, but scared nevertheless. The soldiers looked just as confused.

Hurriedly, Creeps passed Everus another bolt.

Everus leapt to the window, the loaded crossbow in his hands. "*For Xethorn!*" he shouted.

Some in the crowd looked up as he randomly swung the weapon around, as though searching for a viable target. Many ran. Others stood transfixed with fear, staring wide-eyed at the masked, dark-haired man who held death in his hands.

Many of the clergy had scattered, including the high priest, his chariot rattling away down the street. Of his 'Twelve', Everus was only concentrated on Tobias, who now knelt, sacrificing his own safety, in order to assist the unfortunate who lay wounded with the bolt in his leg. With his keen eyesight, Everus could see that the poison was already taking an effect, for the man convulsed and bubbled, black froth dribbling from his mouth.

Everus shot a third time.

Perhaps the kneeling Tobias heard the approaching quarrel, for he half turned just before it struck him in the throat. He raised his hands to his neck and keeled over. Gargling blood, he fell atop the other victim.

"Got the bastard!" Everus threw the crossbow to the floor.

"Right! Let's get out o' 'ere," said Creeps, already at the door. "Out along this corridor and then out that back window. Let's move it afore this place is swarmin' wi' guards."

✝ ✝ ✝

The following morning was bright and clear, though very cold.

The sky was blue and cloudless.

Everus and Creeps walked along the great stone bridge, crossing the River of Weeping Souls, which ran through the centre of Ghavin's Keep. All around them, the day to day bustle of the city went on, albeit to a more subdued rhythm, paralleling in so many ways the commotion of their native Wyrm's Port.

They stopped in order to take in the view.

From where they were, they could see the five stone obelisks that marked the location of the burial palace of Ghavin Truesword, who, according to local legend, was the founder of the city. To either side of the lavishly-built mausoleum were other buildings, each displaying an ornate architectural style which, in many ways, had not been surpassed in some two thousand years. To the left of the burial palace, constructed to look as though it was emerging from the river itself, was the fabled Temple of Weeping Souls. This nine storey pagoda was built from strange, blue-green rock, and looked as though it belonged underwater rather than above it. Beyond, were the municipal buildings; huge timber and stone, many-windowed, governmental fortresses, that had withstood both the battering of the elements and the ravages of unruly mobs, the latter during years of social unrest.

Further away, protruding into the skyline like a dark stiletto, was the spire of the cathedral of The High Three.

A smirk curled Everus' mouth. He wondered what turmoil the place would be waking up to, realising that one of their number had been killed. Already there was an uneasiness on the streets; fear and anxiety that was not there the day before now visible on the faces of many. News of the assassination had spread quickly, flowing through the city like a dark flood which drowned the concerned in despair and worry.

But there was something else. Rumours, in which people had horribly dissolved and vanished, abounded. And whilst most were dismissed as fabricated tales and scaremongering gossip, it all compounded to put the populace on edge. By contrast to the carnival atmosphere of yesterday, it was of no surprise that many chose to stay indoors.

Creeps, like Everus, was unconcerned with much of the gossip. "Some view this." He lit the pipe he had previously stolen from the owner of the inn they were staying at. "Aye, it's summat else. How come ye don't get any o' these swanky buildings around where I live?"

"Wyrm's Port has many finer buildings than you'll see here. Besides, where you live is hardly representative of anything more advanced than a pig sty."

"Where I live ain't fit for pigs. Still, it's home." Creeps puffed out a cloud of smoke and blew it away. "An' talkin' o' which. When are we goin' back? The night? The 'morrow?"

"Tomorrow, at first light. We'll get our supplies in order first and set off at dawn. Hopefully the bastards won't have sealed the gates...what with our recent activities."

✝ ✝ ✝

The weather had changed for the worse overnight so that by dawn, when the two of them prepared to leave, a light sleet fell from the slate grey clouds. They were lucky, however, that a different trio of gate guards were on duty and with a little lying and a fair smattering of intimidation from Everus, the North Gate was opened and they were on their way home.

Wrapped in his long coat and with his scarf wound around his neck, Everus surveyed the unwelcoming terrain. As far as he could see the road stretched on, wending its way over the grey, undulating landscape. Most of the snow was now gone, having withdrawn into the shadows, where it formed a white rime under hedges or around the bases of the few trees. He took in these new sights with faint interest, having traversed this stretch during the night of their arrival two days ago. So much seemed to have happened in so short a period of time. Now he was eager to get home and inform Dae'morogin that his will had been carried out; that Sacrosanct Tobias was dead.

Creeps had spent some of yesterday afternoon buying provisions, clearly not wanting a repeat of their journey south. In addition to a spare pipe, he had also obtained several pairs of socks and a pair of gloves. On his head, he wore a sack-shaped felt hat. Looking skyward, he bit into one of the many oatmeal biscuits he had bought. "Talk about gloomy." He offered Everus a biscuit. "Want one? They're nice."

Nodding, Everus took one and bit it. It tasted all right. He brought out his map, gave it a quick consultation and determinedly set off.

In front of them stretched a tract of desolate country, sparsely wooded with thorn and gorse bushes dotted here and there and with long, unbroken distances of open rock between. It was a place that men would normally shun, unable to support extensive vegetation aside from the tough, wiry bushes that alone seemed to thrive in the harsh wilderness.

They had not been going long when the sleet eased completely, allowing a shaft of golden sunshine through an opening in the grey clouds, illuminating a part of the distant eastern horizon. Far away, in that direction, they could see the wooded edge of the frontier of what appeared to be quite an extensive forest, its dark border, wild and forbidding. The road, however, sloped down a small hill before wending its way towards the north-west.

Leagues passed under their tired feet as they stuck to the road, eager not to venture off the established, worn walkway.

By mid-day, the sky had darkened again, their surroundings becoming rockier and more wooded, towering boulders and craggy tors replacing the flat badlands. Large, fallen slabs of rock lay like grave markers, the trees themselves becoming almost menacing in appearance.

"See when I get ma hands on Weaselnest, I'm goin' to introduce ma 'cutters to his knackers." For the past league or so, Creeps had spent the time by inventing numerous nasty ways to repay his one-time friend for his act of treachery. "Aye, I'm goin' to boil his head in a kettle an' then I'm goin' to feed him to that rat o' his. Never liked that bloody thing, so I hope it chokes. I know what'll do. I'll drag him into the worst bit o' Beggars' Hill, tie him to a post an' put a sign around his neck sayin', 'I'm a rich lawyer, do wi' me as ye please'. They'll skin him alive...shag him, an' eat him."

"I can't see many people falling for that. Weaselnest...*a rich lawyer?*"

"That bastard's goin' to pay, I tell ye." Creeps vented some of his rage by kicking a stone into the undergrowth which grew on either side of the road. "What about yersel', Everus? Are ye goin' to get him?"

"Probably." Everus marched on, senses strained as though wary of something as yet unseen. He did not like the look of their surroundings and memories of their encounter with the death squirrels preyed on his mind. This place looked ideal for an ambush, for there was plenty of cover in which things could hide.

"Aye, I'll show him. He's..."

"Shhh!" Everus hissed.

From behind one of the trees that grew over to their right stepped a warty-skinned giant dressed in an assortment of rank animal pelts. A ridge of knobbly bone sprouted from its forehead, its face was bestial and painted in offensive tribal markings. A shaggy mane of black hair sprouted from its head. Its limbs were long and spindly in comparison to its stocky torso and pot belly. In one of the thing's claw-like hands, it gripped a weighty spiked club.

Creeps reached for his dagger. "Is that...?"

"A bagh'arulk? Yes."

"He's a big bastard." Wiping a trail of snot from his nose onto his sleeve, Creeps pulled back.

"Two of them," said Everus sharply, aware that a second one, somewhat larger than the first, peered out from behind another tree. Drawing his sword, he started to advance towards the smaller of the two, which still stood a full head and a half taller than himself. In the hope of intimidating it, he gave it a quick display of his swordsmanship, twirling his blade in a series of figure-of-eight swings.

What was obviously the younger bagh'arulk paused for a moment and looked back to the bigger one. The adult nodded, urging the other to get stuck in. Warily, it stomped forward.

Fierce as it looked, it was not all that experienced. Its first club swing, which proved to be its last, whistled well clear of Everus' head. For then, even as it cursed its miss, Everus stepped forward and brought his sword down, cutting it open in a violent diagonal slash that ran from one shoulder to its opposing hip. Blood spewed forth in a crimson torrent as, eviscerated, its steaming, dark-red, horse dropping-like guts slopped out. Screaming, it fell backwards and crashed like a felled tree. It was dead before it struck the ground.

"Nice one," said Creeps, approvingly, from a safe distance away.

With a bellowing roar, the adult bagh'arulk stomped forward. It carried a large rock, twice the size of Everus' head, and with a grunt, it hurled it forwards, cursing in disappointment as the missile thudded into the ground behind him.

His sword dripping blood, Everus stood his ground, eyes fixed on the giant-kin.

The bagh'arulk picked up a huge club, its upper length barbed with teeth and banded with metal. Enraged at the death of the other, yet experienced enough not to rush forward, it began growling and slavering its anger. This one was huge, almost double Everus' size both in terms of height and mass. A single curved horn protruded, unevenly, from its skull and a dense growth of black hide covered almost all of its head, neck and chest. Like the smaller one, it too wore a crude assortment of furs and pelts.

Everus moved towards it and swung his blade, hoping for a repeat killing blow. His attack was blocked by the great club, his sword almost knocked from his hands. Retreating, he prepared to follow up with a back swing.

Despite its girth, the bagh'arulk was quick. Before Everus could get in his attack, it swung down, intent on pounding him into the rocky ground. Everus leapt back but not fast enough to avoid getting scraped down his right side by the spikes on the club. His coat ripped and the studded leather beneath tore as the teeth bit deep, lacerating the flesh beneath.

"*Aaaah! Bastard!*" Gritting his teeth, Everus drove a two-handed strike at his attacker's flabby belly. He struck home, the blade sliding a quarter of its length into grossly fat gut. The bagh'arulk howled as he twisted the bloody sword and stepped back.

As the furs it wore above its broad leather belt turned red, it roared again. It then thudded its club against Everus' bloodied arm. The crushing blow sent him reeling, his sword spinning from his grip. A follow up bash sent him careering, face first, into a tree. With a cry of pain, he rebounded off the unyielding trunk. Spitting blood and bark, he crumpled to the ground.

Club raised above its head, the bagh'arulk rushed to attack, desiring nothing more than to smash the man's skull into wet jelly. Despite his injuries, Everus managed to roll to one side. He scrambled to his feet, twisting just in time to avoid getting kicked in the face. He pushed himself forward, ducking under tree branches and tripping over rocks, searching for his sword. Blood ran from his head and flowed down his right arm, dripping from his fingers. It felt as though his arm had been broken. He spat out a tooth.

The bagh'arulk crashed through the bushes in pursuit, seemingly unconcerned about the spreading red patch on its front. Its monstrous bulk oozing blood and malice, it snarled and clubbed everything in its path, cleaving its way towards its prey, knocking branches aside.

Everus spotted his sword. Staggering over to where it lay, he retrieved it with his left hand and turned to face the monster. Ducking to avoid its club, he yelled and lunged at it. With an upward thrust, he went for the thing's lumpy, hirsute face. The edged blade stabbed into warty forehead, not entering as deep as he would have wanted but it was enough to make the thing stagger back and drop its club.

Blood ran into one of the bagh'arulk's eyes.

His green eyes lambent with frenzy, Everus cut the giant brute again, his blade scoring a deep slash along its unprotected left thigh. Viciously, he threw all of his energy into killing; driving his sword repeatedly into his foe, bloody meat rupturing and squelching with each thrust. "*Die! Die! Die!*" he yelled. Blood spattered his face.

The bagh'arulk fell, toppling backwards. In a landslide of flesh, furs and gore, it collapsed onto its fat arse.

It was dead, blood pouring from numerous deep gashes. Wanting to make sure, Everus stood on its grizzled neck and drove his sword through its open mouth, shattering fangs. He pushed down on the pommel, feeling the resistance as metal splintered through the back of its skull. Only then did he pull his weapon free.

† † †

Right arm cradled in a crude sling formed from several lengths of bandage, Everus now limped along the road as darkness descended. With the thief at his side, he had only managed a couple of leagues when the pain became unbearable. As far as he could tell his arm was unbroken, but the ache which pulsated in dark waves through his entire body was excruciating, the pain exacerbated by the sudden drop in temperature as the sun fell behind the western horizon.

Racing black clouds suddenly snapped the last sunlight out of the sky, blotting out the last traces of midnight-blue. Without warning, a wind blew up, followed, almost instantly, by a solid wall of rain that beat against them with a savage force. They lowered their faces in an attempt to shut out the intense force of the falling drops.

In the distance, the first flash of lightning flared in a whiplash of vibrant white over the sky. Then came the racking roar of the thunder, booming and echoing over their heads, seeming to flood in every direction to every conceivable horizon, shrieking back at them from the higher ground with its tors less than half a league to their right.

Everus cursed as he felt the rain soaking through his clothing until it reached the skin. It dripped from his sodden hair and trickled uncomfortably down the back of his neck. It filled his boots and saturated his sling, caressing his bruised flesh and battered bones with all the tenderness of a sadist with ice-cold talons.

The land about them had become open – a desolate heath with few trees to offer shelter from the wind and the rain. Again and again, the lightning flashed before them, bringing the thunder in its wake. There was an elemental fury in the scene that struck both men to the very core, neither having witnessed such a storm before.

"Make for the rocks!" Everus shouted, his face set in a dripping scowl.

"What?" yelled Creeps.

"The rocks!"

The ground had become waterlogged, slippery and treacherous. Streams grew from nothing and came gushing towards them as they left the road and started the uphill clamber. They splashed on as the towering dark cloud masses moved in sinister formations overhead, the wind howling now at their backs. The rocks before them seemed to assume wild, cavorting, eldritch shapes which danced in the lightning.

Trudging through the rain and the mud, Everus raised his head briefly in order to make sure of his direction. The long stretch of moor with its few misshapen, lightning-scarred trees was certainly not a pleasant landscape after dark and there were too many moon-thrown shadows for his liking. There was something else though, an unwholesome feeling that gnawed at his nerves and pulled at his senses. It was as though he was nearing something which had lain asleep for countless ages and he was now in danger of waking it.

"Where are we goin'?" shouted Creeps.

"Just keep moving!"

A sudden finger of lightning smote a tree close by, engulfing it in flames and reducing it to fiery kindling. The air was filled with the smell of ozone and burning wood.

Doubling their pace, they ploughed on, the ground thankfully becoming firmer. The tors loomed high before them, huge flattened rock towers which seemed more artificial than natural. The boulders glistened with mosses and lichens.

"In there!" shouted Creeps, pointing to little more than a crack in the ground. He dropped to his knees, unslung his pack and clambered inside.

Everus watched as the thief disappeared. That feeling of uneasiness grew within him, chilling him to the marrow in a way the rain and the wind could not. He wanted to cry out, to challenge whatever unseen forces were about, to reveal themselves. Sweat now seemed to flow from every pore, mingling with the rain already soaking him. His clothing hung clammily against his cold and bruised flesh.

"Everus! In 'ere!" Creeps peered from the crack, which looked like little more than a wolf's den.

Everus went down to his knees, his sling now soaked and, like his right arm, hanging limp and ineffectual. Gritting his teeth as pain jarred though his body, he crawled inside.

"Don't think it's big enough for a fire. Probably smoke us out anyhow." Creeps hunkered down in his wet gear, his face a picture of misery. "I'm goin' to try an' sleep."

Somehow, Everus managed to get some sleep, surrendering himself to the utter weariness and pain which wracked his body. He had woken some time during the night, aware of a strange dream in which voices had muttered to him of old things; of evil things. He knew that during sleep, the mind had a tendency to unburden itself of the troubles that impressed themselves upon it throughout the day, yet so real had been the sounds that at first he had thought they had come from Creeps, who lay curled up close by, his pack used as a pillow.

When morning arrived, the bleak light from a grey dawn shone outside the cramped cave. The ground was very wet, muddy and strewn with animal crap in which small bones could be seen. Clearly other creatures sometimes used the rock shelter as a lair. Outside, the rain and the wind had stopped although a chill dampness hung in the air.

Creeps stirred. Like a wild vagrant, he lay in a bed of mud and dirt, his body huddled so that his knees were tucked under his chin.

Limbs aching, Everus wormed himself free from the hole. Painfully, he pulled himself to his feet and stretched, easing his cramped muscles back to normal. As nights went, that had to be one of the worst he had ever spent. Drawing air into his lungs, he caught sight of something. He turned to look again. At first glance it was nothing more than an irregularity on the rock. He moved closer, now able to see that it was a small carved face, chiselled into the stone. It was human-like and yet different, more caricature than accurate portrayal. Looking closer, he could discern runic markings inscribed beneath, his eyes widening as he managed to translate some of the words. He turned when he heard the thief clamber out.

"What're ye lookin' at?"

"It's a Mad o' Gadin shrine!" replied Everus, still reading. "A remnant of an old grubban temple. This whole area is no doubt an ancient burial ground. It's no wonder I felt as though the place was haunted. Strange that there's no record of this place whatsoever, at least none that I've ever read. You know, I'd say we've discovered a hitherto unknown site of great historical importance." For a moment he imagined being hailed for this discovery but that kind of aspiration was no longer part of his life. He moved away from the rock.

Prospects of fame and, more to the point, wealth, entered Creeps' mind. "Oh, is that right?"

"No," Everus lied. "I just made it up. Now let's get going. The sooner I get this arm seen to the better. Hopefully, we'll reach Wyrm's Port before sundown."

CHAPTER FIVE

In his private villa, Everus gently padded over to the circular pool and gazed briefly into the clear, turquoise water. Disrobing, he let his black satin gown slide to the floor before descending the three steps into the liquid warmth. As the water rose around his toned body, he closed his eyes, inhaling steam and relishing the relaxing heat. He lowered himself deeper, sinking up to his neck, the water soothing and massaging his weary limbs and scarred body.

Nine full days had passed since he and Creeps had returned from Ghavin's Keep and during that time his arm had almost completely healed.

He tried to erase all memory of that dreadful homeward trudge from his mind, turning his thoughts to the concerns of the day.

Rumours abounded about the assassination of Sacrosanct Tobias, news of his murder having quickly reached Wyrm's Port. Although largely superseded by other events, the nature of the killing had sparked fears of the emergence of a hostile sect now intent on exterminating all followers of The High Three. This belief created ripples of uncertainty, which bordered on paranoia, amongst many members of Utterance's flock. In addition, there had been more stories of people mysteriously dying, consumed by fire or simply vanishing in their sleep. Some believed that the gods were angered at the diminishing levels of human piety and the wanton blasphemy prevalent in society, and were punishing the infidels.

Everus knew however that most were unbothered by such theological concerns.

Of far greater concern was the news that a war band of bagh'arulks and their even larger kin, the Øggarbakken behemoths, had been sighted in the foothills of The Deadmoor Clumps. For many, this could only be a prelude to an imminent attack. As a precautionary measure, Emperor J'hann had ordered the mobilisation of the entire army in addition to the immediate recruitment of volunteers, all in the unlikely event that the giant-kin were foolish enough to launch an attack. Scouts, skilled in avoidance and tracking, had been dispatched to reconnoitre their movements and, whilst preliminary reports did indeed confirm the size of their numbers, their exact motives remained unclear.

Eyes still closed, Everus drifted under the water, letting the warmth bathe his face and hair. After a moment, he surfaced, wiped his eyes and looked casually around at his bathing chamber. Three once-fine statues, carved from white marble, stood in various poses near the entrance. Each was clearly human in appearance but displayed signs of great antiquity and possessed a calm nobility, as though harkening back to a remote splendour now long past. Looking up, he saw the remains of an opulent mosaic on the ceiling, its design faded and yet, in places, the decadence of some of its scenes could easily be discerned. Reflections from the pool danced and rippled across the stone walls, giving them a richly striated appearance.

After a short time, he rose from the pool, his ablutions done. He retrieved his gown and walked barefoot out of the chamber, water dripping from his body. In an adjacent room, he dried himself with a towel. Once done, he sprinkled himself with a scintillating black powder contained in a small bowl fixed to the wall. He put his gown on, fastening the belt around his waist. He then left the room and walked the length of a long hallway, its walls decorated in places with faded murals and small statues set on plinths, housed in niches. Stopping at one of many doors, he reached into a pocket, took out a key and opened it.

The room he entered was dark, its impenetrable gloom only broken by a solitary ray of flickering darkness. Quietly, he closed the door behind him and reverently made his way forward. The darkness in the room was pervasive, like the dark of a totally eclipsed moon, giving the unnerving impression that the room was boundless and insubstantial; a place detached from the physical world of stone and timber. This was a holy place, as far as Everus was concerned; his black chapel. It was here that he had truly found his god and it was here that his god spoke to him.

Bathed in the beam of iridescent shadow was a statue, carved from a single piece of gargoylic stone. The statue depicted a being in a suit of spiked, plate mail armour. It was a truly frightening thing, vaguely resembling a man and yet something far greater. Stone snakes writhed from a head devoid of any facial features, the visage no more than a darkened oval. The left arm was held out, gauntleted-palm upright, whereas the right hand rested atop the pommel of a huge two-handed sword, its edge serrated.

Crossing the nebulous sanctum, Everus began to speak, his words little more than hushed whispers. "Hail Xethorn! O friend and companion of night! He whom many fear and yet unknowingly crave." He went down on one knee before the graven image. "Grant me, thy servant, the strength and the determination to do thy bidding. The moons have darkened. Speak and reveal unto me the location of thy second ward so that I may liberate thee."

✝ ✝ ✝

"Grigalo Shan'alan!" exclaimed Everus, giving the well-built man a resounding slap on his broad back.

Such was the force, the man stumbled forward a step. "What the...?" Turning round, a deep blue right eye lit up in recognition. His left eye was white and blind from an old war wound, leaving him with a long scar which ran from his forehead down to his cheek. He extended a friendly hand. "Everus, my old bastard! How's it hanging?"

Everus grabbed the man's offered hand and gripped it. There then followed a period of uneasy silence as both tried to crush the other's hand. The tension built as both maintained their hold. Through the pain, Everus could feel his biceps bulge. Fixing the man with a piercing stare, he uttered a low growl and gripped tighter.

A hush fell over some of the dozen other patrons in the tavern.

Everus thought he heard someone placing bets. Now was probably not the best time to attract undue attention. "You win."

"Hah!" Grigalo shouted. "You've got a grip like a grubba's arsehole after a bowl of Uttapian chutney!"

Everus smiled thinly. "I may have the grip, but you've got the face."

Grigalo laughed at the retort and began flexing his hand. He was as tall as Everus and equally toned. Years spent as a soldier and then as a mercenary had honed his limbs to athletic perfection. His hair was dark brown and cropped short. "I take it that this ain't a social call, so what brings you here?" Hawking back a wad of phlegm, he turned his head and spat onto a nearby table, much to the displeasure of the sad-looking old man sitting there.

73

"Business."

"Right." The coldness in Everus' stare informed Grigalo not to ask too many questions in public. "Why don't we take a seat and have a drink so as you can tell me more about it?"

"Sounds good." Everus walked to the bar and bought a round of drinks. He then headed to one of the shadowy corners where Grigalo was seated. Sitting down, he raised his drink to his lips, taking a mouthful of the sour tasting brew.

Grigalo took a hearty glug and wiped froth from his mouth. "So...what's it you're after."

"A favour."

"A *favour?* Hmm...what sort of favour?"

"I need your key."

Grigalo shifted in his seat, uncomfortable under Everus' stare. Everus had always been cold and uncompromising, traits which he himself possessed in abundance, but this time there was something else. It was hard to define and that in itself made him uneasy. Just as moments before they had both been locked in a physical contest, they were now locked in a mental one. "What key?"

Everus maintained his unnerving, unsmiling look.

Grigalo Shan'alan; an adventurer and a seasoned warrior, one who had fought countless enemies and had faced down too many dangers to number, now knew what fear was. In his one-time friend's eyes there was evil...pure and concentrated. He looked away, unable and unwilling to hold Everus' gaze for any longer. "Oh...*that key?* The key that'll open any lock? The one we found in the crypts beneath that haunted manor?"

Everus sipped from his tankard.

"It'll only work once, you know. So this had better be worth it."

"I assure you it will."

Grigalo gulped. He had not seen Everus for many a year and it was evident that something had changed him. He was no longer the man he once knew. "And...and just where's the lucky lock?" He smiled, eager to defuse the threat-laden malice of the situation. "No, don't tell me...you want it for Empress Loella's chastity belt, don't you?"

With a grin, Everus acknowledged his victory. There was little need to maintain his iciness. He returned the smile. "From what I've heard that was picked long ago. No, I need your key for something else...gaining access to Araan's Pillar to be exact."

"The Pillar, eh?"

Everus nodded. "Yes."

"I thought it was completely solid. Never thought there'd be anything inside." Grigalo scratched his unshaven face and thought for a moment. "You know, I've been there, three times. Used to offer my services as a bodyguard for the pilgrimages and other weird shit that goes on there." He shook his head. "Don't ever recall seeing an entrance."

"There is a way in. Take my word for it." Everus looked towards the bar and beckoned Creeps over. He waited until the thief had neared. "Let me introduce the man who's going to open it for us."

✝ ✝ ✝

The next morning found Everus, Creeps and Grigalo preparing to leave through the great South Gate. They were all surprised to find that the portcullis was up and the doors were open when they arrived, for a merchant caravan from Ghavin's Keep was entering the city.

In the commotion, the three sneaked out.

Everus and Creeps were both dressed very much as they had been for their previous journey. Everus wore his studded leather jacket, his long coat, his scarf, his dark trousers and his calf-length black boots. Creeps wore a tatty, dark blue jumper and his scruffy brown trousers. A torn woollen jerkin, his peasant's hat and his heavy sack containing gloves, socks, torches, blankets, several bottles of ale, rations and plenty of pipeweed, completed his vagabond-like appearance.

By far the more experienced adventurer, Grigalo wore a suit of light-weight, splint mail armour which hardly hampered his movement. Made of an unusual greenish alloy it could deflect the most savage of blows and ranked as one of his best purchases from the Buyer's Bazaar. He wore an open-faced helmet and in his left hand, he gripped a metal shield on which a green, seven-headed hydra was painted. In a scabbard at his belt was his sword. Slung over one shoulder, he carried a pack, its contents causing it to bulge. His lower lip was busted from a random fight the night before.

The weather was pleasant, the morning bright and cold. As they trekked along the road, a route Everus and Creeps had taken on their trip to Ghavin's Keep, Grigalo would occasionally break into a crude

75

little song or point out something of interest to Everus. For the large part, the thief would remain silent, frequently shaking his head and muttering darkly to himself, clearly unhappy with Grigalo's company.

They had not been going long when, at Grigalo's suggestion, they left the road and headed west across open country. Everus silently cursed the fact that he had returned the map of this area to Dae'morogin, for now he had no idea where they were heading. The notion that the farther they ventured from the road, the more he was at the mercy of someone else was a feeling he did not like. His paranoia was relatively short-lived however, for, upon reaching a slight rise in the landscape, Grigalo stopped and pointed.

"What is it?" Everus asked.

"There! That's the road we want to be on. That's the old caravan route between Wyrm's Port and Trade Peak."

Everus was confused. "Why didn't we just leave by the South-West Gate? We could have been on the road by now."

"Yes, we could've," mused Grigalo. "Then again, we could all be loitering in prison. There's a price on my head these days, one that the guards are quite keen to collect. I knew about the caravan and figured it would be a good distraction, enabling us to get out."

"An outlaw? My, you have gone up in the world," Everus replied.

"You know me. Never one to sit idle and watch others reap the rewards." Looking over his shoulder, Grigalo noticed that Creeps had fallen quite a distance behind and was now out of earshot. "Why do we have to take him along?"

"Because, believe it or not, he's one of the best at what he does."

"And what's that? I mean, I thought we were going to investigate Araan's Pillar...not stand in fields with poles up our arses. Look at him...he's like a bloody scarecrow. Surely we could've got someone a bit better than him? A woman, perhaps? That would certainly have made journeying easier." Grigalo grinned wolfishly. "There's this lovely-looking bit of skirt who works out of the Blackdagger Guild...gorgeous tits. Something to really get your teeth into."

Puffing and panting, Creeps slogged up the hill towards them.

Watching the thief approach, Grigalo frowned with displeasure. "Puh! I'm telling you, that old man's not up for it. One hit and he'd snap. I mean, look at him. He's got a face like a sack of prawns and he looks about as robust as a poofter's wrist."

"Creeps is tougher than he looks," Everus replied. He thought back to the time he had noticed his companion's weird shadow. "There's something else...well, let's just say, don't piss him off. Tread carefully."

"Why's that? Does he shit behind him as he walks?"

If that was meant as dry humour, Everus did not find it funny. "Something like that."

Now that he was near, Creeps eyed the two suspiciously. "So where are we?" It was the first he had spoken since their departure.

Everus nodded towards the west. "Over there is the road to Trade Peak. Once on it, we follow it to the south...and then?" Questioningly, he looked to Grigalo.

"And then we curve back on ourselves, heading for the old road that joins the cities of the Southern Kingdoms with The Dark Sea ports. Beyond, there's a ridge that we need to get to the top of. Once there, we follow the road south."

"How far is it to this pillar-thing?" Creeps asked, dejectedly.

Grigalo shook his head, looking to his boots. "Oh, I'd say it's got to be a good hundred leagues, maybe more," he lied.

"Twelve, perhaps less," corrected Everus, seeing Creeps' crestfallen face. "We should be there tomorrow."

Less than a league of scrub separated them from the road and yet it proved to be one of the worst tracts of terrain either Everus or the thief had ever crossed. The ground was tussocky and dotted with patches of that peculiar, sentient bramble they had seen before. In order to get to where they wanted they had to pass huge, thorny growths which rustled alarmingly, briars grasping and tearing. By the time they reached the road they were cut and scratched, the unarmoured Creeps having sustained the worst of the clawing.

Everus had been along this road once in the past and some of the sights he saw, although largely featureless, reminded him of that first journey. It had been over twenty years ago, when he had been no more than a boy of about twelve, that he had travelled along this way with his father. They had set out for Trade Peak, he recalled, for his father had business to attend to in the city and Everus had pleaded to go with him. The memory stirred up mixed emotions for him. Even after all those years, there was a small part of him that seemed, or rather yearned, to be that carefree boy again. In a sudden flash of memory, he saw himself perched high up on the covered wagon at his father's side as they made their way west, towards the setting sun.

The roads had been much safer in those days. The empire, stronger.

They walked on, stopping once to break out some of the rations they had brought with them before beginning the climb up onto the western ridge. Clouds blew over from that direction, their greyness threatening rain, but it came to nothing. The wind did, however, pick up as they began the climb, the sound eerie and portentous.

Unencumbered, Everus hiked uphill, his walking virtually silent; his breathing constant, his long stride efficient. Grigalo trudged silently beside him, never taking his gaze from the ground beneath him, mentally making each distance no more than a single step. It was a technique he had learnt on the many long marches he had been on as an imperial soldier, when the need to reinforce the frontiers had called for such long-distance treks. The going was slow and laborious for Creeps, who struggled to keep up, each step an effort, the weight of his pack digging into his shoulders.

They stopped near the top, the wind now strong and buffeting at this higher altitude.

Exhausted, Creeps slung off his pack and crumpled to the grass.

"The old road's over in that direction," said Grigalo, pointing. "Providing we can get 'Sleepybones' up, we should reach it before nightfall."

Everus looked in the direction indicated. Sweeping his gaze over the wild and uninhabited countryside, he suddenly stopped. "What's that over there?" Something in the way he said it prompted the thief to sit up.

"Where?" inquired Grigalo.

"There! Beyond those trees."

"Why, it looks like an old tower."

"A ruined outpost, perhaps?" suggested Everus, eyes fixed on the stone-grey shape some league and a half away, its jagged and crumbling silhouette framed against the already darkening sky.

"Could be. Then again..."

"I think we should go and have a look," Everus interrupted. "Besides, it would make a good place to rest. Believe me, after you've been reduced to sleeping in a pit in the ground, covered in shit and lying in a puddle, four stone walls and a roof seems like a top-class courtesan's boudoir."

"I'll take your word for it." Grigalo walked over to where Creeps rested, peering around as he massaged his weary legs. "Give it here." He reached down, picked up the thief's pack and slung it on his back. Now carrying two heavy packs, his shield, his armour and his weapon, he set off, his pace unchanged.

Surprised and relieved, Creeps got to his feet and rushed off in pursuit.

The road had degenerated into an overgrown track. It started to veer slightly to the south and as they walked the rain began to fall in increasingly larger drops. Looking eastwards, in the fading daylight, Everus fancied he could make out the far off urban greyness of Wyrm's Port, its faint lights and skyline a welcome reassurance.

They trudged on for a short time, the rain constant but not too heavy.

Up ahead, they could see that a path left the track and ran for a short distance through an avenue of crooked trees. At the far end of which loomed the dark and truncated tower. From where they stood, they could also see that a shoulder-high, railed fence, its metal bars twisted and warped, secured the grounds in which the tower was set.

"Methinks that's a boneyard o'er there," said Creeps, one scrawny finger burrowing into his right nostril.

"It has the look of one," Grigalo agreed, looking with disgust at the thief. "I wish you'd stop picking your snotter, you filthy bugger. You'd think you were digging for gold or something. You're at it all the time."

Disgruntled, Creeps removed the offending digit and put his hand in his pocket.

Everus looked around at the encroaching dusk, then at the tower. The rain continued to fall. If anything it was becoming heavier. Memories of that terrible night spent under the rocks at the Mad o' Gadin shrine surfaced in his mind. He looked to Grigalo. "What would you suggest?"

"Well, the way I see it, we either keep going for a bit and find someplace else to kip, or...we take our chances in there."

"It could be empty," muttered Creeps, his voice uncertain.

"Could be," agreed Grigalo.

"An' then again...it might no' be."

Grigalo nodded, after all it was a safe bet that one of the thief's notions was right.

Grimly, Everus shook the rain out of his eyes and unsheathed his sword. He started towards the tower. "I say we go and find out."

With a look at Creeps, Grigalo withdrew his sword and went to Everus' side. Behind them prowled the thief, his eyes wide, his dagger gripped tightly. The path they were on was made from crookedly placed flagstones, its surface uneven and in many places overrun with weeds and brambles. Curious black fungi, resembling the seaweed that they had seen adhered to the harbour walls of their home city, clung, parasitically, to the distorted trees that grew on either side.

Everus slowly looked round, seeing Creeps' nervous face. He grinned and resumed walking, his eyes darting now from side to side as he approached the spiked fence. Beyond, he could discern the darkened mass of the tower, its forbidding profile standing tall before them. All around could be seen ruined headstones and leaning statuary, their forms blurred in the deepening gloom.

At the entrance to the graveyard there leaned an old lychgate, its supports twisted and rusty. A heavy chain with a big padlock held the wrought iron gate securely locked. There was a small wooden bench set inside the arch, its wood rotten. To either side of the gate ran the spiked fence.

Everus walked to the side and slung his sword over the wicked-looking railings. With the agility of a panther, he climbed over, landing neatly on his feet on the other side.

Creeps looked at Grigalo, expecting him to vault over as well.

"*Bugger that!* Not in this armour." Grigalo pulled a pained face, imaging what the consequences of a slip whilst clambering over would be. "I don't fancy getting my nethers speared. There're too many whores back in Wyrm's Port who rely on my tackle to keep 'em in business."

Creeps returned his dagger to its sheath and went up to examine the padlock, removing a set of lockpicks from a pouch at his belt.

"Go on. Let's see you do it," said Grigalo.

"Hurry it up," Everus hissed. He had his back to the fence, his eyes looking forward. It was cold inside the cemetery, far colder than it should have been. The repugnant stink of dead things and open graves struck his nostrils.

Creeps started picking the lock, his skill impeded somewhat by the poor light. He worked carefully, twisting and tweaking the lockpick until he heard the lock click. The rusty padlock sprang open in his dirty hands. Returning his tools to his pouch, he then started to unravel the length of grimy chain.

"Such talent! Truly amazing!" Grigalo commented, sarcastically. He was yet to be impressed by the thief. "Now let's get inside."

Squeaking like a nest of dying rats, its sound painful to the ears, the cemetery gate swung open when Creeps pushed it. The two of them skulked inside.

Everus strode over, his sword gripped in both hands. With a nod of his head, he led his two companions through the burial ground, towards the dark tower. The stink of decay became stronger the deeper they ventured, the notion that perhaps camping here for the night was not one of Everus' better decisions strong in everyone's mind.

Now that they were all inside, they were each aware of a preternatural silence, as though a dark and unholy shroud had fallen all around. They followed the short path towards the tower, passing numerous cracked and defaced headstones. The tower now loomed before them, its outer masonry covered with long lengths of strangling vines. A large, wooden door lay slumped against the entrance, its hinges smashed irreparably.

Everus crept up. Inside, he could see heaps of fallen masonry and shattered beams, evidently all that remained of any upper storeys. He raised his left hand. "Torch."

Grigalo slung off Creeps' pack and held it out for the thief, who reached inside for a torch and his tinder box. He lit the torch and passed it to Everus.

With the flaming torch in one hand and his sword in the other, Everus went inside, his shadow flitting ghost-like around the tower walls. Grigalo followed, his shield held before him, his sword raised ready to strike anything unnatural. Creeps hesitated a moment. A sound from outside caused him to spin nervously around. Unable to see anything, he quickly nipped inside.

The interior of the circular-based tower was thoroughly derelict, its floor a jumble of shattered stone and splintered rafters. The wide, curved stairwell that once led to the upper floors had long since collapsed, there being but nine or so steps left on this level. Much of the wall was covered by those twisting, crawling vines which had wormed their way in from outside, damaging the coarse brickwork. Overhead, a few large beam supports leaned precariously, the night sky visible through the countless gaps in what remained of the wrecked ceiling.

"Do you think it's safe?" Everus asked, a light rain falling on his upturned face.

Grigalo followed Everus' gaze and shook his head. "No." It was an honest enough answer.

✝ ✝ ✝

It was just past midnight when Everus heard the scratching sound from outside. He had been sitting at the top of the ruined steps reading, by the light of a dying campfire, a section of graffiti scratched onto the wall; its content lewd and vaguely humorous. At the foot of the steps, Creeps sat huddled, his knees drawn to his chin. Opposite the thief, lay Grigalo, sleeping on an uncomfortable-looking bed of fallen timber. From both could be heard the sound of snoring.

Everus held his breath, eyes staring at the shattered doorway. He got to his feet, his sword a metallic flash in the fire light.

Suddenly a scrawny figure leapt out of the darkness and into the tower, its face and body twisted and cruel. Sprouting from its skull-like head grew straggly grey hair, its tangled length crawling with ticks.

Horror-stricken, Everus retreated.

Red-eyed, the thing hissed and spat. It was completely naked, its cadaverous body covered in festering wounds and scabs. Long-limbed, it looked as though it had been wracked almost to breaking point.

Everus found his voice. "*Grigalo! Creeps!*" he shouted.

The ghoul sprang forward, bounding over a mass of rubble and detritus in a single leap. It landed on the steps and swung out, its clawed hand swiping the air before Everus' face. He stepped back, almost stumbled and dodged a second claw. He swung his sword around in a two-handed arc. With a sickening squelch, the cold metal made contact, slicing the upper half of the ghoul's head off. There was no blood nor any other sort of bodily fluid – just flesh, cold and worm-riddled. Headless from the lower jaw up, it fell to its knees, tugging at Everus' coat. With a cry of rage, he brought his sword whistling down, hacking through what remained of his attacker's head, cleaving its neck and chest in two. His ghastly victim fell, quivering like rancid jelly, a puddle of plump maggots spilling from its enlarged wound.

Dirt-encrusted, long-nailed fingers scraped stone as two more horrors lurked into the tower, their faces canine, their skin stretched and blistered. Serpent-like tongues flicked grotesquely at the prospect of fresh, living flesh. A stink of shit hung around them; visible almost as brown wisps in the firelight.

Everus advanced towards them, eyes on the elongated grotesques, vaguely aware that his companions were scrambling to their feet. One of the ghouls rushed at him, its dog-like maw widening and salivating at the prospect of the kill. He dodged to one side and its momentum carried it forward into the wall, the impact hurting but not stopping it. It snarled and turned to face him.

The other leapt past, howling and cursing, its bony arms upraised like some crazed dancer.

"*Come on!*" cried Grigalo. With a vicious thrust, he ran the ghoul through, his slime-dripping blade rupturing skin and skewering its liver. Still alive, his foe reached out with a claw. Parrying with his shield, he pulled his sword free and took a backhand swing, a great swathe of long dead flesh parting at chest height as his sword cut across. Maggots squirmed from the wound as his enemy tumbled to the ground. He was about to help Everus when the ground beneath him convulsed. He stumbled to one side as a concealed wooden trapdoor, its surface covered with loose rubble, flew open. Another ghoul, with at least three behind it, started to haul itself out.

Everus hacked his attacker down, its body split open. He ran forward and decapitated the first one out of the trapdoor. Its headless body flailed wildly before crashing into Grigalo.

Creeps watched in horror from the relative safety of the top of the steps as more ghouls gathered around the doorway. Even Wyrm's Port cemetery was seldom this lively, he thought.

Grigalo rushed to the trapdoor, slashing the arm off one ghoul that was in the process of pulling itself clear. With a powerful kick, he booted another full in the face, shattering teeth and forcing it back down the way it had just come. With another kick, he slammed the lid closed and stood on it, preventing others from entering the tower by that means.

A hideous throng gathered in the doorway. Snarling, they edged their way in, clearly possessed of some kind of malicious cunning. Some dozen or so now approached, their scrawny and, in places, worm-eaten bodies, crowding the tower.

Everus and Grigalo retreated, backing up the ruined steps that led nowhere. By doing so they were at least provided with a higher ground advantage. The trapdoor was flung wide once more, scabrous hands and arms reaching out.

"Up 'ere!" shouted Creeps.

Everus turned to see the thief dangling precariously from a stretch of vine halfway up the wall.

The advancing horde stopped near the base of the steps and began baying, their unholy cacophony accompanied by the occasional guttural howl. A brick, displaced by Creeps, fell from above, narrowly missing Everus' head. As though that were the signal to attack, the ghouls began bounding up the spiral steps, eager to tear and devour the three men before them.

Unflinching, the two swordsmen stood their ground. They had been in situations like this before – although perhaps not quite as dire. The first five fiends that came at them died quickly, cut wide from numerous slashes; arms severed, chests and stomachs sliced open. Their exposed insides writhed like living wormeries. However, by sheer weight of numbers and complete disregard for personal survival, the ghouls started to gain the advantage. Clawed hands gripped Everus, tearing at his coat and scratching his body. A savage swipe to the head came close to tearing his face off.

Grigalo fared worse. A clawed hand had a grip on his shield arm and even as he tried to shake it free, two more hands reached out and grabbed him, talon-like nails digging through chinks in his armour. Chopping and yelling, he downed one of his attackers only to have another one take its place. The one on the ground was still alive and, unnoticed, it reared back with its head before sinking its teeth into his left shin, chewing armoured greave.

Half a dozen more shadowy shapes massed in the doorway. It seemed as though the entire graveyard's dead had now answered the call of those battling it out inside.

Almost slipping in the maggoty innards, Everus watched in horror as Grigalo was pulled down. Falling first to one knee, Grigalo was then dragged off the ruined stairway, three ghouls leaping at him.

Suddenly a blue phosphorescent flash exploded in the midst of the ravenous pack. Azure-coloured smoke drifted into the air carrying with it the fragrant smell of attar.

Accompanied by a series of high-pitched whines, the flesh-eaters pulled back, shielding their eyes. It looked as though one of them had taken the brunt of the mysterious explosion, for its skin popped and hissed as though from an acid splash. Howling insanely, it leapt high into the air, its muzzle frothing.

Everus sprang down the steps, holding the ghouls at bay and allowing Grigalo to get to his feet. He looked badly scratched but his armour had protected him from any serious injury.

A second flash went off, again in the thick of the pack. As one, the foul horde screamed and retreated further, their horrible faces flinching as though lashed. The scented smoke struck them, causing their eyes to weep a sickly, pus-like matter.

Confused, Everus turned in order to look at the thief. He saw him perched on one of the rafters an instant before he threw down another of the grenade-like missiles. It exploded as had the other two and this time the ghouls yelped in terror and bounded for the smashed doorway, springing away into the darkness. Others scampered like obscene insects, their limbs wan and loathsome, down the trapdoor.

Creeps lowered himself to the ground. "That won't keep 'em away for long. So it's time to get out o' 'ere."

Everus and Grigalo nodded in agreement. Hastily, they grabbed their gear, stuffing equipment into packs and throwing on their remaining items of clothing. By the light of one of Creeps' torches, they jogged out of the tower and back the way they had come, forever looking around to ensure that they were not being followed. They soon rejoined the main road and followed it, largely in silence, for the best part of a league until they found a convenient place to resume their rest. For the remainder of the night they took turns to keep watch, on the off chance that the denizens of the haunted graveyard might pursue them and track them down.

Nothing untoward happened for the remainder of the night, which was probably for the best as Grigalo had drifted off during his watch.

† † †

Everus woke to the sounds of Creeps rummaging through one of the packs. He stood up and stretched, brushing fallen leaves and a silken spider web from his coat.

Creeps came over, a ration pack stuffed with dried fruit, cheese and bread, in addition to some of his left-over oatmeal biscuits, in his hand. He gave it to Everus. "Aye, but that were a close one. I thought we were done for, what wi' spooks comin' out o' the ground an' everythin'." He puffed on the pipe which jutted from the corner of his mouth. "What were they, anyway?"

"Don't ask me." Everus bit into a piece of stale bread. "Ask Grigalo." Curious, he looked at the thief, analysing him, uncertain just how and with what he had managed to repel their attackers. He had spent a troubled night privately deliberating the events and little seemed to make sense. That Creeps had access to weird and wonderful poisons and other concoctions of his own making, he had little doubt, but what he had witnessed surely surpassed such petty alchemy.

"So ye've no idea what they were?"

"Grigalo will know." Everus walked to where he lay and firmly turned the snoring man over with his boot. "Still alive?"

Grigalo snorted and opened his remaining eye. He scrambled to his feet, his face dirty, his short hair unkempt.

"Creeps wants to know about those things that attacked us last night," said Everus, offering his companion a ration pack.

"What?" asked Grigalo, clearly annoyed at having been woken. "Those things."

Grigalo took a swig from a canteen. He swirled cheap ale around his mouth before spitting it out. "Well, they were in a cemetery. So I'd guess it's safe to assume that they were some kind of Dead One. I've encountered similar things before. Piss easy to kill in small numbers but them bastards must've outnumbered us five-to-one. Maybe more." He wiped his mouth and reached for an apple. He looked at the thief, remembering more of the previous night's events. "Well, you've certainly got a few more tricks up your sleeve than I first gave you credit for. Well done! You definitely saved our skins last night. I didn't take you for practicing magery as well."

The thief shrugged his shoulders. "Ye can buy anythin' in Wyrm's Port, if ye know the wrong people."

Biting his bottom lip, Everus looked at Creeps, uncertainly. The situation was becoming stranger; the man more of an enigma. His peculiarities merited keeping a closer eye on, that was for certain.

"I'm hoping that we'll reach The Pillar before the day's out," said Grigalo, getting to his feet and buckling his belt, strapping his sword in place. "So, when you lassies are ready, we'll go."

After a quick breakfast they set off along the south road. They had been walking for some time when they began to see some more ruined structures, their cracked and wrecked shapes littering the landscape like waste discarded by the gods. Getting closer, they could see the ruins of an ancient settlement of some description. Judging from its size it had possibly been an outlying village. A few timber and masonry hulks of once quite substantial buildings still stood, others were no more than heaps of contorted debris.

Striding through, they watched all around, each prepared for an ambush. Their footsteps were the only sound in this ghost town however, for the streets and remaining buildings were long deserted, any trace of their one-time occupation now consigned to a forgotten history.

Soon they left the abandoned village behind, following the road as it turned towards the east. They trudged on for a few more leagues, the ground sloping upwards.

Upon reaching the top of the bluff, Everus called a halt and walked over to the edge. Before him stretched the vast and seemingly unending Southern Plain. With the wind streaming across his cold face, he beheld, still several leagues to the east, the imposing mass that was Araan's Pillar. Like a massive beacon tower, the gargantuan edifice rose high into the sky, its tapered, spiked tip pointing to the clouds. League upon league of predominantly barren countryside lay spread out before him like a huge gaming board, the giant obelisk the only playing piece left.

"There she is," announced Grigalo. "Standing like a brazen trollop. But it's good to see the old lass once more, that it is."

Everus fixed his eyes on the monument, temporarily lost in his own thoughts. He had never seen it before in real life although he had seen pictures of it in numerous books. He shifted his gaze in order to follow the direction of the road. Further along the top of the ridge, it veered to the left before starting a downhill course, meandering through a clump of sparse woodland. Beyond the growth of scattered trees, the road branched. The main route went south, disappearing over the hazy horizon. The eastern path, for that is all that remained, looked bound for The Pillar.

"Come on. Let's put on a turn of speed and we should reach it before nightfall," said Grigalo.

Everus nodded in agreement, his scarf flapping in the wind. He marched at Grigalo's side, eyes focused on the distant edifice, knowing what lay within.

✝ ✝ ✝

It was approaching dusk when the three travellers neared Araan's Pillar. Built on an immense dais of a hundred or so cracked and worn steps, its colossal form was a darker shadow against the darkening sky.

With care, Everus started up, Grigalo on his right.

Creeps came behind, wheezing and spluttering, his face ruddy from exertion. At the top, he suffered a coughing fit, phlegm drooling from his lips.

"You should lay off the smoke," said Grigalo, watching with some alarm as the thief's face turned red.

"I'm...all right. I just need to...to warm up ma lungs." Creeps thumped his chest, hawked up a wad of tobacco-brown phlegm and spat it out. He reached for his pipe and flint and steel. Breeze-blown sparks lit his grubby face.

Disbelievingly, Grigalo looked to Everus and shook his head. Raising his right arm, he marched towards The Pillar. "All hail Araan!" His act of mock piety over, he then went and had a piss against the stonework, his urine steaming in the chill night air.

Everus paced over to another stretch of wall and looked up. Due to his proximity to the stone, he was hit by a sudden dizziness. Reeling, he stepped back. He reached out and ran a hand down one of the countless bricks that had been used in the monument's construction. He searched the wall for a short time before pulling a small roll of paper from one of the innumerable cracks. In the diminishing light, he unrolled it.

"What've you got there?" Creeps asked, intrigued.

Everus did not answer, he merely laughed and crumpled the note in his hand before dropping it to the ground, effectively ending someone's heartfelt wish.

"Got a good one here!" laughed Grigalo, holding another small note to his eye.

"Let's hear it then."

"Blessed Araan..." Grigalo began, reading from the paper. "My husband, Mormo Naff, son of Taitus, Keeper of the Great Vineyards, has fallen in love with our footman. I have travelled far to pray to you and to ask for your guidance and counsel, knowing that only your divine wisdom can provide me with the...something, can't make it out...for it is surely a ruse to...this stupid love cannot be..." He turned the note over.

"Is that it?" Everus asked.

"Well it's gone soggy. I can't make the rest out."

"Never mind. Listen to this one." Everus cleared his throat. "O Araan the Wise! I, Olly Powell of Stranglewood..."

"Where?" interrupted Creeps.

"Shut up and let me finish!" snapped Everus. He continued reading. "...Slave to The Plough and Drinker at The Black Swan, beseech thee. Four days and ten have passed since I woke suffering from Murtle's Rash. I know not how I obtained it but if I am deemed worthy in thy eyes, I beg for healing. The pain is terrible and my pilgrim's burden has become green and runny." He shook his head derisively. "What a load of bollocks!"

"What *is* this place?" inquired the thief.

"You mean you don't know?" said Grigalo, incredulously.

"No."

"Well, Creeps, my old mucker. This here's Araan's Pillar."

"Aye, so I'd gathered. But what're all these things?" asked Creeps, bending to retrieve a discarded petition.

"These things, as you call 'em, are messages, prayers if you like. The faithful come from near and far to leave their messages in the hope that The Pillar will answer them and give them guidance," answered Grigalo. "I guess you'd call it a kind of shrine, or something."

"Hah! What a bunch o' nummies." Creeps shook his head in disbelief.

Grigalo laughed and started to undo the straps on the packs he carried. Lowering the heavier of the two to the ground, he turned to Everus. "So, what are our plans for the evening?"

Everus looked about him, assessing the location. "We make camp here. Tomorrow, we find the way in."

† † †

Everus awoke to find that a light blanket of snow had fallen during the night. By the cold and grey light of dawn, he pulled himself to his feet. He stared up at the imposing stone structure, its pinnacle far, far above him, seemingly swaying due to the movement of the clouds as they gusted overhead. A light snow was still falling. Noticing that his two companions seemed to be asleep, he decided to take a stroll around the massive block.

Walking around each of the four sides of the column, he

counted sixty steps to each side, stopping every so often in order to inspect a note from the thousands of petitions that had been inserted into the very fabric of the towering monument. In spite of his scorn, he found himself somewhat diverted by these windows into people's desires. With the growing daylight, he could see that in many places, the base of the pillar was covered with graffiti. Looking closer, he saw that much of the lower casing of stonework had been chipped away or written over in a hundred different scripts. Names, dates and slogans, in addition to the frequent doodle or cartoon, had transformed huge parts of the edifice into a record of past pilgrimages. Continuing around the square perimeter, he saw three places where metal brackets had been hammered into the surface, creating a ladder of sorts. Looking up, he could see that these had been put in place in order to gain access to premium scribbling space further up.

Walking directly up to the pillar, he reached out with his hand, touching the cold, unyielding surface. Once, long ago, as though in another life, he would have been ecstatic to be here, to feel the tangible aura of history that pervaded the very stone. He had studied everything ever recorded about Araan's Pillar, from its geometrical layout and architectural style to its religious significance. He could have, and should have, been an expert on ancient history. Now, however, it was but brick and masonry; a mere building symbolic of false hope – much like his old dream.

Creeps turned a corner. "So, Everus, how do we get in?" He walked forward, munching on one of his biscuits, a perplexed look on his face. "For I'll be buggered if I can see any doors."

Everus turned. "There is a door and I know where." His voice was as cold as the morning, memories of what he could have been still at the forefront of his mind. His eyes narrowed, his teeth gritted as dark flashbacks to earlier times assaulted him.

"Where?" asked Creeps, looking around. "Is it a secret door?"

"Sort of."

Grigalo came sauntering towards them, his heavy pack in hand. "All right my hearty bastards? And how are we this fine morning?"

"Creeps was just inquiring where the entrance is," said Everus.

"*The entrance?*" replied Grigalo, giving Everus a knowing glance. "You mean to say that this place has an entrance? Well, imagine that! There was me thinking we'd trekked all this distance to take a crap here, that's if you weren't going to make a plea to Araan."

"Is there an entrance?" asked Creeps, unsure of how to react to Grigalo's joking.

"Yes." Everus dragged the thief towards another side of the pillar. "*There! This is it.*"

Creeps stared at the ancient, crumbling masonry, its surface masked with the recorded pleas of past and present generations. Tentatively, he approached as though half-expecting a portal to magically appear on the scrawled surface.

"*There,* you fool!" exclaimed Everus, pointing upwards.

Stepping back, Creeps gazed up to where Everus pointed.

High above them, barely visible, was a ledge – a feature which the many pilgrims had failed to see, blinded by their own petty needs and mundane desires.

"That's the only way in," revealed Everus. He could now see the very faint outline of an arch which seemed to have been intentionally bricked up. It was almost impossible to tell from ground level.

Creeps was getting a crick in his neck from staring up. "How the...? How're we goin' to get away up there?"

"*We?*" Grigalo grinned and passed him a length of coiled rope and a grappling iron from his pack. "I think you mean, *you.*"

"*Eh!?*"

"That's right," said Everus nodding. "You're going to go up. I know you can do it, so don't give me any crap. Now's not the time to get cold feet. Once at the opening, I'll send up the remaining gear. Just think of all the treasure inside. You'll be able to smoke yourself silly with the amount of coin we'll get from this one."

Rheumy, sick dog-like eyes lit up in Creeps' ugly face. "What's inside? Gold? Magic? Dead pilgrims?"

"The latter," replied Everus, impatiently. "Come on, up you get. The sooner you get started the sooner you'll be..."

"*Dead?*" Creeps interrupted. "Splattered to the four winds?"

Everus' eyes narrowed.

"All right, I'll..." Creeps took a step back and looked up at the north face of the pillar. "*Shit!* That's high." Testing the weight of the rope, he then slung it over his shoulder. Nodding his head slowly from side to side, he studied the stone wall, skilled eyes planning his route of ascent.

"Good luck. You'll need it," said Grigalo, patting the thief on the shoulder. He strode over to stand by Everus. "Ten gold he falls," he whispered.

The thief started the climb.

The first stage was relatively easy, newly-inserted brackets providing strong and reliable hand-holds. Beyond that the going became harder, his movements hindered by the weight of the rope he carried. Muttering a curse, he cast a wary glance over his shoulder, the ground now far below. Slow and steady, he reached out with his right hand, fingers searching for a crevice in the brickwork that would support him. He dug his fingers deep, before shifting his right foot to a corresponding toehold. Loose chippings fell away. Holding his breath, he clung like a limpet as a buffet of wind tried to pry him loose. For agonising moments he dared not move.

Bile rose in Creeps' throat as he tried to regain his composure. He reached out and carefully pulled himself upwards. Once more he looked over his shoulder, the forms of Everus and Grigalo now looking tiny. Unaware that they had placed bets on whether he would make the climb or slip and hurtle to his death, he paused before continuing his slow progress up the north face of Araan's Pillar.

Five times he came close to losing his footing, twice dislodging bricks from the crumbling wall. Thus it was with a huge sigh of relief that he reached out with his right hand and grabbed the base ledge of the concealed archway. Carefully, he worked his feet, finding decent leverage, before pulling himself up and onto it.

"*Creeps!*" shouted Everus from far below. "*Drop the rope!*"

"Remember to keep hold of one end!" Grigalo added, peeved at having lost the wager.

Removing the rope, Creeps gripped the grapple iron and let it drop.

Slithering down, a length of slack hit the ground.

Grigalo ran over, eager to examine it. He stared, angrily, at a small green ribbon which had been tied as a marker around it. In his temper, he began to wrench the rope in either hand as though in a game of solo tug-o'-war.

Everus walked almost silently up behind him. "Eighty-two arms! Just as I said. That makes it twenty gold, I believe. Ten for the rope length and ten for Creeps' success."

Cursing under his breath, Grigalo threw down the rope and reached into his pouch for the coins, which he counted and grudgingly handed over. "*Shit on a blind tart!* Where did you find out about this entrance anyway?"

"It's mentioned in Wyrmius' Second Letter to Scrûbba, Chief of the A'bar-Donians."

"*Who?*"

"Scrûbba. Chief of the A'bar-Donians. They were a race of desert nomad people akin to the present day Mzaahi of Mzaah. They lived far to the north of The Dark Sea." There was unashamed smugness in Everus' voice.

"Never heard of 'em," replied Grigalo, his albeit scanty intellectual pride taking a bruising.

"Not many have. You see they were wiped out ninety-four years after the scribing of the Second Letter at the Battle of Bonfire Scar by the emir of Umm-Dabba, who, with the assistance of a troglodytic, demi-human coven of Uhu'giaggothian cultists, instigated the first of several cataclysmic battles that rendered much of their homeland..."

"Well there you go...you know, I sometimes wonder if you make that stuff up," interrupted Grigalo, now bored with the current topic of conversation. He looked at the pack at his feet. "Come on. Let's get this kit up to the scarecrow."

High above, 'the scarecrow' sat on the narrow ledge, looking down, his matchstick-thin legs dangling over the side. He reached into his jacket, removed his pipe and lit up. From up here, he could see for quite some distance across the mainly snow-covered landscape. A sudden violent tug on the rope almost pulled him over the side. "*Ye bloody nummies! Watch what ye're doin'!*" he yelled down.

"You'll get him next time," muttered Grigalo to Everus, who had just finished fastening the pack.

"*Creeps!* Pull it up!" shouted Everus, hands cupped to his mouth. He watched as the pack was hauled into the air. He turned to Grigalo and held out his right hand, palm up. "Your key."

From a chain around his neck, Grigalo produced a silver key. It looked plain enough, but both men were well aware of its enchantment. For a moment, Grigalo seemed loathe to give it away, the desire to just keep it obviously strong within him. Stronger however was the unspoken demand that bid him hand it over. After a deep breath, he gave it to Everus.

Everus took it and placed it in a pocket. He looked up at where the thief sat huddled like a human spider. "Fasten the grapple hook. I'm coming up," he shouted.

"Right ye are," came the faint reply.

With the aid of the rope, Everus climbed relatively easily to the ledge. Once there, he found the thief hunched against the narrow alcove, his pack hanging from a spike he had hammered into the wall. "Well done. You've won me ten gold."

"Eh?"

"Never mind." Everus looked at the stone façade of the sealed archway. Its ornate decoration was now faded and displayed clear signs of weathering. Yet he could see numerous different scenes, carved in miniature, their execution painstakingly fine. He felt the age-old texture of the masonry, its surface untouched by human hand for almost two and a half thousand years. Set in the middle, on a raised boss, was an iron lock. It was big and complex-looking, its exposed, rusty cogs and tumblers arranged like an insane artificer's puzzle. Five separate bands of stone dial, each with over a hundred different symbols, were set around the centre, providing well over a million different combinations. Each wrong one would probably trigger some deathly trap.

"Hmm." Following Everus' gaze, Creeps stared at the lock. "Don't like the looks o' this. Never seen anythin' like it."

Everus took a deep breath and inserted the key into the central keyhole. For a moment nothing happened and then the various tumblers began to revolve, the panels shifting to the correct combination. The lock pushed out. The key melted. He waited, prepared for any eventuality. Then, with a deep grinding noise, the decorated archway started to recede, dragged back into the pillar. Dust and brick powder rained from the tunnel ceiling as the niche elongated. At the far end, barely visible, was the beginning of a shadowy flight of spiral stairs leading down – the sole access to the core of Araan's Pillar.

Creeps unhooked his pack and pulled out a torch which he proceeded to light. "What about yer man? Is he comin' up?"

"*Grigalo?* No, he's scared of heights. Besides, he has trouble enough climbing out of his bed in the morning, never mind making his way up here." Everus made his way to the far end of the passage, the low ceiling causing him to stoop.

"So, what do ye know about this place?" asked Creeps as they paused at the top of the steps, peering down into the sunless depths. "I mean, traps an' such."

"Who knows what horrors we may find? Wyrmius wasn't all that well disposed towards tomb-robbers, nor was Araan, come to think about it."

The two adventurers slowly descended. Creeps went in front, torch raised, eyes darting over the many broken steps and the glyph-covered walls. Twice he paused, noticing loose stone pressure pads and after pointing out their location to Everus, they avoided them and continued down. Deeper and deeper went the sepulchral stairway, the air becoming stale and humid.

"We must be near ground level by now," whispered the thief.

"Or beneath it."

Eventually the stairs ended and both men found themselves in a large octagonal chamber, its ceiling vaulted and supported by two great pillars. They could see over a dozen large stone sarcophagi stood upright against the walls. At first glance they looked more like squat statues, such were their stylised, anthropomorphic forms.

As the two walked further into the chamber, and the torchlight drove back the shadows, they could see that at the far end stood a large stone idol, easily three times as tall as the stone coffins. The statue was of a kingly man, dressed in a cracked and archaic suit of plate mail armour. In one hand he held a now snapped stone lance. A spiked stone crown was expertly carved on the statue's head and the face was that of someone both stoic and aloof.

"Wyrmius," muttered Everus, moving closer and snatching the torch from Creeps. "The founder of Wyrm's Port."

"Looks a bit like ye."

Ignoring the thief's comment, Everus wiped away a thick layer of dust which partially obscured a rectangular stele at the statue's feet. Inscribed on this plaque were many lines of text. Squatting down on his haunches, he started to scan the written information. Shortly after, he let out a private laugh.

"What's the joke?"

"No joke," Everus answered. "Just an affirmation that I was right and others were wrong."

"Eh? What're ye on about?"

"Never mind," said Everus, keeping to himself whatever hitherto unknown knowledge he had just discovered. "You came for gold, did you not?"

Creeps looked about. "Aye, but there's nothin' 'ere."

"You haven't looked in the coffins yet."

"No' yet, but I was goin' to." Removing a crowbar from his pack, Creeps headed off to the nearest sarcophagus. Just as he was about to wrench the lid off, he turned to Everus, something remotely resembling an intelligent look briefly contorting his unwashed face. "Everus. If that's Wyrmius," he said, nodding towards the idol. "Who's this Araan fella?"

"Araan." Everus hesitated for a moment. "Araan Maelarian was Wyrmius' high mage and chief architect, the designer of this pillar. This was to have been the southern cenotaph to the dead emperor, located as it is roughly halfway between the twin cities of Wyrm's Port and Ghavin's Keep. Turns out that it is more than a symbolic burial site though."

"Eh? Ye've lost me."

"Never mind. It's...no longer important." Once it would have meant everything to him, but now Everus had gone a different route. To think that he was here and that he stood by the actual sarcophagus of the infamous ruler. *No!* He shook his head. Such thoughts were now damaging. He was no longer the scholar he had once been.

"So what became o' this fella?"

"Why don't you ask him? He's in that coffin over there," Everus answered, pointing.

"All right! I bloody will," replied Creeps, heading over to the sarcophagus in question, figuring out that this one may hold the most loot. "I'll ask him where he's stashed the gold. These emperors an' folk always have loads o' it lyin' about."

"Creeps, do be sure to check these other coffins and remember to collect some gold for Grigalo, we did make use of his key after all," said Everus, coldly. "Also...in that far one over there, you should find a gold amulet. It'll be circular in shape with an inset triangle. Quite distinctive. When you find it, hand it to me."

CHAPTER SIX

Several days later, Everus strode down the long and shadowy passage, his boots padding gently on the black marble floor as he passed by wan-faced, black-cowled figures. With an air of trepidation, he approached the immense double doors which gave access to the inner high temple of Xethorn. Each door was carved from stout wood with an obsidian overlay and adorned with a pale, grinning skull motif.

Two dark-robed sanctum custodians armed with huge, execution-style axes, stood aside, bowing slightly as he neared. By unknown means, the huge doors swung open, permitting him entrance. From the doorway, he could see the long aisle before him, flanked on either side by six double rows of highly polished, black marble pews. Between the ranks of seats stood several narrow dark pillars, their slenderness somehow making a mockery of their function. In sconces secured to the pillars, guttered an uncountable number of black wax candles which gave off a repellent and oleaginous perfume.

Unaware that the temple doors had silently swung shut behind him, Everus walked reverently down the central aisle. Directly before him, on a raised dais, he could see a man-sized statue of a helmeted being clad in plate mail armour, a huge two-handed sword held before him. On either side, dark candles flickered, illuminating the statue in an infernal glow. Behind it, there was a large bas relief, its myriad scenes contorted into a chaotic whole. He walked over and sat next to a cowled figure in one of the front row pews.

"Everus," said Dae'morogin, eyes focused on the images before him, his voice little more than an echoing whisper.

"You have a new assignment?"

The high priest nodded, his face bathed in shadow. "That is correct...but, before we speak of that, I wish to hear more about you.

You remain an enigma to me, Everus. You kill without question and accept comparatively little in return. *Why?*"

"Are my actions not in keeping with Xethorn's decree?" countered Everus, defensively.

"Take no offence, my friend," replied the high priest, his tone as comforting as a death sentence. "Your actions have been sanctioned by Xethorn Himself."

"Then...?"

"It's just that I merely wish to understand you better, to fully comprehend the gifts that...our god has given you," Dae'morogin interrupted. "Since that day when high priest Dae'dicus first introduced you to our order, the brethren were quick to recognise your potential. *I saw, what Dae'dicus saw.* I saw your strength. But he was the true visionary. He knew that you would be no ordinary follower of Xethorn and that you needed a more...arcane form of guidance. He warned me to be vigilant and cautious in harnessing your hatred. In order to control and channel your murderous nature, Dae'dicus invented a plan, so simple, and yet, so ingenious. You've never asked me *why* the order wishes these people killed. Have you never wondered?"

Everus was feeling clammy and uncomfortable. He always did when he came into this most holy of chambers. Strange. It was a feeling that something was wrong somehow; that for some reason his god was no longer with him. He looked briefly at the idol of his deity, but the graven image provided him with no answers. It was cold and lifeless.

Dae'morogin reached for a heavy tome at his side. With some effort, he lifted it onto his knees. "Through this book..." he said, patting its grotesque cover, "Dae'dicus found the means to...fully concentrate your abilities." He opened it, the pages parting reluctantly like tortured flesh.

A sulphurous reek made Everus recoil slightly, whether it came from the grimoire or elsewhere he was unsure. "I...I'm not sure I understand." He stared at the opened pages, his eyes drawn to the foul gibberish inscribed within. He knew many of the ancient languages and writing styles but what he saw in that blasphemous codex was unlike anything he had ever seen before. It looked as though it had been written in burnt blood.

"Mahaff Salu, 'Bearded' Bryan, Trallo Fatts, Egor Waetsop, 'Big' Gee, Fanny Nayler, Harigold Mutton, 'Dobbs', Sharl the Keek..."

announced Dae'morogin, reading aloud some of the names written within, "Basil Scroff, Umpho, Sadie Farlan, Ulrus-Wit-Waloo, Ae'demoth Nun'chala, Fop of Distant Foppery, Tarquin Snell." He looked up from the book and straight at Everus. "*Well?* Do they sound familiar?"

Everus shook his head. "No."

"*No!?*" The high priest feigned surprise. "What about...'Spud', Tim Cockman, Harry Haigh, Oni Patroni, Linda Myers, Sammy Kerr, Tracy Anne Garbble, Kuntz, Moss Farrel, Dribble Crowthang, 'Wee' Roy?"

"I've no idea who these people are."

"But you should, Everus. For you killed them." A ghost of a smile flickered for a moment on Dae'morogin's cadaverous face. "Let me explain. Dae'dicus went to great lengths to fashion this holy book, knowing that to do otherwise would produce little more than a random list of random victims. And so, with a little help..." he shuddered suddenly as though at a bad memory, "he found a way in which, by killing a few, it would result in the death of many. *The Book of Dead Names*, is what he called it. An apt title. For you see, normally each death is *unlinked*. When any given individual dies, their death shouldn't *directly* bring about the demise of another. Within this book, however, Dae'dicus bound a spider's web of interconnected death, each death the agent of causation of another and so on. A 'reaction of mortality', he called it."

Everus was not feeling well and he was having trouble getting his brain around things. His head was beginning to spin like a hanged man. "So, what you're telling me is that..."

"What I'm telling you is that through your deeds, many hundreds, if not thousands, have died. It is *you* who are responsible for the alleged strange deaths which have been happening. They are not mere deaths, Everus. They are not normal. They have purpose and as such are murders and are holy in our god's eyes. *You*, my friend, are one of the greatest mass murderers this world has ever known. I congratulate you."

Everus had been executing these sanctioned assassinations for nigh on three years. During which time he had probably killed thirty. But how many had that escalated to? Just how many 'innocents' had died as a result? He stared into Dae'morogin's doll-like eyes, drowning in their seemingly abyssal depths. For an instant, he saw his own reflection mirrored in the inky darkness and then nothing, as though his soul had been snuffed out. For an unknown time, he sat motionless, his mind reeling from the high priest's revelation. There was something intrinsically wrong with this, something which grated against his personal code of murder – he killed with the sword, the dagger, the crossbow, poison and on one memorable occasion with his bare hands, *not* through infernal sorcery. It seemed to run contrary to Xethornite dogma.

"But there's still work to be done," said the cowled figure, his chill words breaking his hypnotic grip. "For as you can see, the book remains unfinished. The tale of death is not fully written."

Everus found his voice again. "And...when the pages are filled?"

"My friend, we will deal with that wondrous day when it comes to pass."

"And my next...?"

"Why of course! Your next assignment." Dae'morogin turned a wedge of gluey, slime-covered pages and looked down at the last name visible. *Roach Weidenreich*. Under the hood, his skull-like face tightened. With a trembling hand, the colour of bleached bone, he rubbed his chin. There was something wrong; something corrupt. The name was *different* from the others; the inhuman letters from which it was composed, squirming in a way that he had never seen before.

† † †

It was a cold and foggy night when Everus and Creeps made their way towards The Drowned Man theatre. This was the oldest part of Wyrm's Port, not far from the harbour itself. The narrow streets were cobbled. On either side of them, dilapidated buildings and decaying shop fronts loomed up like towering shadows. Ghostly figures, going about their unknown business, drifted by as the two stalked their way through the warren of foul-smelling alleys, their presence heard, rather than seen, in the deepening fog.

Everus felt a growing sense of unease. A feeling of nausea had festered in his stomach ever since venturing into these gloomy streets and now, with the visibility decreasing, seemingly with every step, he felt sure he was going to vomit. The reek of foul seawater added to his sickness. From some way off, he could hear the painful groaning of a church organ, its baleful tones full of melancholy. In his mind, he likened the sound to that of a babe being strangled. With each creak and squeak, it did not take long for his imagination to start conjuring up all manner of nameless horrors lurking in the fog.

Gripping Creeps by the scruff of his ripped leather jacket, he guided the thief towards a doorway.

"What is it?"

"Let's wait a moment. I think I'm going..." Everus leant against a wall and threw up. Once done, he wiped the spittle from his lips. He started taking deep breaths, the air he was returning to his lungs not of the highest quality, tainted as it was with the smell of dead fish as well as other things.

"Ye all right?"

Everus nodded. "Better now."

"Do ye think they'll let ye in wi' yer sword?"

"Maybe, maybe not." Everus cleared his throat and spat. "I had planned to strike when he came out, but in this blasted fog..." Visibility was now so poor, he could hardly see the thief standing before him.

"Aye, it does make things a bit trickier, an' ye still haven't told me who it is that we're after."

"I know."

An uncomfortable moment passed between them. Hidden figures, partially shrouded in the mist, walked by, paying them little heed.

"*Well?* Are ye goin' to?"

"He's called Roach. Roach Weidenreich."

"*Roach?*" queried the thief.

"That's what I said." Everus' voice was harsh and unfriendly. He did not appreciate Creeps' questioning. The thief was there solely to provide backup, if any was needed and to open any locks that might hinder him. It was *he* and *he* alone, who did the killing.

"Nob'dy I know."

"That matters not," said Everus. "What matters is that he is removed; *permanently*. You'll get your hundred if that's what worries you."

"Why's he at the theatre?"

"He's a performer; a puppeteer. A ventriloquist to be precise."

"A *what?*"

"A ventriloquist. A voice-thrower. One who entertains simpletons, like yourself, by...projecting his voice, so that it seems as though someone else, rather than he, is talking."

"Oh?" replied Creeps, dumbly. "Never heard o' that before. Is it like magic?"

"No."

"Still, it sounds like a good trick to do when it's yer turn to get the drinks in."

"*Does it?*" Everus replied, dryly. He had had enough of the thief's banter. The man was really beginning to get on his nerves; from his off-putting appearance and his pedestrian humour, to his downright scuzziness. He was the archetypal, uneducated lowlife that Everus despised; the embodiment of the grown-up guttersnipe, fit only for licking his boots. And yet – and this was the thing that *really* got to him – he knew, deep down, that he needed Creeps. There was, and always had been since their first encounter, an unfriendly, inseparable bond between them.

"Well, just imagine if ye'd to buy..."

"*Shut up!*" Everus spat up the last dribbles of sick, relieved at how much better he now felt. He had to be on top form, for he had been warned by Dae'morogin that this assassination may be unusually dangerous and that it merited extra care. As they had made their way through the fog, he had carried the suspicion that they were being watched, a sensation he had felt, to a much lesser degree, on some of the other sanctioned murders he had committed. Privately, he considered the possibility that his actions were being spied on by fellow Xethornite agents – a notion which provided some comfort.

† † †

"*Pathetic,*" Everus muttered, watching as five handaxe-juggling, grubban acrobats stumbled across the creaking stage. Dressed in their dark-grey leotards, the quintet cavorted around, performing acts of none-too-great dexterity. Honking on squeeze-horns and crying profanities, they leapt and cartwheeled. One walked on his hands, his fat backside wobbling for all to see.

"They're no' bad," voiced Creeps, staring fixedly from where they sat near the back of the dimly-lit fleapit.

On stage, the grubbas formed an unsteady pyramid of flabby limbs. The precarious flesh-work effigy held for a moment, teetered and then buckled, the stocky performers landing atop one another.

Sporadic laughter broke out from some in the forty or so audience.

"Get off! Ye're rubbish!" jeered one heckler.

"Give us our money back!" complained someone else.

"Give us Tarby!" cried a voice from a side aisle.

As the grubbas retrieved their props and scrambled to get off stage, a tall, thin man, dressed in a dark, frilled coat and top hat, entered from the other side. He strode out onto the stage, hands clapping the now finished act in a doomed effort to encourage the disgruntled spectators to do likewise. "*Ladies and gentlemen*. Let's hear it for *Ozgo... and the Boys!* Weren't they great!?"

A man in the third row stood up. "Let 'em hear this!" He belched raucously, the sound reverberating around the shabby interior. "Bastard grubbas! We should send 'em all back to the slave-pits!"

Suddenly the lead grubba stormed out from the side of the stage brandishing a hatchet. "*Who said that!?*" The stumpy, bearded figure looked around, his wild eyes searching the crowd, settling on the one who had burped. "Whit're ye sayin' aboot me an' ma boys? Ye swine that ye are!"

"This could prove to be better entertainment," Everus whispered to Creeps, sitting upright in his uncomfortable seat.

The irate grubba ranted on. "Get oot o' ma way, ye bastard!" he barked, roughly throwing the spindly compère, who had tried to intervene, to the floor. Like a runaway bull, he charged to the front of the stage and hurled his handaxe. It flashed end over end towards the heckler, before embedding itself into his right shoulder with a meaty thwack.

The man hollered his pain to the ceiling.

Some in the audience screamed as the handaxe-struck man, in his desperation, scrambled over the seats to get away. With blood pouring down his arm, he made a break for it along one of the empty rows of seats. He had reached the end of the row, when a second handaxe thudded with deadly accuracy into the side of his head. The force of the blow catapulted him into the next row, where he fell, upended.

Everus watched, smiling grimly as the victim's legs twitched before the body slumped down into the space between the seats.

Ozgo cursed to himself and stomped off stage, followed by the compère and a smattering of nervous applause.

The stained, moth-eaten red curtain fell.

An unsettling silence followed, during which the lights were lowered. A couple of stagehands fetched the dead body, carrying it out through a side door.

"Do ye think that was part o' the act?" Creeps whispered.

"Probably not."

"It's good this. I used to think these places were just for poofters an' arty-farts. If I'd o' known I'd o' come 'ere before." Creeps was clearly enjoying the violent cabaret. "Aye, well, whatever else, we've certainly got our money's worth, an' yer man's no' even done his turn yet."

"Yes...and to think some say theatre is dead."

After a short time, the compère returned, mopping his sweating brow with a handkerchief. It looked as though Ozgo had given him a black eye. "Ladies and gentlemen! Boys and girls! Tonight's final act and the one you've all been waiting for, is, somewhat...*unusual*." He cast a surreptitious glance over his shoulder as though fearful of whatever was behind the curtain.

"Get on with it!" yelled a haughty-voiced individual.

Booing and rhythmic clapping began to come from the crowd. Many in the audience began stamping their feet. The noise built up, until it sounded as though a thousand hammers were battering at the decaying building. Dust drizzled from the ceiling.

The compère raised his hands in an effort to placate the mob. "Please, kind people!"

Suddenly a woman's shrill scream broke the echoing din.

The clamour from the crowd ceased.

The scream came a second time.

"Don't be alarmed!" cried the compère, his eyes drawn to the hideous, corpse-green face that peeked through a parting in the curtain at one end.

A shocked hush fell over the theatre-goers.

Everus sat up, watching as the grotesque thing looked around, its bulging red eyes falling disturbingly on an individual, before drifting elsewhere. It was hard to tell whether the face was formed from flesh or something more akin to papier mâché. It was as equally hard to ascertain exactly what it was – a very ugly, heavily battered midget being perhaps the closest estimation. Straggly, jet black hair trailed down either side of its head.

"For your amusement, may I present...*Uncle Tarby!*" With that, the compère sprinted to one side, returning with a high chair which he set down on the stage. He then ran off again as though chased by a pride of invisible lions.

"Good evenin'," Uncle Tarby rasped, its voice harsh and guttural.

Creeps nudged Everus. "*What's that?*" His face creased in a wince, as though he had just found a dead bullfrog having a crap on his knee. Despite having seen more than his share of the macabre, he was clearly somewhat repulsed by what he saw. Obviously seeing a man slain before his very eyes was of little concern when compared with the downright weird and unsightly.

"It's foggy outside, ain't it?" said the bogeyman. What looked like saliva drooled from its open, fanged mouth. "It's a good night fer a killin'. Did ye see that fella get axed? *Bloody great!* Anyhow...I'll see ye all later." It grinned wickedly before retreating back behind the tattered covering.

Suddenly, from the opposite end of the stage, a flash of light and smoke announced the arrival of someone else. Striding out from the side, came a middle-aged individual with slicked-back black hair and a beaming, pearly smile. His face was tanned a vibrant mahogany with theatrical cosmetics. Dressed in an expensive, glittering cloak festooned with sequins and jewellery, he reached the middle of the stage; dark, piercing eyes surveying the crowd. "Ladies and gentlemen," he announced grandly, his words eloquently spoken yet heavily accented, "I'm the one, the only...*Roach Weidenreich*, your entertainer for this evening." He brought his hands together as though in prayer, before holding them out to either side. Breathing deeply, he started to rise into the air. He levitated higher, maintaining his pose.

Now presented with a good target, Everus watched, yearning for a loaded crossbow.

Many in the theatre gawped, open-mouthed.

"Now *that's* magic," whispered Creeps.

Everus looked for the wires, but due to the rather conveniently poor lighting, he could see none. It could be magic, he had to concede, and there did seem to be an air of authenticity about it, but surely only a third grade sorcerer would eke out a living performing parlour tricks for the lowlife masses?

"Allow me to introduce you to my world of phantasm." Vivid orange flames leapt from Roach's outstretched palms, winning a round of applause from the crowd. He descended, tracing mystical patterns in the air before him. A smoky curtain formed, concealing him completely. It dissipated in amber-coloured whirls.

Roach had vanished!

"Where's he...?" muttered Creeps.

In a blinding flash, the illusionist reappeared at the other end of the stage, drawing a second round of applause. Sequins flashing, he rubbed his palms together before pulling them apart. In between, stretched like webbing, was a warped face of shimmering light. Hands now chest-width apart, the phantasmal face mirrored his own, down to the finest detail. Its mouth opened, breathing forth a gout of red fire. It then disappeared.

Everus watched, pulling at his bottom lip. If Roach was a true magic-user then this was going to be difficult. Obviously Dae'morogin had been correct in issuing his warning.

Preening his hair like a cat, Roach strolled casually towards the high chair. With nothing more than a stare, he summoned forth a tall, gaunt individual, who came out from one side, trundling a tall and sinister-looking guillotine. The being pushing it was ugly and lean, a truly bizarre-looking creature, barely human in appearance.

Once the beheading device was in place and the ugly prop assistant had left, Roach smiled, staring up at the heavy blade. He turned to his audience. "Now is normally the time I ask for a vict...I mean, volunteer."

"Go on, Everus. Now's yer chance," whispered Creeps.

"No? No takers?" said Roach, eyes panning the reluctant crowd. "Ah well, probably for the best." Eyes sparkled as he gazed out, smiling. "You wouldn't believe the mess this caused last time. *Blood everywhere!*" Turning his head from side to side, he walked up behind the guillotine. He stopped, one hand resting on the framework. "This stunt is one that very few of my fellow magicians will dare attempt. It's fraught with danger, none more so than for yours truly and the idiots who chose to sit in the front row." He grinned madly at those in question, displaying his insane demeanour to full effect. "And so...without further ado." He knelt down and thrust his head into the chopping-hole, pulling down the restraining block.

Everus stared.

Suddenly the repulsive head burst through the curtains. "I've fixed it, ye bastard! Yer bleedin' head's comin' off this time."

"*What!?*" Wide-eyed, Roach stared, fingers scrabbling at the board behind his neck. "*No!*" Legs kicking, he tried to free himself from the structure, fingers now desperately clawing at the locking mechanism. The guillotine rocked to one side.

The crowd were screaming, horrified at this turn of events.

Grinning, the ghoulish head retreated behind the curtain.

Then, the blade fell, chopping through air, then flesh, then bone; decapitating Roach. His head tumbled to one side, unleashing a torrent of blood which sprayed out over the stage in a bright crimson fountain. Yells of horror filled the auditorium. Some rose from their seats and, having seen enough, edged towards the exit doors. This was certainly not a show for the squeamish.

Intrigued, Everus watched as the headless conjuror then got to his feet, an obscene amount of blood jetting from his severed neck. *This was bizarre*, he had to admit.

"Down here!" cried the blood-covered head, guiding the shambling body. Roach walked drunkenly to one side, blood continuing to squirt. Reaching down, he retrieved his head and messily slopped it back onto his neck, as good as new. Madly, he held his arms out, awaiting the applause.

None came.

The lights dimmed further.

The gaunt assistant came out to remove the bloody prop, wheeling it off stage.

Addressing the remaining audience, Roach continued as if nothing untoward had happened. "For the second part of my act I would like to introduce you all to an old friend of mine." Removing a silk handkerchief from an inside pocket, he wiped at the blood which smeared his face. "However, he's a little shy when it comes to eating, I mean, *meeting*, new people. So, I'm going to nip backstage, get cleaned-up and hopefully see if I can coax him out. And if, in the meantime, you could all just say...'*come on out Uncle Tarby*', I'm sure he'll hear you." He smiled creepily as he pranced to one end. "And...if you're *really* lucky, he might just appear in that empty seat next to you." On that comforting note, he gave an insane laugh and slipped behind the curtain.

A disgruntled-looking man came on stage with a mop and bucket. Muttering darkly to himself, he began cleaning up the copious blood spill.

A time of general uneasiness passed.

Some stared nervously at the empty seat next to them.

"Well, what do ye make o' this?" Creeps asked Everus, who had so far sat in virtual silence throughout the illusionist's weird show.

"Different."

"Aye, it's summat else, ain't it? It seems almost a pity that ye've got to...well, ye know."

Everus was thinking up a suitable response, when he noticed movement behind the curtain, the mopper-upper having now cleared off.

The heavy drapes rose, albeit clumsily, and Roach stepped out from beyond, impeccably dressed in a glittering evening cape and bow-tie. Cradled in his right arm was something straight from a child's nightmare – the dummy, Uncle Tarby. It was dressed as a scruffy court jester; the woven, patchwork garment of dull mixed colours, frilled cuffs and collar and three-pointed jester's cap, complete with jingle bells, giving it an even more macabre look. Red and black striped leggings covered its short legs. On its feet it wore a pair of turned-up slippers, a small bell at the end. The outfit was dirty and dusty as though it had been stored in an old chest or an attic for a considerable time. The dummy had been fashioned to look stunted and deformed, however its arms and hands looked like normal human arms and hands and moved accordingly. In one hand it held a marotte – a jester's stick – which was topped at the end with a head not unlike its owner's.

"Good evenin' once again," Tarby spat as Roach walked towards the high chair and sat down.

Two rows from the front, a woman fainted and had to be helped out by a couple of men nearby.

"I *said* good evenin', *ye insolent bastards!*" the dummy croaked, its voice gruff and grating as though Roach had swallowed a hot coal.

"Good evenin' Uncle Tarby!" called back a handful of drunks, all of them pissed out of their heads.

"That's more like it," Tarby growled.

"Ladies and gentlemen! May I introduce my old friend and fellow performer, everyone's favourite uncle...*Uncle Tarby!*" Roach rested the dummy on his knee. With an odd jingling, he brushed dust from the dummy's sordid motley and straightened the hat on its head even as it growled, unhappily. "Oh Tarby, one could've at least made an effort. Nonetheless, tonight, what a show we have in store."

"Have we?" the dummy responded, head turning towards its controller.

"Have we what?" queried Roach, over-the-top fake confusion on his face.

"A show?"

"But of course, Tarby. For tonight..."

"*Oi! Missus!*" Tarby interrupted, eyes drawn to a horrified woman who was hurriedly getting ready to leave. "Buggerin' off are ye? An' there were me thinkin' ye were the kind o' tart that'd go backstage fer a little bit o' rumpy pumpy. Aye, I thought I were in there. Mind ye, now that I can see ye in the light, I'm no' so sure. My, ye're ugly. Wi' a face like that I'd teach ma arse to talk. Go on, fart an' tell us yer name. Ye know what? I'd sooner kiss a grubba's hairy dangler. I'd have to be starvin' to feed on yer sag-bags, missus."

"*Tarby!* Decorum, please."

"Oh shut up ye old tit! Do ye think I've got nothin' better to do than sit 'ere wi' yer hand up ma shitter? Besides, there's some nice bits o' skirt in tonight. *Look!* Look at her o'er there! Her wi' the massive wabble-yazzers." Leering, the dummy pointed straight into the audience, singling out another not very attractive woman. It gave her a wave. "Aye, missus, I'm talkin' to ye. Get yer stinkin' knickers off! I could just imagine smotherin' ye in freshly-chopped onions. Along wi' a nice little mustard coatin', a white wine sauce an' a sprig o' parsley. Ye'd like that, wouldn't ye? Phwoar, I'd give ye a good stuffin'." It gave a lecherous, knowing nod. "I can see ye smilin', ye dirty hussy. Ye wouldn't be the first bird I've pulled in 'ere, I'll tell ye that. Aye, they've been queuein' up fer me in the past. I'll be needin' to get 'Tit-Face' 'ere stitch us on a bigger todger soon."

The drunks thought the dummy's salacious banter hilarious and burst into fits of laughter.

"*Tarby!* Now, I've warned you before. Whilst on stage you are on your best behaviour. Understood?" Roach admonished, wagging a finger with his free hand. "And, sir, I don't appreciate being called..."

"Piss off! '*Tit-Face*'!" Tarby croaked, a mischievous grin now on its face. "Ye talk a load o' codswallop ye do an' I'm sure these folk don't want to listen to it." Nodding, it looked at its marotte. "Ain't that right, Mister Shittyarse? What's that? Aye. Ye're quite right. They'd much rather hear about the time that big-titted lass asked if she could have a rummage in ma funny-bag. I said, sure missus, but do ye mind if I first butter yer sweaty dumplin's?"

Some chortled at the innuendo.

"Enough of that!" Roach cleared his throat, a look of genuine embarrassment on his face. "Ladies and gentlemen, please forgive my rather crude associate, but you must understand that, for someone who spends most of his life in a box..."

"I'll put ye in a box, ye old bastard. A wooden one wi' brass handles attached," the obscene puppet-thing rasped, winning some more laughter. It turned to the audience. "*Ye think I'm bad? Ye should get him to tell ye what he really gets up to...what he really is. I'm lucky if I get a little bit o' scrawny arse thrown ma way now an' then, but this bugger, he gets the full works, tits an' all. Ye should see how he munches on 'em. Only other night we were wi' this blonde trollop we'd bumped into down by the docks. She were a big woman. Ye know the kind. Belly an' buttocks on her like an Ullerby Slapper. Anyhow, she'd these huge, an' I mean huge, pair o' right juicy melons on her. They were that big we almost ran out o' garnish.*"

"Ahem, as I was saying," Roach continued, his voice raised. "Please forgive my lewd associate..."

"Aye, that's it, blame me! It's no' ma fault ye're a murderin', man-eatin' tit, now is it? I'm no' the one who's feastin' on whores like there's no tomorrow. That's right folks! Big, small, fat or skinny. He'll have 'em all."

Roach sprang to his feet. "You sir, have gone *too* far."

"*Ye sir, have gone too far,*" the dummy parroted, in a mocking, almost child-like voice.

"I'll put you back in your box," threatened the crazy ventriloquist.

"*No! Anythin' but the box! I promise to be good.*"

"Promise?"

"Yeh, I promise. I suppose." Its face went tearful; eyes watering, mouth drooping. "I'll be a good Tarby." It gave a pathetic little wave with its jester's stick.

"Very well! On with the show!" Ecstatic, Roach did a little tap-dance.

The bulk of the act was carried off in the same, surreal vein. The foul-mouthed dummy would insult the audience or its operator, whilst Roach himself kept up the facade of a crazy, if well-mannered, gentleman. Amidst the horrible comedy, the ventriloquist would sometimes participate in a little one-handed prestidigitation, often with hysterical outcomes.

The performance now coming to a close, Roach was walking back to the high chair when, to the surprise of everyone watching, the dummy threw aside its jester's stick and turned on him. With its human-like hands, it reached out and grasped him around the throat.

Roach's eyes bulged like a squashed toad's. Feebly, he pummelled at his ghastly, shrunken assailant as the two staggered across the stage. Horrified screams, in addition to outbursts of laughter, came from the spectators as the incongruous grapplers crashed against the high chair and clattered to the floor. In the brawl, Tarby's cap was sent flying.

With legs kicking, and the dummy now astride his chest, Roach pulled out a dagger with his free hand. Twice, he stabbed the berserk puppet – if that is what it was – red blood squirting with each hit. On his third attempt, Tarby released its strangle hold and instead grabbed its controller's wrist. Writhing like a thing possessed, the dummy shook the bloodied dagger from the ventriloquist's hand.

Near the shadowy rear of the theatre, Everus sat up, his eyes fixed on the anarchic puppetry. Curious, he watched as, with murderous intent, Tarby retrieved the dagger.

The remaining spectators then witnessed the brutal, frenzied stabbing of Roach at the hands of his dummy. Screams resounded around the building as the thing known as Uncle Tarby maliciously butchered its controller, the dagger descending again and again.

People rushed to get out. This had now gone too far.

Astride Roach's gutted body, the blood-spattered dummy turned to stare at those strong-stomached ones remaining, a maniacal glint in its eyes. "*Who's next? Come on, ye pieces o' shit! Who's next?* If I'm no' gettin' any crumpet tonight, then neither's he."

An exodus of theatre-goers was now underway, people clamouring to escape. The main doors were flung wide, inviting in the cold and the fog from outside.

"*Lower the curtain!*" the compère shouted, his frightened face peering out from one side.

"I'll get ye too, ye scrawny bastard!" cried the vicious dummy.

The drapes fell. From behind the covering, there came the sounds of a scuffle, followed by a croaky curse and then a scream.

"*Well I'll be buggered!*" Creeps stared, wide-eyed. He had hardly moved throughout the show, captivated by the gory slapstick, eager not to miss a thing. "Now what do we do?"

"We complete what we came here to do," Everus answered, rising from his chair.

"But...that Tarby, or whatever it's called, has beaten us to it."

Everus smiled and headed for the exit.

Apart from a drunk who had somehow slept through tonight's

performances and was now snoring loudly in the row behind them, they were now the only two left inside.

"Where're ye goin'?"

"To retrieve my sword. I had to leave it with the man at the front door. Then I think we should take a look backstage."

† † †

They walked around to the rear of the rundown theatre, their forms cloaked by the thick fog. Down a squalid side alley they turned, its decaying walls covered with rotten posters advertising past attractions. From all around they could hear the sound of rats as they squeaked and scurried amongst the numerous heaps of garbage that clogged parts of the dirty passage. A sickly stink of piss and dead cats hung thickly in the air.

"Are we goin' to kill Tarby? Is that what we're goin' to do?"

Ignoring the thief's questions, Everus drew up short, gripping Creeps by the collar and pushing him against a nearby wall. "Quiet! I hear voices. Wait here." He crept forward, clinging to the shadows, his eyes drawn to the light up ahead. Hugging the wall, he neared the alley corner.

"*Whit dae ye mean? Whit dae ye mean?*" an angry grubban voice shouted.

"I mean you're under arrest for public disorder. Now how many times do I have to say it?" replied another voice, this one definitely human.

"*Why?* Whit've I done?"

"We've been informed that you *killed* someone in there tonight."

"It were an *accident*. Ma axe slipped."

Peeking around the corner, Everus saw five men, each dressed in the cheap armour and poor outfit of the city watch. Two of them held large poles from which hung several bright bullseye lanterns. Another pair restrained the short-arsed performer he had seen earlier.

"Fayther!" cried one of the grubba's sons in a high-pitched voice. "Whit's goin' on?"

"It's these bastards. Get aff me!" screamed the held grubba, kicking and spitting.

What seemed to be the head guard strode up and clapped a pair of handcuffs on their prisoner. "Quick now! Let's get this mad bugger back and in a cell before he causes any more trouble."

"*Bastards!*"

"Shut it!" said the head guard, jabbing his captive in the gut with a clenched fist. "Call me a bastard once more an' I'll..."

Everus stepped out into the light. "I wish you gentlemen would keep the noise down, you'll be giving this neighbourhood a bad name."

"Who're you?" the officer asked, eyes drawn to the sword Everus held.

Ignoring the question, Everus took a few steps forward, sizing them all up.

The officer drew his sword. "State your business, citizen!"

"*Go on!* Kill the bastards!" shouted the grubba.

"I said, state your business! Do so or I'll have you arrested."

"My business is exactly that...*my business.*"

"Men! Apprehend this arrogant sod."

The two guards threw the handcuffed grubba to the ground. They then ran forward. One held a sword whilst the other charged Everus unarmed.

"Surrender or die!" the officer commanded.

Everus calmly cut down one guard and then another. They slumped, red and groaning, to the cobbles. He sprang at the two lantern bearers, slashing one open in a crimson spray as the other threw down his pole and ran screaming into the fog.

With a snap, the grubba broke his bonds and hauled himself to his feet.

The officer retreated in fear, surveying the carnage Everus had wrought. Three of his men were now dead and he had no wish to join them.

"Stubb!" the grubba shouted to his son, who stood in a doorway. "An axe b'gods!"

"Right ye are fayther!" Stubb squeaked, his tossed hatchet deftly caught by the enraged Ozgo.

It was at that moment that the remaining guard decided to make a break for it.

Ozgo threw his weapon at him even as he disappeared into the fog. A thud and then a cry followed, his aim as true as it had been in the theatre. He walked over to where Everus stood and gave him a friendly slap on the arm. "Cheers pal."

"Don't think I helped you out of the kindness of my heart," Everus responded, sheathing his sword on his back. "I need information."

"*Information!? Whit* information?" Ozgo asked suspiciously, his voice cracked and gruff.

"Where's Roach?"

"*Roach!?* Who's Roach?" Ozgo replied, his tone becoming more belligerent.

"The voice-thrower."

"Whit're ye on aboot?" Rage now flared on the grubba's broad and whiskered face.

"Fayther. He means that nutter wi' the ugly doll," piped Stubb in his reedy voice.

"Oh, that stuck-up freak?" Some of Ozgo's anger began to dissipate. "He's got a face on him has he no'?"

Now that the combat was over, Creeps decided to sneak into view.

"Will someb'dy tell me whit's goin' on?" cried Ozgo, watching the thief. "An' who's this b'gods, creepin' aboot wi' a face like a well-slapped arse?"

"I need to find Roach. *Where is he?*" Everus would wring the information out of these grumpy midgets if that is what it would take.

"*I don't know!*" barked Ozgo, shaking his head, bearded jowls wobbling. "How should I know where he's away tae? Dae ye think I'm his mutha or summat?"

"Mister. Listen tae whit ma fayther's tellin' ye. The man wi' the puppet's away," added Stubb. "He buggered aff sharpish. I think he'd a carriage or summat waitin' fer him."

"*Jammy bastard!*" Ozgo grumbled. "Us poor buggers have tae walk hame. An' who's tae say that oor show's no' as good as his, eh?"

"That's right. Ye tell 'em fayther."

Everus cursed under his breath. He stood staring for a moment, aware that Creeps was already in the process of garnering whatever loose change the dead guards may have on them. His target had got away and to some extent it had been his fault; his poor planning. If only he had got here earlier he might have been able to ambush Roach upon arrival.

The remaining three members of the axe-throwing, acrobatic act emerged from the back door. Dressed in ratty, woollen ponchos, they started to pack up the last of their props, readying to set off home.

"Stubb! Ûmmy! Pack them axes up! *No! No' like that!* Dae it like

I've telt ye!" ordered Ozgo, accompanying his commands with the occasional slap or boot. Just as they were about to set off, he walked up to Everus. "Cheers a' the same. Next time we're daein' a show I'll see tae it that ye get a free ticket. How's that fer ye?"

"Fayther. Next show's the day efter the 'morrow," added one of his sons.

"Do any of you know where Roach lives?" Everus asked, unmoved by Ozgo's proposal. As far as he was concerned, the grubba could take his offer of a free ticket and stuff it somewhere seldom washed.

"No. I cannae help ye there, chief. I telt ye, I don't know nothin' aboot yon arse wi' the puppet. Yer boss man inside the theatre might."

"Fayther. I ken where the puppet man stays," revealed one of the others.

Ozgo stomped over and cuffed his youngest son. "*Whit?* Why d'ye no' say so afore? Ye wee *bastard* that ye are! Well c'mon then, tell the man afore I kick yer arse a' the way hame."

† † †

Later that night, Everus and Creeps skulked along the foggy streets, twice passing separate groups of violent late night revellers. Screams, drunken shouts, and the occasional line of a poorly sung tavern shanty accompanied them as they wound their way through the gloomy city. Following the directions given to them by Ozgo's youngest, they headed out of the dock-side slums and into a relatively wealthier residential quarter.

Brick-built houses, many with their own stretch of garden, lined either side of the long avenue they had turned on to. Lanterns, suspended from tall stone posts, lined the roadside and in the fog they bathed much of the place in a dream-like glow, illuminating the many garden statues and small pools in an enchanting, faerie radiance.

"Everus. Do ye think Tarby might've brought what's-his-name back to life?" Creeps asked.

"Roach?"

"Aye, him."

"Roach never died. It was staged...a part of the act."

"Ye mean...?"

"I mean it was all faked. The knife. The blood. Probably the audience's reaction for all I know."

"An'...Tarby?"

"That's nothing more than a pile of assorted junk...an old costume with a cabbage head. Ugly, yes. Dangerous, no." Everus looked at the thief. "A lot like yourself."

"So it's no' alive?"

"It is *not* alive," Everus said, shaking his head in frustration. Since leaving The Drowned Man he had had to reassure the thief numerous times that the dummy was nothing to be afraid of. Roach, on the other hand...

"What a relief. For I don't mind tellin' ye, see when he first came out, I nearly curried ma crackers."

"*Nearly?* From the smell, I thought you had."

The road started uphill, high garden walls towering on either side, the shadowy outlines of much larger buildings behind them. Then, seemingly from out of nowhere, the sinister-looking house at the end of the road suddenly loomed up before them. Rambling and disjointed, clearly the product of an insane architect, the building looked every bit the home of someone as weird as Roach. They paused directly across from it, surveying the forbidding property with a cautiously heightened interest. In spite of its obvious age and decrepitude, the place still retained something of its past grandeur.

Looking up, Everus saw peaked turrets and a sloping, angular garret, crowned with a spiked metal border. Over a dozen dark, small windows peered out from the spooky, lop-sided mansion. Moving up towards the main gate, he could see, annexed to the main building, a low-roofed coach house.

Creeps chuckled to himself. "*I knew it!* I just bloody knew it!"

Everus turned. "Knew what?"

"Well, just look at the joint. I'll bet ma back teeth that that's haunted."

"*Hah!*" Everus snorted. "Ghosts or not, we're going in. So quit whining like an unpaid tart and let's get the job done." Stealthily, he made his way to the gate and, surprised to find it unlocked, quietly opened it, signalling for the thief to get inside. "We'll try the back door first."

Clinging to the shadows and using the wicked-looking statuary in the garden as cover, Creeps scampered towards the rear of the house, Everus not far behind. Upon reaching the back door, the thief started on the lock, diligently probing and tickling with his lockpicks.

Everus watched from behind a statue.

A light appeared in one of the upstairs rooms.

From where Everus crouched, he saw one shadow and then another cross the window. He hissed a warning to Creeps, who instantly melted into the shadows. Shortly after, the light was extinguished, and with a signal from Everus, the thief resumed his task. The lock was proving a swine to better, frustration growing each time Creeps thought he had it. He was just about to give up when, with a click, he heard the door unlock. He waved Everus over.

Whilst Creeps put his lockpicks away, Everus slowly eased the door open. From the distant light of one of the street beacons, he could see a corridor, its floor tiled and well swept, stretching before him. Silently, he drew his sword.

In the semi-darkness, the murderer and the thief edged their way inside.

Up ahead, they saw two doors.

Everus reached for the handle of one and after finding it locked, he tried the other. Opening the door as quietly as he could, he peered into a shadowy room, its myriad contents little more than darkened blurs. A musty smell as of dusty furniture and old wood filled the air. With his sword gripped firmly, he slid into the room like a venomous snake ready for the kill.

"What were that?" asked Creeps, startled.

"What?" Everus whispered back, eyes straining to see in the darkness.

"Thought I heard summat. Summat upstairs."

"Don't worry. It's probably just Roach putting Tarby to bed."

"Don't joke like that. This place is bad enough."

In the dark and the silence they waited and listened. Carefully, they then navigated the cluttered room and headed for one of the three exit doors. They soon found themselves in another corridor, its floor carpeted. Along the walls, they could just about make out the dark outlines where paintings hung, their quality shadowed.

A dull thud sounded from directly overhead. It was followed by the barely audible sound of jingling bells.

Again they waited.

"This joint is givin' me the heebies. I'm shiverin' like a dog wi' the shits."

"Why didn't you bring your lantern, fool?"

"Well I thought..." Creeps began, his words cut short by the noise of a door slamming followed by the sound of running feet from overhead.

Everus hurried down the carpeted corridor and opened the door at the far end, believing that their intrusion had been detected – and, if so, there was little reason to maintain their secrecy. He found himself in what was clearly the entrance hall. In the dim light, he could see that the room was richly decorated with more statuary, a dozen or so large and variously shaped paintings and at least two full-length tapestries. To one side, an ornate stairway, its steps made of beautifully polished wood, curved upwards towards the first floor above. Gold-framed mirrors reached to the ceiling and a large chandelier hung from above; the place reeking of extravagance. He was just about to call Creeps over, when the whole room lit up as dozens of small candles, held in several large and ornate brass candelabras, suddenly blazed.

Surprised, Everus' initial reaction was to retreat into the doorway he had just stepped from, pulling back into the shadows. He gazed up to see the dark-eyed ventriloquist slowly descending the stairs. Roach wore an indigo, velvet smoking-jacket and a matching pair of upturned slippers. On his head, he wore a black tasselled cap. In one hand, clasped between his fingers was a cigarette-holder, its end trailing purple smoke.

"Who invades my privacy?" demanded Roach.

Everus strode out into the lit room, his blade glinting in the light. "I invade your privacy, fool!"

Roach leaned casually against the marble banister and took a draw of the slender pipe. "And you sir, are...?"

"*Your death!*"

"Ah, another scoundrel," said Roach, upon seeing the thief peer from around the door. "I should've guessed. A dog and his master. But which is the dog...and which the master? Hmm."

"Spare me your questionable wit." Everus stalked towards the staircase.

"You show signs of learning. Such a pity, for this will be your last lesson." With unnatural quickness, the puppet-master reached into a pocket, muttered something arcane and hurled a small glass globe down the stairs. The spherule shattered against the tiled floor of the hall whereupon it burst into a choking cloud of foul-smelling, green smoke.

Coughing and temporarily blinded, Everus staggered across the hall and threw his shoulder against the front door. With a crash, the door splintered open and he stumbled out, falling down a small flight of steps and onto a patio. Green smog cascaded out in voluminous clouds behind him. Lungs bursting, eyes streaming, he got to his feet and staggered further, falling to the grass.

"Everus! Ye all right?" shouted Creeps from inside. "*Everus!*"

Everus was finding it hard to breathe, the smoke forcing him to be sick. It stank of rotten eggs and maggot-ridden food scraps. With a painful convulsion, he retched green slime.

"*Everus!*" Creeps came running through the toxic cloud, a hand clamped over his mouth. He rushed over to where Everus lay and helped him to his feet, dragging him away. "The dirty bastard! That stinks. It's enough to make yer soil turn soggy!"

Now clear, Everus watched with stinging eyes as the smoke started to fade, dissipating into a mist and then vanishing completely. He waited for a moment, before gritting his teeth and marching back.

The hallway was empty.

Watchful and ready for anything, the two of them sneaked to the top of the stairs. Once there, they found themselves on a long gallery, its wood-panelled walls decorated with paintings and ghastly memorabilia. Posters detailing past performances and plaques highlighting Roach's none-too-illustrious career covered one section of wall, whilst the other was devoted to a series of poorly painted portraits. At the far end stood a suit of antiquated plate mail armour. Opposite it was an upright, stuffed bear.

"Some joint this," muttered Creeps, nervously staring around. "I bet he's worth a..."

"Shhh!" Everus started to sneak towards the nearest of three doors on the landing. Once at it, he turned the handle and with a push, he flung it open. Light from outside revealed dozens of marionettes and puppets of every description. Over two score of the horrid little things hung in twisted poses from the ceiling whilst nearly double that number lay scattered, like massacred infants, on the floor.

"What's in there?" whispered Creeps.

"Dolls," answered Everus, shutting the door.

The thief threw a nervous glance at the portraits on the near wall. "I don't like the look o' them pictures."

"They probably don't like the look of you." Everus made for the second door.

Suddenly one of the painted faces let out a heart-stopping scream.

Startled, Everus and Creeps watched in utter disbelief as the canvas face tore free from its frame on a sinuous, rubbery neck. Before their eyes, the painted face morphed into a solid head. "I'll have ye know I'm a masterpiece, ye ugly bastards!" it gargled in a weird voice.

Creeps screamed and retreated.

Hesitant, Everus pulled back, watching as a second portrait began to undergo its obscene transformation. Necks elongated. Faces stretched. A clawed hand crept like a spider from around one of the frames. On their snake-like necks, the bizarre abominations snapped their sharp teeth and screamed profanities, blocking the way further into the house.

"*Xethorn, preserve me!*" cried Everus, charging to meet them. Ducking and parrying, he did battle, slashing the head off one of the grotesque abnormalities. The headless neck flailed wildly, bile-like fluid spraying from it with the sound of a deflating bladder.

The second monstrosity was harder to dispatch, for it weaved like a cobra. Its head was that of a monocled elderly man with flaring sideburns and a swooping, handlebar moustache.

Gnashing like a ferocious guard dog, the thing launched itself straight at Everus. He dodged at the last moment, but not fast enough to prevent its sharp teeth from biting into his left shoulder. It fastened itself, tearing at him.

Everus dropped his sword. Fighting back the pain, he managed to grip the creature by the hair, which, to his surprise, felt perfectly normal. He pulled, yanking the head off his shoulder and then fell, maintaining his grip. The portrait-monster bucked like a wild mule under him. Locking the head in a strangle-hold under his left arm, he thumped in several punches with his right fist, bursting the thing's nose. Still it tried to snap at him. Mustering his strength, he got to his feet and repeatedly rammed the head into the wall.

After the eighth such battering, the neck went floppy and the strange thing slumped to the floor. Then, even as Everus withdrew and retrieved his sword, both of the weird adversaries vanished in a blue flash; their necks, heads, hands and even the stains all over the floor and along Everus' blade vanished. All that remained were the grim-looking oil paintings on the wall and the bite marks on Everus' shoulder.

"Foul trickery," muttered Everus.

"Magic," replied Creeps.

After discovering another room crammed with scary puppets and devilish stage props, the two of them came to another flight of stairs. At the top, they found themselves on a much wider landing, at the opposite end of which could be seen yet another staircase. Nearly a dozen doors led to further rooms, giving Roach more than enough places to hide, if indeed that was what he was doing.

Everus no longer cared for stealth. His shoulder hurt from where he had been bitten. Systematically, he kicked in each door, and then leapt into the room beyond, sword raised to hack down anything before him.

All the rooms were uninhabited but contained all manner of strange objets d'art. In one of the rooms, nearly every bit of wall space was covered by grinning masks and more unnerving portraits of dour-looking men and women, giving the chilling impression that all those eyes were staring out at them. Another room was filled, almost to the ceiling, with theatrical props of all shapes and sizes, from blade-filled trunks and a foldable rack, to cabinets of mirrors, a strange-looking pendulum contraption and a guillotine device not unlike the one they had seen on stage. Maybe it was the same one.

They were in the process of exploring the final room on this level when, from outside, there came the loud sound of horses whinnying.

Dashing to the window, Everus looked out and saw, by the light of the street beacons, a horse-drawn carriage wheeling its way out of the coach house. "*Shit!* The bastard must've doubled-back. He's escaping." Pushing the thief out of his way, he turned and sprinted for the stairs.

"Everus! Get back 'ere!"

Everus stood, heart thumping. "What?"

"Get back 'ere."

Eager to be off and in pursuit of his quarry, Everus stared back at the room where the thief was. He rushed back. In his temper, he kicked the door wide, its frame shattering against the wall with a resounding crack. "*What!?*" He advanced menacingly towards Creeps.

"Those nags ye saw..."

"What are you on about?"

"Well...they didn't cast any shadows."

Confused, Everus made for the window. He peered out into the gloom at the courtyard below. Even in the poor light, he could see the faint outlines of the stationary carriage. Briefly, he contemplated the notion that Roach owned two carriages.

"I think it was just another o' his magic tricks," said Creeps, noting the uncertain expression on Everus' reflected face in the glass. "Ye know...he makes it look as though he's buggered off when really he's crappin' his crackers upstairs."

"Hmm. Maybe." Peering out into the darkness, Everus was still unconvinced.

"Well, even if it wasn't, there's still someb'dy upstairs, for I heard 'em movin' about."

Everus was still staring down towards the coach house when a sudden movement caught his eye. A carriage door opened and something seemed to hop out. Its movements were bizarre and when it started across the courtyard towards the house his heart missed a beat on realising that it was the Tarby-thing. Eyes wide with horror, he found himself unable to look elsewhere. Under different circumstances, its idiotic skipping and capering could have appeared funny, but now, looking down as it neared the house, it sent a shiver of fear right through him.

"What is it?" asked Creeps.

"It's..."

Suddenly the horrible jester-like dummy appeared at the window.

Its grotesque features were separated only by the thickness of a pane of glass from Everus. Horrified, he pulled away, as the ghastly, crumpled face, with its bulging red eyes and straggly black hair, grinned in at him.

"*Who's next?*" Uncle Tarby seemed to float, one hand rapping at the window, the other clenched around a blood-streaked dagger. It gave a hideous laugh.

Then it vanished.

Just at that moment, one of the doors behind them was flung open and a tall and gangly figure, dressed in a pair of blood-stained labourer's overalls, loped out. There came the click and the twang of a shot crossbow.

The bolt lanced through Creeps' left shoulder and flung him back against the near wall.

To the sound of the thief's whimpering, Everus leapt forward as their attacker dashed his crossbow to the floor and reached for a vicious-looking weapon that resembled a cross between a scythe and a large axe.

Just then the entire landing lit up in a haze of glowing, multi-coloured balls of illumination.

Like flickering fire-flies, the incandescent globes bobbed and danced, constantly changing colour. In the magical, chromatic glow, Everus could now see that his opponent was none other than the loping, misfit prop-man from the theatre. Up close, he could see that the individual did not appear human at all but was rather a loose patchwork creature of sewn up body parts, as though a mad mortician had taken up needlework. He was completely bald; his face a flesh-work tapestry of haphazard stitch marks.

Scarred gums stretched back to reveal misshapen, horse-like teeth as the abomination grunted and thrust forward.

"*Die!*" Everus cried, dodging to one side and forcing the thing back with a series of masterful swings. Parrying a vicious swipe, he stabbed home, catching his foe high in the chest. Stunned, it staggered and fell back, thick dark fluid leaking from its mouth.

The thing spat blood, a vacant look on its otherwise grim face.

Unmercifully, Everus moved forward and drove his sword deeper, taking pleasure in the tearing sound as the red blade emerged out the other side. With the sound of the thing's dying gargles in his ears, he withdrew his weapon.

Twitching, the cadaverous freak fell to the floor.

"*Everus!*"

On hearing the thief's cry, Everus turned in time to see Roach at the base of the stairs. There then came a flash of white light and the next thing he saw was a series of strange missiles flying through the air straight towards Creeps. Expecting to see the thief go up in flames, Everus was astonished as, with the sound of breaking glass, they seemed to evaporate against a shimmering barrier before him.

Roach cursed.

Before Everus' eyes, the ventriloquist spread his palms apart, fanning open a magical deck of playing cards. With uncanny speed, the conjuror then removed a handful and threw them, like shurikens, straight towards him. With unerring precision three of them struck him full in the chest, embedding themselves into his coat and skin.

With a pained roar, Everus staggered back against the near wall, his face blood-spattered.

Roach laughed and ran back up the stairs.

Gritting his teeth, Everus plucked the cards out. They had struck as though made of sharpened metal but now in his hand, they became as soft as tissue paper. "Let's get him!"

"Aye," muttered Creeps murderously. Blood poured from where he had been hit by the crossbow bolt.

Wounded, the two slowly made their way up to the third floor.

Once again they were in near darkness, but within the shadowy confines they could just about make out a short landing leading to a corridor, from which four or so doors gave access to other rooms.

"Show yourself!" shouted Everus, his echoing call his only answer.

"Aye, come out so as we can kill ye," muttered Creeps through clenched teeth.

Everus walked over to the nearest door and kicked it open. In the gloom, lit dimly by the outside street lights, he could see the shapes of assorted furniture and nothing else. He walked over to the door opposite and booted that open, his nostrils recoiling from the stench that emanated from beyond. Consequently, he was not entirely surprised by the sight which greeted him.

Hung neatly on large meat-hooks from the sloping rafters, were over ten cadavers or portions thereof, all of them in varying states of decomposition.

Everus stepped back, noting the gnawed bones and grisly puddles of viscera that lay strewn on the bare stone floor. Not far from where he stood, he could see the Uncle Tarby dummy sitting at a table, a wooden bowl, filled with what could only have been a sort of bloody stew, set before it. Its jester's outfit, in addition to several other outlandish costumes, hung from a row of pegs nearby. The corpse of a scantily dressed young woman had been dumped in a corner. From her wide-eyed look and the frozen scream on her face it was fairly safe to assume she had died of fright.

"*Gads!*" exclaimed Creeps, as curiosity got the better of him and he looked in. "What kind o' fella is this?"

Eyes on the dummy, Everus stepped inside, ready, and more than willing, to hack down *anything* that moved. He was struck with a disturbing mental image of the now naked dummy stirring to life and tucking into its gory dinner. *What was this?* Had the bogeyman he had seen at the window been just another frightening trick? In this house of horrors nothing was as it seemed. With each room he explored, this place and its odd owner became increasingly mysterious. There was something *really* strange going on...and then there was the thief again – was he invulnerable to magic?

"Look at that poor tart. I bet this bastard brings 'em back 'ere an' scares the shit out o' 'em before eatin' 'em. Do ye think that'd make 'em taste better? Anyhow, that's what Tarby said at the show! He was tryin' to warn us. An' look at this," said Creeps, presenting Everus with a heavily gnawed bone. "They ain't normal teeth marks."

Before Everus could respond there came a noise from out on the landing. Dropping the bone, he rushed out. Silhouetted in the open doorway at the end of the corridor stood Roach, his cigarette-holder in hand. For a moment, it seemed as though the conjurer's eyes glowed yellow.

"Welcome to my lair," sneered the ventriloquist.

"You're going down!" Everus charged at the spell-caster.

Roach raised one hand, shouted something and stepped forward, his hand now crackling with blue fire.

The two of them clashed.

Hatred fuelled Everus' swings, his blade slashing with the kind of lethality that would have killed a tavern-full of normal men in no time. But Roach was far from normal. With his burning hand, he reached out, dodging Everus' attacks and trying to score a hit of his own.

Weaving and parrying, Everus managed to force his opponent back into the room from which he had just emerged. The room was exquisitely furnished, a stark contrast to the cannibal's larder, which he had just exited. A fire blazed in a grand fireplace and in one corner there was an elaborate four-poster bed. Plush drapes, a lavish sofa, various expensive animal skins, a couple of ornate wardrobes and over a dozen portraits on the walls all added to the high level of opulence. The air was richly perfumed.

Retreating, Roach tripped on the head of a large, white, bear-skin rug. He fell backwards and then, with the agility of a wild cat, he sprung back, righting himself.

Everus pushed his slight advantage. With a cry, he pounced forward, bringing his sword down in a powerful, overhead swing.

Roach looked up, just in time for the sword to cleave his head in two. Each side fell apart like a sliced melon.

The spell-caster continued to get to his feet, his head flapping.

"*What the...?*" cried Creeps from the doorway.

"Another illusion!" shouted Everus, pulling his sword free. He watched with morbid fascination as the two parts of Roach's head jelled together again.

"Now you *have* pissed me off..." Roach began, his words cut short as Everus slashed across and severed his head from his body.

Everus stood over his decapitated foe, noting yet again the distinct lack of any blood. Unsure what kind of creature Roach was, he was about to hack down again when, with a cry, he felt a burning grasp on his left ankle. Jolting pain pulsed up his leg as the mystical blue energy which encased the ventriloquist's hand sparked and sizzled.

Electrocuted, Everus was thrown back, his hair bristling.

With a sickly squelching sound, a new head coalesced onto Roach's neck. Squealing like a new born babe, he started to undergo a gruesome transformation. Black striped, orange-coloured hair sprouted from his hands and face. His eyes yellowed and became cat-like, their vertical pupils, dark and evil. His ears grew pointed and his nose became a whiskered snout. His mouth was stretched back, becoming a gaping, fang-filled maw. Razor sharp claws burst from his slender fingers. A striped tail sprouted from his rear end.

"*Shit!*" screamed Creeps, backing away out onto the landing.

"I'll devour your flesh!" the Roach-thing snarled, its tiger-like head turning towards the retreating thief.

Still smoking, and with his hair standing upright, Everus hauled himself to his feet. Small, fiery electric-blue sparks danced around his lower legs. His teeth tingled.

The monster's head darted round, eyes staring at him; all claws and teeth wrapped up in a dark velvet smoking jacket.

"*Rakshasa!*" cried Everus.

"*Yes!*" the thing snarled. "Remember it well as I feast on your mangled carcass!" With a roar, it pounced forward, claws slashing wildly. Its first swipe raked Everus across his left arm, blood instantly filling the five parallel grooves.

With a cry of pain, Everus instinctively fell back, a claw flashing past his face. With a well placed kick, followed by a swift right hook, he managed to scramble away from the corner in which his foe tried to trap him. Knocking over a stand with a crystal decanter, two goblets and a pitcher of what might have been red wine, he made a dash for the door, now aware that he faced an enemy far beyond his ability to do battle with. He reached the door when the man-eating illusionist pounced on him. Claws raked across his back, scoring his flesh and shredding his coat.

The rakshasa snarled triumphantly.

Again, Everus managed to shake the thing from him. *"Run! Downstairs!"* he shouted at the thief. Turning, he tried to close the door, but a striped paw, its retractable claws as sharp as daggers, came round the edge. Throwing his shoulder against the door, he crushed the paw against the wall, but even as the smirk of satisfaction died on his lips, the wood cracked with a tremendous thud.

"I'll gorge on your brains!" the shape-changer roared, thumping the door a second time with its free paw.

With blood trickling down his face, Everus tried to contain it.

Again came the hammering and this time the frame splintered.

"Creeps!" Everus shouted, straining to crush the thing's paw as well as keep the door from being opened. Looking around, he could see no sign of the thief.

With the beast's fourth blow its clawed hand smashed through the door.

Everus leapt back and darted for the stairs as the monster tore the door from its hinges. With a growl, it chased after him, the aroma of fresh man-blood fuelling its need to kill. Crashing down the stairs, his legs muscles still quaking from the electrical jolt, Everus thought he saw the thief's frightened face peer from a doorway at the end of the landing.

In an orange and black blur, Roach leapt down in pursuit and sprang on him.

Screaming, Everus felt the beast tear and rip at him. He felt its hot breath on his face even as its jaws widened and closed in on his throat. In desperation, he gave a final push, and somehow managed to struggle free once again. He was badly mauled, blood pouring from his ragged body. A smack to the back of his head sent him reeling towards a marble plinth. Falling back, he landed with a crash on the floor, his vision already blackening as he struck his head off the wall. Through glassy eyes, he saw the tiger-headed beast leaping at him, its arms extended, its fanged maw open and ready to chomp. Then he passed out.

† † †

They struck during the night, their clinking armour and shouted commands accompanied by the barking of dogs.

He woke to the screams. Springing out of bed, he threw on a cloak. Listening at the door, he heard one of the mysterious assailants questioning a servant as to his father, Iwain's, whereabouts. When the servant refused to answer, there came a pitiful scream and then a thump.

Taking a display sword from the wall, he kicked the door open and leapt out, ready to confront these attackers. Were they thieves come to raid the villa, or assassins hired to kill his parents?

"Drop the weapon, boy!" shouted a hooded man holding a bloody sword.

"Intruders! We're under attack!" he cried.

A second man came forward, carrying a lit torch. "That's his son, Everus. We've to take him as well. They're all wanted for questioning."

"Who are you?" he asked.

"I have orders from Antonio De'carla, High Overseer of The Watchful Eye, to take you and your parents for questioning. Failure to surrender will result in your deaths. Don't force me to kill you."

"Everus, son. Do as he says. We cannot win this battle."

He turned on hearing his father's voice. Seeing his father being manhandled like a common criminal sent a wave of anger through him. His grip tightened around the sword handle. "Father?"

"We know what's been goin' on here," announced one of Iwain's restrainers. "We know you've all been involved in some kind of heresy. Demon-worshippers all of you."

"What rubbish is this?" he asked, still in two minds about fighting his way out and rescuing his father.

"Drop the weapon, boy!" ordered one of the men. "I won't ask again."

He looked at his father. Seeing the resignation on the older man's face, he then, helplessly, threw his sword to the floor.

† † †

Everus awoke when a pitcher of cold water was poured over his face. He found himself lying flat on his back in one of the rooms he had previously explored. Creeps' unpleasant visage, his ratty hair and moustache, accompanied by his cracked and stained teeth, hovered nearby.

"Ye alive?"

Everus thought about it for a moment. "Well if this is paradise, I pity us poor bastards."

"Aye, I thought ye were dead meat for sure, certainly after that whap ye took to yer bunnet."

"What happened?"

"Aye, but I thought ye were away this time," replied the thief, evading the question.

"*Roach?*" muttered Everus, suddenly remembering the rakshasa.

"He's out there," said Creeps, indicating to somewhere out on the landing. "But ye don't need to be worryin' about him any more. He'll no' be scarin' whores to death or doin' any more o' his tricks in a hurry."

"Did you...?"

"Aye. He were just about to get ye an' all."

"How did you...?" Groggily, Everus tried to get to his feet.

"Ye'd be better off just restin' a bit. Look, there's a nice bottle o' wine. How's about I pour ye a glass?" Creeps offered Everus a filled glass, which he readily accepted.

With what remaining strength he still stubbornly possessed, Everus pulled himself upright.

"Nice enough," Creeps commented, downing half the wine bottle and emitting a hushed belch.

"I...I don't understand." Everus started towards the door, his movement slow and uncomfortable. "How did you...?" His mind in a blur, he lumbered against the room door and then out onto the landing. Sprawled out, some five steps away, a crossbow bolt protruding from its throat, lay the tiger-headed fiend that had gone by the name of Roach Weidenreich.

CHAPTER SEVEN

He paced the room nervously, waiting for Katryna to arrive, desperately hoping that she would believe him – believe the truth. The door opened and she entered, her slender form enveloped in a rough, dark cloak, so different to her usual, light-hearted self. From the forlorn look on her face, he could see she was troubled.

"Kat," he said, embracing his lover before closing the door behind her. "I think this place is safe for a while, but I can't be sure."

"Everus, I...I can't stay for long. Aunt Xenobia will miss me." Katryna looked around at the almost bare room, her tear-filled eyes resting on the parchments strewn on the bed.

Following her gaze, he picked a handful of them up. "I've been trying to think of all the people who might've wanted to hurt my father but so far I've had no success. Why he's been accused of this accursed demon worship I don't know...but if I can just find out who's done this then I can clear him and bring an end to this nightmare."

Sorrow-laden doubt showed in Katryna's eyes. "But why did you leave the house, Everus? Your mother needs you...you're all she has. Surely you could do this at home? It pains me to see you here all alone." She was close to sobbing.

He shook his head. "I can't risk it, Kat. The Watchful Eye only let me go last time because they couldn't find a suitable excuse to lock me up...but if they can falsify evidence against my father, why, they can set me up too. It's only a matter of time, believe me. Out here, I've been able to dig around. I've bribed some and threatened others and yet I still can't find out what's going on. None of this makes any sense. I'm sure that someone in The Watchful Eye or maybe one of their bastard lawyers is manipulating all of this. I just can't find out who or why." He slammed his fist against a wall, anger and frustration twisting his good-looking features.

"But Everus...are you sure, absolutely sure, that this isn't just an *honest mistake? I mean, your father traded with so many strange merchants, maybe one of them gave him the statuettes...and, he didn't know what they were."*

"Katryna. I was in his study shortly before they searched it. They weren't there. Someone placed them there to be found. It was a clear set-up."

"Oh Everus, what's going to happen?" Katryna sobbed, burying her face in her hands.

Some of his anger melted away. He hated seeing her in pain. For all he now cared, the world could burn and everyone, but her, with it. He put a comforting arm around her, not knowing how much it would help. "I...I don't know...but we'll get through it. As long as we've got each other I'm sure that..."

"But Everus, can't you see? I can't come here again." She looked up at him, her pretty face tear-streaked and desolate. "Watchmen visited my home last night. They warned father that if I was seen associating with you they would assume that my whole family approved of...your behaviour. I know that you have nothing to do with this but...they said that your father has confessed."

He staggered back, a look of utter confusion on his face. "Confessed?"

"That's why I had to risk coming here tonight. I had to tell you." Katryna stared blankly at her hands. "And..." She gulped and wiped tears from her eyes.

"And what?"

"I...my parents have decided to send me away. Aunt Xenobia's escorting me tomorrow."

He stared at her bleakly. "Where?"

"I don't know. She won't tell me."

He clasped her in his arms, his green eyes fixing her. "You can't. You said we'd always be together. Stay with me, Kat. I can't deal with this on my own. I'll find somewhere safe for us until..."

"I'm sorry, Everus." Tears were now streaming down her face. "I'd put everyone in danger if I did...and I..."

"Then I'll come with you. I'll find out who did this and..."

"You'd be seen. Oh, Everus, this is terrible, a nightmare. I just want to wake up and find that everything has been a bad dream. That you were still at The Academy and..."

"Well I'm not." A coldness crept into his voice. "I was thrown out, remember? I guess they don't like the son of an accused

'demon-worshipper' studying there." He tried to fight the dark thoughts that now plagued him. He loved Katryna. None of this was her doing. He had to make her stay with him. Without her, without his academic dreams and without his family, there was no longer any future for him – he may as well throw himself on his own sword.

"Everus, please..."

"Kat, you've got to understand. That life has been taken from me. You're all that I now hold dear. Together we can make a new life, away from all these false allegations. I'll find out who did this and..."

"I can't," Katryna interrupted. "You know I can't. Even if I could, there's nowhere we could go. People are talking, Everus. Don't you know what they're saying? They say that you're...evil."

His eyes narrowed as he let go of his beloved. "Evil?" He had been called many things over his score of years; talented, handsome, obsessed – but never evil. Deep down, some part of him smiled. This was an epithet he could grow to like.

"I can't stand it...it's driving me mad. I have to go." Katryna looked up at him and for the last time their eyes met.

His mind raced through the possibilities, trying to find one that would allow them to be together but he knew that nothing could change the facts. Whoever had framed his family had effectively damned him, destroying his life with Katryna – for even if they were to defy everyone and steal away somewhere, he was too different now. He felt as if he were molten wax, shifting and flowing into new shapes as the hatred, bitterness and pain worked upon him. Love Katryna though he did, it would not stop him from pursuing vengeance in any way he must and it was better that they part now so she would remember him as he was, rather than who he felt he was becoming. For a moment it felt as though time itself had stopped, the agony of that parting gaze hanging with the poignancy and weight of a guillotine blade.

† † †

Roach's severed head rolled across the stage.

Body shivering, Everus sprang awake.

He lay in his bed, his mind alive with the memories of that night when he and Creeps had broken into the ventriloquist's house and fought with the rakshasa. He remembered regaining consciousness and staggering out onto the landing to see the dead beast but everything after that was largely blank. He had no recollection of getting home.

His mind swam with questions as he remembered the thief.

How had Creeps killed such a powerful enemy, an enemy who seemed to be invulnerable to normal weapons? Why, and how, had the spell Roach hurled at the thief been negated? Had Creeps somehow cured him as he lay, torn and ragged? Although he was a naturally fast healer, from the looks of things, his wounds, which had been grievous, were all but healed.

Slowly, Everus climbed out of bed, unaware that he had been asleep for nearly three full days.

† † †

Thirty-three hooded monks followed in procession behind Dae'morogin, their chants dark and malign, filled with blasphemous phrases which no sane person would care to hear. Entering a dark cavern, the demonic brethren filed out, forming a semi-circle before a natural stone podium. Their foul hymn came to an end as the high priest strode up to a wooden lectern.

Dae'morogin peered into the throng of shadowy figures massed around, relishing the eagerness with which they waited for his words. "Our time nears, my brothers." His words echoed and dripped like slime down the subterranean walls. "Soon this world will bathe in the Great Nothingness that will usher The Daemon God forth. And whilst each of us has attained the necessary level of enlightenment, we must still prepare, by praying to the darkness within our own souls. For on that blessed day, none will be spared, except those chosen few who are deemed worthy." He opened a thick grimoire which rested on the stand.

A dark red smoke billowed from the tome, slowly cascading out to cover the floor.

"From the Ninth Prophecy of Cyrvilus," Dae'morogin began, reading from the unholy bible. "I have seen the dark universe and out of that Chaos, I witnessed the Second Spawning of Uhu'giaggoth at the hands of a mortal born on the Third Alignment of the Third Moon. Raised by the priest of a fallen god, his death will summon forth the first of the spawn which will be but the catalyst for my own rebirth."

More and more hellish smoke belched from the book, threatening to shroud its reader.

The high priest continued, paying it no heed. "The spawn of Uhu'giaggoth will return when the last of the Ranters of Disas-Taurus have been cast into the fiery cracks of Zeth and the Øggarbakken behemoths stand on the brink of extinction." He looked up, surveying the congregation. Having read from the chosen passage, he closed the book. "As you all know, the last of the bastard heretics from Disas-Taurus have now been cleansed in the purifying fires of Zeth. The great furnaces and crematoriums have been working flat out and I am told that the smoke was of the sweetest grey." He closed his eyes for a moment and inhaled, imagining, with some delight, the scent of charred flesh and bone. "As I speak, the behemoths are mobilising for war, readying to attack our cities. They are being drawn to their doom, like moths to the flame. Their eradication is inevitable for it is as foretold by our messiah." He raised his arms. "All praise Cyrvilus!"

"All praise Cyrvilus!" came the sibilant reply.

His short sermon over, Dae'morogin descended from the smoky pulpit and paced over to a bloodstained statue nearby. In the gloomy light, cast from hundreds of black candles, the high priest dropped to one knee and muttered his own private prayers. Once finished, he rose to his feet and exited the murky shrine.

Hood raised, Dae'morogin headed down one of the countless labyrinthine passages that twisted throughout the subterranean temple complex. At the bottom of a long and tortuous stairwell, he made for another passage, its walls adorned in places with faded mosaics. In near darkness, he edged his way deeper into the bowels, the air becoming colder with each step.

Soon, he came to the yawning mouth of yet another flight of steps. From the confines of his robe, he removed a small torch, which he lit with but a wave of his hand. In the light from the guttering green fire, he paused for a moment in order to look at the malign and deviant images which stared out at him from the crumbling brickwork all around.

Slowly and carefully, he began down the steps, glad to be away from the dark scrutiny of the evil, mosaic-faces. Deeper and deeper he went, into the very foundations of the old Xethornite temple, eventually arriving at what appeared to be a dead end, its walls carved, relatively recently, with abominable shapes. He stopped and reached into a pocket for a key. After a brief moment spent searching for the keyhole, he inserted the key and unlocked the secret door.

An unholy chill gusted over what little there remained of

Dae'morogin's soul as he stepped into the large, vaulted chamber beyond. By the light from his torch, he saw the many stone sarcophagi that had been used to house the corporeal remains of many bygone high priests of Xethorn – undead slaves to an impotent, mundane orthodoxy.

He hated this place as much as many within hated him.

Striding down the central aisle of the dreary mausoleum, Dae'morogin was aware of that hatred with each step he took. Like a dark flood, it seemed to spew out in waves from some of the carved granite and black marble coffins, drowning all it touched in its bitter embrace. There was no doubt the inhabitants therein could turn nasty, violent even, launching psychic attacks which could prove dangerous, as indeed they had in the past. For the time being, however, they remained cowed by the essence of the one whom he was going to invoke.

In the hushed silence, Dae'morogin knelt before one particularly grimly-carved reliquary, his breath now steaming as the air in the catacomb became colder. The torch hissed and spat before going out, plunging him into complete darkness. He waited in the disturbing silence that followed, his eyes failing to accustom to the impenetrable gloom, despite the fact that he had spent most of his life underground. That this was a preternatural darkness, he had no doubt. A dark bluish light began to appear in a beam around the sarcophagus, bathing the stone funerary container in an indigo glare. Shadows slowly coalesced into rigid, discernible shapes. He watched as the glow began to shift and transform.

A spectral face, lined with loathing, blurred into view.

"Dae'dicus." Dae'morogin lowered his head in respect.

"Dae'morogin!" screeched the ghostly visage in a tortured voice. The doomed soul's eyes flared a deep crimson. "I take it this is about Everus?"

"Yes. I beseech your counsel." Dae'morogin stood up.

"What do you wish to know?" asked the disembodied wraith, each word laden with malice.

"I fear your protégé is...becoming suspicious. You were right to warn me of his prowess, for he possesses a rage that is proving hard to contain. I think now is the time for you to tell me more about him. And if he is 'The One'..."

"Everus is 'The One'. Of that there is no doubt. And as such, it is imperative that *he*, and *he* alone, is the author of the book. It must

135

be *his* deeds which fill the pages. The blood *he* spills must be its ink."

"And what of him?" Dae'morogin asked from the shadows. "For he still remains closed to my divinations."

"That's because you are weak," spat the ghost, disparagingly.

Dae'morogin swallowed and a deathly sensation froze him to the core. Deep within, a part of his human self screamed and cried out to his common sense to leave this unnatural place.

"Nonetheless, I will tell you. Everus Dragonbanner was once the most talented scholar of all things past this city has ever seen. I saw in him a great passion, an almost religious desire to unravel the mysteries and the puzzles of ages long since gone. Such energies were ideal for tainting. Such desires were perfect for destroying...or rather, redirecting and channelling anew. He was broken and turned to our cause by the brutal ruination of his ambitions and the sadistic corruption of his dream. With the aid of our accomplices, I commissioned his downfall. I was the great architect of his destruction, or his deliverance, depending on how one elects to see it." Dae'dicus smiled, a horrible sight to behold, before continuing. "His refocused energies we have harnessed and used to our advantage. His misdirected bitterness, fuelled by the lamentations for his lost dream, have proved to be ideal for our cause. He will make the perfect sacrifice, for his soul will soon be blackened with the deaths of thousands."

Dae'morogin shivered. There was something he had to say and yet he feared saying it. "I..."

"What is it?"

"As high priest, I need to know what you did, for he's an extremely volatile individual. He follows orders implicitly and yet...I sense a duality within him. He disguises it well but I feel he's keeping something from us. My agents are keeping watch on him whenever possible, but still I fear he could be...problematic."

"Do I detect an element of self-doubt? Are you perhaps not equal to this task?"

The high priest stared at the spectre with a mixture of distrust and fear, unsatisfied with the scant explanations but unwilling to continue in this vein. After all, there was something else that needed answering. "Regarding the book..."

"*The Book of Dead Names?*" the ghastly face cried, its features contorting cruelly. "What of it?"

"One of the names has been corrupted. A minor demon, possibly a rakshasa or an impshaga, has infiltrated, slain and adopted one of the names in the book. From what I can make out, the creature was destroyed. However, there does seem to be something strange, an anomaly I've not encountered before. So what are the...ritualistic implications?"

"Dragonbanner...destroyed it?" asked Dae'dicus sounding surprised.

"It would appear so."

"Then there is no problem. The book will be satisfied all the same."

"But Dae'dicus, could it not be that the chaotic nature of the demon bound within is itself beginning to wreak its power by warping the very fabric of the tome? Is it becoming unstable?"

"Perhaps. But remember, the book was fashioned with the greatest care. I personally oversaw its creation. Your task is simple. See to it that Dragonbanner continues to fill its pages. If you think that he is beginning to question *why* he is doing what he does, then provide him with an alternate motivation. His allegiance is to Xethorn and He alone...so inform him that his actions are geared towards his false deity."

"But Dae'dicus, my friend. I..."

"*My friend?*" snapped the spectre. "I am no friend of yours. Wasn't it *your* poison that filled my chalice? *Your* blade that sank into my back?"

"Yes...but, I only did it to..."

"To usurp my position? For you never could have earned it!"

"I have knowledge!" cried Dae'morogin. "I have power! I have life!"

"*Hah!* You're but the bastard son of Cardinal Ghuss! Remember who it was who took you in. Remember who it was who guided you in the worship of Uhu'giaggoth and who guides you still. The only power you have is that which I choose to give you. As for life...there are many here that are long dead that could destroy you ten times over. Life is but a moment encased in a prison of weak flesh. Death, if mastered, is an eternity of unlimited possibility. Now...be gone from my sight, unworthy one, before I unleash some of The Others."

Dae'morogin reeled away, the noise of the dead high priest's mocking laughter gnawing at his tortured mind.

✝ ✝ ✝

"A rakshasa, you say?" Cu asked. "Nasty things. Did you know that back in my old adventuring days, I met up with a whole caravan of the beasts out on the Stonesea Plateau? Me and my group thought we'd have ourselves a little fun with some of the pretty young things in the headman's harem. I only survived because I remembered a little of their native tongue and managed to impress the top man with a few conjuring tricks. So they let me go. Ate all the other poor buggers though."

"An interesting tale I'm sure..." started Everus.

"Yes, that it was," interrupted Cu, nodding at the memory. He was a bald-headed character of medium size and build with a small, black and grey striped goatee beard. His face was wrinkled and sun-bleached and had a lived-in look that clearly belonged to someone who had experienced life beyond the city walls. His clothing was weird and baggy, typical mage attire, brazenly decorated with stars and crescent moons. Around his neck, there dangled a necklace made from teeth and other miscellaneous bits of scrimshaw.

"All the same, I was informed by someone that you could tell me more about them. Specifically, their destruction. For my weapon seemed ineffective." Everus thought back briefly to his meeting with Grigalo two days before. If any of his acquaintances knew about these demons then surely he would, but it had been Grigalo who, after confessing his ignorance, had informed Everus about the reclusive wizard in whose wigwam he now found himself.

Reluctantly, Cu Cthonos rose from his pile of stuffed cushions and walked over to one of several heavy-looking oak chests. He opened it and spent some time rummaging through its contents, removing an array of weird and wonderful objects and pieces of clothing before returning with a scrappy old book. He took a seat at the table across from his inquisitive guest.

"What's that?" Everus asked.

"Why, this is one of my old notebooks. A bestiary if you prefer, listing some of the many monsters I've devoted the best part of fifty years to studying."

"And what does it say about rakshasas?" Everus asked, violently knocking aside the wizard's small, monkey-like familiar as it tried to leap onto his lap.

Cu looked up, a glint in his eyes. "I wouldn't do that if I were you."

"Do what?"

"Black Jinx. He don't take kindly to your treatment."

"Is that so?" Everus asked, eyeing the sorcerer's imp as it slunk out of the tent.

"Aye. He'll remember and then he'll pounce on you when you're least expecting it."

"Well, in that case, I suppose I'd better kill it now." Everus was in two minds about following his threat through, of just marching out with his sword and slaying the irksome thing. He knew better though. Even by saying what he had, he may well have put his life in danger. On the whole, wizards tended to be tetchy individuals, strongly attached to their associated imps and homunculi.

Cu laughed. "Hah! You don't even know how to kill a rakshasa. What makes you think you could kill an elder groglin?"

"I could always devote my life to trying," Everus replied, coldly. "Anyway, enough of that. What does your book say about rakshasas?"

Cu studied the index at the back of the book. "Rakshasas. Here we are. Page one hundred and forty-three." He turned to the correct page and began reading. "Malign, often insane, shape-changing illusionists that possess an insatiable hunger for human flesh. The first recorded encounter is described by the famed explorer and self-styled missionary, Hamman Azif, who reports meeting a man who became like a jackal in the ash deserts of Uttapia, close to the ruins of Ancient Qadang-Mo."

Everus nodded. "Hmm. That may explain the human sacrifices and demonic cults that sprang up around Qadang-Mo during the time of the Fifth Uttapian Uprising."

"Yes, I suppose so. Anyway, the report goes on to say that half of Azif's men fell battling the demon before realising that their weapons were not harming it. Spells from their accompanying mage likewise proved ineffective. Indeed it was only when..." Cu looked up. He slammed the book shut. "Hmm. Well would you believe it? It seems as though I must've forgotten to write up the full account. Such a pity but not really all that surprising."

"What do you mean? Have I come here for nothing?"

"This is strange." Genuinely confused, Cu stared at his book. "I could have sworn that I had all of my early encounters compiled and up to date. Anyway, why don't you ask me about something else...a Galgauntian Ghoul, a Shivering Teether or a loup garou for instance?"

"I came here to find out about rakshasas. Someone I know killed one with a crossbow. Does that mean *anything* to you?"

"Oh?" Cu's eyes widened. "Did he now?"

"That's what I said." There was an unconcealed iciness to Everus' words.

"And...how did he achieve that? I mean, did he shoot it or did he club it to death?"

"Guess."

"So, I take it you're saying he shot it dead with a crossbow?" Cu stroked his goatee. "Interesting. I'll have to do some research on that. Clearly it must've had something to do with the bolts he used. Perhaps they were magical?"

"Hmm. Perhaps." Realising the futility of discovering any further information from the colourfully-garbed wizard, Everus stood up and prepared to leave. He stood at the entrance to the untidy tent, considering whether to pursue the matter further. With a shake of his head, he changed his mind and left, still none the wiser.

† † †

That evening, Everus left his villa and decided to talk a walk. It was a surprisingly peaceful night and by the light of the dying sun, he fought with the dual emotions that were constantly threatening to pull him apart. Whereas there was a part of him that desired to kill, there was another part, an older part, that belonged to nothing more harmful than an inquisitive child. A child who had grown to be a man. A man, who, through no fault of his own, had become bitter and twisted. A man who had been forced to walk through the destruction of his past.

His perambulations brought him onto one of the many bridges which crossed the Great River that ran through the middle of Wyrm's Port before spilling out into The Dark Sea down by the harbour. He leant against the waist high stone parapet, gazing pensively at the scummy water as it swept past, trying to bring some clarity to his confused emotions. It was common at times such as this, and more so during the long and lonely nights, that his thoughts turned to the dreams of what he could have been and what had been stolen from him. He smiled briefly to himself as memories of Katryna surfaced in his mind. His thoughts then passed to his time at The Academy. He could have been the best scholar the city had ever seen, of that he was convinced.

Then, just as easily as the notions of what could have been surfaced, he found himself asking why they had not. *Why?* A question he had posed to himself hundreds of times during countless sleepless nights and tortured days.

It was all that bitch Julia's fault.

She had ruined his academic career. *She* had discredited his family. *She* had driven his mother to an early grave through illness and his father to commit suicide in a Wyrm's Port cell. *She* had caused Katryna to abandon him. *She...*

With difficulty, Everus wrenched his mind away from the well worn dark cycle of his thoughts.

Suddenly he was struck over the back of the head with something heavy.

"We've to take the bugger alive!" croaked an angry voice from somewhere close by.

With a pained cry, Everus turned, his right hand instinctively reaching to his battered head. With his fingers, he felt the dampness of blood. Stumbling against the parapet, he was struck a second time from behind, the blow glancing off his back. His vision swimming, he fell to his knees even as two more blows rained down. Shouting his fury, he shrugged off the pain, got to his feet and punched one of the two blackjack-wielding louts who were attacking him. His clenched fist struck home, shattering teeth and bursting lips.

Whimpering, one of the thugs fell to the ground.

Everus rushed forwards and kicked his standing assailant full in the crotch. He grabbed the unfortunate by the hair and introduced the man's face to his rising right knee before taking hold of him and hurling him head first over the bridge.

A round of applause came from a group of spectators as the man splashed to the water far below.

Things had happened so fast that Everus had been unable to fully take in what was happening. Now that the initial bout of pain and the surprise of having been attacked had subsided somewhat, he steadied his nerves, surveying and assessing the scene. One of his attackers still lay on the ground, a hand clasped to his bleeding mouth. He was just about to go over and see if he could lend a helping hand by throwing him over the side as well when a shout from behind stopped him in his tracks.

"*Oi! 'Bastard-Face'!* You an' me."

Everus turned to see a large, powerfully-built man moving towards him. This individual was outfitted in the attire of an executioner. On his legs he wore a pair of black breeches. His chest was bare, tattooed and strongly-muscled. His face was masked by a black hood, complete with eyeholes.

The hooded man took a step forward and cracked his knuckles. "I'm goin' to kick the shit outta you. An' you know what? I'm gettin' paid to do it. Life don't get any better, now does it?" The brute lunged forward, one vice-like hand clamping around Everus' left shoulder, thrusting him to the ground.

Everus cried out as he was then kneed under the chin. A huge boot then stomped down, clipping an ear and drawing blood.

"It's lucky for you that you're wanted alive," shouted the bruiser.

Rolling to one side, Everus scrambled to his feet. Narrowly dodging a haymaker swung by his opponent, he stepped to one side and jabbed in two hard punches of his own straight into the man's solid torso.

The large man grinned, pain hardly registering. With a meaty hand, he reached out and dragged Everus forward by the hair before cracking a punch into his stomach. Everus instantly doubled over and collapsed in agony, having felt as though he had just been struck by a battering ram.

"Kick him while he's down!" cackled an old woman from the small crowd that had gathered.

"Stomp on his bloody head!" yelled someone else with equal enthusiasm. "I want to see his brains on the cobbles."

The brawler needed no such encouragement. Bending down, he grabbed Everus and held him aloft, pushing him back against the parapet.

Struggling to escape, Everus kicked the man hard on the left shin, causing him to release his hold and howl in pain. He then smacked a punch into the hooded face.

With a roar, the tattooed grappler locked his arms around Everus' chest and raised him off the ground. "You're comin' wi' me!"

"*Never!*" Everus gasped, his ribs beginning to strain under the fierce bear-hug. Gritting his teeth, he spread his fingers wide and drove his thumbs into the mask's eyeholes. He gouged his thumbs deeper, puncturing the gelatinous wetness and popping eyeballs.

Screaming in agony, the brute flung Everus to the ground, blood and vitreous fluid soaking his black hood. Hands raised to his face, he tilted his head and tried to replace one of his dislodged eyeballs which now hung by its optic nerve. Hollering in pain, he stumbled as Everus drew the dagger he kept concealed in his right boot and stabbed him in the back. Using his raw strength, he managed to throw Everus off before turning and making a blind dash for it, the dagger still stuck in him.

From the ground, Everus watched as his attacker ran and stumbled, bellowing and bleeding like a harpooned sea monster.

✝ ✝ ✝

The next day, before sunrise – not that there was any sunlight down in these abyssal depths – found Everus in Dae'morogin's office. Curious, he watched as the high priest removed one of his numerous relics from a locked cabinet before placing the obscene artefact on the desk before him.

"Been fighting again, have we?"

Well aware of his bruised face and cut lip, Everus nodded. "Just some drunken louts who chose to mug the wrong person. Nothing to worry about." Privately, he was worried about the attack the night before. It had sounded more like an attempted abduction.

"Good," replied Dae'morogin, distantly. "Anyway, I take it you recognise this piece."

Everus reached across and picked up the small, almost shapeless, figurine. Its composition was an open affront to all that was natural and it felt slick and moist as though covered in invisible frog spawn. Carefully, he examined its exterior, noting that there were vague patterns within its seemingly featureless design. Looking closer, he saw that a few abominable visages had been carved into it. He returned it to the desk before looking up.

"Well?"

"I'd say it's a rather crude rendering of The Great Evil from Beyond, The Devourer of Life; Uhu'giaggoth. Made from black laval chaostone, I'd surmise it was probably fashioned in Zeth sometime during, or perhaps before, The Hellspawn Cataclysm."

"Which was?" prompted the high priest, grinning like a skull.

"A time of great chaos. A time when The High Three themselves were nearly defeated. It was only by rallying the other gods that The

High Three managed to expunge Uhu'giaggoth from our time. From what I remember of my teaching, it was Our Lord, Xethorn, who, aware of the implications of ultimate chaos, lent His powers to The High Three and the others so that chaos would be defeated."

"Although that is true, if one believes in the Ancient Prophesies, particularly the Writings of the heretic, Cyrvilus, a time will come when Uhu'giaggoth and his followers will return. Only this time they will be victorious."

"Why tell me this?" asked Everus, eyes fixed on the vile relic before him.

"Because you, my friend, are the only one who can...prevent Uhu'giaggoth's return."

"*What?*"

Dae'morogin sat back. "Long ago, Dae'dicus saw in you and in you alone, a strength, a burning power. Knowing that his time was short, he compiled *The Book of Dead Names*, which, once completed, would serve as a channel through which Xethorn could return."

"And Xethorn could defeat Uhu'giaggoth?"

Dae'morogin's answer was little more than a weak, uninspiring smile.

"But I'm..." Everus was just about to inform the high priest about his own divinely appointed quest to discover and return the three magical amulets and of how only one more was needed, when an inner voice told him to say nothing. This was his secret and the time to reveal it was not now. "I..." He stared once more at the foul stone before him. It seemed as though it wanted him to divulge his secret, to tell Dae'morogin all he knew and what he was attempting to do. What harm could it cause? Perhaps now was as good a time as any? Should the high priest of Xethorn not be made privy to what Everus was doing in Xethorn's name?

"You've something to tell me?" Dae'morogin asked, his dark, raven-like eyes pecking at Everus' will.

"Yes. I...I've been..." Everus was about to tell Dae'morogin about his private rapport with his god and all about his own attempts to emancipate Xethorn, when there came a firm knock on the door.

The high priest looked up. "Enter."

The door opened and a cowled hunchback looked in, his face wrinkled and sallow. Like an aged mole, he peered about, almost blindly. "High priest, forgive my intrusion, but...I think there's something you should have a look at. One of the prisoners is...well, he's..."

"Spit it out man!" snapped Dae'morogin, clearly annoyed at the interruption.

"Well...he seems to have come back from the dead. We killed him earlier and when Brother Murgo went in to remove the corpses we found him alive."

"Zombification?" Dae'morogin asked.

"No, high priest. He appears to have retained all of his faculties. We think it may have to do with a ring he's wearing, but we can't be sure, nor can we remove it."

"Very well. I suppose I'd better look into it," Dae'morogin sighed. Like an animated corpse himself, he rose stiffly from his chair. "Everus, stay here. I'll be back soon."

After the door had closed behind the two clerics, Everus sat back in his chair and looked about the room he knew so well. Now that the high priest had left, the great need to reveal his secret left him as well. As he looked around his surroundings, memories of the many conversations and discussions he had shared with his mentor, Dae'dicus, came into his mind. Countless times had he sat in here, debating and learning all about the nature of religion and the inadequacies of justice. It had been Dae'dicus who had suggested that he should train as an active agent of Xethorn as opposed to becoming one of the brotherhood.

As Everus waited for Dae'morogin to return, his mind drifted back to an earlier time.

† † †

After the demise of his parents and the death of his academic dream, he turned his abilities in a new direction. He was practicing his swordsmanship within the cavernous training room as his trainer, a slim, battle-scarred veteran from distant Tarnech, barked commands and pushed him to the limit of physical exertion. Swinging and dodging, weaving and parrying, he obeyed his trainer as all around him other young men, dressed in a variety of armour types and armed with an array of weapons, rehearsed their deadly skills. Dodging one of his instructor's padded maces, he landed a blow, much to the armoured man's surprise. His trainer grunted and withdrew.

He spun round and dealt out a twirling flurry of blows, forcing the man back and out of the circular training area.

"Now you're showing off," claimed a familiar voice.

He turned, sweat dripping from his forehead, and saw the stooped, robed figure of his mentor. "Dae'dicus!" Running to meet the man, he knelt before him. "I thought you weren't due back for many days."

"Rise, my son," replied the aged, grey-haired high priest. "My mission went better and passed faster than I had hoped."

He got to his feet, handing his sword back to his disgruntled trainer.

"When you've finished here, come to my room for there are things which you must hear."

Hurriedly, he bathed and dressed, keen to discover what news the old man had for him. Dressed in his black, hooded robe, he made his way down the darkened passage towards the high priest's private chambers. With growing apprehension, he paused outside the stout wooden door, his mind troubled at the undercurrent of concern he had detected in his mentor's voice.

"Enter," Dae'dicus announced from inside.

Turning the handle, he opened the door and strode into the room beyond. Seated in his chair, his lined face barely illuminated by the burning candles on his desk, was Dae'dicus.

"Everus. Please, close the door and be seated."

He walked in and sat down in the offered chair.

"Tell me my son, tell me what you sought to find within these walls. For when I brought you here over seven years ago, you told me that you had lost everything and now I wish to know what you have gained."

Hesitating a moment, he glanced at the wall behind the seated man, taking in the collection of bizarre and macabre masks the high priest had on display. Many of them were priceless works of art gathered from the dark and uncivilised corners of the empire, places only spoken about in wild rumour. "Xethorn returned my will to be. Our Lord gave me focus and restored my belief. It is due to Him and you, that I live at all. You...were the one who gave me the strength to continue after..."

"After your expulsion from The Academy? And after the untimely death of your mother and father?" Dae'dicus gently prompted.

"Yes."

The old man stroked his chin. "I remember you telling me, when we first met, that your father, Iwain, took his own life. Was that so?"

"That's true. He couldn't cope with the constant accusations. They believed him to be a worshipper of Uhu'..." He struggled with the name.

"Uhu'giaggoth?"

"Yes. He was tried as a traitor and a deviant. A demon-worshipper. He committed suicide rather than face a public execution."

Dae'dicus nodded. "I remember now. Yes...I remember you telling me about the crusade you went on to try and clear your family name. How you tried to prove their innocence and yours."

"My wasted years," he said bitterly, sinking once more into the haunted memories of the past.

"Wasted? But surely, avenging your parents was a worthwhile cause?"

Battling to keep his emotions in check, he tried to switch his attention to something else. He stared at the masks once more as though compelled to do so. Every time he came here it was always the same. He felt the rage, deep inside as it began to boil within him. The agent of his downfall, the nameless culprit who had falsified evidence, started the preposterous rumours and who had persisted in the slanderous campaign against himself and his father had always remained hidden; faceless, and without a target to unleash his venom against, it had just welled inside him. "Wasted, because I never succeeded. I never found out who was to blame."

"And that continues to pain you, the fact that whoever did this is still out there, unpunished? Those who've crippled you...you want to see them burn, yes?"

He nodded, slowly.

"Good. It's as it should be. It's as Xethorn would want." Dae'dicus' smiled, his face shrouded in shadow. "Then you'll be pleased to know that I can tell you who did it."

"You know?"

"Yes, indeed. I've travelled far and wide to assist in alleviating your torment and obtaining the justice your heart craves." The old man's smile widened, revealing his stained and cracked teeth. "After all this time, revenge will be yours, young Dragonbanner. The one you are after was once a student at The Academy. Her name..."

"Her!?"

"Her name is Julia Camberra. Once a lawyer, she is now a captain of The Watchful Eye."

✝ ✝ ✝

The door was flung open, jolting Everus back to matters at hand.

Dae'morogin strode in, wiping his hands with a cloth. "Can you believe it did not occur to them to cut his finger off? Still, I do believe we've acquired a nice little ring with rather amazing regenerative powers. No doubt the brotherhood will squabble over who gets to keep it." He went to his chair and sat down. "Now then, where were we?"

"You were about to..."

"Ah, yes. As I was saying, through *The Book of Dead Names*, it's hoped that you can create the means for Our Lord to return, in order to prevent..."

"The return of Uhu'giaggoth?" Everus gazed at the small demonic figurine once more. "Ultimate murder as opposed to ultimate chaos? Sanctioned assassination and death with a motive...or the senseless eradication of us all."

"Which would *you* prefer?"

Everus picked up the slimy-feeling figurine and studied it once more. Certain of its poor workmanship and worthlessness, he crushed the friable piece in his fist and dropped the powdered crumbs on the desk. "My allegiance is to Xethorn."

Dae'morogin flinched. His face trembled, masking a spasm of hate. Under the desk, his right hand began to shake uncontrollably. Tinged crimson, his pupils dilated. He was finding it hard to contain his anger. Like a stretched mask, skin visibly tightened on his face.

Startled, Everus watched, transfixed as the high priest seemed to battle with himself. He rose from his chair, half-expecting him to transform into something unnatural as a certain ventriloquist once had.

Dae'morogin gripped his shaking hand and began to laugh, insanely. "*You...*" His apoplectic fit began to subside. He took a few deep breaths, seemingly mesmerised by the powdered fragments before him. He then looked up. "You...suspect that your, what shall we call him...*accomplice*, has latent magic abilities?" he asked politely and in stark contrast to his attack of madness. There was a look now of genuine interest on his pale, sickly face.

"Possibly," Everus answered, guardedly. "Anyway, that thing almost killed me. He was a rakshasa...and he was immune to my attacks."

By the flickering candlelight, Dae'morogin peered at Everus, his hollow-looking face showing signs of sudden ageing. "I did warn you about Weidenreich. But what matters is that you saw it through...*you* did kill him, didn't you?"

Everus choked back a nervous gulp. Was everything now doomed to failure because *he* had not killed the demon? What were his chances of leaving the temple alive if he admitted his failure? Was the high priest insane? "Hard to believe, I know."

"With a magical bolt, you say?"

"Yes," lied Everus. "At the last moment my accomplice gave me the crossbow. Where he got it from, I don't know."

"But it was *you* who killed it?" pressed Dae'morogin.

"Yes. I've told you."

"A most useful ally," mused Dae'morogin, relaxing a little. "Perhaps you should introduce us one day. His talents, from your own accounts, could prove useful to us."

"He's just a nobody, a common thief."

"What of this...darker shadow that you've mentioned before? A most intriguing ailment, and one of which I've never heard."

"I don't know. I could be mistaken."

"Hmm. Very well." The high priest's eyes narrowed to black slits. "Your next victim is another grubba, one Oodle Gaggs. She should be easy to find and easy to kill. Easier than Roach, that's for certain." He stood up, preparing to usher Everus out. "You know, we're getting near the end. Great things are nearing, Everus. Great things indeed." He opened the door and steered Everus out.

Uncomfortable with Dae'morogin's behaviour and disturbed by his uncharacteristic tone, Everus was relieved to be leaving.

† † †

Everus entered his private shrine and solemnly walked over to the dark, faceless statue of his god. After a moment's silent meditation, he raised his head. Within the darkened oval, he saw his own face as though the surface had become a mirror. Then the reflection disappeared. "Hail Xethorn! Lord of Night. Widow-maker. He who rejoices in the baying of dogs and spilt blood. Make thy servant worthy, so that I may succeed in thy task. The moons have darkened. Reveal unto me the location of thy final ward."

Suddenly the reflection returned. "Everus," it spoke.

Dropping to his knees, Everus bowed his head in supplication.

"The remaining amulet is to be found in the tomb of Khorgo Wulvargen."

Everus looked up. The face had gone. Still, he knew what had to be done. Leaving his private temple, he headed down the corridor, towards the room which now served as a study. He entered. Numerous bookshelves, crammed with tomes and obscure, bound manuscripts ran around the length of the walls and more books were kept in locked bookcases at one end. Directly across from him there was a great stone fireplace, now chipped and crumbling. To his immediate right was a large wooden table, its surface covered with rolled maps and many more books.

It took him some time to locate the book he was after. It was a large, clasp-locked tome, part of the works he had salvaged from his old home before it had fallen into the hands of those who had ousted his parents.

Grubban runes were never easy for a non-grubba to decipher and Everus' problem was compounded by the antiquity of the grammar and the worn nature of the book. Consequently, it took him a long time before he discovered that Khorgo Wulvargen had lived some two and a half thousand years ago. This came as no surprise, for it tallied well with the age of the places where the other two amulets had been found. The brief extract on the grubban warlord's life was interspersed with accounts of his glorious deeds and how certain engineering marvels had been introduced during his short lifetime.

Most of the details no longer interested Everus but, resisting the urge to just throw the book on the fire, he continued to peruse the time-worn pages. Eventually, he found, contained in one of the obscure fragments on grubban burial lore, a mention that the warlord had been entombed some league or so north of the now ruined and abandoned city of Durgan's Rock, close to the even older ruins of Disas-Taurus, the ancient stronghold of the demon lord, Bhûl-Mara'gorcho.

✝ ✝ ✝

"Do ye like ma new chair? It's the dog's bollocks, ain't it?" asked Creeps, rocking back and forth. "Got it from a man whose nephew snuffed it the other day. He said that I could have it for helpin' him shift some o' the rubbish that the..." Belatedly noticing that his guest was not in the least bit interested, he decided to change the topic of conversation to something a little more pertinent. "So, who're we to bump off this time?"

"Oodle Gaggs," Everus answered.

"What a name," chuckled the thief. "Wi' a name like that he should o' been put down at birth."

"She."

"Ye mean he's a woman? A bint?"

"A grubba."

"Another bleedin' grubba! This is gettin' weirder. They must be some real sick bastards ye're workin' for. All these different folk. One moment it's a nobody, then it's a priestly chap, then it's some nutter who turns into some kind o' cat monster. Now it's another grubba, an' a female one at that! What next I wonder?"

"I follow instructions," said Everus, icily. "Besides, what should it matter to you, so long as you get your money?"

Creeps shut up. He rocked back on his chair and puffed at his pipe, blowing smoke rings towards the discoloured ceiling.

Everus stared, scrutinising his associate, convinced there *was* something strange about him. He had come to confront the thief about his strange powers, but for the time being he was content to stand and wait. He paid close attention, looking to see if the thief wore any unusual trinkets, be they a ring or a necklace, which could explain his bizarre abnormalities. Tattoos were another possibility, for he had once read about a race of people who had developed such a means of periaptic bodily adornment. However, he had no real compulsion to see any more of the thief's naked flesh. Such sights were not fit for human eyes.

"What is it?" asked Creeps, aware of Everus' scrutiny. "Am I showin' signs o' the pox?"

"Who are you?" Everus asked, his words hushed as though his mouth had tried to veto the question his brain wanted to ask.

"Eh? What's that?"

"Nothing. Just thinking to myself."

"Seems as though that pummellin' ye took the other night might've..."

"*Might've what?*" snarled Everus, rising from his chair. "*Damaged my senses!?*" Turning his back on the thief, he strode over to the window and gazed out at the grim cityscape. Why did he keep coming back here? Why didn't he just go it alone? Could he go it alone? He spun round and looked Creeps dead in the eye. "Account for thyself."

"Ye what?"

"Who or what are you? Are you some kind of lay wizard?"

"Eh? What're ye on about?"

"Come on, Creeps. Don't think I haven't noticed your shenanigans."

"What shenanigans?"

"You know perfectly well." Everus' eyes narrowed. "Your magic."

Creeps went on the defensive. "There's no magic in openin' doors or climbin' walls."

"I agree. But how did you kill the rakshasa and...?"

"The what?"

"You know exactly what I'm on about. The crossbow bolt. The magical defence."

"I haven't a clue what ye're..."

"Tell me," interrupted Everus, threateningly.

"But, there's nothin' to tell."

"I'll ask *once* more."

Seeing the menace in Everus' eyes, Creeps finally gave way. "Ma magic," he blurted, clearly worried. "It's a curse. I was cursed when I was a nipper. Aye, that's it. Ye see, ma dad, from whom I learnt the tricks o' the trade, he found some old thing. A ring..."

"*Bullshit!*"

"No, it's true. Honest. This old ring used to belong to a wizardy chap. Anyhow, it were cursed, for shortly after ma dad gettin' it, he fell ill an' died."

"You told me your father was hanged."

Creeps scratched his head, cogitating. "He...he was. But he'd been ill...for some time before we, he...went to the gallows." He was clearly flannelling. He grinned broadly, the sight not a nice one. "An' anyhow, that ring's brought nothin' but grief an' ill-fortune to all ever since. Take me for instance. I've lived a sad an' lonely life an' I'll no' live that much longer." His grin had died now, replaced with a pitiful expression that looked false somehow.

"Quite true," Everus acknowledged, reaching for his sword.

"*Wait!* Just give us a mo so as I can tell ye more o' ma story. Ye see, just afore ma dad passed away, he used the last o' his money in gettin' some priestly nutter to come round an' pray for us all...to try an' break the curse. Summat went wrong however, an' I ended up gettin' this magic protection-thing on me instead. It's kept me safe a few times, I can tell ye."

"This ring. Where is it?"

"It was flung into the sea."

"How convenient. And your shadow?"

"Ma shadow?" Creeps looked confused. "Oh aye, that. Well, I suppose that must've summat to do wi' the curse. Might be eatin' away at ma soul, or summat."

"So you're not cured?"

"Well...no' fully."

"And Roach? How did you kill him, for nobody I've talked to seems to know how to destroy a rakshasa?"

"Aye, well. I remembered a tale I was told as a nipper. It was about one o' them rak-thingymabobs. An' they killed it wi' a crossbow bolt that'd been dipped in holy water...ye know, that stuff that the priests use to clean their arses wi' afore they go into the temple." Creeps gulped. "I always carry a little bottle o' the stuff wi' me in case I meet any spooks. It's a habit I got into when I used to work the boneyards wi' Matt. Ye never knew what ye'd run into out there. One time I saved Matt from one o' 'em bloodsuckin' things. It's true, I swear."

Dubiously, Everus stared at the thief anew, wondering whether to believe him or not. "You could be telling the truth, I suppose. Although, knowing you, it's most likely pure fabrication."

"*Fabric?*" Creeps shook his head. "Is that summat to do wi' clothes? I don't make clothes."

"Well, perhaps you should. A shroud for instance."

"*What do ye mean?*" Creeps whimpered, tears brimming.

"Creeps. You're forever the lowlife; the dung on my boots. What a predicament me and thee now face. Do I let you live? Or do I kill you?"

"Don't kill me," the thief pleaded. "It's true, all I said."

"It's not just that. I mean, can I afford to operate with someone like you any more? It's bad for my image."

"I've been loyal."

"Up to a point."

"An' I've saved yer hide once or twice," said Creeps, uncertain how Everus would respond to such a truth.

"You've been lucky."

"Come on, Everus. Me an' ye go back a long way. Ye know I've always..." The thief's words were now bordering on the pathetic.

"*Shut up!*" Everus' look darkened. "Know that you're living on borrowed time." He pointed straight at Creeps to emphasise his threat. "Know also that you live only because I still have need of your services. This Gaggs, or whatever she calls herself, could well be another tricky customer."

"Ah, don't worry. We'll put her in the book all the same."

Everus stepped back, the thief's particular choice of local euphemism causing him to stare at his unkempt associate anew.

† † †

Two days later, Everus walked into the small shack and brought death to the elderly grubban matriarch that lived therein, slaughtering her in her bed. The high-pitched screams of her young fell deafly on his ears as he sliced his sword down again and again. A sudden desire to butcher them all – to transform this squalid hovel into a complete bloodbath – filled his mind. Something other than his allegiance to Dae'morogin seemed to be guiding his actions, something which instructed him to kill; a remorseless, savage hunger that fed on merciless slaughter. Somehow, he reigned in his need. He turned his back on the wailing. Outside, he casually wiped the blood from his blade before walking over to where the thief stood on lookout.

"Ye all done?"

Nodding, Everus sheathed his dried blade on his back.

"That were easy. Now, how's about goin' for a drink? If ma memory serves me right there used to be a good alehouse near 'ere. The Dripping Kipper, or summat like that. Used to serve a whole load o' drinks from foreign parts; Uttapian Rum, Wee Agg's Whiskey, Ullerbian Funny Sauce, Grubban Goat Shandy, High-Balls, Stinkin' Pussy Liquor. Ye name it, ye could get it there."

"Sounds good."

In silence, the two headed to the tavern in question.

During that short walk, Everus had to fight to keep the images of the recent murder out of his mind. Normally, it was something he could do with comparative ease; blotting out the viciousness of his attack and pushing it to the back of his mind, where it would soon vanish. This time it was different though and the faces of the helpless grubban infants, as they screamed and pawed at their dead mother, played constantly on his mind.

They reached The Dripping Kipper and went inside.

Finding an empty table, Everus sat down and waited for the thief to return with the drinks.

"Captain Mung's Special Ale. Get that down yer thrapple," said Creeps, passing across a tankard of purple-frothed beer. "Ye know ye've got blood on yer coat?"

The question broke Everus' chain of dark recollection. Casually, he looked at the small offending stain.

Creeps raised his drink to his lips and took a greedy glug.

"I'm planning another venture."

"Eh? Where to?"

"The Deadmoor Clumps."

"*The Deadmoor?* What're ye wantin' to go there for?"

"A...friend, wants something brought back."

"Bad place The Deadmoor, from what I've heard. What wi' all 'em big wild men an' things. It's just no' safe. Ye go in there, ye don't come back."

"Very well. I'll find others." Downing his drink in one, Everus stood up and prepared to leave.

"Hold on! I didn't say I wouldn't go wi' ye. All I said was that it's a bad place."

"So am I to take it that you're in?"

Creeps drew his stool closer, eager at least to adopt the pretence of an equal partner. "Providin' the price is right."

Everus grinned. "Well, I might put off killing you by a couple of days. Is that good enough for you?"

"Go on then. Count me in," the thief muttered, darkly.

"Of course, we may need others."

"Eh? No' that daft git, Grigalo, or whatever he's called?"

"No. Grigalo has departed for Ghavin's Keep. If we're going to The Deadmoor, and especially considering the recent reports about Øggarbakken behemoths in the area, I think we need someone with...different talents."

"Who?"

"I've someone in mind. And, thanks to you, I've some information that may prove of interest to him."

✝ ✝ ✝

Later that day, as the snow fell and swirled through the streets in white whirlwinds, Everus made his way towards the abode of the wizard, Cu Cthonos. Dressed in his long coat and with his scarf wound tightly about his face, he came to the stretch of wasteland on which the eccentric wise man had set up home. He stopped for a moment in order to look around, noting the discernible lack of other houses, or indeed people. That this was one of the more remote and least populated parts of the city, he had no doubt, facts abundantly clear from a casual glance at his surroundings.

Everus disliked all who practiced magic. It was not just as a result of his encounter with Roach Weidenreich, his inherent paranoia or, for that matter, the fact that he did not like dealing with anyone more powerful than himself, but because he had been brought up within a sacerdotal environment, one where sorcery was largely frowned upon as blasphemous and ungodly; a pseudo-religion – one based purely on deceit and trickery. He had been brought up to believe in the dishonesty of magic. It lacked the courage and, to some extent, the nobility, and indeed, romance, of combat.

Striding up towards the tent, he was thinking of how to present his proposal when, suddenly, he trod on an old mat that the wizard must have left outside. It had been half-buried under the snow and just as he raised his right foot from it a blinding blue flash of icy cold power blasted him off his feet. Flying backwards, he landed with a crunch on the snow, the freezing numbness paralysing his entire body.

Cu came rushing out, a broom held above his head, his spangled gown flapping in the wind. "*Got you! You little...*" He stopped and stared. "*Oh?* It's you."

"Aaaah," moaned Everus, his eyes staring blankly.

The wizard walked over and helped Everus to his feet. He half-dragged him inside and sat him down in one of the skin-covered chairs.

From its cradle, Black Jinx stared.

"You should be more careful in future," warned Cu, pouring a shot of mead. "I don't know, creeping around my tent at this time

156

of day. I was hoping to catch one of them wild dogs that keep sniffing around here." He gave Everus the filled cup. "I've had no end of trouble with them bloody scavengers."

With a shaking hand, Everus accepted the drink.

"Don't worry. You'll live."

"I...came...to...ask..." Everus began, his voice weak, his teeth chattering.

"I'd just take it easy for a time if I were you. I've seen dogs turned into chunks of ice after succumbing to that spell. However, if you survive...as you evidently have, the effects will soon wear off," informed Cu. He reached into a drawer for a potion of orange-coloured liquid.

"What's...that?

"This'll heat you up, bring you back to your senses," answered the wizard, shaking the bottle vigorously.

Everus watched as Cu uncorked the potion and gave it to him. He drank the liquid, feeling the warmth as the syrupy fluid crawled down his throat. It tasted slightly of cured pork.

"You may feel a touch light-headed for a while." The bald-headed wizard sat back in his chair. "So, what are you after this time? Need to know how to tackle an ice hippo or a Sawerrean three-headed horror?"

Now that the magical drink had taken the edge off his freezing, Everus relaxed a little, taking a sip of mead. It was strong stuff and he now felt a fire in his throat. He shook his head. "No. I've come to ask if you'd care to join an expedition I'm organising...into The Deadmoor Clumps." From its cradle, he could hear the snoring familiar.

"Why would I want to go there? There's nothing out there but bagh'arulks and Øggars. Lots of them."

"Oh, there's much more than that. I know where there's a forgotten grubban tomb. Who knows what magical treasures may lie within?"

Cu emitted a fruity mead belch. "My adventuring days are over. No, I'm fine and comfortable where I am. Why don't you ask one of them young whippersnappers at The Wizard School? I'm sure you'd find someone willing to jump at the chance."

"I need the service of someone...experienced."

"Well, I've done a bit of adventuring in my time, boy." Cu raised his chin and scratched at his odd-looking, little beard. "But what makes you think I want to risk my neck out there?"

"As I said, I've done some research and I've discovered the location of a hitherto unknown grubban tomb. One of the old warlords. The gold..."

"I'm not interested in money," Cu interrupted.

"Magic, then. I guarantee it. A place such as this will be brimming with magical items. Just think about it...an undiscovered grubban tomb. There could be arcane artefacts that have not seen the light of day for over two thousand years."

"How many others are going?"

Everus hesitated, unsure how to answer. "Just one."

"*Just one!*" Cu cried, astonished. "What is he, Wyrm's Port's greatest warrior?"

"Hardly, but he's one of the best at what he does."

"And what is it, he does?"

"He's a thief...of sorts," answered Everus. "Oh, and he also knows how to kill rakshasas."

CHAPTER EIGHT

Two of the moons had darkened since Everus had slain Oodle Gaggs and during that time the citizens of Wyrm's Port experienced some of the worst snow falls ever recorded. They had come, harsh and unforgiving, leading some to believe that Krüshe, the god of the freezing winds, had left his icy palace of Jarlnabâd and taken up permanent residence somewhere in the city. Others turned their furore at the Øggarbakken behemoths, believing that their wicked shamans and witchdoctors had unleashed the blizzards from their far off mountain peaks, in order to wreak havoc, weaken and isolate the city prior to an attack.

Everus gave that possibility more credence and, as he gazed out of the window of Creeps' room onto the near-glacial cityscape, he cursed the giants for their possible mischief. The expedition he had planned had been postponed twice already and with each day that passed he felt an inner urgency to retrieve Xethorn's third and final amulet. Looking down, he could see a ragtag group of misfits, wrapped-up in woollens, heading down the street, their faces red and puffy, their breath white and wispy.

"Are ye sure ye want to go out there? It's bloody freezin' outside."

Everus turned. "Yes. The sooner we leave the better. So come on and hurry it up. I had hoped to leave sometime this morning."

"I'm just goin' to stash some extra woollies." Creeps turned and reached for a heavy-looking pack which, with some effort, he lifted and dumped on his bed. He started to rummage through various drawers and cupboards, filling the pack with all manner of clothing and other things. Eventually, he completed his packing. "Right. That's me." He grabbed his jacket and hat and threw on a scarf.

"Ready?"

"Ready." The thief checked that his pipe and flint and steel were

159

in his jacket pocket. "Now, where are we to meet this wizard o' yers?"

"At the North East Gate," answered Everus, striding towards the door, pleased to be leaving.

After leaving Creeps' 'apartment', the two trudged through the snow-filled squares and the muddy streets. The few people out eyed them curiously, and wherever possible gave them both a wide berth. Icicles hung from the eaves of many of the ramshackle buildings and the ground was slippery.

It was bitterly cold.

They were nearing the North East Gate when, suddenly, a snowball flashed in a white blur before Everus' face. Turning, his green eyes fell on a cheeky-faced, bedraggled urchin. The kid poked his tongue out before scampering down a side street, his childish taunts fading as he made good his escape.

Creeps walked over to the small guard hut built at the side of the great gate. After looking through a dirty window, he turned to Everus. "Looks empty. There's nobody 'ere. I wonder if I should nick in an' see if they've got anythin' worth takin'? There's some..."

"Creeps," Everus interrupted. He stared blankly in the direction the child had ran. "Did you...did you see that boy?"

"Which boy?"

"The one that just threw the snowball. I'm sure it was the same kid we saw as we were going to Ghavin's Keep. The one sat at the rear of the pilgrim caravan." Everus frowned. "Just a strange coincidence, I guess. Maybe I'm wrong."

"I didn't see anyb'dy. I were too busy..."

Suddenly a group of armed militia men rounded a corner and came marching straight towards them.

"What're ye nosin' about in, ye miserable little maggot?" yelled the sergeant, his stern face studying the thief.

"Nothin'," answered Creeps, shaking his head and failing to look innocent.

"*Then bugger off*, the pair o' ye!"

Everus walked over and joined the thief. "We need to get outside. *It's important.*"

The sergeant strode up and stood directly in front of Everus, his mood adversarial. He was a big man and it looked as though he could probably handle himself in a fight. His bravery and confidence were undoubtedly bolstered by the dozen or so armed men with him. "This gate opens for no one. The emperor's orders."

"Surely no one would notice..." At this distance Everus could almost taste the man's halitosis.

"*Are ye deaf or summat?* Didn't ye hear what I just said? Don't piss me off...I've had a bad day an' I'm runnin' out o' places to hide the bodies as it is."

"Are we gonna have to bounce these stiffs, sarge?" asked one of the other guards, his right hand twitching on the pommel of his sword. "Please. Tell me we are."

Everus retreated a couple of steps, his nostrils glad to put some distance between himself and the malodorous sergeant. It was abundantly clear that there would be no reasoning with the likes of these men and he doubted whether he could fight them all. Besides, reinforcements would be here in no time.

The thief took his shot at negotiation. "Mister. We need to get out to see ma dyin' granny."

"Oh, aye? An' where's this granny o' yers live? In a bog in The Deadmoor?"

"So ye know her do ye?" Creeps grinned. "Look, pal. We need to get out. She's no' got long to go an' I'm her only survivin' relative. I've heard that she's loaded, so how's about we give ye a few coins for yer trouble now, an' when we get back..."

"Bribery now, is it? It's five years in the dungeons for that an' from the looks o' ye that's where ye belong. But believe me, if I had ma way I'd be only too happy to kick the pair o' ye out an' let ye freeze to death...along wi' all the other scum in this city."

"All right." Everus had had enough. Time for talking was over. His eyes slitted, his gaze fixed on the small, obviously bloodthirsty, platoon of infantrymen before him. "So much for doing this the nice way."

"*Sarge!* Let's just waste 'em," one of the guards cried. "We can stash their bodies in the bunkhouse. Take off their heads an' use 'em as target practice."

"Aye. I think we'll need to..." The belligerent sergeant stopped in mid-sentence, a daft grin forming on his harsh features.

"Sarge?"

"We'll need to...*eh?*" muttered the man, more to himself than anyone else. He struggled to speak, words unwilling to leave his wide-mouthed smile. "What's...?"

"Sarge!? Ye all right?"

Everus looked at Creeps, as confused as to what was going on as, no doubt, the sergeant was himself. It was then, however, that he noticed Cu leading a pack mule on the other side of the square.

"Aye. Well. Hello," muttered the militia man. Beaming away, he walked forward and shook Everus by the hand.

Cu led his mule across the cobbled square. "We need to get out. Would you kindly raise the gate?"

"Sure. No trouble," said the sergeant, as some of the other guards voiced their disapprovals. "Anythin' for a pal. Come on lads, let's jump to it."

The wizard winked at Everus. The three of them and the mule then waited for the gate to be raised, before heading north-east, out of the city.

✝ ✝ ✝

The first couple of leagues were covered with relative ease, their hopes buoyed at having left the city and venturing into the unknown. Their optimism was short-lived, however, for just before mid-day the snow began to fall in heavier flurries and the chill, biting wind howled across the snow-covered plain, blinding and cold.

"Everus. It may be best to camp here," Cu shouted, his words blown back at him.

"I agree. But where?"

"What're ye sayin'?" shouted Creeps, his hunched form appearing out of the blizzard. "I can't hear ye." He cursed to himself and pulled tight the woollen poncho that he now wore, his baggy hat already sodden with snow.

"We're going to camp up," answered the wizard.

"Where?" cried Creeps. Blinking sleet and the wind from his eyes, he peered around. There was no shelter to be seen. Everything was shades of white and grey.

"Here!" shouted Cu, reaching into a pocket. "Stand back!"

Everus and Creeps watched as the wizard took ten steps or so and planted something into the snow. He quickly retreated, his form emerging once more from the near whiteout. Cu muttered something and then, up from the frozen ground, a small, stone building emerged, complete with a door, two small glass windows and a chimney.

"Well, *what do ye make o' that?*" cried Creeps.

Cu turned to the thief. "Surely you didn't expect a man of my age to be kipping under the stars now did you? Come on, let's get inside before we freeze to death."

+ + +

"How's that food coming on?" asked Cu from the small bed on which he sat, watching as Creeps stirred and tasted the bubbling soup contained within a pot which hung over the fireplace.

"Lovely. How do ye like it?"

"Hot and sloppy and doused in onion sauce. Just like my old missus," answered the wizard.

The thief ladled out three bowls of the steaming broth, handing one to Everus and one to Cu. He reached for the one set aside for himself, accidentally spilling half of it. "*Bastard!*" he cursed as he was scalded.

"Ah, the joy of travelling once more," said Cu, dipping bread into his meaty soup. "Adventure. That's what it's all about." He took a mouthful.

"I like your house," commented Everus, looking around the austere interior. It was a genuine comment, for he really did appreciate the shelter, despite the fact that the furnishings consisted of no more than three small beds, a fireplace, one small cupboard and the cooking pot.

"I am pleased," replied Cu. "I considered bringing a tent, but they can be such a nuisance to put up, especially in these conditions." He popped another bit of dipped bread in his mouth. "Besides, I've lived in one of them for so long now I quite like the change." He looked admiringly around the single room. "It's been a while since I last spent a night in here but I like it all the same."

"Aye," nodded the thief, refilling his bowl. "There's no doubt about it, this is the way to travel. Sure beats campin' under a bush or lyin' in a hole wi' crawlies creepin' in yer crackers."

Cu smiled. "I'll take your word for it."

Everus finished his soup and poured himself a second helping, pushing the mule out of the way to get to the pot. He could hear the wind howling against the small cottage. Every so often a particularly violent blast would rattle the panes in the windows and occasionally a fall of snow would drop from the chimney above and land with a hiss in the crackling fire.

"How long's it goin' to take to get to this place?" asked Creeps, greedily tucking into his broth.

"If the weather improves, four, maybe five days," answered Everus, returning to his bed.

"An' if it doesn't?"

"Much longer."

Finishing his soup, Creeps looked up, taking in the confines of the small room, not particularly relishing the fact that he may be cooped up in here for some time to come. He was also concerned about what would happen if the cottage were to revert back to miniature whilst they were inside.

"Tell me, Everus, what's your interest in coming out here?" Cu asked.

"Gold, and lots of it," Everus lied. "I'm tired of scratching a living as a hired bodyguard, constantly having to do battle in order to sustain my wealth."

"That makes sense, I suppose." Cu turned to the thief. "And what of you?"

Creeps looked up from his bowl, still lost in his private worry, his chin dripping with steaming soup. "Eh? What?"

"What do you seek from this expedition? Gold also?"

"Aye," nodded the thief. "Gold, gold and more gold. I was thinkin' o' gettin' some gold teeth put in but I'm goin' to hold off till I'm a bit richer. What do ye think? Do ye think they'd suit me?" He gave a ghastly, largely toothless, open-mouthed grin.

The wizard winced.

"Shut your mouth, I'm eating," complained Everus.

"But just gold? What about knowledge?" asked Cu.

Creeps shook his head. "Nah! That's no good. Besides, I know everythin' I need to know."

Cu sat up. "Is that so?"

"Aye. Ask me summat an' I bet ye I..."

"How does one destroy a rakshasa?" the wizard interrupted.

Everus looked across at the thief.

Creeps hesitated, eyeing the mage and then Everus suspiciously. "Are ye on about that Roach fella? Well I shot him wi' a crossbow. The bolt I'd dipped in holy water."

Cu stroked his beard. "*A blessed bolt!* Well I never." He looked towards Everus, his eyes flickering with the light of knowledge. "You know, that's a vital piece of information your friend's given me. For

164

if you remember at our first meeting, I'd lost the exact details regarding their destruction. I did a little research of my own and nowhere could I find such information. There was a brief mention, again related to that account of Hamman Azif's, which mentioned the use of divine magic, but..."

Suddenly Creeps let out a startled cry.

Instantly, Everus sprang to his feet, reaching for his sword.

"*What's that?* cried Creeps as Black Jinx, the wizard's familiar, materialised on the mantelpiece.

Everus relaxed, somewhat amused at Creeps' dismay. "*That*...is something possibly even sneakier than you," he said.

✝ ✝ ✝

After two cold and lugubrious days spent trudging across the frozen wilderness, the three travellers entered the low foothills of The Deadmoor Clumps. Rocky tors and craggy outcrops of stone thrust out from the ground, and here and there stood the dying hulks of huge, gnarled trees. Now that the snow had finally begun to thaw, rivulets of melt water added to the already sodden ground. In places, bogs and fast-flowing, muddy streams made movement treacherous.

"*Bloody place!* This is gettin' beyond a joke. How long have we been walkin' through this shit?" complained Creeps, trying his best to coerce the mule across a narrow, water-swollen gully.

"We're not even in The Deadmoor yet," said Cu.

The going got harder as the ground became soggier. The land here was desolate, a barren landscape barely touched by the passage of anything remotely civilised and as such there were no roads to follow. Reaching higher ground, they could see the distant shimmering of The Dark Sea far to the north and east, whilst before them and to the south, the hills loomed, threateningly.

"Away over there is Øggarbakken. Home of the behemoths," announced Everus, surveying the grim panorama. "Over to the east, the land becomes swampier. From what I've read, Durgan's Rock lies in a mountain gorge beyond."

They soon came to the edge of an extensive stretch of marshland. Dripping trees, covered with net-like growths of trailing weed and glistening, green algae grew on some of the tussocks of firmer ground. Giant bullrushes and huge, reed-like vegetation sprouted from some of the deeper-looking pools and bogs, and a knee-high mist covered much of its watery surface.

Snakes and lizards slithered rapidly from their path as they pushed on.

"There must be another way," moaned Creeps, now forced to dragging the reluctant mule. "This bloody quag looks like it goes on forever."

"I dare say there is. But this is the only way I know of," replied Everus. "Remember, I've never been here before and the only map of the area I managed to find didn't reveal much either. I don't think the swamp's that extensive though, so hopefully we should be free of it before nightfall."

The fetid water became deeper the further they went.

The fog thickened, swathing them in its ghostly shroud, smothering them in its chill embrace.

From all around could be heard plopping sounds, as foul marsh gases belched and bubbled. Winged, unseen creatures flapped and screeched from overhead and on several occasions the sounds of splashing nearby brought all three of them to an abrupt halt. The odd, looming form of a stunted tree would sometimes emerge before them as though possessed of its own malign spirit.

It was getting dark as well.

Everus' hope of being clear of the mire before sunset was looking increasingly unlikely and he tried not to consider the possibility that they had become lost. Without a map, or any other means of navigation, it would be so easy for them to have deviated off course. He swallowed a lump in his throat when he thought about having to spend a night here, for there *were* things out there, beyond the wall of fog, of that he had no doubt. They had to hope that...

"*What's that?*" cried Creeps.

Everus turned round. "Where?" Following the line of the thief's pointing hand, he noticed a flickering up ahead. The spark seemed to sway from side to side, making it look as though someone was approaching with a torch.

Suddenly the thing flared up, for a moment its incandescence blinding. It sped straight for them, shooting past before coming to an abrupt halt some distance away.

"What is it?" asked Everus, his sword already in his hands.

"Is it a ghost?" queried the thief.

"I think not," said Cu. Raising his hands, he muttered something arcane and unleashed a torrent of magical power at the glowing ball. The orb pulsed a bright yellow as the energy was absorbed, then zoomed for them a second time.

Everus swung out as it streaked past, his blow going well wide. "It's an Evil Eyeball!" shouted Cu. "Beware its..." The weird ball stopped high above him, glowing a vibrant violet. Suddenly a bolt of crackling white light shot from it and struck him full in the chest. Blasted, he flew backwards, his smoking form splashing into the stagnant water.

With unbelievable speed, the malign sphere zipped past another swing from Everus and came to rest, hovering well out of striking distance.

"Bastard thing!" Everus shouted.

The dazzling ball of evil energy flashed a bright green, now bathing the surrounding marsh in its lurid, eldritch effulgence.

Somehow Everus knew the devious thing was taunting him, daring him to come and get it. With a buzz, a halo of electric-blue light spread from it, filling his mind with anger. Snarling, he splashed through the muddy water towards it.

"Everus! Don't!" shouted Cu, struggling to his feet.

Another two steps and Everus plunged up to his waist in the reeking bog, its dank water icy cold. Cursing, he slid in further, the water now rising to chest level. He looked up and saw the Evil Eyeball bobbing towards him.

Suddenly a second volley of magical bolts zapped into the thing, causing its colour to change to a dull amber. It whizzed away as, with Creeps' help, Everus began to drag himself free, his lower body soaked and stinking.

With an unfathomable hatred, the orb buzzed around once more, circling them like a bizarre satellite. It changed course and weaved towards them, speeding over the surface of the swamp before rising high above their heads in an awesome display of manoeuvrability. It then unleashed a blast of energy from its crackling nucleus. The lightning arced down, exploding close to Everus. Flaming mud erupted all around, knocking him and Cu off their feet.

"Bugger this!" yelled Creeps, diving for cover behind a wet and rotting tree stump.

Pulsing a ghostly green, the Evil Eyeball descended, hovering about head height.

"I think it's replenishing its energies," Cu shouted from where he lay sprawled in the mud.

Everus scrambled to his feet, his coat and trousers black with filth. Swinging his sword dexterously, he ran towards the glowing sphere. Crazily, the thing danced around him, making a mockery of his swordsmanship. It weaved and zigzagged with such speed that it began to generate numerous after-glows, their multiple images confusing and painful to the eye. The thing seemed unhittable.

But then, just as it was about to fire a third energy blast, a final stream of magical darts cast by Cu cascaded into it. Instantly, the ball exploded in a rainbow of colours. Caught in the blast, Everus was once again knocked back, his eyes stinging from the sudden pyrotechnic display.

"*Everus!* Look out!" shouted Creeps.

Half-blinded and struggling to his feet, Everus backed away as a huge lizard-like creature, obviously enraged at all the commotion, lumbered towards him. Twice the length of man and with teeth that could shred flesh to the bone in a single bite, the large crocodilian charged forward on its four stumpy legs, bearing down on him. His vision still a haze of fantastic colours, he pulled back. The ferocious reptile was nearly on him when, from Cu's fingertips, there shot a spray of magical fire which jetted through the air, engulfing it and wreathing it in flames. Burning and with its skin beginning to pop, the beast rapidly crawled away, sinking back into the morass from whence it came, any ideas of an easy meal now far from its mind.

† † †

"You can stuff adventure!" said Cu, morosely. He was making a great show of removing a curative poultice from his bare chest. Underneath, where he had been struck by the Evil Eyeball, the skin looked raw and singed.

"We all knew it would be dangerous," replied Everus, uncaringly. He sat upright on his bed, nursing his own wounds.

"Aye," agreed the thief. He sat on his bed feeding small biscuits to Black Jinx. "Besides, I thought ye wizardy-types liked goin' to weird places an' seein' strange things."

"We like reading about them, not necessarily experiencing them at first hand. At least not at my time of life." Cu grimaced as he tore the last of his makeshift bandage free. "*Shit!* That's sore."

"Well, we should soon be clear of the worst of the swamp. And if all goes well, this time tomorrow we should be standing in the ruins of Durgan's Rock itself," said Everus, hoping in some way to raise the wizard's battered morale.

"Perhaps," muttered Cu, sullenly reaching for his hipflask. He drank till late into the night.

After a poor supper, they settled down for sleep.

✝ ✝ ✝

Everus was correct with his prediction, for early the next evening, after a harrowing day's journey through the remainder of the swamp, they reached what was left of the ancient grubban city of Durgan's Rock. Built on either side of a yawning canyon, long before the rise of the giant-kin and the renaming of the land to Øggarbakken, the fabled city was once home to generations of royal grubban households. Great and honourable were the grubbas of old, the builders of this once-great city, but that age had long since crumbled, along with the temples and palaces. Hewn from the rock itself, pillars and weathered statues protruded vertiginously from the sheer cliff faces. High above, there were many openings in the cliff wall, whilst all around, on ground level, were thousands of jumbled architectural elements including shattered columns, leaning archways and collapsed walls. A colossal statue, now badly eroded, but still standing, stood in the middle of the canyon, its outstretched arms bridging either side, enabling, in times long past at least, passage across.

As the three got closer, a huge flock of hideous, black winged creatures cawed from high above, before sweeping past and flying to a darkened roost high up on the cliff face.

"Are we stoppin' 'ere the night?" asked Creeps, warily looking around.

"We'll get to the top of that ridge," replied Everus, pointing to the place in question. "That looks quite defensible and secure to me." Crunching loose rock underfoot, he set off towards a steep track which wound its way up the cliff face. Every so often, he would signal the others to an abrupt halt, certain that he could hear things moving around, as though they were being followed.

Eventually they reached the top and Cu conjured forth his magic cottage. The cold and the snow of but a few days before had vanished completely so that now the sky was painted with a garish sunset which bathed the ruins in a hellish glow.

Sitting on the edge of one of the beds, which he had carried outside, Everus stared down in wonder and partial disbelief at the strange beauty he now saw. From up here, he could see virtually all the surface remains of the city spread out before him. Reaching for his sword, which he had resting nearby, he started to sharpen it with a whetstone.

The thief strolled out of the cottage, puffed on his pipe and headed towards the cliff edge for a better look.

Cu led the mule inside and came out soon after. Looking skyward, he staggered to where Everus sat. The wizard had spent most of the afternoon drinking. "Most peculiar, this weather we've been having of late. It's as though the year has become sick or something. I mean, who would've thought that only a day or two ago we were tits-deep in snow? Most unnatural." He took a swig from his hipflask.

"I guess so," replied Everus, turning his attention to his blade.

"But the view is quite something, is it not? Quite spectacular."

"Yes. I suppose it is."

The wizard leant back, resting against the cottage wall. There was a strong smell of drink on his breath. "You seem troubled, my friend."

"*Do I?*" Sparks flew as stone sharpened metal.

Cu nodded. "I'd say so. You've said little all day and you've not eaten much. Is it the prospect of finding this tomb, perhaps empty, that concerns you? Are you worried about what tomorrow may bring?"

"Tomorrow?"

"Or perhaps the day after?"

Something in the nature of Cu's questioning and the odd, knowing glance the now bleary-eyed wizard gave, caused Everus to sit up. Could he confide in this man all of his past troubles and tribulations. Where would he begin, if he so started?

"You know, when I was younger, I was a bit like you. Worried about what the future held and whether or not I could alter it. I wrestled with myself, worrying and debating, chewing myself up day after day over whether or not I had any control over my actions."

"And?"

"And, well, I came to realise that the past is..." Cu took a glug from his hipflask, wincing as the fiery liquid burned his throat, "much more frightening than the future." He finished with a hiccup.

"How's that?"

"Well. With the exception of one individual, a great sorcerer I knew long ago, our pasts are fixed. We can't change them...only learn from them," Cu slurred. Eyes closed, he took another slug. He shook and opened his eyes. "Your past is like an incurable illness. It's something you've got to live with. Like it or not. Then...one day, that illness'll strike you down. And that's it...you're dead!" He belched.

"So what are you saying? Are you saying that our past contributes to our death? That one causes the other?" Everus watched with some alarm as Cu poured more mead down his throat. How much longer would the man remain lucid?

"No. Not at all. It's just that our actions in the present create our pasts tomorrow. And that, seeing how our pasts have already gone, by the time we stop to think about them in the present...therein lies the danger. The danger...the, you know?"

"*What are you on about?* What danger?" asked Everus, unsure whether he wanted to know the answer. His own past was an almost constant source of turmoil and bitterness. He had been raised by the wheels of fate to the relative highs of life, only for everything to subsequently fall apart, plummeting him to the darkest depths. And, as far as he was aware, one woman – Julia Camberra – had been the cause of it. Why? He did not know, for she had carried her motive to the grave he had put her in.

"Why, isn't it obvious? The danger of trying to create one's past by altering one's present. For therein, lies the path to...self-delusion and lunacy of course." Cu stopped and gazed blankly at the sky as though either looking for the answer or the will to carry on. He must have found inspiration from somewhere. "You end up going down that route and you're certain to end up as mad as a cart filled with woolly breeches."

"*What!?* You're speaking in riddles old man and your wisdom is only as deep as your flask."

Cu gave a private giggle. "But what are riddles? I'll tell you what a riddle is. Here, look at this hipflask." Unsteadily, he passed the container to Everus who looked at it before taking a quick whiff at its potent contents. It was strong stuff. "Now then. If this hipflask is, let's say *you*, and we put it here..."

"*Everus!*" cried the thief, his shout interrupting the drunken wizard's ramblings. "There's folk down there an' I think they're comin' our way!"

Springing from the bed, Everus dashed to the cliff edge. Looking down to where Creeps pointed, he saw some two dozen dark figures making their way through the ruined city below. He watched as they headed towards the track that led up to where the cottage stood. Fading sunlight glinted, revealing that many, if not all of them, were armed.

"What're they?" asked Creeps, peering from behind a large boulder.

"Not sure. But whatever they are, I doubt they're friendly." Everus' right hand tightened around his sword hilt. "Go and tell Cu."

Like a rat, Creeps scampered back to warn Cu, who was sitting on the edge of the bed singing quietly to himself, his drunkenness obviously having progressed to the next, merry stage.

Everus watched as Creeps nipped inside the cottage, returning with a battered satchel.

"Yer man's as pissed as a fart."

"*Shit!*" Everus' keen eyesight could now discern that the approaching humanoids were baazelgrigs, a brutal, primarily subterranean race. He had never seen one of them before in the flesh but he had read enough to match their description.

Each of the creatures was clad in dark grey mail and over half their number carried metal shields. Some were armed with spears, while others carried vicious-looking axes.

"What's going on?" mumbled Cu as he wobbled over.

"Baazelgrigs," muttered Everus. "Twenty or so...coming this way."

"*Baazelgrigs?* Twenty you say?"

"Are you capable of doing a spell?"

"Sure. I'll blow them all to..." The wizard was unable to finish the sentence, never mind work magic. Drunkenly, he staggered back a few steps, a vacuous look on his face. A small rivulet of drool seeped from a corner of his mouth. Suddenly his cheeks swelled up and with a sideways lurch, he vomited, undigested ham and eggs splattering in a sickly, stringy, slightly-steaming splash.

Creeps grimaced, his face contorting at the offensive stink of fresh puke. "*Gads!*" He looked at Everus. "That's all we need! Ye should o' told us he was one o' the Bubblin' Gob's lot."

"*Drunk bastard!*" Looking towards the thief, Everus shook his head in disgust. "Come on. We're going to have to take them."

"There's a lot o' 'em. Why not hide?" asked Creeps, reluctantly drawing his dagger.

"Because they might just notice that there's a bloody house up here! Besides, look at the state he's in! Get him inside and I'll see if we can find a good place to launch an ambush." Turning his back on the two of them, Everus dashed for some large rocks that lay over to one side. Crouching, he took cover, watching and waiting. All was clear, for the time being, but he knew that would soon change. It was only a matter of time before the baazelgrigs appeared.

Keeping low, Creeps scampered across, his satchel slung over one shoulder. "Ye see 'em?" Reaching into his bag, he removed two liquid-filled bottles with short wicks.

"Not yet. But they'll be here soon."

Still some distance away, three baazelgrigs came into view, their pudgy, pale orange faces, harsh-looking and tusked. All were completely bald and, despite being stocky, none stood any taller than the thief. Another dozen brought up the rear. One of their number held a length of taut leash at which two slavering, sabre-toothed hounds strained. Upon noticing the incongruous house at the top of the rise, the leading armoured creature raised a hand and shouted something excitedly at those behind.

In grating voices, the baazelgrigs cried out and started to jog up the track.

Near to where Everus and Creeps were hiding, fifteen baazelgrigs now stopped and stared, perplexedly.

"*Now!*"

At Everus' command, the thief leapt from his hiding place and threw the first of his grenade-like missiles. The baazelgrigs looked up, clearly surprised as the hurled flask exploded on a rock nearby. Flaming oil rained down on the three nearest. One of them staggered back, clawing at its burning face as the other two dived for cover.

With his enemies in complete disarray, Creeps' second improvised bomb exploded. His aim was better this time and two of the stocky monsters suffered the full impact of the blast and fell, burning, to the ground.

Cries of rage and panic erupted from the baazelgrig band as Everus rushed out, beheading two of them before they could react. The next nearest started to shout orders, before it too fell headless to the ground. Swinging his sword two-handedly, he hacked down another, its thick, purplish blood spattering his coat and face. With the bodies of his felled foes now beginning to pile up around him, he looked up just in time to see the two mutant hounds come tearing towards him. Knocking one aside with his sword and dodging the other, he sidestepped and chopped down. Throwing all of his killing power into the swing, he sliced one of the beasts in two. Steaming entrails hung from both halves as the bisected animal writhed in its death throes, snapping out with its powerful teeth and spilling unborn pups in a visceral splat before dying.

With jaws like a bear trap, the other hound gnashed and snapped, forcing Everus back, its handler content for the time being to let it do the fighting. Narrowly avoiding a vicious bite, he kicked it full in the ribs. He then skilfully reversed his grip on his sword and drove it down, skewering the quadruped between its shoulder blades. Blood spurted as he drove the blade deeper, pushing it through its chest.

The fanged beast died instantly.

But just as Everus withdrew his sword, a thrown spear sped towards him, catching him a glancing blow, the impact still strong enough to knock him off his feet. A stab of blinding pain surged through his body. Biting back the pain, he got to his feet, just in time to parry a downward spear jab. His baazelgrig attacker chuckled sadistically as it prodded again, catching him on his left shoulder. The rivets on his studded leather jacket helped deflect the worst of the stab, but it was still enough to draw a cry from his mouth.

A second spear-wielding baazelgrig stepped up and together the two of them tried to keep Everus at bay with their longer weapons. One gave a curse and advanced, throwing its weight behind a savage thrust. Parrying the barbed pole-arm, Everus swung his sword up with blinding speed. Recently sharpened metal struck just below a fleshy jaw line, gorily cleaving a baazelgrig face in two. His remaining opponent now pulled back, its morale clearly shaken.

A sudden, mighty explosion nearby shook the ground and cliff walls and the air suddenly stank of sulphur.

Unaware of what had caused the blast, Everus nonetheless put the distraction to full use, decapitating his confused foe, its spear hitting the ground shortly before its head. He looked down the track to see another dozen or so baazelgrigs charging towards him. As he flinched from the wound in his side, there came a second explosion, somewhat louder than the first, from up on the scree slopes above him. Lumps of blasted rock rained down and black smoke billowed out, forming a small mushroom cloud.

Out of the smoke staggered Creeps, his face sooty, his eyebrows singed, his jacket scuffed, torn and smoking. His hair was smouldering and patches of skin on his hands and face were raw and blackened.

Everus rushed to the thief. "*Creeps!* Get back to the house! There's more coming!"

"*Bastard!*" cried Creeps. "That's the last time I use one o' them pots o' explosive mix. Look at the state o' me!" He coughed and spluttered, small flames still licking at the back of his jacket.

Two thrown spears clattered harmlessly nearby.

"*Quick!* Back to the house!" cried Everus.

The two men turned and sprinted back up the track, a small army of angry killers charging after them.

"Inside!" Everus shouted, pushing the thief through the open door. He dodged to one side as a spear sparked off the wall just by his head.

Two baazelgrigs charged forward, axes raised.

Everus cut them both down, their bloody corpses falling to either side of him. Yet another spear flew past, going straight through the doorway and thudding into the back wall of the cottage, just missing the mule. Rocks smashed through windows whilst three of the enraged besiegers went around to the rear of the building and clambered, in an ungainly manner, up onto the roof. With crude jeers and taunts, they tried to goad Everus out from the doorway, knowing that if they could do so they could quickly surround him and overpower him.

Leaping inside, Everus slammed the door shut, just as several heavy stones battered against it. "Any suggestions?" he asked, tensely. He might as well have been talking to the mule, for Creeps seemed preoccupied with something in his pack and the wizard was far too drunk to do anything.

Four rocks shattered through the windows, one striking Cu on the head as he cowered and gibbered by the hearth.

The door juddered as the baazelgrigs tried to force it open, pushing Everus forward a little. He gritted his teeth and pushed back, trying to keep them out, well aware that once they created a bridgehead then all would be lost.

Suddenly one of their attackers crashed through one of the small windows. With a snarl, it began to clamber in. The thief sprang up and thrust his dagger deep into the thing's throat. Gargling, the baazelgrig tumbled forward, its hands at its squirting neck.

Again the front door buckled.

Booted feet clomped overhead.

Then...silence.

The late evening sunlight which streamed through the ruined windows darkened noticeably.

Shifting shadows lengthened.

Shoulder to the door, Everus listened. Shivering at a sudden drop in temperature, he waited, straining his senses, readying himself for the next onslaught.

There then came a cacophony of raised voices and there was no longer any pressure against the door.

Risking a glance outside, Everus peeked from behind the door, dismayed at what he saw. "*Shit!* They've got reinforcements." He watched, as the ones gathered outside began to retreat, his initial thought being that they had been instructed to do so, probably in preparation for a fresh assault. But then, as the 'reinforcements' drew nearer, he saw that all of them were badly mutilated. Two or three had missing arms and one stumbling along at the back was headless. A further cold shiver passed over him as he realised that these walking dead were none other than the baazelgrigs he had slain only moments before.

"What's happenin'?" asked Creeps, now at the other window.

"Don't ask me," answered Everus, confused. He opened the door wider and stepped out, watching as the dead staggered and crawled in pursuit of their fleeing, living kin.

† † †

Now that night had fallen and the sky was cloudless, all three of the world's moons were visible, shedding their various lurid glows across the broken land, creating weird, moon-thrown shadows. An eerie silence had fallen over the ancient city and the deep gorge in which it nestled, broken only by the distant howling of some wild creature.

"Such strange goings on," muttered the now sober Cu as he and Everus sat outside on watch. "I mean, where did those dead come from and who created them?"

Everus stared, eyes fixed on the celestial tapestry of stars. Astronomy and cosmology had never appealed to him, although that was not to say that he was ignorant of either. He turned to the wizard, as sure as he could be that he would not find the answers to the many questions his mind asked by looking skyward – leave that for the astrological charlatans. "All I can think is that perhaps the grubban gods intervened."

"A possibility. But why? I mean, if they're as omnipotent as you mortals like to assume, then would they not know what we plan to do? I mean, robbing a grubban warlord's tomb is hardly the most pious of deeds, now is it?"

"Perhaps we're being kept alive in order to discover something." Everus knew it was a lame argument, but right now, he could think of no better explanation.

"Hmm. An interesting notion. But, surely that would beg the question...what will they do once we've unearthed it?"

"I guess we'll find that out soon enough. And, in the meantime, I would suggest that you stay off the booze. Your inabilities nearly cost us dearly...*old man*."

"*Old man?*" Cu laughed. "Remember when you said that my wisdom was only as deep as my flask? Well, watch this!" Removing his slim hipflask, he began to pour.

Everus watched in silence as the golden liquor streamed, unceasingly, from within.

† † †

Cold morning sunlight filtered through the grey clouds as they made their way across the rugged landscape. Along narrow tracks they hiked, their path obstructed in places by tumbled rocks from past landslides. That there remained tracks to follow was something that surprised Everus, aware as he was that this territory had been uninhabited by any civilised race for many centuries.

Deeper into the craggy badlands they ventured, until they came to a place where they saw many scattered and weathered stelae, inscribed in ancient variants of the grubban, runic script. Thousands of the stone plaques lay shattered on the ground as though intentionally desecrated in a remorseless act of iconoclasm.

"This is all that remains of an exceptionally ancient Mad o' Gadin temple," commented Everus, looking around and taking in his surroundings. "Judging by the references on some of these stones, I'd guess that the place we're in must be over two thousand years old."

"Do any o' these things tell ye where this tomb is?" asked Creeps. He was tired and more than a little hungry, their supplies now having reached the rationing stage. In addition, he was missing his drink. As far as he was concerned, it was high time to get back to the city.

Everus gazed from side to side. "Not really, although...I'm sure we're on the right track." What he was looking for was a marker, some kind of indication as to where Khorgo Wulvargen was buried. He was certain that once they reached Disas-Taurus, he would have a much better idea as to where to go, providing the snippets of information he had amassed were correct. He pointed to a ridge on the northern horizon, less than two leagues away. "If we're where I think...the tomb is somewhere over there, just on the other side of those cliffs. It must be..." He stopped, noting the strange and slightly disturbing look upon the wizard's face. Surely he had not been drinking again? "Are...you all right?"

"*What?* Yes. Fine."

"All right. Come on."

The rough terrain was deceptive, and in order for them to get to the ridge they first had to make their way down a treacherous slope into a rock-filled gorge. Few springs gushed up in this largely dried-out country and the ground they had to traverse was rugged and inhospitable; a broken land, wild, vast and untameable now that the grubbas had gone. By the time they started the climb out of the gorge, the sun had risen sharply to its zenith. They were now on a terrible trail, one that was scarcely ever used.

Fluted, spined vegetation, three times the size of a man, sprouted from the bare earth on either side.

A foul stink, like that from rotting meat, wafted down from above.

Everus remained constantly vigilant, knowing that death could lie in wait at every bend of the trail. Venomous snakes and scorpions lay coiled and hungry in the shallow holes they passed, ready to lunge out. He was well aware of the many different breeds of both, having studied the finer arts of poison preparation as part of his training in the service of the Xethornite brotherhood. Consequently, he knew that once a man had been bitten or stung by either, it would only take a short time before he died, his body swollen and puffy, his limbs afire with agony.

Eventually the trail levelled out and the going became easier.

The path led between tall, rearing pillars of rock, lofty pinnacles of eroded stone that had been twisted by the rain and the wind into strange shapes, until there, before them, they could see what had to be the remains of Disas-Taurus; the ancient stronghold of Bhûl-Mara'gorcho. It was both impressive and terrifying and it was clearly the place from which the terrible smell originated. It was of no surprise that it stank, for the stronghold was, in itself, one huge carcass – a massive, dead, practically skeletal, horned creature, its remains half-buried in the rock. If what they were looking at had once truly been a living thing then it would have been gargantuan in scale, dwarfing the countless high tors and pinnacles with ease.

Everus stared in wonder, half-expecting the sight before him to melt away as though it were a mirage brought on by exhaustion, but like the stink, Disas-Taurus remained, mocking him with its refusal to go. In amazement, he looked, noting the monstrous shreds of gore and ancient flesh, the unscavenged scraps, which hung to parts of the bones. A huge span of leathery, ragged skin stretched tightly across part of the enormous ribcage, forming some kind of crude covering. Desiccated meat still clung to a giant, protruding leg and cloven hoof which, due to its raised angle, gave the thing the appearance of dynamism, almost as though it were about to haul itself up in order to once again rampage across the land. Its eye sockets were empty and cavernous; dark holes set within the bleached and red-stained bone.

"Well...would you look at that?" said Cu, staring wide-eyed.

"Now there's summat ye don't see every day," voiced Creeps.

Everus ran a hand down his unshaven face. "Ancient Disas-Taurus! That's where we're going. Come on." Hope fuelled his steps and much of the ache and the fatigue which had dogged him for the past many leagues seemed to leach from his limbs. Striking out across the wastes, he led them on, the ground here becoming firmer, rockier.

Soon they came to an area of ground cracked wide by gaping fissures which zigzagged like crazy lightning across the destroyed earth. Looking down one such crevasse, they saw that it fell away into the deeps; small, barred, cell-like openings visible half-way down, set into the chasm walls. Everus thought he could make out ledges, whether natural or otherwise, on which some form of primordial, grisly totem poles had been erected. He turned away and headed for the ossified ruins.

The going was hard, the presence of the chasms often causing them to backtrack and retrace their steps. Like some infuriating maze, the ragged rifts in the earth seemed almost intentionally laid out, forcing them further from their goal. They would get near, certain that this time they would be able to reach the entrance to the stronghold, only to find that they had to go further out, and must once more make their way back in. There was only one true approach, the numerous other routes leading to abrupt cliff edges. Yet slowly, patiently, they made their way, picking through the natural labyrinth, until, there before them, they saw the giant, open, fanged maw; the entrance to the demon lord's demesne.

"This is it," announced Everus, staring up.

"*Bugger that!* We're no' goin' in there, are we?" asked Creeps.

"It doesn't seem to go anywhere," added the wizard, straining to keep the mule under control. The smell and the unnaturalness of the whole area was making it fretful.

"So I've noticed." Stiffly, Everus walked up to the massive skull, steely determination overcoming the sense of paralysing fear which seemed to have affected the others. He remembered one of his teachers once telling him that true strength was derived from knowledge...yet, as he approached, he realised that knowing too much was just as deleterious, for he knew that the fanged opening once gave access to the hellish dimension ruled over by the demon lord, Bhûl-Mara'gorcho, one of the great fiends summoned by the arch-demonologist, Cyrvilus. Hesitantly, he took a step nearer, the stench becoming increasingly sickening, almost as though it was a rancid breath exhaled by the putrid skull. The fearsome jaws, although open wide, gave one the uncomfortable impression that at any moment they would clamp down.

A wind picked up, blowing red dust and sand high into the air. Small tornadoes whirled and spun, whistling against the bones and the rocks, creating an unpleasant piping as they gusted through thousands of crannies.

Everus walked into the gaping maw as prepared as he could be for whatever might happen. An uneasy moment passed. Then, he started to count the teeth on the lower right-hand side of the skeletal mandible. Each was as big as himself. Stopping at the ninth tooth, he squatted down. There, just as his studies had informed him, was a hole, through which he could see the specific pinnacle of rock he was looking for; the tomb of Khorgo Wulvargen.

† † †

Barely discernible bands of runic inscription had been carved all over the finger of stone that reared before them.

"*Is this it?*" asked Creeps, looking unadmiringly at the squat obelisk. "Doesn't look much like a tomb to me. An' I've seen one or two in ma day."

"Yes." Everus nodded. "This is it. This is an ancient grubban tomb." He paced up towards it in order to examine the faint archway chiselled into the rock's surface.

Cu finished lashing the mule's lead around a nearby rock. "How do we get inside?"

"Ye watch an' learn, Cu, old pal." Creeps unslung his pack. "Watch an' learn." The thief started pulling out his tomb-robbing gear; his stone-corroding acids, his kettle, his crowbar, his spikes and hammers. He covered his nose and mouth with a ratty handkerchief before chemically treating the stone doorway – a thoroughly smelly affair which prompted Everus to take several steps back.

The wizard stood his ground, seemingly unbothered by the noxious fumes.

Creeps passed Everus the crowbar. "It looks a thick bugger this one..."

"*So?*"

"Well, I just thought ye might be able to..."

Everus tutted. Taking the crowbar, he waited a few moments before hacking into the rock. It was hard work. Soon he was ankle-deep in excavated fragments, the rock seemingly becoming harder the deeper into it he quarried.

"How thick's this bastard?" queried the thief, smoking kettle in hand. "Are ye sure that it's no' solid all the way through?"

"It goes back a way yet," said Everus, a dull ache in his arms.

"Do ye want more o' ma magic tea?" asked Creeps.

"Go on then. Give it another shot." Everus stepped back in order to allow the thief in.

The rock sizzled and smoked as a further dose of the green, caustic fluid was liberally poured over it.

181

His eyes watering, Everus renewed his attack on the sealed archway. With each strike into its surface, he now imagined he was driving deeper the sharpened crowbar into Julia Camberra's twitching body. He may have killed her over three years ago but what he would have given to have been able to repeat it. Shortly after, he breached through into an opening. "At last! Creeps! Get your lantern ready!" Hacking through the last layer of stone, creating a hole wide enough for himself to gain entrance, he clambered inside. He stood within a small, hewn chamber which had been hollowed out of the very tor.

Creeps passed him the lit lantern.

Lantern held before him, Everus looked around. At first glance there was not much to see; a few bones scattered on the floor and the shadow of a grubban-sized sarcophagus. Light glinted off something and his immediate sense of excitement vanished as he saw that it was just a small pile of ancient coins. Grubban coins, probably of no value to speak of.

"What can ye see?" asked the thief, clambering in.

"Nothing of interest on the ground." Everus was about to make for the stone coffin, certain that therein he would find the final amulet, when a gust of wind from somewhere blew the lantern out, plunging him into darkness.

"Hang on!" cried Creeps.

Everus heard the thief fumbling in the darkness. The lantern was taken from his hands.

"Let's get that bastard thing goin' again." Sparks were struck and Creeps lit the little wick. "Now then, what have we got?"

"There's a stone sarcophagus and...looks as though there was an explosion in here. Look at all of these bones." Now that his eyes had accustomed better to the lantern-lit gloom, Everus started to see things he had initially missed. There were many more bones than he had first assumed, some charred and snapped. "They've been blasted out against the walls."

"Aye, an' ye're right in the middle o' it. Remember what I've told ye about traps. Ye could've triggered summat." Creeps headed towards the sarcophagus. "Still, I think we're safe. Whatever happened 'ere happened a long time ago. I'd say that..."

Everus pushed the thief to one side in his eagerness to investigate the sarcophagus. His heart sunk as he reached it, for it had clearly been smashed and damaged, whether from the ancient explosion or from the act of previous tomb-robbers he knew not. Frantic, he rummaged through the debris.

"Aye, aye. What's this then?" Creeps bent down in order to retrieve something that lay on the ground. "This what ye're after?" He stood up, holding aloft a gold amulet.

"Give me that!" Everus snatched the amulet from the thief's hand.

There came a low growl from outside.

Both men turned round.

Reflected light shone from a pair of emerald green eyes as the vaguely human-like head of a black panther stared in through the broken opening.

A ripple of fear spread through Everus' body as he realised that whatever this creature was, it stood wearing Cu's travelling robe.

"*Hah!*" the thing hissed, its teeth large and very sharp. A red tongue licked across its fangs. "You've no idea how hard it's been to maintain my masquerade, knowing that you morsels slew one of my kin. Now I have the chance to avenge one of my brothers."

"*Everus! Yer man's turned Roachy on us!*" yelled Creeps, drawing his dagger.

"Rakshasa!" cried Everus. He unsheathed his sword, temporarily forgetting how ineffectual his weapon was against such demonic shapeshifters when, with nothing more than a flick of a paw, a wave of magical energy from Cu sent him flying against the far wall. He struck stone hard and fell to his knees.

The rakshasa repeated its conjuration. A torrent of bright azure bolts flew in, homing towards the thief. Instinctively, Creeps pulled back even as the spell dissipated in a chromatic blast around him. The Cu-thing growled its displeasure and prepared another spell.

In agony, Everus crawled behind what remained of the stone coffin, eager to make use of whatever cover there was. He had just managed to duck down in time as a fiery blast, like a dragon's breath, engulfed the small tomb. The heat was terrible but mercifully short-lived. Yet he knew that had he been caught in the midst of that conflagration he would surely have perished.

Dust and rock drizzled from the ceiling.

Somehow Creeps seemed relatively unscathed, despite the fact that he should have been cremated. With a worried look on his blackened face, he scampered over to where Everus sheltered.

"We've got to escape or else that bastard's going to burn us like clay in a kiln." No sooner had he spoken than Everus rose to his feet, the amulet gripped tightly in his right hand and with a running leap sprung out through the gap he had made earlier. He struck the Cu-thing as he went through, catching his shoulder, his sword knocked from his hand. Rolling painfully on the ground outside, he barely had the time to look up when suddenly the rakshasa's shadow fell on him.

"Everus, Everus. All out of blessed bolts are we?"

"You! But you were injured...the Evil Eyeball..."

"Hah!" growled the demon. "I barely felt it." With lightning speed, it reached out and hauled Everus to his feet by his hair, its other paw swinging up and clamping around his throat.

Hot breath, with a distinctive animal odour wafted unpleasantly against Everus' face as the rakshasa gazed, mesmerisingly, into his eyes, all the time licking its lips in expectation.

"I *will* kill you; tear out your throat and force you to watch as your own life spills out before you. Then I will eat you. But before I do, know that your little runt of a friend is not all that he seems."

"Meaning...what?" blurted Everus. His head was being held back and he was forced to stand on tiptoes, slowly being asphyxiated. It felt as though he was drowning, melting into those luminous, hypnotic green eyes with their gold flecked motes and their black vertical-slit irises.

The rakshasa suddenly turned its gaze away.

Barely conscious, Everus heard Creeps clamber from the tomb. He was dying and somehow it no longer mattered. Nothing mattered any more. The portal to oblivion opened before his darkening mind.

"Stay your distance, weird one, or I'll rip him open," the panther-headed wizard snarled, its warning hushed and warped as though it came from the bottom of a pool to Everus' ears.

"Let him go," replied Creeps.

"To think that I've come all this way and there's nothing in there but a few paltry coins. Such a waste of my time. I should've killed you sooner. At least I'll have the satisfaction of feasting on your mangled carcasses. You should..."

Suddenly a burning sensation emanated from the amulet Everus still held. The pain became intense, blotting out the fact that he was as close to death as it was possible for any who yet lived to be. For what seemed an eternity, yet in reality could have been no time at all, the burning went on. There then came a whirling vortex of dark flame and fire and he was sent reeling to the ground. For a moment, he imagined he saw spectral figures hacking and slashing within the mystic firestorm...and then, darkness took him.

† † †

"Everus Dragonbanner. You've been brought before us charged with the cold-blooded murder of our own beloved law-giver, Julia Camberra of The Watchful Eye . Do you have anything to say before we are forced to sentence you to death?"

"The bitch deserved no less. I did for her what she did for me." Defiantly, he stared into the face of the High Overseer, Antonio De'carla. He would have his moment, his chance to tell those who listened. Of that he was determined. "She destroyed me. She ruined my life. She took away my only love. It was she who incriminated my father." His face hardened. "For that, she died."

"And where is your proof? What evidence have you to support your claim?"

He hesitated. How could he tell these uncaring, supercilious and law-enforcing lickspittles that he had been informed by a high priest of Xethorn as to whom was responsible for his downfall? To admit such would be just as punishable as the charge he now faced.

"As I thought," sneered Antonio. "You have no proof. You killed her and her children out of the evil in your heart. You are a murderer and as such I sentence you to..."

"Wait, I..."

"Silence! I've heard enough. Remove this vermin from my sight. On the morrow you shall be executed. May the gods deal out the true punishment that we cannot. For know that whereas your time on the gallows may be fleeting, your soul will burn for an eternity in the fires of the dead. Take him away."

Gauntleted hands gripped him. He was frogmarched out of the courthouse and taken down a dank subterranean passage; a low-ceilinged tunnel, which led to the extensive city jails which housed hundreds of inmates and fellow undesirables. Through a warren of twisting, labyrinthine corridors he was shoved and steered, the wails of the condemned echoing all around.

The guards came to a halt at a stout wooden door. One started to turn a key in the lock.

"Hope it's warm enuff fer ye," said one of them.

"An' I hope ye freeze in there, ye murderin' bastard," added his friend.

With such pleasantries over, the door was opened and he was shoved inside. The door was slammed shut and he heard the key locking it behind him. He was in a small dungeon cell. The cold stone walls dripped a greenish moisture and the dank brickwork was in places covered with unreadable graffiti and patches of wet moss. The only light in the room came from a small, grilled opening near the ceiling, well clear of head height. Dirty straw and filthy puddles of what looked like water but in truth could have been almost anything, covered much of the floor.

Huddled in a corner, failing to look inconspicuous, was a thoroughly wretched-looking man. Despite the fact that he did not have a beard down to his feet, he looked as though he could have been imprisoned within for several decades. His clothes were torn and dirty.

Ignoring his fellow prisoner, he turned and kicked the door. In his rage, he kicked it again. It was then that he heard the obviously feigned snoring coming from his unwashed cell mate. He strode over, reached out and pulled the shorter man to his feet by his hair.

The man yelped in agony as he was hoisted upright, tufts of his tangled hair, wrenched from his scalp, coming away as he stared about with wild eyes.

"Come now, let me introduce myself. I am Everus and you..." he said, staring deep into the stranger's frightened eyes, "why, you are mister sleepy at times, awake at others, are you not?"

"Aye. I mean no. Just tired." The man yawned as though to prove his point.

"What are you in for?"

"Nothin'."

"I see, a classic case of Watchful Eye justice." He smiled and the man grinned back. Suddenly he grabbed the stranger around the throat with one hand and began to squeeze. "Answer my question or I'll see to it that your execution is brought forward."

"Grave-robbin'."

He let go of the man and stepped back. "Of course, I should have guessed from your appearance and your stink. And what do they call you? O pilferer of tombs? O friend of rats?"

"Creeps. Adolf Creeps," the man answered, fear evident in his quavering voice.

186

"Well, Adolf."

"Creeps. Call me Creeps."

"Well, Adolf," he began again. *"Any ideas about getting out of here?"*

† † †

Completely unscathed, Everus awoke to find that night had settled over the world and that he lay alone on the rubble strewn ground. At first, his mind was empty, as though his past memories and experiences had simply been poured away, decanted from the vessel that was his consciousness. Slowly, that vessel began to fill up and as he lay, gazing at the dark skies, his memories started to return, filtering back into his troubled mind.

He picked up the amulet.

Looking around, he could see, blasted beyond recognition, the remains of what he assumed was Cu, now reduced to nothing more than a scattered assortment of blackened bones and dark ash. Further away, no more than an imprinted shadow on the rocks, was the powdered remains of the mule. A smaller smudge, probably that of the demonic wizard's familiar, was nearby.

Of Adolf Creeps, nothing remained.

CHAPTER NINE

The twenty or so gate guards sat huddled around glowing braziers, exchanging lewd jokes and bottles of cheap grog. They were supposed to be on active duty, but the night was cold and they were all bored and tired. One of them yawned and started for the crude latrines, unbuckling his pants before he even reached them. He was just considering whether or not to have a piss up against a nearby wall when he thought he caught sight of movement out beyond the great portcullis. Curious, he held in his immediate need and paced over in order to take a better look.

Out of the dark, there charged an Øggarbakken behemoth. Raising its clawed hands, the giant mustered its foul sorcery, channelling unholy energies into a sudden wave of power, which it unleashed against the iron gate. The frame juddered and the gate buckled even as the guard dropped his halberd and unloaded more than piss into his underpants.

Shouting orders and crying the alarm, the sentries leapt to their feet as the portcullis rattled a second time.

Then, with a clang, the East Gate broke and the behemoth shaman, with a tribe of thirty behind it, stormed into Wyrm's Port. The bloodthirsty monsters slaughtered all who stood in their path; trampling many where they stood or hacking soldiers in two with single blows from their massive swords and axes. They hurled boulders and corpses, bowling over armoured men like nine-pins. Guffawing and screaming, they charged down streets and thoroughfares in a violent, unstoppable, unruly tide of terror.

Their shaman, Gharagas Barü, caused the greatest havoc. Hurling terrible curses, he instilled fear into the hearts of all before him. With bolts and storms of dark sorcery, he slew many.

Bells and screams rang out as though heralding the city's doom.

In numerous barracks men donned armour and readied their weapons as, all about them, buildings were torched and torn down.

Mutilated corpses littered the streets as the militia brought in reinforcements from all over the city to try and repel this ferocious incursion. The battle raged well into the night and it was only as dawn's light was approaching that a final, white-feathered arrow pierced Gharagas Barü's thick skull and brought him down, bringing an end to the behemoth's punitive raid.

Over two hundred and fifty citizens and seventy militia men had perished.

Thus it was to a grim, if not entirely inappropriate, homecoming, that Everus, weary, soaked and half-starved, returned, thanks, in part, to the guiding glow of the city's numerous fires. Much of his return journey had been trudged in a grey-black haze, each step taken more painful than the last. He had been unable to find the 'magic cottage', not that he had the power to activate it anyway, and as such he had gone largely without sleep and food for over four days. It was only as he neared the ruined city gates that the notion that perhaps something other than his steely will and determined character had guided him home, flickered uncomfortably in his mind.

† † †

Everus' reflected face appeared on the faceless statue as he reverently approached it. The dark light which bathed it seemed to grow in intensity, illuminating half the chamber in its preternatural glow. From within the confines of his robe, he removed the third gold amulet, noting for the briefest of moments the flame-like flickering within the three small rubies. "Xethorn! My master. Lord of Shadows and Slayer of Foes! I have completed the last of your tasks." He stepped forward and placed the final ward on the statue's open palm.

With a scarlet flash, the amulet vanished as though consumed by the graven image. In that same instant, the reflection changed.

Everus watched as the face warped and melted through a thousand different faces – murderers and killers all – until only one, that of a bullish-looking, scarred man of indeterminable age, appeared on the statue. There was nothing exceptional or out of the ordinary about the visage – it could have belonged to a hundred thugs and bruisers – and yet, a sense of great evil emanated from it as though it itself possessed the wickedness of a thousand nameless mass murderers. He dropped to his knees and bowed his head, knowing that he was now in the presence of his god and that through his deeds he had finally restored a face to that which had been faceless. That which up till now had been but a reflection of himself.

In a voice laden with dread, the image spoke. "I have one further request. I charge you, Everus Dragonbanner, my most loyal of servants, with the destruction of Uhu'giaggoth and those who support its foul creed. For know that what you have so long believed to be true, is false. All of your life has been naught but a preparation. A preparation for a sacrifice. A sacrifice, it is hoped, that will result in the awakening and subsequent rebirth and summoning of Uhu'giaggoth."

Shocked, Everus raised his head and stared directly into the face of Xethorn.

"Dae'morogin, Dae'dicus and the man you know as Creeps are all apostates, followers of The Daemon God as was the succubus you once knew as Julia Camberra. Through Julia's actions, Dae'dicus managed to destroy your parents, your career, your life and your love for the woman, Katryna Hapsburg. I charge you to destroy them. Destroy them all before you yourself are destroyed and offered as a sacrifice to Uhu'giaggoth. Fail, and the world you know ceases to be."

His mind reeling from these revelations, Everus felt as though he had been psychically stripped and his essence laid bare. It was all he could do to ask one question. "How?"

"When the time comes, I will aid you, as I have aided you in the past. Until that time, my intervention must be limited. My energies will take time to grow. The power you know as The High Three seeks to maintain the balance, yet it has been reduced to little more than an impotent puppet." A sneer flickered briefly across the statue's cruel visage. "You must return to Dae'morogin. Execute his final deed. Slay his last victim. Complete the book. Once this is done, return to me. It is *imperative* that you do this before returning to Dae'morogin, for without my intervention you will be destroyed."

"Complete...the book?" asked Everus, hesitantly.

"Yes. For only once Uhu'giaggoth stirs can I intervene directly." The face vanished.

Revelation after revelation crashed tumultuously through Everus' confused mind. His life had been engineered, cleverly and deviously orchestrated so that he would, unwittingly, assist a chaotic cult whose doctrines were, by definition, ones of unimaginable discord and horror; horror on a scale that the mortal mind could barely comprehend. Certainly, he had murdered for Xethorn, but murder was on a human scale; The Daemon God's cult's aims were both insane and inhuman. And yet, as such thoughts assaulted his mind, he began to wonder whether or not there was a part of him that had always known, or at least suspected. Was it possible that somewhere in the shadow of the darkest pits of his mind there was a part of him which had colluded with or at least acquiesced to this plot, operating on a level below his conscious awareness?

A long time later, he got to his feet and somehow made it to his bedroom.

When he did eventually drift into tortured sleep, he dreamt; always the same cycle of events – the false accusations, his expulsion from The Academy, his loss of Katryna, his parents' untimely deaths, the unbearable grief and the burning hatred swelling within.

† † †

The snow had largely melted, leaving behind a cold, grey slush that still clung like a bad memory to many of the houses and hovels. Muddy puddles were everywhere. Although the morning had dawned bright and crisp, by the time Everus had awoken, bathed and dressed in preparation for his divinely approved rendezvous with Dae'morogin, more grey clouds had gusted over, bringing with them a chill wind which cut like a blade through any amount of woollen layers.

Walking down the cold streets, Everus wondered how he would be received by the high priest and, for that matter, whether he would be able to contain his own venom. Knowing what he now knew, he felt the bitterness which had festered within him for many years boil inside. It would take all the self-restraint that he could harness to keep from killing the bastard on sight.

Lost in his own thoughts, Everus headed for the slums from which he could gain access to the subterranean temple. He was striding down the road when two large horses, pulling an odd-looking carriage, thundered out from an arched opening on his right. Cracking his whip, a hooded driver steered them straight towards him and it was all he could do to leap aside as they careered past, creating a huge splash as they went through a deep puddle. He slipped on the cobbles and fell.

Suddenly the carriage door was thrown wide and four surly-looking men scrambled out. They were a rough lot, each was thick-set, their faces scab-ridden.

"That's him!" cried one, fists clenched around a stout club.

"*Quick!* Get the bastard!" barked another.

Before Everus could get to his feet a blow landed on the back of his head. He pitched forward onto his knees and was kicked full in the face for his efforts. Blood erupted from his nose and lips. Catching a raised boot that was headed for his face a second time he twisted it and brought one of his attackers down. Grabbing the lout by the hair, he smashed the man's skull off the hard ground, silencing his curses with one savage blow. He was then forced to roll into a ball as more attacks battered down on him. Heavy clubs were now striking hard and he tried to protect his head. A vicious kick to the groin knocked the breath from him.

Suddenly everything went black as a hood was roughly forced over his head. Flailing madly, he tried to tear it free, oblivious to the repeated thumps and kicks he was being dealt. A rib was broken. With a crack, a club smacked off the side of his head and for a time he knew no more.

✝ ✝ ✝

Darkness.

Then from within the darkness, Everus thought he could hear squeaking. Rats, he thought, trying to peer into the gloom. Pain crept into his body, letting him know that he was very much alive, although for how much longer, he had no idea. His head ached and it was with considerable effort that he managed to crane his neck to one side, straining his senses to detect anything that might provide a clue as to where he was. His ribs hurt and had he been able to see he was certain that his legs, face and torso would be a mass of bruises. He had lost all sensation in his arms and it was only after a time that he slowly began to feel a cold dampness against his back.

With rising panic, he realised he was manacled; arms outstretched on either side. Alone in the darkness, he tried to make sense of this latest twist in his life. Who had imprisoned him? Where was he? And, as always, *why?* It was as all these thoughts were going through his head that he began to hear the sound of voices coming from nearby.

The voices became louder.

Approaching footsteps could be heard just outside.

A key turned and the door to the small cell opened.

The first man through the door wore a scuffed leather coat, its collar turned up. He carried a lantern by the light of which Everus could see that he was in an untidy cellar filled with rotting boxes and pieces of decrepit furniture.

"Here he be," said the man in a gruff voice, turning to the men behind him.

Wooden wheels turned as Otha Camberra, sitting in a modified wheelbarrow-like contraption, was pushed through the doorway by one of his cronies. He looked up at Everus with an ever so slightly malicious grin growing wider all the time he beheld his captive. Despite now having to be wheeled most of the places he wished to go, the white-haired, ex-knight of The Watchful Eye still possessed a certain amount of dignity. He wore a white tunic decorated with dark blue stars over his chain mail armour. Protruding from the back of his chair was his sword and a pleasant scent of undoubtedly expensive masculine perfume did something to counter the stench of the stale cell.

"How's the leg?"

Otha ignored Everus' remark, instead fixing him with his cold, blue eyes.

"I thought I cut your leg off. Not your ears."

"Defiant even in death. I like that and I suppose I would've been foolish to think you'd be anything other." From his wheeled-chair, Otha continued to stare at Everus, his gaze almost as potent as a basilisk's.

"So, the tables have turned. For you, once again with hired help..."

"Help or not," interrupted Otha, "unfortunately for you, the facts remain the same. You're my prisoner."

"Why not kill me? Get it over and done with. We both know that only my death will satiate your twisted sense of justice."

"*Kill you?* Oh, don't worry I will. But let's not be too hasty. I've looked forward to this day for so long that I don't want to spoil it all by disposing of you too quickly. After all, wasn't it you who said something about killing me only after you'd tortured me first?" Otha patted his stump. "My recovery has been slow and painful. So...I think it's only fitting that your death is the same. You see, I've done my share of suffering. But for *you*, I've got some real tortures in store."

"I didn't think torture was your style. Thought it went against the grain for you Watchful Eye types; seeing the prolongation of another's misery. I always thought torture grated on your perverse code of morality. But then again, your bitch lived for that, didn't she?"

Otha's face hardened and it was all he could do to quench the sudden rage that flooded through him. He took a deep breath. "As you know, my days with that institution are over."

"Did you know that she was a follower of Uhu'giaggoth?"

The question struck Otha like a crack from a mace. "*What?*"

"I said, *she* was a demon-worshipper."

"*Lies!*" roared Otha. He drew out his sword, his body trembling with rage. "*Lies! Lies!* By the gods you'll suffer for your defamation, you bastard!"

"You *knew* she worshipped Uhu'giaggoth!"

Suddenly a part of Otha did snap and, gritting his teeth, he swung out with his sword, slashing his chained enemy viciously across the chest. It was a savage slice, though mercifully not too deep. Everus screamed in pain as blood sprayed from his body. Blood welled in his mouth and his head drooped. Bile rising to his gullet, his last sight before losing consciousness was of his own blood pooling around his bare feet.

✝ ✝ ✝

In pain-wracked dreams, Everus saw the face of the man he had once respected more than any other – Dae'dicus. In his dreams, he appeared as Everus had known him in life – considerate and helpful, the only person who had really understood him, who had fostered and guided him through the wreckage of his shattered dream.

It had been Dae'dicus who had informed him that Julia Camberra was the one responsible for bringing about his destruction. He had strongly persuaded Everus to obtain his vengeance, insidiously suggesting and indeed indoctrinating him, telling him that only through killing her would he ever know emotional and spiritual solace. For each day that she lived, Everus would continue to suffer. 'She has to die', the high priest had oft repeated, vehemently reinforcing his inculcation. 'Slay her, Everus. Whatever the risks...she has to die...Julia has to die.'

Yes, thought Everus. Dae'dicus had been that guide; the light which had revealed the darkened path. The path which had now been revealed by his god for what it was and where it led. A path that led inexorably to chaos.

As Everus dreamed he saw that the former high priest seemed troubled, as though something had gone seriously amiss. It appeared that his old mentor was frantically searching for something and it soon became apparent to Everus that that *something*, was him.

✝ ✝ ✝

A bucket full of cold water was sloshed over his battered body. With bleary eyes, Everus saw one of his captors, empty bucket in hand, walk out of the cell. The man was whistling a tune.

A moment later, Otha was pushed in. "Awake, I see. Good."

The diminutive man who was doing the pushing was dressed in a garish purple robe, festooned with glinting trinkets. He was completely bald with a strange, green, rune-like tattoo on his forehead. Inquisitively, this stranger looked Everus up and down as though examining a dodgy purchase.

"May I introduce my friend, Schraeggaenello."

The bald-headed weirdo bowed slightly. He *was* odd-looking. His eyes were almost too large for his head and each stared in opposite directions. His nose and chin were unnaturally long, ideal for picking pickles out of a jar, if he ever had the mind to do so.

"Schraeggaenello's a thought-reader, a telepath," said Otha, obviously trying, but failing, to impress his prisoner. "He's also an expert in mind torture."

Everus sneered. "Stop! Please...the pain. It's too much."

"Please...a little demonstration for our ignorant friend here." Otha gestured to the telepath to move into position.

Schraeggaenello closed his eyes. His bottom lip began to tremble.

At first Everus could feel absolutely nothing. His pain seemed to just vanish as though all of his senses had become numb. There then came a sudden surge of agony. It was internal, as though his guts were cooking. A fire spread throughout his body and he felt as though he were about to implode. Sweat bubbled to his skin's surface and blood trickled from his nose. He thought he could feel his brain leaking out of his ears.

195

"Enough!" cried Otha.

Instantly, the pain stopped as though it had never been.

"*Again!*" shouted Otha.

And once more Everus screamed.

And so the torture went on.

† † †

Otha saw to it that Everus was kept alive, ensuring, with the psychic's help, that the pain level was just enough to inflict intense agony but not enough to kill. He had also seen to it that his captive was given fresh water and basic food, not wanting him to die from either dehydration or starvation.

After one such session, Otha dismissed the psychic so that he and Everus could be alone.

Everus now hung against the wall like a broken, ravaged doll. His ribs and limbs ached and his body was a mass of blue-black bruises. The scar across his upper torso still bled and, despite the salt that his captors frequently rubbed into it, seemed infected. One of his eyes had been badly punched and it was now closed and puffy. Through the other, he painfully watched as Otha sat up in his 'wheelbarrow', as Everus thought of it, and toyed with a dagger.

"Such a strange turn around, don't you think?" said Otha, running his thumb along the edge of the blade.

"What?"

"Fate or destiny. I guess they're one and the same when you think about it. You know, for so many moons I've been forcing myself to deal with what you did. In some way I owe you for giving purpose to my life. You see, it's just that...life. Life is what separates us, what makes us different. For, whereas I lived for living, all of my life devoting myself to protecting others and upholding values, to bring justice and fairness, you...*you* sought only to destroy and corrupt. We're like two chess pieces. One white...one black."

"You're just a pawn," groaned Everus. "Your life and your loves have been lies."

"Oh, you think so, do you?" Otha studied the dagger for a moment longer before looking up. "I know more about you than you think. I know that you loved once, did you not? Katryna. Yes, that was her name. Katryna Hapsburg. Old Xenobia's niece. By the gods she was something, if I remember rightly."

196

In a part of Everus' heart, now dark and devoid of any emotion, he felt a slight stirring as memories of the young woman he had once loved flooded back to haunt him. His already punished mind reeled as he thought of everything he had lost. His parents. His academic ambitions. Katryna. Even his own sense of humanity. Everything had been taken from him. *Everything.* And it had all been down to Julia Camberra, Dae'dicus and their scheming ilk. They were the ones who should now be hanging in fetters awaiting the red hot brands and the thumbscrews. He had slaughtered her and her demonic offspring quickly and efficiently. If he could go back now he would have been sure to see *their* pain linger. Even if he had not been aware of their demonic nature at the time of killing them, he had easily justified murdering them to himself. And that, as far as he had been concerned, was where it counted.

"It hurts, knowing what you've lost, doesn't it?" asked Otha.

Everus could feel the rage within him grow. "*Bastards!*" He strained, succeeding in pulling one of his restraining brackets loose a little. "Your bitch worshipped Uhu'giaggoth! She wasn't even human!"

"Shut up!"

"She was a succubus!" cried Everus. He no longer cared whether his enemy would hack him to death there and then. Life and death were the same as far as he was concerned; each as dark and miserable as the other. "*You fathered hellspawn!* Ask your telepath if you think I'm lying! *I dare you!*"

Otha no longer listened to his ranting captive. He wheeled himself out of the cell.

As soon as he had gone, Everus lapsed into a wracked sleep. It brought him no comfort, however, no respite from his torment. For once more he was aware of Dae'dicus, only now in his dreams his fiendish mentor seemed menacing and terrible, his face cadaverous, his eyes tinged red with loathing. And again, it seemed as though, across the gulfs of nightmare, the former high priest was searching for him.

✝ ✝ ✝

How long had he been chained here, Everus no longer knew. Wherever he was, there were no days or nights, nothing to enable him to guess the normal passage of time. There was pain, interspersed with food and water and his torturers' goading banter, and that was all. He hung against the cold, damp wall, the sounds of things rustling amidst the litter and the constant drip of leaking water all he could hear. If it had not been for the noises and the constant hurt, he would have gambled his blackened soul on the odds of him having died and gone to whatever afterlife the gods had reserved for such as him. In the darkness, perhaps reminded of the last time he had been incarcerated in a dungeon such as this, his thoughts turned to Creeps and the expedition into the badlands that were The Deadmoor Clumps. It now seemed as though it could have been a year ago and yet he knew it could not have been anywhere near as long ago as that.

Creeps – a man whom, more than anyone else, he had come to rely on, if not fully trust, in a strange sort of way. Yet now, he too had been revealed as a follower of Uhu'giaggoth. The more he thought about it, the clearer the picture became. No doubt he had been assigned by Dae'morogin to keep an eye on him, to make sure he carried out his sanctioned, ritualistic slayings. He should have suspected it earlier. For surely it had been no coincidence that Creeps, a highly skilled lockpicker, had been in *that* cell *that* day he had been tried and sentenced to death by Antonio De'carla, the High Legal Overseer. No doubt Dae'dicus had seen to that. He had never thought to question just why his fellow inmate had kept a single lockpick in his shit-streaked underpants without having ever used it.

And yet, thought Everus, why had Creeps assisted with his quest to obtain the amulets for Xethorn? Was it just another part of the man's duplicity and ambiguity; something to mask his charade, to give an element of credence to his disguise? Or was the thief just ignorant of the facts? Also, how long had Creeps been a demon-worshipper, an agent of Uhu'giaggoth? In the end, it no longer mattered, for, as far as he knew, the bastard was dead. Good riddance.

† † †

"It's all lies," moaned Everus as he was taken from his cell and dragged into a larger room by two of Otha's men. It was clearly a training room of some description for various weapon racks, target boards and stuffed mannequins had been pushed back against the walls.

"Come on, pig-shit," jeered one of the men. "It's time for a little bit o' fun."

The two of them threw Everus against a heap of old crates. Striking his aching ribs against a hard edge, he roared with pain and fell to his knees.

"Steady boys," said the once-honourable ex-knight of The Watchful Eye from his wheeled-chair. "He's no good to me dead...*yet*."

Everus' two man-handlers hauled him to his feet and frogmarched him towards an upright flogging board that had been set up in the middle of the room.

About a dozen other men stood around, watching with measured interest.

"Now then," announced Otha as more of his lackeys entered the chamber. "As you all know, I'm a merciful man. However, the nature of the heinous crimes that this one has committed leave me with no alternative but to prepare his soul for whatever afterlife the gods, in their mercy, have seen fit to grant one such as him."

"Just kill the bastard, I say," shouted a gruff voice.

"Silence!" ordered Otha. "Before I mete out his punishment, I'd like to tell you all of this one's crimes. Some three years ago, he murdered my wife and my two young daughters, slaying them in cold blood as they slept. He's a coward, a child-killer and a malefactor of the highest order. He was caught, tried and sentenced to death, but somehow he managed to escape."

"They weren't human...they..." moaned Everus, his words drowned out by the sounds of outrage from the gathered men.

"And so...in order that we don't sink to his level of depravity, we must purge the evil from him. Only through sustained suffering can his tortured soul be saved. A process, which, although unpleasant, in his case I deem utterly necessary."

Craning his neck, Everus could see the robed telepath, Schraeggaenello, and at least five other men.

Otha continued. "Such purification is a process that may take some time. So...in order to keep you bloodthirsty jackals happy and to repay a friend, I think a little extra purification is in order."

Men cheered, voicing their approval. They had come to see blood and torture and it now looked as though they were going to get their wish. None of the gathered men held any allegiance to The Watchful Eye and consequently none had any moral objection to witnessing a wholesome dose of cruelty. As far as most were concerned, the bloodier the better.

Everus heard the sound of a door opening, followed by the clomp of heavy footsteps. The footsteps came closer and he tried in vain to turn his head in order to see who was approaching. Suddenly, he was gripped by the hair and his head was pulled back so that he was forced to look into the black and ragged eye-sockets of a loutish-looking bruiser.

"Remember me, pretty boy?" the barrel-chested man croaked. Spittle flew from his mouth, spattering Everus' face.

"You looked better with the hood."

"Go on! Flay the bastard!" someone shouted even as Otha handed the big blind man a nasty-looking barbed whip. And flay him the big blind man did.

Everus' back was lashed raw, each sting of the scourge tearing the flesh from him. Lapsing in and out of consciousness on the agonising waves of torture, he mumbled prayers to his dark god, begging for his forgiveness; believing that he had failed in his quest. With a mad laugh, born of despair, pain and hysteria, he realised that if he died, as was now almost certain, then Dae'morogin and his demonic cult's schemes would also fail.

After a while, Otha took over. Laughing sadistically, he became possessed with the bloodlust and the brutality. Lashing, cursing and spitting – any vestige of his former self now gone completely – he intensified the scourging. Despite having to be supported by one of his cronies, his hatred drove him on, fuelling his violence.

Everus was dying now. In his mind, he saw Dae'dicus. The old man's face was contorted with rage as he scried for his wayward protégé and...just as death finally took him, he was convinced the evil face laughed in triumph.

† † †

His eyes opened. Staring at the high-roofed ceiling, his numbed hearing faintly registered sounds. They came from everywhere as though a hundred invisible spirits were cavorting around him. Clangs, shouts and screams all added to the din in a diabolical melody.

Then the noise faded until, for a time, there was nothing.

For a long time, it remained that way.

Out of the darkness, faces suddenly flashed through his mind;

Weaselnest, Dae'morogin, his mother, Julia and Otha Camberrå, each image forever imprinted on his mind, forever locked away in some dark recess. And as the faces appeared and then vanished, it seemed as though he was being given an insight into some larger machination, some contrivance for which he was not yet fully prepared.

Out of the darkness screamed his soul. Transcendent, the amorphous, ethereal entity which formed the dead man's essence howled from the clutches of something terrible, obeying the unnatural power that was tugging it, drawing it away from a writhing nest of rapacious, slimy, black tentacles.

In his mind's eye he saw Dae'morogin, dressed in his full clerical attire, standing over his own battered corpse. The smell of unpleasant incense was strong in the candle-lit chamber. His vision blurred so that he could just about discern two of the high priest's attendants standing to either side, gripping his cold and clammy arms.

The high priest read passages from a large tome in a language as dead as the man laid out before him. Once done, he removed his headgear and began running his pale hands over the lifeless flesh. Solemnly, he paced over to a grotesquely-carved font that was filled with a murky, foul-smelling liquid in which he washed his hands before splashing some of it over his face. His unholy ablutions complete, he strode around Everus' corpse and gripped it by the head.

More prayers and dark mutterings came from the two acolytes.

Demonic wails filled the air as phantom wraiths partially materialised and were dispelled by the high priest's protective circles of power.

Dae'morogin had performed this rite of resurrection to the letter, taking inordinate care over the many steps required. He knew that only twice before had this particular feat been attempted by the priests of Uhu'giaggoth. On both occasions they had failed, with consequences that still brought a shiver to those who had participated in it.

With a final prayer, the high priest cried out and, in that instant, Everus' heart began to beat once more.

† † †

For two days, Everus had lain on the flat, cold altar, barely aware of his surroundings. He could do little but stare at the curiously half-hewn ceiling, only vaguely aware of the countless stalactites which hung high above, threatening at any moment to come raining down upon him, impaling him in a lethal barrage, killing him once more. Twice, he had been aware of Dae'morogin's presence, as the high priest checked on his progress, but apart from these brief visits he had been left all alone as though he was undergoing a ritual of purification which necessitated his partial removal from all others.

Either that or he still reeked of death.

From what he had pieced together as he lay at death's door, it would seem that he had been located probably via some form of divinatory magic and that once his whereabouts had been traced to Otha's villa, a small army of cultists had been dispatched and had stormed inside. The battle had undoubtedly been fierce, both sides taking high numbers of fatalities. But through their magic and the advantage of surprise, the hooded assassins had gained victory, killing Otha and his men and retrieving his own dead body.

It had taken him a surprisingly short time to accept the fact that he had been brought back to life. Rumours of such feats being performed successfully by priests of The High Three were relatively well known to the educated, and Everus himself had long suspected that such resurrections were far more common than many expected. According to local rumour, many members of the imperial family had been brought back from the dead on several occasions. If gossip on the street were anything to go by, the current emperor, J'hann, had long out-lived his mortal life span and yet the ruling elite had seen to it that he remained in power, probably for their own political reasons rather than out of any sense of affection.

However, there was a limit to how far wealth and power could buy immortality. For Everus had heard tales of such feats that had gone horribly wrong, producing insane, hybrid monsters – abominations – which were but travesties of their former selves. From what he remembered of his readings, one of the greatest mishaps was the risk that the deceased's soul could become host to a demon from beyond, who, according to the studies of the numerous demonologists he had flicked through at The Academy, prized such things above all else.

And now, here he lay, knowing that the sole reason he had been brought back to life was so that he could be slain once more, ritually sacrificed in order to invite Uhu'giaggoth into the world. With that thought, much of what he had forgotten came flooding back and he remembered all that Xethorn had told him.

† † †

The door to his charnel chamber opened and two hooded monks entered. Noting that he was awake, they moved closer. One of them carried a robe and offered it to him.

"The high priest wishes to see you now," said the other, impassively.

Everus slid his legs from the cold marble and took the offered robe. He dressed quickly, aware of his own nakedness. It was then that he saw the scar across his chest where Otha had cut him. Most of the bruises seemed to have faded and there was little pain from his back, despite the severity of his lashing. He tightened the sash and followed the two out of the room and down the long corridors towards the high priest's office. Opening the door, he stepped inside.

"Ah, Everus. Back with the living. Excellent. You're extremely fortunate that we managed to locate you in time. Another day or two and your friends may have seen to it that returning you would've been impossible," said Dae'morogin. He sat in the chair behind his desk, and had obviously been expecting him.

"I have no friends," replied Everus, flatly. Now that Xethorn had exposed the high priest's deceitfulness, revealing him to be a Uhu'giaggothian worshipper, respect and cordiality were no longer warranted. "Any friends I once had, died with me long ago."

Dae'morogin frowned and leaned forward, his elbows resting on the desk. "But, surely we're your friends...your fellow worshippers, Dae'dicus, myself?"

"Dae'dicus is dead." It was only a matter of time before Dae'morogin joined him. From the doorway, Everus stared at the seated man with eyes that had now seen the other side, eyes that had witnessed the horrors of beyond.

Dae'morogin eventually broke from Everus' gaze. "Anyway, to business. Come in and take a seat." He was clearly unnerved, unwilling now to meet Everus' stare. He reached for *The Book of Dead Names* which lay nearby and opened the tome as Everus sat down.

Curious, Everus leaned across the table, keen to see as much of

203

the book and its demonic contents as possible. Scribbled lines of text were intermingled with bizarre illustrations and diagrams, the meaning of which he could only guess at. Drawings of obscene things and nameless, tortured entities, many winged, others amorphous horrors, stared out from the final few pages. With a shudder, he forced himself to look closer and he saw that the sketches seemed to move and shift as though trying to free themselves from the confines of the book.

With a crunch, as though a nest-full of cockroaches had just been crushed, Dae'morogin closed the book. "It's best that you don't look too closely." He had no sooner finished his warning when the book seemed to convulse under his shielding hand. "It's a little lively today. I think it too can sense that great things are imminent. For, as you can see, it is almost complete."

"Who?" asked Everus, icily.

"A little eager are we not?" There was an element of suspicion in the high priest's tone. "Anyway, your next victim is a man called 'Bloody' Magruder."

"*Magruder?* Who is he? Where do I find him?"

"He's a cutthroat, a pirate, a rogue. He's the gang leader of a group of scum known as 'The Wild Breed'. He can be found most nights in one of the many alehouses down by the city docks. You'll be sure to recognise him. Just look for the meanest scoundrel this side of The Dark Sea. Failing that, you could always ask someone as to his whereabouts. From what my sources tell me he has numerous enemies eager to watch someone like yourself cut him down to size."

"And when the deed is done?" Everus asked, knowing full well what he would do.

"Why, return to me with full haste so that we can complete the preparations for the return of Our Lord."

† † †

Down in the depths of the old Xethornite temple, Dae'morogin walked over to the stone coffin which contained his predecessor's physical remains. Strained from the necromantic powers he had expended over the previous days, he leant wearily against one of the pillars in the chamber. The twisted face of Dae'dicus formed before him.

"I sense your success." There was blatant mockery in the

unearthly voice. "Dragonbanner lives once more?"

"Yes. He's weak and confused, but he will recover."

"Excellent."

"We got to him with little time to spare. Any longer and it would've been beyond my abilities," said Dae'morogin. "As it was, his soul was only recently detached. Nonetheless..."

"It must be *his* soul. We've no use for a mindless zombie. Only *his* soul will suffice."

Dae'morogin nodded, wearily. "It is his soul."

"Of this you're convinced?"

"Yes."

"Good. It's fortunate for you that we are back on track. As soon as he is fit, you must see to it that he carries out the final murder."

"Those orders have already been given."

The ghost's eyes narrowed. "For I sense something...something else."

"You foresee...complications?" asked Dae'morogin, tentatively. The last thing he wanted to do was offend Dae'dicus when he himself was not at his full power. He was only too well aware of what the wraith was capable of, for he could feel his icy presence wherever he went. From the likes of him there was no escape. Even when death finally took him he knew it would offer his damned soul no respite.

"Hmm." Dae'dicus' spectral head moved from side to side like that of a dragon atop its hoard, scanning the shadows for a thief. "There is a great change taking place in the fabric of existence. From a dead sleep Uhu'giaggoth stirs. Soon this world and those before and yet to come will bask in the darkness of a new sun. As prophesied by Cyrvilus, the waiting of generations will soon come to a close and with it the end of that pestilent canker...*humanity!*"

CHAPTER TEN

The Crossed Bones had to rank as one of the dirtiest taverns Everus had ever seen and, thanks largely to his past acquaintance with Creeps, he had seen more than his fair share. Created from the remains of an old cargo vessel, it jutted from the many reeking, dilapidated buildings that lined the city's northern wharf as though it had inadvertently run aground and smashed though the houses behind it. Its initial impressiveness was, however, diluted by the fact that much of it was heavily wrecked and falling apart, its countless loose timbers still covered with barnacles. It was a favourite haunt of the many freebooters and piratical thugs who plied the river and the coastal trading routes; a place where shady deals, murders and all manner of illicit cargoes changed hands for the right price. It would have suited Creeps down to the ground.

From across the street, Everus watched as several unsavoury types entered through the leaning prow of the weather-battered ship. He heard a shrill whistle and turned to see two drunken whores come staggering towards him, their faces dirty, their lipstick smeared.

"All right, luv?" said one of them.

"You're handsome. How's about two for the price o' one?" giggled the other.

"Sod off! Trollops." Pushing away the two whores as they tried to cajole him into accompanying them, Everus marched determinedly for the tavern doors. As he neared he was struck by the almost overpowering stench of dead fish given off by the rotting boards. Fighting back a strong need to vomit, he pushed the crude bat-wing doors open. The first thing to hit him was the smoke-filled fog of the interior. The second was a ring-studded fist. With a smack, the blow seemed to come almost out of nowhere, landing squarely on his chin. Reeling, he staggered back through the swing doors and fell on his backside. From his sitting position, he saw the man who had struck him being grabbed by two burly bouncers and flung outside, whereupon he started to hurl curses at anyone and anything, stomping up and down in his drink-induced madness.

"*What're ye lookin' at, slag?*" the aggressive drunk slurred, an empty bottle in his hand. "Ye want some o' this?" He raised the bottle and flung it at one of the tarts.

The bottle cracked off her face and shattered at her feet. She started screaming.

Springing to his feet, Everus grabbed his violent attacker by an arm, spun him around, stuck out a boot and tripped him up. Two swift kicks were then delivered to the man's head, silencing him. He was just about to kick the unconscious man a third time when an unmistakably familiar voice called out. Looking over his shoulder, he watched as two grubbas hailed him from across the street and began to make their way over.

"A'right, ma pal?" the more bearded of the two asked.

"I'll live," Everus replied, rubbing his aching jaw and trying to remember where he had seen the two before. Then it came back to him. They had been part of the crap act he had seen at The Drowned Man theatre the night he and Creeps had battled with Roach. Handaxe jugglers, or something as equally rubbish, he seemed to remember.

"Did he try tae mug ye?" inquired the younger grubba, looking down with some interest at the sprawled body at Everus' feet.

"Something like that."

"Aye, well, it's a good job me an' the boy were 'ere tae help ye oot. Ma name's Ozgo." The grubba stepped back, scrutinising Everus anew. "Hang on. Ye're...it's ye is it no'?"

"What?"

"Ye're the man fae the flea-pit, are ye no'? Aye, ye were efter someb'dy," Ozgo croaked in his barely comprehensible dialect. "Stubb. Ye remember, don't ye?"

"Aye fayther, ye're right. It's yon man who helped us oot that night the watch tried tae nab ye," squeaked Stubb.

"B'the gods! How're ye daein', ma pal?" inquired Ozgo, painfully slapping Everus on the arm.

"Surviving...just."

"Well how's aboot ye get me an' the boy a drink?" Ozgo gripped Everus by the arm and began to amiably drag him towards the tavern. "Ye see, it's the boy's birthday, so I was plannin' on gettin' him a wee strumpet fer the night. Summat tae play wi'...ye know whit I mean?" He gave Everus a sly wink.

"But fayther! I don't want a strumpet!" protested Stubb in his high voice.

"Whit dae ye mean ye don't want a strumpet!" Ozgo rolled his eyes at Everus who was fast becoming increasingly uncomfortable with the whole experience. He started to wish he had settled for the whores' company.

They were now by the tavern doors.

"I don't want a strumpet." Stubb's pleas sounded pathetic.

"Well I've no' come a' this way tae go away wi' nuthen. I'm goin' tae get ye the fattest strumpet ye've ever seen as a wee treat, whether ye wants it or no'." He looked up at Everus. "An' whit aboot yersel', mister? Whit've ye got fer the boy?"

Everus paid the obstreperous grubba no heed. Extricating himself from Ozgo's grip, he entered the tavern. It was similar in many ways to a hundred other dens of iniquity he had been in and, like unpleasant smells, he soon found out that wherever he went, the two grubbas were sure to follow. Ozgo became drunker and more belligerent, twice threatening him for not buying his share of booze and for 'forgetting' to buy his son a birthday present. For the most part Stubb sat, seemingly stuffed, in a corner, sipping from a tankard of diluted wine.

As the evening wore on and The Crossed Bones filled up with more 'skullduggerists' – as Ozgo called virtually everyone – Everus' keen ears began to pick up useful snippets of information. Although the majority of the news and the gossip he overheard was of no interest whatsoever, he did note one conversation about how another Øggarbakken behemoth raid had been repelled along the South Wall. Again, a tribe of the giants, led by a shaman, had caused serious destruction. It was likely that Emperor J'hann was going to impose tax increases as well as possible conscription in order to assist in the defence of the city.

After coming to the conclusion that he was not going to find his quarry in this particular tavern, Everus made a brief excuse to Ozgo, telling him he was going to get more drinks, and nipped outside. Into the cold and unfriendly night he went, doing his rounds of nearly a dozen more rough alehouses.

It was in The Throttled Squid that he eventually tracked his man down. Leaning at the bar, a tankard of ale at his elbow, he watched, surreptitiously, as a man whom he had ascertained was Magruder, and a gang of seven others, ate, drank, gambled, swore at one another and occasionally groped the several young serving wenches that had the misfortune of having to serve them. They were a motley bunch of ugly misfits and murderers.

Magruder was tall and wiry. The right side of his wolfish, dirty and unshaven face was decorated with a series of three claw-like scratches, the central one of which extended from his jaw line to his forehead, appearing either side of his right eye. His hair was long and spiked up with grease at the front. Like a prize hog, he sported a large gold ring through his nostrils.

Everus watched and continued to sip from his tankard. Catching the barkeeper's eye, he beckoned him over. "Who's the big shot? Is that 'Bloody' Magruder?" He looked over to see one of the uglier ones at the table suck in his thick lips before spearing a hunk of roast meat on a long-bladed knife and tearing at it avidly with his set of strong, pointed teeth.

The barkeeper raised a finger to his lips, signalling to Everus to keep quiet. It was obvious he was scared.

"I asked a question." Everus reached into a pocket and placed a gold coin on the bar.

The man looked around before pocketing the coin. "Don't know."

Everus smirked and shook his head. "Wrong answer." He stood up and turned to face the gathered disreputables, knocking his stool to the ground in order to get their attention. "I'm looking for Magruder."

Two of the nearest pirates stared at him. One looked more baazelgrig than human, probably one of the mongrel types Everus had heard of, while the other's face was terribly scarred. From the looks of it he had lost a fight with some piece of heavy mining machinery.

Magruder thumped the table in lazy acknowledgement.

Everus fixed him with a stare. "If you're the one they call 'Bloody' Magruder, I'd like to join your group."

"We don't take pretty boys," snarled one of the thugs. "Except for ballast."

"Or shark bait," laughed another.

"So bugger off, or I'll splice yer gizzard, ye landlubber scum," growled the mongrel, gripping a dagger.

Magruder cracked his knuckles. "Steady boys. Let's hear what he's got to say before we kill him and feed him to the gulls." He looked Everus up and down. "Now tell me. What do I want with the likes of you?"

"As I said, I'd like to join your group. I'm a half decent swordsman and I know The Dark Sea like the back of my hand."

"The Wild Breed ain't open to just anybody...so maybe I need a demonstration. You show me how good you are, and I'll consider it." Magruder nodded to one of his men. "If you beat Keef, I might let you join." His men started to snigger, obviously reckoning that Everus may as well jump on the man's blade and speed up the inevitable. As far as they were concerned he was already dead.

Coldly, Everus watched as one of the more normal-looking of the ragtag group gave a smug nod to his cronies and rose from his chair, reaching for a huge sword nearby. But before any of the group could react, Everus unsheathed his sword in a blinding flash and two-handedly swung out at Magruder's champion. Unprepared for the suddenness of it all and expecting the fight to take place outside once the group had gathered around, Keef could do little for the brief moment of horror before his head was chopped from his body.

"*Kraken's Teeth!*" someone shouted.

The pirates roared, almost to a man as, with a red spraying, the two parts of their accomplice's body fell back and landed on their table.

Those in the background screamed in shock.

Everus grinned wickedly. "Now can I join?"

"Kill him!" shouted one of the buccaneers, rising from his chair, a hook for a hand.

"*By the Tentacles of the Deep!*" cried Magruder. "*Get him!*"

Upon hearing the pirate leader's order, and now sure that any chance of subterfuge was gone, Everus opted for his contingency plan. With a cry, he sprang forward, cutting and hacking with abandon. Two of the cutthroats fell almost immediately to his attacks, whilst the rest retreated, scrambling for their weapons.

'Hook-hand' got as far as drawing his cutlass before Everus ran his sword straight through his belly. He was pulling the blade free when the mongrel cracked him with a large hammer-like weapon. Stunned, Everus' next swing went wild, allowing his opponent in for a second attack. Close to crunching his skull like a nut, the blow smote painfully off his left shoulder. Numbed from the hammer blow, he withdrew across the rapidly emptying, dimly-lit tavern, whirling his sword defensively with his right hand.

"Kill the son o' a sea troll!" someone shouted.

The baazelgrig-faced individual and another two, 'Shredded-Face' and a hook-nosed man with an eyepatch, closed in.

Springing up onto a table, Everus swung down at his foes, parrying and dodging their by and large untrained attacks. He ducked as a bottle flew past his head. Transferring his weight, he delivered a powerful kick to the man with the many scars, catching him full in the face. The man careered back, blood trickling from between the grimy fingers clamped to his mouth.

"Up-end the bastard!" yelled the one with the eyepatch, grinning maniacally as he reached for the table and began tilting it.

Everus half-leapt, half-fell as the table was pushed over. Now on the floor, he began to scramble to his feet when suddenly a heavy, hobnailed boot cracked into his ribs, knocking the air from his lungs. He let out a pained wheeze as the boot struck home again. The mongrel stood over him, pulling back his foot for a third kick.

Everus moaned as the boot connected with the pit of his stomach, driving a stab of pain through him. He looked up at the cruelly sneering thug and the shifty-looking pirate with the eyepatch. Both were toying with him before going in for the kill. Then, as he tried to drag himself to his feet, a bottle was slung from the other end of the bar, shattering over the man with the eyepatch. The unfortunate screamed and pulled back, blood leaking from his gashed forehead.

"I telt ye tae go fer the ugly bastard! Whit did I tell ye?" cried Ozgo, reprimanding his long-suffering son and cuffing him about the head.

The 'ugly bastard' looked up even as the irate, wild-eyed grubba charged straight into him, both of them crashing back over a table.

Stiffly, Everus got to his feet, retrieving his sword.

"Fayther!" cried Stubb. "Hit him, fayther!"

Looking around with a grim face, Everus saw a crowd of onlookers gathered at the back of the bar and a few interested faces peering in through the windows, but there was no sign of Magruder. Nearby, fighting like savage dogs, were Ozgo and the mongrel. Although the cross-breed was the taller of the two, the old grubba, spurred on perhaps by too much drink and his over enthusiastic son, threw all caution to the wind, kicking, biting and gouging as though this were a typical evening's activity – as perhaps, for him, it was.

Preoccupied with the fight, Everus did not notice the scarred man creep up behind him. The next thing he knew a thin leather garrotte had been looped around his neck and he was hauled back. The cord bit tighter as, in vain, he tried to reach for his would-be assassin. His eyes began to weep, veins bulging at his neck. Tongue protruding, he waved frantically at Stubb who mercifully came to his aid.

Swinging the mongrel's hammer, Stubb cracked Everus' attacker, shattering a kneecap.

Releasing his hold on Everus, 'Shredded-Face' fell to the ground, allowing the young grubba to crack him once more, smashing his skull open.

Catching his breath, Everus saw that Ozgo and the mongrel were still grappling on the floor. At least two bottles had been smashed over the grizzled grubba's head but still he fought on. Then, with a crack, Ozgo broke his attacker's arm by wedging it under a chair leg and dropping a knee on it. The half-breed roared in pain as the grubba, now cut and bloody himself, rose clumsily to his feet.

"Bastard!" cursed the half-breed.

"Stubb, ma boy!" Ozgo shouted, gesturing to his son.

"Aye fayther!" Across the length of the bar room Stubb slung the hammer. Gracefully it flew, spinning end over end, before bypassing his father's hand and crashing onto an overturned table.

"Whit kind o' throw was that, ye wee bastard?" roared Ozgo. He was then hauled to the floor by the mongrel, who, despite his broken arm still had a lot of fight left in him.

That fight, however, was soon to end.

Sword in hand, Everus paced over to where the two grappled. He held his sword point against the side of the mongrel's brutish face. "Tell me where Magruder's gone!"

The battered pirate shook his head as though not understanding the question.

"Unsatisfactory." With a grinding squelch, Everus thrust the blade through the half-breed's head. Upon hearing movement, he turned in time to see the lanky, eyepatched man come charging at him with a raised dagger. Parrying the attack with ease, he turned his blade and disarmed the man. He advanced, and with a vicious smack punched the pommel of his sword straight between his attacker's eyes, knocking him out, cold. Surveying the battlefield, which had once been the main room of The Throttled Squid, and content that there was now no immediate danger, he began to drag the unconscious man into a side-room.

"Whit're ye goin' tae dae wi' him?" asked Ozgo, rubbing his arm.

Everus looked up. "Probably kill him." He flung the man into a chair. "Go and see if the barkeep's got any rope," he shouted back to the grubba.

The pirate was stirring by the time Ozgo returned with some rope. "Let me go!" he blurted, eyes wide with fear. There was glass in his hair and dried blood covered his face.

"Not until you tell me where your leader's fled." Pulling the knots tight, Everus finished binding the man to the chair and picked up his sword.

"I don't know. I'm a new member o' the gang...this was ma first meetin'."

Menacingly, Everus looked along the edge of his sword, pausing for a moment to examine his reflection in the highly polished steel. "I'll ask once more."

"I don't know."

Conscious of the fact that there was not the time for a full interrogation, Everus just picked up his sword and prepared to run the man through there and then. It seemed to get the desired effect nonetheless.

"*No! No!* Wait! I...I think I remember hearin' him mention summat about a place down by the old lighthouse, the one at the far end o' Damp Street."

"*You think?* Well I'm afraid that's not good enough either." Everus thrust his sword deep into the man's chest. Removing his blade from its human scabbard, he wiped the sword clean before leaving the side-room. In the bar, Ozgo and his son were helping the tavern owner do a bit of tidying up. Even in this short time, he could see that they had managed to return the bar to some semblance of its former self, although it was hard to be sure, for the place had been a bit of an eyesore before the skirmish had erupted. At least the bloody corpses had been disposed of.

"Bloody good birthday present!" shouted Ozgo, limping over in order to look up at Everus through beery and bruised eyes.

"Aye," agreed Stubb. "Thanks mister. That were much better than a strumpet."

"I try to please." Everus himself ached from the disturbance but such things he did his best to ignore. Magruder had escaped alive and only when he was dead, his god freed and Dae'morogin and his demonic cult eradicated, would he permit such feelings to get the better of him. "Have you ever heard of Damp Street?"

The grubba ran a cut hand through his tangled beard. "No. Never heard o' it."

"*Damp Street?*" piped up Stubb. "I ken where that is."

Everus turned to face Ozgo's son. "*You* know of it?"

"Aye. There's an ol' lighthoose oot there. Me an' ma brothers used tae go there tae fish an' hunt crabs."

"*Hunt crabs!?*" cried Ozgo. "Whit dae ye mean, *hunt crabs?* Ye don't hunt crabs."

"We did," replied Stubb.

"No ye didnae!" roared Ozgo, stomping over and cuffing his son. "Ye didnae hunt crabs, ye hear me? Naeb'dy hunts crabs. *Naeb'dy!*"

"But fayther..."

Ozgo smacked his son some more. "This man doesnae want tae know aboot that, ye wee bastard that ye are!"

"Just tell me how to get there," said Everus, trying to curtail their meaningless bickering. Once informed, he left the tavern and, like the highly trained assassin he was, he stalked the poorly-lit streets in search of his prey. Down filthy alleys, accompanied by the occasional distant scream and the chittering of unseen vermin, he went, his mind focused on getting the deed done. His quarry had evaded him once. He would not let that happen a second time.

Crossing one of the ramshackle bridges that crossed a series of canals in an area of the city commonly known as The Rat's Wharf, Everus made for the rotting dockside warehouses that loomed up ahead. On the other side of the bridge, he saw that some of these buildings seemed to be in a far better state than he had first thought. There was little doubt in his mind that some were undoubtedly storage places for illicit goods.

Now that he was heading into areas that were by and large completely unlit, he removed the small hooded lantern he had taken from The Throttled Squid and lit up. The scant illumination it provided revealed to him the utter inhospitality of his surroundings, leading him to wonder what Magruder would be doing out here. Dark ideas entered his mind. The more he pondered, the more his mind began to create notions that perhaps the pirate leader was not a normal man. Perhaps he was akin to Roach and Cu, or more likely, considering his whereabouts, a wererat or some other kind of night horror. He was now in a part of the city in which he had never been before.

Over to his left, there ran a largely ruined harbour wall, the ground beyond sloping down to the lapping waters of The Dark Sea. The tide was in, and the salty stink it brought with it nipped at Everus' eyes. He was beginning to think that he had come all this way for nothing when, up ahead, he could see the shadowy outline of the old lighthouse Stubb had mentioned. He was just about to start sneaking up towards it when he heard voices over to his right. Darting quickly to one side and hooding the lantern, he crouched behind a protruding part of the wall, blending into the shadows. Not far away, he saw the outlines of three men, one of whom looked either dead or asleep, for he was supported by the other two.

"I'm sure I saw someb'dy up 'ere," said a gruff voice. "Sure I saw a light."

"Nah. Ye're just imaginin' things," replied another, lighting a lantern of his own.

"Do ye think it's the boss?"

"Nah. Boss said he won't be back till sun up. He's gone drinkin' wi' some o' them new lads. Ye know, them ugly nutters we picked up in Ullerby. I imagine he'll grab himsel' a tart or two so we might no' even see him till 'morrow afternoon."

"Aye. Well, I suppose we'd better get this shit into his pit afore he hurls his innards all o'er his shirt. That's the last time I'll go drinkin' with him. I don't know, these bastards that can't handle their ale."

The three made their way towards the lighthouse.

Concealed in the shadows, Everus waited for them to move on. Using the various piles of crates and half-repaired boats as cover, he sneaked towards Magruder's hideout. There were several lights on in the lighthouse, enabling him to see that the tower-like building was in a reasonable state, far better than that of the many smaller outbuildings which clustered around it.

Now hiding in a small forecourt area, which was evidently used for excess storage, Everus could see all manner of bits and pieces scattered around like flotsam. Old anchors, a pile of cannon balls, several stacks of crates under an old cargo net, the remnants of at least three rowing boats, a peeling, naked female figurehead and dozens of large barrels cluttered the area. Stealthily, he made his way across this mariner's stockyard, heading for the door that gave access to the tall, conical building. Looking up, even in the poor light, he could make out the domed roof.

He tried the door and was both pleased and surprised to find it unlocked. He opened it. The area beyond was in darkness. There was no sound, so he risked unhooding his lantern and peered inside. From where he stood at the doorway, he could see before him a circular entrance chamber. Round to his left, a narrow staircase with an iron banister curved its way up to the floor above. Directly opposite, there was a small unlit hearth. Various pieces of junk and crude furniture, largely salvaged from old boats, filled the hallway.

Quietly, Everus entered and closed the door. He knew that there were at least three pirates somewhere within; one drunk and two relatively sober. Hopefully they had gone to their beds. With near silent steps, he crossed over to the stairwell. He was halfway there when he heard the sound of footsteps directly overhead, followed by the creak of a door opening. Looking around, he hooded his lantern and darted to a large stuffed armchair, crouching behind it.

A lantern was lit and the long shadow of a man armed with a curved sword began to slink down the stairs.

"Who's there? Snotty, is that you?"

Everus held his breath and remained hidden, watching as a man came to the bottom of the stairs.

"Is there anybody there?" called out a voice from further up.

"Can't see anythin', boss," the man replied. He turned and began the climb back up.

"Are you sure?"

It was definitely Magruder's voice and with that realisation Everus sprang from his hiding place and charged forward, cutting down the lantern-bearer even as he turned in surprise. Screaming, the man slumped to the steps, an arm, now a stump, jetting blood. He convulsed, feebly trying to stem the pumping blood with his remaining hand.

"*Intruders!*" yelled Magruder, eyes wide in shock. He was dressed only in his nightshirt and breeches.

"Shut up and I'll make this quick," snarled Everus, looking up. A dagger hurled by the man above sparked off the wall by his head. Forcefully, he pushed his way past his bleeding victim and started up the steps in pursuit of the retreating pirate leader. Heart thumping, he found himself on a timber-floored landing, its walls decorated by many paintings of mermaids and ships. At the far end, he saw

Magruder shin up an iron ladder before disappearing through an opening in the ceiling. "Get back here and face me!" he shouted.

The loud ringing of an alarm bell suddenly shattered the relative silence as though announcing the rise of some horror from the deep.

That was the last time he kept anyone alive, one hand or not, Everus thought as he heard sounds of movement from downstairs. With no time to investigate its source, he sped over to the ladder and began to pull himself up. It was just as he was nearing the top that, with a barrage of curses, he heard the sound of an angry mob in the hallway below and looking over his left shoulder his heart sank as he saw some dozen or so ruffians come charging their way up the stairs. They had come from their sleeping quarters under the lighthouse. Some had been awake, informed about the fight earlier at The Throttled Squid. Others were still getting dressed, not too appreciative at having been woken in the early hours of the morning. All were armed, vicious and very pissed off.

There was only one way now for Everus to go. Throwing open the trapdoor, he pulled himself up through the opening. He found himself in what had once been the cupola. It was a large, circular, domed chamber with windows on all sides and it was reasonably well illuminated by five lanterns suspended from brackets around the walls. It was well furnished. Over to one side was a large bed of carved dark wood, to either side of which were small dressing tables. Beyond the bed, flush with the wall were an array of wardrobes, full-length dress mirrors and three cabinets. The floor was covered with several expensive rugs.

From behind the bedsheets peered a nervous woman, her dirty blonde hair long and tousled. Standing beside her, a sword in one hand, was Magruder.

Everus wiped a trickle of sweat from his forehead.

"What do you want?" demanded the pirate leader.

"I want to kill you," replied Everus, coldly. With a quick look around, he noticed a large wardrobe and with a great heave he pulled it over, crashing it down on top of the trapdoor.

"Who sent you? Tell me that at least."

"A priest of Uhu'giaggoth." From down below Everus could hear the hammering as the pirates tried to get through.

"Who? What?" cried Magruder. "What have I...?"

"*Enough!* You die!"

"Come on then, bastard!" Magruder tore open his shirt.

It was not so much the pirate's rippling, muscled torso that caused Everus' heart to sink, but the sight of the prominent black octopus tattoo that he had on display. For it was a design he knew and recognised immediately. Before him was a fellow worshipper of Xethorn.

"I'm going to cut you in two!" With a bellow, Magruder charged at Everus. His first swing went wild and Everus quickly brought up his own blade, catching the pirate a glancing blow on his left arm. Magruder cursed as he dived back, narrowly avoiding Everus' backward swing.

Frantic shouts and hammering resounded from below as the mob tried to break in.

Magruder cursed, dashing furniture to the floor as he and Everus battled around the screaming woman in the bed, each of his swings answered by Everus' blade. Suddenly one of the lanterns in the room exploded. Like a small fireball, glass, spiralled metal and fiery oil jettisoned into the air. Magruder turned, cut from a piece of shrapnel, his lean and angular face red with blood and rage. It was at that moment that, down below, his men's cries of rage turned to cries of fear and horror.

For a moment the whole building shuddered as though struck by an earthquake.

Everus stumbled to one side. The pirate-leader took advantage, lunging forward with a whistling slice which hit Everus at the top of his right thigh. Falling back, Everus rolled over a small table, decanters and goblets smashing on the floor.

The building trembled once more. The screams from downstairs were becoming terrible to hear, like the sounds from a torched orphanage.

Neither man knew what was happening, but this was Magruder's domain and he was now fighting for his life. Sword raised, he hacked down, his eyes ablaze. It was all Everus could do to parry the deadly attack. With a kick, Magruder booted the sword out of Everus' hands.

Another two lanterns exploded, the flames from one quickly igniting a set of curtains.

"*By the Wytchfires!* What sorcery is this?" Magruder cried out.

With a crash, the heavy wardrobe blocking the opening juddered and jumped briefly into the air, as though some superhuman strength from below was trying to break through.

Assuming that he was about to be overrun, Magruder grasped his sword and prepared to run Everus through. He would at least take one of his attackers with him. He suddenly stopped as though frozen. A glazed look came over his eyes and another face, a face Everus had seen before on the statue in his private shrine, seemed to flicker over his sharp features.

A commanding voice came from the pirate leader's lips. *"Kill him now, Everus!"*

Magruder dropped suddenly to his knees, offering his blade. *"Do it!"*

Knowing what had to be done, and yet confused as to what was happening, Everus snatched the pirate leader's sword from his hands and cleanly beheaded him with it. In a red fountain, the severed head cartwheeled over the squirting body.

The wardrobe behind him crashed once more as it landed. Turning round, Everus was surprised to see Ozgo's grizzled face grinning at him through the narrow gap.

"You all right?" The grubba tried to force his way through.

"How did you...?" There was disbelief all over Everus' face.

"Me and the boy thought you..."

"Everus, run! Escape this place!" An unearthly voice shouted, causing Everus to spin round.

There was no one to be seen.

"Come on by gods!" Ozgo tried to get his gnarled hands around the side of the wardrobe and it appeared as if he was going to rip the whole thing apart.

Everus retrieved his own sword. He was just about to go over and assist the grubba when a thud from behind caused him to turn round once more.

The sound had been caused by Magruder's severed head falling from the chair on which it had landed. With almost pleading eyes, the grisly face looked straight up at Everus. *"Flee!"* it cried.

"Everus, my pal," shouted Ozgo. "Give us a hand!"

"Don't!" The severed head shouted. "It's a follower of Uhu'giaggoth. An agent of Dae'morogin. Listen to his voice."

"Who's in there with you?" barked Ozgo, now beginning to haul himself through.

"Flee!" insisted the head.

A severed head, or a crazed grubba – what a choice. Everus decided to trust his instincts, for the grubba's accent was relatively refined, clearly not the one that had been annoying him all night. Rushing over, he slashed out, his blade cutting the grubba's left arm to the bone. Blood spurted as the grubba roared in pain. With a swift kick, that caught him high in the chest, Everus knocked him back down through the floor, whereupon the grubba fell, catching a leg in the rungs of the ladder. Suspended, upside-down, he then swung back, banging his head off one of the metal uprights before crashing, head first, to the floor below.

Flames licked up one wall of the chamber as pieces of furniture started to ignite, bathing the room in an orange-red glow. From where Everus stood, looking down with disbelief at the mad grubba, he could feel the burning heat on his face. Of the woman, he could see no trace, guessing that she had probably hidden under the bed. There she would die.

"*Everus, flee!* The powers here you cannot defeat!" the bloody head shouted.

Everus sprang to one of the windows and looked out. Some distance below he could make out the shadowy forecourt. Darting to another window, close to the flaming curtains, he saw what looked like the outline of a low wall. Far away, he could see the beacons of a sailing ship some league or so out to sea.

It was at that moment that the wardrobe exploded. Splintered wood flew everywhere before dropping like so much kindling. The blast rocked Everus on his feet even on the other side of the chamber.

"The window!" shouted the head. "I'll protect you!"

Clambering up onto the window ledge Everus looked down at the shadows far below.

Suddenly a window on the opposite side of the cupola shattered and a dark figure leaped through.

Everus looked over and was astonished to see Adolf Creeps rise to his feet, brushing glass off his dirty jacket.

"Ye'll die, ye fool!" yelled the thief, casting a swift glance at the grubba who was pulling himself in; his head lolling, his neck clearly broken.

"By Xethorn, you'll never take me!" Everus shouted.

"*No!*" shouted Creeps. But his warning came too late, for in that instant Everus smashed through the window and dived out into the night sky.

For agonising moments Everus felt as though he had become

suspended in mid-air, then gravity took hold and he plummeted towards the ground. For a time that seemed longer than it should have been, he wondered whether this was how it would end, indeed, *should* end. Faster and faster the old, smashed rowing boat below raced up to meet him, before a darkness swept over him and everything changed.

At first, he thought he had smashed through the wooden wreck and was now descending through the bowels of the world. Air gusted past his body, alerting him to the fact that he was travelling at great speed. He began to see a strange flickering, as though a thousand will-o'-the-wisps, or perhaps Evil Eyeballs, had come to speed him on his way. The lights grew in both number and intensity until the dark void was illuminated, allowing him to see that he was in some sort of giant tunnel, the likes of which his soul had been swept along during his recent resurrection. Yet as he watched, he became convinced that it was the tunnel that was moving, not him.

No sooner had he reached that observation than, with an almost blinding flash of light, he found himself face to face with the statue in his private chapel.

CHAPTER ELEVEN

Only a few moments had passed since Xethorn had delivered Everus from the burning lighthouse and yet, as Everus knelt in silent, fervent prayer at the statue's base, he felt as though an aeon had elapsed.

"*Time* will soon have little meaning," spoke the statue, reading Everus' thoughts. "Uhu'giaggoth has now awoken and is preparing to enter your world. Together we can stop it."

Everus raised his weary face. Of all the strangeness he had seen, for some reason, it was the sight of Creeps that haunted him the most.

"You must slay them, Everus. *Slay them all!*"

"They're too many."

"Not single-handedly," intoned the statue. "*I* will provide whatever assistance is needed."

† † †

Dae'dicus' twisted face blurred into vision. With malign eyes, he surveyed the high priest standing before him with open contempt. "So. Your agents have failed?"

Dae'morogin choked back a lump in his throat and felt a clammy wetness in his palms. "Dae'dicus, you must hear me, there were others. Dragonbanner was rescued by an equal force. We tried our best."

"But *Dae'morogin*, your best was evidently not good enough and now Dragonbanner has escaped. You must see to it that he is found and brought here. *Do so now!*"

"Those orders have already been given. He won't get far."

"I take it you know where he is?"

"We have an idea."

"Where?"

Dae'morogin could feel the burning stare of the ghost's red-rimmed eyes as they bored into his soul.

"Where?"

"My agents report that no body was found outside the tower..."

"WHERE?"

"I have despatched some of my best to his villa. If he is there, they *will* bring him back."

"I hope so, for your sake" cried Dae'dicus. "For failure is not an option you will want to consider."

† † †

Slay them! Slay them all!

The voice rang in Everus' head, causing him to break free of whatever trance he had been in, its content already forgotten. Disorientated, he looked around, finding himself still in his private shrine. He looked up at the blank-faced statue before him.

Everus! I will avenge you! Every wrong done to you will be returned a thousandfold.

Unsteadily, Everus rose to his feet, his body responding to commands that were not his own. He watched, willing, yet at the same time helpless, as a dark red glow emanated from the statue and fell about him, wreathing him with its hellish, incarnadine light. Fighting back a strong desire to scream, he felt a deep, almost spiritual, burning as though his very soul was on fire.

At that moment, Xethorn took up residence in the well-prepared shell of Everus' body.

Suddenly Everus ran to the exit, his sword drawn. His muscles obeying orders that were no longer his own, he stepped out into the gallery beyond, just in time to see a trio of cowled men sneaking down the hall.

One of them called out, before launching a spiked ball from his hand. The ball imbedded itself in the wall just over Everus' left shoulder, whereupon it exploded in an orange gas. Another man stepped back, muttered something, raised his hands high above his head and unleashed his spell. From his fingertips jetted a sticky web-like net. With lightning speed, Everus dashed forward, the viscous web falling behind him.

The first of the three, the one who had thrown the gas-filled orb, reached for a professional-looking blackjack, but before his hand even touched it, Everus swung out with his blade and with superhuman strength cut the man in two. Such was the speed of the attack that for a heartbeat his victim's upper-half remained supported on the lower. Then, spewing blood and squelching organs, the upper-half slopped to the floor.

The remaining two men pulled back, blackjacks raised.

Everus looked down at the writhing halves of the man before him as the hapless forms convulsed in their puddled mess. Eyes narrowing, he stared at Dae'morogin's remaining agents, images of blood and mayhem alive in his thoughts. Psychically, he directed the chaos of the battlefield towards the men, attempting to bend their minds to madness.

One of the two began to hastily mouth the words of power necessary for unleashing magic. The other stepped back, adopting a fighting stance.

"I see Dae'morogin has taught you well," voiced Everus, now aware that his attempts at mental domination would be far harder than he had hoped.

Suddenly the cleric completed his incantation, unleashing a magical attack which seemed to compress the air around it, before rushing towards Everus like an oncoming mammoth. Raised off his feet, Everus was pushed back. Down the length of the hall he went, before crashing through a wall and sprawling against an old fireplace. None the worse for wear, he sprang to his feet even as another gas-filled missile went off nearby.

With the room rapidly filling with soporific smoke, the only effect it was having on Everus was to obscure his vision. Having a god possess his body certainly had some benefits. He strode to the door and flung it wide, noting one of the hooded attackers at the other end of the gallery preparing another spell. Stepping through the doorway, he instantly pushed his sword to the right with one hand, whilst applying pressure with the other. With an unpleasant sound, the blade plunged through the guts of the assailant hidden by the door, just as he was about to swing down an attack.

The man collapsed to his knees as Everus withdrew his blade. He looked at the remaining agent. "One against one."

The cowled fanatic reached for a grotesque, unholy symbol, one which had been fashioned from the fused remains of a dozen butchered babes, and muttered a prayer to The Daemon God.

"I don't think so," shouted Everus, as a reddish glow began to form around the evil cultist. With superhuman speed, he tore up the hall and chopped at the man, who was beginning to fade away, attempting to translocate to the safety of the temple. Blood fountained, spraying beyond him as the partially phased-out man crumpled to his knees.

✝ ✝ ✝

Dae'morogin raised his bloodshot eyes from the hefty tome and surveyed the dark-cowled assassins before him. He had given them their final orders and each man knew exactly what had to be done. They had all devoted their souls to this cause, each having been dehumanised long ago by listening to the high priest's demonic liturgies and readings, for contained within the pages of their unholy bible, *The Cyrvilus*, were dark and terrible passages contrived and written with the principal aim of instilling madness. More effective than a drug and more damaging than mass indoctrination, the writings within the foul grimoire actually subverted the will through its very being, forcing the reader to read more, to become one with its insane web of demonic didacticism.

There remained but one task left for the fanatics – to capture Dragonbanner and sacrifice him. They had no other purpose.

When the dark brotherhood had left, Dae'morogin walked over to a ghastly statue of The Daemon God. It was an amorphous mass of writhing tentacles and bulging eyes. Fresh blood from countless victims had leached into it, discolouring the foul, misshapen rock. He knelt before it and offered up his prayers, begging for guidance. Seemingly in response to his pleas, he began to feel a prickling sensation as though the dank air within the cavern had become statically charged.

With a red flash, the kneeling outline of a man appeared.

The apparition solidified.

Dae'morogin stepped back, knowing that one of his agents had returned. He was just about to question him, when, to his horror, his agent's head simply slid from his shoulders and rolled to his feet. Dae'morogin stifled a cry and stepped back as the headless body fell prone, blood pooling around it.

The high priest raced from the shrine, his dark robes flapping behind him. Down torch-lit corridors he ran, shouting and screaming. He went as fast as he dared, down into the deeper dungeons, his way lit by the guttering torch he held aloft. Twice, he stumbled, but on both occasions he managed to save himself from serious injury with his free hand. Nearing the mausoleum, he slowed down, the only sound that of his shallow breathing. With a trembling hand, he unlocked the secret door and stepped into the crypt beyond.

Dae'dicus was waiting for him. "*And?*"

"Dae'dicus. I..."

"Let me guess," interrupted the ghost. "Your men have failed once more? Dragonbanner still eludes you. Would I be right?"

"He has slain those that I dispatched," replied Dae'morogin, his heart pounding. "What should I do? Should I send more?"

"I would guess it's a little *late* for that, wouldn't you?"

A desperate frown creased the living high priest's brow. "Meaning what?"

"Meaning that Dragonbanner...wait, I sense something."

"Uhu'giaggoth?"

"No...something else," answered the spectre.

"Could it be that the immanency of Uhu'giaggoth's return has acted as a catalyst for..."

"*For what?*" snapped Dae'dicus, his wrinkled face contorting in the indigo glow.

"I don't know. A resurgence? Another power? One that we had not foreseen?"

Dae'dicus' evil visage tightened as though stretched and a baleful moan escaped his dead lips. "There *is* something else. You must act quickly. Get Dragonbanner and bring him before me! *Do so now!*"

† † †

Down filthy streets strode Everus, his body now an extension of Xethorn, The Dark Slayer, the Lord of Murder, a mere gaze from his pitiless green eyes causing even the bravest to back away. Animals kept well clear, and plants withered and died at his passing. Children began screaming as though suddenly troubled by a hundred nightmares, each one worse than the one before; for where he walked, death and darkness followed.

With vengeance on his mind, he determinedly entered the slum area, bound for the entrance to his own debased temple. He stopped as he turned a corner, his heightened senses acutely aware of the two cultists on look-out duty as they tracked his movements. He knew they were armed with crossbows and he also knew that they dare not harm him; could not harm him.

To the obvious surprise of both, Everus suddenly looked straight up at them, his sight lancing towards them with unimaginable lethality. With a wave of his hand, he influenced one of the men to turn and suddenly shoot his companion point-blank in the face. Dropping his crossbow, the survivor then clambered from his hideout and proceeded to the roof edge, whereupon, at Everus' beckoning, he lunged and plummeted, head first, to the street four storeys below, his skull splattering off the cobbles like a hurled egg off a pillory.

Everus smiled and continued on his way.

He was nearing one of the many entrances to the subterranean cathedral.

Kicking open a door to a rather non-descript house, he made short work of the three cultists on guard within. Striding over their bloody corpses, he entered a back room and flung wide a hidden trapdoor before climbing down a long ladder into the secret temple below. At the bottom, he pulled his hood over his face before pacing menacingly over to a junction in the passageway and heading down a shadowy corridor, its walls buttressed. Up ahead, coming towards him, he saw one of the dark brotherhood leading, by a length of chain, another man who was naked apart from a grubby leather loincloth. From the blank, expressionless look on the prisoner's face, it was clear that he had been drugged and that he was probably now being taken for experimentation.

The cultist gave an almost imperceptible nod as he and Everus passed, clearly preoccupied with his own duties. No sooner had he done so than Everus drew his sword and chopped him down from behind. Sliced open from shoulder to belly, the man fell to the floor.

With eyes that now registered nothing, the deranged unfortunate looked up at Everus, drool and spittle leaking from between his blackened lips.

Everus turned and walked on, leaving the captive, who began to paw childishly at the dead body before him. At the far end of the passage, the god within changed His mind and, with nothing more than a gesture of His hand, the chain leash animated, wrapping around the scrawny prisoner's neck, strangling and constricting him like a metal python.

As far as Xethorn was now concerned the punishment was death for most that lived.

And justice would prevail.

Walking on, the god within Everus crossed a gloomy chamber, stopping briefly to look up at an ancient stone idol that jutted out from one wall. That it was a representation of Himself, or rather His true persona, He was certain, and yet it had been defiled, desecrated by those that had once worshipped Him, their allegiance now pledged to The Daemon God. It was the same everywhere. His temple was no more and now it was time to reclaim it; to rebuild it atop the bloody corpses of those apostates and denouncers, those heretics, infidels and demon-worshippers who had turned their backs on the one religion...for the beauty of a turned back was that it was ideal for stabbing.

In his rage, Everus' eyes became little more than glowing, emerald slits.

Suddenly a loud gonging, followed by the clamour of alarm bells, echoed around the temple complex, announcing that an intruder was at large.

Everus smiled as, in his mind's eye, he saw the many cultists dashing to the various armouries, frantically donning their armour and grabbing their weapons. Come to me and fight, he thought. Come to me and die.

The sound of clanging portcullises reverberated all around as parts of the temple were sealed off.

Stretches of passageway were intentionally blacked out as activated magical glyphs extinguished torches.

Stepping out into a cloistered area which ran around the perimeter of a cavernous vault, Everus saw a bizarrely-carved fountain, shaped like an obscene, ruptured heart, its bubbled blood collected in a shallow pool around it. Bats squeaked and flew past, their dried guano sticking to the rough ground and twisted architectural elements. The cavern into which this part of the temple had been built stretched upwards into the pervasive darkness and as he stared up, his mortal self recalled a time when Dae'dicus had once told him how several worshippers had been snatched by some hidden horror which lurked up there. At first, he had thought it was just one of his mentor's apocryphal stories, but, when regurgitated body parts began to turn up, he had quickly changed his mind. Now, however, imbued with Xethorn's power, he knew the nature of the beast that laired up there, and, as he walked along, he sensed its fear.

Like a revenant's shadow, he stalked through the labyrinthine hallways, heading ever closer to the inner sanctum where he was certain Dae'morogin and his forces would be waiting. The sirens had stopped now, the dark brotherhood no doubt prepared for the final battle. He knew they were insane; crazed zealots who would sooner die than surrender or turn from their cause. Which was how it should be, for death was the only blessing he was now willing to bestow upon them. The sound of their foul chants and prayers echoed disturbingly down the tunnels before him; an unholy chorus of woe and impending chaos.

† † †

Silently, Creeps sneaked down the long twisting passage, his form seeming to cling to the shadows with an almost unearthly ability. Unnoticed, he had observed Everus as he had stalked the city streets and he had witnessed the cultist plunge from the rooftop and the ease with which Everus had killed the sentries in the derelict house. He had followed him down into the underground temple. Now, with dagger drawn, he crept along behind him.

Distant cries resounded through the tunnels.

Stepping around the two corpses that lay on the floor, he was about to move on when his keen ears detected the sound of approaching footsteps. Darting into deeper shadows, the thief crouched and waited.

Two dark-robed men came running. One stopped to examine the corpses, while the other looked anxiously about. Kneeling down at the body of his slain fellow worshipper, the cultist said something to the other man, who then darted off from whence he had come. Almost instantly alarms began to sound. Looking about but failing to notice Creeps, the cultist then withdrew back round the corner.

Creeps listened, his ears detecting the man's retreating steps above the din. Rising to his feet, he then proceeded along the tunnel. There came the clang of a portcullis falling some distance behind. The sudden sound of turning cogs alerted him to a mechanism nearby. Running forward, he just managed to roll under an iron gate as it dropped, blocking off the way back. Getting to his feet, he dusted the dirt from his jacket before leaping once more into the clinging shadows.

Darting from pillar to pillar, he ventured further into the underground complex.

† † †

Some two score armed and highly trained worshippers of The Daemon God, their only creed – to die in the service of their chaotic deity – amassed in the inner temple. Dressed in their sable cassocks, under which each wore a chain mail haubergeon, they gathered and offered their final prayers.

Dae'morogin stood before them, his frame emaciated and deathly. "The time comes, my brothers. *He's here!* Like the fool that he is...he has returned. Go forth and fetch the sacrifice!"

Mobilised, the unholy congregation shifted – a dark and murderous horde; acting as one entity. The footsoldiers of Uhu'giaggoth cried out their praise and raised aloft their weapons.

Without warning, the huge double doors at one end of the sanctum crashed open, metal and timber bindings cascading through the air in a sudden and violent explosion. A cloud of yellow-red smoke billowed forth, clearing rapidly.

Framed in the doorway, sword in one hand, a blood spattered head in the other, stood Everus.

"Ah, Everus..." Dae'morogin began.

"*Defilers!*" roared Everus, his cry deafening. "How dare you break away from me!? How dare you think you can find salvation in the arms of another!? *I am Xethorn! And I condemn you all to death!*" With a berserker's lust, he threw aside the severed head and rushed to meet the demonic brethren – and the clash, as he and the first of many collided, was melodious to his ears.

† † †

Creeps followed the trail of bloody, butchered bodies that Everus had left in his wake. Up ahead, still some distance away, he could hear the sounds of combat as though two armies were battling it out in this subterranean hell.

Screams and shouts erupted as well as the occasional explosive blast of magic.

With a growing sense of urgency, the thief sprinted in the direction of the clamour. Stepping over two decapitated bodies which lay on the floor, he peered from behind the remains of a shattered doorway and gazed at the extraordinary carnage in the chamber beyond.

Stood with his back to him, knee-deep in gore, hacking and slashing at anything that moved, was Everus. Around him were scattered many bodies. Bodies that had been sliced, eviscerated, beheaded and blasted asunder by magic lay all over the place. Some were still ablaze, wreathed in indigo flames, burning with mystical fire. Many were unrecognisable as having once been men, mere chain mail-wrapped gobbets of strewn bloody flesh, like the leftovers in a gladiatorial arena. And as Creeps spied on the grisly events, more Uhu'giaggothian devotees added their corpses to those spread out over the sanctum floor. By sheer weight of numbers they tried to subdue Everus, outflanking him and swarming from all sides. But each time, with superhuman reflexes and swordsmanship, Everus thwarted their attempts.

Suddenly the chamber was ablaze with arcane power as some of Dae'morogin's chosen unleashed their spells. Scarlet lightning danced and crackled, striking chaotically, wreathing Everus for a moment in a vortex of clashing light. Shadows shrunk as the whole chamber lit up, illuminating the massacre, the bloodbath, in a lurid glow. With a low roar, a pillar of green fire blasted downwards in a vertical stroke, engulfing Everus in its unearthly conflagration.

Unaffected, he continued to kill, heaps of screaming gore now piling high around him.

Slay them! Slay them all!

With a triumphant roar, Everus waded through the chopped and quivering human remains, eager to engage the next wave of suicidal fanatics.

✝ ✝ ✝

Flushed with fear and exertion, Dae'morogin rushed from the chamber, the pulsating tome gripped tightly under his arm. He rushed for the catacombs, hoping against hope that Dae'dicus would be able to offer an explanation and a course of action. That Everus had somehow become possessed by Xethorn and was now meting out retribution, he had no doubt. The question was how to combat him and, more importantly, how to proceed with the ritual. As though in response to the high priest's feelings of imminent dread, the tome kicked and juddered against his body.

Torch in hand, he raced down into the deeps. At the bottom, he opened the secret door and leapt inside, slamming it shut.

"You appear troubled. What is it? Things go badly?" queried the ghost.

"Dragonbanner...Xethorn...things are bad," stuttered the high priest, his back to the door. He was too scared to enter further, yet at the same time he dared not leave.

"*Xethorn?*"

"*He's here!* What are we to do? Now, more than ever I..." Dae'morogin was interrupted by the sound of explosions.

The very walls shook, even way down here in the innermost foundations. Loose rocks and powdered masonry drizzled from the vaulted ceiling. A cloud of dust blasted from one corner.

"Dae'dicus!" screamed the high priest, wildly staring about.

Rubble crashed down, burying several of the ancient sarcophagi.

More tremors shook the chamber.

Dae'morogin staggered and fell to one knee, the clutched book almost leaping from his hand, as though in its own desire to be free. Righting himself, he watched, mesmerised, as the book, now rippling with fibrous, throbbing veins, opened at the final page.

† † †

"*Dae'morogin!*" yelled Everus, crashing his sword, two-handedly, through another hapless attacker. Blood, bone and entrails sprayed into the air. "*Dae'morogin!*" He was now bathed from head to foot in blood, none of it his own. Three cultists armed with katars charged him. Two collapsed headless, their weapons spiralling from their hands, while the third was sent reeling in a bloody flurry of blows.

The air was thick with the clogging stench of fresh blood and spilt innards, the floor a mass of butchered men.

Everus stared about. For a moment he stood motionless, searching for the high priest.

Over to one side a pillar crashed.

As if in reply a horde of screaming monks came rushing through an archway.

Everus turned, dodging and parrying a volley of gas-filled orbs. His green eyes turned crimson and suddenly a fireball exploded in the midst of the dozen or so demon-worshippers before him.

Burning bodies raced around in agonizing pain, before falling, ablaze to the floor. Some escaped the worst of the blast by leaping or rolling clear, but those fortunate few were then struck by the blast of a second fireball.

Dense orange and green smoke began to fill the chamber.

Everus leapt into the fray, slaying the stunned and burning survivors, his sword slashing in moves as yet unrehearsed by the world's finest swordsmen.

A second pillar cracked and fell.

The chamber quickly filled with the stink of roasted flesh.

Hatred burned in Everus' eyes as, trampling smouldering, cowled bodies underfoot, he strode on.

† † †

Creeps cast a wary glance at the ceiling. Twice so far he had been forced to dodge falling masonry and rubble.

More pillars collapsed as bricks and rocks crashed from above. Dust billowed in great clouds as arches buckled under the strain of the titanic forces now preparing for battle. Doors fell in. Metal gates warped and twisted even as gargantuan idols teetered on their bases.

There were dead bodies everywhere.

Things were very messy, even by the thief's standards.

With morbid interest, Creeps noticed that some of the human remains in one such tangled heap were still moving. His grip tightening around his dagger, he watched as a hand, attached to a bloody and severed arm, scuttled from beneath the pile. Intrigued, he stared as the arm, with its knob of bone and raw gristle, crawled over the many leaking bodies as though in search of the torso from which it had been amputated. He noticed the sparkling, green ring on one of the fingers. Suddenly an inner voice told him to take it and put it on. Walking over, he brought a foot down on the arm, watching as the hand splayed out and then tried, like an upturned cockroach, to right itself. He reached down and cut off the ring finger before tugging free the ring and examining it. Pleased with his new find, he twisted it onto one of his own fingers before going, once more, in pursuit of Everus.

† † †

The open book began to convulse and spew a sickly, purple goo. The pages shook and started to turn a grotesque green, whilst the demonic illustrations contained therein danced and screamed. A frogspawn-like slime started to seep all around. Everything it came into contact with immediately started to bubble and melt.

"*Dae'dicus!?*" cried the high priest, backing away.

"Dae'morogin? Yes, now I see...it is..."

"Do something. You can..." the high priest started, his words cut short by a blow from a piece of tumbling brickwork. He stumbled and with a tortured screech was dragged by an unearthly force towards the spurting tome. Kicking and screaming, he was pulled closer, the spraying matter from the book now drenching his body and eating through his robes like acid.

Uncaring, Dae'dicus watched.

"*Help me!*" Dae'morogin's face was now a festering mass of bursting blisters. His fingers had melted away like molten candle stubs. With eyes that had now turned to a dribbling mush, he failed to notice the sudden alteration in the configuration of the final page as, with a dark flash, the name, *Everus Dragonbanner,* was replaced with his own.

A stone coffin nearby cracked and splintered. With a clatter, a heap of mouldy bones exploded across the floor.

Dae'morogin screamed, his cry accompanied by Dae'dicus' cruel laughter. Then, with a nauseating squelch, the high priest was hauled, head first, into the cursed book. What remained of his arms flapped to either side as he frantically tried to pull himself free.

Captivated by the scene before him, Dae'dicus watched as the book, denied of its promised victim, began to swallow the high priest instead. The high priest's withered limbs danced in spasmodic judders as, like a constrictor snake with its prey, *The Book of Dead Names* began to expand as it drew him in further. Blood poured from its hungry pages. With a loud slurping noise, Dae'morogin was engulfed from head to waist, his lower half continuing to melt as the bizarre digestive juices quickly set about dissolving him. Somehow he was still alive and somehow he staggered to his smoking stumps, blood and purple ooze covering what little there remained of him. Then he fell against a pillar.

With a final slurp, the foul book devoured him completely.

For a while, there was silence. Even the crashes and explosions from high above ceased.

Dae'dicus stared, transfixed, at the tome, which lay on the floor before him, steaming and belching like some gorged, fat toad. It shuddered, like a diner after a gargantuan and repulsive meal. Obviously, it had not found the high priest all that palatable. It began to emit gaseous, noisome odours. Odours that would eat the skin from living flesh like acidic vapour.

With a sudden, watery fart-like squelch, a purplish, puckered tentacle ruptured from the tome along with a red, soupy mass that Dae'dicus had to presume was all that remained of the high priest. With a splat, a second tentacle burst forth, dislodging more of Dae'morogin's runny remains.

The heartless spectre flinched as he sensed the unsettled stirring of two or three of The Others, those dead high priests of Xethorn whom he had cursed and yet shared the crypt alongside him. He could feel the almost holy hatred that these true Xethorn worshippers had for him.

A third, then a fourth, sinuous, slime-covered appendage snaked forth.

In the feeble light from Dae'morogin's dropped torch, Dae'dicus watched as a writhing, squirming mass, like a multitude of ravenous maggots, vomited from the book as though it were some abominable afterbirth. Amorphous and horrible beyond mortal comprehension, a lesser spawn of Uhu'giaggoth slithered from its extra-planar dimension beyond the furthest visible star.

Tentacled, the alien, shapeless mass of chaotic jelly extricated itself from the book.

"*Uhu'giaggoth!* I have returned ye!" cried Dae'dicus, ecstatically.

The entity raised and extended two of its dripping tentacles on detecting the dead voice. Defying gravity, the pulsating blob sprang up and landed on the dead high priests' sarcophagus. Like a mantis, two pseudopods shot from it and engulfed the ghost. Within the beat of a heart, Dae'dicus' ethereal form was absorbed into the demonic amoeba. Briefly, the chaotic mass ballooned out as though, inside, Dae'dicus' spirit struggled to escape. After the bloating had ceased, the horror disappeared in a black flash.

✝ ✝ ✝

The god within Everus was suddenly hit with a wave of nausea. So strong and unexpected was it that He staggered against a door. His vision swimming, He leant against the wooden frame, trying to fight the rising surge within His gullet. He threw up, His vomit splashing in a steaming puddle at His feet.

Uhu'giaggoth has come.

Wiping free the strings of spittle from his mouth, Everus headed for another passage.

Another bout of sickness coursed through his guts, causing him to double over in pain. Gripping his sides, he heaved and spewed forth a torrent of grey, sticky sludge.

Slay The Daemon God!

Staggering, Everus entered a large, many pillared hall.

Statues and gargoyles leered from numerous shadowy places. At one end a fire burned in a huge pit. Rays of dark-tinted daylight shone down through a score or more hideously-crafted stained-glass windows.

Supporting himself against a pillar, Everus unleashed a further bout of bodily sewage from his mouth. It felt as though he was retching up barrel loads of hot tar. No sooner had he recovered than, at the opposite end of the chamber, the sickly mass that was one of the innumerable lesser spawn of Uhu'giaggoth, appeared.

Slay it!

With a roar, Everus charged the demon.

The lesser Uhu'giaggothian spawn responded with a psychokinetic attack which struck Everus full on. Blasted, he was flung back, crashing through a pillar as he went. Rubble crashed from above as the support splintered and collapsed.

Painfully, Everus rose to his feet before charging the vaguely squid-like monstrosity a second time. Before he got near, another blast of unseen energy yanked him off his feet and began to draw him into the air. Hurling curses, he was raised higher. Nearing the stalactites at the roof of the cavernous chamber, he narrowed his eyes, unleashing a fireball at the demon. The fiery ball exploded close to where the oozing evil lay quivering.

Slay Uhu'giaggoth!

Suddenly Everus plummeted. With a cry, he hurtled towards the ground, smashing off the unyielding floor. The force of the impact shattered his left leg, driving bone through flesh in a ragged, bloody tear, yet still, he got to his feet, the power of Xethorn forcing the body to operate in ways no longer physically possible for a mere mortal.

A hail of rubble crashed nearby as the very chamber began to convulse.

Portions of the ancient walls caved-in as huge rents appeared, making it look as though some chthonic denizen from the deep was attempting to claw its way up from below. High above, many of the widows cracked and shattered, their myriad, multi-coloured glass fragments raining down in a prismatic cascade.

The lesser spawn of Uhu'giaggoth sprang forward. Like a blasphemous, malign polyp, a hundred stinging tentacles shot out towards Everus. They never reached their target, striking an invisible barrier before him instead. The slimy horror writhed, its multiple graspers seemingly unable to breach the force field around it. Pseudopods slid along the transparent surface of its sphere-like cage, smearing the inside with its sticky secretions.

Mystified, Everus moved forward and reached out, placing his palm on the smooth surface.

Like a caged animal, the chaotic jelly on the other side obviously sensed his presence for it went into a frenzy of action; squirting vile, purplish fluids and thrashing wildly from side to side.

A sudden sound from behind made Everus wheel round, sword at the ready. He saw Creeps, leaning nonchalantly against a pillar a short distance away. Despite the fractured leg, he leapt into a forward roll and tumbled to one side, leaping to his feet in the same fluid motion.

"Xethorn," acknowledged the thief.

"I know of you."

"Then ye know that yer bein' 'ere is no' permitted. Yer fight is over."

"You would be foolish to think that *you* can stop me," Everus smiled, wryly, his face and body drenched with the blood of others. "For now is *my* time. For over two and a half thousand years I have been imprisoned...left to rot. *I* shall govern over these imbecilic mortals, teaching them the new order, showing them the glories of hate and the divinity of murder."

"The High Three have decreed otherwise."

"*Hah!* What care I of them?"

Behind Everus the slimy demon slithered within its impenetrable globe of force, as though searching for a weak point.

"Yer fight is over," repeated Creeps.

"No, I'm afraid not. Now it is time you died." Before Everus could launch an attack, a huge hand materialised before him. He swung out at it, his sword slicing through it as though it was not there. With a gesture from the thief, the ghostly fist smacked into him, knocking him back against the magical barrier. Battered, Everus fixed Creeps with a gaze that would have reduced a normal man to ash.

From the other side of the transparent sphere, the tentacled thing flew into a rage.

The spectral hand clenched again, blue light framing its hefty knuckles. It struck Everus a second time, even as he was recovering from the first punch.

"Do ye yield? Will ye go?"

"*Damn you!*" Everus roared, his *own* blood trickling from his nose and lips. The giant fist struck again, pounding him to his knees. This was beginning to hurt.

"We can go on for as..."

"*Die!*" cried Everus. The god which possessed him mustered His own magical powers and detonated a fireball at the thief's feet.

The fiery explosion destroyed much in its immediate blast radius, scorching stone and incinerating a headless corpse nearby, but for all its fierceness, Creeps emerged from it totally unscathed, a pale blue barrier shielding him from the devastating spell.

Suddenly the giant hand grabbed Everus around the body and hoisted him off his feet.

"Return to yer imprisonment," ordered Creeps.

"*Never!*" Everus' face contorted in pain as the fist began to crush. "This is not your fight! Why have you interfered?" he managed to blurt.

"The High Three won't permit this world to be destroyed in a new Cataclysm. Yer vendetta against that which ye believe resides in the magic sphere has turned many against ye. Ye had yer time an' ye became unstable."

"Return to The High Three and tell them that *I, Xethorn*, will see them and Uhu'giaggoth slain. I promise this."

"Ye fool," Creeps shook his head and pointed straight at The Daemon God's lesser spawn. The sphere in which it was trapped began to glow. Suddenly the abomination within the globe exploded, spattering the inner walls with lumps of grotesque matter and dripping membranes. "That wasn't yer nemesis! Did ye think The High Three would permit such a thing as Uhu'giaggoth to return again? As ye undoubtedly recall, it was hard enough to get rid o' it the first time."

Everus studied the jellied remains. "Not...The Daemon God?"

"I'm afraid no', just one o' its dribblin' blobs. Its offspring, I guess ye'd say. Ye see, I had to be on hand to ensure that these stupid clerics ye've so efficiently disposed o' didn't succeed. That's why I made sure Everus wasn't the author o' all the deaths in that bloody book they were usin' to try an' summon it." With a dirty nail, Creeps scraped something away from one of his few teeth before wiping it on his jacket. "So...that leaves us wi' only one thing left to take care o'."

"And what is that?"

"Ye know full well." Creeps grinned. "As I've said, ye're no' to be allowed to reign on this world. It's ma task to see that this is so. I'm afraid ye've got to go. Return whence ye came, Xethorn. A time may come when ye'll be allowed free. But that time is no' now."

The deity within Everus thought things over for a moment. Confined and trapped within a mortal's body, He knew His powers were limited. Would it be best to go and prepare for a fresh escape in another five hundred years or so...or would it be better to go out in a blaze of glory? Without His full powers, *could* He take on an agent of The High Three?

"Ye decided? Are ye goin'...for look about ye, ye've got yer revenge."

"*Have I?* For centuries I have languished. Banished. Reviled. The world has moved on in my absence and *you* have the audacity to tell *me* that I have obtained my vengeance. I was there, remember, when Uhu'giaggoth rent the Heavens asunder and spilled its chaos over the world. I fought against it, sending its demonic taint back to the Netherworld whilst others cowered and fled. I battled Cyrvilus. And how was I rewarded?"

"Ye became unmanageable."

Everus laughed, the hand still gripped around him. His face hardened once more. "Tell me. Why did you assist the mortal in gathering my wards?"

"What these?" Reaching into a pocket of his scruffy jacket, Creeps withdrew three gold, circular amulets. "Oh, please...don't look so surprised. Ye surely didn't think I'd let Everus use the originals, did ye? I couldn't let him return ye wi' all yer powers, now could I?"

Everus scowled, waiting for the thief to continue.

"All I had to do was switch false ones wi' the real ones. Quite easy really."

"Cunning bastard."

"That's me," replied Creeps, with a nod.

With growing frustration, the Lord of Murder stared through Everus' eyes directly at the thief, wondering whether He could destroy him or not. The fact that Creeps now held the authentic wards reinforced the opinion that such an act would not be without its risks.

Suddenly the *entire* ceiling collapsed.

Mouth agape, Creeps looked up.

Everus pulled back, darting to the far wall as jumbled blocks of stone and brickwork rained down in a lethal deluge.

The cave-in created a huge cloud of dust and debris, burying the bubbling remains of the Uhu'giaggothian lesser spawn within its magical prison.

Get the wards! Get the wards!

Everus peered through the cloud of dust, his heightened eyesight noting the huge pile of rubble that now lay where Creeps had been standing. Smiling sardonically, he paced over, his cat-like eyes searching. Eagerly, he began to tear into the mass of stone, searching for the thief's body and the wards he had so foolishly displayed. Clambering to the top of the cairn-like mound, he began plucking at the rubble, heaving shattered masonry away with ease. Excavating deeper, he unearthed the thief's crushed remains.

Get the wards!

Sadistically, Everus dragged the moustachioed man from the rubble, delighting in the way his head jarred and snapped against the sharp rocks. Once clear, he briefly examined the battered body, shaking his head in feigned sympathy. He then ransacked the corpse, searching for the amulets.

Creeps' fingers twitched.

Mine! At last! Now I can finally escape this pathetic mortal's body and...

A mumble escaped the thief's lips.

"Hmm. Still alive, are we?" Everus took hold of a weighty rock. Smiling, he raised it in one hand and dashed the broken man's brains out, cracking open the skull in a bloody smash. He rose to his feet, the three wards grasped in his free hand. With a cry of exaltation, he raised his arms as a crimson glow emanated from his body, its light illuminating the ruined chamber. A shaft of blood-red light fired from him and ripped through the wrecked ceiling, shooting up into the grey daylight.

Of no further use, Everus' body crumpled to the ground like a puppet whose strings had been cut. The critical wounds he had sustained whilst possessed by Xethorn now took a massive effect; severe and crippling.

Above, in the mortal world of light and hope, people set about one another; killing each other with whatever weapons were at hand, responding to Xethorn's successful rebirth. House fires erupted. Mothers slaughtered their children. Husbands killed their wives. Animals ran mad, biting and snapping.

And distant dark clouds gathered as, far away in The Deadmoor Clumps, the Øggarbakken behemoths, aware of the calling, mustered in great numbers and began their final march towards the city.

CHAPTER TWELVE

Deep within the dark and destroyed temple, Creeps opened his eyes. Blindly, he felt around to assess the weight of rock that had buried him. Torn and bloody, he dragged himself free, his body aching from numerous cuts and bruises. He muttered an incantation and a glowing orb of white light flashed in his hand, illuminating the scale of the utter destruction all around him.

Collapsed pillars lay shattered. Large parts of the cavern wall and ceiling had disappeared entirely, the spaces beyond seeming to vanish into an underworld darkness. Gaping fissures zigzagged their way across the floor and heaps of smashed statuary lay everywhere.

After he had coughed the last of the dust from his lungs and wiped it from his eyes, Creeps got to his feet. In the stillness, he waited for the voices, listening for what they would say and how they wished him to proceed. They came in hushed whispers that only he could hear, instructing and informing, telling him their plan. His eyes widened with surprise as he raised his hand in order to take a look at the ring he wore. Such had been the severity of his injuries that it had taken a full two days for the ring to restore him to life; fusing his brain matter and knitting his cranial bones back into shape. He felt his right ear, half of which had been eaten by a death squirrel, but was disappointed to note that it had not regrown – apparently there were some limits to the ring's power.

Now all he had to do was find Everus' body and see if he was still alive. The voices informed him that he would be. Clambering over the mountain of rubble and ruined architecture, he soon came to where the dark god's battered, manipulated and discarded disciple lay.

† † †

Underneath the imperial Southern Palace, Emperor J'hann sat at one end of the war council table, his military, wizardly and religious advisors gathered round. A state of emergency had been declared after a sector of the city, long known to house undesirables and troublemakers, had exploded in a turbulent frenzy of riotous anarchy. What was more, the madness was spreading like wildfire. In a relatively short period of time, much of the city had been transformed into a seething pit of violence, with many of its greatest monuments torn down and reduced to smouldering ruins. According to the most recent reports, almost half of the city had fallen from within as though some kind of social decay had taken root. Wyrm's Port's problems were doubly compounded by reports of increased Øggarbakken behemoth and bagh'arulk activity. It appeared that the giants were massing for an all out attack. An offensive was already under way.

With sleepless eyes, Emperor J'hann looked at the half dozen, mostly grave faces around the table. Gone now was the experienced, if somewhat ruthless diplomat. In its place was the shell of a weary old man who realised that the demise of his city and perhaps the world he knew was close at hand. He turned to the stern-faced general seated beside him. "What news?"

"Sire. We *must* strengthen our eastern defences. Our reports would indicate it is there that the enemy will make their next attack," said General Adamian, the senior commander of the imperial army. "Our forces have fought a few running battles out on the Eastern Plain but despite our best efforts and the brave work carried out by our elite troops, in addition to numerous enlisted mercenary companies, we are on the retreat. We've heard nothing from the two infantry divisions from Ghavin's Keep and the behemoths have breached a part of the northern defences. Commander Tymor of The Watchful Eye has successfully led a platoon of his finest swordsmen deep within the enemy ranks and his report should provide us with more information regarding their numbers and planned tactics." He swallowed dryly. "However, I have to also report that preparations are in place for a full-scale evacuation, if it comes to that."

"My lords," started archmage Olron, speaking from behind the elaborate beaten gold face-mask he always wore. "What we now face is not a conventional enemy. Swords and arrows may help us stave off the behemoths and their ilk but it is the disease which runs rife within our city that is by far the greater danger. I have no doubt that behemoth sorcery is behind it all. Therefore, what is needed is understanding...we need to discover what it is that our enemy needs. If we can establish that, then we have a hope of discovering what it is that it fears."

"*Nonsense!*" Pope Benignus snorted. He was a little drunk and very sleepy, having spent most of the night interpreting omens and praying to The High Three. "There is no doubt in my mind, that what we face is a calamity of godly proportions. It has nothing to do with those blundering, giant lummoxes." Reaching over for the wine jug, he refilled his goblet and took a sip. "I'm convinced that the rash of unexplained deaths that've been taking place over the last few years have been intentional immolations. Although they've appeared random, I'm certain that they've served a purpose. According to my divinations and based on peculiar celestial movements..."

"Get to the point!" interrupted the general, his dislike of the pompous, fat cleric boiling over.

"I am getting to the point, you hot-headed oaf," shouted Benignus, his sweaty face reddening. "*As I was saying*, I believe our current troubles stem from some kind of divine schism. It's as though two, or more, godly entities, although probably not true deities, did battle. One obviously lost, whereas the other..."

"Remains?" interrupted the emperor.

"It would appear so," answered Benignus.

"So what do we do? Challenge a god?" asked Adamian, his tone of voice demanding answers.

"Don't be so foolish," said Benignus. "That would only lead to the obliteration of us all. No, we must seek other solutions. We have to find out what it is that this divine being seeks. Then, perhaps we can negotiate."

"Half our city is destroyed! The other half may well soon follow. Many of our people are dead, missing or have gone stark raving mad. The behemoths are about to attack our city in numbers never seen before and you want us to parley!?" Adamian smashed a gauntleted-fist on the table.

"If we don't, we're all finished," replied Benignus with a sorrowful shake of his head. He opened his mouth, about to speak and then went quiet. He nodded to himself and seemed to fall asleep, his double chin and jowls resting against his chest.

Adamian rose from his chair, looking every bit the warrior, resplendent in his highly polished field plate mail armour and long blue cloak. "Well, I for one won't stay here and listen to your doom-

mongering. We've a war to fight...and already you talk of defeat."
He turned to leave.

"*General!* Please, return to your seat. I have need of you."
Emperor J'hann gestured for Adamian to sit.

Slowly, Adamian turned around. "Sire, with all respect, this is
not the time to...to listen to such defeatist ranting. I am a religious
man, but the enemy we face is a flesh and blood one. We've a saying
in the army, 'if it bleeds, we can kill it'. This madness that has
befallen many of our citizens may well be due to some foul sorcery
cast by the behemoths." His face hardened. "So I say, we go out there
and we kill them. Rid ourselves of their menace once and for all.
This has nothing whatsoever to do with a religious conflict."

"Once again, the general is wrong," interrupted Benignus,
stirring to life. "For I'm not merely theorising. I now know the
identity of our enemy."

Something in the way the chubby pope made his announcement
caused all the other seated council members to sit up. With baited
breath, they waited as Benignus poured himself another glass of
wine and took a sip.

"*Well?*" prompted the emperor.

Benignus cleared his throat. "Honoured friends and associates.
It is Xethorn, the Lord of Murder, who now walks amongst us."

"*Xethorn?* But that's preposterous," said Olron. "He was
banished hundreds of years ago. What few worshippers He had
crawled into the deepest recesses of our society long ago. And, as far
as I remember, most of those were rounded up and sent to the
gallows." The archmage shook his head in disagreement.

"It *is* Xethorn," replied Benignus. "Through the gift of
clairaudience I have just this moment learned from some of my own
operatives that they've discovered the ruins of a hidden Xethornite
temple underneath a part of the Old Quarter. Within the rubble,
they've found numerous slain members of that creed. The fools
probably performed some ceremony or other to bring The Dark
Slayer back. No doubt He was none too happy with the summoning
and He thus set about killing His worshippers. Quite fitting I
suppose."

"And, assuming that you're right, what can we do?" asked
Olron.

"I fear our options are limited," replied Benignus, finishing his
drink.

"What are they?" asked the emperor.

"Well...we either order a full-scale evacuation..."

"Or?" interrupted Adamian, arms crossed, still not believing any of it.

"We die," said Benignus, aware of the nervous faces on many of his fellows. "Either way, I can't take my wine cellar with me, so, if you gentlemen don't object, I intend to drink as much of it as possible before we leave. After all, waste *is* ungodly."

✝ ✝ ✝

That evening, as much of the city burned and many of its crazed citizens maliciously attacked one another, fighting their own running battles in the streets, Everus and Creeps sat in a derelict, burnt-out, third-storey room, discussing their next move.

"Aye, so ye see, Xethorn used ye in order to battle what He thought was The Daemon God."

"Yes, yes, I've grasped that fact. But what do we do now?" Everus sat on what remained of an old table, the screams and shouts from several streets away dying in his ears. His mind was in constant turmoil, no longer knowing who to trust any more. He had been lied to and deceived by almost *everyone* he had ever known; manipulated, he had served as nothing more than an expendable pawn. His religion was assuredly false for it had no doubt been warped by Dae'dicus. His god had abandoned him, leaving him for dead. Now, it seemed, he had to put his trust in perhaps the most dubious of them all – Adolf Creeps.

"Well, first off, we try an' find where the bastard's gone. That shouldn't be too difficult." Creeps took his smoking pipe from his mouth and tapped out its contents.

"What about the wards? What can you tell me about them?"

"Ye mean ye don't know?" answered Creeps, with a knowing look. "An' there was me thinkin' ye were the expert on 'em."

"All I know is that they were fashioned some time after The Hellspawn Cataclysm. Each contained a part of Xethorn's life-force."

"Aye, that they do. But they also contained a part o' each o' The High Three, for it was them that made the wards, if made's the right word. Anyhow, when Xethorn became a bit too big for His breeches, it was decided that He should be..."

"Imprisoned?"

"Aye. Ye know how it goes."

Everus remained confused. So much had happened, most of it outside his control, that it was now proving hard to rationalise all that had transpired.

Outside, the cries and shouts were getting louder.

Somewhere, out in the chaos, someone or something was being tortured, perhaps murdered.

"We've caused quite a stink, have we not?" said Everus, listening to the dreadful sounds.

"*We?*"

For the first time, Everus realised the gravity of the situation and the role he had played in it. And, for the first time, he felt a pang of guilt. After all, it was he who had set out to obtain the wards and thus free Xethorn. He had been so intent on pursuing his own dark desires and obsessions that he had not thought his way through the implications. True, his manipulators had probably encouraged him in his self-centred view, but he could have looked beyond his own priorities, could have wondered what would happen when Xethorn was restored to power. He did not even have Dae'morogin's excuse of insanity to lessen his guilt. Limping over to a broken window, his leg still painful despite the healing effects of the magic ring, which he had now returned to the thief, he peered out at the unfolding pandemonium.

Half of the city now seemed to be on fire.

"Bit o' a mess, ain't it?"

"What can we do? Anything?"

"Well," Creeps began, relighting his pipe and taking a puff. "We can either sit it out, hope that Xethorn tires o' this place an' leaves..."

"How likely is that?" Everus interrupted, returning from the window.

"Well, some o' the minor gods have been known to get a bit bored wi' life 'ere. They hang around for a bit, stir up a bit o' mischief an' then bugger off. Then again, some don't."

"Let's assume that Xethorn is here to stay. Then what?"

"Well...then I guess we have to force Him. But for now I think it'd be best if ye try an' get some sleep."

"Maybe you're right, and besides this place looks safe enough for the time being." Looking about, Everus spotted a half-wrecked bunk which looked as though it would suffice as a place to rest. Lying down, he pulled a ratty blanket close to fend off the worst of the night's chill. He fell asleep quickly but spent an unpleasant night, for in his dreams tortured faces cried out to him as, with withered arms, wizened beings sought to drag him down into whatever hell they had emerged from.

✝ ✝ ✝

Everus awoke in a cold sweat, his nightmare visions' fading wails still crying out in his mind. Stretching uncomfortably, he gazed across the room at the anaemic, almost shadowy, sunlight outside the window. Countless dark thoughts ran through his mind as he got up and went to the window.

Despite the fact that it must have been early morning, a dark gloom, far darker than the grey smoke which hovered everywhere, had descended over everything, as though even the life-giving powers of the sun had abandoned Wyrm's Port.

"Creeps!" Everus cried, continuing to stare out off the window.

"Aye?" replied the thief, emerging from the shadows.

"The sky...?"

"Aye, it's Xethorn. His powers are growin'. Each day it'll become darker, until it's continual night. When it gets to that stage...well, let's no' think about that, eh?"

"Can the bastard be stopped?"

As way of answer, Creeps just shrugged his shoulders. "Come on, best we get goin'."

Abandoning the demolished house, they headed out into the litter-strewn streets. It was deathly quiet now, the marauding gang members having either died or moved on to plunder other areas. Not even a dog or a cat moved and yet all around they could see the results of three days of Xethorn's handiwork in the smoking corpses and the burnt out buildings which formed the ruined urban environment.

"Surely not all of the city's like this?" muttered Everus, staggered at the sheer scale, and the relative suddenness of the destruction.

"Nah. I wouldn't think Xethorn'd kill everyb'dy," answered Creeps. "I don't think that's His style. I mean, if He were to do that then there'd be nob'dy left to murder."

"Looking at this, perhaps it would have been better to bring Uhu'giaggoth back instead."

"Had that been the case we wouldn't be 'ere, neither would anyb'dy or anythin' else for that matter. Everythin' would be dead.

Look on the bright side..." Creeps shifted his head, gazing about. "*There!* There's a couple o' crows up there. If The Daemon God had come back there'd be nothin'. No, at least Xethorn can be reasoned wi'. He still possesses some o' His human traits. He was mortal once."

"*Once mortal?*" Everus stopped in his tracks, gripping the thief by the shoulder.

"Aye. Why, I'd o' thought a man o' yer learnin' would o' known that."

Everus shook his head. "No. None of the books mention it. Tell me more."

"Well, many o' the minor gods, the so-called demigods, were mortal once. Beings who had incredible powers, magical or otherwise. Through their abilities, they...transformed, an' became like deities."

Everus removed his hand from the thief's shoulder, suddenly remembering just how powerful his associate was. It was going to prove hard to stop ridiculing and patronising the smaller man, whom he had maltreated for so long. "And...are you one of these beings?"

"*Me?*" Creeps chuckled. "No. I'm just...I'm just the sorry soul that ends up havin' to clean up the shit."

A sudden flash of memory struck Everus. "When we went to Durgan's Rock, was it you who created the undead baazelgrigs?"

Creeps shrugged his shoulders. "Had nothin' to do wi' me." It was a good lie.

Turning a corner, the two men saw up ahead the scattered human remains suggestive of a great fight. Bodies lay sprawled by the roadside, their faces contorted into rictuses of pain. The stench was appalling.

"What happened here, I wonder?" said Everus, approaching.

"Look! There's one o' 'em dead giant-things o'er there."

Everus strode over to the huge corpse. Numerous cuts and several arrows, one still lodged deep in its grizzled face, gave ample evidence of how the brute had met its end.

A cloud of large, black flies buzzed from one of the corpses Creeps turned over. Waving them away in disgust, he began to unceremoniously rummage through its pockets.

"Are the behemoth attacks related to Xethorn's appearance?" asked Everus, covering his nose.

Creeps ignored the question, too busy pilfering from the corpses that lay around. He examined a battered leather purse, emptying a few coppers into his hand before tossing it nonchalantly over a shoulder.

"Creeps. Are the attacks...?"

"Aye. The bastard things have rallied together in order to destroy the city. The fact that they've banded together in such numbers, coupled wi' the fact that there are many different clans workin' as one, is a sure sign they're bein' guided."

"Why? For what purpose?"

"I'd guess that they've come to pay some sort o' homage, in addition to obeyin' some kind o' summonin'. They've got some tribal shaman or such who worships Xethorn. An', like ye were, they'll be the muscle wi' which Xethorn'll spread His will."

"So, what's your plan?"

"Well, I think we've got little option but to confront Him. To wait this out would be daft."

"And are you sure you can take Him?"

"No, but it's been laid on me to try. As I said afore, I'm the poor bugger that ends up havin' to do the dirty work. You wouldn't believe the shit I get dealt."

Everus tried to understand some of what had happened as the two men continued their way down the derelict streets. They passed many more bodies and destroyed houses. Not surprisingly, the majority of the dead were the common citizens, mostly the sick and the elderly, those poor bastards who had neither the means to run, nor the strength to fight.

They entered a large public square.

Strewn before them were the mutilated bodies of armoured fighting men at which a flock of crows now pecked and tore.

"Ye may want to arm yersel'," suggested Creeps. "I've a feelin' things might get nasty from now on in."

Taking the thief's advice, Everus rummaged amongst the dead, equipping himself with a fine longbow, a half-full quiver of goose-feather fletched arrows and a fire-blackened sword. What shields and armour he saw were too battered to be of any real use.

"Is that ye ready?" questioned Creeps.

Everus nodded grimly. "Where now?"

"Well, I think He's gone where all the other bastards once lived. The Southern Palace."

† † †

General Adamian had been correct in his belief that the eastern area of the city was in need of reinforcing, for it was here that the Øggarbakken behemoths and their bagh'arulk allies waged a formidable offensive. Undoubtedly assisted by the evil darkness and the disintegrating morale of the defenders, they had stormed the city, laying waste to its citizens, its army and its buildings on an apocalyptic scale. By the time the emperor's army had regrouped in the heart of the city, over three thousand had been lost. Many soldiers had fled, knowing that to surrender meant death – for the behemoths did not take prisoners, they ate them.

In an attempt to maintain some kind of authority, and acting on the advice of Pope Benignus, Emperor J'hann had abandoned the Southern Palace late on the second day of the siege. He stood on the steps of the much smaller and less grand Northern Palace and gazed out at the ravaged ruins. Despite his objections, his advisors had put into effect a great evacuation procedure and his heart sank as he gazed out at the columns of miserable-looking refugees, their wagons and caravans heaped with all that they held dear, shuffling and trundling towards the West Gate and perceived safety. Many others were being shipped out in a flotilla of boats, bound for new and unpredictable lives in one of the distant cities on the coast of The Dark Sea. For this was an exodus – the beginning of the rout of Wyrm's Port.

"Sire, my commanders tell me that the entire Eastern Side has fallen. Now...might be the best time to leave," recommended Adamian.

The emperor tore his gaze away from the sorry lines of shambling, downcast people, turning to face his tired and battle-worn general. "But...but I've poured no end of gold into this damned city! Do you think I want it to fall into the hands of these behemoths, these overgrown savages?" It was clear he cared far more about the city's wealth than he did its people. He turned once more to look at the long lines of those desperate to escape. *Cowards!* Why did they not come back and fight? If he had been more like some of his tyrannical, despotic ancestors he would have whipped them to the front lines. Women and children as well. His grandfather, old Emperor Hann'ah, would not have tolerated this craven-hearted desertion.

"Sire, if you stay, you'll die. Look upon our retreat not as a defeat but as a tactical withdrawal."

"Don't make me laugh. This is a rout, pure and simple."

"Our allies across The Dark Sea, in addition to the extra troops being sent north from Ghavin's Keep, will enable us to recapture the city. Who knows, perhaps the behemoths will depart after they've completed their bout of pillaging. With reinforcements, we'll return and annihilate the bastards. You've my word on that."

"Look about you general. Have not the gods deserted us?"

"No, my lord, whatever Benignus says. What you see is the work of the behemoths, not gods."

"But..." The emperor never finished his particular reply for suddenly an almighty explosion shook the ground as a huge fireball detonated far away to the south of the city. A large black mushroom cloud billowed skywards.

Adamian stared, open-mouthed.

"The Wizard School! I feared it would be targeted. I tried my best to warn Olron."

"He...he may have escaped," said the general, knowing full well that no one could live through such a calamity, be they a sorcerer or not.

✝ ✝ ✝

They had not been walking long when they arrived at the Southern Palace.

From the outside, the impressive building showed signs of only superficial damage, its finely wrought iron gate and its colonnaded forecourt still standing proudly. Skulls now adorned the spiked fence. Thirty or so armed figures milled about the grounds. It seemed as though Xethorn had already begun attracting His own crowd of human followers. What men Everus could see would not have looked out of place in Magruder's 'Wild Breed' gang. The place was heavily guarded and unwelcoming.

"You reckon He's inside?"

Creeps nodded.

"So how do we get in?"

"Hmm. What we're needin' is a di..."

Suddenly a terrific blast lifted both men off their feet. Together they were buffeted to one side as neighbouring buildings shook and crumbled. Everus shielded his head as loose bits of debris rained down. A dense black smoke billowed out and covered them in a layer of hot, black ash.

Coughing, Everus rubbed his stinging eyes. "Creeps," he moaned.

"I'm 'ere," came a reply.

Like tephra from a volcanic eruption, lose chunks of masonry and black, sulphurous dust showered down, almost burying the two men.

Still coughing, Everus rose to his feet, accepting the thief's helping hand. Blackened, yet relieved to be alive, he cleared the soot from his eyes and wafted some of the foul-smelling, eye-watering smoke away from his face.

"Methinks we've been given our diversion. Come on, let's make the most o' it."

Shrouded in the black smoke that had been generated by the explosion from The Wizard School, they crept their way past the reeling guards and into the palace. Past stately statues and regal portraits they sneaked, heading down long, marble-tiled corridors. In front of them, was a huge set of gilt-edged double doors, which they assumed gave access to the throne room.

It stood to reason that Xethorn would be within.

Everus heard a door unlocking behind them. Quickly and quietly, he nipped behind a tapestry. He peeked out to see a short man striding down the corridor, a pole arm held out before him. He was squat and solid, his long black hair hanging over one eye and draping wildly about his shoulders, lips pulled back under a drooping moustache to reveal a mouthful of black teeth. A dented and blood-smeared plate mail breastplate, undoubtedly scavenged from some dead infantryman, had been tightly fitted onto his upper torso.

"*Oi!* Who're ye an' what're ye doin' in 'ere?" the stocky man asked, looking Creeps up and down, suspiciously.

"We, um...I'm 'ere to offer ma services," Creeps replied, grinning. "I'm a good cook."

"*Ye what?* Well, ye'd better get back outside. We don't want any old snot-picker just wanderin' about in 'ere. The big boss man gave orders no' to let any weirdos in. So, go on, get..."

Before the man could finish, Everus silently grabbed him from behind, tilted his head and cut his throat with a horizontal draw of his sword. Blood spurted forth. It was a messy way to kill a man, but that no longer concerned him. Little did any more. Hardly making a sound, he let the still gargling man slide to the floor. With little more than a nod to the thief, he wiped his blade clean on the tapestry, sheathed it at his side then picked up his longbow before striding determinedly towards the double doors. Before he got to them, the doors swung wide, allowing him to see into the large throne room beyond.

Creeps looked at Everus. "Watch what ye're doin'."

Removing an arrow from his quiver, Everus notched it and drew his longbow.

Once the seat of the emperors of Wyrm's Port, the throne at the far end of the pillared chamber was now occupied by Xethorn. Standing by the seated demigod was one of the Øggarbakken behemoths; a towering form of murderous savagery.

"Everus, what a pleasant surprise," cried out Xethorn in a voice as chill as death.

Limping across the threshold, Everus pulled back the bowstring and launched an arrow straight at the seated figure. The arrow flew straight and true but then seemed to curve unnaturally away and ended up well clear of where Xethorn sat.

"*And you!*" said Xethorn, on seeing Creeps sneak in. "*The flunkey!* I must admit, I admire your resilience."

"I told ye to leave," shouted the thief.

A second arrow from Everus went the way of the first.

"And, what if I don't want to?" asked Xethorn, His form dark and shrouded.

"*Then you die!*" roared Everus. Notching a third arrow, he pulled the string back to his ear, channelling all of his hate and rage into this one action, desiring nothing more than to send the arrow, fletching deep, all the way into his deceitful god's black heart. He released the string.

Xethorn caught the arrow in His hand with about as much ease as taking an apple from a tree. "Everus. Is this how you repay my benevolence, my kindness?"

"*Kindness?* What kindness have you shown?" Everus demanded.

"Have I not avenged you? Are not those who destroyed your dream now no more?" Xethorn rose from His throne. "*I* have done this. *I* have blessed you with my rage, my anger, my power. It was I who gave you the will to persevere, to live where others would have laid down and died. And now...now you turn on *me*?"

Everus gulped. There was undeniable truth in the words that the demigod had spoken. "But...you used me. You twisted my thoughts."

"I gave you the power and the conviction to do what your heart desired," replied Xethorn. "Without me you would have become nothing; your life and future no more than a pitiful existence in which you would have forever remained a victim. I enabled you to rise above the laws of your impotent society, to kill those who deserved to die. Can't you see, we are kindred spirits Everus, you and I."

"Don't listen, Everus. It's..." began Creeps.

"Slay him, Everus, and join me! Together we can rule this city, this world."

Everus could feel the mental pressure inside him grow as both entities began to battle within. The darker, murderous part of him began to swell, filling with the seduction and the promises offered by the egotistical demigod. The allure grew stronger and with it the desire and the willingness to turn round and shoot an arrow straight at Creeps, hopefully killing not only the man but everything he represented.

"Fight Him, Everus! Ye must!" Creeps shouted.

Time seemed to have become suspended, frozen, as Everus continued to struggle against Xethorn's will. Memories, dark and unwelcome, flooded through him, each more painful than the last. Memories of his academic aspirations and what he could have, should have been. Memories of his parents; Katryna, Julia and Otha Camberra, Dae'dicus, Dae'morogin. The agony within was crippling, far greater than the worst physical pain he had ever known. Then, deep within, a part of him broke through. The obstinate, sociopathic, censorious, misanthropic, bitter and intractable bastard that others had made of him, tore through the guile and the lies. He raised his eyes from the floor. "*I DENOUNCE YOU AND ALL GODS! DAMN YOU ALL! FROM THIS DAY ON I, EVERUS DRAGONBANNER, WILL SWEAR ALLEGIANCE TO NONE BUT MYSELF!*"

Everus' declaration echoed around the throne room.

"Hmm." Xethorn looked unimpressed. "Then you have chosen your path. That is unfortunate. Now...you die!" With a mere snap of His fingers, He ordered the giant bodyguard down from the raised platform. "I shall give Dread Jungora, Lord of the Behemoths, the privilege of taking your life."

Everus unleashed an arrow, thumping it deep into the approaching giant's right shoulder.

The behemoth snarled and rushed forward, a huge falchion –

half sword, half meat cleaver – in its hands. The monster was tall and gaunt, its limbs elongated. Its swarthy skin was painted with white and red tribal markings, giving it the macabre appearance of a living, raw skeleton; its face was whitened with powder and pigment in order to resemble a skull. What clothing the giant wore was crude and filthy, fashioned from grim-looking beadwork and black and white striped hide. On its back, it carried a bow which was almost as long as itself, a spear, a quiver containing thirteen black-feathered arrows and a sling from which a shrunken, hideous-looking infant gawped with hungry eyes and filed teeth. Around both of them, as though their skin and hides had been rubbed in excrement, hovered a swarm of flies.

Dashing his longbow and the quiver to the floor, Everus withdrew his sword, his blade looking feeble in comparison to Dread Jungora's falchion. He dived to one side as the monster's great blade swung down and scored a deep groove, in a haze of sparks, in the tiled floor. With a cry of rage, he chopped into one of the behemoth's legs. Blood spattered.

The stinking giant bellowed.

Everus stepped in to swing again, but suddenly his only recently healed leg buckled under him and, slipping, he fell to the floor.

Bloated flies buzzed everywhere.

Growling hungrily, the behemoth was just about to hack down, hoping to cut Everus in half, when an arrow, shot by Creeps, struck it in the right arm, just above the elbow. The arrow sunk deep, embedding itself to the bone. The mighty behemoth lord dropped its weapon.

From where He stood watching, Xethorn grinned cruelly.

Before Everus could scramble away, Dread Jungora reached down and hefted him aloft by his damaged leg. The behemoth raised him higher, intending to either smash him against a pillar or else just wrench his head off. An arrow smacked into its face, piercing the flesh of its left cheek as though it were canvas. Howling, it dropped its catch and staggered back, the feathered shaft protruding from between the warty claws clamped to its face. Another arrow then pinned a hand to its bestial face.

His body aching, Everus crawled free of the melee, snatching up his dropped sword.

Screaming, the behemoth plucked both arrows free. Blood ran in rivulets down its painted face, making it appear even more grotesque. On its back, its shrunken infant snarled and stared about.

Getting to his feet, Everus wearily staggered over to do battle with the monster once more. The flies swarmed around him, but his insatiable rage spurred him on as he set about hacking and cutting, throwing every bit of his strength and anger behind his attacks. So much hate had been allowed to fester inside him that now he no longer cared what happened. He had been crafted in Xethorn's image and now it was time to supersede that; to become something even more lethal. Dodging under Dread Jungora's weakening blows, he thrust upwards with his sword, impaling his foul adversary in the groin.

The behemoth reeled and crashed to the floor.

Everus continued to hack and butcher, blood spraying above and beyond him.

"Not bad! Not bad!" Xethorn cried out.

In the heat of the battle, Everus had forgotten about his spectator, too concerned with slaughtering the behemoth and keeping himself alive. He looked across at the demigod who stood, arms crossed, as though nothing of consequence had happened. Then, noting that the giant was still alive, albeit more or less helpless, he took his sword and beheaded the emaciated infant. Raising his sword, he then drove it down through Dread Jungora's open, fang-filed mouth.

"Very good!" Xethorn gave a mocking clap. "Such swordsmanship. Now then, regarding our little..."

"*You're next!*" shouted Everus, pointing. Wiping away the blood from his face, he began to advance on the shadowy figure.

For the briefest of moments a sensation almost akin to worry flickered across the Lord of Murder's mind. Then it vanished, leaving the demigod time to put facts into perspective. How dare an insignificant mortal challenge Him? A blade of glowing fire appeared in His right hand. "Come then Everus. Meet thy doom."

Eager to engage, Everus hobbled forward, his sword raised.

The two clashed, the demigod and the mortal, their blades ringing.

Xethorn cut across with His fiery scimitar, His blow slicing and burning across Everus' chest. Staggering, he fell back. A second attack from the demigod would have severed his head from his neck, had he not parried with his sword. Crimson splinters flew from his blade as the force of the swing forced him back again. A third attack sent the sword spinning from his hand.

Laughing, Xethorn effortlessly rose into the air, swirling His flaming scimitar in movements that defied emulation. From within the vaguely human-shaped mass of unholy plate mail armour and shadow shone a pair of glowing red eyes.

Suddenly a large, spectral fist appeared above Everus.

Turning, Xethorn looked to see Creeps skulking from behind a pillar. "*Hah!* You think your childish attempts at magery can stop me now? I will take a great deal of pleasure in watching you *burn!*"

The ghostly hand reached out, its grasp passing straight through the armoured demigod.

"Your spells are useless against me now! I am no longer trapped in a mortal shell and my powers are almost at their peak. *This is my time.*"

The hand reached out and again it grasped nothing.

Rising painfully to his feet, Everus leant against a pillar, breathing heavily.

"*Now to finish this!*" roared Xethorn, a second tongue of fire suddenly blazing in His other hand. He descended to the floor and advanced on Creeps. Preoccupied with the desire to chop the thief to fiery, burning pieces, the demigod failed to notice the spectral hand raise the slain behemoth's falchion in readiness to strike from behind.

The magical hand brought the falchion hurtling down. With incredible speed, the heavy, cleaver-like weapon sliced through the air like a guillotine blade. Xethorn seemed to sense something, for He began to turn around but was too slow. The blade severed the shadowy form in two, crashing through the rune-adorned armour and the wraith-like essence contained within.

A blinding flash of dark light blasted from the bisected demigod, buffeting the thief off his feet. He recovered quickly and ran over to where Everus lay sprawled, having been knocked flat.

Dark smoke began to gather as the demigod, although hurt, began to reform.

The thief helped Everus to his feet. "Come on. We've got to get out o' 'ere."

Everus snatched up his sword. "*What?* Why not finish the bastard?"

"Come on, move it! We've got to get out. We can't..." Creeps was interrupted by the sound of a set of doors crashing open as a horde of dangerous-looking men came charging in.

They were clad in dark mail and all were armed with swords and axes. Matters were made worse when, with a cry from the regenerating Xethorn, the floor on which Everus and the thief were standing began to transform, its marble-tiled surface becoming black and oily.

"*What is this!?*" cried Everus, slowly sinking into the floor.

As though he were standing on water, Creeps seemed oblivious to Xethorn's transmutative spell. He raised his scrawny arms as though offering up a plea to whatever powers watched over him.

Everus heard the harsh laughter and the malice-laden voice of Xethorn and he thought that, for him at least, this was the end. There would be no escape. He sank up to his chest only vaguely aware of the blue shimmering light which seemed to fall, like stardust, around him.

✝ ✝ ✝

Low in the water, the ship gradually pulled away, leaving many on the dockside to search desperately for an alternative means of escape. Jostling through the crowds of injured, weary, heart-broken people, Everus and Creeps reached the main deck. There they watched as Wyrm's Port burned.

An evil darkness blanketed the city.

On the northern wharf, chaotic scenes played out as citizens fought their way to get aboard any of the diminishing number of sailing vessels leaving the city. Grief-stricken parents clawed their way through the masses in search of their children as others shoved and killed for their passage to safety. In the bedlam, the weak were trampled and many more were drowned as they tried to cling like limpets to departing, overburdened boats.

A cry went up as a group of behemoths rampaged into the thick of the mob, driving a killing wedge through men, women and children alike.

Fires raged everywhere.

"I thought we were dead for sure," said Everus.

"Aye, so did I," agreed Creeps, pipe in mouth.

Grim-faced, Everus continued to watch.

A few hurled timbers splashed into the water, but for the most part, the behemoths were too busy butchering those unfortunates left behind.

"Ma stomach's startin' to complain," said Creeps. "This is the first time I've been on a boat."

"Same here."

"Do ye know where we're goin'?"

"No. But I guess anywhere's better than here."

"Aye, guess so."

"So now what do we do?" Everus asked, trying to find some way to alleviate the strangely apathetic feeling that had enveloped him since their divinely-assisted flight from the Southern Palace. He had been so sure of his impending death, that when he had suddenly found himself aboard an evacuation ship, he had felt almost cheated. He believed he could have killed Xethorn. But now, the bastard was still alive and *that* really pissed him off.

"I'd say our options are limited, unless ye're a good swimmer. I mean, we're on this damned boat. We go wherever it takes us. Once there, who knows, maybe there's a call for grave-robbers. At any rate, I think it'd be best if we lie low for a while."

"And Xethorn?"

Creeps shrugged. "I imagine He'll stay for a bit. Become a divine ruler, instigate a few wars, that kind o' thing."

"So much for The High Three."

Creeps grinned. "Aye, well, there ye go. Such are gods, I guess. Fickle buggers. No doubt they've got some kind o' plan in mind." They certainly did, and the thief knew some of what that plan entailed. "In the meantime, they'll let us stew for a while. It's the way o' things."

"Bastards," Everus blasphemed, half-heartedly. He fixed the dying red glow of the city he had come to hate with a pensive stare.

The thief looked strangely at the sword Everus still absently gripped. "I wouldn't think ye'd be attached to that, all things considered."

"Why?" Everus lifted the sword and looked at it. On the dirt-smeared pommel was emblazoned the symbol of The Watchful Eye. He gazed at it, seemingly struggling with conflicting emotions before casting it into the water. "I'll get a new one when we reach land."

"A new sword...or a new grudge?"

Something in Everus' cold smile seemed to answer that question.

CHAPTER THIRTEEN

Shafts of early evening golden sunlight shot through the open window, baking the air in the small room. A large, orange and red-striped desert wasp buzzed inside, its loud droning disturbing the blanketing hush. Zigzagging in an almost hypnotic dance, it flew around before landing on a small wooden table, clearly attracted to the clay bowl heaped with old and particularly unappealing fruit. The size of a finger, the stinging insect was just about to climb up the bowl when a leather shoe thwacked down on it.

"Got ye, ye little bastard!" Creeps examined the squashed wasp before using the edge of the table to scrape it from the sole of his shoe. He drew the dagger from his belt, skewered the dead insect on it and disposed of it out of the window before turning round. "I'm tellin' ye, this is becomin' unbearable."

"What do you want me to do about it?" asked an unsympathetic voice from the shadows.

Creeps shook his head, retreating into the shade. There, dressed in the scantiest of clothes, the unkempt thief sank his head dejectedly and began to whimper.

"What's up, can't handle a little sun?"

"It's too bloody warm! I can't stand it," complained Creeps. "An' these bloody wasps are *really* gettin' to me! Last time I was stung by one o' 'em ma arm came up like a slattern's tit. I can't take this any more. I want to go home."

"*Home?*"

"Aye. Wyrm's Port...somewhere where it rains."

"You know as well as I that..."

"Course I know, but that don't stop me wantin'." Creeps slouched back towards the window. Shielding his eyes from the sun's blinding glare, he peered out over the white-washed adobe walls and the narrow, straw-strewn streets of Umm-Dabba. Off to one side, he saw an almost naked individual disappear into an arched doorway.

Far off, an ill-treated animal grunted and bellowed. "It's no' normal. All these folk walkin' about wi' next to nothin' on. It's disgustin'."

Looking at his companion, Everus silently agreed. "Umm-Dabba's far from being a normal city. At least not by our reckoning. Nonetheless, it's the one that we're in, so get used to it."

"I don't think I can, Everus. Ye know me, too much sun brings me out in a bad rash. Look at ma bloody arms an' ma face! Ma skin's all peelin' away! This bastard place is too hot for the likes o' me. I can't sleep because o' the heat, an' I'm sweatin' and stinkin' like a tanner's armpit."

"It'll get hotter as the year goes on," said Everus, reaching for the water bag the thief had recently filled from the outside well. Dressed in a loose, pale-red robe of fine material, he sipped from the container and dabbed some of the precious moisture onto his face and neck. Closing his eyes, he lay back and stretched out on the low bed, conserving his energies.

Both he and the thief had now been in the desert city for many days. After their escape from Wyrm's Port across The Dark Sea – a voyage that had not been without its own adventures – they had disembarked at The City of the Glittering Spire. There they had easily avoided the emergency refugee re-housing operation, quickly and illegally disappearing into the foreign city proper.

Penniless, the two had resorted to theft and murder.

Dark days had dragged into darker months as the two continued their nefarious trade. Yet, always at the forefront of Everus' mind, there remained Xethorn, his evil and deceitful deity who had proclaimed himself divine ruler of their native city. Coins, whores and the thrill of violence could not satiate the burning hatred that surged within him whenever his thoughts turned in that direction. Just knowing that Xethorn existed stirred murderous, destructive feelings within him, just as they had once done when Julia Camberra, the agent of The Daemon God, Uhu'giaggoth, had been the focus of his bitterness. Julia was now gone, for he had killed her. All that remained, as far as he was concerned, was to ensure that Xethorn shared a similar fate.

In time, his investigations had taken them to Umm-Dabba.

"*Eleven!*" cried Creeps, his shoe slapping against a wall.

"What?" mumbled Everus, stirring from his thoughts, unsure how long he had been only half-awake. Within the small room shadows had lengthened and it was now slightly cooler.

"That's the eleventh bastard so far."

"Well, you're unlikely to better your record today. Twenty-three, isn't it?"

"Aye," answered Creeps, flicking the crushed wasp from his shoe. "Anyway, I hope when ye see yer man ye'll tell him that this place stinks. Ye tell him from me that this city's one o' the worst shitholes I've ever been in."

Everus sat up. "Don't worry, I'll be sure to pass on your regards. Who knows, if I'm really lucky, he might have you dragged from here and publicly beheaded." He got to his feet and ran a hand through his black hair. He paced over to the window and looked out at the sun-scorched city, watching as torches and lanterns were lit in some of the many houses.

"I doubt he'll see ye."

"He will."

"Well, just watch yersel'. Ye don't know what these foreign folk get up to. An' whatever ye do be sure no' to eat anythin' dodgy. I'd a bad case o' the shits after eatin' some o' that spicy crap we got the other day."

Escaping Creeps' incongruously paternal advice, Everus vacated the room via the only door. He made his way down a well-worn flight of steps, descending onto the street below. Looking up, he could see a fantastic astronomical landscape contained within the heavens, its brightness alone illuminating his path. He strode on, stopping once in order to look back to see whether the thief was following him or spying on his progress. When he saw no one, he continued on his way. It was warm, for although night time made living in Umm-Dabba slightly more tolerable for himself and Creeps, the air still retained much of the day's heat, enveloping all in its stifling embrace.

Down cobbled, sand-swept alleys and streets he went, conscious now of his alien appearance in the eyes of the numerous passing Umm-Dabbites he saw. For although he had made some effort to dress in the typical attire of the common citizens, his height, piercing green eyes and stern look singled him out as foreign. Veiled women muttered and warded themselves with superstitious waves of their weathered arms at his passing, whilst he looked on with complete indifference.

The sound of weird music alerted him to the fact that he was nearing his destination. Turning a corner, he saw the large, mud-brick, dome-shaped building. In its numerous arched openings, shadowy figures could be seen moving about. Outside, one on each side of the stepped entrance, stood a huge, ebony-skinned man. Both were naked apart from a wide, red sash across the groin. Like basalt statues, each stood silent and intimidating, huge curved scimitars in their hands.

Calmly, Everus crossed the wide courtyard before him and approached the two. Eyes trained upon the two sentinels, he climbed the steps. "I'm Everus Dragonbanner. I've come to meet Emir Ibirem."

Neither guard uttered a word, merely looking on with their vacant eyes.

Unsure as to whether their silence indicated his unchallenged admittance, Everus prepared to pass by when he saw another figure arrive at the main entrance.

"So you are *Iv-ir-us*?" Like many Umm-Dabbites, this stranger had trouble pronouncing his guest's name. "Well met. The emir has been expecting you for some time now. Come, my friend. To business." The man was old, short and bald-headed with an eyepatch covering his left eye. He wore a tatty, russet-brown robe and carried what looked like a shepherd's crook in one hand. A small and scrawny, grey-skinned gibbon-like creature perched in an ungainly manner on a shoulder.

Everus tried hard to smile, friendliness and trust in others no longer coming naturally to him. He followed the man past the guards and in through the entrance. They walked down a vaulted tunnel before entering a large chamber in which some dozen men and perhaps twice as many women were seated on silken cushions, sipping from goblets, eating from expensive platters of chilled fruit and intimately fondling one another.

The air in the chamber was thick with the reek of incense, exotic perfumes and smokeable hallucinogens, and to Everus' senses it was sickening and almost overpowering. Conscious of the many pairs of dark eyes which were surreptitiously following his every move, he stuck close to his guide, ready to grab him and hold his concealed dagger to his throat if anything untoward transpired.

Parting an arras which concealed an opening, the small man Everus had been following bade him enter a chamber beyond. Inside, he could see that this much smaller room was, if anything, even more lavishly furnished than the one he had just exited. Plush silken cushions and priceless wall-coverings adorned the room. Superb rugs covered the floor and several small, finely wrought gold ornaments and exquisite carvings made from exotic materials were housed in numerous niches and alcoves. A scintillating light, cast from a rotating colour-filtered lantern transformed the fabulous interior into myriad, ever-changing prismatic hues.

"I welcome you to my humble home," came a mellifluous, child's voice. "Or as we say, '*tzcah'ca-whaz nu-hi-hi qawa.*'"

Half-hypnotised by the kaleidoscopic lights, Everus had initially failed to notice the small figure seated atop a huge heap of cushions in one corner. He squinted before bowing slightly. "Emir Ib-irem. *Wa-ghyis shawwerabb izi-u ta'wa'qwi.*" Greeting formalities over, he entered and sat down on a mountain of pillows, awkwardly sinking into their deceptive softness.

Ib-irem laughed and reached for a large, ornate hookah from which he took a deep puff, filling the room and his lungs with eye-watering purple smoke.

"Most exalted one. It has taken me many moons to..."

"I can help you," interrupted Ib-irem, drawing once more on the pipe. "But first I require a boon from you."

"Name it."

Emerging from the chromatic-tinged shadows, Ib-irem leant closer, permitting Everus to make out what appeared to be a wizened child of no more than ten years. His face however had the texture of a peach stone; cracked and burnt as though from a century spent under the harsh and unforgiving glare of the desert sun. His eyes, although bright and blue, revealed him to be someone who had experienced a life of toil for they showed signs of great weariness as though his soul, rather than his body, had sustained the greater burning. The clothes he wore looked very expensive. "You must first seek out Jazzraeli, for far from here, deep within the sands, there is an ancient ruin..."

"*Khasekh?*"

The emir's eyes widened. "*Yes.* You know of it?"

"A little. Khasekh was once home to a race of serpent-worshippers. Rumour has it that their city was engulfed by the desert over fifty centuries ago when the gods became angered at the..." Everus smiled slightly, "let's say, more demonic aspects of their religion. Their last ruler, Möthcra'aba..."

"*You know of Möthcra'aba!?* You are indeed a scholar! Few

265

outsiders know of anything outside the confines of their own city walls." The emir's eyes sparkled like oases in the desert of his face. "Within ancient Khasekh there is a library, a repository of ancient scrolls. One particular scroll I seek. Obtain this for me...and I will tell you how to defeat your god."

✝ ✝ ✝

Early the next morning, Everus followed an aged dragoman down the filthy, reeking back alleys of the city. Into an ancient warren of twisting back streets and through a maze of decrepit, crumbling buildings they went until eventually arriving at a shadowy doorway.

Out from a dark opening above them there scrabbled a bizarre, ape-like creature. It was the size of a man, certainly no larger; its brown-grey hide bristling, its pronounced fangs bared. It wore a thick, bone-studded, brown leather bandolier and an obscene codpiece which did little but exaggerate the parts it was meant to conceal. Around its long tail it had hooped dozens of small rings. Curled, ram-like horns sprouted on either side of its head. The strange creature looked at the drop beneath it, before jumping down. It landed nimbly and started to make its way towards them, its bandy-legged gait making its movements almost comical.

Like a slaver showing off his best muscled wares, the scrawny, leathery-skinned guide extended an arm, indicating to Everus that this is what he had come to see. So this strange creature was Jazzraeli. His task done, he then left the two staring at each other.

Everus stepped towards it. "I've been told that you know the way to Khasekh." It was neither a question nor an assumption, just a statement of fact.

With a rattle of its tail, the thing sprang into an upright stance. "By whom?"

Its voice sounded strangely cultured and yet it was clear that human speech was not native to its race. It was certainly not the kind of voice Everus was expecting to hear from the thing. He watched, uncertain how to respond as the scruffy baboon-like beast scratched its neck. It perched nonchalantly on a low wall, its bauble-festooned tail curling behind it. There was neither friendliness nor malice behind its amber eyes, only a sense of watchfulness, as though it was weighing him up.

"Who has said that I know the way to that accursed place?" inquired Jazzraeli.

"Emir Ib-irem."

"Hmm...then you've been informed correctly. I do indeed know the way. However, I have no intention of going back there again. Once was bad enough."

Everus had been told to expect such a reply. He reached into a pouch and removed a handful of rainbow-hued pearls. "I can pay you well. A hundred pearls. Thirty now, the rest..."

Jazzraeli's feral eyes lit up. "And when do you want to leave?" He began scratching at his furry hide. He removed a handful of fleas and popped them into his mouth.

"Soon." Everus answered. "There are several more things to prepare and then we should be all set. A day or two at most."

"Very well." A hairy paw extended. "The pearls."

For a moment, Everus considered the possibility that this bizarre creature would take its payment and scamper away, never to be seen again. Then, albeit reluctantly, he tipped what pearls he had in his hand back into the pouch and handed it over. He had little option but to put some measure of trust in Jazzraeli, knowing only too well that without a reliable guide there would be no way he could reach the desert ruins.

† † †

Two days later, preparations for the expedition into the sandy wastes came to a close. Everus and Creeps sat in the sweltering heat on a low wall outside the building where Everus had first met the emir. Two laden camels, piled high with all the necessities for a journey into the desert, stood nearby.

The thief sat kicking his heels and mopping sweat from his brow, a crude parasol made from two sticks and a torn shirt offering scant shade. He fixed the camels with a disparaging stare, reflecting on just how much he disliked them. It was not only their stink, but the fact that he always associated them with the dark-skinned, Uttapian merchants who had plagued the Wyrm's Port markets, selling their junk and letting their beasts shit all over the place.

"I can see you're not too happy about this, are you?" asked Everus, lacing a boot.

"Huh! Ye already know the answer to that."

"You don't have to come. In fact, perhaps it would be better if you didn't."

Creeps shook his head and muttered something Everus failed to catch. He got to his feet and finished securing a pack to one of the camels before turning around. "So what about this guide o' yers? When's he goin' to turn up? If ye ask me, I reckon he's done a runner wi' yer loot."

"He'll be here." Despite being assured of Jazzraeli's reliability by Ib-irem, Everus harboured his own doubts. On first appearances the hirsute guide had looked even sneakier than Creeps, if such a thing was possible.

"An' what is he? An' what's his name?"

"He's called Jazzraeli. As to what he is I haven't a clue, but he claims to have been to Khasekh before."

"*Claims?*"

"I've no reason to doubt him...as yet." Everus lowered his tone of voice. "Besides, the brat suggested him." He looked around in order to make sure that no one else had heard him. It was then that he noticed the bandy-legged ape-thing approaching them from the other end of the square.

Creeps followed Everus' gaze. "Is...is this him?"

Everus nodded and waited for their guide-to-be to join them.

Jazzraeli wore a baggy, light, brown and grey mottled outfit. The clothing was tightened by a belt worn around the waist, but elsewhere it was slack and airy as though several sizes too big for him. Covering most of his head and face was a wrap of similar material, one end trailing over his left shoulder. On his back, he carried a small pack which was mottled in the same camouflage colours, from which containers and other bits of miscellaneous desert survival gear hung. In his right hand, he carried a slender, carved, wooden staff which was topped with a small horned skull and several green and red feathers. He bowed slightly. "You all set?"

"We're getting there," answered Everus.

The thief eyed the creature that was going to be their guide disapprovingly.

"You got water, food, torches, oil, rope, sacks, tents, camel provisions?" asked Jazzraeli, his questions directed to Creeps, who was seemingly the one responsible for loading up all the equipment.

"Yeh, we've got the lot," Creeps replied, finding it hard not to stare. He had seen many strange things but most he had never got round to talking to. Everus had usually killed them before they reached the dialogue stage.

"Salamander oil?" asked Jazzraeli.

"What?" inquired Creeps.

"Salamander oil," repeated Jazzraeli, reaching into a pocket and tossing a small, sealed blue pot to the thief.

Creeps caught it. "What's this for?"

"*What's this for?*" parroted Jazzraeli, unbelievingly. "*Stone my mother and leave her shattered!* I can see I'm going to have my work cut out getting to the ruins with you two."

"Why's that?" asked Everus.

Jazzraeli grinned, his upper lip pulled back to expose a set of nasty-looking incisors. "Because you're not going to last a day in the desert without your salamander oil. Humans, especially outsiders, don't take to the heat all that well and out there in the fiery heart of the Inner Dunes you two will crisp and burn up...unless you put some of this on your pale, tender skin."

Once the camels were ready and Jazzraeli had contented himself with their final preparations, the three set out, leaving Umm-Dabba via the South Gate. Everus thought that the emir may have been on hand to provide them with some extra words of caution or at least to wish them well, but he never turned up. Upon departing the walled city, they circumvented the wastes and the middens on its western side before striking out in a north-westerly direction.

Before them stretched a broken land of red rock and sand. The road they had set out on dwindled to nothing more than a barely discernible track. Within the first league, had it not been for Jazzraeli's expert navigation, Everus and Creeps would have soon been helplessly lost. Their surroundings seemed by and large featureless, the high stone walls of Umm-Dabba now no longer visible on the hot, shimmering horizon behind them.

As they walked, Everus quizzed their guide over his past visit to the ancient city of the serpent-worshippers. It was with some reluctance that Jazzraeli told him what little he remembered; about how he had gone there hoping to find wealth and fame but had instead found nothing but horror. His group of fellow explorers had been slain by some invisible monster which had tracked each of them down. One by one his associates had been devoured. Jazzraeli went on to say that he alone had survived only because he had access to a magic potion which had enabled him to fly for a limited period of time. It was thus, with a certain pang of guilt, that he divulged how he had been forced to abandon his friends. When asked about the journey itself, Jazzraeli informed Everus that they had to reach an ancient caravan trail which, once on, they had to follow for perhaps six or so days until they reached the half-buried colossus of Shaab-Utu. From there, they would leave the trail and enter the flaming heart of the desert. It was from then on, warned Jazzraeli, that the going would get hard for they would be entering into the realm dominated by the Blood Orb, which, according to him, was in actuality a false sun, the cruel light and the heat from which was focused solely on that one area of desert.

✝ ✝ ✝

After another three tiring days, Jazzraeli climbed to the top of one of the many sand dunes, calling for the others to come and join him. He was by far better suited to this kind of terrain, his feet splayed and ideal for walking on the hot, shifting sand. In addition, despite his mammalian appearance, he was cold-blooded and his clothing seemed to exude a certain coolness which kept him comfortable despite the increasingly ferocious heat.

Everus raised his tired eyes to look up. "What? What is it?" Slowly, he clambered up. Upon reaching the crest, he shielded his eyes and squinted towards where Jazzraeli pointed. Many leagues away, on the horizon, he could make out the outline of something gargantuan.

"That's what we're heading for. The colossus of Shaab-Utu."

The thief staggered up towards them, leading the two camels. "Are we there, yet?" he asked, dejectedly. His limbs ached and his face was raw and peeling. Dried blood caked his blistered bottom lip. Despite having carried the parasol and having smeared much of his skin in copious amounts of the salamander oil as advised by Jazzraeli, it still felt as though he was on fire from toes to scalp.

Eyes narrowing to mere slits, Everus scanned the far horizon. Above the rugged line of the land, the sky was a clash of vibrant red, orange and purple colours, as though the heavens had been sliced open, spilling blood and their chaotic insides.

Jazzraeli held his staff out and waved it. "Beyond you can see the outer limits of the Blood Orb. One must be wary of its rays for they can corrupt the flesh as sure as the strongest poison."

"*Great!* Just what I wanted to hear," mumbled the thief. "Right now, I feel as though I want to lie down an' die."

270

"How long will it take us to get there?" asked Everus.

"I would guess, at our current rate, two days. Maybe less. There's water," said Jazzraeli, pointing to a shimmering pool not that far way. "Let's make our way and be sure to fill our canteens, for from then on there will be no more. Drink well here, then sparingly hereafter."

They rested for a short time before heading for the small oasis. Eagerly they drank, before filling their numerous containers with the vital liquid. The camels drank heartily, filling their lean bodies and storage humps with enough to sustain them for many days to come.

At Jazzraeli's suggestion, they pitched tent and sheltered from the blazing heat of the midday sun.

In the small tent, Creeps sat cross-legged, scooping another mass of the salamander oil from one of the small pots Jazzraeli had provided and smearing it over his face and neck.

"Make sure you don't use it all up," cautioned Jazzraeli, rummaging through a pack and unrolling a sealed packet of beef strips. "So far we've been lucky in the sense that it hasn't become too hot but that'll all change as soon as we venture beyond the colossus...and remember to save enough for the return journey."

"Shaab-Utu," said Everus, digging sand from his nails with a dagger. He looked towards Jazzraeli. "She of a Thousand Teats. She was supposed to have been an early fertility goddess, an earthly representation of the heat of the sun if I'm not mistaken."

Jazzraeli nodded.

Everus looked at Creeps, suddenly reminded of the fact that the burnt, scruffy, exhausted man slumped before him, his face dripping obscenely with foul-smelling, snot-like gunge, was, or certainly had been, an agent of The High Three – the supposed omnipotent creator gods. That the thief once possessed powers and abilities of his own, Everus had no doubt for he had seen them in action. While Everus had been powerless, trying to battle Xethorn within the Southern Palace in Wyrm's Port, it had been the thief who had saved his life, beseeching his gods to deliver them from impending death. And yet, since that day, Creeps had vociferously claimed that he had lost complete contact with them. Certainly, he had not displayed any unearthly powers since that time. At least none that Everus had witnessed. However, the thief's shadow still remained somewhat darker.

"The worst of the day's heat has passed. It's time we should get moving," announced Jazzraeli, breaking Everus' train of thought and getting to his feet.

They packed up and were soon off again.

Jazzraeli led them on, striking out for the dark silhouette on the horizon. The going became more difficult and Everus and Creeps soon found themselves having to trudge through what seemed like a mire of shin-deep, wind-blown sand. The old caravan trail they had been following had, at least to Everus' eyes, long since vanished, the desolation which stretched in every direction broken only by the dark shape of the colossus before them.

The late afternoon sun-blast was like a furnace which struck at them without mercy, pulsing down at them in great waves of heat which pressed and enveloped them, dredging up every last drop of moisture from the surrounding sand and their bodies. It seemed to Everus that the sun was cooking them, readying them like meat in an oven in preparation for a god to devour and despite the fact that the day was now waning, the heat increased, piling up over the baking flats behind and before them, the lurid, reddish light of the Blood Orb reflecting off the desolation all around.

To the south, a dust storm had blown up and they could make it out quite clearly as it scudded over the desert, the sand whirled high by the wind, lifting it into the brazen crimson heavens like an army of infernal devils off to do battle. Jazzraeli commented that so long as it did not switch course and head in their direction they had little to fear. He watched it worriedly, tracking its movements through experienced eyes, relating that he had encountered such sand storms before and that he knew the danger as well as the general discomfort they could bring with them; the millions of tiny, stinging grains, whipped along by aeolian forces, able to permanently blind and scour exposed flesh until it bled raw.

It was getting dark by the time they reached more traversable ground, the sand now only ankle-deep. A vibrant tapestry of stars and all three of the world's moons shone down from the deep indigo sky, lighting their way. Still Jazzraeli pushed them on, eager to cover as much ground as possible during the cooler phases of the day. He would stop every now and then in order to consult his position in the great heavenly map above him.

"He's no' right," commented Creeps, walking alongside Everus.

"You think so?" Everus replied, eyes fixed on their guide's back as he strode on tirelessly.

"Aye. There's summat funny about him. I don't trust him an' I don't think he sleeps."

"I've heard him snoring."

"Aye, but all the same, that doesn't mean he's sleepin', now does it?"

To some extent Everus shared the thief's suspicions, but he had come to the conclusion that there was little he could do but follow Jazzraeli. His life was now devoted to destroying his dark god and the only way he could do it, as far as he knew, was to complete Ibirem's mission. Consequently, he had to reach Khasekh. He was giving this some thought when suddenly the sky lit up further as a blazing asteroid shot earthwards, its fiery trail streaking through the heavens with a vermilion glow.

The three travellers watched, stunned, as the flaming chunk of space debris then vanished beyond the distant horizon like a god-fired catapult stone.

† † †

After another day and a half, they came to the massive stone effigy – the mysterious idol of Shaab-Utu. Sloping up out from the sand, the towering, steatopygous statue was worn with age, making it hard for them to fully discern its sun-scorched features. That it was supposed to be female was evident from the many large, almost shapeless protuberances on its chest, but the cracked face was more leonine than human.

They took shelter from the midday heat in the statue's giant shadow.

When late afternoon arrived, they set off again, departing from the track and heading out into the realm of the Blood Orb.

† † †

On the second day out from the Shaab-Utu colossus, the world Everus thought he knew altered. It was not just the terrain which changed, transforming as it did into an alien realm of shattered, striated cliffs, sand-scoured sculptured rocks and huge pools of bubbling, plopping magma but the sky itself, dominated as it was by the fiery gaze of the Blood Orb.

The long, russet-brown cloak he wore was streaked with dust

and grime, the flesh underneath chafed and burning. With each step, the sand seemed to become hotter, burning through the very soles of his boots, the initial discomfort of having walked many leagues now giving way to utter agony. His face was cracked and blistered, streaked red with exposure to the Blood Orb, which scorched the dunes and the rocky deserts of this land with its blazing rays. Yet, even as he stared up at it, defiance ignited in his piercing green eyes. Exhausted and badly burned, he mustered the will to hold its image. For a moment, he managed to discern its shimmering outline, noting the crimson, fiery corona which encircled it. Just as quickly, he pulled his gaze away. He had not been quick enough. Like tears, blood dribbled from the corners of his eyes and ran down his burnt face. His vision swam, the image of the fiery disc seared into his brain as though branded there. Like a stream in a gulch, blood trickled down a furrow in a cheek, collecting on his swollen, split bottom lip. His tongue tasted it, relishing the moisture, no matter its source. He could no longer remember when he had last drunk, time itself seeming to warp and stretch, not assisted much by the fact that there were no nights. The Blood Orb never moved – never rose or set – nor did the light which emanated from it create any shadows. There was no longer any shelter, for their flimsy tents proved ineffective. Nothing escaped its hostile, ferocious radiation.

Not that there was much life in this blasted, cratered landscape. Apart from his companions and the two camels, Everus had seen nothing but rock and sand ever since leaving Umm-Dabba. There were no lizards or scorpions. No snakes or vultures.

The land was seemingly devoid of life.

Time blurred, along with his own consciousness. All Everus clung to was the mission and the fact that he knew he came from elsewhere – that there *was* something else, something beyond this apparently unending wasteland of blistering heat and pain. And yet, despite his training and his background, this thought also gave rise to his greatest fear – that he would lose all notion of his past and become one with the desert and vanish out of existence; forgotten, doomed to a life of emptiness within this desolation and that, despite his actions, Xethorn was now laughing at his futility.

It was for that reason he had accepted this perilous mission. He *would* trek the empty leagues on ragged stumps if need be. Revenge and bitterness empowered him, fuelling his determination; stubbornly raising each foot from the ground before bringing it down again. In this manner, pain was viewed as something to embrace, something to focus on. It provided the means needed to anchor him to his diminishing sense of reality. Without it, he was sure he would go insane. He would either die, or he would kill Xethorn – as far as he was concerned, there was no in-between.

Like a melting mirage, the image of the Blood Orb dissipated from behind his bleeding eyes, leaving once more the cliffs and the dunes. Directly before him and on either side, crumbling away like a sea of dust, lay a vast expanse of trackless desert, broken here and there by high dunes and the occasional shattered up-thrust of rock. Everything was bathed in that horrid, alien-red glow, tinted more so by the crimson wetness of his already drying tears.

"I can't go on...I..." Feebly, Creeps crumpled to his knees.

Everus looked back. "Get up!" He trudged over and hauled the thief to his feet.

"Ma legs." Moaning, Creeps went floppy, sinking to his knees once more. Much of his face and hands were now heavily scabbed over and despite the fact that he had been coating himself with the protective salamander oil, he looked as though he had crawled from a crematorium's oven. Patches of hair and his short moustache looked singed.

"Get up, damn you!"

"Everus...I'm done for," the thief whimpered. "I'm dyin'."

"Get him on one of the camels," cried Jazzraeli. "We'll load up the other one and divide the excess between us."

Harshly, Everus dragged Creeps to one of the camels, which Jazzraeli was already in the process of unloading. Jazzraeli brought the camel to a kneeling position and, with some trouble, the thief clambered onto it.

Everus was tightening a securing strap which fastened one of the bulging saddle bags when, with a terrible hiss, a fearsome-looking monster burst from a large fissure nearby and came bounding straight for them.

It appeared more insectoid than anything else, having several rows of segmented, smaller, hooked arms, in addition to a set of huge claws. Its head was beetle-like, a vicious pair of mandibles clacking in readiness to feed. Large and scrawny, its desert-toughened flesh resembling burnt bone, its blistered head spiked with rows of cactus-like needles and twin antennae, the wiry horror sprang at Jazzraeli. With a swing from one of its claws it dashed him to the ground before taking a grip with the other and hefting him into the air.

Creeps screamed from atop his camel even as the second pack animal bolted.

Drawing his sword from amidst the baggage fastened at the remaining camel's side, Everus ran to engage their attacker. Two-handedly, he chopped into its chitinous hide, cutting deep.

Dark yellow blood squirted from the wound.

On a pair of spindly, spined legs, the monster stood up to its full height, its many, bulging, bug-like eyes on a level with Creeps on the camel.

Bleeding, Jazzraeli crawled to his feet, reaching for his staff.

Everus hacked again and again, severing one claw and then the other, driving the thing into a spasmodic rage. A host of nippers and pincers shot from an abdominal opening, along with a spray of acidic digestive juice which jetted forth from a further freshly-sliced open wound.

Ducking away from the fierce mandibles, Everus sidestepped and chopped a deadly two-handed slash into the thing's main trunk, almost cutting it in two.

The monstrosity crashed to the ground. It quivered for a moment and then went still.

Grimacing, Jazzraeli limped over to examine the mutilated corpse.

Everus poked it with his sword, ensuring it was dead. "Any idea as to what it was?"

"No." Jazzraeli looked about him, searching for the missing camel. It was nowhere to be seen. Not a trace. Either it had fallen into a fissure or else it had been snatched by another one of these predatory creatures. "Come on, we should be gone from this place."

"What about the other camel?" inquired Everus, looking about.

Jazzraeli started to go. "I'd guess it's already dead."

Everus had to concede.

† † †

How long they had been going, Everus could no longer tell, the fact that there were no nights any more making it nigh on impossible to keep an accurate track of time. The supplies of water were beginning to dwindle even as the discomfort and the pain brought on by the rays from the Blood Orb began to increase. He was growing increasingly concerned that if they did not soon reach a watering hole then getting back to Umm-Dabba was going to prove impossible.

There seemed to be no end in sight.

League after painful league passed agonisingly slowly beneath his tired feet as, head down, Everus trudged on, Creeps on the sole remaining camel behind him. Dismissing the niggling uncertainty that he had felt for some time – that perhaps there was nothing here, no ancient city and no repository of scrolls – he staggered behind the seemingly indefatigable Jazzraeli to the base of a large dune. Following his guide, he began the slow and arduous climb up, the sand shifting under his feet. He sank deeper the higher he got, the sand now rising to knee level.

"Behold, cursed Khasekh!" announced Jazzraeli. With one hairy paw, he pointed towards what lay beyond the dune.

A mad, relieved laugh escaped Everus' parched mouth as he crumpled at the top, for, through red-rimmed eyes, he could see, stretched out before him, the mud-brick ruins of the ancient city. Huge mounds of sand covered most of its walls and cracked structures. Close to the centre of the predominantly buried settlement, there rose a weathered, stepped monument – the ziggurat of Möthcra'aba. If Xethorn was dead and vanquished, a part of him would have been content to die here and now, for such sights were surely not meant for human eyes.

"*What a place!*" muttered Creeps. He dropped from the saddle and went to stand by Everus, one hand gripped around the camel's stout leather leash.

"Well that's me done my bit," said Jazzraeli. "The rest is up to you two, for there's no way I'm going inside. I'll set up camp and I'll wait here till you've done what you came here to do but I'm not going another step."

"What's in there?" asked Everus, surveying the seemingly desolate city before him.

"That's for you to go and find out. But whatever you do, be sure not to entice anything back here." With those words of reassurance, Jazzraeli loped towards the camel and started to set up camp.

† † †

After they had rested, Everus and Creeps set off to explore the crumbling city. Walking down the steep dune, they saw that Khasekh extended much further than they had, on first sight, believed. In numerous places could still be seen the remains of a fairly substantial perimeter wall, its sun-bleached stones reddened by centuries of exposure to the Blood Orb. Several large, shattered towers still stood, rising from the burnt earth and sand in open defiance to time and the cruel blaze.

"Do ye think there'll be monsters in 'ere?" asked Creeps, his eyes shifting from one sundered ruin to the next.

"Who knows?" replied Everus, his drawn sword reflecting the red rays, making it look as though it was already awash with blood. "So keep your eyes peeled."

"They're already peeled. Feels as though they've been clamped in a vice an' scraped wi' a chisel," cursed Creeps, scratching at his flaking scalp. He had ditched his makeshift parasol several days ago after discovering its ineffectiveness.

The going was slow and difficult; broken walls and huge drifts of wind-blown sand impeding their movement. Cautiously, they made their way towards the great stepped ziggurat – the old temple dedicated to the foul Möthcra'aba. Beneath this, Ib-irem had informed Everus, lay the old repository wherein the scroll he was after would be located.

Finding the entrance to the ziggurat was easier than either of them had anticipated. Fallen columns and large statues of mythical beasts now lay defunct and half-buried outside the almost collapsed entrance. It was deathly quiet as Creeps retrieved a torch from his pack, lit up and stood beside Everus, who peered into the darkened tunnel.

Together they made their way down, their sun-damaged eyes welcoming the darkness.

"Seems like old times," said Creeps. Torch held high, he led the way, vigilantly on the look out for anything out of the ordinary, especially traps. "Aye, back to what we do best."

Everus ignored the thief's comments. With shoulders stooped, he followed close behind.

The air was hot and dusty. The tunnel was narrow and low-ceilinged and the further they went the more confined their surroundings became. Every so often crumbling brickwork would drizzle down, giving the impression that the entire structure was about to collapse about them, burying them at any moment.

The stale air was stifling, catching at the backs of their throats.

Everus was about to suggest they turn back and see if they could find an alternative entrance, believing that the one they were in must have been a dummy passage, probably excavated in order to fool tomb-robbers, when part of the tunnel behind him collapsed, crashing down in an avalanche of rubble and sand. A cloud of dust blasted out as the entire tunnel seemed to disintegrate before his eyes and what looked like half of the desert sifted in to fill the exit. Pulling himself low, he shielded his head with his hands.

"Come on!" cried Creeps.

Crawling free of the cloud of dust, Everus coughed and dragged himself onwards.

"Eh...where now?" asked Creeps, staring bemusedly at the dead end before him.

Everus cursed. It seemed as though there was no way forward and now, no way back. "There must be a secret door...or a switch of some kind."

"An' if there isn't?"

Everus thought about it for a moment before answering. "I guess we die." He could think of others he would rather spend his last few days entombed alongside – all of them female. He started to examine the walls. "Start looking. You're better at this than me." He looked back, considering whether or not they should start digging.

It was the draft from the parallel passage which caught the thief's attention, the torch guttering as he moved it up and down one length of wall. There was definitely a void beyond, it was now just a matter of finding the entrance.

"You found something?" asked Everus, his words tinged with growing desperation. Not surprisingly, he did not want to rot down there.

The thief neared with the torch. "I wonder what this does? Stand clear." He pushed a stone block and a portion of the wall began to slide back.

Beyond, Everus could see that the opening in the wall led to a small chamber. Looking in, he saw numerous niches inset around the walls in which lay some of the mouldering, desiccated inhabitants of Khasekh. They were a grisly lot, most of them barely human in appearance. What exposed skin he saw looked scaled and rough; their faces elongated, angular and disturbingly serpentine.

Thankfully, none of them showed any signs of motion.

A shadow-filled archway over to their left allowed deeper access into the core of the ziggurat.

Cautiously, Everus clambered inside, his sword held out before him. A general feeling of uneasiness formed in the pit of his stomach. An unidentifiable smell hung in the stale air. Raising a finger to his lips, he gestured to Creeps to be quiet. He waited for a moment before waving the thief inside and pointing to the archway.

Creeps moved towards it. He was just about to enter the tunnel beyond when, with his left foot, he stepped on a concealed pressure pad. Instinctively, he leapt to one side as a huge spiked ball, attached to a length of rusty, linked chain hurtled from a recess above his head and smashed into the wall. "*Buckets o' blood!* What's this place tryin' to do, kill me!?" he shouted.

Everus grinned and briefly examined the spiked trap, trying to understand the ancient mechanism behind its triggering.

"Are ye sure there's another way out o' 'ere?" asked the thief, rubbing his shoulder.

"We find the scroll first. Then we find an exit. Come on."

Deeper into the crumbling labyrinth they went, the stink of age-old bone and musty brickwork strong on their nostrils. They came to a corbel-vaulted chamber, its inner walls lined with dark stone. Scattered all over the ground and stored in countless hewn alcoves and niches around the walls were thousands of dried scrolls in addition to hundreds of clay tablets, most of which lay shattered.

Raising his torch, Creeps stood staring, surveying the ancient library with something akin to awe. "There's thousands o' 'em."

For someone who, from his own admission, could neither read nor write, the thief seemed genuinely dumbfounded, leaving Everus to wonder whether the thief thought there might be some money to be made from this discovery. As a one-time scholar of ancient history, Everus knew that what he was now looking at was historically priceless, for herein were contained countless written accounts, ranging from the chronological ordering of some of the truly ancient kings to the mundane descriptions of daily life for the working populace.

"We'll be 'ere for..." started Creeps. He stopped upon witnessing Everus remove a pair of strange and ornate optical devices from a wallet and attach them to his face. "What're they for?"

Ignoring the thief, Everus began scanning the chamber. He advanced further, bending occasionally to search under a heap of pages or rummage inside a decaying casket.

Creeps watched and waited, a confused look on his face.

After a while, Everus removed the weird spectacles and rubbed his eyes. "It's got to be here somewhere."

"Do they things let ye see better?"

"No," answered Everus. "But according to Ib-irem, they'll reveal the scroll that he's after. It's either this or I sit here and read every one of them. And if it comes to that, I think Xethorn will have died of old age by the time we get back." He put the glasses back on, his vision now dark and hazy.

Crossing the chamber, his eyes meticulously combed the many recesses and it was not until he felt the dull thud in his head that he saw the tell-tale red glow from under a large pile he thought he had already searched. Frantically, he scattered the other pages, now no longer caring about their historical importance. Eyes drawn to the single sheet of glowing papyrus, highlighted by means of the emir's magic lenses, he carefully picked it up.

"Ye got it?"

Everus removed the spectacles and, with his own sight, examined the page, verifying to himself that this was indeed what he was after. From a quick glance, it looked like some kind of territory deal or an ancient land deed. The language was unfamiliar. He returned the lenses to their case before delicately rolling the sheet of papyrus and tucking it away in a leather scrollcase he had been given for that very purpose.

"Now what do we do?"

"We get out, return to Ib-irem and..."

"*Behind ye!*" yelled Creeps.

Everus turned round, pulling his sword from its scabbard. By the light from the thief's torch, he saw a large, shadowy creature enter the chamber directly behind him. As it neared, he saw that its lower half consisted of the trunk of a monstrous snake which tapered to a rattling tail, whereas its upper body was that of a withered and partially mummified man. Dead serpents hung like dreadlocks from its head. The hybrid's face was repellent; its flesh flaking like an ancient mural. Dirty grey, orb-like eyes, stared malevolently. On its head it wore an ancient peaked crown. In its right arm, it carried an equally ancient weapon which seemed to be a cross between an axe and a hooked spear.

Creeps darted like a shadow to the archway from which they had entered, his fleeting movement drawing the monster's attention as, with a terrible hiss, the horror slithered further forward.

Everus rushed forward, his two-handed swing slicing naught but air as the abomination withdrew. He sidestepped to counter his over balance, his backhand swing parried by the thing's weapon. He was struck by a potent stench akin to festering carrion. Now that he could see the horror more clearly, he could see with revulsion how its putrid flesh glistened with an oily pus. Fighting back the urge to vomit, he narrowly dodged a powerful downward hack that would surely have cloven his head.

A disgusting forked tongue wagged from its gash-like mouth as words neither Everus nor the thief could understand were hissed in a sibilant voice.

Everus renewed his attack, his blade striking home and cutting open a long layer of rubbery flesh just above the meeting of its human and snake-like parts. Spitting its agony, the mutant ophidian withdrew. Sensing its vulnerability, Everus leapt at it, his forward lunge parried once again. He was about to swing once more when, suddenly, the thing's long tail coiled around his right leg and pulled him roughly to the clay tablet-strewn floor.

Upon seeing Everus' predicament, the thief dashed forward, torch in one hand, dagger in the other. Frantically, he dodged and parried, occasionally finding the breath to hurl insults.

Unable to effectively use his sword from the floor, Everus threw it aside and withdrew the dagger from his boot. He rolled and dodged, twice narrowly avoiding the downward thrusts from his attacker's weapon as repeatedly he stabbed into the scaly tail.

For his part, Creeps did his best to distract the horror's attention, even managing to slash it down one arm with his dagger. His short cry of triumph was short-lived however, for, with a rapid jab, it struck him painfully in the left shoulder, driving him from the fray.

After being repeatedly stabbed, the punctured tail uncoiled from Everus' leg.

Dexterously, Everus sprang to his feet and darted behind his attacker. The battered crown was knocked flying as, with one hand, he pulled the gruesome head back and sliced its throat open with his dagger. The thing went berserk as it tried in vain to shake him loose. Still he clung on, cutting again and again, severing stringy veins and butchering elastic tubes of long-dried vocal and respiratory pipe-work. Flaps of leathery flesh hung from the unsightly wound.

Gargling obscenely, the horror flailed wildly and tried to grab Everus with its hands, its weapon now lying on the ground before it. Savagely, Everus drove the dagger into the thing's head.

Metal squealed against bone as the cranium was punctured. Dark, gelatinous brain matter hung in thick loops like molasses from its ruptured skull as, with a final violent death spasm, the thing collapsed, twitched for a moment and then lay still.

Everus, spattered with its dark cranial juices and other foul, leaking, bodily fluids bent down in order to examine the ancient crown. "*Möthcra'aba!?*"

"Eh? What's that?" asked Creeps, moving closer now that things appeared safe once more.

"This crown. It's the crown of Möthcra'aba. I therefore assume that..."

"*Möthcra-what?* What's that...a name or summat'?"

"This is...*was*, Möthcra'aba." Everus pointed with his oily dagger to the gory corpse. "He...*it*...ruled this place long before the sands took control. He was a diabolical tyrant...a king who instigated a cult, a religion based on snake-worship. From the looks of him I'd guess he probably offered his soul to some snake-demon or other in order to obtain power or some such."

"He might o' been born that way," Creeps suggested. "After all, I've seen worse. Anyhow, if ye've got what ye came for methinks it's high time to try an' find a way out o' 'ere. That stink's terrible."

Everus retrieved his sword.

They left the chamber the way the dead serpent-king had entered and headed further into the labyrinth.

"Ye sure there's another way out o' 'ere?" asked Creeps, searching for traps. Since leaving the library chamber he had found two deep pit traps, thus saving himself and Everus from almost certain death and impalement on the numerous rusty spikes below.

"No."

The thief gave Everus a nervous grin, the nagging ache in his shoulder getting worse with every forward step. He was about to say something when an unexpected gust of air almost blew the torch out. Curious, he looked about him and saw the narrow chimney above his head. It looked like some kind of ancient vent.

"What is it?" asked Everus.

Creeps stared up. "Looks like a tunnel. It might lead out," he added, hopefully.

Everus nodded in agreement. It made more sense to go up, rather than down. Securing his sword on his back, he looked about for suitable handholds before pulling himself up. It was dark and narrow and, despite the inrush of air, it smelled terrible. Sand drizzled down from above and the further he ventured, the more confined it seemed to become. He could hear the sounds of Creeps' scrabbling not far behind and he had to blot out the possibility that this was a bad idea – that it would lead to a dead end. He was certain that reversing would prove nigh on impossible.

"This shaft's goin' to disappear up its own arse," complained Creeps.

In places, the vent levelled out, enabling them to crawl on hands and knees before rising once more at an acute angle. Slowly and carefully, they wormed their way ever higher up the shaft until they came to a tiny area, its ceiling and the potential exit from their bolt hole blocked with a huge stone.

It was difficult work, the confined space impeding his movements but, with a final heave, Everus managed to shift the great stone block. Violent, red heat from the Blood Orb and an inrush of sand greeted him. Wearily, he crawled free of the ziggurat, dragging himself forward on his hands and knees. Dust and red sand covered his face. It was in his hair and inside his clothing, making everything itch. Shielding his eyes from the intense light, he could see that he had come out about a third of the way up one of the tiers of the great edifice.

With a grunt, Creeps crawled free. At first sight he could easily have been mistaken for one of the Khasekh dead. "Never again," he vowed, lamely. "From now on, I'm goin' to become a gardener."

"Sure...and I'm going to take up ballet." Everus' voice was hoarse, his throat dry. "Come on. Now all we have to do is get back to camp, rest up a bit and then return to Umm-Dabba."

† † †

That evening, Everus stood on the high dune, watching as the crimson light from the Blood Orb soaked the dead city in its fiery blaze. A desert wind picked up, billowing his robes. From the other side of the ridge, he could hear the sounds of his companions as they moved about the camp. Now that he had Ib-irem's scroll, part of him could not believe where he now stood. To actually be here, at the site of Khasekh, filled him for a moment with a sense of long-forgotten awe and as he looked about him at the ancient city of sand-encroached buildings, he was reminded of his time at the Wyrm's Port Academy. He had done much research on many of the lost desert kingdoms; the books he had studied tracing their development over the millennia – from village to empire to dust. And whereas the academics could pontificate all they liked, arguing over the petty details, their widely-held beliefs no more than bombastic conjecture spewed from the mouths of those who never ventured further than their comfortable studies, they would never experience or know history – *real history*. Standing here, however, with the dust of Khasekh in his lungs and the dried blood of Möthcra'aba on his sword, he knew what history was, for in a place such as this it was almost tangible. Yet, to a large degree, he no longer cared, for the academic world was one on which he had been forced to turn his back. Pensively, he started back down the dune, knowing in all likelihood that he would never be here again.

† † †

The heat was now intolerable, a sweltering inferno which scorched clothing and skin alike, and it felt to Everus as though his brain was drying up. He was weakening, the meagre amounts of water they now had to ration out no longer enough to hydrate his heat-tortured body. Unless the camel could somehow carry both Creeps and himself he did not see how they were all going to escape this hellish place. Getting back was going to prove difficult, if not impossible.

Jazzraeli informed them that it was going to be at least another three days before they would get back to the Shaab-Utu colossus. Occasionally their guide would stop and gaze back, ears pricked up as though he had detected something closing in on them, but whenever Everus turned to look he saw nothing. Despite the ongoing ache and the almost crippling tiredness in his body, he could discern that their guide was becoming increasingly detached and agitated, pacing far out in front.

The sands soon gave way to a stretch of rough, the way onwards rocky and uneven. Scoured rock formations, their surfaces marked in places with ancient fossil imprints, stuck up from the ground.

Creeps snored and sat slumped in his saddle.

Indefatigably, Jazzraeli led them on.

After another two leagues or so, Everus had to call a halt. Exhausted, he threw himself to the baking-hot ground. Not for the first time, he wished he had just threatened Ib-irem into telling him how to destroy Xethorn when he had the chance, rather than having to bust his balls and wear his feet to the bone playing fetch. From past experience, he knew how persuasive a blade to the throat could be. "Jazzraeli!" he shouted. "We need to stop for a while." On his knees, he watched as their guide turned and began to head back. He had never felt so weary in all of his life. Every muscle seemed deadened and the pain from the Blood Orb, staved off only slightly by the salamander oil, seemed to have drained him of energy. His mind was swimming in pulsing waves of flashing red agony. If they could just get out from this blasted light.

"*We must go!*" screeched Jazzracli. "Something stirs in the desert. A great evil from Khasekh follows us." He stared, wide-eyed at the unending, broken wastes they had just covered. "You must get up."

His face chaffed and blistered, Everus turned to look. All he could see was wavering red rocks and red sand. There was nothing else. Nothing. Nevertheless, unsteadily, he got to his feet – that still cogent part of his mind telling him that he could not rest. Not yet. "How much further?" he groaned.

Before Jazzraeli could answer, something erupted from the ground nearby in an explosion of stone and sand. It was partially invisible and yet Everus could sense that the thing was huge and that it emanated an animalistic evil and a desire to devour. Fear fuelled his actions, his survival instincts temporarily lending him the energy to flee. Screaming, he leapt over a loose pile of rocks, lost his footing and tumbled painfully into a small ravine. Grazed and bleeding, he desperately scrambled to his feet.

He heard the sounds of Creeps shouting and Jazzraeli screeching.

A camel's bray was cut short by a horrible rending, rasping sound.

Heart racing, Everus pulled himself clear of the crevasse. Rocks cracked and fell away as the entity rushed towards him, compressing the baked air around it. He began running, aware that the partially invisible predator was in pursuit, as though it exuded a tangible menace; a solid wave of terror, which precipitated its arrival.

Staggering and stumbling, he fell once again, crashing down in a cloud of dust into a shallow-lipped crater. His palms were bloody from the landing and the pain in his knees and his left leg in particular was excruciating.

For a moment all was quiet.

Everus lay silent, knowing full well that such a monster was beyond his abilities to battle, especially in his current condition. He could only hope that it was not now chewing up his travelling companions for, by the sounds of it, the camel had already been devoured. Aching, he crouched low, unable to see anything beyond the rim of the bowl-shaped depression. He thought he heard Jazzraeli's voice once again and then nothing. Somehow, he had to escape, but first he had to clamber out of the crater. He was just about to start the climb when, to his horror, the giant, barely visible snake-thing slithered down into the crater over to his right.

It hissed and sped towards him, hesitating a moment as though savouring its triumph over the one who had defiled Khasekh by his mere presence and slain its undead ruler. Briefly, its transparency darkened, taking on a deep crimson hue. Then, with a sickening retch, it vomited the remains of the camel directly at Everus, plastering him to the crater wall with gobbets of gruesome gore.

Horror-stricken, Everus scrabbled to wipe the worst of the sticky mess from his face and pull the camel's ropey intestines from his chest.

The entity sped forward, its blood-spattered, lamprey-like mouth gnashing.

"Catch it an' drink it!" shouted Creeps from above.

Through the blood-drenched chaos, Everus looked up, his will and reflexes tested to the extreme as he caught a small glass vial. Without hesitation, he flipped out the loose cork and poured the watery liquid down his throat, not knowing or caring what it was. Instantly, he rocked back and his feet rose from the ground.

The invisible horror rushed to get him, colliding with the rock face as he ascended above it. It reared higher but Everus was now clear of it.

Now well above the crater, Everus was surprised to see the thief floating unsteadily close by.

Swimming through the air with wobbling strokes, Creeps drew closer. "*Gads!* Ye're all covered in innards!"

With some difficulty, Everus began to propel himself forward.

There was a weird, weightless feeling in his stomach and he felt as though he was going to spin, unable as he was to anchor himself to anything. Peering down, he could see traces of the massive, multiple-headed worm-like fiend below as it scoured the desert and created huge 'sidewinder' tracks in the depression below. The terror drained from him as he realised they were safe. He looked in vain to spot Jazzraeli. "Where's...?" he asked.

"Yer man?" replied Creeps. "This is his potion we're usin'. I think there should be enough to get us back most o' the way an' it'll be a damn sight easier than walkin'." He reached into a pocket and looked at the small amount of liquid left in a bottle. "There's no' that much left. I think he was keepin' it to himsel'."

"Is he dead?"

"Aye...the thing swallowed him. It took the camel an' all. It were bloody horrible. Anyhow, yer man went for his potion an' tried to fly away, but guess what? Ye'll no' fly on piss an' water." Creeps gave an unpleasant smile.

"What do you mean? You'd switched them?"

"First thing I did when I overheard ye an' him talkin' about his last trip out 'ere. Thought to masel', aye, I bet ye've got some interestin' things in yer bags, an' sure enough, look what I found."

"What a bastard. You're becoming as bad as me." Everus flew into a thermal, the heated updraft spiralling him skywards. He found the heat no longer crippling, a side effect of the potion. Additionally, his strength was returning. He levelled out once more, eyes scanning the far off horizon for the Shaab-Utu colossus; a landmark for which to steer. He saw it and started out, rapidly getting the hang of this unnatural locomotion.

"Steady on! I'm no' used to this," called Creeps. "An' don't fly too high in case the blasted magic runs out. I don't want to end up fallin' an' breakin' ma neck after all we've been through."

CHAPTER FOURTEEN

"Yes, yes. This is it." Nodding to himself, Emir Ib-irem examined the age-worn sheet of papyrus, his eyes darting over its many lines of miniscule, pictorial script.

Standing upright, his arms folded across his chest, Everus waited.

"Many thanks for obtaining this for me. With this I will be able to legitimise my rule over the Western Tribes...and possibly the ghâr-ghârs as well. And, as promised, I will give you the information that you requested." Ib-irem paused for a moment and cleared his throat, clearly thinking how to proceed. "As you will know, killing gods is not easy, in fact, I reason it to be impossible, or at least, beyond the powers of a mortal. However, Xethorn, whom my people call The Dark Efreet, is not a true god. He is one of many who were once mortal, yet due to their powers and abilities they were elevated to the position of demigods. Each of these demigods was given a sphere of power; a domain to rule, by The High Three. The Dark Efreet, Xethorn, was given murder, one in which hate and vengeance run hand in hand. His worshippers are assassins and cutthroats...scum of every description."

Everus contained a smile.

"I know of but two ways to vanquish such an entity," the emir continued. "The first, and by far the easiest, is to do direct battle with Him. In order to succeed you will need access to a vast amount of magical protection."

"And the second?"

"The second would necessitate you...or someone else, becoming a demigod. Thus, in effect, having The High Three substitute another for Xethorn. In which case Xethorn will be obliterated from memory. It will be as though He had never been."

Everus was interested. "And...in order for someone to become a demigod, to replace Xethorn, what would they have to do? How would one attract the likes of The High Three? Go on an unstoppable killing spree? Murder the inhabitants of entire countries?" Even before he had asked his questions, he thought about Creeps and the latter's connection with the omnipotent creator gods. Did he know about this and if so, why had he not mentioned it before?

"Probably...that is why I would strongly advise the first alternative. That is, if you're as dedicated to this cause as you seem to be, for I take it your journey to Khasekh was not all that pleasant?"

"It could've been better."

"Understandable." Ib-irem reached to one side and drew his hookah towards him. Once within reach, he fed the pipe into his mouth and inhaled, his azure eyes blurring temporarily. He removed the mouth-piece. "Are you familiar with the legends of Cyrvilus? For only something as potent as the hand of Cyrvilus will grant you the magical protection needed to face Xethorn, although obtaining it may prove...difficult."

Everus nodded, for he knew only too well the unholy fables and the dark myths which surrounded that name. According to legend, it had been Cyrvilus, a powerful demonologist from Zeth, who had breached the planar boundary in order to invite The Daemon God, Uhu'giaggoth, into the world. It had been he who had initiated the divine conflict which had culminated in The Hellspawn Cataclysm. To many, he was the first of the Uhu'giaggothian worshippers; the progenitor of that unwholesome, demonic cult.

The emir continued. "Then you will undoubtedly know that it was Cyrvilus who all but finished Xethorn. Indeed, had it not been for the intervention of The High Three, The Dark Efreet would have been slaughtered there and then. However, if the tales are true, even as Cyrvilus turned to face The High Three, with The Daemon God, Uhu'giaggoth, rending the Heavens asunder, Xethorn severed Cyrvilus' hand, forcing the demonologist to flee. Alas, the fate of Cyrvilus remains a mystery. Some tales relate his later murder at the hands of Xethorn, prior to His own imprisonment. Others tell how he escaped and fled back to Zeth and the other ravaged lands, rebuilding his forces for a Second Summoning. A third tale, a rumour I overheard when I was..."

"I deal with facts, not rumour. Just tell me where I can find the hand. It wouldn't be nearby would it?" Everus interrupted, a wry grin on his face. He seemed to remember that at least part of it used to be on display in The Grand Repository in Ghavin's Keep.

"Well, yes and no. We're talking about a powerfact, a relic from the time of The Hellspawn Cataclysm, not something likely to be haggled over at the local bazaar." The emir laughed to himself as he took a date from a tray nearby and slipped it between his leathery lips. He reached for something within the confines of his gown. On a length of chain, there dangled a knobbly lump of bone, yellowed with age. He snapped the chain and presented it to Everus. "The forefinger. Only it, in conjunction with its composites, possesses the magical power needed to do battle with a demigod."

† † †

Drawing the entry curtain to their small room aside, Everus stood, framed for a moment in the archway, his face set in a brooding scowl as though something was very wrong.

Creeps took his pipe from his mouth. "And? How'd it go?"

"Well. This is going to be fun," snarled Everus. He entered the room, paced over to the window and stared out at the gathering dusk, his eyes lynx-like. He watched and waited, gathering his thoughts before turning around. "According to the brat, Xethorn can be defeated..."

"Well, that's all right then," interrupted Creeps.

"I haven't finished," said Everus, harshly. "In order to defeat Him we need to obtain the hand of Cyrvilus – a potent magical relic from the time of The Hellspawn Cataclysm. Only its power will ensure success against the bastard."

"An'...I take it yer man told ye where ye can find this thing?" guessed Creeps, tentatively.

"No. He suggested we should just walk out into the desert and hope it finds us," Everus replied, sarcastically. "Of course he did, you idiot! Part of it's in The Grand Repository in Ghavin's Keep."

"What do ye mean, part o' it? A hand's a hand." The thief looked at his own right hand and flexed it as though to make sure it was still there.

Everus shook his head, clearly annoyed. "That's the problem. It was broken into several pieces. Part of it's in Ghavin's Keep. Ib-irem said that another part is now in the possession of a Sawerrean sisterhood. They rule from a nunnery or some such in Wathang-Hu, many leagues south of Ghavin's Keep."

"*Wathang-Hu?* Never heard o' it."

"*Shut up and let me continue!*" snapped Everus. "Another fragment belongs to a Hyadean warlord called Bhubbaal. He now rules over a citadel in the old grubban land of Gossothus, east of The Deadmoor Clumps. A dangerous place and a dangerous character, by all accounts. I remember reading something about his ancestors. They were a degenerate bunch of demon-worshippers who allied themselves to the followers of Uhu'giaggoth."

Creeps scratched his head. "So, what do we...?"

"I haven't finished yet." Everus flinched as a desert wasp buzzed past his face. "Another piece is known to lie somewhere in the vicinity of Stranglewood." Angrily, he swatted the irksome insect away.

"Quite the quest we've got in front of us," muttered Creeps. "That's if ye still plan on goin' for Him."

It was a pointless question for it was abundantly clear from the look in Everus' eyes that he was. "Do you think *you're* up for it?" he asked.

Creeps slouched down onto his bed with a sigh. "What choice do I have? Ye know that Wyrm's Port's the only home for me. There's nothin' for me 'ere...nothin' but this blasted sun an' dust. The ale tastes like camel piss. The food's all curried an' covered in spices that give me the shits. Ye can't get any decent smoke an' the stuff that ye can get makes yer bloody eyeballs crawl. It's enough to drive a man mad."

"Can we count on your...*helpers?*"

Creeps scratched his neck, his skin peeling in places. Like Everus, he too had been badly burned by the Blood Orb, but thankfully the red streaks on their faces were now diminishing. "How many times have I told ye? I've lost all contact wi' 'em. Ye could say they've used me, abused me an' left me for dead. It's as if they've no need o' me any more. Ye see, things were obviously different when 'em nutters ye worked for tried to summon The Daemon God. Aye, they needed ma help then. But now, well, they seem to be content wi' lettin' Xethorn rule Wyrm's Port. I guess in the big scheme o' things He's fairly insignificant. Who knows, maybe it's in their interests to let Him remain there?"

Everus gave a grim smile. "Well, I guess they're going to be disappointed." Keeping his eyes on the circling wasp, he lashed out and caught it, crushing it in his hand.

† † †

That night, he dreamt of blood. He watched as the world he knew turned red, as it was embraced in a viscous, frothy ichor. Everywhere he looked, from his vantage point high in the sky, he could see the world transforming before him into an incarnadine ocean. Soon, all that remained above, marooned on its own island, was the city of Wyrm's Port.

He stared in awe, as from out of the city he knew so well, there poured more and more blood. A seemingly endless flood spewed from its many gutters and gargoyle spouts. The red fluid belched forth from reeking vents and, geyser-like, shot high into the air from countless chimneys.

Fascinated, and yet not of his own will, he was drawn closer. With agonising clarity, he saw, within the blood-drenched city, a skeletal army of giants brewing and stoking, butchering and processing. People were dragged to their knees and slaughtered like cattle – their blood drained, cycled and segregated through an elaborate system of pipes and columns. Like effluent, the blood from some was discarded. That not wasted was further treated and...

✝ ✝ ✝

Everus sprang awake, lathered in a cold sweat, his skin damp and clammy. The nightmare visions refused to fade from his mind and it was only when he heard Creeps rise from the bed opposite that he felt his own senses returning. Rubbing his eyes, he heard the thief stumble to the window, before being violently sick. He watched as the shorter man's shoulders heaved as, convulsing, he purged his innards. *Was he retching up blood?* he thought to himself.

After a few more heaves, Creeps turned around, his face ashen. Spittle drooled from his lips. "*Gads.* I don't feel well." Moaning, he dragged himself back to his bed and, unsteadily, slumped down, his head in his hands.

Everus sat up. "What's the matter?"

"Bad night. Bad dreams."

"What sort of dreams?" For a moment, Everus wondered whether Creeps had seen what he had and, if so, what was the meaning, if there was one, behind it? Was it possible for two people to dream the same dream? Despite his own bizarre experiences, his common sense quickly forced him to dismiss that notion. Things were weird enough, without having to go down that route. He had to remain focused, otherwise he may as well just abandon everything here and now.

"Horrible things. Monsters. It were bad." Creeps' shoulders shuddered and it looked as though he was going to be sick again. "I'll be all right." Raising his head, he started taking in a few deep breaths. However, he had no sooner wiped the spittle from his lips and chin when he leapt to his feet and dashed to the window once more. After spewing up whatever was left, he turned with a certain look of relief on his face. A look of relief which quickly turned to surprise on seeing that Everus had already dressed and was now buckling on his boots.

"I plan on leaving as soon as possible." The nightmare had Everus rattled, for he clearly believed there was some significance, some catastrophic meaning behind it. He rarely dreamed, or rather, rarely remembered their content and even now, fully awake, he could still see in his mind the bloody images before him. Whatever the explanation, it acted as a catalyst to get him going. "We'll join one of the trading caravans bound for Ullerby. Once there, we should be able to get a ship to take us to Trade Peak."

"Don't talk to me about ships." Creeps' face took on a distinctly greenish hue at the mere thought.

"If we don't go by boat we're looking at a journey of a thousand leagues or more, across some of the harshest terrain this side of the cracks of Zeth. We'd have to circumnavigate the entire western shore of The Dark Sea from here to the Falls of Sin-Dracotho. No, it has to be by ship."

Creeps groaned at the prospect.

† † †

They left Umm-Dabba shortly after midday and, four days later, they eventually left the desert, bound for the eastern port city of Ullerby. The caravan they had joined was a small one run by an aged and withered merchant by the name of Hajee, who, along with his three sons, had made this journey several times. It was a hard way to scratch out an existence, never mind a profit; the constant travelling and the threat of raiders making it all the more dangerous. Hence, when Everus had offered to act as a free bodyguard for the trip, Hajee had jumped at the proposition.

One night, as they sat around the blazing campfire, the old merchant asked them why they were so keen to reach Ullerby, a city that, for some reason, it was clear he held in low esteem. "For we'll be there in another eight or nine days and, believe me, it's the pits. It's a wreck. A nothing. A blight on the face of the empire. I only go in order to sell some of my rugs and spices," said Hajee, his words having to fight their way through a cloud of eye-stinging cigar smoke.

Finishing off another mouthful of undercooked stew, Everus reached for the canteen of cheap ale, a slightly confused look on his face. "Drugs...*and rices?*"

Hajee laughed. "No. Rugs and spices. Cinnamon. Paprika. Widow's Whiff. That kind of stuff."

Everus finished drinking and corked the container. The ale he had drank not so much washing down the stew but rather diluting it, taking away the sour taste it left in his mouth. He was convinced it was dog. "We need to join a ship. We've got...*business*...in Trade Peak."

The old merchant grinned and gestured to one of his sons. The youth scurried forward and gave his father a small wooden box in which he kept his potent, Mhaazi-cactus cigars. "Now Trade Peak's a nice town. Well at least it used to be. Don't know what it's like nowadays after that business with the Øggars and things." With a shake of his head, Hajee lit up. "I don't have any truck with those southern cities any more."

"What about Gossothus?" Everus asked. Every bit of information he could find out now was going to be a bonus.

"*Gossothus?*" Hajee pulled his poncho tighter, his old bones feeling the chill of late evening. "What makes you think I've been out that way? That's a bad place, by all accounts."

"Do you know of anyone who has?"

"Well, it's funny you should ask because there's a man in Ullerby who may be able to tell you a bit about that wild place. I'm pretty sure he once mentioned something about going out that way once...or maybe it was something to do with where he came from? Can't think for the life of me what he was doing out there. Probably adventuring or some such."

"I may be interested in meeting this man."

"Well I could introduce you, but I should warn you, he's one of them magic-men. He knows spells and things. Somebody once told me he kept demons in his cellar. Of course, I couldn't comment. As long as he pays good money, I'm more than happy to provide him with whatever he needs. Why, business is bad enough without me going around angering my customers."

As Everus was giving this some thought, wondering whether it was an avenue worth pursuing, Creeps arrived. The thief had spent most of the evening cheating at dice and 'winning' a small fortune from the merchant's sons.

Hajee reached into his cigar box for a cigar, lit one with the one he was smoking and gave it to the thief. "Were you lucky?"

Creeps patted his pouch and grinned. Puffing on his cigar, he sat down next to them.

"I hope you're not leading my sons into bad habits. They can ill afford to gamble their hard earned money away."

"*Bad habits?* From this man?" Everus laughed. He wafted away a cloud of stinging cigar smoke. "By this time tomorrow night they'll be picking their arses and stealing the wheels from your wagon."

✝ ✝ ✝

Fortunately for all concerned, neither of Everus' predictions came true and eventually the small caravan crested the hill above Ullerby. The journey had taken only six days, thanks to the improving terrain, the more temperate weather and the fact that Everus encouraged the merchant to keep going that little bit further each day, eager as he was to be off on his quest to find the pieces of the hand of Cyrvilus.

Ullerby was a small port, now living in the shadow of its once-prosperous history. Ten years ago it had been a bustling town, one that could commercially hold its own with the other imperial trading ports dotted along the coastline of The Dark Sea, namely; Wyrm's Port, Chid-B'hara, Trade Peak, Port Laafaenburg, Um-Kombo and The City of the Glittering Spire. Founded by pioneering seafarers close to the rich veins of marble a short distance inland, its early rulers had capitalised on the port's unique location, ensuring a steady flow of wealth and trade into the town. Perhaps the rulers' most famous achievement and one of which Ullerby was justly proud, was the construction of an entire temple, which had been transported, by sea, to Wyrm's Port.

Its glory days were long gone, however, and as Everus gazed down on the fog-wreathed hulk of the town below him, he wondered what had caused its decline.

"Welcome to sunny Ullerby. A paradise to rival any other," announced Hajee, presenting the town to them.

"What a place." Creeps puffed on one of the merchant's cigars. They were hit by the tang of strong sea air.

A change in the direction of the wind began to disperse the fog, allowing weak sunlight to filter down from the clouds above, and enabling them to better discern the old buildings, with their rotting timberwork and faded colours. Looking down, they could see the occasional marble building – providing some proof of the port's affluent history – but for the most part, Ullerby was a wreck. It made Everus think of some great ark which had run aground on a desolate island, only to have been forgotten about and left to decay.

In the distance a bell began to toll, the sound strangely eerie and unsettling, as though it announced feeding time to rows of dark, gibbering, shambling things. Things like the dreaded, rag-covered Scabby-Daggy men, who haunted the plague-ridden alleys of folkloric coastal towns. In his mind, Everus could see the batrachian zombie-folk with their blank, fish-like eyes and their wide, drooling mouths, as they skulked down twisting alleys or crawled from cellars, their appetites now awakened.

They entered the town's main gate, receiving nothing but a grunt and a nod from the sullen, sour-faced guard on duty.

Arthritically, Hajee got down from the driver's seat of his covered wagon. "Here we are my friends, the end of the road...and here we part." He shook Everus' hand. "I hope you get your ship to Trade Peak, though I'd warn you, after the invasion of Wyrm's Port, it may prove harder than you think." He hugged Creeps. Fighting back the urge to choke from the man's stink, he managed a smile. "You've taught my sons a valuable, if expensive, lesson. Goodbye, my friend."

"Aye, good riddance."

The old merchant read the humour in the thief's face and laughed. By contrast, Everus' face was cold and unsmiling, as though he were waiting for something. "Yes, yes. I nearly forgot. My customer. If you still wish to find him, his name is Mhoon. Ask for him at The Beached Kraken tavern on the seafront." With a final wave of his hand, Hajee and his sons headed off further into town, leaving Everus and the thief on their own.

"Now what?" asked Creeps, surveying the squalid buildings around the square in which they stood.

"We find this tavern he spoke of," answered Everus. He sniffed. "I guess it's this way."

Heading for the seafront, they made their way towards a fairly large market area. It was a hub of activity, densely packed with dour-faced men and women, all busy either preparing this morning's catch of fish or selling vegetables and other day-to-day goods and commodities. One nearby alley was completely blocked by a team of women shucking oysters at a ferocious pace. Elsewhere, people walked to and fro, buying and haggling, doing their best to stretch their measly coppers as far as possible.

A thick, clogging reek of fish guts and cat piss hung in the air.

At one end of the market was a garishly painted, poster-covered, wooden caravan with a smoking chimney. From an open hatch, a bald-headed grubba was preparing and selling all manner of foodstuff.

"Dram's Delicacies," said Everus, eyeing the caravan and reading aloud the bold legend painted over its door. He was hungry for something other than Hajee's dubious stew. "I wonder what unpalatable rubbish he has on the menu?"

"Aye, I'm starvin'." With uncanny adroitness, Creeps pick-pocketed a passing vendor of his recent takings. "Let's get summat to eat."

Dressed in a stained apron, the grubba smiled broadly as Everus and Creeps walked over. He was fat and ugly and, like most of his breed, he had a substantial growth of dark beard which bristled like a wire brush. Behind him, a large pan of onions smoked and spat, filling the crammed interior with eye-watering fumes. "How're ye doin' mateys? So, what'll it be ma happy, smilin' friends?" He rubbed his greasy hands. "I've got onion pie. Eel sausages. Garlic buns. Onion stew. Mushroom pie." He ticked off each on his fingers as he spoke. "Chipped dungsticks. Pickled toads. Badger bollocks...or maybe ye want to go for an Ullerby Special, summat to really get yer...?"

"*Everus!* Look, it's..." Creeps stood rigid, as though paralysed, pointing to one of the posters on the caravan.

"*What!?*" Everus turned to look. There, amidst the other tattered and yellowing posters, he saw the face of a man, and something else, something so grotesque it would be sure to put the squeamish off their food.

"It's Tarby. Tarby the man!"

"Indeed it is. The dummy with the tit obsession...and Roach."

Suddenly reminded of the monstrous ventriloquist and his bizarre puppet, Everus joined the thief in an almost trance-like stare. It was only when the bearded takeaway owner leaned over to see what all the fuss was about, that he broke from the pair on the poster's gaze.

"What is it? Ye seen summat o' interest on ma hut?" inquired the grubba. "I'm sponsored by some of 'em folk."

Creeps pointed at the poster. "Ye see *him*? We've seen him in Wyrm's Port...aye, an' we killed him."

"Was his act that bad?" asked Dram, nonchalantly picking his nose.

"It were bloody brilliant," replied Creeps. "Best thing I've ever seen. I chuckled so much I wet ma pants. That Tarby ended up stabbin' him. Ye should o' seen the mess. Blood an' guts all o'er the place. Anyhow, what about summat to eat?"

"Yes. What about one of your...Ullerby Specials?" said Everus, a look of disgust on his face.

"Of course. Good choice. Two Ullerby Specials comin' right up." The grubba delved a little deeper into a nostril, extracted a runny bogy, looked with some alarm at it and then rather embarrassingly rubbed it on his apron. He grinned before turning his back on them to start making their snack. A short time later, he turned around, two large buns filled with damp fried eggs, mushrooms, pickled herrings, mushy peas and rat livers wrapped in fatty bacon, in his dirty hands. "There ye are gents. They'll be sure to get yer mouths waterin'. Smell good, don't they?" He handed them over. "That'll be four copper."

Everus gave the grubba the money. With faint revulsion, he studied the leaking, oily, smelly bun in his grip. Tentatively, he raised it to his mouth, the stench and the sound of Creeps' munching contributing to its overall unpleasantness. He was about to take his first bite when Creeps let out a startled cry.

"*Gads!* It's lookin' at me!" Creeps had peeled back his bun and was staring at what looked like a watery, bloodshot eye. Revolted, he threw it to the ground and began stomping on it as though in order to make sure it was dead.

"What's up?" asked the grubba, busy cutting a string of mouldy sausages. "Ye don't like it?" He then had to shield himself with a frying pan as Everus' hurled bun came flying back at him.

✝ ✝ ✝

The food and the service at The Beached Kraken was a slight improvement, even if the tavern itself was untidy and filled with all manner of unsavoury individuals – and that was *before* Everus and Creeps entered. The tavern was the oldest in Ullerby and looked it. It had stood opposite the old, barnacle-encrusted pier for some twelve generations, its name having originated from the day, some three hundred years ago, when the unsuspecting Ullerbians had woken one morning to find an immature kraken washed up on the beach. A team of twenty or so locals had dragged the bloated, slimy thing from the beach with the intention of taking it to the local taxidermist, who, it was claimed, had keeled over and died the moment he saw it.

The giant, squid-like sea monster was now housed in a large tank behind the bar. It was both an awe-inspiring and a repulsive sight, and on more than one occasion a tipsy patron had sworn that he had seen its plate-sized, inky eye move.

"Some beast," said Creeps, tucking into his plate of cod, crab and wild lettuce. He washed his mouthful down with a glug of ale. "It's a funny lookin' thing all the same."

Everus turned in his chair so that he could see it better. On the ceiling above him was stretched a huge cargo net in which smaller stuffed and imitation sea creatures; lobsters, giant starfish, large crabs and lesser Ullerbian crocothrashes, were trapped. It was a crude form of decoration, but at least it served to camouflage the smoke stains.

"I'd bet that beak could give ye a nasty nip."

"I think it's dead." Everus rose from his chair. "I'll get some more drinks. If I scream then you'll know it's got me."

The barman saw him approaching. "Same again, sir?" He was a tall and spindly man attired in a fairly expensive dinner jacket that was more than a little incongruous in these surroundings.

"Yes." Everus sat down on one of the high stools, next to an old drunkard who stared forlornly into his tankard.

"She's quite somethin', is she not?" The barman nodded to the preserved carcass in the tank behind him as he finished pouring the drinks. "Used to draw in the crowds from all over she did. Folk'd come from far an' wide just to say that they'd seen her." Sadly, he shook his head. "Not many come nowadays."

"They found it on the beach?"

"Well, it sure wasn't under ma bed." The barman laughed at his own joke. "It were just out there, near to where the pier now stands.

Must o' been some job gettin' it off the beach an' in here." He rapped the display case with his knuckles. "Ye see this? A wizard made this. Tougher than stone it is."

"Impressive." Everus rested his tankard on the bar. "I'm looking for a man named Mhoon."

"*Mhoon?* Why...that's him, there." The barman nodded to the seated drunk.

Oblivious to their conversation, Mhoon continued to stare into his empty tankard. His face was lined and slightly tanned and there was little doubt it belonged to someone who had lived a strange and varied life, far removed from the rest of the other Ullerbians. His hair was long, greying and looked as though it had probably never been combed or brushed. The hand that gripped the tankard was intricately tattooed, the fingers dirty but delicate, confirming Everus' impression that they belonged to someone who cared little for heavy manual work. He had all the hallmarks of a down-trodden wizard.

"I'd like a word." Everus looked into Mhoon's eyes. There was more life in the solitary eye of the tentacled monster of the deep on display.

"Ye're wastin' yer time," commented the barman. "He's been like that for quite a while now. Won't talk to nob'dy."

"Then he might talk to *somebody*. *Me*, for instance." Everus waved a hand in front of Mhoon's blank face, getting no reaction whatsoever. "Does anybody know what's happened to him?"

Nervously, the barman looked about. He leaned closer, his words little more than a whisper. "First off, ye didn't hear this from me. Right?" He gulped. "Rumour is, the hag at the end o' the pier has put a spell on him. Cursed him. Some say that she's stolen his mind. Course, nob'dy plans on goin' to find out if it's true. I mean, we all like Mhoon...but, well, it'd take someb'dy wi' a bit more bottle than what we've got to face *her*."

Creeps walked up and snatched his drink from the bar, clearly annoyed at having to wait for it.

"Creeps...meet Mhoon. Mhoon, meet Creeps," said Everus.

"Aye, glad to know ye." The thief poured half of his drink down his throat, pleased to be back on his regular ales and beers rather than the weak, heavily-watered, camel piss drinks he had been forced to endure in Umm-Dabba. Questioningly, he looked at Mhoon. "So, who's this? Is this the man ye're lookin' for? An' what's up wi' him? Looks as though he's swallowed a turd or summat."

301

Ignoring Creeps, Everus turned to the barman. "What else can you tell me about this...*hag?*"

"Not so loud." The barman winced and fluttered with his hands, clearly rattled.

"What hag's this?" asked Creeps.

"*Shhhh!* Gods preserve us!" With a pained look, as though he had just crossed a room of broken bottles barefoot, the barman muttered a prayer and grasped a small, fish-shaped talisman that hung from a chain around his neck. "Like I told ye, she lives in a small shack at the end o' the pier. It's said that she eats babies an' things raw from the sea."

"Why has no one gone after her? What about the militia?" inquired Everus.

"Gone," answered the barman, flatly. "Most o' what militia we had we sent south to help wi' the troubles in Wyrm's Port. No one ever returned. On top o' that, our remainin' defences were wiped out by those bloody pirates from Tavocos. Now you look big an' strappin' an' I see that ye've got a sword. So, if ye wanted to go an'...well...see what ye can do, then be my guest. I'd warn against it though."

Creeps finished his ale. "What say ye, Everus? Do ye think we should go an' have a word wi' this bitch? It's been a couple o' days since I last put on ma arse-kickin' boots."

Purposefully, Everus made for the exit.

† † †

The tide was coming in, bringing with it the strong stink of the sea. Gulls called out to one another and circled overhead, landing occasionally to devour some leftover. Dark grey clouds gusted from the north, bringing with them the threat of heavy showers.

The sight of the old pier made Everus think of some dead and rotting creature – something that, like the beached kraken, had been vomited from the dark, cold depths. Built almost entirely from timber, its skeletal, barnacle-encrusted supports and framework creaked and groaned as though at any time the whole rickety structure was liable to collapse. Parts of it already had. The remnants of decaying arcade-like booths and ramshackle funhouses still stood at its entrance, revealing that it had been modified into a place of entertainment, as opposed to one for the mere harbouring of boats.

"What kind o' place is this?" asked Creeps.

"The Ullerby Pier," answered Everus, striding forward. "It used to be quite famous as a place where people came in search of pleasure and thrills. Though by the looks of it, I'd guess those days are long past. It started as nothing more than a jetty...where fishermen and the like would moor their boats. Over the years, and as the town became wealthier, it transformed...into this." He stopped short of the main entrance and looked up at the large, wind and rain battered jester's face that stared down at them ominously from the huge facade above the archway. Despite the poor state it was in, there remained something deeply unsettling about it – something about the eyes and the menacing smile.

Everus crossed under the jester's grinning face and strode out onto the pier proper. The wooden, seagull-shit-covered boards groaned under his feet. "I'd watch your step. Some of these old timbers may not be that safe." All around was a realm of decaying madness. To his right, he saw a boarded-up building. A crooked sign over the door identified it as Creepy Geezer's House of Horrors. To his left leaned a row of small vandalised booths. From the fading paintwork on their facades, he could tell that they had at one time been stalls where people could participate in minor feats of skill in order to win small prizes.

"There's some *real* weird shit 'ere." Creeps lit one of his cigars; he had filched a couple of boxes from Hajee's supply. "There's nothin' like this in Wyrm's Port."

Turning the handle to the House of Horrors, Everus found it to be locked, a row of peeling, shrunken heads peering from a lattice window seemed to look outraged at their intrusion. Everywhere he looked, he could see more tattered and unsafe structures, the sheer level of decrepitude making him wonder once more just how rapidly the town had degenerated.

Posters on the walls gave details of past attractions – highlighting the importance the pier had once played in the life of Ullerbian entertainment. From this evidence, it appeared that Roach and Uncle Tarby had featured here frequently during the city's heyday, starring alongside such renowned comics as The Ullerby Slappers and Wormdoddy the Knobbly Joker.

One of the boards Creeps stood on cracked. He managed to leap aside, but only onto another rickety part. Immediately, the damp planks buckled and gave way and, with a snap and a cry, he fell through the gaping, jagged-edged hole. Luckily, he managed to grab the sides, saving himself from a nasty drop onto the litter-strewn shingle far below. Hauling himself clear, he scraped his left arm on one of the many protruding nails. Biting down on his cigar, he grimaced and tentatively made it to a safer stretch of boardwalk.

"You all right?" asked Everus.

"Aye. Just cut ma arm. Bastard place!" The thief walked over and joined Everus. His arm was badly grazed and he walked with a slight limp. "Ye any idea what ye're goin' to say to this bint?"

"I'll ask her to reverse the enchantment. If she proves uncooperative…" A sudden bloodcurdling wail stopped Everus dead in his tracks. Paralysed, his heart temporarily stopped beating. Wide-eyed, he stared at the ghastly thing floating down towards them, the repugnant stench of dead fish and brine-soaked algae making his eyes weep.

The Ullerby hag was draped in long lengths of glistening seaweed, its dried pods and nodules alive with small crabs and sea lice. Her face, along with the rest of her loathsome skin, was a nauseating green, broken in places with patches of mottled olive. Her eyes were black and soulless and yet within them there burned a hatred for all living things. "Who is this?" she gargled. "More warm flesh come to feed me?" The fiend bared needle-sharp teeth, rivulets of watery fluid dribbling from her mouth.

Everus could now feel the gradual reawakening of his senses. Body trembling, he fought against the sheer, almost overpowering horror the witch exuded.

"Oi! Missus! Have a bit o' this!" cried Creeps, hobbling forward and stabbing out with his dagger.

The hag flinched away, swinging up her claws in defence. Clumps of seaweed crumbled and fell about her scabrous feet.

Free now from the hag's powerful gaze, Everus spurred himself into action. Withdrawing his sword, he rushed past Creeps and barged into the crone, sending her flying to the damp floor. He kicked her hard in the stomach and, two-handedly, raised his sword high above his head.

The hag vanished.

Bewildered, Everus looked about, his eyes searching.

"Get yer back to a wall!" shouted Creeps.

Violently, Everus was grabbed from behind, nails like sharks' teeth at his throat. His sword was knocked from his grip.

Dexterously, he flipped the hideous bitch over his shoulder, crashing her to the boards once more.

Creeps stabbed her in the back as she began to get up.

The hag screamed, the terrible sound filled with undercurrents of darkness and doom-laden anguish.

Although he had only once been to sea, Everus' mind was flooded with haunting images of rock-shattered wrecks and drowning sailors. A wave of nausea struck him and he staggered, failing to get in the death blow, for in that moment's hesitation, the hag vanished a second time.

"Where's she away to now?" asked Creeps, ready with his dagger.

Everus shook the disturbing images from his mind. "I don't know."

"Gnaw ye raw, I will," came a snarling voice from atop one of the rotting booths. She laughed and spat, fish tails and dark drool dripping from her mouth. "Aye...I'll chew on yer marrows." A clawed hand rested on one of the many horrible, wooden clown cut-outs.

"Come on then!" challenged Everus. "Get down here and I'll slice you to pieces."

"Why don't ye come an' get me?" she taunted, shaking her unsightly, flabby breasts and throwing a kiss like a street corner harlot. Tilting her head, she gave a horrible laugh – which sounded more like lumpy sewage gurgling down a drain.

"Now's the time I wish I'd a bow an' arrow," muttered Creeps.

"Catch this!" Fast as a striking snake, Everus reached into his boot, removed his dagger and threw it. The weapon struck home, thudding into the hag's left hand, pinning it to the laughing clown's head. "Hah! Who's laughing now?"

Cursing, the witch painfully pulled free the blade. Whimpering, she sucked the wound before disappearing once again.

† † †

"No luck?" asked the barman of The Beached Kraken, pouring an ale.

"We'll get her." Creeps gripped his tankard. "Aye...we'll get her."

Blankly, Everus gazed at the monstrous display. Even his cold-heartedness had unprepared him for the gruesome discoveries he and the thief had made in the hag's hut. There they had found human

305

remains crawling with sea lice and other decaying, slithering, reeking things. And as for the pincered abomination the thief had disentangled from the witch's cauldron...Everus doubted whether he would ever eat lobster again.

"She'll rue the day she ever met us," threatened Creeps.

"So what are ye goin' to do next? If ye'd take ma advice, ye'd leave well alone. Ye don't want to be makin' her mad," advised the barman. "Let her stay there an' we'll stay here. That's what I say."

Chewing his bottom lip, Everus gazed into his drink, the booze doing something to erase the foul memories. Was it worth trying to confront the hag once more, in the hope that he could free Mhoon from his bewitchment and thus learn more about Gossothus, where part of the relic he sought resided...or should he just focus his attention on getting passage to Trade Peak? That the witch had powers, he had no doubt.

"Are we goin' to get her?" asked Creeps.

Everus looked at him, then at the slumped figure of Mhoon in his chair, and then at the thief again. He nodded. "Though next time I think it best if we opt for diplomacy."

"Eh?"

"Has anyone ever seen her about town?" Everus asked the barman.

"Why...no. I remember Mhoon once sayin', before he...well, ye know what...that she couldn't leave the pier. It's her home, ye see. I remember him sayin' it'd be like a fish livin' on the land. Don't know what he meant by it though, cause I ain't ever seen no fish on the land. Ye get some women down the market who look like flat-bellied snappers but that's a different matter."

"Hmm." Everus took a drink.

"Ye got an idea?" Creeps asked, patting out the ash from his cigar on the floorboards, an act that did not go unnoticed by Everus. With a nod, he beckoned the thief to follow and together they exited the tavern.

The skies were darkening and the tide was receding as they stood outside, gazing at the cursed pier once more. A chill wind gusted in from the sea and on the storm-lashed horizon they could see flashes of lightning.

Everus strode out towards the entrance, shivering slightly as he passed under the jester's wide-smiling visage. He dropped to one knee in order to feel the planking. On finding the boards damp but not saturated, he nodded to himself.

"What're ye plannin' on doin'?" asked Creeps, despite the fact he already knew.

"Let's say I'm going to make a little bargain. You get back a bit. In the shadows." Everus turned towards the ramshackle booths and arcades. "Listen up, bitch! Return Mhoon's soul or I'll burn this pier to the ground!" he yelled.

For a moment the only response was the groaning of the structure itself as though it had taken offence to the threat. Then the hag appeared. "Ye wouldn't," she growled.

Everus smiled. "*Wouldn't I?* What have I got to lose?"

"Ye daren't."

"Enough of this." Everus turned his head. "Go and get the oil!" he shouted.

"Aye, right ye are," replied Creeps, collaborating in Everus' bluff. "Ye want all forty barrels?" He pulled back out of sight.

"Yes. That should do."

The witch growled, uncertainly. In the poor light, Everus thought he could detect a certain amount of unease in her unsightly features.

"The lads want to know where they've to put 'em?" queried the thief, stepping back into view. "An' how many are they to put underneath?"

"Release Mhoon from your foul enchantment," ordered Everus.

"*Never!*" Wildly, the hag looked about, searching. She became invisible only to reappear elsewhere. Frantic, she ran the length of the pier, looking over its railings every now and then, trying to detect any of the spurious arsonists.

"Is she bitin'?" asked Creeps.

"Not sure. Don't know where she is."

Suddenly, with a scream, the hag appeared no more than five steps in front of them. "*Liars!*" she spat, spraying slimy spit. "Ye think to fool *me!* Ye've no burning water. Ye'll not have soul." She disappeared even as Everus prepared to swing out with his sword.

"Nice try...now what do we do?" asked Creeps.

"We burn this pier to the ground."

"Oh aye? How?"

Everus merely smiled.

✝ ✝ ✝

Everus spied on the grubba, watching as he served his last late night

307

customer and began scraping fatty residues off one of his frying pans.

"Are ye just goin' to kill him?" asked Creeps, pulling his swollen bottom lip. He had previously put the wrong end of a lit cigar into his mouth, much to his discomfort.

Everus thought about it for a moment. "No...let's keep it civil. You stay here." He waited for a group of singing drunks to disappear out of earshot before making his way across the nearly empty market square. Silently, he approached the small caravan, the reek of burnt and oily food extremely off-putting. "An Ullerby Special, please."

"*Eh? What?*" Surprised, Dram dropped his pan and spun round. "Oh...I was just about to close for the night." The grubba's eyes widened in recognition.

"The Ullerby Slappers." Everus gazed intently for a moment at one of the handbills on the side of the caravan. A drawing of four, fat, bare-bellied men grinned out at him, their hands held as though about to smack their enormous guts. Shifting his scrutiny, he looked directly at the grubba. "Are they any good?"

"Eh...never seen 'em," answered Dram, suspiciously. As a late night vendor he *had* seen and dealt with more than his share of drunk and unpredictable characters, and on more than one occasion he had been physically attacked – hence the club and the loaded crossbow under the counter.

Everus sprang forward, giving the grubba no time to use either. Grabbing Dram by an arm, he pulled violently and hauled him out, manhandling him to the cobbles.

"*What the...!?*" Dram cursed, landed awkwardly and was greeted by a leather boot in the face. Stunned, he was then kicked once more before being lifted and slammed hard against the side of the caravan. He was only vaguely aware of two hard punches landing on his chin before blacking out.

Signalling the thief over, Everus then slung the unconscious cook over his shoulder, carried him to a nearby side street and left him slumped in a doorway. By the time he had returned to the caravan, Creeps was already inside, fidgeting with the small iron stove and sniffing at some of the foodstuffs.

"That bastard was packin' a crossbow. I wonder what else he's got?"

Everus looked in the small rear door. It was way too cramped for both of them to be in at the same time. "Can you figure out how that stove works?"

"Aye. It looks easy enough. Ma old man used to have summat similar."

"Good." Everus walked around to the front of the caravan and examined its coupling. With a grunt, he raised it, tilting the whole thing back a little. From inside came a surprised shout. He smiled to himself and went to the hatch. "You're going to have to give me a hand."

"Right ye are." The thief got out and, whistling jauntily, he helped Everus to drag the mobile kitchen along the empty streets towards the pier.

It did not take them long to get there.

"You go inside and get that oven fired up."

"Aye." Creeps entered the untidy caravan, crouched down and lit the stove. Soon a merry blaze was crackling. On a shelf, he found numerous spices, napkins, cloths and several bottles of cheap ale. In a cabinet, he discovered a large tub of cooking oil, more grimy pans and pots and a wooden box with the grubba's takings.

Everus looked inside. "How are we doing?"

"Do ye think this'll work?" asked Creeps, filling his pouch with coins.

"It's worth a try, even if it only succeeds in scaring the bitch."

"Do ye want a sausage or summat afore we start? I could murder a burger."

Everus shook his head. "No. Come on, let's hurry it up and get this going. We need to do it before the tide comes in so she won't escape."

"All right." Liberally sloshing oil inside and scattering flyers, Creeps started to ignite anything that would burn. Once done, he leapt outside and with Everus' help, they trundled the caravan onto the pier.

Here was something for the painted jester to laugh at, thought Everus.

They stepped back and watched as black smoke began to appear from the hatch and chimney. In no time at all the whole interior seemed to be ablaze. With a loud *whoomph*, the whole caravan was wreathed in fire. Flames leapt to adjacent structures, greedily dancing and darting up already ruined woodwork and balustrades. Soon the whole front of the pier was ablaze. Creepy Geezer's

House of Horrors went up next. Fiery clown faces blackened and melted. Peeling paintwork curled and burnt.

Flames now consumed the front of the hag's realm.

The heat from the fire prompted Everus and Creeps to pull back.

A crowd of onlookers began to gather, most of them regulars from The Beached Kraken. The barman walked over to stand by them, a look of utter disbelief on his face. Other folk gawped and pointed, mesmerised by the conflagration before them.

The hag appeared, her form a dark silhouette behind the crackling red and orange. Frantically she howled and rushed about, her actions futile against the advancing, remorseless wall of fire.

"It's the witch!" someone shouted. "*Burn her! Burn the bitch!*"

"Ain't that Dram's kitchen?" cried someone else.

"Aye, he's cookin' tonight," replied Creeps.

A strong stink of burning wood and smoke gusted out towards the spectators as a structure collapsed in a large cloud of embers.

Uncontrollable, the fire raged for the best part of the night, and by early dawn, with the tide beginning its slow encroachment, the pier had been reduced to a blackened, smoking, burnt-out husk.

Sometime before sunrise, Everus and the others had heard the hag's final, soul-wrenching wail. She had been forced back to her small shack at the end of the pier. There she had been trapped and cremated.

With her death, the malediction that had held Mhoon for so long suddenly broke. With a glazed and confused look in his eyes, he stumbled out of the tavern to join those now gathered facing the smoking wreck.

✝ ✝ ✝

"Ah, ye're the man who burnt down the pier, aren't ye?"

Everus stopped. He turned to look at the wrinkled old man who sat on a doorstep, eating from a dirty bucket filled with unsightly whelks. "What of it?"

"Nothin'. Nothin'." The man extracted one of the small shellfish with a pin and sucked it off the end. "Just thought I'd say good on ye. It's always been a bloody eyesore, since before I was a nipper."

Ignoring the praise, Everus continued on his way. He and Creeps had now been in Ullerby for eleven days and, after their destruction of the once-famous pier and their rescue of Mhoon, they had mainly concentrated on trying to obtain passage to Trade Peak. As the merchant, Hajee, had warned, such a venture was proving much harder than anticipated, and it seemed as though no one was willing to travel south, despite Everus' generous offers.

The smell of salt and old planking grew stronger as Everus strode towards the docks. He looked about, trying to see if any new ships had arrived since his visit two days ago. Several fishing boats bobbed in the scummy water of the marina and two large cargo vessels rested at their respective moorings. The crew from one of them was busy loading her up, their calls and snatches of ribald shanties adding to the cries of the gulls overhead.

Passing several small wooden cabins and weathered fishermen, Everus arrived at the harbourmaster's lodge. He entered the building and headed over to the grizzled old sea dog at the reception desk.

"Ah, ye're back? Still tryin' to get to Trade Peak, right?" growled the harbourmaster, his words having to fight their way through his seagull-shit-coloured beard. On the timber wall behind him there hung a ship's wheel and several tacky, nautical maps. The overall effect was of a man who was trying too hard and Everus strongly suspected the harbourmaster had probably never left dry land.

"Yes. Anything going?"

"Nah. Not fer next couple o' days...weeks, maybe." Noting Everus' displeased look, the grizzled man reached for a thick ledger on the desk before him. With a callused hand, he opened it and studied what looked like a crude timetable. "The next southbound ship'll be..." He tapped the page, thinking things through.

"When?" asked Everus, impatiently.

"Well...not fer some time." The harbourmaster scratched his head, trying once more to cross-reference the timetable. A moment passed before he looked up. "To be honest wi' ye, I think ye're wastin' yer time tryin' to get to Trade Peak from 'ere. I'd say yer best bet is to see if ye can jump on that ship out there. That one...Ye Olde Typhoon." He pointed out the window at the waiting cargo vessel. "That lot are bound fer the 'Spire' in a day or two. Ye'd 'ave a better chance o' gettin' a ship fer Trade Peak there."

"Hmm. Perhaps you're right. I'll go and make some inquiries."

✝ ✝ ✝

Mhoon waved as Everus entered The Beached Kraken and walked over to the table. "My friend, once more I'd like to offer you my sincerest thanks. What you and your companion did for me will prove hard to repay."

"Forget it," said Everus, pulling up a chair and sitting down. There was a tankard of ale waiting there for him and he took a drink.

A faint smell of attar came from the much cleaner clothes Mhoon wore and his eyes now sparkled sharp and clear, like sunlight reflected off the sea. His long, greying hair was tied back in a ponytail. "Although I'm the one in debt, there are a few things I would like to ask you, if I may?"

"Ask."

"You've mentioned the hand of Cyrvilus. Would you mind telling me *why* you seek it?"

"In order to kill a demigod."

"Xethorn, perchance?"

"Do you know of another?"

"Well, perhaps not a true divinity. Not strictly speaking anyway. I speak of Bhubbaal...for he is almost as powerful. He is one of the *ul-garu*."

"The *ul-garu*?"

"Part man. Part demon. He's one of those lifeless beings who dwell beyond the shadows. They are dangerous and malign. Their hatred for the living is as legendary as is their evil." Mhoon's face tightened as his eyes burned with an inner hatred of his own. "Bhubbaal's cruelty..."

Mhoon was interrupted by Creeps' sudden return from the bar area. There he had been playing a round of cards with some of the regulars. Ever since their torching of the pier and their killing of the hag, both he and Everus had become overnight celebrities. With a brusque nod to Mhoon, he sat down, a slightly dissatisfied look on his face. "*Cheatin' bastards!* I'm the only one supposed to cheat!"

"Did you lose?" asked Mhoon.

"Aye. Thirty gold. Bastards!" The thief threw a dark look towards the bar. One of the men there, a scruffy-looking individual with an eyepatch, grinned and gave a cheeky thumbs-up. "They're some o' the men from that boat we're takin' the 'morrow. Ye see that old hopalong waste o' space wi' the wooden leg? He says that we'll have to sleep wi' the bilge rats."

"What joy," commented Everus, sarcastically. He took a sip from his ale before resuming his conversation with Mhoon. "Would I be right in guessing that you know more about this Bhubbaal? Something in your eyes tells me that you have a particular hatred for him."

Creeps looked across at Mhoon, hanging on a response.

"Is...is it so obvious? Is the hatred so strong?" Mhoon slumped and held his head in his hands. He sobbed quietly before looking up, his eyes watering. "He...he killed my wife. It was long ago, but still...still I feel her torment. He prolongs her suffering. She's become a thrall. Her life is long gone, but still she..." He closed his eyes, trying to blot out whatever harrowing images his imagination had created.

"Then join us. Come with us to Gossothus. Together we'll bring Bhubbaal's rule to an end," urged Everus, aware of Creeps' surprised look.

And, despite the tears, Mhoon smiled. Deep in his heart, he had hoped for such an invitation, an opportunity to adventure once more and avenge his wife. He felt a surging resolution – a chance to embark on a crusade Everus himself knew only too well; the pursuit of vengeance.

CHAPTER FIFTEEN

The voyage to The City of the Glittering Spire took eight days. On the third day out, the monotony was broken by the sighting of another fiery rock in the sky. Apart from that, the time spent aboard had been largely without incident and, for the most part, the weather had remained clear and favourable. Even so, life aboard Ye Olde Typhoon was rough and cheerless.

When the call went up that land was sighted on the starboard side, Everus sprung out of his cabin and rushed to the main deck. There, he looked out across the waves at the barely visible horizon. At first sight, he could see little but the blanketing sea fog, but then the clouds shifted, revealing the magnificent edifice after which the city port had been named.

Needle-like, the giant spire rose from the urban greyness. It had been constructed from thousands of highly polished interlocking cubes of various metals, causing it to glint, even in gloomy daylight.

"Amazing, isn't it?" commented Mhoon, walking over and standing next to Everus. "The Spire of King Mazacar I."

"Mazacar II," corrected Everus, his eyes fixed on the towering, metallic structure. "Although his father commissioned the building, it was the son who lived to see its completion. Hence it is to him that the credit for its construction belongs."

"Come on, move it ye landlubbers!" growled one of the roughest, foul-mouthed, foul-smelling sailors onboard. He forcibly pushed past Mhoon and made for the main mast. "Some of us 'ere have to work fer a livin'." Despite his bulk, he shinned dexterously up the rigging towards the crow's nest.

"Hmm. Mazacar II." Mhoon brushed himself down, the damp imprint of a beefy hand on his light grey cloak. He flung a disparaging look at the fat sailor's ascending backside. "I'll be glad to get off this boat. That's no lie."

Everus wiped a sheen of sea spray from his face. "I'll go and let

Creeps know we're nearly there." Fighting back mild nausea, he staggered across the swaying deck and made his way down into the small, low-ceilinged galley, where the thief was busy gutting mackerel. He waited for a moment before giving a whistle to catch his attention.

Creeps turned, knife in hand. The apron he wore was stained and bloody.

"Didn't you hear the cry? We're getting close to land."

"*Well thank shit for that!*" Angrily, Creeps threw the cutting implement to the floor and pushed the stinking chopping board to one side. For the past two days, he had been slaving away; ordered to work in the ship's kitchen after having been caught by the captain having a sneaky cigar in his cabin. After a severe lecturing on the dangers of a fire at sea, his treasured cigars had been confiscated and he had been set the odious chore of preparing the day's catch.

"I see you're still enjoying yourself."

"Yeh, whatever." Creeps tore off his apron. Mischievously, he looked about before leaning over a tray of freshly prepared fish and vigorously scratching his head over it. Clumps of dandruff fell from his ratty hair. Once done, he faced Everus. "Seein' as we've ran out o' salt I'd stick to the apple puddin' for lunch if I were ye."

"I might just do that."

✝ ✝ ✝

The landing board creaked as the three travellers disembarked. It was late evening and a chill sea breeze gusted through the docks as they left the ship and her unappealing crew. Following the directions provided by the first mate, they headed down one of the many side-streets before arriving at a public square. Situated almost directly across from them they saw the welcoming sight of The Dragon and Anchor tavern.

Whores of varying levels of attractiveness milled around outside.

Approaching the tavern, they could hear the painfully cheerful sounds of someone playing a squeeze-box.

"I don't know about ye, but I feel as though the bloody street's swayin' from side to side," said Creeps, wobbling slightly. "It wouldn't be so bad but I haven't even had a drink."

Mhoon laughed. "Don't worry, the feeling will soon disappear." With a tug of a strap, he readjusted his pack of belongings. "Well,

315

here we are. The Dragon and Anchor. Doesn't look too bad."

"Ye shouldn't judge an alehouse on its outer appearance," replied Creeps. "There's probably all manner o' weirdos inside."

"Do you think so? I do hope it's not like The Beached Kraken."

Ignoring his companions' banter, Everus opened the main door and entered.

The raftered, low-ceilinged tavern room was warm and cosy, its patrons illuminated almost too well by the many lanterns hung inside. Some folk turned as the three of them came in, but for the most part their entrance went unnoticed, as most of the patrons were captivated by a roguish-looking accordionist who sat playing in one corner.

Creeps winced at the sound.

A group of nearby locals winced at Creeps, the stench of chopped fish still strong on him.

The three of them made their way to the bar.

"Good evening to ye. How may I be of assistance? Are ye after some rooms or perhaps a little drink to take away the chill o' the night?" asked the thick-set man behind the bar.

Everus was about to answer when, mercifully, the music came to an end. Claps and cheers broke out. A voice was raised as someone called for an encore.

"First class!" shouted the barman, clapping with the rest. "Absolutely first class. Now, where were we? Ah, yes...what'll it be?"

Everus threw a dark look at someone who had inadvertently bumped into him. The thin, curly-haired man quickly apologised before backing off.

"We'd like a room each," said Mhoon.

"By all means. Three rooms it is. An' what about a round o' drinks? On the house o' course."

"Free booze?" queried Creeps, suspiciously.

"I don't make a habit o' it, believe me." From a large cask on the wall, the barman began filling three tankards. "But as you can probably tell, we're all celebratin' tonight. I just made myself a little fortune, ye see."

"Oh?" Creeps' suspicion was now replaced with interest.

"Aye. They're appointin' me mayor in the mornin'. Can ye believe it? *Me? Mayor?*" The barman grinned broadly as he finished pouring the third ale. "Well there you go. Enjoy."

"And the rooms?" asked Everus.

"Oh, aye. I were nearly forgettin'." The soon-to-be-made mayor reached for a bunch of keys on a hook behind him and put them on the bar. "There. I'll just get the missus to give the rooms a quick once over and then ye can go on up. But for now, why don't ye all grab a spare table an' listen to the music? He's summat else, isn't he? Cost a fortune to hire, ye know. But worth every penny."

It was only when they were on their third ale that the music thankfully came to an end. The accordionist, resplendent in his frilled jacket, tight, emerald green leggings and tricorne hat packed away his instrument, doffed his hat to the barman and headed out into the night. Now that the 'entertainment' had departed, so too did many of the patrons, each offering their thanks and congratulations to the owner before making their respective ways home.

"I'd a bad feelin' that bastard was goin' to go on all night," muttered Creeps. "I've heard caterwaulin' better than that. There was this one wall, near to where I used to live in Wyrm's Port, where the cats would gather every night. An' every night I'd hear 'em, screechin' an' hissin'."

Yawning, Mhoon sat back in his chair. "Oh, I don't know. I've certainly heard worse. There used to be a group of minstrels in Ullerby...can't remember what they were called but believe me they *were* terrible. I once considered paying them to help me..." His voice trailed off as though he had already said too much.

"To help ye do what?" asked Creeps.

Mhoon's gaze darted warily towards Everus as though the secrets he had were guilty ones.

"Just what is it ye do anyway?" pressed the thief, leaning forward.

Before Mhoon could answer, the barman noisily slid three heavy bolts across the front door, sealing the now all but empty tavern. "Well that's me closin' up for the night, gentlemen. I've got a big day tomorrow but by all means stay right where ye are if ye wish." He blew out several lanterns, waved a goodnight and began climbing a flight of wooden steps. "I've got a lovely big pork joint for breakfast. I'll do it nice an' crispy so there'll be plenty o' cracklin'. Ahh! I can almost smell it. Anyhow, sleep well."

With the creak of the barman passing overhead, Everus took up Creeps' questioning. "First off, Mhoon, there are no secrets between us. I've told it to you straight. I used to work as an assassin for the cult of Xethorn. When I finally realised the extent of their manipulation, I turned renegade. Creeps claims to be an agent of The High Three, a claim, that, due to what I've seen, I've no real reason to question."

"The High Three?"

Creeps finished his drink and winked.

Everus nodded. "Yes. You see it all started when Xethorn revealed to me the location of the three wards of binding, which The High Three had used to imprison Him. Through them, I managed to free Him...hence the current problem with Wyrm's Port. And before you ask, don't think for a moment that I feel any guilt. Wyrm's Port meant nothing to me. Its people were weak-willed and insignificant. For many, death was a blessing; an end to their shallow, mundane lives. When I was young, I quickly learned the nature of the many; the way in which to be an individual is to be an outcast from so-called social norms. Even then, I fell into a trap set by my supposed mentor, Dae'dicus, and his Uhu'giaggothian cult."

"Uhu'giaggoth?" mumbled Mhoon, his eyes aglow with interest.

"The Daemon God. You see, the old high priest, Dae'dicus and his successor, Dae'morogin, had both fallen from Xethorn's darkness, seeking enlightenment within the doctrines of demonic worship. Their attempts to reawaken Uhu'giaggoth and plunge this world into a new cataclysm were thwarted by..." It pained him to admit it aloud, so Everus merely nodded towards Creeps.

Mhoon's face was a portrait of incredulity. "And...Xethorn?"

"That bastard remains. Together, Creeps and I did battle with Him in one of the imperial palaces, but He was too strong. Creeps believes that The High Three reconsidered their decision to have Him expelled, almost as though they were playing some kind of game with us." Everus' face hardened. "But the way I see it, games have rules. Some play by them, some don't. I don't."

"And...you plan to destroy Xethorn? Even if it's against the judgement of The High Three?" asked Mhoon.

"I care nothing for them," Everus spat, venomously. "Where were they when I knelt before my mother's bedside, praying for her recovery? Or when Dae'dicus and his succubus, Julia Camberra, orchestrated my downfall? And as for those I've murdered..."

"They got ye out o' the palace that time. Remember?" interrupted Creeps, his face half in shadow.

Everus hesitated for a moment, unsure how to counter the thief's irrefutable statement. "Yes, only in order to make me recant – to live to see the destruction my vengeance had wrought and to change my ways. But they have failed, as they have always failed. Gods or not, they will rue the day that they kept me alive."

The colour seemed to drain from Mhoon's face and he leaned back as though Everus had just announced he was the carrier of a virulent disease. For a while, it appeared as though he was holding his breath, then, after expelling a lungful of air, he spoke. "It's a dangerous life you lead, my friend. I mean, it's one thing not to believe in the gods, but to...to say what you have, why, you're asking for trouble."

"Spare me your eschatological concerns. I see no lightning bolts. I hear no cries filled with divine malice. I dare the gods to strike me down, to throw me into their hellish dungeons." Everus grinned, harshly. "I have known death...the gods, I no longer fear."

There followed an unsettling silence in which Mhoon studied Everus' cold face, almost as though he was half-expecting the darkly charismatic, profane and undoubtedly sociopathic man before him to be consumed in a sudden pillar of godly fire. Recorded in those intense, green eyes, he could see the pain and the bitterness, the stolen potential and the now all but forgotten dreams.

Creeps yawned. "Well, if I can manage 'em stairs, I'm goin' to ma bed." He rose from his chair.

"Manage the stairs?" Everus laughed. "This from the only man to have ever scaled Araan's Pillar."

"Aye, but I wasn't drunk then."

"Well, it has been a long day." Mhoon also stood up, slinging his pack over a shoulder. He was halfway towards the stairs when Everus called him.

"You still haven't answered Creeps' question."

"Oh? Which one?"

"What it is you do?"

Mhoon smiled and lifted a lantern from a hook in order to light his way. "Why, I'm an exorcist."

✝ ✝ ✝

Blood. Only this time the blood he saw was his own – at least it came from inside him. He was bound to a table, around which several strange-looking devices sucked like mechanical leeches. Screaming, he strained and struggled, his actions futile. Small, sharp barbs in his shackles painfully drew more blood. Above him, a glistening, blood-soaked contraption slowly lowered, its many tubes and siphons eager to draw out his life.

Puckered pipes latched onto his bare skin. A whirring sound started up from somewhere. Body thrashing against the vampiric tubing and its collecting bladders and globes, he caught sight of shadowy movement nearby.

A grinding, twirling mishmash of teeth and suckers descended from above. Then everything went dark.

† † †

It was the smell of burning that woke him up. Throwing his blankets to one side, Everus leapt from the bed, fortunate not to have bothered to get undressed. Shocked, he noticed thick, dark smoke creeping around his door. Dark swirls crawled and coiled their way towards him.

Cries could be heard from outside in the main square.

Dashing to the window, he threw it wide and looked out to see a couple of men pointing with some alarm at the orange and red flames that now licked up two sides of the tavern.

There came a loud crash from somewhere inside as the stairs collapsed.

Screams and coughs broke out from those trapped in adjoining rooms.

The heat now emanating from beyond the wooden door was ferocious and Everus knew that escape that way was impossible. The inner surface of the door began to warp and char, black patches spreading like a voracious mould. Eyes stinging, he gathered up his sword and forced the window wider before clambering up and jumping out. It was a considerable fall and he landed with a thump on the ground, pain jolting through his ankles and up his legs.

"Ye all right, mister?" cried out one of the onlookers, rushing over and helping Everus to his feet.

Everus coughed and wiped his eyes. Before him the whole front of The Dragon and Anchor was now ablaze. It was like The Ullerby Pier all over again. Looking up, he saw Creeps' worried face appear at an upper storey window. From the looks of it his whole room was ablaze. With a cry, the thief smashed his way through the glass and tumbled out along a sloping veranda, his leather jacket on fire. Like a human torch, he fell to the cobbles, rolling to extinguish the flames. More people joined them. From all around the square they came, watching helplessly as the tavern became engulfed in fire, for the time being too stunned to try and douse the flames or save those still trapped inside.

Creeps stumbled over to where Everus stood. Blood ran from his cut forehead and his face was black and sooty. His clothes smouldered and reeked of burnt leather.

"Mhoon's still in there," said Everus. "Poor bastard."

Suddenly from inside there came another loud crash as flaming timbers gave way. A portion of the roof, directly above the room in which Creeps had been lodging, collapsed in a cloud of fiery embers and flaming rafters, as the entire tavern began to fall in on itself.

The heat was ferocious.

Folk screamed and pulled well clear, leaving Everus and Creeps silhouetted like harbingers of doom against the conflagration as flames leapt hungrily to nearby buildings. Now realising the greater threat posed by the fire, a general alarm went up. More and more people, dressed in hastily flung on clothes, sleep-sodden and gripping their children and prized belongings, ran shrieking from neighbouring houses.

"*Ye nutter!*" The thief spat and threw Everus a black look. "This is what ye get goin' about pissin' off the gods. Ye shouldn't o' done that, ye know. They'll only let ye go so far." Shaking his head, he reached into his smouldering jacket for his pipe. "Pah! We're lucky to be alive."

Before Creeps could light up, Everus sent the pipe spinning from his hands with a backhand slap. "More likely the fire was caused by some idiot smoking in bed. *You stupid bastard!*" Eyes flickered with growing rage. He was about to lambaste the thief some more, when Mhoon patted him on the shoulder.

"My friends! What's happened? I'm so pleased to see you're not harmed."

"I...I thought you were still inside," said Everus, his rage now giving way to relief.

"I couldn't sleep so I decided to take a walk in the moonlight. I saw the flames and came straight back."

"Come on," said Creeps, bending to retrieve his pipe, which he guiltily concealed in a pocket. "There's nothin' to stay 'ere for. Let's go." No sooner had he finished than a great cry went up from those gathered around as the shell of the burning building and two houses on either side crashed to the ground in sheets of flame.

+ + +

It was early afternoon when they boarded a much smaller, unnamed cargo ship bound for Trade Peak. The captain of the vessel was a tall, bearded ex-pirate named Garoth, who had a disconcerting habit of scratching his well-weathered face with his hook-hand. During their initial meeting, when Everus had paid for their passage, Creeps had watched in the somewhat questionable hope that the captain would try and pick his nose with it. He had been disappointed.

From the main deck, they could see the large plume of black smoke that now hovered over a large part of the city. The fire had been far more devastating than they had at first assumed, for it had spread quickly and uncontrollably, strangely altering course in order to inflict the greatest damage. In many places it was still burning.

The ship began to pull away.

"At sea again," moaned Mhoon, leaning against the gunwale and gazing out.

"Aye. I feel as though I'm goin' to hurl ma guts up an' we haven't even left the dock yet." With his back to the railings, Creeps watched idly as some of the ship's crew began lowering a huge crate of merchandise into the hold.

Cries and shouts echoed from the darkness below.

"At least it's a shorter voyage this time. Old 'Hook-Hand' reckons we'll reach Trade Peak within five days," said Everus. "And once we've done this leg, we don't have any more sea journeys to make...just several hundred leagues of hard terrain by foot."

"Just what we need...summat to really boost the morale," chirped the thief, sarcastically. "So, once we get to this place...then where?"

Everus did not have any clear strategy, content for the time being to take things one step at a time. "Not sure...yet." He was wrestling inside with a strange, slightly disorientated feeling which had been with him ever since waking in the burning tavern.

"You know, I've been thinking about what you've told me...about your desire to vanquish Xethorn and about this hand of Cyrvilus,"

Mhoon said. "And, well, I think it would make more sense to go for the part that's kept in The Grand Repository in Ghavin's Keep first. For if we do it in that order, not only will it enable us to skirt Wyrm's Port...from a safe distance, it will also, hopefully, give us the power needed to confront Bhubbaal. Once we've got it, I think we should then head south for Wathang-Hu, before heading back north towards Stranglewood and Gossothus."

It sounded a workable approach. Everus nodded and turned to Creeps. "What say you?"

Creeps shrugged his shoulders. "Whatever, as long as it's no more boats."

"Very well. Ghavin's Keep it is."

The ship began to rock beneath them as it pulled further out of the great stone-walled harbour. Sailors called out to one another, busily going about their duties. The ship was brought around and was soon heading out to the cold and capricious expanse of The Dark Sea, its prow cutting through the choppy waters of the tidal pull.

With the huge glinting spire still in sight on the landward horizon, the unease Everus was feeling began to grow within him. It was more than just the jangling of his nerves or the nausea brought on by the rocking of the boat; it was a strange, unsettling feeling, as though in his mind he was living with the certainty that he would soon die or perhaps a part of him had already died. Like his room, earlier that day, his godless soul seemed to be filling up with dark, suffocating smoke, both numbing and surreal. He was relieved to find out that his condition was not unique to himself when Mhoon offered him a drink from his canteen.

"Want some?"

Everus declined with a shake of his head.

Mhoon tried a smile, but it appeared false and hollow and did nothing to alleviate his troubled look. As though he were about to vomit, he leant against the railing and looked down at the constantly churning sea. The strong glare from the reflected sunlight on the water caused him to squint.

"Where'd Creeps go?" asked Everus, aware that the thief had left them.

Mhoon looked up, a tired, very ill look on his face. "I think he went back to the cabin for a rest. I think he mentioned catching up on some sleep."

"Looks like you could do with some," remarked Everus.

Yawning, Mhoon took a sip from his canteen. A gull flew down as he corked the container, landing on a pile of crates nearby. He shivered. "There's something strange going on. I can feel it, deep down." Lightly, he patted his chest. "What's more, I can tell it isn't normal."

"What do you mean?"

Mhoon sighed. "Well, that's just it. I don't know. There is something though, a..."

Suddenly the doors leading to below decks were flung wide.

"There'll be no turnin' back till we reach Trade Peak, ye hear!?" barked Garoth, forcibly pushing aside another thick-set man with a flaming red handlebar moustache. "An' it'll be twenty lashes fer the next man I hear bellyachin'. Ye got that!?" Angrily, he stomped towards the poop deck.

"Looks as though the captain's none too happy," whispered Mhoon.

The man Garoth had pushed aside shook his head and threw them both a withering look before making his way back downstairs.

† † †

The captain's quarters were finely furnished, if a little cramped. In one corner of the cabin lay a small four poster bed, which looked particularly inviting to Creeps who had spent most of the afternoon and early evening on an uncomfortable, wooden-planked cot. Two wardrobes, a small dressing table, several ornamental stands and a large, broad-leafed plant growing from a bucket all helped to make the cabin seem relatively pleasant.

With a noticeably shaking hand, Garoth poured two shots of hard liquor from a decanter and passed one to Creeps. "Nob'dy else?"

Everus and Mhoon shook their heads.

Garoth took a swallow, wincing as the liquor burnt his throat. "Well I've called ye all 'ere tonight to ask some questions. Now, contrary to what ye might've heard about me, I'm a fair man an', seein' as ye've paid up front, I'm prepared to hear ye out. Still, seems that some o' the crew seem to think ye're nothin' but jinxes, the lot o' ye."

"Why's that?" asked Everus.

324

Garoth coughed. "Well I guess ye've got to see it from their side o' the coin. I mean, everythin's fine an' dandy...then we take on ye three swallybuckets an' before we're even on the open sea things start to go belly-side up. I'm sure ye've noticed the drop in the wind an' the weird tiredness that seems to have come o'er everyb'dy. Now, I've been at sea fer o'er forty years an' I've seen some strange shit...but I've never known anythin' like this afore."

"So...how do we proceed?" asked Everus, coldly.

Refilling his glass, Garoth slumped back in his large, padded chair. "Relax, ma friend. I've got no intention o' throwin' ye o'er the side, if that's what ye're thinkin'. Nonetheless, ye've got to understand the situation I'm in by keepin' ye. Now I'm no idiot. I know that ye three swallybuckets aren't the problem."

"We're not?" asked Mhoon, somewhat relieved. The thought of being stuffed into a sack and thrown to the sharks had played strongly on his mind.

"No." Garoth downed half his drink and reached for the decanter once more. Silence fell as he topped up his glass.

"Then who or what is?" asked Everus.

"It's this," answered the captain, clinking his hook against his glass, a slightly mad smile on his lips. Drunkenly, he mumbled something into his drink before taking a sip.

"*Eh!?*" Creeps stared at his own glass.

"Aye...it's this all right. No doubt about it." Garoth took another drink. "We'd enough fresh water aboard to get us to Trade Peak an' back. But, it isn't water any more. It's booze...good old booze." Raising his glass, as though in a toast, he then finished the lot.

"So, what are you saying? That we've no drinkable water aboard?" Everus asked, his lids drooping. It was hard for him to believe that earlier that morning he had been forced to escape from his burning room in The Dragon and Anchor tavern. So much had happened in the space of one day. For some strange reason, his thoughts turned to the landlord of the tavern, which was now a smouldering ruin, wondering whether or not he had escaped, or whether he now resembled nothing more than the crispy pork joint he had intended to serve them for breakfast.

"Has the water become contaminated?" added Mhoon, wearily.

Garoth hiccupped. "Aye. I'd say it's summat like that. To let ye into a little secret, I blame it all on that bloody stone thing we've got in the hold." His head drooped and he hiccupped again. "I never should've agreed to take it."

Everus shook the feeling of lethargy away and tried to focus. "What stone thing?"

"It's...it's in a crate. The landlubber I got it off looked a right regular swallybucket, all hooded an' shit...a bit like yersel'. Anyhow, he paid good money. Said if I were to take it to Trade Peak someb'dy else'd collect it." Once more, the captain reached for the decanter. "Ye sure I can't be offerin' any o' ye some? It's damn good stuff an' I'm all on fer gettin' shit-faced."

"Why don't you go and get this thing so that we can have a look?" mumbled Mhoon. Although he had not touched a drop, he felt as though he had gone drink for drink with the captain.

Clumsily, Garoth rose from his chair. "Tell ye what." Unsteadily, he reached for a hung-up jacket and removed a big bunch of keys from a pocket. "Why don't ye go an' have a look fer yersel'?" He tossed the keys onto the table.

+ + +

By the light from a rusty old lantern, Everus and Mhoon slowly climbed down a metal ladder into the shadowy, reeking hold. All around they could see many crates, boxes, barrels and sacks, each filled with an assortment of cargo, some bound for legal customers, some not.

At the bottom of the ladder, Everus took hold of the lantern and made his way into the belly of the ship. Kicking aside a large rat, he headed over to the largest collection of piled crates, panning the lantern around. Many of the containers had hastily scratched writing on them, indicating both the nature and the provenance of their contents. Advancing further into the low-ceilinged area, he stepped into a pile of wet faeces.

Something hissed.

Raising the lantern, he shone it towards a crack in the timber wall. Cautiously, he approached, his right boot raising strings of squidgy shit. Within the dark recess, he saw a tusk and a solitary, watery eye staring back at him. There was something in there, a small, blubbery, ugly-looking thing. It did not appear aggressive.

"What is it?" asked Mhoon.

"There's something in there. You see it?"

The thing had pulled back into its recess, but it seemed reluctant to retreat any further, obviously well aware of its plundering hole and the proximity of the stored foodstuffs therein. Well, that being the case, thought Everus, perhaps a little forcing was needed. Looking about he was pleased to see a bundle of poles and gaffs propped between two old casks. He withdrew a hooked pole and with a quick thrust, he jabbed at the skulking beast.

Steel snagged mottled flesh.

Everus pulled and flesh parted, torn as easily as a wanton whore's knickers – the sea creature's blubber the texture of wet putty. It chattered and hissed, emitting a strong, vinegary stink. A pinky-red tentacle shot out of the hole and thrashed wildly for a moment, almost dragging Everus' pole from his hand. He stepped back and prepared to stab it a second time, but, before he could, the sludgy animal withdrew further, out of reach. With a wounded hiss, it tumbled back into a further cavity within the hold.

"Do you think it's gone?" asked Mhoon, nervously looking around in case others were waiting to slither from the shadows.

"I don't think it'll be back in a hurry. Come on, let's find that crate." It did not take too long for Everus to find the container he was looking for. Catching Mhoon's eye, he beckoned him over. "Here. This is it. Pass me the keys."

"There's a mighty strange feeling coming from this box," said Mhoon, handing the keys over.

Everus began unlocking the three padlocks which secured a tight length of chain wrapped around the crate. He grabbed a small prybar from a hook nearby and began to prise the lid open. When the final nail popped free, he flung the lid aside, half-expecting something unpleasant to leap out at him, the Uncle Tarby dummy for instance.

The crate was filled with what appeared to be old bottles. Some had obviously smashed in transit but many were surprisingly intact. Now open, the container and its contents reeked of stale ale and drink-induced vomit, the stench blasting out as though it had been a trapped, living thing.

Mhoon gagged and reeled back a couple of steps.

Having spent more time with Creeps, Everus coped better with the smell. "Bottles? Ale bottles?" Briefly, he wondered whether he had opened the right box. Carefully, he began to clear some of the grimy glassware out of the way in order to see if there was anything else inside. Removing the bottles and placing them on the floor, he soon uncovered what he was looking for.

Wrapped in a roll of damp leather was a rough chunk of dark stone about the same size and shape as an infant's skull. On one side, carved in order to conform to the natural lumps and bumps was a bizarre, yet slightly jocular, face. Its goggle-eyes were far too big and the nose was squashed and slightly upturned. Like the eyes, the mouth was large and disproportionate and from between the puffy, fat lips leaked a small amount of green, gelatinous fluid.

"Oh shit! *A Bubbling Gob!*" cried Everus.

☩ ☩ ☩

Through a drunken mist, Garoth tried, and to a large extent failed, to focus his eyes on the cursed stone that now rested on the table in his cabin. With mouth agape, he covered one eye with his hand and stared hard, trying to make the stone's liquor-induced twin disappear.

"There's something really unusual about this rock," slurred Mhoon, almost to himself. He turned to Everus, who stood gazing at the thing as though he were examining the internal workings of a freshly dissected demon. "How do you explain this?"

"Like I said at the time, it's a Bubbling Gob, one of only a few known to exist. How it ended up here, is anyone's guess." Everus stroked his unshaven chin, deep in thought. After a while, he moved closer in order to better study the strange relic.

Hand shaking, Creeps poured himself another drink and raised his filled glass. "To the Gubblin' Bob. Aye, hats off to it."

Everus threw the thief an annoyed glance.

"What do you know about it?" asked Mhoon, struggling to remain sober.

"The Bubbling Gobs...where to begin? No one really knows what they are or where they come from. Some suggest that they have always been; neither made nor formed – that they transcend time as a result of their own paradoxical lunacy. Some believe they are the debitage from the time of Creation – the unwanted excesses from the formation of other worlds. Others hold them to be living entities, emissaries from a demi-plane ruled over by a solitary mad drunkard." Everus smiled sardonically and shook his head. "I seem to recollect Creeps once telling me that there used to be a tavern in Wyrm's Port that sold imitation ones. It was called, not surprisingly, 'The Bubbling Gob'. This, however, is no replica."

Garoth slid from his chair and landed with a thump to the floor, his glass rolling from his hand.

Loud snores came from the sleeping captain.

From Creeps, there came an almost unintelligible, crude little song about his 'old an' dirty mother'. The odd line that Everus could make out stirred up images of ragged people living, ten to a family, in squalor and filth.

Mhoon resisted the temptation to try and hum along with the tune. Like Everus, he had had no sleep, but from some reserve, he managed to draw the willpower to stay awake. "I'd say that you don't hold any of those theories in much esteem."

Everus shook his head. "I think it's more likely that they were fashioned by an archmage in order to sow disorder and apathy. I'm of the view that they contain some kind of trapped demon or spirit. That they contain power, is unarguable."

"Why not just get rid of it? Throw it over the side?" Mhoon suggested. "Then we'll be free of its effects...*won't we?*"

"Legend tells that once found, the Bubbling Gob couldn't easily be disposed off. Any attempt at discarding it would prove futile. Give it a go if you don't believe me."

The exorcist declined Everus' invitation. From his own knowledge of sorcery and arcane items, he suspected he was right. "Can it be destroyed?"

"I don't know how."

"What about cracking it with a lump hammer?"

"I'd doubt it'd be anything so easy." From outside the captain's cabin, Everus could hear the sounds of drunken sailors singing, cursing and fighting. They had been at sea less than a day and already many of the crew were becoming insubordinate and reckless. The time for turning back had passed. Now it would be only a matter of time before all semblance of normality and discipline broke down and control of the ship would be in the hands of madmen. The ship would become a floating asylum. Increasingly, his thoughts turned to a possible escape on the jolly boat.

"Well, let's see about putting your theory to the test." Mhoon rose from his chair in order to look down directly on the stone head. More goo dribbled from the mouth, as though in some way it were reacting to the conversation of those around it. The dribble formed a small rivulet which ran to the edge of the table. The sway of the ship then caused it to flow back on itself.

"What're ye up to?" asked Creeps, a vacuous, inebriated look in his eyes.

Mhoon rolled up his sleeves. With both hands, he grasped the stone skull. He closed his eyes and began mumbling words in a strange voice. In response to his glossolalic mutterings, two things happened – the more noticeable of the two being the increased volume of spew that now began to ooze from the head as though the exorcist was squeezing it out; the second was that the tattoos on his hands began to glow and shimmer.

Startled, Everus took a step back.

With a violent shudder, Mhoon threw his head back, his hands still gripping the Bubbling Gob.

More and more sticky, snot-like fluid sprayed from between the stone lips.

The exorcist's whole body began to tremble. His cheeks puffed out and for a moment his face mimicked that of the stone, his head thrashing from side to side. Still he held on and continued his occult mumblings. Then, just as Everus was about to try and separate the two, Mhoon's bizarre convulsions subsided and with a final cry, he let go and staggered free.

Wide-eyed, Creeps started to wipe away some of the viscous yellow discharge that had hit him.

"Trapped inside the head are many loyatwats. From what I could understand from their garbled pleas, they're desperate for release," said Mhoon. He peeled some of the slime from his hands, the glow from his tattoos now beginning to dim. The motion of the ship caused him to sway for a moment but he quickly recovered.

"*Lawyer...twats?*" queried Everus, unfamiliar with the name. It brought a smile to his lips nonetheless. As far as he was concerned all lawyers *were* twats. The scum of the earth who deserved nothing but a slow and painful death.

"Loyatwats. They're tiny, for the most part innocuous, invisible spirits. However, in large concentrations and when held against their will, they become...unfriendly. Apparently, whoever created these Bubbling Gobs seemed to take delight in capturing them. Several of these stone 'skulls' were fashioned for such a purpose."

"So what do we do?" asked Everus. The sticky yellow leakage had decreased considerably, almost as though, now that its secret had been revealed, the skull no longer had to draw attention to itself. "Can you free them?"

Mhoon stroked his chin. "No. Regrettably, I lack the power.

Whatever magic was used to create these bizarre prisons is beyond me."

"Can you converse with them? Tell them to cease their...?"

"Their what?" interrupted Mhoon. "There's nothing particularly malign in what they're doing. It's simply their proximity which is causing our misfortune and affecting our water supplies. You may as well ask a rain cloud not to rain, or a...a stone cast into a pool not to sink."

"All right. That leaves only one course of action left to us. Get our gear together and I'll see about getting us off this ship."

✝ ✝ ✝

With the help of two drunken crewmates, Everus managed to get the small rowing boat lowered to the water. He waited with the two mumbling sailors as Mhoon steered the almost paralytic Creeps forwards. Over to one side, another sailor was violently throwing up, whereas the one up in the crow's-nest was blissfully pissing down from on high.

"What about provisions?" asked Mhoon.

"Already loaded." Everus looked at the thief, wondering just how they were going to get him down the precarious rope ladder that gave access to the bobbing clinker-built boat.

As though he had read Everus' thoughts, Creeps managed to stand upright on his own. The thief looked over the edge and then gingerly made his way down.

"You sure about this?" asked Mhoon.

"We've no choice," answered Everus, looking around and taking in the complete apathy and disorder that had befallen most of the others. Like a zombie, one of the sailors who had helped him with the jolly boat stood rigid, staring out to sea with empty, drink-addled eyes. The other was sitting on a large coil of rope, sobbing, a pathetic look on his grizzled face, which was almost child-like.

Over on the far side of the ship a knife-fight had broken out.

With the crazed eyes and grin of a potential pyromaniac, another sailor sat sparking a flint and steel, occasionally conversing with the three flasks of oil before him.

One sailor sat atop the starboard gunwale, talking to a glove puppet.

Mhoon looked over the rail. Seeing that Creeps was already seated in the boat, he carefully clambered over and began the climb down. The rocking of the ship made it difficult but, shortly after, he

331

too was sat hunched next to the thief.

Everus went last. Halfway down, from inside the belly of the ship, he heard the sound of dull thudding – like an axe on wood. For a moment, he kept his position, hands tightly clenched around the rope, boots anchoring himself to the side.

"Come on!" cried Mhoon.

"There are strange sounds coming from inside. I think…" said Everus, his words cut short by his sudden plummeting as the rope ladder was cut. With a startled cry, he fell for several frozen heartbeats before crashing into the rowing boat and her two passengers below.

"*Ye bastards! Ye bloody bastards!*" screamed the handlebar-moustachioed first mate, waving a cutlass. "We should've keel-hauled the lot o' ye!"

Dazed and bleeding, Everus looked up. His landing had been particularly sore – not just for him but also for the other two, who had, to some extent, broken his fall. As his vision righted itself, he saw the crazed first mate dart to and fro along the main deck above him. The madman was grabbing anything heavy he could get his hands on and throwing it down at them.

With a splash, an old barrel landed nearby.

"*Look out!*" cried Mhoon as a second barrel was hurled down, cracking off the port side of the boat.

"Start rowing!" ordered Everus, craning his neck to look over his shoulder as the berserk first mate cursed and emptied out a box filled with pots and pans and other cooking utensils. A cleaver gashed his shin, causing him to grit his teeth with pain.

Creeps moaned as a bottle shattered off his head.

A cutlass struck the back of the boat before spinning harmlessly off into the sea.

His arsenal now empty, the irate sailor threw the only thing he had left – himself. With a cry and a splash, he hit the water close by.

"Crazy bastard!" exclaimed Everus. He rose from his position and waited for the man to surface. As soon as he did, he viciously cracked an oar down on his head, killing him instantly.

† † †

Everus sat upright in the gently rocking boat and looked pensively at the stars. Across from him sat Creeps. Uncomfortably huddled in the space between the two was Mhoon. Occasionally the sleeping exorcist would moan or flinch, a sign that whatever powers governed his life were not content with confining the horrors they had in store for him to the waking world.

Creeps took his pipe from his mouth and tapped out its contents. "*Puh*. This is fun." He looked dejected and thoroughly bored.

"Do you remember much about Wyrm's Port?" asked Everus.

"Aye, sure I do. After all, it's no' like it's been that long since we were last there."

Everus shifted his legs, carefully avoiding Mhoon. "You know it's strange, but to me it seems a long time ago. It's as though the more I try to remember, the less I actually can."

"Oh?" Creeps began picking his nose.

"Well, take that dump you used to live in. I can hardly remember it now." Despite, or perhaps because of, their present situation, Everus managed a rare smile. "For some reason, I remember the smell though."

"Well, so ye should. Stink adds to a place's character. It took me years to get it smellin' so good. All the best houses have a reek, ye know. It gives 'em a certain..."

"Ambience?"

"Aye...whatever that means." Now having disentangled a juicy treasure from his face, Creeps popped it into his mouth and started to chew. "It's like ma old dad used to say, 'a house wi'out a stink, is like a dug up corpse wi'out a trinket'. It don't make sense to have one wi'out the other."

Everus looked out across the placid waters, his thoughts, like the sea, unusually peaceful.

"What about Xethorn?"

The thief's question instantly shattered Everus' sense of tranquillity. "What about Him?" he snapped.

"Do ye remember much about Him?"

"Not really."

"Come on, ye must remember summat," the thief pressed. "What about that time we had that scrap down in the temple?"

"For which I wasn't really there...I'd been possessed, if you recall. Even the fight in the imperial palace is hazy."

"Aye, it's a strange, strange world we live in, an' that's no mistake." Creeps turned his gaze out to sea, pulled his torn, woollen blanket tighter and took a puff of his pipe. "We've been through a fair bit, have we no'? I mean, monsters an' things, gods an' demons, Bubblin' Gobs an' deserts. Aye, we've seen more than our share o' weird things. An' summat tells me there's more to come."

Everus reached into a sack for an apple. He was about to take a bite, when he saw a spark of light in the dark sky. At first he thought a star had blinked into vision, but then the light increased in magnitude and with a tremendous roar an immense meteor fired past. The whole sky was lit in various glowing incarnadine colours as the sea churned and became like frothing blood, reflecting the myriad crimson glows. Reds and oranges violently clashed as the dark was torn asunder.

The thief screamed and covered his face.

Everus covered his ears.

Then the great glowing extraterrestrial rock was gone. In its wake, like a huge scar in the sky, was a gigantic smoking trail.

"What was that?" asked Mhoon, blearily staring skyward.

The sound faded until, with a dull explosion like a far off thunderclap, a part of the distant western horizon lit up in a bright yellow-green glow. The night air suddenly began to crackle as dendritic lightning spread from the epicentre of the unseen impact. Soon the whole sky was illuminated with powerful electrical discharges, which spread out like a living, violet web.

All three of them in the boat stared in awe, mesmerised at the inexplicable atmospheric light show.

"Gods preserve us! What...*was* that?" asked Mhoon, his words struggling to escape his quivering lips.

Neither Everus or Creeps provided an answer.

† † †

Everus awoke to the cry of gulls and the splash of the oars. It was daybreak and, with the sun just beginning to peek over the eastern horizon, he stretched his legs and massaged his stiff neck. High above him, he could see a few burnt out vapour trails etching the sky with traces of fading crimson.

"Get up an' give us a hand wi' the rowin'," said Creeps, gritting his teeth and pulling back an oar. "There's land or summat o'er there."

Everus peered in the direction the thief was taking the boat and, sure enough, there in the distance, he saw the tenebrous forms of crags and forests. He gave the huddled exorcist a nudge. "Get up. We're nearing land."

"Eh? What?" mumbled Mhoon.

Everus took the seat next to the thief and together they began rowing. The land was much further away than he had first gauged and the going was both slow and laborious but soon they built up a workable rhythm and with each stroke they decreased the distance between themselves and the shore. Soon they had to navigate the rowing boat around barnacle-encrusted rocks that jutted out of the water and scraped against the hull of the craft.

Then the tide took a full hold of them and the going became easier.

With limbs aching, Everus gave a final few pulls, driving the boat onto the pebble-covered shore. Pleased to be on land, he leapt from the boat, eyes fixed on the dark cave mouth further up the coast, from which the stench of rotting meat wafted.

"Does it never end?" said Creeps, wearily looking around.

Everus turned. "What do you mean?"

"Well, look at that." Creeps pointed toward the dark opening in the crags. "There's bound to be a monster o' some sort in there."

"Well, so long as it stays there. Go and give Mhoon a hand and don't forget to pack those extra water bottles. We're going to have to find somewhere to refill as many containers as we can."

The thief nodded and trudged back in order to help Mhoon. After a short time, the two completed their packing and came over to join Everus.

"Any idea where we are?" asked Mhoon, absently taking in his surroundings. He looked very tired.

Everus looked about him, momentarily ignoring the question. To what he assumed was a westerly direction, the unbroken line of the coast continued for at least a league. It then ran north-westwards for as far as the eye could see. To the east, there was a small cluster of broken boulders beyond which the beach continued for perhaps half a league before ending, abruptly, at the foot of some high, fractured cliffs. With the sun now cresting these crags, he could see, at their base, a dozen or so tall sea stacks protruding out from the shoreline into the water. To the south, emerging like a great natural barrier, rose a high cliff wall, its rugged, sea-battered surface scoured and cracked. The Dark Sea lay cold and threatening to the north.

"Well? Do you know where we are?" Mhoon looked gaunt and

exhausted, a desperation in his voice. Like an ineffectual scarecrow, he seemed powerless to do anything but stare; a demoralised, almost forlorn look in his bloodshot eyes.

By contrast, Everus was sharp and focused; continuing to take in his surroundings, searching for a landmark – some feature, be it natural or otherwise, he could use as a marker. Sniffing the air, his nostrils only picking up the stink of rancid meat and the pungent smell of the sea, he turned to Mhoon. "Not sure. You?"

With a hollow laugh, Mhoon shook his head dejectedly and crouched down. The weariness he now felt was crippling. With some effort, he picked up a damp pebble and idly began to examine it.

Creeps stood, silently digging the dirt from his nails with his dagger.

If this was how the two of them were going to be for the remainder of the quest, then Everus knew they may as well give up now. "Well, what do you want to do?" He looked hard at his companions, a great deal of impatience and annoyance in his voice. "Do you want to just stay here and live on seaweed for the rest of your days? Or maybe you can sit on this beach and wait for whatever lurks in that cave to come out and eat you. We're not going to get very far unless you..."

"What's the point?" interrupted Mhoon. Flicking the pebble away, he got to his feet. "I mean, where do you plan to go? For all we know we could be on some uncharted island in the middle of the sea. Marooned, with no hope of rescue."

"Nonsense," replied Everus, dismissively. "The ship was only a day, a day and a half at most out of The City of the Glittering Spire. We were on a south-westerly course for Trade Peak when we made our escape. If my reckoning is right, yesterday and most of this morning we've drifted south across The Lyhussian Straits. That being the case, then we're some forty, maybe fifty leagues east of Trade Peak and perhaps thirty west of Wyrm's Port. If I'm correct, then we've been rather fortuitous, for we've actually shortened our initial journey. Now all we have to do is get over those cliffs and head inland. Somewhere out there is the old trade road that joins Wyrm's Port and Trade Peak. Once on that, we go east, take the road south past Araan's Pillar and then head cross-country on one of the 'pilgrim paths' for Ghavin's Keep."

"An' no more boats...ye promised," said Creeps.

"No more boats." Everus kicked a large, one-pincered crab away.

After his experience in the hag's shack back in Ullerby, things with pincers now put him on edge. He turned to survey the route he planned to take when, suddenly, he saw movement within the opening of the dark cave. His sword was free from its scabbard in an instant.

Like a sewage spill, a horde of naked, man-like degenerates came pouring out of the cave. They were a grisly mob, their faces blood-covered and dirty, their hair wild and long. Some were armed with primitive weapons – bone clubs and stone-bladed axes – but most came screaming, unarmed.

"*Run!*" shouted Everus as more and more charged forth.

Loping and cursing, the almost watery surge of cannibalistic horror flooded across the beach towards them.

Creeps dropped his pack and was off like a shot. Sprinting across the sands and weaving between the boulders he went. Mhoon, on the other hand, spent a dreadful moment rooted to the spot with fear and it was only when Everus dashed past him and he saw the approaching killers that he found the strength to flee. Like Creeps, he too flung his pack to the sand.

"Split up!" ordered Everus, dashing towards the cliff edge, his eyes searching for a means of ascent. Unable to see a direct route, he started springing up the rocks that lay at the cliff's base. Slivers of rock fractured beneath his boots but somehow he kept his footing. Two hurled chunks of stone shattered nearby. Looking down, he saw at least half a dozen of the man-eating troglodytes clambering up in pursuit. Some wore crude facial paint, daubed on, no doubt, by bloody fingers – fingers that were well used to tearing flesh from corpses and cracking bones for marrow. One snarling face looked as though it had been ritually defleshed. Far beyond them and way over to his right, he saw Creeps and the exorcist tearing across the beach towards what appeared to be a dense cloud of incoming fog, a second group of ten or so bloodthirsty man-eaters close on their heels.

Guttural howls and yells came from both packs.

With heart thumping, Everus leapt from rock to rock, knowing that a slip here could well provide his pursuers with an easy meal. One of the cannibals launched himself forward and just missed grabbing him. With a scream, he fell into a jagged cleft between the rocks.

Everus came to an abrupt drop, his forward momentum almost causing him to overbalance. Desperate, he looked about. Far beneath him was the rock-jumbled beach, a few discarded bones and little else. Above him and separated by a span way too far to even consider leaping, was the lip of the cliff, its edge crumbling and eroded, roots and rocks jutting out from the side.

Growling, one of the slavering cave-dwellers clambered up onto the high rock Everus had just leapt from. It bared teeth that had undoubtedly torn many an unfortunate to swallowable gobbets before looking at the gap that separated it from its prey and making the jump. It managed to land with both feet but even as it began to scrabble for a suitable handhold, Everus' sword whistled down and chopped it open. Blood sprayed as the cannibal was dashed from the rock.

"Come no closer!" Everus threatened, doubting whether these throwbacks would understand a word of what he said.

One of the cannibals bounded down in order to feast on the one that had just fallen.

Another leapt the rocky divide.

With a slash of his sword, Everus beheaded it. A fountain of blood sprayed up the side of the rocks as the headless body thumped to the shingle below. A small hunting party of carnivorous crabs, sensing blood, were on it in no time.

Another ugly faced savage, a bone through his pierced nose, was about to leap to attack when there came a loud, deep roar from somewhere in the direction Everus had seen Creeps and Mhoon flee. Clearly agitated, the remaining attackers exchanged glances.

The roar came a second time.

Like the wild monkeys Everus had once seen his old mentor, Dae'dicus, hex at the Wyrm's Port menagerie, his attackers broke off and ran, leaping and screaming, back to their cave. He waited until they had all gone, the blood pounding through his veins, his survival instincts rooting him in place. Whatever beast had made such a noise must have been of considerable size. A sea monster from the deeps, perhaps?

A great swathe of thick fog now shrouded the stretch of shoreline that Creeps and Mhoon had fled towards.

Moments passed.

Now judging that the immediate threat had gone, Everus clambered down from his rocky vantage point. Tendrils of wispy fog seemed to rise from the very sand before him. Just then, he saw the fog-wreathed form of Mhoon stagger out from behind a large rock. He rushed over, just as the exorcist crumpled to the ground, blood streaming from a nasty-looking head wound.

Sinking his sword into the sand, Everus crouched down. "Mhoon. Can you hear me? Come on, I've got to get you out of here."

Mhoon mumbled and groaned. Clearly concussed, he muttered something and then went quiet.

From the looks of the injury, Everus rather suspected he had been struck by a rock. Tearing strips from his cloak, he moistened them in one of the many rock pools and then dabbed at the wound. Taking one of Mhoon's tattooed hands, he applied it to the already bloody cloth. "Hold this."

Wincing, the exorcist did as instructed, blood now running down his arm.

"What happened? Where's Creeps?"

Mhoon shook his head and groaned.

"Where's Creeps? Is he still out there?"

"We...we split up. I fell and..." Mhoon's face screwed up in a rictus of dripping, blood-streaked agony. "The fog...Creeps...I heard him...screaming."

Retrieving his sword, Everus gave a quick look in the direction Creeps had gone. Due to the fog, he could hardly see more than ten steps in front of him. "Stay here. I'm going to look for him. If anything happens, give a shout."

The expanse of thick, mud-like sand which separated the shingle from the mass of grey, glistening rocks was, at first glance, featureless and empty. However, as Everus strained his eyes and tried to follow the muddle of damp footprints, he began to see that some sediments were dotted with drips of blood. At first he thought they may have been made by Mhoon, but the direction seemed all wrong. Eyes down, he followed the trail past a large dried-up jellyfish and on towards a high, seaweed-covered outcropping of rock. Lying nearby, he could see the body of one of the troglodytes.

The thief's dagger protruded from its filthy chest.

Pulling the dagger free, Everus wiped the blade clean and tucked it into his belt. He heard a thick splash, the sound coming from over to his left. Cautiously he set out in that direction, the wet sand becoming alarmingly thicker and deeper with each step. Up ahead, a short distance away, he could make out the shadowy outline of a small ridge of rock, which emerged from the wet ground like some half-embedded monster's backbone.

There came another splash.

Boots squelching, Everus headed over. He clambered up onto the rock. When he reached the top, he looked down in time to witness Creeps beginning to drag himself free from a pool of sludge-like quicksand. A cannibal's corpse lay to one side.

"Creeps!" Keeping to the firmer ground, Everus carefully made his way down the small ridge and around the edge of the slurping pool.

Creeps hauled himself to safety. Covered almost entirely in the clinging, tar-like mess, he rolled over onto his back, and gave a laboured thumbs up.

CHAPTER SIXTEEN

Two days had passed since their escape from the tribe of coastal cannibals and the noisy sea monster Creeps claimed had resembled a 'sort of upright giant fish-thing wi' a face like a strangled rat'.

They headed inland across a barren expanse of wasteland. Their progress had been slow, for every so often Mhoon held up a weary hand, signalling the fact that he was close to collapse. A blood-stained bandage was wound around his head, and one side of his face was caked with dry blood. In his eyes was a pained, almost tortured look. For the most part he walked along like a dead man – or so thought Everus, who had seen dead men walk.

Yet, even in this punctuated manner, they covered the dreary leagues that separated them from the old trade road.

"There it is!" announced Everus. "I knew we were on the right track."

Creeps and Mhoon staggered to his side, eyes wide, regarding the narrow stretch of greyness that wound like a stream over the landscape, as though their guide had just pointed out the best free whorehouse in the land. Despite their aches and tiredness, their hearts leapt somewhat.

"From here, we head east." Everus stared in that direction, studying the lie of the land and tracing the route of the road as it disappeared and reappeared over the course of the undulating terrain.

Like Mhoon, Creeps looked almost dead on his feet. "How far are we plannin' on goin'?"

"Well...if my memory serves me right, about two leagues from here there are the remains of a Mad o' Gadin ruin."

"*Mad o' Gadin?* One of the old grubban deities?" asked Mhoon, his naturally curious nature getting the better of his crippling exhaustion. "That'll be one of their old temples, yes?"

"That's correct. I'm sure I saw one out here the last time I came along this road."

"And when was that?" asked Mhoon.

Everus thought for a moment, his mind swept back to that hot, almost sultry day when he had been much younger. Just a boy, he had accompanied his father, Iwain, to Trade Peak, for his father had some mercantile business to attend to. Despite all that had transpired since then, he could still almost feel the sun burning on his happy, upturned face, revelling in the thrill of adventure that time, and all that he had experienced, had, to some extent, failed to dampen.

"Well...?" Mhoon prompted.

Shaken from his daydream, Everus answered. "Over twenty years ago. I came out this way with my father. We travelled along this road." The images of his childhood were fleeting, vanishing quickly in a dark haze before his mind's eye. In vain, he tried to cling to them, to draw them back from the morass of his embittered soul. His face hardened. "However, the land is different now...as am I."

Seemingly in response to Everus' change in mood, the sky overhead began to darken. A belt of slate grey cloud gusted in from The Dark Sea, which now lay behind them, several leagues to the north.

Creeps shivered and stared skyward. "Come on, let's hurry it up afore we get pissed on." He set off, his head bowed like a supplicant.

The rain struck them before they reached the next horizon. It gave no warning – no spits or spats to announce its arrival – rather it came down in torrential, blinding sheets that soaked the three of them before they could even begin to rush for shelter. It was as though The Dark Sea had risen in one almighty tide and was now venting its anger on those who had escaped its clutches.

Everus gritted his teeth, his face set in a dripping scowl. Head down, he trudged on, the wind-whipped rain lashing him to the bone. He turned once, making sure that Creeps and Mhoon were still behind him. When he made out their saturated shadows, he trudged on, the many wagon-marks in the road now fast becoming overflowing pools of mud. At this rate, they would probably be better off making a canoe and paddling.

Fortunately, The Dark Sea's wrath was mercifully short-lived, the deluge seeming to disappear with the same unnatural suddenness with which it had struck.

They regrouped by a fallen tree. There they stood, staring and shivering like drenched rats. The land about them seemed to have changed, almost as though the unexpected shower had provided it with a much needed draught of regeneration. Flowers, green and dappled, appeared at the summoning of nature's magic, as a plethora of hitherto unnoticed wildlife came into view; hares bounded from the grasslands, insects and spiders crawled out to taste the dampness and birds now ventured into the air. Two small grass snakes slithered from a fallen log nearby.

Coughing, Creeps spluttered and spat. Cursing to himself, he squeezed an arm of his jacket, wringing out water. "*Shit!* I'm soaked to the bloody skin! Bloody place! Bloody weather!" Sniffing, he looked at Everus, an almost accusatory glower in his eyes. "Now what do we do?"

"We keep walking."

Mhoon backed away from an over-curious grass snake. "Everus, be reasonable, we're soaked through and we've already covered a fair distance this day." With a grimace, he tightened the wet bandage around his head.

"But not far enough." Grimly, Everus looked about him. "I've a feeling that Xethorn's somehow aware of my intent – that He's exerting His will and purposefully throwing everything He's got at us. Consider that rain storm. It didn't seem natural to me, and what about all those strange happenings in the sky?"

Mhoon frowned and gave Creeps a quick look before turning back to Everus. "What do you think it means? Is it some kind of omen?"

"Who knows? In fact, who cares? If Xethorn could destroy me, I think He'd have done it by now, don't you? And why warn someone who no longer cares? No. He's impotent, powerless to stop me and, what's more, I think He knows it." Everus presented his face to the sky. "You're going to have to do better than that! *Bastard!*" he yelled into the heavens.

With a fluttering of feathers, a few startled birds took to the air.

Creeps gave a scornful, half-hearted clap. "Very good. Let Him know where we are. Maybe He'll strike us wi' an earthquake or summat next. That'd be fun, wouldn't it?"

"As if I care." Everus fixed the thief with a cold gaze before turning his back on his companions and striking out, each step sodden and squelching.

Wet and aching, they trudged on, passing the old, largely overgrown grubban ruins, stopping at nightfall for some sleep and refreshment.

† † †

After another day and a half of steady travelling they arrived on a high bluff from which they could view dark-shrouded Wyrm's Port. Ever since Xethorn had usurped control of the imperial capital, an unearthly darkness had fallen, transforming it into a city of perpetual midnight. A tenebrous smog now enveloped much of the surrounding countryside for several leagues in every direction, reducing the area to a dense, contaminated blotch. Even from where he stood, Everus could feel the evil and the wickedness that emanated from within the cursed, death-ridden city.

Slack-jawed, Mhoon stared. "What...what happened? The extent of this darkness is beyond anything I'd..."

"That's where we're going. That's where the final showdown will take place," interrupted Everus. Defiantly, he stared at the blighted scene before him, his wound up nerves hungry for a fight. "Yes, Xethorn. Hide behind your wall of shadows if you must, but know that I'm coming for you."

Mhoon looked at Creeps with a face limper than a hag's tit, and just as wrinkled.

"Don't ye worry. Xethorn's all talk an' no trousers. Soon as we turn up wi' this hand-thing, He'll shit Himsel'." The thief took his pipe from his mouth and scratched his stubbled chin. "An' if He doesn't...then I sure will."

Everus set off along the road, the others close behind. They walked for some time before a natural darkness, the dark of evening, began to fall. After looking about for a while they decided to camp up by a small leafy glade just off the road. A small stream flowed nearby and, after Creeps had confirmed its safety, they all drank and filled their water bottles.

What provisions they had left were now beginning to dwindle.

"We tighten the belt from now on in. Ghavin's Keep is at least another two days' journey." Everus sat with his back to a tree and chewed on a strip of salted meat, his face half lit by the glow from the small campfire.

Creeps returned from where he had been rooting about in the foliage. "What about this?" he ventured, holding aloft a ragged, lumpy stretch of fungal matter he had pulled from a tree bole. He sniffed at his find. "Looks good to me. Smells a bit, but I've smelled worse. A bit rancid."

Mhoon sat cross-legged, tenderly stroking his bruised forehead. "What've you got there? It looks like iballswabbs."

"Can ye eat it?" asked the thief, dangling the slimy length. He walked over and held it before the wounded exorcist.

"Why yes, it *is* iballswabbs. I wouldn't have thought you'd find any of that around here. It's primarily a subterranean fungus... although it does grow in shit."

"Yeh, but can ye eat it?"

"Certainly, although it doesn't taste too good...a bit like offal," Mhoon answered. "You'll have to boil out its impurities and toxins first. Otherwise you might start to talk gibberish and see things...I mean, hallucinate."

"*See things?* As though I don't see enough." Happy that he had some supper for this evening, Creeps set about getting a pan of water on the boil.

Everus was clearly not interested in feasting on glorified mushrooms – probably because he had unpleasant memories of Creeps cultivating both edible and smokeable fungi in a bucket of horse dung back in his old room, and during their time in Umm-Dabba, the thief's habits had become even worse. He had been unlucky to bear witness to him cramming all sorts of foul-smelling things into his smoking pipe. He would not have been surprised to learn that the thief had taken to smoking camel dung itself – apparently many did. Spitting out a piece of gristle, he looked towards the exorcist. "Mhoon, what else can you tell me about this Bhubbaal?"

"Bhubbaal. Hmm." Mhoon flicked a twig into the fire. "Well, like I told you, he's one of the ul-garu – part demon, part man. His ancestry is as black as night. His heart as cold as ice. Defeating him will not be without its risks."

"I take it he *can* be destroyed?"

"Well, according to legend, the ul-garu could only be permanently destroyed by means of a lengthy ceremony performed by an exorcist. Once the physical body had been slain, an exorcism or a similar rite of purging was needed to expel the demonic essence within. However, from my own research into the matter, I've come to the conclusion that such a theory derives principally from *their* own accounts. In other words, the ul-garu have exaggerated their own legend of invulnerability in a desire to promote their power."

"So what are you saying?" asked Everus. "That they are defeatable? That this Bhubbaal character will be easy to take out?"

Mhoon nodded. "Yes...and no." For a moment, he stared emptily at Creeps, who was still busy preparing his supper. "Bhubbaal has the powers of an archmage. In addition, he's an expert warrior. I guess someone who has lived as long as he, has a lot of time to train. That aside, I think a well-placed sword will drop him just as well as it would a normal man. But that's not going to be our main problem. You see, he'll have servants and bodyguards – a whole host of protectors. What's more, they, like him, won't be human. They'll never surrender. His stronghold is a bastion of pain and evil."

"You've been there, haven't you?"

"Yes...once." Mhoon stared bleakly at the fire for a long moment. It appeared as though he was waging an inner war, battling with his own personal demons. He shifted his gaze to study his left hand.

"And?"

Mhoon stirred. "The memory is a dark one and one that I'd rather not talk about...not tonight anyway." He pulled his cloak tighter and resumed staring, deep in thought, into the flames.

After an uneasy period of silence, Creeps spoke up. "Everus, ye should try some, it's quite nice, help keep yer strength up." He sucked a wad of the snot-like gunk from his fork. A lump fell from his chin onto the ground. He scooped it up. "Would ye care for some?"

"Not while I've still got boots to eat."

† † †

Like soldiers on a forced march, they packed up and were off before sunrise. The sky was grey and an icy wind blew from the north-east. It seemed as though whatever evil enchantment had befallen Wyrm's Port was deliberately seeking them out, for every so often Everus would stop, certain that he could hear pained voices carried on that ill wind.

If either Creeps or Mhoon heard them, they did not say.

At mid-morning, they passed through a ruined settlement, its buildings now reduced to little more than heaps of rubble and splintered rafters. Here they sheltered from a brief rain shower in the remains of an old windmill before resuming their trek.

They were now heading south and, with each league, the wind began to fade. Leaving the damp and the chill behind them, they walked much of the afternoon in pleasant sunshine, and for a time their spirits lifted. Creeps even took to whistling one of his tunes.

Everus led them down into a wood. At its back was a narrow rift in the hillside. The rift did not close, but its upper reaches were so crooked that they could not see out the top. Under their feet, a layer of damp, dead leaves muffled their steps. A musty smell of age filled their nostrils, as if the packed leaves had been rotting for generations.

"This place is startin' to look familiar," commented the thief. "Aye, we've been 'ere afore, haven't we?"

"You're right," Everus agreed. "We came this way with Grigalo."

Soon they left the wood and followed the course of the road, hiking back up the slope of the escarpment. From here, they continued for another league or so until arriving at a high, flat expanse from which they could see far over the surrounding countryside.

Like a madman's smile, all looked peaceful, yet not quite right, and as Everus scanned the wilderness before him it did not take him long to see just what was wrong. In utter disbelief, his eyes settled on the mass ruin that had once been the mighty monument known as Araan's Pillar. Constructed under the reign of Emperor Wyrmius some two and a half thousand years ago it was now a scene of complete destruction. It appeared as though the once-towering, four-sided edifice had exploded. Huge mounds of rubble and brick formed artificial hills and a low-lying cloud of dust still hung over everything.

"What's happened 'ere?" asked Creeps, shaking his head in disbelief.

"*Xethorn*. It has to be Xethorn," replied Everus. He could see the remains of the four external walls protruding from the great mountain of architectural debris; the prayers and the pleas of thousands, reduced to rubble. Once a focus for pilgrimages, the monument now only paid testament to the ferocity of Xethorn's wrath – targeted, undoubtedly, because it had been here that one of the three amulets used by The High Three to contain Him, had been secreted.

"Do ye want to go down there an' have a look about?"

Everus thought about it for a moment. "No…I think we should steer clear. If we keep on this road for the rest of the day, we should arrive at one of the pilgrim tracks around dusk. We'll camp there.

Tomorrow, if all goes well, we should reach Ghavin's Keep."

"Or what's left of it," muttered Mhoon, gloomily.

✝ ✝ ✝

It was late afternoon and the sky was awash with streaks of gold and mauve as the three 'pilgrims' crested a low rise and looked down at the great walled city of Ghavin's Keep – the city founded by the renowned warrior Ghavin Truesword. The conurbation had grown up around the fertile banks of the River of Weeping Souls. Initially, it had served as a stop-off point for imperial advances into the Southern Kingdoms, where few now dared venture, but over time and with the decline of the empire, under the long reign of Tychanna III, the despotic father of Wyrmius, Ghavin's Keep had grown from a town into a city. Now, with the annexation of Wyrm's Port, it had assumed the mantle of imperial capital – even though none now knew the whereabouts of the emperor, J'hann, himself.

"Well, here we are," said Mhoon, wearily. The side of his head was bruised and yellow, like a bad apple.

"Aye, I remember this place well enough. Doesn't look as though it's changed much," replied Creeps.

"Oh, it has." Everus pointed. "Look at those towers and defences. They're all new. Look at the glacis and the refurbished crenellations. Look at all of those mangonel positions and the catapults lined along that girdle wall. Over on that side, they're building a ballistae tower and from the looks of it they've even begun to shore up the earthwork ramparts. Yes, I'd say it's changed since last we were here."

Mhoon scanned the defences. "Do you think they're expecting...?"

"An attack?" Everus interrupted. "Well, I'd say it has the looks of it, wouldn't you?"

"Well, let's hurry this up then. Let's get inside, get this thing an' go," said Creeps, using the same words his thieving father had often spoken.

Despite the enhanced security and the increased number of armed guards stationed outside, they managed to enter the city unchallenged. Every other building they passed as they made their way deeper into Ghavin's Keep had been turned into a barracks.

Hundreds of infantrymen thronged everywhere they looked.

Advancing further into the city, the militarised quarters faded

348

and their surroundings became more urban. The streets narrowed and filled with grumpy-faced people going about their day-to-day business. The air was heavy with an anxious pessimism as, from the tall and shabby buildings on either side, folk shambled forth, downcast and worried, believing perhaps that the end was about to come.

Cats, dogs and children all added to the smell and cacophony of city life.

"We'll stop there for the night," said Everus upon eyeing a faded tavern sign down a side-street. Pushing a foul-smelling beggar aside, he headed towards the poorly-lit building.

Inside, the tavern was empty apart from the owner. He was a fat, repulsive-looking man, his face covered with leaking pustules and an unsightly rash. As soon as all three of them were inside, he lumbered towards them, a toothless grin on his chubby face. "Greetings. What can I do for ye?" With two fat fingers, he burst a lump below his puffy bottom lip.

"Some food and drink for a start. Followed by three rooms for the night," Everus answered, looking the owner up and down with open distaste.

"I'm sorry gents...but we've got no food. No ale either. It's the rationin', ye see."

"No food?" queried Mhoon.

"*No drink!?*" added Creeps.

"Ye be strangers to the city, aye?" The fat man pulled a sorrowful face, his bulldog-like jowls juddering below his bleeding chin. "Thought as much when ye came in. Said to masel', Stoddard, these be strangers to yer fair city, so ye've got to look after 'em. But like I said, I've nothin' left." He presented to them his empty, upturned hands as though to prove the point.

"Well, that's no bloody good," Everus cursed.

"Good sir, where *can* we get something to eat?" asked Mhoon, slightly more tactfully.

Stoddard dabbed at his bleeding sore and examined the discharge on his fingers. "Well, like I said, what wi' the rationin' an' all, ye might have a bit o' a problem...unless, that is, ye've got plenty o' coin on ye. Ye see, a lot o' the taverns an' whatnots have had to close. I hear tell that some o' 'em o'er on the West Side, down by the Imperial Gate aren't doin' too bad, what wi' the garrison based there an' all. An' then there's those in the Noble Quarter...*rich bastards!*"

"Ye must've summat?" said Creeps. "A couple o' ales an' a bacon roll'll do me."

Mournfully, Stoddard shook his head. "Nope. Sorry."

"Let's try elsewhere." Everus did an about-turn and headed for the door, Creeps and Mhoon close behind him.

They left the tavern and its unhygienic proprietor and headed towards the Noble Quarter. Through a veritable warren of cobbled streets and bustling squares they went, stopping once or twice to ask for directions. They then crossed a stretch of bridge and passed under a colossal triumphal arch, their surroundings becoming increasingly grandiose and opulent. The houses they now saw were built on the scale of small palaces, their many annexed shrines and adjoining buildings ornate and fabulously decorated. Built on a rise before them, overlooking many of the wealthier residences, was the great temple precinct, where, among the many towers and minarets, stood the great stiletto-like spire of the cathedral of The High Three.

"Some o' these streets are lookin' familiar," commented the thief. He turned to Everus. "Aye, I remember this. Ye shot that priestly nummie wi' a crossbow from one o' these windows around 'ere, didn't ye?"

Everus gazed to where Creeps pointed. "It was around here somewhere. Can't be exactly sure."

"It was a good shot. Anyhow, let's hurry it up an' find a place to eat. I'm starvin'," complained Creeps.

"Yes. I'm dead on my feet," moaned Mhoon. "When are we going to rest?"

Everus drew them to a halt. He had led them at quite a fast pace through the city, at times not even bothering to look round to ensure that they were keeping up. "We'll rest as soon as we find a suitable place, somewhere that sells food for starters. A drink or two wouldn't go amiss either."

"I've got very little in the way of coinage." Mhoon unstrung his money pouch and looked in. "Three silver and some copper pieces. I doubt whether that will get us much around here."

Everus looked at the thief. "What about you?"

"Eh?"

"Stricken deaf, are we? How much money do you have?"

Creeps muttered darkly to himself and reached into an inside jacket pocket. Obviously peeved, he withdrew a leather wallet he had previously liberated from a passing Ghavin's Keep resident and took out a handful of gold coins.

"That'll be plenty," said Everus, snatching the coins from the thief's hand. "Now let's find somewhere that serves food, and I'm talking about decent stuff. None of that inedible Ullerbian crap."

✝ ✝ ✝

With Creeps' coins they enjoyed a sumptuous meal of roast peacock, cockatrice steak and slivers of grilled Uttapian camel buttock, all washed down with copious amounts of fine Quarunnian brandy. It crossed Everus' mind that the Ghavin's Keep zoo may have contributed to the nobles' efforts to avoid rationing. Nevertheless, it was highly tasty. The service was outstanding, even if the cherub-faced clarsarch player, who went from table to table, strumming various notes, was more than a little annoying.

"What's this place called again?" asked Creeps, stuffing his face. Bits of uneaten meat sprayed obscenely from his mouth. A trickle of snot leaked from his left nostril, becoming matted in his short moustache. Tiny, winged things hopped from his hair.

Mhoon winced at the thief's distinct lack of table manners.

"Ghavin's Keep," Everus answered. He looked about before raising his goblet to his mouth and taking a sip. Near the table where he and his companions sat were some forty or fifty wealthy patrons partaking of the bountiful fare that was reserved for the city elite. The dining hall in which they feasted was lavish and perfumed with a honey-tinged incense. At one end, near the entrance, a tall artificial waterfall cascaded into a turquoise pool filled with large fish and other aquatic livestock. Crayfish and strange luminous jellyfish were occasionally fished out and flambéed on a spit nearby.

In all, the restaurant represented the physical epitome of indulgence.

"No...I mean, *this place*. This eatery." With a dirty fingernail, Creeps scraped a bit of food from a tooth before briefly examining it and popping it back into his mouth. At such exorbitant prices he was going to make sure he did not miss anything. He would get his money's worth by hook, crook or dirty fingernail.

"Triton's Bounty."

Creeps belched and looked about him, taking in the sheer lavishness all around. It was abundantly clear to all and sundry that

351

he was completely out of place – like a leper at a palace ball or a shit stain on a princess' perfumed panties. Not that his incongruity seemed to bother him in the slightest. "It's some place all the same. Aye, an' the grub's no' bad...no' bad at all. Mind ye, at five gold each, it bloody should be. No wonder yer average plobs don't eat 'ere."

"You never were one for the high life, were you?" Everus asked. Smiling, he tilted his head slightly in order to peer to one side, aware that a gorgeous, classy brunette seated not far away was giving him the eye.

The thief finished his drink and set about pouring himself another. "*At these prices!?* Hah...ye can stick yer fancy livin' an' yer glass o' wine wi' yer cheese an' crackers where ma old dad used to hide his baccy."

Mhoon gave Everus a wry smile. "I won't ask if you won't."

Bleary-eyed, Creeps leant forward, an elbow on the covered table as though slouching at a bar. "An' I'll tell ye summat else. See all these rich nummies tuckin' into their beef an' syrup an' whatever?" Drunkenly, he waggled his finger at those in question. "Well, in ma book, they're no' worth piss." Hiccupping, he helped himself to another drink.

Seated within earshot, a disgruntled couple, dripping in jewellery, looked across, clearly unhappy.

Distinctly embarrassed, Mhoon smiled and gave them a wave.

The thief leapt to his feet and glared across. "Aye, ye heard me right! *Bastards!*"

The rich couple muttered to one another and rose from their chairs. A ripple of unease passed through several others sitting nearby, a few of them also getting to their feet and fixing the thief and those on his table with unfriendly looks.

"*Creeps!* Shut up and sit down!" ordered Everus, through clenched teeth.

"No!" The thief's body was trembling with hard to contain rage, his face flushed red and obviously a little worse the wear for the drink. "If there's one thing that really gets on ma nipple ends, it's seein' all these rich bastards crammin' their faces wi' all sorts, when there's poor buggers outside wi' nothin'." Face livid, he turned to his angry spectators. "*Bastards!*"

"*Waiter!* Be a good chap and remove this undesirable!" a corpulent man, sweating like a frightened porker, shouted.

"Get them out of here!" cried a sour-faced woman, wafting the air as though shooing away a lingering fart. "Such lowlifes."

Ranting like a madman, Creeps kept up his tirade. "*Stuck up bastards!* I don't know how ye've all got to where ye are but I bet ye're all bloody inbred halfwits. There's better folk than ye outside havin' to eat rats to stay alive. We should hang the lot o' ye an' feed ye to the crows!"

Shocked and startled diners stared with utter disbelief.

Everus' admirer looked dumbstruck.

Two of the serving staff cautiously advanced, clearly uncertain what action to take, for nothing like this had ever occurred here before. Triton's Bounty was for the refined, cultured echelons of Ghavin's Keep, the prices alone enough to exclude the hoi polloi from entering. What little trouble they had experienced before usually concerned a momentary lapse of service or polite dissatisfaction over an underdone steak.

"*Go on!* Get back to yer well-groomed chambers an' yer..." Creeps broke out into a coughing fit, his face now beetroot-red in colour. Tears streamed from his eyes.

"Sir. Kindly desist or we'll have to ask you to leave the premises," interrupted one of the waiters.

"Don't worry, we're leaving." Rising from his chair, Everus grabbed the now doubled over and coughing Creeps by the shoulder and began to forcibly escort him out through the disgruntled crowd. Folk muttered and shook their heads as he frogmarched the thief towards the exit.

"Everus, I..." Creeps staggered and nearly lost his footing, having to hold out a hand to support himself on the grand, polished glass and gilded doors.

"Mhoon. Go and get our gear. Looks like we're going to have to find somewhere else to stay." Everus glowered at the thief. "All thanks to..." He stopped, suddenly noticing figures approaching in the reflective glass. He turned round as the thief exited.

"*Uncouth swine!* How dare you defile the best dining establishment in the land?" a young, effeminate fop taunted. Due to the abundance of make-up he wore, it was hard to tell what gender he was supposed to be, although his voice sounded vaguely masculine. He wore purple lipstick, a strange-looking powdered wig and had a large, mole-like beauty-spot on his left cheek. One hand rested on the hilt of a slender rapier. Like strutting turkeys, four other lanky, long-necked pretty boys, all dolled up in their fineries, packed closely behind him. "I ought to have you stripped and flogged, but seeing as you look like you've just been dredged out of the nearest sewer, may I instead suggest a bath? Your appearance is positively barbaric." He talked with a lisp.

"At least unlike you I'm wholesome to look upon." Everus stared pointedly at the traces of rouge and powder visible on the young man's face.

"Gentlemen," the fop addressed his cronies. "I do believe we've a comedian in our midst. And there was I thinking the entertainment was over for this evening."

Oblivious to the potential trouble brewing, Mhoon exited a garderobe and gave Everus his sword. Slinging his pack over his shoulder, he went outside and joined Creeps.

"Why don't you and your girls return to your embroidery, faggot?" said Everus idly.

"*You cur!*" With one hand on his hip, the young man drew out his rapier. "*How dare you insult me?* Do you even know who I am? I'm Prince Mallory, son of King Braith of Torl; suitor of Princess Ugeena and very close personal friend of her brother, Prince Umphrey. I'm the twenty-fourth in line to the..."

"Shut up!" Everus swung out with his sword and cut the princeling down in one violent hack.

King Braith's only son lay twitching on the floor, his wet, bloody, cleaved flesh gaping. Blood and bone glistened where moments before a frilly, shirt-covered shoulder had been.

The gathered dandies gave out shrill cries.

Everus stared at them, that cold, uncaring gleam in his eyes. Foolishly, one of them made to draw a dagger, so he advanced, swung out with his sword and severed a braceleted hand.

The young aristocrat stared dumbstruck at his squirting stump before collapsing.

Screams erupted in the main dining hall as horrified people retreated.

Everus pulled back, his eyes never leaving the remaining three young nobles before him. One of them bent down and with the use of a fine silk handkerchief tried to stem the blood pumping from his friend's wrist. "Bastard!" he whimpered. "Oh, you'll swing for sure. Look what you've done."

Surveying the scene with a measure of grim satisfaction and

quite content with what he *had* done, Everus kicked the doors wide and joined his companions. "Come on. Let's go," he said, aware of their confused looks.

✝ ✝ ✝

The clientele inside The Jealous Baboon were much more to Creeps' liking, for although the tavern was but a relatively short distance from where he had started the fracas, it was blatantly clear that none of the Triton's Bounty patrons would have condescended to patronise it. There were the usual group of drunks singing raucously in one corner and a dozen or so foul-mouthed infantrymen gathered around the bar. Five grubbas and a very drunk man dressed as a jester were just finishing a game of tabletop-thuggery whilst upstairs, some tasty-looking whores leaned provocatively over a balcony, giggling to one another. One raven-haired beauty threw Everus a kiss and called out something obscene as she wiggled her huge breasts to full effect.

"Now this is more like it." Creeps gave a dirty grin and rubbed his hands.

After they had got their drinks and paid for three rooms for the night, they managed to find a quiet corner in which to sit.

"We should o' come 'ere first," said the thief, lighting his pipe.

Everus looked cold and annoyed. The face of the pretty brunette he had seen earlier was still in his mind and since leaving the upper class restaurant, his mind had entertained the idea that she could have been his childhood sweetheart; Katryna – a woman he had last seen well over ten years ago. It could be that she had perished when Wyrm's Port fell, although many did escape.

"Now don't tell me ye liked that other joint." Creeps scratched at his grimy face and twisted a finger into an ear.

"We've only just arrived in this city...and already I'm a wanted man, and not just by the tarts. Perhaps I should just walk about with a noose around my neck." Everus gave the thief a dark look. "Let me know next time you plan on starting a fight, arsehole."

"Feelin' guilty, are ye? That's no' like ye. I bet ye enjoyed cuttin' them toffs down to size." Absently, Creeps examined the wad of dry earwax he had extricated, rubbing it between his thumb and forefinger. "Anyway, what're our plans now? What's our next move?"

"We get what we came for. The pieces of Cyrvilus' hand."

"Any idea how?" asked Mhoon.

"Well, if The Grand Repository here is anything like the one in Wyrm's Port then it'll be heavily guarded." Everus flicked a beetle off the table. "Once inside, we'll have to find out where it's kept...no doubt it's lying forgotten in some cabinet or other. Tomorrow morning, we'll go to The Grand Repository and have a look around."

"Would it no' be better goin' at night?" inquired the thief.

Everus was finishing his ale, so Mhoon answered. "I think Everus means we just case the joint tomorrow."

"Is it one o' them places ye've to pay to get in?" Creeps inquired, concernedly. The very concept of having to pay to get into a place when there was hardly a lock in the known empire he could not pick, certainly grated.

"They sometimes ask for a donation." Everus put his empty tankard on the table and rose from his chair. "Well, it's been a long day and it's been a while since I last slept in a proper bed." He made his way towards the stairs, two rapacious whores latching on to him before he even started the climb, their smiles and whispered promises, irresistible.

It may well have been a long day but at least it looked as though it was going to be a good night.

† † †

They set out after breakfast.

Following the directions given to them by the landlord, they crossed the mighty River of Weeping Souls and walked down several long avenues before entering a wide plaza close to the highly decorated civic building – the seat of political power in Ghavin's Keep. In the centre of the square, built atop a great marble platform, stood a giant statue of Ghavin Truesword. With sword raised high and a stern, almost bullish look on his face, the exaggerated, stone likeness of the city's founder stared defiantly down at them.

Beyond and to the right of the colossus was the approach to The Grand Repository. At first glance, it could easily have been mistaken for yet another governmental building or perhaps a palatial mansion, but as they moved closer, they saw that this was only its external entrance; its gateway to wonder. For what lay beyond, at the end of a wide, grove-lined concourse and at the top of a slight, stepped rise was much more like a bizarre temple in appearance. Domes and spires, flying buttresses and acute-angled towers seemed to sprout from it almost as though its construction had been an organic phenomenon – as though it had heaved itself out of the ground in a fit of crazed exuberance.

Much more than a mere museum, the building was also a working academy solely dedicated to the unravelling of a largely ignored and forgotten age. It was a focus for hermetical archivists and a nexus for esoteric heurists.

Almost three leagues of cluttered passageways, some of them underground, ran like warrens throughout the arcane storehouse. Dusty display cabinets lined the walls, their contents ranging from the fairly mundane and uninteresting to the strange and exotic.

Hundreds of windows gleamed in the bright early morning sunlight as Everus and his companions stood in the shade of the massive statue and looked across.

"Ye say there's summat like this in Wyrm's Port?" Creeps asked, staring in wonder.

"Yes. However, surprisingly, this one looks much more extravagant. That is not, however, necessarily a reflection of the quality or even the quantity of the treasures inside."

"Treasure, ye say?" Rheumy eyes lit up in Creeps' face. History was all well and good he supposed, but easily portable history that had a good market value was so much better. "I always thought it was just old junk they kept in these places. Ye know, out o' date coins an' granny tokens."

"*Granny tokens?*" asked Mhoon, confused.

"Aye, ye must've heard o' granny tokens!" The thief looked genuinely dumbfounded. "Everus, ye tell him."

Everus obliged. "There used to be a tradition in Wyrm's Port whereby a certain number of tokens were distributed to the hags of the city in order to enable them to get prime viewing spots at public executions. Those who had a token – they resembled wooden coins with their own individual marking – were entitled to a seat and a free loaf..."

"A biscuit," Creeps interrupted.

"Yes, whatever. No doubt you'd know. I can imagine you with a shawl over your head jostling to get to the front. Anyway, once the hangings were over, the officiator would draw a symbol on a blackboard and whoever's token matched the symbol was dragged forward and joined those strung up."

"You mean they were hung?" queried Mhoon.

"*Hanged*," corrected Everus.

"Hmm. A rather strange practice...and more than a little barbaric," mused Mhoon. "Whose idea was that, I wonder?"

"Saraq's. Saraq I," Everus answered sharply. "He came to power shortly after the brief rule of Jamba Bastardborn the Unfavourable. Three hundred and thirty-nine years ago." He noticed two custodians approaching the immense wrought iron gates which gave entrance to The Grand Repository grounds. "Looks like they're opening up."

As a group they headed over. At the gates they were instructed to hand over their weapons and informed that admission would cost them one silver piece each. Everus paid with one gold coin and told the gatekeepers to see that the change went to the furthering of academic research and the maintenance of the building. Cynically, he suspected it would end up either in a pub landlord's safe or a whore's purse.

It was strangely quiet as they headed down the tree-lined avenue towards the entrance proper. Until, there, now looming high above them, they saw The Grand Repository in all its majesty. A gargantuan stone minotaur-like head glared down at them from above the huge entrance archway.

"That's some sculpture," muttered Mhoon, staring up.

"It's not a statue." Everus was likewise staring up, a grim intensity in his eyes. "It's the petrified head of G'garochi-Kaggh, the dark lamassu." With no further talk, he passed under the monstrous trophy and entered the main hall.

The chamber was cavernous in size and design, with several balustraded galleries on higher levels.

Held together by magical means, the fractured, sulphurous, stained skeleton of some enormous, upright creature dominated the hall. The monstrous remains towered up towards the high domed ceiling, the jaws wide enough to accommodate any one of them.

"Well bugger me wi' a broom handle!" commented Creeps. "Would ye look at that!"

"What is it?" asked Mhoon, eyes wide with awe. "A dragon?"

"Yes. *That*...is the skeletal remains of Xethorn's steed, the brimstone dragon, Magmabreath. Impressive, is it not?" Everus looked about, his eyes catching sight of a couple of robed custodians shuffling towards them.

"Welcome to The Grand Repository. A finer collection of wonders you'll not see anywhere else," said one of them, his voice echoing. "Are you scholars or just curious visitors?"

"Scholars," answered Everus.

"Hmm." The old man who had welcomed them stared uncertainly for a moment at Creeps. "And, is there any way I can help you? I'm Geffreys, archivist and relic keeper of the Ground Floor. If you have any questions, by all means ask."

Before Everus could respond, Creeps stepped forward. "Was that a real dragon?"

Geffreys turned to his bespectacled companion. "Moorby, would you...?"

Moorby cleared his throat. He waved a hand up towards the massive bone colossus. "What you can see is the skeletal framework of the mighty brimstone dragon, Magmabreath, who ravaged the lands south of here some time before The Hellspawn Cataclysm. The last and most powerful of the brimstone dragons, Magmabreath was possibly used as a steed by the Lord of Murder, Xethorn, who as you may know has returned and taken control of Wyrm's Port to the north." The scholar straightened his glasses and continued with his spiel. "Held together by a mix of special resins and a form of magical, fungal-based glue created by one of the conservational teams based at our Academy for Ancient Relics, the remains are now entirely complete, down to the smallest detail. Close examination of the skeletal structure and in particular the taphonomic wear visible along both primary and secondary scapulae, indicate quite incontrovertibly, that the dragon was, at least in the past and perhaps only during the initial proto-development stages of its lifetime, capable of flight. As you can see, the wings have now long since gone. Unlike most dragons, and especially those which originated within the Zethian lava fields, we believe Magmabreath was capable of speech. Such a deduction is based both on the surviving written accounts from that time, which are admittedly ambiguous and open to debate, and on the recent examination carried out by Professor Glee on the draconic vocal architecture, in particular the distinct dentition patternation and arrangement of the..."

"An aye or no would've done," Creeps interrupted, certain that the man would have gone on all morning if permitted.

"I'm looking for the bones of Cyrvilus," Everus quickly

inquired, aware that Creeps' offhand manner was likely to blow their cover. "I understand that parts of the preserved hand are stored here."

Geffreys raised his eyes to the ceiling and stroked his chin. "The hand of Cyrvilus. Hmm...not sure, but if you just wait there a moment, I'll see if I can locate it for you." He strode over to a small annexed office and disappeared inside. Shortly after he came out, a roll of vellum in his hand.

"You've found it?" Everus asked, excitedly.

The old scholar unrolled the scroll and looked at it. "Ah, I'm sorry to disappoint you but unfortunately the relic pieces in question have been temporarily removed, possibly for further study. We've a lot of other similar material however, including some as yet unidentified skulls from Zeth itself."

Everus clapped his hands together and sighed. "Look. We've travelled all the way from The City of the Glittering Spire to examine the bones. Now, surely there's some way we can get to see them? If you would be so good as to tell me where they are, then we can complete our research. It's very important that we...have the opportunity to compare the skeletal erosion on the remains with the...the..." He was clearly flannelling.

"The works o' Wormdoddy o' Ullerby," added Creeps.

Suddenly reminded of the poster of the skinny jester in the knobbly motley he had last seen in Ullerby, Everus fought to choke back a laugh. "Ahem...why, yes. Wormdoddy of Ullerby. Apparently it was he who carried out much of the early research on the Cyrvilian pieces and...it was he, who...postulated the connection between the nature of black laval chaostone as a working medium and its links to the reawakening of Uhu'giaggoth, The Daemon God." As lies went, this was undoubtedly one of his best – a true classic.

Geffreys and Moorby looked quizzically at one another.

"So, are ye goin' to tell us where it is?" prompted Creeps. "Or are we goin' to have to beat it out o' ye?"

† † †

"Utterance's cathedral to The High Three. Why here?" Everus inquired. Night had fallen and the street was more or less empty as he and his companions skulked in the shadows and made their plans.

Across from them, the dark, angular building rose like a darker shadow into the sunless heavens.

"Safekeeping, perhaps?" suggested Mhoon.

"Possible." Everus gently chewed his bottom lip.

"Aye. Could be them priestly nutters know summat we don't, summat that fart back in Umm-Dabba didn't tell ye," said Creeps. "Maybe the bones are cursed."

"Or more likely they've discovered their connection to Xethorn, and they fear that He'll come for them...hence the city defences," reasoned Mhoon. "And if I'm right, then obviously it's imperative that we get to the hand before Xethorn does, which could also explain why He destroyed Araan's Pillar. Perhaps He thought that part of the hand was kept there."

"So what do we do now?" asked Creeps.

Everus remained silent for a moment, his mind running through the limited options available to them. Should they launch an all out assault on the cathedral, hoping that whatever resistance they met would be light? Or should they opt for a more subtle approach – perhaps create some kind of diversion to draw out whatever guardians were inside and then sneak in, locate the remains and steal them with minimum bloodshed? Were they accomplished enough thieves to do that? He was still thinking things through when a light appeared in the immense cathedral doorway.

"Look!" hissed Mhoon.

Two shadowy figures exited the temple. A moment later, two huge beacons on either side were lit by magical blue fire. The illumination was brilliant, transforming the night sky like the sudden genesis of two small, azure suns.

Blinking, Everus recoiled slightly. Still temporarily blinded from the effect, he reached out and steadied himself against a nearby wall.

"There's folk comin'," whispered the thief. "They look like wizardy-types."

Shaking the vestiges of the sudden flash from his vision, Everus peered to where Creeps pointed and saw three men dressed in robes – one vermillion, the other two purple – come striding down the main approach to the cathedral. With barely perceptible nods to the two priests on gate duty, they entered the building. Even as the last of the trio vanished inside, a splendidly decorated carriage drawn by two black stallions pulled up outside and another two purple-robed men got out.

"A wizard's convention?" suggested Mhoon.

"It would appear so," Everus replied, a plan developing in his mind. On the periphery of the blue glow, further back along the street, he could see two approaching forms – one dressed in a plain grey robe and the other, somewhat shorter in height, in a purple-coloured robe decorated with black stars. "Hmm. From the looks of things it's an invitation only do." He reached for the dagger he kept secreted in his right boot.

"*What?* Are you nuts?" muttered Mhoon, understanding exactly what Everus had in mind.

"Why don't you return to the inn? We'll meet you later." Everus looked to Creeps, who grinned wickedly and nodded.

† † †

From his podium, high priest Utterance IV dramatically whisked away the black cloth from the plinth before him to reveal the intricate brass ossuary in which resided several small bony fragments. Some in the forty or so congregation emitted hushed cries of awe, others stared wide-eyed, whilst still others stepped closer for a better look – their eyesight poor from decades devoted to reading arcane scrolls.

Everus' eyesight however was perfect and even from where he and Creeps stood near the back of the crowd managing to look inconspicuous, he could see the cursed container better than most now almost within touching distance of it. He could still feel the damp spot where he had cleaned the blood from the robe on his lower back. Creeps had fared better – not only had he claimed the fancier robe but he had also used his belt to strangle the unsuspecting, bespectacled boy-wizard.

Utterance was tall, bald and gaunt, with sharp, almost hawk-like features. He raised a hand, silencing the majority of the observers. "And so...as prophesied, a time of chaos once again draws near. A dark day is about to dawn for the people of our world. I've gathered you all here tonight to this council to decide what should be done." He turned to a fat, lavishly dressed man standing nearby. "Pope Benignus."

Wiping a sheen of sweat from his ruddy forehead, the fat, greasy-faced pope swaggered to the podium. "As I'm sure you're all aware, and despite the differences in our...beliefs, the events of the past year have given rise to our need for unity and full co-operation. Now, more than at any other time in our past, we must be resolute in our steadfastness. We must set aside the petty bickering that has plagued our respective, and at times, disparate, teachings. Magic and religion must combine if we're to defeat the greater evil."

"Why?" asked a red-robed wizard, a crimson glow encircling his raised hand.

Benignus and Utterance, not expecting an interruption this early in the proceedings, raised their eyebrows in shared confusion.

"I ask again. Why should we join forces with the very cause of our predicament?" The wizard was young, but the red colour of his robe signified his importance. "Without religion there would be no gods. The Cyrvilian bones thrive off the power that the misguided sacerdotal collectivity has bestowed upon them. It's that which has made them dangerous." A handful of his fellows murmured in agreement.

"And Xethorn?" queried Utterance. "Are you naïve enough to believe that His power is derived solely from His worshippers?"

"That's exactly what..." the wizard started.

With a wave of his hand, Benignus extinguished the querying wizard's light. His fat face hardened as he glared at the disgruntled crowd around the young mage. "Xethorn has no worshippers left. Now that He has assumed an earthly mantle He has become unworshipable. He has become undeified."

"How do *you* know?" asked a different red-robed man, the scintillating pale yellow crescents on his robe brazenly displaying his affinity to lunar magic and shape-shifting.

A solemn, almost downcast look came over Benignus. "Through commune."

"I see," said the wizard, even as some of his cohort gasped with amazement and disbelief. "So...what has our esteemed despiser told you? Or, more to the point, what have *you* told Him?"

Benignus brushed aside the accusatory undertone, even as Utterance made to complain. "We've until the morning of the High Festival to hand over the relic pieces kept here. Failure to comply will result in the destruction of the city."

Creeps nudged Everus.

Like a single entity, the crowd around them muttered.

A wizardly glow from the side silenced the council. "You say Xethorn will use force...yet, He has no worshippers. How exactly does He intend to take the city? After all, it's not as though we're without defences," asked a voice.

"Aye, an' what about the Øggars? Tell me, what's become o' them?" came the gruff demand of a hunchbacked grubban necromancer. The short staff he gripped was topped with a grinning skull, his ugly face not that dissimilar. "I've heard they've all been killed."

"The Øggarbakken behemoths *are* dead," answered Benignus. "As are all who rallied to Xethorn's call; pirates, berserkers, assassins. All dead."

"Who killed 'em?" asked the grubba.

"Xethorn."

"*Why?* Why kill yer supporters?"

"For fuel." Benignus stared hard at the garish gathering, noting the open mouths and the confused stares. He whispered something to the high priest beside him before turning to face his audience once more. "As you know, there's always existed a great enmity between Xethorn and The Daemon God that we know as Uhu'giaggoth. And, ever since His reawakening, Xethorn has been attempting to breach the planar boundary that The High Three created to imprison His nemesis."

"Hence the meteoric activity of late?" called out a voice from the crowd.

"Yes," Benignus answered.

"But why would Xethorn seek to free Uhu'giaggoth?" inquired the young, red-robed mage.

"In order to do battle. In order to vanquish The Daemon God once and for all. It's our belief that Xethorn feels cheated of His victory. He's angry and bitter at having been rescued by The High Three during the final battle of The Hellspawn Cataclysm. Despite claims to the contrary, Xethorn was all but annihilated by The Daemon God. His efforts were, by and large, futile. His actions no more than a wasp sting to a mammoth. Perhaps He resents His humiliation. In truth...we don't really know."

A hulking, black-skinned sorcerer levitated himself in order to see better, his high-collared crimson robe radiating heat. "And what of this fuel you mention?" His voice was thunderous and conjured up the image of roiling lava flows and erupting calderas.

"The fuel I speak of is blood. The blood of His enemies. The blood of those who followed Him. Xethorn is collecting their blood in order to lure Uhu'giaggoth," answered Benignus.

"Will He prove successful?" the sorcerer boomed.

"That, I cannot answer. However, we both hold the view that...if this goes unchecked, then yes, Xethorn *could* breach the celestial prison. Besides, if we do nothing to intervene and Xethorn gains the part of the hand in our keeping, then, for us at least, what does it matter?"

"And it's your belief that the Lord of Murder seeks the hand to assist in summoning Uhu'giaggoth?" asked someone else.

Benignus nodded. "As I'm sure many of you are aware, the hand of Cyrvilus is a highly potent relic and, although the remains are scattered and their exact whereabouts remain a mystery, if they were to be found and united, I've no doubt they could be turned to great evil. Cyrvilus was, in some ways, himself a demigod – the first of the Daemondamned – a mortal spawn of Uhu'giaggoth." He shook his head. "It must never fall into Xethorn's grasp."

"Xethorn will never take Ghavin's Keep without an army. His powers may be considerable, but surely we possess the combined might to keep Him at bay," called out one of the mail-clad militant wizards.

"But He has an army," replied the pope.

"Ye said that the Øggars are dead," cried out the deformed grubba, cracking his staff on the cathedral floor. "What has He done, re-animated 'em?"

"It would appear so. His army is now composed of the bones and residues from His sacrificial soup. The blood, as I've said, has been drained and collected. Some has been used in perverse experiments, creating monstrous hybrids and unspeakable abominations. Even as we speak, His unholy creations are preparing for war," Utterance answered.

"So what do we do?" someone at the front asked, his voice tinged with panic.

"Without a better suggestion, it's our belief that we should try to stem Xethorn's power," said Utterance, his voice slow and surprisingly calm despite the gravity of the situation. "He seeks the hand. He knows that part of it's here. Despite our endeavours, we've failed to destroy it, nor have we been able to utilise its powers, thus, we cannot use it as a weapon against Him. Our pleas to The High Three have so far gone unanswered. Consequently, from three options...we're left with but one." He stared down at the casket before raising his sleepless eyes to the assembly of troubled wizards. "It must be taken from here. The further the better. Who among us will take it?"

CHAPTER SEVENTEEN

"Well, that was easier than expected," growled Everus, sitting down on the edge of his bed.

"Did you end up having to steal it?" asked the exorcist.

"No...the daft nummies gave it to us...for safekeepin'." Creeps laughed, the sound cracked, laboured and unpleasant. Reaching into the dirty sack he carried, he removed the small casket and rested it on a table. "They said we could look after it...so long as we leave the city." He looked over to where Everus sat and hesitated a moment as though gathering the courage to talk to him. "Where'd they say they wanted us to take it again?"

"Nowhere specific."

It was clear to Mhoon that something had Everus irked. Running a hand down his chin, he looked at the small box. "I can't believe that they just gave it to you. I mean...are you *sure* it's the real thing?" Tentatively, he reached out as though he were about to open it.

"I wouldn't if I were ye," warned Creeps.

Everus raised his right hand, around which he had a tightly wound bandage. "It burns."

The exorcist withdrew his tattooed hand. He squatted down to examine it. "Hmm. Very curious. It seems to be generating its own heat. It's as though there's a small internal fire or something inside. Almost as though it's volcanic."

"Demonic," corrected Everus, lying back and gazing at the raftered ceiling of his small tavern room. "On our way here, I added a finger bone given to me by Emir Ib-irem, a boy-sage from Umm-Dabba. The bones conjoined, giving off more than a little heat."

Mhoon stood up. "Demonic, you say? Well I suppose that would explain..."

"*It explains nothing!*" Everus sat up. "Does it explain the way in which Creeps managed to lay claim to it? The way in which he was suddenly able to sway the entire assembly of gathered priests and

366

wizards!? The way in which he passed Utterance's tests of truth? *No! It explains nothing!"*

Confused and uncomfortable with Everus' outburst, Mhoon took a step back and looked at the thief.

"You ask him!" shouted Everus. *"Ask him how he does it!"*

Guiltily, Creeps looked to the floor.

"Ask him!"

Mhoon hesitated. "Er...Creeps. How did you...?"

Creeps looked up, his body visibly trembling although whether from rage or fear it was hard to tell. "It just sort o'..."

"Cut the crap Creeps, and tell it like it is," Everus interrupted, angrily. He pointed straight at the thief. "Back in Umm-Dabba, you told me that whatever gods you worked for had deserted you. Now, after what I witnessed this evening, I know that what you told me then was complete bullshit. How else could you've done what you did?"

"Does it matter?" said Creeps.

"What do you mean? Does what matter?"

"Well, we've got what we went for, haven't we?"

"That's not the point! I'd have sooner fought my way through an army of wizards than rely on your constant lies. You see, I, for one, have had enough of being a god's plaything – but you, on the other hand, seem to thrive on your little secrets and so-called abilities." Removing his stern gaze from the thief, Everus looked across at Mhoon. "Yes...I'm surprised our little liar here wasn't made the next pope, what with his intimate knowledge of The High Three theology and spiritual flimflam."

"But we do have the part of the hand. Surely that's what counts?" said Mhoon, trying to act as a mediator.

"Aye, Everus...look at it that way," Creeps added.

"Oh...why don't you two just leave me alone for a while?" Everus had heard enough. He fell back on his bed, his thoughts in turmoil. Yes, they had been successful in obtaining a piece of the relic and yet, deep down, he felt betrayed – such a common emotion for him, what with all he had been through. And yet, even as weariness crept into his body, it felt as though a power, an external force, something beyond his control, was smothering that feeling of betrayal as someone would extinguish a fire.

He did not hear Creeps and Mhoon leave.

Gazing at the ceiling, lost in his spiral of dark thoughts, a wave of intense anger flashed through Everus like a jolt of electricity. It was a dark anger which told him to kill...and then kill again. He closed his eyes and gritted his teeth as, in his mind, tormented, wraith-like visages swam before him. Five or six, then twenty or so and then hundreds. He seemed trapped in a horrible living nightmare – a phantasmagoria – in which twisted beings span around in a morbid, ghostly carousel, their pleas pitiful. He tried to scream but his cry was strangled.

And still the doomed whirled around, their eyes hollow, their limbs withered, their bodies no more than spectral husks.

And...when the time for horror and sorrow had passed, he laughed. He laughed for he knew that he had damned them and that they suffered because of what he had done.

† † †

When he awoke, he was surprised to see that the small room was partially lit with rays of early morning sunshine. He stretched and went over to the window for a look outside. Below him was an untidy back yard in which lay a covered wagon from which two bearded, broad-shouldered men were noisily offloading several large beer barrels. A small boy was playing around them, and assisting, in a childish way, with the ale delivery.

Suddenly the child stopped his playful antics and stared up at the window Everus was looking down from.

Everus froze. He had seen this child before – once accompanying the pilgrims to Araan's Pillar and, almost certainly, once in Wyrm's Port.

A sudden knock at the door startled him, causing him to spin round, his eyes darting to where his sword rested.

The knock came again.

"Enter." Everus edged back, reaching for his sword.

The door was opened by a tall, curvaceous beauty. She was outstandingly pretty; from her long, rippled hair which was a striking blend of rich lilacy-purple with flaming red highlights, to her eye-catching figure and modest but close-fitting clothes – all contributing to make Everus think she was a classy and highly expensive courtesan. She looked about his age.

"You look a little surprised," she said, her voice slightly husky.

"I...I was expecting someone else." Tilting his head, Everus glanced over her left shoulder, checking that there was no one else with her. It was then that he was pleasantly struck by the mild scent of exotic perfume. The aroma was delightful and highly arousing.

"Oh?"

Everus found it hard to take his eyes off her face. She was perfect. Deep blue eyes. Full, cherry-red lips. He swayed slightly on his feet, captivated by her beauty.

"But I told you I was coming." She took a step towards him, a hand reaching out in an offer of friendship.

He fought against the attraction he was feeling – the desire in his heart to just abandon everything right here and now and run off with this woman he had never seen before in his life. Somehow, he managed to shake himself free of her enchantment; her spell, her magnetism, her whatever it was – cast it aside and flung it into the dark pits of his heart, to rot there if need be. It would not be for long though.

"What's the matter?" she asked, concernedly.

"Who are you?"

The woman stood her ground, her radiant eyes fixing Everus with their mesmerising power. "My name's Carrie Orlandis." She turned her gaze over to the where the casket rested on the table. "I've been appointed by the Grand Archmage of Ghavin's Keep to see to it that your...associate, fulfils his duty. You see, not all of us wizards trust either the pope's or the high priest's decision making, or judgement."

Everus tutted. This was all he needed. He should have guessed that things were bound to get complicated. So far, it had all been too easy. Looking at her again, a strong wave of lustful thoughts flooded through his mind. She was *absolutely* gorgeous.

"I also know that you're not all that you claim." Carrie walked over to stand near the table.

Everus gulped. "Oh?"

"Yes. I know a lot about you." Smiling, Carrie walked up and circled Everus, even as he fought with the lascivious need to just lock the door, throw her down on the bed and strip her naked.

Just at that moment the door was pushed wider and Mhoon entered. Surprised at seeing Carrie, he faltered in the doorway, his mouth agape. "Eh, I...I hope I'm not...um..." he stuttered, embarrassedly. He turned to leave.

"Mhoon. Get back in here," commanded Everus.

Clearly confused, Mhoon stood at the threshold.

"Ah, an exorcist, I see." Carrie turned and smiled at Everus. "You can tell a man by his hands."

"Where's Creeps?" Everus asked.

"He's out. Getting money, I think he said."

Everus nodded, guessing full well what the thief-cum-deity's-servitor was up to. "This is Carrie." He nodded to the woman, who in turn smiled at Mhoon. "She's been assigned by the Grand Archmage of the city to make sure that we perform our task – that we take the Cyrvilian remains as far from here as possible."

"Ah...yes," Mhoon mumbled, patting his bottom lip with a finger.

"And your name?" Carrie asked.

"I am Mhoon." The exorcist bowed. "At your service."

"Well, I thank you." Carrie turned, and for a disconcerting moment that lingered longer than intended, her eyes, sparkling like sapphires, locked with those of Everus. "And...yours?" she asked.

"Everus." In that brief clash, it seemed to him that she was trying to melt his icy exterior, trying to breach the defences he had built about himself over the years since his beloved Katryna had abandoned him. Defences he had honed with distrust and reinforced with the mortar of bitterness.

Her smile faded but refused to die as their eyes parted.

"You said you told me you were coming? How can this be? I've never seen you before today," Everus asked, his voice cold despite the sexual yearnings that stirred within him. To bed *this* woman would be to know paradise.

"I told you in your dreams," Carrie answered. She lowered her voice till it was little more than a whisper. "I saw...what you saw."

"And what was that?"

"Dark things. Dead things. The spirits of those you've damned."

† † †

"So, who's the tart?" Creeps asked, nodding to the far table at which Everus and the sorceress sat talking. He accepted some change from the barkeeper and received a packet of *Erbert Toad's* finest baccy and a pipe.

"Her name's Carrie," answered Mhoon. "She's been appointed

by some wizardly high-up to make sure that we don't just run back to Xethorn with the bones or make off with them for our own goals. I gather from what she's said that there's more than a little distrust between the wizards and the religious order here in the city. Hence the safety measure, I suppose."

"Hmm. Rather buggers things up, don't it?"

"Well, yes...I guess it does."

Shiftily, Creeps looked over and lowered his voice to a hushed mutter. "Unless o' course, she were to just disappear." He rolled a wad of the brown, dung-like *Erbert Toad* between thumb and forefinger and sniffed at it.

"*Eh?* You..." Before Mhoon could finish, Everus and Carrie rose from where they were seated and walked over to join them.

"So...what's the plan?" Creeps asked, nonchalantly sprinkling some of the now powdered baccy back into its pouch. "Are we leavin' or what?"

"I think it'd be for the best, don't you? After all, we still have a certain demigod to battle." Everus looked at the thief, darkly. "Besides, if we don't, I think we're liable to be on the receiving end of some tough questioning from those who've entrusted Cyrvilus' bones to us. If you remember, we, or should I say, *you*, did agree to self-imposed exile." Grimly, he looked about the half-empty tavern, confirming that only his companions were paying attention. "In addition, Carrie has told me that the archmage has placed a spell on the relic so that he can track its movements. We venture too close to Wyrm's Port with it, we'll be detected...and attacked. Similarly, if we loiter here for too long."

Carrie nodded, her long hair cascading in purplish-red curls. "I'm afraid this is true. And, even though Everus has confided in me, telling me the true nature of your quest, I would suggest that we leave as soon as possible."

The thief shook his head, muttering to himself. It was clear he did not approve of Carrie being made privy to their attempt to destroy Xethorn. It only served to complicate things.

Mhoon looked questioningly towards Everus.

"*Well?* What did you want me to do?" Everus argued, defensively. "Creeps lies to all and sundry. One moment he plays the ignorant, claiming he knows nothing about what's going on. The next, he's so high and bloody mighty he might as well march on Wyrm's Port and take on Xethorn himself. That reminds me, that time on the beach

371

when we were chased by those headhunters or whatever they were...how come that sea monster you *claimed* you saw never ate you? I think there was no such thing. It was just your magic...or your gods...or whatever, coming to the rescue once again."

Guiltily, Creeps looked about, then settled on staring out of a nearby window, keeping his thoughts to himself.

"I...get the feeling that I'm not entirely welcome," said Carrie.

If she was not so damned charismatic and attractive, Everus would quite probably have told her to piss off – would have taken his chances with the archmage and his cohort. As things were, however, he would much sooner tell Creeps and Mhoon to take a hike. He turned to her. "Don't worry, you'll soon get used to it." He looked down at the pack lying at the thief's feet, inside which was the brass casket. "So...are we going to Sawerrea to get whatever pieces are there, or are we going to sit here and wait for Xethorn to put in an appearance?"

"I may be able to find some horses for us, but many of them have not survived the siege precautions," Carrie volunteered.

"Don't bother. I don't know about Mhoon, but Creeps can't tell one end of a horse from the other and I admit that I'm not that proficient at riding, myself. I guess I trust my own feet too much. They've brought me this far."

"You know, going by horse isn't that bad an idea, Everus," Mhoon added. "I *can* ride and it would speed things up."

"I can't ride," said Creeps. "I'd have to sit behind someb'dy. Although, there's good eatin' on a horse."

Everus' mind was already made up. "We walk."

✝ ✝ ✝

"Looks nothin' like ye," said Creeps, looking a little too blatantly for Everus' liking at a nailed-up wanted poster. "That drawin's got blue eyes an' yet ye've got green. I could do better. Ye know, had things worked out different for me I could o' been an artist."

"Really?" Everus raised his hood and walked over to where Carrie and Mhoon waited by the South Gate.

"What's your friend looking at?" asked Carrie, curiously.

"Oh, I don't know. I think it's a recruitment poster, asking for volunteers to join the army or something. Personally, I think they should reinstate conscription. That'd get some of the scum off the streets. Throw them in the army and kill them off. Anyway...are we all set?"

Mhoon nodded.

Carrie smiled.

Creeps jogged over.

✝ ✝ ✝

The skies were darkening by the time they reached the last hill which provided a view of the city. Atop its windblown summit, they gathered and looked back at the winding road they had spent the better part of the day walking along.

"Farewell, Ghavin's Keep," Carrie whispered, her words carried on the growing breeze along with the dead leaves all around.

Everus had heard her words and a slight pang of sympathy stabbed his otherwise pitiless heart. Since their first meeting, he had found it hard to take his eyes from her, almost as though a part of him desired nothing more than to keep her safe, to ensure that she was always nearby. His sense of sympathy grew stronger as he watched her staring forlornly back towards her home city, probably thinking, as was he, about what would be left standing if Xethorn were to turn His rage against it.

Creeps had obviously heard her as well, but he shook his head uncaringly and rubbed his hands together. "So, how long's it goin' to take us to get to this place?"

"Several days," Everus answered. He gazed back at the city, which was now little more than a rectangular silhouette on the far horizon. He took a deep breath and started down the hill.

They walked on for a short time until the road they were following reached a crossroads. Here they stopped for the evening, and as Creeps set about preparing a campfire, the three others started to rummage through their packs for their provisions and bedrolls and other pieces of camping gear.

A chill wind wailed through the camp, causing the now lit fire to dance and gutter.

"It's goin' to be a cold one the night," commented Creeps, walking over to where he had left his pack. "Good job I managed to get the fire goin'." He crouched down and removed a bottle of ale and a pack of sausages.

"What've you got there?" inquired Mhoon, peeling an apple.

373

The thief slyly patted his nose with a finger. "Ah, these be mine." Reaching into his pack, he withdrew a grimy frying pan, into which he dropped the sausages. He walked over and rested the pan on the fire. "Aye...these be mine." In the firelight, his eyes lit up greedily.

Everus returned from taking a piss.

"Creeps has got some sausages," said Mhoon.

"*So?*" Everus replied, flatly. Unbothered, he headed over to where Carrie sat at the base of a tree, huddled in a thick poncho. If anything, in the firelight, she looked even sexier, brimming with a primal comeliness that he was finding it very hard not to respond to. He had to wonder whether she had the same effect on the other two men. "Are you cold?" he asked.

"A little...but I'll cope."

Everus stared for a moment longer before looking skyward. "Have you ever been to Umm-Dabba?"

"Why do you ask?"

"The stars...in Umm-Dabba, they're very different; brighter. It's said that a man can navigate the vastness of the Great Desert of Chul-ta by the stars alone...that The High Three locked a map in the heavens in order to lead the famed hero, Ma'qata Dunestalker, to safety."

"Oh? Do you believe that?"

For a moment longer Everus' eyes lingered on the heavens – no longer knowing what he believed. Then he looked down at her, and, as he looked into her eyes and saw how the firelight danced over her face, he felt himself being transported back to an earlier time, a time when everything he *had* believed in and everything he had desired had been pure and innocent. He dreamily remembered a time when he and his beloved Katryna had been out all night on a romantic sojourn in the grounds of her aunt's estate. He had been in his mid-teens, she a year younger. They had talked for most of the evening, pledging their undying love to one another, discussing their plans for the future after he had become a high scholar. And, as the night had gone on...

"Everus?"

Carrie, calling his name, brought him back. He blanked the memory from his mind, knowing that to do otherwise would be to give in; to surrender to the emotions that would just as readily tear him apart as a quartet of mad stallions.

"Everus!" This time it was Creeps. "Ye want a bit o' ma meat?"

Mhoon looked across quizzically, the slightly camp look on his face somehow exacerbating Creeps' unintended innuendo.

"Maybe for breakfast." Everus turned once more to Carrie, silently cursing the presence of the other two. "Well, you know what we're up against. Do you still plan on seeing this through? After all, you could just as easily return to your order and tell them that we left you behind or disappeared during the night." He paused to think for a moment. "I guess what I'm saying is, I can't vouch for your safety."

"I know."

"And?"

"And...well, I'm in on this now. If this is the only way to defeat Xethorn once and for all, then how could I not be?" Briefly, Carrie look distractedly over to where Creeps and Mhoon sat bickering with one another, their heated exchange concerning the latter's right to a portion of the thief's supper. "Besides, do you remember back to our first meeting?"

"What about it?"

"Do you remember me telling you that I'd seen you in your nightmare? That I'd been there? That I'd witnessed what you'd seen?"

Everus looked confused. "I remember you saying something to that effect."

A sudden chill in the air prompted Carrie to draw her poncho closer. "Well, I've been trying to fathom its meaning. You see, in addition to my, albeit limited, magical prowess, I've some skill in interpreting dreams and auguries." Her eyes focused on him, noting his restrained scepticism. "A darkness has befallen you, Everus. Death has embraced you as would...a lover."

"You're beginning to sound like a two copper soothsayer." Everus' words were cruel, but his smile showed that he did not mean to offend.

Carrie brushed aside his remark. She drew her knees closer to her huddled form. "You've had other dreams. Ones in which you've seen the creation of Xethorn's blood-drained minions and..." She paused, trying to bring order to the images she had seen in her mind. "There's something else, something darker, but I can't see what. A...veil, or a mist has descended. It's as though you yourself have blotted it from your mind."

"Then that's probably for the best." Everus gazed pensively at the fire. "My mind is filled with many things that aren't particularly nice."

"Has anyone any idea how we're going to get this next part of the Cyrvilian relic?" asked Mhoon.

Stirred from his dark reflections, Everus looked over. "I thought we'd just send Creeps in to get it. He seems to have a certain flair for such things."

Nonchalantly, the thief looked up from his plate of steaming sausages.

With no further talk, Everus then settled down and tried to get some sleep.

When he awoke, it was almost dawn. To the east, the sky was streaked with grey, but over to the west, it was still dark and the last stars were just visible as he got to his feet, rolled up his blanket and built up the fire, blowing on the red embers to bring it to life again. From the looks of it, his companions were still sleeping, so he warmed up the leftover sausages and ate a hurried breakfast on his own. Once finished, he strolled over to the edge of their campsite, his eyes taking in the rugged stretch of country that lay before them. It was a land of which he knew very little; a land of rising buttes and mesas, where great red and grey sandstone rocks had been etched and fluted by long geological ages of wind and storms, naturally fashioned into twisted sculptures of strange, eerie beauty.

✝ ✝ ✝

After five more days of travelling along empty roads and lonely stretches, where the rare sight of some strange herd of giant, rhinoceros-like herbivores or an ancient ruin did little to alleviate the tedium, they eventually entered the vast cinder fields and baked basalt flows that signalled their arrival in Sawerrea.

Built almost entirely from large blocks of local lava crust, the town of Wathang-Hu, which lay on the northernmost fringe of Sawerrea, was a dreary place. The stink and the dust from the great piles of ash and refuse that all but buried the outer walls was enough to dissuade most casual visitors and if that failed, then the approaching road, lined on either side with crucified criminals, usually did the trick.

Although never considered a part of the empire that included the more 'civilised' settlements of Ghavin's Keep and the former Wyrm's Port, many of the northern cities had, certainly in the past, carried out much commercial activity with the multiple Sawerrean communities. As it did not fall under the imperial judiciary, many of its laws and customs tended to border on what outsiders could only describe as barbaric – with death being rated as one of its more lenient sentences.

Rising from the centre of the stinking settlement was a great rocky mound – an ancient tell formed from the centuries of accumulated building phases. Perched on top, was a crumbling edifice – an artificial eyrie; a filthy, desolate dwelling fit only for the truly depraved.

Over everything there hovered a dirty, red smog.

"Wathang-Hu. The Town of the Burnt Waste," announced Everus, gazing down from where they stood on an overlooking ridge.

"What do you know about this place?" asked Mhoon, staring at the rows of macabre wooden cross-pieces and their unfortunate occupants, many of whom now served the many circling carrion birds. "I must say, it doesn't look too welcoming."

"I agree with Mhoon," added Carrie, nervously.

"This place is as new to me as no doubt it is to you." Everus swatted at a bloated grave-fly that had landed on his sleeve. Its flattened body left a red smear before falling to the hot ash at his feet. "However, I think it goes without saying that you all need to be extremely vigilant and keep as low a profile as possible once we pass the city gates. That's if we get in, of course."

Carefully they made their way down the shifting slope of knee-high ash. At the bottom, they staggered over to the road, the stink from the crucified corpses rank and disgusting in the hot sunshine. A cloud of large black flies buzzed around the ragged remains, laying their eggs in what putrid flesh remained.

"Do ye think these are crooks...or visitors?" asked Creeps.

"They could be lawyers," Everus replied, brightening up slightly.

Creeps chuckled. "Place can't be that bad then."

Everus strode on, heading for the cracked opening in the outer wall, towards which the grisly avenue led, his companions following nervously behind. Every so often, he would look up at a rotting face or pecked-clean skull; the ragged skeletons seemingly arranged to instil as much fear in approaching newcomers as possible. At least three of them had been nailed up upside down; their skulls, having long since fallen from their spines, now lying at the base of the upright.

The main entrance to Wathang-Hu looked as unwelcoming as the avenue. Dirty and smoke-shrouded, the askew archway looked as though it had been clawed from the wall by something desperate to get out. On either side, was a chained skeleton; bones blackened and snapped as though the remains had been dragged out of a fire. Beyond the entrance, they could see a veritable hive of tumbledown huts and lean-tos as well as a decrepit tower of some sort built from rickety, wooden scaffold.

A thickset humanoid, its hide as black as coal, stepped forward. It wore a mismatched suit of darkened chain-linked armour on which, at the elbows, knees and along the forearms, had been fastened several pieces of sharpened horn. It stood, bandy-legged, slightly taller than Everus. The slight height advantage being increased by the curved-horned helm it wore almost rakishly on its prognathous, fierce-looking face. From under the helm sprouted dirty-red, matted dreadlocks. Held in its strong grip was a savage-looking, hooked weapon that, from its appearance, had tasted blood on more than one occasion.

Instinctively, Everus' right hand went for his sword. He knew that the brutish humanoid before him was a yogroo, and that, by and large, they were not only exceptionally stupid but also highly unpredictable. They could just as easily tear one's throat out as offer a helping hand. They were the sort of creature that only the truly desperate would ever think of employing as a gate guard.

The yogroo snarled and slavered, making threatening gestures with its weapon.

"We mean no harm," said Mhoon, raising his hands. "We only wish to..."

A shorter yogroo, clad in a similar suit of armour and carrying a similar weapon, stepped into view. "Ach. Humans. What...ach...do...ach...ye want?" Its words were more coughed out than spoken, almost as though they had lain as dust inside its chest. It seemed visibly relieved when its question was complete.

Everus had already prepared his introductions. "We're merchant agents from the north," he answered, stepping forward. "We've come to see what profits can be made in establishing a trading venture with your city...and indeed with the land of Sawerrea as a whole."

The guard looked pained. A yellowing tusk appeared briefly from its jutting lower jaw as it pointed to itself, signalling that it was going to try and speak once more. "Ye wait, ach...ach-ach." It coughed violently, before thumping its chest as though in order to pound the words out. "Wait...here!" It pointed to where they stood and finished with a hoarse snort. It then turned its back on them and loped off to one side, vanishing from sight.

"That's a bad cough he's got," muttered Creeps.

"Are we going to wait for it to return?" asked Mhoon, uneasy under the intimidating scrutiny of the remaining larger yogroo.

Everus was about to reply when three more yogroos leapt out from the side. Jumping about like baboons on heat, they growled and brandished their spears. One of them advanced towards them, its pudgy nose sniffing.

"*Dra-drac-dra-ba! Worc-no-carabba!*" cried out a chilling voice.

Clearly agitated, the guards turned round, their hides bristling.

Gliding into view through a cloud of dust, its feet slightly above the ground, there came the bizarre, transparent image of a shrunken, cowled man carrying a short, crooked sceptre, the yogroo that had conversed with them, albeit painfully, by his side. Like an evil mirage, he seemed to shimmer with an inner dark light.

"Aye-aye. What's this then?" said Creeps.

"*Drac-dra-ba!*" With a wave of a hand, the spectral entity shooed the remaining yogroos away. It stared pointedly at the four travellers, its face worn and wrinkled like sun-baked mud, its eyes tinged crimson. Lengths of untidy grey hair sprouted from either side of its head. "Greetings. I welcome you to Wathang-Hu." It bowed slightly, a sly and somewhat devious look in its eyes.

"It is an honour to visit your city," replied Everus, staring hard to try and discern just what it was that he was conversing with. He was about to speak again, when his eyes noticed that the ramshackle construction visible through and behind the wraith-thing was beginning to tilt dangerously to one side. "It's going to..." Along with his companions, who had likewise seen what was happening, his eyes widened in growing alarm.

Then the whole structure seemed to sag like a dying beast. Wooden planks and ropes snapped. Crashing and clanging like a collapsing armoury, the tower fell apart. A great cloud of dust billowed into the air as several figures ran screaming from neighbouring doorways. A wind then caught it, blasting it out further, straight through the apparition and out towards Everus and his companions.

They coughed and shielded their eyes from the airborne grit.

Nonchalantly, the strange gate-warden glanced over its shoulder. It seemed that it had neither felt nor heard the tower collapse, but was actually just responding to what the others had seen. It tutted and turned around, as though such mishaps were daily occurrences, before turning to face them once more. "You're merchants, I understand. What is it you wish to trade?"

"Well, at the moment our main aim is just to gauge the potential. To see what benefits there may be. To gauge whether or not such an enterprise would be mutually profitable." Everus stared through the transparent image, watching the chaotic scenes as people – largely human from what he could tell – raced about shouting, wailing and digging at the contorted jumble. "We're agents from the north...prospective customers, if you like, sent by the various mercantile guilds to assess..."

"Wathang-Hu has not traded with any of the imperial cities for some time now," interrupted the unnerving image. "We've little need *now*...for your northern baubles," it added with a sneer.

Fangs bared, the yogroo sniggered, hoarsely.

"What about slaves?" asked Everus.

Mhoon butted in. "Weapons? Spices? Textiles? All going cheap."

"Aye, that's right," added Creeps. "A lot o' the stuff from Wyrm's Port was salvaged, and...if ye know the right people..."

A knowing smile flickered briefly over the image's ugly face. "Slaves...perhaps. We've little need for any other such things." The wizened face scrunched further, eyes slitting. Gliding towards them, he began to sniff the air, a claw-like hand extended. "You've something else?"

At first Everus thought the thing was going to start pawing at Carrie, but it drifted past, heading towards Creeps. It was disconcerting to watch its movements, for although it appeared aged and arthritic it moved so smoothly, nothing hindering its passage.

"I've got nothin' for ye," said the thief. "So keep yer dirty mitts to yersel'."

It looked Creeps up and down before turning its attention to the thief's sack in which was stowed the brass casket.

"There's just some o' ma dirty socks an' a couple o' old pans in there, pal."

For a moment the group was silent.

Then the gate-warden, or whatever it was, smiled, nodded, turned round and hovered away, before seemingly melting into nothing. "Enter. I welcome you to Wathang-Hu," came a disembodied voice from all around.

† † †

That evening, with the sky a dismal shade of tangerine, Everus, Mhoon and Carrie stood on the roof of a small, crude, nameless tavern and surveyed the ramshackle shanties and smoking middens that constituted Wathang-Hu. In every direction, they saw deplorable squalor and poverty. To the north, east and west, the town was especially run-down; the many dwellings visible, bordering on the uninhabitable. To the south, in the direction of the huge artificial mound which dominated the town, lay an expanse of smoky huts and shallow pits, in which the occasional figure could be seen moving about.

As they looked about, the sun sank further into the horizon, its descent seeming unnaturally fast. As darkness encroached, a sinister-looking half-moon peeped out from the tarnished clouds as though reluctant to bear witness to the spoiled earth below.

"I didn't think this place would be quite as bad," commented Mhoon. "I mean, it really is an eyesore. Even the worst areas of Ullerby, and I expect Wyrm's Port, have some saving graces, some beauty amid the squalor. Here, it's as if no one even tries to make their lives any better. It's a wonder people can live in such a place."

"I don't think they do so out of choice," Everus replied.

Carrie stared towards the crumbling monastery atop the tell. "There's something up there. I can sense it."

Running a hand down his unshaven face, Everus turned his gaze towards where she looked. "Hmm. Me too." There *was* something up there...*something evil*. The very building itself looked evil; from its ruined spires and shattered walls to its domed, smashed roofs and cracked arches. It looked utterly deserted, the only approach tortuous and winding; a trail only a mountain goat would dare ascend. What looked like vultures or very large bats circled high above it.

"You weren't serious about suggesting we just send Creeps in to get the bones, were you?" asked Mhoon.

"I'm thinking about it. Where is he anyway?"

"Last I saw of him, he was chatting to that strange barkeeper," answered Carrie.

"I think we should all keep an eye on him." Everus looked towards the opening in the floor, through which they could gain access to the tavern's communal bedrooms, making sure that the thief was not skulking within earshot. "There's something weirder than normal going on with him. Did you all see the way in which that spectral gatekeeper reacted to him? I've no doubt that he suspected that there was something of value in Creeps' bag. What I can't understand is why he didn't insist on searching it. I think..." He was interrupted by the sound of the tavern door down below them on the street being flung open. He dashed to one side in order to look down – just in time to see Creeps rush inside.

At least two angry voices could be heard shouting downstairs.

Then the entrance door to the roof was opened. Creeps entered, dragging a miserable-looking man behind him. "*Oi!* Guess who I've found?" he cried.

The thief's prisoner was scrawny and unkempt. His hair was grey and lank and looked as though it had never been washed or brushed. His long face was ugly and covered in sores and soot. He wore a filthy pair of tattered leggings and a ripped, blood-stained vest. He looked and smelled like someone who had spent their life milking pigs and living under a dung heap. Blood trickled from his nose.

Creeps threw him forward and he stumbled into their midst, his eyes darting.

Startled, Mhoon and Carrie backed away.

Everus advanced, grabbed the ragged man and stared hard into his dirty face. "Well...if it isn't Mister Weaselnest. How nice of you to join us."

† † †

Everus looked across the table at Creeps. "And?"

"Matt says that ye'll never be able to get in from the top. It's an impossible climb an' it's too heavily guarded. However, he says that there's an arse-route way into the mound." With a dirty hand, the thief picked at a small bowl of nuts. "He says that inside, it's a bit o' a rat-run. There's holes an' tunnels all o'er the place. He said he could lead us...show us the safe way in, past all the traps an' other

382

things. From the sounds o' it the whole place is trapped to buggery. There's spear traps an' pits filled wi' crawlies. There's..."

"What about its inhabitants?" Everus asked sharply.

Munching on his nuts, Creeps shook his head. He waited until he had swallowed. "Nob'dy in town seems to know much about 'em. Matt said that once a year some o' 'em used to come down from that church-thing at the top...as part o' some religious festival or summat. But, sayin' that, nob'dy's seen 'em for some time. He says they're a fairly secretive lot."

"Who is this Matt? Is he an old friend of yours?" Carrie inquired. She sat, her back to the wall, her long legs resting on a stool, her face flushed with the sordid late night heat of the tavern.

"*Puh!* Hardly." Creeps turned to face her. "All ye need to know about him, missus, is that he's a bastard." His look hardened. "Aye...nothin' but a traitorous, lyin', backstabbin' bastard. He dug up his old mother the same night she was buried just so as he could make a pan o' soup out o' her bones. Make o' that what ye will."

"Charming. Although, perhaps, not the most informative of answers. Everus, can you...?"

Everus watched, temporarily lost in his own wandering thoughts as Carrie unbuttoned the top two buttons of her blouse, revealing the beginning of her tanned cleavage. He shifted his gaze back to his tankard of heavily-watered ale. "Weaselnest's a thief...a duplicitous grave-robber from Wyrm's Port."

"Aye...no' a very good one." Creeps grinned at some memory or other. "He's one o' the worst in the business. Did I ever tell ye about the time he...?"

"Shut up. We're not interested." Everus poured his ale out over the stone floor.

"Is he dangerous? I mean, will Mhoon be all right guarding him?" asked Carrie.

"He's tied up, isn't he?" Everus replied, his words not so much a question as a statement of fact. He turned to Creeps. "How did you know he was here?"

The thief scratched his head. "Well, I'd a feelin' that the bastard had escaped Wyrm's Port, ye know...when all the trouble started. An' I've been askin' everywhere to see if anyb'dy had heard about him." He looked about, a mischievous glint in his eyes. "An' first time I clapped eyes on that barkeeper downstairs I knew that he'd taken a shine to the old spade an' shovel work. I mean, he'd done a bit o' grave-robbin' in the past, so I thought that I'd ask him. Turns out that Matt's been slummin' it 'ere for some time." He began picking his nose. "He's been stayin' at some crappy shack near that mound-thing."

"So, what do you plan to do with him?" asked Carrie, her gaze on Everus.

"Kill him," replied Everus, casually.

"But...we could get him to lead us into the mound. I mean, if he's been there before, he may, as Creeps said, know a safe way in."

Everus smiled at her. "A nice idea...but, as with Creeps here, he can't be trusted. Besides, I've the matter of a little personal debt to settle with him. So, if you'll excuse me." He rose from his chair, unsheathing his sword. "I'll go and finish him now." At the top of the stairs, he kicked open the door to their grubby, communal living room. The air inside was stale and humid – more like a leper's cave than a tavern room – all of this despite Carrie's best attempts to try and make the place more fragrant by using some of her minor magic and by insisting that they keep the window open at all times. Everus strode forward, noting Mhoon's startled face and the horror on Weaselnest's.

Weaselnest writhed, his eyes wide, his arms and legs bound with rope to a high-backed chair.

"Time to die." Everus raised his sword, one hand ready to apply pressure to the pommel in order to drive the blade through the face of the bound man.

"Don't!" Weaselnest cried, tears in his eyes.

"You pathetic excuse for a man! You set me up back in Wyrm's Port, didn't you? You and Otha tried to..."

"Everus. I..." Mhoon began.

"*What?*" Everus heard the sound of Creeps and Carrie racing up the stairs behind him.

"I'd hold off killing him if I were you," advised Mhoon. He bit his lower lip, unsure how to continue. "He's..."

"*He's what?*" spat Everus acerbically.

Mhoon grabbed Weaselnest's hair and yanked his head back. He spat lightly on the index finger of his other hand and smeared away the soot and the grime from their captive's forehead, revealing a small, red, tattoo-like mark. "Look!"

Everus' confusion did not last long. "*So?*"

Mhoon released his hold on Weaselnest's hair and wiped his hand down his cloak. "This, is a sigil of possession. It's a potent device used to keep individuals under the control of whoever put it there."

Everus' gaze drifted from Mhoon to the little curved triangle on Weaselnest's brow.

"You recollect the Ullerby witch, the hag on the pier? Well, this is what she tried to do to me. I was fortunate. Her spell was only strong enough to render me powerless."

"Why would anyone want to possess a wretch like this?" Everus asked.

"In order to trap us?" suggested Carrie from the doorway. "Perhaps whoever did this was trying to get this...man, to lure us into a trap."

Everus' eyes narrowed, the murderous anger returning. "All the more reason to end his miserable existence. The sooner he's..."

"Before you kill him, as you seem intent on doing, may I just make a suggestion?" Despite Everus' cold glare, Mhoon continued. "If we assume that he, like the odd stooge at the gate, is being controlled by someone or something, and that we are being scrutinised, then I think it safe to guess that it's being overseen by those who have the bones we're after."

Weaselnest moaned, his tear-filled, crossed-eyes fixed on the sharp point of Everus' sword, which still hovered before his face.

"What I'm saying, is that it could be that he has been commanded to lure us into a trap," Mhoon reasoned. "However..." he turned to face his companions, a smile forming on his lips, "if one were to break the hold that's on him, then not only will we be severing contact, but we could also gain whatever *true* information he may have." He looked questioningly at Everus. "Perhaps the real *him* knows the safe way in."

"And do you think you can break the spell?" Everus asked.

Mhoon nodded.

Everus stared hard at the grave-robber, battling with the desire to just run him through there and then. He knew he would take great delight in finishing the bastard off; in slaking his thirst by slaying one of the many who had wronged him, no matter how slightly. One of the prime tenets of the Xethorn creed he had once lived by was that murder was a permanent solution to a temporary problem. Here was his problem. Murder would be the solution. His eyes slitted. His grip tightened.

Silence fell.

Weaselnest screwed his eyes shut.

Everus thrust the blade forward.

The sword point tore through Weaselnest's right ear, mangling it and pinning him to the back of the chair.

Weaselnest howled in agony.

Twisting the blade before pulling it free, Everus turned to Mhoon. "Do what you must. But if he crosses me once more, I'll hold you both accountable." Scowling, he turned and headed for the door.

✝ ✝ ✝

Well into the night, the exorcist chanted over the bound grave-robber. The tongue was unintelligible but soothing at first, sending Weaselnest into a semi-hypnotic state, then Mhoon's voice took on a harsher, more commanding tone and Weaselnest twitched and grimaced as the forces within him battled against the exorcist's will. Finally, Mhoon's tattooed hands glowed as though on fire and the sigil on the grave-robber's forehead steamed, waking him with a scream of pain and rage. Cursing and panting, Weaselnest struggled as the mark of possession was burned away, until, exhausted, he slumped back, falling into a near comatose stupor.

Mhoon took several deep breaths, the tattoos on his hands fading to their normal state. Once he regained his composure he called for Everus.

"Success?"

"Yes." The exorcist ran a hand down his lined face. "I know you hate him, but if you can manage to question him neutrally, in this condition, he cannot lie to you."

Everus considered the traitor with disgust but spoke with cold precision, reigning in his murderous impulses. He heard of how Weaselnest had been possessed and set as a lowly scout for his mysterious, dark-cowled master. The gaps in his knowledge were substantial but he did seem to know a safe way into the mound. For the moment that would suffice.

✝ ✝ ✝

The streets were empty. The hovels were dark. Every now and then small, bat-like creatures would flap out of nowhere; their wings dark and leathery, their eyes green and horrid.

386

Everus stopped and listened. With a wave of his hand, he signalled Mhoon and Carrie over. Up ahead, he could just make out the thief's shadow, that of the equally disreputable grave-robber crouched beside him.

"I can hardly see a thing in this light," whispered Mhoon.

"Stay here." Everus dashed like a shadow across the street. He had only just reached the concealment of the crooked building where the other two hid, when, not far away, he saw approaching torch light. Half a dozen shambling figures came round a corner. Three carried flaming brands and from the light shed he could see that they were yogroos. Frantically, he gestured to Mhoon and Carrie to get out of sight.

The armoured brutes snarled and grunted to one another. Soon they had passed, their rank odour remaining long after they had gone.

Everus grabbed Weaselnest by the throat. The weird mark of ownership was no longer branded on the ugly man's face, although dirt and caked blood from where his ear had been torn apart still covered one side of his face. "One step out of turn and you're dead," he warned. He released his grip and turned on hearing Mhoon and Carrie rush over to join them.

"Where now?" asked Carrie.

All eyes turned to Weaselnest.

"There's an old house up 'ere a bit. I used to kip in one o' the back rooms. There's a trapdoor that we can nip in. It leads to the tunnels below the mound."

They followed their unwholesome guide as he led them deeper into the largely derelict centre. They saw no citizens, leading Everus to wonder whether people feared going out at night or whether there was some kind of imposed curfew in place. Twice, they had to backtrack on themselves in order to evade the yogroo patrollers. Soon, however, they arrived at the shack the grave-robber had spoken of.

Like moths from a skinflints money bag, a swarm of the leathery bat-things suddenly fluttered out of an opening, prompting Everus to quickly clamp a hand over Carrie's mouth in order to silence her startled exclamation.

"Farty, flappy-things!" muttered Creeps in annoyance, waving his hands in an attempt to shoo the winged things away. Ten or so of them circled around him, attracted by some smell or other. "Go on! Away wi' ye!"

"Shut up!" hissed Everus, releasing his hold on Carrie. "Come on, let's get inside before the watch return." He moved forward and pushed the door open. When they had all entered, he gestured to Mhoon to shut the door. "Let's have some light."

For a moment they stood in utter darkness, the sounds they could hear unsettling – the sense of fear exacerbated by the stink of rotting flesh.

Then a torch was lit.

The interior of the hovel they stood in looked worse than what they had been able to discern of it outside. The walls and ceiling looked particularly unsafe – buckling rafters ready to give way at any moment. The floor was made from discoloured planking, many of the boards rotten or missing. Rubbish and filth, generated by its previous scuzzy inhabitant lay strewn everywhere, leading Everus to think that the place had probably been used as a communal tip.

Amidst the detritus in one corner, lay a half-eaten corpse. Looped, rubbery intestines protruded from a grisly tear in its abdomen.

"Gads!" cried Creeps, looking with measured disgust.

Everus walked over. After examining the body and finding nothing of interest or value, he spent a moment looking through the rubble nearby, before pointing to the doorway which gave access to the rear of the hut.

Nodding, Creeps gripped Weaselnest by the scruff of the neck and pushed him forward, so that if anything lurked beyond, odds were it would take the grave-robber first.

"What do you think happened to...?" asked Mhoon, pointing towards the body.

"Rats." Everus answered. Although to be honest, he had his doubts. It was more likely that their 'guide' had turned to cannibalism in his desperation to stay alive.

Carrie shivered and looked about, her mouth forming a silent 'rats'. In the poor light, it now seemed as though every shadow had taken on a life of its own. "I hate rats," she said.

"We've found the trapdoor!" Creeps called out.

Everus entered the littered back room; the grave-robber's secret hideaway. Amongst the heaps of rubble and the piles of what looked like gnawed bone, he could make out an old bed roll and, as Mhoon entered with the light, he could also see a ripped water-skin lying alongside a dented kettle, a pickaxe and a spade. Propped up against the near wall stood two smashed wooden caskets – coffins, seemingly made either for small creatures or children. Hanging on a hook opposite was a length of coiled, knotted rope.

The stench was terrible – a squalid mix of rot and musty bone.

"This be it." Weaselnest stood in one corner, a hand holding open the wooden cover to the tunnel he had dug. From the opening, there came a centuries old odour of putrescent corpses.

"What a stink," commented Mhoon, pinching his nose.

Snatching the torch from Mhoon, Everus walked to the hole, his boots crunching over the loose gravel on the floorboards. Looking down, he could see a roughly hewn pit about his own height deep, wide enough for only one person at a time. At the bottom a crude tunnel had been dug. It looked as though it ran in two directions – a smaller passage leading back under the floor of the hut they were in and a slightly wider one burrowing into the nearby artificial mountain. He turned to Weaselnest. "What's down there?" he asked.

"Eh...bones an' things. Lots o' stiffs."

"What else?"

"Don't know...but the warrens twist an' turn into the mound itsel'." Weaselnest snorted up a wad of phlegm. "I didn't fancy goin' in too far."

"Why?"

"I...I could hear things movin' about."

Everus looked into the shallow pit. It was all too easy to imagine Weaselnest down there, tunnelling away – unearthing all manner of dead things; frantically burrowing like a maggot into a rotten apple as he scoured the mound for corpses and trinkets.

"Where does it go?" asked Mhoon.

"Into the bowels of the tell. From there, there's hopefully a way up." Without warning, Everus turned, grabbed the grave-robber and dragged him to the hole. "You're going in first." Deaf to Weaselnest's pleas, he forcibly pushed him down through the opening.

The grave-robber slid and then fell further, skidding like a dry and reluctant turd down a latrine. Something cracked as he landed with a cry and a thump on his backside.

Everus looked about, before taking hold of the rope. He pulled on it to test its strength and then dropped the excess down the pit. "All right Creeps. You next, then Mhoon. Down you go."

Unquestioningly, the thief crouched down and clambered in. He looked down between his shoes before dropping, the rope he held used to control his descent.

Everus stared down. By the light from the torch, two ugly faces, both equally cadaverous in the shadowy glow, gazed up at him. He drew his sword. "Now to put something to the test." With a hack, he sliced through the rope.

"*Everus!* What...!?" cried Mhoon.

Everus crouched down. Ignoring Mhoon's protests, he reached for the trapdoor lid. "Well, Creeps, it's up to you now. I'll give you till sunrise to..." There was a sudden noise outside as something tried the front door. Everus looked up. "Keep quiet!"

Mhoon and Carrie held their breath.

The hovel door creaked open and torchlight flooded the derelict front room.

A monstrous shadow crept along the wall, announcing the arrival of a huge yogroo. It stepped forward, its face somewhat fiercer-looking than most they had seen before, for it bore more scabs and scars than a long-lived alley cat and one eye was a dirty blind-white. Grasped in one hand was a heavy, iron chain-linked flail.

Mhoon backed away, his hands raised like a common thief held at crossbow point.

The yogroo growled, its hair bristling. Its one good eye fixed them with a malice born of years of bitter servitude to humans and whatever other powers ruled Wathang-Hu.

With a thud, Everus dropped the trapdoor lid, plunging Creeps and his one-time, good-for-nothing associate into darkness. Rushing forward with his sword, he took a swing at their grizzled interloper.

The yogroo ducked away. With a roar, it pulled back, the boards creaking under the weight of its large hairy feet. It raised its weapon in time to parry an attack, then another.

Everus pushed the offensive, harrying the yogroo with a combination of skilful swipes and thrusts.

Carrie shouted a warning as another guard reached the main doorway.

A thrust to the guts caused 'One-Eye' to double over and crash to the floor, yet, even as Everus ducked away from the other yogroo's flail, his heart sank to hear the calls and howls from outside. He chopped down, felling his hairy foe with a two-handed blow that severed one of its arms at the shoulder. Blood, fur and fragments of chain and horn epaulette flew in a red explosion.

Snarling, a third yogroo sprang through the doorway. No sooner had it done so, than Everus rushed forward and cut it open. It howled in agony and reeled back into the street, its barbed spear falling from its hand. Still standing, it went for a knife sheathed in a leather bandolier, its thick red blood spewing from its barrel-chest.

Beyond it, Everus could see another six bounding up the road, their loping gaits accompanied by their howls and whoops of excitement. He flung the door shut and set his shoulder against it.

"What now?" asked Mhoon, bending to pick up one of the fallen flails.

The door cracked, budging Everus forward a step.

"Down the hole! It's the only way," shouted Carrie.

"*Hurry it up then! Go!*" Everus shouted. Without warning, a heavy axe blade punched through the door, narrowly missing his right shoulder. He sprang back and the door fell in, revealing a huge yogroo, already pulling back for a second swing. Rushing through into the back room, he saw Mhoon lowering himself into the pit, Carrie having presumably already gone. He spun around, just in time to leap aside as the yogroo missed him, instead hacking into the wall with its axe.

Stocky, shaggy figures massed in the doorway.

With a bellow, the yogroo swung out, its axe striking Everus' sword and knocking it from his hand. Frothing at the muzzle, it then smacked him with a ridge of knuckles and sent him crashing against a wall.

Stunned, somehow Everus managed to dodge another swing, his sword now lying behind his attacker. He dived to one side, snatching the old pickaxe. With the stout wooden handle, he parried another attack. For an instant, he contemplated just leaping down the pit, hoping he would not break his legs upon landing. Again he blocked the yogroo's axe, trapping the blade.

The two, now locked in a desperate tussle, battled over possession of their weapons. Everus, knowing that he could not match the yogroo's strength, moved fast and pushed the handle away from himself, in effect intentionally breaking the hold.

The yogroo clumsily fell back, all of its strength, expended in pulling, now causing it to overbalance.

With a cry, Everus swung the pickaxe down. The heavy tool

passed but a cat's whisker from the yogroo's heavily armoured chest, but Everus continued with the downward swing, letting the tool's weight carry it on. Its pointed edge punched straight through one of the beast's hairy feet, impaling it to the boards beneath. Bones splintered. Blood squirted as though from a punctured underground pipe.

The beast went berserk, throwing its head back and howling its pain to the ceiling. Its axe fell from its hand. Effectively nailed to the spot, it flailed about in its agony, preventing the others from getting in.

Knowing there was no other means of escape and that his companions had already gone, Everus dashed to one side and scrambled down the trapdoor.

CHAPTER EIGHTEEN

His back hunched, Weaselnest scurried along the narrow tunnel like an overgrown rodent. Every so often, he would stop and sniff, before changing direction and half-crawling down another passage. Behind him came Everus, Mhoon and Carrie, with Creeps bringing up the rear.

The 'rat-run' as Creeps had called it, seemed to go on without end. No sooner had they crawled to what appeared to be the end of one tunnel, than Weaselnest would lead them down a hole into another. It was hot and claustrophobic, the air filled with the dry taste of decaying brick. They were soon covered in age-old dust and crumbled bone, the tunnels they were worming their way through; the very strata of past habitation and burial.

Everus spat dust from his mouth and kept crawling, the torch held before him, the sight of Weaselnest's scrawny backside about the limit of his vision. At times he found it hard to keep up with the grave-robber, but somehow he managed to keep him in sight. As they went deeper, he wondered just how many times his untrustworthy guide had been here – how many times had he crawled into the mound searching for his ghoulish trinkets?

Weaselnest came to a stop and looked over his shoulder. "Up 'ere." He started shinning up a near vertical crack, his wiry body contorting to squeeze inside. Like a lizard, he began to pull himself forward, soon disappearing from Everus' sight.

"How much more of this?" cried Mhoon. His hands and knees were grazed and bleeding.

Everus pulled himself forward, relieved to see that the chimney which Weaselnest had just climbed up seemed to be wide enough for him to get in. Torch held above his head, he began the ascent, using his free hand to grasp the many ledges. Higher and higher he went, the complaints and scrabbling of his companions below, combined with the dust and the grit drizzling from above, making him think that perhaps an all out assault on the main entrance may have been a better tactic, assuming they could have got there in the first place.

"Nearly there."

Everus looked up to see the grave-robber peering down at him.

"Do ye want to hand me the torch?"

"Just so you can run off with it? I think not." Everus scrambled awkwardly for the ledge and pulled himself up. Looking around, he could see that he had come out on a rise overlooking a small, hive-like village of empty streets and mud-brick walls, all contained within the core of the great hollow of the tell. From where he stood, he could make out the half-buried skeletons of men and beasts lying in the ancient streets, their remains twisted and desolate.

"Some place, ain't it?"

Everus did not reply. He moved to one side, almost skidding from the ledge they were on. For a heart-stopping moment a wave of vertigo rippled through him as he envisaged himself tumbling over the edge and falling in a heap of bones, spider webs and dust to the dead streets below – adding his bones to the many already there.

"Ye should mind yer step in 'ere. It's a bit unsafe." Weaselnest turned, offering Mhoon a helping hand up.

"Amazing!" muttered the exorcist, staring around with awe-struck eyes. "Absolutely unbelieva..."

"Shhh!" hissed Everus. Carefully creeping to one side, he looked over the edge, the light from the torch illuminating the giant scrawny spider crawling up the rocky surface. The thing was hairy and repulsive, each of its eight legs as thick as the torch he held, its body grey and mottled. A watery venom dripped from its palp and fangs as it slavered and made obscene squelching sounds.

"What is it?" asked Creeps, he and Carrie now having reached the top.

"A bloody big spider!" Everus pulled back. Swordless, he held the torch like a club, ready to attack as soon as the huge arachnid scuttled over the edge.

Like horrible feelers, two spindly legs crept over the side, then four, then six. Now that they could all see it better, they noticed how shrivelled and emaciated it appeared, even considering its size. If it had not been for the growths of bristle-like hair which covered most of it, it would have looked almost skeletal.

The torch Everus gripped swung down, a trail of smoke and embers left in its wake. The spider recoiled, obviously repelled by the flames. Again the torch swung out, singeing hair and causing the thing to hiss and spray venom.

Mhoon and Creeps leapt up to the attack.

The exorcist tripped and fell, rapidly scrambling to get to his feet before the spider could bury him under its shrunken, grotesque abdomen. It hissed and spat, its two front legs raised in an offensive stance. It sprayed some of its deadly and pungent venom all over Everus' dust-covered shirt and his already tattered coat. The stink and the mild burning sensation prompted him to stagger back, his torch blow accidentally catching the thief's right shoulder.

Creeps howled in pain and annoyance.

With a teeth-clenching thwack, Mhoon's flail shattered one of the spindly legs. Grinning, he happily crippled another leg, causing the thing to temporarily slump to one side.

"*Look out!*"

Rapidly tearing his coat and what remained of his smouldering, poison-pocked shirt from his body, Everus wheeled round to see what had prompted Carrie to shout her warning. Out of the darkness descended another spider; a smaller one, but no doubt just as deadly. Judging from the damage done to his clothes, one good bite from either of these horrors and that would be it.

Weaselnest picked up a rock and threw it.

Carrie raised her right hand and shouted out a word of power. With a turquoise flash, a bolt of magic sped from her hand and struck the smaller spider even as the grave-robber's stone hurtled past. For a moment the spider danced spasmodically, its legs twitching uncontrollably. It then retracted in on itself and recoiled back, the magical burning illuminating it as it withdrew, seemingly reeled back up its line.

The bigger of the two still held its ground against Creeps and Mhoon, lunging forward with its fangs and preventing either of them from getting in for a killing strike.

Bare-chested, Everus snatched up the torch he had earlier flung to the floor and joined the fray.

The spider quickly scurried around, trying to stay away from the flames. It darted forward and made a lunge for Carrie.

The sorceress screamed, more in revulsion than outright fear.

Hair singed as Everus thrust the torch into its wiry mass. He drove the flaming brand deeper, threatening to extinguish it in the spider's hide. Flames erupted as the spider swung around, dripping venom, several of its eyes now scorched and bleeding black pus.

With a sickening squelch, Mhoon's flail whistled down onto its head, ending its miserable life. Yet, even as he stood over it, ready to crack it again if its twitching became too great, the smaller spider fell from above, causing him to leap aside in fright.

Everus rushed forward and, with a powerful kick sent the now frazzled remains hurtling over the edge.

The fight with the spiders over, Weaselnest led them down a narrow, twisting defile that came out close to what Everus recognised as a ruined shrine of some sort. Formed from a warped knoll of hard rock, the large formation bore crude carvings and many bones were scattered around its base.

"What's this?" asked Mhoon, tentatively approaching.

"I'd guess it's a shrine of some sort. It probably served as the religious focal point for this strange, fossilised settlement." Everus walked up to it and ran a hand down the cracked surface. Old blood stains could be clearly seen.

"They must be a nice lot, these nuns or whoever live here," commented Mhoon, sarcastically. "Bones, spiders, blood sacrifices, twisty tunnels. Whatever happened to the scantily clad virgins willing to take care of your every need? I could just do with lying back in a cool pool, getting fed grapes, whilst a nubile young girl massages my feet."

"Well, tough," Everus responded, brusquely. He looked to Weaselnest. "Where now?"

"There's a tunnel o'er there," said Weaselnest, pointing. "But it's clogged up wi' stiffs. Ye'll need to do some shiftin' if ye want to go that way."

Everus looked to where the grave-robber pointed. The stink and the stale, unwholesome air conspired to create images of heaps of decaying corpses crawling with rats and spiders in his mind, even though all he could actually see was a dark and shadowy mass.

"There's a bad aura surrounding this stone." Mhoon crouched by the old shrine, running his tattooed hands over its crumbling contours. His face had taken on a ghastly pallor and it looked as though he was about to be sick. "A great evil. Something subterranean...awakens." He let go and shook his head, momentarily dazed.

"Ye all right?" Creeps asked, supporting him.

"Yes. Come on, let's get away from here."

Everus had to agree. In the torchlight, shadows shifted on the periphery of the illumination. More spiders, no doubt. "I think it best if we see about making our way up and out of here." He looked in the direction of Weaselnest's 'clogged-up' tunnel. "We'll go this way," he said, pushing the grave-robber in front of him.

Through the shadowy, dust-filled streets they went, the dim light shed from the torch Everus held allowing them to make out the almost cavernous surrounding walls, which had been created over the centuries by phases of continuous building and collapse.

Disconcerting sounds came from all around, eerily echoing within the strange vault. Obviously larger things than bats and spiders lurked up there in the shadows.

"This is it." Weaselnest stood staring towards the dark opening, his long face grinning madly in the torchlight. "Ye see this openin' up there? That's where all the stiffs are."

Mhoon groaned, supporting himself against a protruding rock. "Everus. This is getting beyond a joke. I mean, we don't even know if we can get into the temple from down here. And where that tunnel goes, I don't want to know. The smell's terrible."

Weaselnest's grin widened; his teeth cracked, crooked and stained from gnawing on bones.

"Get moving." Everus gave the grave-robber a push, wiping the unappealing smile from his face.

It was a relatively easy climb to the tunnel entrance. And, despite the stink, Everus for one felt heartened to be leaving the ancient, hollowed-out settlement behind. With a last backward glance, he gazed over the preserved ruins, the light from his torch somehow seeming to illuminate much more of the long-dead dwelling than should have been possible, bathing what he could see in an infernal glow. Briefly, he wondered just how old this place was. For how many unrecorded centuries, if not millennia, had this precursor to the present Wathang-Hu been here?

"Better keep movin'. There are more spiders an' things back 'ere."

Everus heard Creeps' recommendation. At least eight very large spiders could be seen, crawling down the walls and dangling from their web-lines. "*Quick!* Everyone, into the tunnel."

The tunnel they entered was noticeably different from the largely cavernous, disorderly twists and turns they had followed earlier. The floor was much smoother, formed as it was from large, tessellated, square stone slabs, worn with age. The walls were similarly constructed, their uniformity broken only by the occasional protruding buttress. The ceiling was high enough for them to walk without having to stoop, the flames from the torch Everus held aloft singeing the many small webs on its cracked and arched surface.

A stinking mass of web-wrapped husks, scattered bones and shrivelled corpses lay in a tangled heap at the far end. Beyond the ghastly pile, they could see the passage continuing.

Carrie gagged and coughed into her hand.

Grimly, Everus took a couple of steps forward. The desiccated remains were crawling with normal-sized spiders and bugs. The clogging stink caused him to wince and raise a hand to his mouth.

Creeps stood staring, his eyes skilfully picking out the odd copper ring or gold tooth his one-time associate had overlooked.

Everus turned his back on the dead. He pointed to the thief and the grave-robber. "You two! Start clearing."

Creeps had already guessed what he was going to have to do and, together with Weaselnest, he set about clearing the horrendous obstacle. It was disgusting work; the bones snapping, the skin flaking, parts of bodies crumbling to dust when touched. The unceremonious dumping and the rapid disposal was given a sudden sense of urgency when something black and hairy scurried out from beneath a pile as though eager to partake of a bite of living skin.

Soon the two had established a working rhythm – with Weaselnest burrowing into the thick of the dead, before drawing one out and manhandling it to Creeps, who then flung it to one side. The thief started piling the remains in an alcove, stopping only to brush away the odd spider or remove a stretch of web from his hair.

After a time, the grave-robber stepped into view. Dusting himself down, he turned to where the others waited.

"Finished?" asked Everus, coldly.

Weaselnest nodded. "Aye. Ye can..." He began twitching uncontrollably as something crawled down the back of his collar and bit him between the shoulder blades. Grimacing, he flung himself against a wall, back first, crushing whatever had done the damage.

"Well?"

"Aye...ye can get through now. Seems to be goin' up."

Forcefully pushing the grave-robber to one side, Everus moved forward, the light from his torch revealing that the passage did indeed appear to be sloping up. Suddenly, a spider dropped from above, scurried quickly off a shoulder and dropped to the floor. His boot squashed it. Determinedly, he led them past the heaped cadavers, the torch held before him as though it were a talisman to keep the dark and whatever lay within it at bay.

The incline they soon reached was not very steep, and as they started up the gradient, leaving the stink and the bones behind, they soon noticed portions of the wall with faded paintings and strange murals, depicting bizarre rituals. Shrunken cowled beings resembling human vultures and giant bats featured strongly, their preponderance increasing the further they traversed, until whole stretches of brickwork were thus covered.

Everus called a halt so that he could examine the ancient diagrams in better detail. That whatever they meant to portray was some kind of narrative, he had little doubt. The more he studied its composition, the more he began to decipher some of its story. For in its own visual way, it was informing those who could 'read' it, the tale of the genesis of Wathang-Hu; describing how the settlement had arisen, collapsed and been re-built, all under the watchful eye of these seemingly venerated cowled beings. For these were the sisterhood, an evil race of harpy-like monsters who ruled the city through fear and demanded human sacrifices. Their whole story seemed laden with violence. There were many scenes of mutilated enemies and tortured people.

"Anything of interest?" asked Carrie.

Everus turned, for a moment the images he had been looking at swimming before his eyes. "Not much of relevance to our task."

"What are these things?" She pointed at one of the small hooded figures.

"Not exactly sure. Although I think they're the old rulers of the city." Everus pointed at another scene, above which some crude-looking symbols had been scrawled. "This, however, is a representation of some great earth kraken, possibly Whaggustraag. One of the dead chthonic gods. Some say that they've dwelt deep under the earth in their cavernous burrows since the beginning of time. It's said that they contain all of the souls of those dead who've been buried. It's also..." Creeps' sharp whistle brought him to a halt.

"There's a light up ahead."

Everus strode up to where Creeps and Weaselnest slouched in the shadows.

"There!" Creeps pointed.

Sure enough, Everus could see light beyond that cast from his own torch. It seemed stationary, as though the light came from some fixed source. He quickly discounted the possibility that it was merely a reflection.

"Could be that we've reached the entrance to the temple-thing," reasoned the thief. He looked about him with wide eyes, as though half-expecting some wrapped horror to shamble out of the shadows. After all, he had seen enough of them.

"Take this." Everus handed the torch to Creeps before sneaking forward. He passed a side passage which curved around to his left, before being able to make out that the fiery glow came from an archaic lantern that appeared almost embedded into the wall just above head height. Several others, now unlit, had been set at equal distances on either side of the wall.

Mhoon approached, his cloak and outer garments grey with dust, Carrie not far behind him. Behind them came the shadowy figures of Creeps and Weaselnest.

"Well, at least the air's marginally fresher here," commented the sorceress, getting little more than a lecherous nod of agreement from Weaselnest.

The passage before them widened, opening out into a moderately-sized chamber. Rusty lengths of chain, large, dead spiders and heaps of rubble lay near the centre. A quick glance also revealed a larger pile of detritus in one corner – the result of a ceiling cave-in. Sharp chunks of shattered statuary, many more bones, the odd rusty weapon and countless pottery shards also littered the uneven floor.

Across from where they stood was an arched opening and Everus was just about to lead his companions towards it when, from out of the darkness beyond, there stepped a skeleton clad in a ragged chain mail shirt and carrying a rusty blade.

"Give me that." Everus grabbed the flail Mhoon carried. He took a step forward.

With a wicked grin, the skeleton also moved nearer. Behind it there stepped a second, similarly armed. They then rushed forward, their sickly white bones bound together in places by molten resin and thick leather straps.

Everus ran to meet them. Wrong footing the first, he let it rush past. Then, with a whistling, two-handed swing, he cracked it over the back of the skull. The spiked metal ball shattered the empty braincase and sent his foe reeling into the arms of Mhoon, who fell down with a scream and a clatter, the battered skeleton's sword scraping his left arm.

The other skeleton thrust forward at Creeps, who nimbly dodged to one side. It was about to strike out again when Everus gave out a cry of rage and smashed it asunder; clavicle and ribcage exploding in a violent blast as his weapon crashed through its bones, creating a rent that ran from what was left of its shoulder to its pelvis. A follow-up elbowing knocked the skull flying.

Sounds erupted in the dark archway.

Suddenly, several more animated, bony remains came charging into the chamber. All were in an advanced state of decay, the bones mouldy, discoloured and rat-gnawed. There was both a great evil and a horror about them, as though they were created from the reanimated leftovers of the thoroughly wicked. Bugs crawled from empty jaws, nostrils and eye-sockets.

The first fell under a barrage of hurled rocks, its pummelled, fleshless torso all but disintegrating.

"*Take the bastards!*" shouted Everus, wading forward and swinging his flail furiously. Bones cracked and flew into the air as the heavy, spiked weapon struck home. He whirled and swung low, shattering leg bones and knocking his enemies to the floor.

More armoured skeletons rushed in, crowding the archway, their already battered features ironically alive with a hatred for all that lived.

One or two crumpled beneath the hurled rocks from Weaselnest. Others were dispatched by the dagger of Creeps and the torch, swung like a club, of Mhoon. Carrie blasted a group to oblivion with a small fireball that briefly illuminated the wrecked chamber in its golden flash. But it was Everus, with the flail that Mhoon had taken from the felled yogroo, back in the world of the living, who did the most damage. Despite the fact that this had been the first time he had ever handled a flail in combat, much preferring edged weapons, wave after wave of skeletons were smashed to bits under his devastating swings, so that, by the end of the skirmish, he reckoned they had destroyed over twenty five of them. An exact tally was nigh on impossible, for parts were everywhere. In addition, some of the horrors had been seemingly fused together, their bones interlocked, separated only through brute force.

They themselves had not gone without injury.

A vicious stab had almost finished the grave-robber and, indeed, for the latter part of the battle he had lain prone and bleeding. Mhoon and Carrie each carried their own minor cuts and bruises and even Everus had received a stinging slice down his left arm. A lesser cut on one cheek had already closed over, leaving little more than a bloody streak down the side of his face. From his own admission, Creeps had not been injured. 'Expert swordplay,' he put it down to, even though he had fought with a dagger.

Everus was not entirely happy with the thief's explanation.

Carrie and Mhoon went over to where Weaselnest lay groaning.

"Just leave him," said Everus, staring with pitiless eyes. "He might keep the spiders off our backs for a while."

Creeps set about rummaging through the many scattered bits of their shattered enemies, stooping occasionally to retrieve some minor treasure. In this fashion, he collected over a dozen small, probably worthless rings and three reasonably valuable silver bracelets.

"Come on. Hurry it up." Everus walked over to where the grave-robber now lay propped between Mhoon and Carrie. In the torchlight, he looked more dead than alive. Every so often he would shiver uncontrollably and there was a lot of blood.

Mhoon looked up, an already crimson-soaked rag in his hand from where he had been dabbing. "He's cut quite badly. Lost a fair amount of blood too."

"You're only saying that to please me." Everus grinned and moved closer to have a better look for himself. "I've cut myself worse shaving. Come on! Get up!" Reaching out, he sadistically dragged the wounded man to his feet.

Weaselnest groaned aloud and slouched, almost collapsing in Everus' arms.

Everus had no desire to sully himself with handling such a wretch more than he had to. Not only was there blood pissing out of him, but there was absolutely no telling what this one had been in contact with. It could be virtually anything. He stepped back, allowing the grave-robber to slump forward.

Creeps caught him. "We should see about gettin' him to a healer."

"Oh, where exactly!?" Everus looked about at the dereliction and the darkness, hammering home the fact to the thief that there were no helpful herbalists or skilled surgeons waiting to step from the shadows and come to their aid. There was nothing friendly down here. "Let's get moving before more skeletons arrive." Snatching the torch from Mhoon, he turned his back on them all and strode over to examine where the skeletons had come from. He saw a rubble-strewn passage heading on and up, extending away beyond the radius of flickering light. Fallen brick and shattered masonry lay everywhere, but there did at least seem to be a navigable route through.

Mhoon walked over and stood beside Everus. "It's gone quiet"

"That's what scares me."

"Oh?" There was a note of unease in Mhoon's question.

Everus turned and smiled uncheerily. "There's something else up there. In the dark...in the shadows." He peered in that direction, eyes scanning the edge of the light for any movement. "Skeletons are mindless. They've no will of their own. Hence, someone or some*thing* controlled them."

"What do you think it is?"

"The keeper of the bones, perhaps?" Impatiently, Everus turned and stared at Creeps and Carrie, the wounded grave-robber supported between them like a straw dummy – a recently stabbed and bleeding straw dummy at that. "Ready?"

Together, the two of them helped Weaselnest forward. His head hung low and his feet dragging, he continued to groan in pain.

The length of passage they were now on continued its gradual incline. In places lay more heaps of broken bone and smashed pottery vessels. Parts of the wall were blackened from relatively recent fires, the soot easily smeared free. Dusty webs hung from the ceiling, their wispy strands hanging like ghostly hair.

"The torch seems to be burning low," said Mhoon.

Snorting his displeasure, Everus took several steps forward. Three small spiders scurried underfoot and another disappeared into a crack in the wall. Up ahead, the passage turned again and, for a fleeting moment, he was sure he caught sight of a shadow retreating on the far corner wall.

"See anything?" asked Carrie.

Everus did not answer. Instead, he rushed for the corner, the torch and the flail in either hand. He found himself at the entrance to a huge chamber, its ceiling supported by half a dozen squat pillars. Even in the limited light from the now dwindling torch, he could see that in the centre of the chamber there rested some kind of cairn-like structure, its tapered point reaching halfway to the ceiling.

A quick look revealed many more strewn bones and piles of bricks. A torn open, badly battered suit of old plate mail lay over to one side; the now rusty shell from which a once living creature had been hauled and no doubt eaten. He could see nothing else and was just about to wave the others forward when, from a ledge above him, a small, hunched thing sprang down on him. Surprised, he fell back, the torch knocked from his grasp. Screeching like a crazed baboon, his attacker lashed out, one scrawny arm locking around a thigh, talon-like nails digging deep.

A bolt of white light sped up the passageway and blasted into them both, bathing half the chamber in its preternatural glow. Little motes and stars of sparkling purple twinkled within.

With a cry, Everus staggered back. Torn and ragged in the light from the sorceress' spell, he looked as though he had spent half the day wrestling an angry cave bear.

Mhoon, Creeps and Carrie rushed to his aid.

The shrunken ambusher howled and went into a frenzy. Illuminated by the magical light, they could all see its grisly repulsiveness far too clearly. What face it had was scabrous and decayed; the blistered warts, the exposed bone and the rotten, yet sharp, teeth, along with the hideously hooked, almost beak-like nose, adding to its overall grotesque appearance. Its eyes were filled with malign promise; jelly-like and independently roving, threatening to pop out at any moment.

"*Kill it!*" yelled Everus, stepping in and lashing out. The flail struck home and knocked the thing, whirling, against a pillar.

It gave a ghastly scream and fell, the filthy cowl it wore beginning to disintegrate in Carrie's scintillating light.

"*Die! Die! Die!*" Again and again, Everus swung down the spiked metal ball, hammering the foul thing that now slithered at his feet, trying to escape. With each sickening crunch, parts of it seemed to collapse internally. Still it moved – its clawed, filthy hands dragging it away, seeking to escape the light that was beginning to fry it.

Snatching up the torch, Mhoon rushed forward and tried to set it alight. To his dismay, the now all but spent torch did little more than singe its cowl before burning itself out.

"*Shit!* The bastard's not even feeling these hits!" More blows from Everus battered its slowly rising form to the floor. "It's shrugging off these blows as though they..."

With a maniacal roar, the thing sprang to its feet and, with a powerful backhand smack sent the exorcist flying. With its cowl now ashes around its feet, it leapt back, withdrawing to the fringe of the luminous area.

Everus swung out. The flail's chain link wrapped around the thing's scrawny neck, the spiked ball crunching into the side of its face.

Slavering, it reached with both hands for the chain.

With a heave, Everus dragged the thing back into the circle of magical light. He kept his grip, fiercely battling with the ghoulish midget, holding it in the light, knowing that this was the only thing that seemed to be doing any real damage.

The bizarre tug-o'-war went on for a few moments, the thing roaring in agony as large parts of it popped and blazed. One eye burst, obscenely splattering like a crushed snail. Then, in a searing flash, the heat from which almost made Everus release his hold, the horror combusted. Blue fire wreathed its body, burning it to the core.

The chamber filled with the stench of corruption and cremated soul.

The smoking remains collapsed, permitting Everus to whisk back his weapon. He stepped back and watched as parts within the quivering heap, now reduced to glowing embers, still struggled to get away. This time, however, there would be no escape. The brightly burning undead creature rapidly became as ashen pages, and soon a breeze from nowhere mysteriously blew them away. Nothing remained.

"Aye...but that were nasty," said Creeps. He had obviously found time to light his pipe whilst Everus had been locked in desperate battle, for it now jutted from one corner of his mouth.

Everus winced at the pain in his thigh and a few lesser scratches on both arms – the ache remembered now that the imminent threat was over.

"Any idea what it was?" asked Carrie.

"I think it was a cryptwight," answered Mhoon, limping towards her. "And that," he pointed to the burial mound towering over them in the centre, "is probably where it came from. As to just what something like this was doing down here I've no idea."

"Creeps! Get in there and see if you can find anything of interest," ordered Everus, his eyes drawn to the crooked, arched opening in one side. "Could be that this cryptwight, if that's what it was, guarded the remains."

"It's no' goin' to be easy tellin' which is which. There's bones all o'er the place. It'll be like findin' a nit wi' yer name on it." The thief skulked over. After checking that there was no way Everus could lock him in, he crouched down and disappeared inside. He was not inside for long. "Couldn't see much. It's too dark an' the light don't go in that far." He shook his head. "Didn't seem to be much o' interest. Just bones, bones an' more bones. They were as numerous an' as common as a lawyer's lies."

"Now where?" asked Mhoon, rubbing an injured shoulder.

There was no further point in asking Weaselnest. From the state he was in he probably did not even know his own name. Besides, it seemed as though this was probably farther than the grave-robber had ever ventured.

"This way." Everus strode towards another arched opening, the only other suitable exit from the chamber. There were several cracks in the wall leading to other chambers but none of them looked all that inviting. Beyond the archway, the passage widened. It wound its way further on and up, its walls decorated with many more murals and strange carvings. Ruined lanterns, embedded into the walls, like those they had seen earlier, did nothing to light the way. More bones lay scattered on the rough floor.

"The bloody torch is dead," cried Creeps, holding aloft the burnt out stick. The remnants of sooty tallow and rag fell from it to land at his feet. Their only illumination came from the stationary light spell that had destroyed the cryptwight – and that was now fading. "I might be able to rig us a makeshift torch out o' some bits o' cloth an' stuff but it'll no' last for long." He set about improvising, making a crude light source out of some bound cloth donated unwillingly from Weaselnest's shirt. He lit up, using his small flint and steel.

"Let's move it. I don't fancy getting stuck in here without a light." Everus signalled for the thief to start moving, he then fell in line beside him, aware that the others had drawn in behind in order to keep as close as possible.

Weaselnest staggered along like a zombie.

After walking down the passage, they came to another chamber. At one end, a cracked flight of stone steps led up into the darkness. Smashed pillars and huge piles of detritus formed small mountains of rubble which, in places, reached up to the ceiling. Niches and alcoves around the walls housed many age-worn statues, giving the adventurers the unnerving sense that they were being watched from the shadows.

Creeps' primitive torch guttered and spat, its light flaring and then diminishing.

They crossed the chamber and made for the steps, Mhoon assisting the barely conscious and bleeding Weaselnest.

Creeps stopped and pointed out the location of a particularly nasty-looking shallow pit trap that was lined with downward pointing spikes. Had anyone been unfortunate enough to step in it they would never have got their foot out again without amputating it first.

At the top, they entered a smaller chamber, the air somewhat fresher and colder now that they had left the labyrinthine catacombs behind. Two ruined openings, one on either side of where they were gathered, gave partial access to darkened spaces beyond.

"Which way?" muttered Creeps.

Everus looked about. "Hmm. What do you think?"

"Let's try this one." The thief crept towards one of the openings, the torch dying with the same speed as Weaselnest.

Everus and the others followed.

The room they entered was much larger than expected. Looking around, they could see many places where the walls had been blackened by fire, and as they moved further in, a mass of charred skeletal remains, that had been all but reduced to carbon, became visible. Cremated ribs and large, bird-like skulls rested in the incinerated heap alongside taloned hand-bones and heaps of scattered ash.

The air reeked.

"By all the gods!" exclaimed Mhoon. "What's happened here, I wonder?"

"I'd say there's been a purge." Everus looked about, noting the charcoal frameworks of small pyres which lay amidst the remains.

"A purge? What do you mean?"

"Well, this has been a deliberate burning. You can still see where the bonfires were." Everus moved towards one of the cremated skeletons and looked down at the blackened, beaked skull. Irreverently, he kicked it to one side. "I reckon that this is all that remains of that sisterhood I was told about."

"You think so?"

Everus nodded, absently scuffing the sole of a boot in the ash. Was it possible that someone else was after the hand? *Had Xethorn been here?*

"So, it's possible that the piece of the hand may be in this room somewhere," said Mhoon, hopefully. It was obvious from his voice that he wanted to be gone from this unhallowed place as soon as possible. It was a feeling shared by them all.

"I doubt it."

All eyes turned to Carrie.

"I think it's more likely that whoever did this now has it."

Weaselnest stumbled to his knees, his face screwing up in a rictus of pain.

Everus paid him no heed. Instead, he walked further into the room, knowing that Creeps, who carried the only light source, would follow. They passed another dozen or so charred remains before arriving at the base of a ramp, at the top of which stood a set of large stone portals – one cracked and ajar, the other tightly shut. On either side reared a large, vulture-headed statue, their features now moulded more by the passage of time than the sculptor's chisel.

From the space beyond there came an ominous green glow.

"I've a feeling this is it," cautioned Everus, his knuckles whitening around the flail's handle, reassured by its solidity. There was a sudden tightening in his stomach.

Slowly and quietly, those of them who could crept to the top of the ramp.

Everus looked in. The chamber beyond was like the interior of a vast mausoleum, its ceiling domed and shadowy, its walls decorated with many faded frescoes and murals. Window-like slits pierced the walls in places and it was with some relief that he noted the occasional star in the night sky outside, affirming to him that he was now free of the mound – their harrowing journey from the base to the top now more or less complete.

Broken statuary and shattered offering tables lay heaped here and there; inanimate witnesses to a violent act of iconoclasm.

Near the middle of the huge area, standing upright, surrounded by the lurid green glow, was a figure.

Cautiously, Everus entered, his companions close behind.

As though it had detected them, the figure shifted slightly, its frame small but its shadow huge and menacing on the curved inner walls.

"Mhoon. Creeps. Get to either side. We'll flank the bastard." Everus gestured for them to take up their positions. Reluctantly, they agreed.

Creeping closer, using rubble for cover, Everus could see that the figure inside the light was neither Xethorn nor a netherworld demon, but a man. He was short, shorter than the thief. His face was deeply wrinkled, his skin sallow and dry-looking, as though he had spent most of his many years away from the sun. His wispy grey hair was long, straggling over his ears, and his body seemed frail, ready to deteriorate like an archaeological find removed from its hermetic deposit. His eyes were black and dangerous, like tar pits. The dark cowl he wore was scuffed and bloodstained as though he had seen recent action. In one hand, he held a thin, black cane. In the other, pressed to his chest, he held a small, portable ossuary, not unlike that which now lay in Creeps' sack.

He was the man they had seen at the entrance to Wathang-Hu.

"So, Everus, you've arrived. Took your time didn't you?"

"Who are you?" demanded Everus, unnerved by the stranger's use of his name.

The wizened man laughed, the sound unpleasant and mocking. "I've many names, but you can call me Blackmorg."

Cautiously, Everus moved closer. He could see that the green glow emanated from some sort of mystical prison, in which the man was enclosed. "You've something I want."

"Then take it. I am, as you can see, unarmed." Blackmorg grinned and held out the ancient reliquary. "Take it!"

Seeking assurance, Everus looked across at Mhoon.

"It's got to be a trap," warned the exorcist. "I can sense a great evil about this one. The fact that he's been imprisoned within this protective circle is in itself cause for caution."

"Be careful, Everus," seconded Carrie. "I too can sense evil. There's an incredible amount of magical energy here. It's highly potent. Who or what created this prison did so for a reason."

From within the glowing aura, Blackmorg smiled, the offered casket still in his hand.

"You would give it to me freely?" Everus asked, staring hard at the grinning man. Somewhere in the back of his mind, a memory began to stir. Tenebrous images and half-thoughts swam, but failed to form a coherent picture, almost as though some other power was preventing him from reaching a conclusion; a definite identification. The harder he tried, the lower the murky veil of forgetfulness seemed to descend.

"It's what you've come for, isn't it?"

"After all I've battled through to get here, do you think me stupid enough not to suspect something? Explain why you're here. Are you the one responsible for the destruction of this temple and the deaths of the sisterhood that once dwelt within?"

Blackmorg sighed with feigned pity. "Ah...the daughters of Whaggustraag. How sweet the stench of their burning." A mad gleam came to his eyes as he inhaled whatever air there was in there with him. "The answer to your question is, yes. I did so enjoy watching them cook. Their wings I tore from them first, and their screams were most...palatable."

"So you're the one responsible," said Mhoon.

Blackmorg turned his gaze on the exorcist before turning back to address Everus. "*Who*...is this that dares speak to me?" His words dripped, venomously.

"You would do well to show me proper respect, 'Trapped One'," replied Mhoon. "For the way I see it, it is we who hold the key to your freedom. Unless you wish to spend the next age imprisoned in this circle..."

"*Silence!*" For a moment the barrier shimmered. Icy green flames shot forth and the ground shook slightly. "My incarceration will not be for long." Blackmorg's voice mellowed slightly. "After all, you need what's in the casket. Only by breaking the wards that bind me will you be able to take it."

"How do you know my name?" Everus asked.

"He who walks in shadows..."

"*Xethorn!*" interrupted Everus. "You're a Xethornite!"

The diminutive man smiled and gave a mocking clap. "Excellent! I knew we'd get there in the end."

"Blackmorg! Why of course, now I remember." Everus scrutinised the man anew. "Dae'morgus. You were one of the early Xethornite high priests of Wyrm's Port."

"*Dae'morgus?* Now there's a name from the past." The Xethornite stared vacantly for a moment, lost in his own unholy recollections. "Dae'morgus...yes, that was my name. *Once.*" He spat out the last word. His eyes refocused on Everus, an open malignancy born from all the evils he had ever committed – and there had been more than a few – discolouring them and making them momentarily blaze crimson. "Dae'morgus is dead! *Do you hear me!?* I...I have been born anew!" His body trembled with a paroxysm of fury. With a sudden lunge, he reached out and beat at the barrier from the inside, even as the magical fire scorched his hands. Despite his

410

actions, it was apparent that his efforts were futile. He screamed in anger and frustration as he tore and burned.

"So what are we goin' to do?" asked Creeps, rather nonchalantly, from where he sat atop a heap of ruined masonry.

Blackmorg ceased his useless clawing and turned. "So, this...this feeble excuse for a man is the best The High Three can do? My master warned me about you. But now that I see you, I know how impotent you truly are. To think that *you* had us worried. *Ha!*" He looked about, for the first time really taking in the rest of Everus' companions. "And just what else do we have? What other fools have deigned to join thy foolish quest?" His eyes fell on Weaselnest, not that he noticed. "Ah...my little grave-robber friend, I see these bad people have hurt you and somehow removed your mark of holding. Don't worry, I will soon return you to the fold." His smile became wolfish as his gaze settled on Carrie. "Hmm. Very nice. I wonder what I should do with you?" His eyes widened. "*What are you...!?*"

The sorceress made a motion with her arms. "You're not a very nice person, are you?" she interrupted.

Within his prison, Blackmorg flinched as though stung, his hideous face contorting further. "I...I..." He was struggling to speak. "I..."

Everus looked to Carrie, for it was clear she had put some kind of spell on the Xethornite.

With a shake of his head, Blackmorg seemed to break her hold. "There will be time...fear not. We *will* get to know one another. But in the meantime, what should I do?" His tone had changed somewhat.

"The first thing you can do is thank your bastard god that you're in that circle, for if you were out here I'd cut you to pieces," snarled Everus.

"With a flail?" Blackmorg laughed. "My...that'd be something to see, wouldn't it?" His gaze returned to Carrie. "You'd love to see your hero here cut an old unarmed man to pieces with a flail, wouldn't you?"

To Everus, the Xethornite's words seemed false somehow, lacking the authority with which he had earlier spoken.

"What should we do?" asked Mhoon.

Blackmorg joined with the others and turned to face Everus. "Yes, Everus. What *will* you do? I have the casket. You want it. And, as you've probably guessed, by taking it, you set me free." He gave a cruel laugh, the lines on his face making it appear more like one of the many ancient, evil and flaking mosaics Everus had seen deep within the old Xethornite temple in Wyrm's Port, than actual flesh. "What a quandary you now face. In order to get that which you need, you must release me. But, the cost of my liberation is, as you've no doubt guessed, the death of you and your friends. Such a pity."

"What if I just leave you here? I can make do without it."

Blackmorg saw through Everus' bluff. "Don't make me laugh! We both know that's not an option. So cease your little games."

"Tell me, Dae'morgus..."

"*Dae'morgus is dead!* You *will* call me Blackmorg!"

"Very well. I take it that you've been dispatched to reclaim the hand for Xethorn. If your god is so powerful, why does He fear me so? After all, He's going to rather inordinate lengths to stop me from acquiring it."

"*Fear you?* My master fears no one."

"Then why seek the hand of Cyrvilus?"

"To assist in the summoning."

"Uhu'giaggoth?"

"That is but one name for it." Blackmorg's face screwed up as though in discomfort. "With the hand, my master will summon and slay The Daemon God once and for all. With any luck, the greater part of this world will also be engulfed in the resulting cataclysm. But that matters little."

"You're as insane as He is!" cried Mhoon.

"*Insane?* Where's the insanity in fulfilling one's destiny – a destiny that was thwarted by the intervention of others."

"How come you're trapped?" asked Everus, offhandedly.

"So you've noticed?" replied Blackmorg, sarcastically. "So kind of you to take an interest."

"Answer my question."

"I think I pissed off Whaggustraag." Blackmorg's grin turned into a smile, his rotting teeth displayed to full effect. "Hardly surprising I suppose, when you think what I did here in this temple. But these things happen, and besides, when my master comes for me..."

"What makes you think He will?" Everus interrupted.

"He will." The Xethornite smiled, assuredly. "His armies may be approaching Wathang-Hu as we speak. The part of the hand from Ghavin's Keep may already be in His possession."

"I wouldn't count on it, pal," said Creeps. "Ye see, we've just come from there an' we've got it wi' us." He reached into his pack and brought out the small casket. Instantly, crimson flames shot forth, bridging the gulf between himself and the green light surrounding the trapped Xethornite. With a flash and a crackle, the barrier began to vibrate.

Everus, Mhoon and Carrie pulled back in alarm.

With a muffled explosion that filled the air with green smoke, the barrier stretched and broke, sucked into the curious container in the thief's hands. Energy crackled between the two caskets.

With a cry of victory, Blackmorg sprang free.

Everus was the first of the group to react. Rushing forward, he swung out with the heavy flail, his blow going well wide.

Nimbly, Blackmorg leapt away. He scampered to one end of the chamber, his cast shadow that of a terrible giant's. Raising his cane high, he uttered a word of magical power and suddenly the whole area was bathed in a sickly, yellow light.

A stink like an old vomit-filled drain clogged the air.

Everus felt the strength drain from him. Magically sapped of energy, the flail became as heavy as a ship's anchor and fell from his hand. He pushed his way towards his enemy, each step taking considerable effort, as though he were wading through a pit of molasses.

"Now you die! You all die!" Blackmorg screamed, his ugly face bathed half in shadow, half in the bilious glow. A crackling stream of energy fired from a taloned hand. But his cruel smile of victory changed to a growl of displeasure as the force of his spell was dragged towards Creeps' outstretched hands and absorbed by the reliquary the thief held.

Suddenly the chamber convulsed like a starved dragon's stomach.

Plaster and bricks fell from the ceiling.

With manic eyes, Blackmorg stared around him.

Mhoon leapt at the small man from behind and both of them crashed painfully to the ground.

Thrashing and biting like an adult crocothrash, Blackmorg flung the exorcist free. He then cried out in pain as a rock, flung by Everus, cracked off his head, knocking him to his knees.

The chamber shook again. Larger chunks of masonry, carved roof supports and arches broke away and tumbled to the floor. A great fissure opened in the floor, venting foul fumes from the dead warrens beneath.

"Someone get the casket!" Everus shouted. He just managed to crawl to one side as half a pillar shattered nearby. Dust billowed, stinging his eyes and obscuring his vision.

Blackmorg stood atop a desecrated, all but destroyed, altar, the casket clutched tightly to his chest. He raised his left hand and muttered a dark prayer. Although much of the strength behind the spell was absorbed by the thief's casket, Everus and Mhoon were still repulsed and flung backwards; tossed into the air as though struck by the full force of a hurricane.

Painfully, both of them collided with the far wall.

Suddenly, a huge, dirty-grey tentacle burst through the ground. Earth-encrusted scales and puckers the size of serving plates covered the unsightly appendage as it reared like a serpent towards the ruined ceiling. It coiled around a pillar before reaching out, seeking a greater prize.

"*Shit!*" cried Everus, getting to his feet. "*What's that!?*"

Blackmorg turned to face the new threat.

Creeps took advantage of the Xethornite's surprise and preoccupation. Unaffected by the strength-sapping enchantment, he ran forward and snatched the container out of Blackmorg's hands, his thieving talents used to full effect. "I've got the bones!" he cried jubilantly. "I've got the bones!"

"Now get out!" yelled Everus. "Everybody out!" Shielding his head from falling stonework, he moved as fast as he could for the temple exit, no longer caring what happened to Blackmorg. His vision darkened and seemed to pulse in and out in surreal waves as he began slowly clambering over piles of debris and dodging collapsing walls. Somehow, he reached the exit, stumbling to his knees, as dull explosions shook the ground. Turning, he saw that the entire temple had been transformed into a chaotic battlefield. Monstrous tentacles sprouted from the shattered floor, crushing and grasping whatever they fell on, constricting and crushing stone columns; pulverizing them to powder.

Bizarre lights and purplish-green fumes all added to the maelstrom.

Inside, Blackmorg could be seen leaping from side to side, his spells blasting randomly. Sometimes he targeted the great tentacles, his magic causing them to recoil as though in pain. Other times he went for Mhoon or Carrie.

On hands and knees, Everus crawled back further, the scene playing out before his weary eyes, his distorted vision, a living nightmare. Seven massive tentacles could now be seen, bashing and crushing anything and everything in their path. Two burst through the already collapsing ceiling as Whaggustraag, the ancient chthonic burrower from below, ravaged its own temple. In one agonising moment, Everus saw Mhoon thrown into the air like a rag doll. The exorcist's body bounced off the temple roof and fell to the ground with a sickening thud.

Electric blue flashes and more muffled explosions shook the mound. Fissures cracked open, venting noisome gases and covering the ground with the ancient dead.

Screaming and wreathed in green flames, Weaselnest staggered out, Carrie behind him. The grave-robber fell, his body charred and smoking. Carrie looked about, her pretty face blackened by ash and smoke.

Everus crawled over to where Mhoon lay.

"I..." Blood drooled from a corner of the exorcist's mouth.

"Keep still. We'll get you out of here." Everus' words were hollow and lacked conviction, knowing as he did that Mhoon's wounds were grievous. It was a wonder the man was still alive. Blood soaked his crushed body and his lower left leg bone protruded bloodily through his torn leggings.

"*Aaaagh!*" Mhoon cried, feeling his fractured bone. "Everus...go to...free my wife..."

"I will..." Before Everus could complete his oath, with another violent upheaval, the top half of the mound, temple and all, started to subside, sinking in on itself in a great implosion of rock, debris and dust. Blinded, he felt himself falling, but instead of being devoured by the mound and the nest of giant, searching tentacles, somehow he managed to stagger to one side, so that, as the tell collapsed, he slid and tumbled on the terrible avalanche of rubble and sand that was formed. Crashing and screaming, an artificial mountain of debris in pursuit, he continued to fall, his world darkening and flashing through his brain in one almighty, all-smothering, descent.

Choking, coughing, spinning – his nightmare seemed to go on and on until, crashing through the timber roof of a neighbouring hovel, he struck the bottom.

CHAPTER NINETEEN

For what seemed like an age, Everus existed within a realm of
darkness. It was a world of torment, one in which light and laughter
had long been extinct – if they had ever existed at all – and where the
only hope left was the hope that death would bring with it the
cessation of such an existence. He felt no pain, no agony from the
crushing rocks, no burning lungs from the suffocating dust. What he
did feel was a gnawing emptiness, as though he had become a
vacuous shell, a drained and lifeless container.

In time, images, malign and dreadful, assaulted him.

Each subsequent visitation was powerful enough to drive a clear-
thinking man to madness or to cower in fear for the rest of his days.
Perhaps it was because Everus was unable to perceive them in their
full horror, his consciousness mercifully blurred and unable to
blend their forms into finished products, that he did not.

✝ ✝ ✝

It was the noise that woke him – the clatter of wheels beneath him.

Gradually, his eyes managed to focus and he saw that he was in
a small covered-wagon, its walls formed from tough canvas, its floor
from planking. Dull daylight entered the opening in front of him,
revealing the drab interior. He was lying in a narrow bed, from which
he could see a small stool, an open chest filled with clothes and boots
and, to one side, a collection of crates stuffed with food; meat,
bread, various vegetables and a few bottles, which clinked as they
bounced along.

With a groan, he stretched his arms.

"Ye up?"

Creeps! Everus' mind and vision swam; a wave of nausea
triggered on hearing the voice.

"Everus! Are ye up?"

Where am I? Where am I? Where am I? Like a lunatic in chains, an inner voice rattled in his mind. *Who am I?* He gripped his now pounding head, a cold sweat damp on his fingers.

The wagon came to a halt.

Confused, delirious, concussed, motion sick and dazed beyond belief, Everus slumped to one side as his body lurched to a standstill. Yet, in his mind, he was still moving; free-falling into a dark abyss. Everything else seemed unreal. Reality became delusory. Crying in bewilderment, he tried to sit upright – succeeding only in falling from his cot. There was no shock or pain as, with a numbing thud, he landed on the floor.

Breathing shallowly, his vision clouded and painful, he began to haul himself to his feet, his surroundings pulsating with each throb of garbled message to the brain. Using the bed as a crutch, he managed to stand. Unsteady, he watched as the canvas flap before him widened.

"Everus. Ye should be restin'. Ye're no' fully recovered."

"Who? Where am I?" His own voice sounded alien and distant.

"It's me." The thief moved forward and steered Everus to the bed. Sitting him down, Creeps stooped and picked up a small bottle. This he uncorked and gave to his patient. "Drink."

Wearily, Everus accepted the bottle.

"How're ye feelin'?"

"Eh?" Everus responded, his mind seemingly a thousand leagues away. His hand shook with the strain of holding the water-filled container. He stared at the bottle, unsure as to what to do with it.

"Ye should have a drink."

Everus looked up at the thief. Who was this? Creeps. *Creeps?* He struggled to remember, his teeth gritting in frustration. *Where was he? What had happened? Who and what was he?* A sudden flash of darkness clouded his consciousness further, making him flinch and bring a hand to his face. The bottle fell from his trembling fingers and bounced off the planking, its liquid contents spilling out and darkening the boards.

And as the darkness passed, he found his eyes drawn to the spreading stain at his feet. Oblivious to the sounds of the man beside him, he gawped at the spreading dampness. Only now it looked like blood; a dark, viscous stain that seemed to spread and bubble of its own will. He tried to scream, but no sound escaped his lungs.

The stain was forming a face. His face.

And, before his eyes, the blood continued to seep and crawl, taking the semblance of a living horror.

✝ ✝ ✝

"*Creeeeps!*"

A gentle hand fell on Everus, calmly pushing him back, as though returning him to the grave from which he had just risen.

"Be still, Everus. Be calm."

"Carrie?"

The sorceress smiled and gently dabbed his forehead with a damp cloth.

"Where...am I?"

"All in good time. Rest now."

Carrie sat down at the edge of the bed in which Everus lay. She reached out with a braceleted hand, gently prompting him to lie back, to cease his agitation.

"How did I get here? Where's Creeps?"

"He's on guard." Soaking the damp cloth in a small basin nearby, Carrie then dabbed it against his brow.

With a sigh, Everus surrendered himself to the sorceress' ministrations. There were far worse things in life to do. From outside, he could faintly hear the sounds of birds chirping. Either that, or Creeps had added bird mimicry to his growing repertoire of unusual talents.

"Are you hungry?"

"Starving."

"Good." Carrie reached for a small basket at her feet. "What would you like? There's some bread, there's cheese...I know." She gave him a sexy, mischievous smile, opened a wicker container and took out a sealed packet. "I made these myself. They're my own recipe. They'll be sure to get you back on your feet in no time. Here." She presented him with a flat, biscuit-like cake.

"Thanks." Everus took the cake and bit into it. The crunchy exterior tasted of cinnamon. The inner core was a delicious creamy blend of blueberries and spiced honey. There was more than a little mead in it as well.

"Help yourself." Carrie rose to her feet.

Everus could feel his strength and sense of lucidity return with

418

each mouthful, thanks in large to the beneficial properties of the cake. He scoffed down several more.

"You know, it's no wonder that you're hungry."

Swallowing, Everus reached for another. "How long have I been out?"

"Like I said..."

"Tell me."

"Very well. This is our eleventh, no twelfth day out of Wathang-Hu."

"*Twelve days!?*" Mouth agape, awaiting the poised cake, Everus stared disbelievingly. "*Twelve days?*" he repeated.

Carrie nodded. "Yes...although it feels a lot longer, believe me."

Suddenly a shadow fell against one side of the wagon covering. A moment later, Creeps stuck his unpleasant face through the opening. "Ah...so ye're up? I thought ye were goin' to sleep forever."

"I hear I've been out for some time." Everus managed a laboured smile although it was directed more at the sorceress than the thief. "Twelve days."

"Aye. Now that's what I call kippin'. I was sure ye were dead."

"Perhaps I was." Everus knew that such a reply was bound to make the thief uneasy, for it carried with it the implication that perhaps Creeps had invoked his divine acquaintances in order to restore him to life. Satisfied with the thief's grumpy look, he turned to Carrie. "Tell me what happened. The last I remember I was outside the temple having escaped from Dae'morgus."

So Carrie told him. She told him how they had both tumbled down the side of the tell as, all around, the great earth kraken, Whaggustraag, with its gargantuan tentacles, had destroyed all. Her account did not dwell on the death of Mhoon and even less on the fates of Weaselnest and the cruel Xethornite. She went on to relate how, after the collapse of the mound, which incidentally had destroyed much of the town, they had both been dug free by a gang of townsfolk. She had been rescued, barely conscious, whereas he had been taken for dead. Along with scores of others, he had been carried to an established tented area which had served as a makeshift morgue. There he had lain for two days, amidst the flies, the lamenting and the corpses, until she had found him. It had been about then that Creeps had turned up, much to her surprise, for she had thought him amongst the dead and buried.

Everus sat up. "Do we still have the bones...the hand of...?"

"Yes, Creeps hasn't let them out of his sight."

With a crooked grin, the thief nodded.

"But I think it best that you sleep now, Everus. Sleep." Carrie drew a hand over his face and muttered words in a strange, arcane tongue.

Everus' head instantly hit the pillow and he was asleep in no time.

† † †

The rain came down in heavy sheets as the small wagon, driven by a cold and thoroughly soaked Creeps, trundled down the track towards the town of Stranglewood. The sky darkened as the rain became heavier, the track now degenerating into a deep-rutted quag.

Everus peered out into the damp gloom. A sudden flash of lightning illuminated the timber palisade they were now approaching. For a moment, he saw the outlines of a few large buildings beyond and what looked like a watchtower.

"I'm gettin' bloody pissed on 'ere!" cursed Creeps. It was a fair comment, for he was drenched, his bedraggled hair hanging in saturated strands around his wet and miserable-looking face. Rain and snot dripped from the end of his nose. He belched and threw away the bottle of ale he had been drinking from.

"We're nearly there. Look! There's a gate up ahead," said Everus, pointing.

The last stretch was sluggish; the mud and the rain making the going especially arduous. More flashes of lightning rent the murk asunder, allowing both of them to discern that on either side of the track stood great straggling trees of a variety neither had seen before. Thunder boomed ominously, the noise indicating that the storm was yet some leagues distant.

"She still sleepin'?"

Everus looked over his shoulder to where Carrie lay on the small cot which had served as his sickbed for many days. With some interest, he watched the rhythmic motion of her chest as she breathed, part of him wanting nothing more than to just slide in beside her. "Yes," he answered.

"I'll be buggered if I know how anyone can sleep through this racket." The thief coughed and spluttered before spitting out a wad of phlegm. He sniffed and wiped the sodden hair from his eyes.

They were now nearing the entrance.

The rain had slackened slightly.

On one side of the high wooden gate there was a small bothy. From its windows came the welcoming sight of lantern light. A door opened and a figure wrapped in a long coat and wearing a wide-brimmed hat stepped out, a lit lantern in one hand. His other hand held a length of rope, at the end of which was a fierce-looking dog. Parts of the man's face were puffed and dribbling.

"Hullo!" Creeps called out.

"What're ye wantin'?" shouted the stranger, his voice gruff, his tone surly.

"We thought we'd stop 'ere." Now having brought the wagon right up to where the man stood, Creeps brought the horse to a halt. "It's a bloody lousy night to be on the road."

"Aye, it is that."

After a moment of awkward silence, during which the man made no sign of either moving or talking to them, Everus jumped down from where he sat beside Creeps and walked over to the bothy. "So, are you going to open the gate or are you just going to stand there?"

"*Open the gate?* Do I look like a baazelgrig?" It was clear there was something not right with the man and as though to emphasis the point, he raised his lantern and pointed to his face. A green rash covered most of it. Boils and warts sprouted on his cheeks and forehead and over his hands. His face looked more like a fungal patch. "Openin' the gate ain't ma job. Ye'd be needin' to speak to them bastards inside."

Everus did not like the man's attitude any more than his appearance. "I guess you're right...I suppose you don't."

"Eh? What're ye on about?"

The hound the man held growled, foam frothing from its muzzle.

"I said, I suppose you don't."

"Are ye tryin' to be funny pal?"

"No...not at all. I was just agreeing with you. You don't look like a baazelgrig." Everus stared pointedly. "A baazelgrig's arse, maybe."

"Bugger off, ye cheeky bastard!" The diseased man took a couple of steps back. "Or I'll have to set dog on ye. Go on, just bugger off! We've got no time for strangers 'ere. It's bad enough me havin' to live out 'ere wi'out buggers like yerselves ticklin' ma onions." He pulled back into his hovel and slammed the door shut.

Up on the driver's seat, Creeps chortled to himself. "I see ye've made a new pal."

Briefly, Everus considered battering the door down and pounding the unfriendly soul senseless. He decided otherwise and, after a bemused look at Creeps, he strode through the rain and the mud to the main gate. A flash of lightning lit up the large sign above it:

WELCOME TO STRANGLEWOOD

"Hurry it up, will ye?" cried Creeps.

Before Everus got to the gate, a hatch was pulled back and a bearded face, clearly grubban in appearance, glared out.

"State yer business." The grubba peered about. There was a mad look in his darting eyes.

"We're looking for somewhere to rest for the evening."

"Ye haven't got the scabs, have ye?"

For a moment, Everus did not know how to answer. Confusion showed on his face as he looked down at the slit from which the grubba stared. "Not last time I checked."

"All right, in ye come." The bearded face disappeared. A moment later there came the sound of two large bolts being drawn back and then the gate began to swing inwards.

Everus signalled to Creeps to head over. He turned to see the grubba standing before him, a loaded crossbow in his hands. From the look in his eyes, it appeared that he would have taken great delight in pulling the trigger there and then.

"Welcome strangers."

It was the first time Everus had been welcomed at crossbow point.

The stocky gate guard waited until the wagon had entered. He flung a hasty look towards the small hut. "Ye've to watch out fer that ol' bastard. He came down wi' the scabs a couple o' days ago. That's why we put him outside." Pushing the gate shut, he secured the bolts. "Anyhow, ye both look clean to me." If Creeps' appearance was anything to go by, the grubba had obviously seen a lot of unclean people. "But afore I allow ye into town, I just need to make sure that ye aren't carryin' anythin'...illegal or otherwise in yer cart. There's been a run on contraband armaments an' shit recently."

"There's just one of our companions, a woman, in there," said Everus, not wanting the grubba to search inside.

"Oh aye?" The guard's eyes widened.

"And I don't think she'd take kindly to you waking her up."

"Ah, bugger it!" The grubba stepped back, his crossbow still raised. The unnerving look in his eyes made Everus think that perhaps he was going to start something. Despite his size, he looked a highly unpredictable, volatile and dangerous character. "Go on, on ye go. Just don't go causin' any bother...or else I'll have to introduce ye all to 'Bertha'." Grinning like a psychopath, he raised his crossbow and made a clicking noise with his teeth.

Everus' eyes narrowed. "*Really?* Sounds interesting."

"So where can we stay?" asked Creeps.

"Ye'll find a few good taverns, although most are probably full, what wi' 'The Slappers' bein' in town an' all. Now get goin' afore I change ma mind. An' remember, I ain't kiddin'. Ye piss about on ma watch an'...*click-click!*"

† † †

The rain battered off the window. The storm continued to lash the town, the frequent flashes of lightning enabling Everus to get a view of the surrounding structures as well as the strange, dark forest that lay all around. From the window, he watched as the shapes outside were lit up, briefly appearing like startled ghosts, before vanishing once more into the darkness. From downstairs, he could hear sounds of revelry as patrons drank and made merry in anticipation of tonight's main event.

After a time spent gazing out at the rain-battered rooftops and the dark street below, he walked over to the small bed and sat down.

There came a knock at the door.

It opened a little and Carrie looked in. "Can I come in?"

Everus nodded and watched as the sorceress, dressed in a brown peasant girl's skirt and white cotton chemise, glided in, the simple clothes accentuating her sensuality. She had tied her long hair into a fetching ponytail and her smile sent his pulse racing. On a chain around her neck hung a small amulet he had never seen her wearing before. It looked like a small piece of white glowing mineral set within a golden locket.

Carrie noticed his interest. "It's *lunarite*. It was given to me by my mother." She held it for a moment and gazed at it, temporarily lost in her own thoughts and whatever memories it was associated with. "It's supposed to..."

"Protect you from shapeshifters," interrupted Everus. "I know,

423

I...I used to have something similar." A sudden memory, one that had lain dead for many years, flooded back. Choking back a strong desire to weep, he screwed his eyes shut and held his head.

"Everus? Are you...?" Carrie moved close to him, reaching out so she could offer whatever comfort was needed.

Everus breathed deep. "I'm all right." Absently, he looked away from her, his gaze taking in the floor, the walls, the furniture – anything but her. To some extent she was too beautiful, too desirable.

"What's the matter?"

Everus exhaled, as though to expel whatever recollection she had inadvertently triggered. For a moment, his face hardened as though another memory, a darker one, had come into dominance.

"What is it, Everus? Tell me." Carrie sat on the bed next to him and tenderly stroked his hair.

"Where to start?" Everus turned, all of his past's torment and pain visibly clear, the look of a long-lost innocence in his eyes. "What's happened to me...to what I should've been? There's now nothing left. Nothing but hate." He shook his head. "That's all there is for me."

"I...I don't understand."

"I've lost her. Katryna, the only woman I've ever loved. It was she who gave me an amulet just like the one you wear. It was a birthday present. She'd always been particularly afraid...of shapeshifters, so she..." He swallowed a lump in his throat. "She..." He bowed his head, a hand grasping his hair, threatening to tear it out. "*What's happening to me?*" he asked through gritted teeth.

"Did she...did she die?"

Everus shook his head. "No." A coldness entered his voice. "She abandoned me, as did others. Deserted me when I needed her most, destroying my chance of leading a normal life."

"I'm confused. I thought you said..."

"Had she stayed, I might've been able to cling to something. To live for something, something other than hate and revenge." Everus feigned a smile. "I guess, such a life was not meant for me."

"Did you and she meet at The Academy?"

"The Academy! *Huh!*"

"You studied ancient history, didn't you?" Carrie asked, hoping to change the subject, somewhat concerned at the state of depression Everus was wallowing in. "That must've been so interesting. All those remote places and kings from bygone days. It all sounds so intriguing, so mystery-laden...so...romantic. It's all so..."

"*Rubbish?* That's all it is."

"*How can you say that?* Surely you studied it for a reason? That's why you're a high scholar, isn't it?"

"I'm *not* a high scholar. I never sat the final examination; *the academica.* I was denied the opportunity."

"*Why?* Why was that?"

"You wouldn't believe me if I told you."

"Yes I would."

"Very well. A succubus named Julia Camberra conspired with others to destroy me. First my family, then my ambition to become a high scholar, and finally Katryna. They took it all from me. *Bastards!*" Once more Everus sank into the depths of his inner turmoil. He flexed a fist and then closed it, willing all of his undying bitterness into that action as though in so doing he could contain it there and crush it. In reality, in his mind, he was crushing Julia Camberra's neck. His knuckles whitened and he seemed close to erupting into a rage. A sudden loud burst of laughter from below broke him from his dark thoughts. He waited for the noise to subside. "But being a high scholar isn't what it's cracked up to be. Passing the academica isn't a measure of intelligence – only a measure of whether one can endure three years of a scholar's existence. In the end, thanks to others, I couldn't."

"I'm so sorry. I didn't know."

"That's just the start. There is more, much more, but perhaps it can keep for another time." Everus stood up. "Come on." He smiled reassuringly at her. "Let's go and see what all the noise downstairs is about."

They left the room together and headed for the stairs.

Well over a hundred people had crowded into the tavern's large main hall. They were an untidy assortment, the slatternly womenfolk barely discernible from the men. All were shouting and drinking, their voices echoing around the high stone and timber walls. Grubbas and other odd-looking, barely human, characters all added to the unwashed, obstreperous gathering.

Everus and Carrie descended the stairs at one end of the room, their entrance going unnoticed amidst the general hullabaloo. At the far end from where they stopped, halfway down the stairs, they could see a crude stage had been erected, a hastily flung up dark red curtain screening whatever lay beyond it from the eager audience. A crumpled banner proudly carried the legend:

THE ULLERBY SLAPPERS

"Now that I'm here, I'm not so sure I want to watch this," remarked Everus.

"Well...we could go back to your room," Carrie replied, suggestively.

Everus felt his heart leap. He knew by the look in her eyes and the curl of her lips exactly what she was inferring, and deep down, he knew it was what he was wanting, needing perhaps. That she was different from the countless whores he had lain with, he had no doubt. To begin with, she was far, far more attractive, and he had shagged some beauties in his time. Yet still, somewhere in the dark pits of his mind, he knew he could not. For to give in, to surrender to her charms, to become passionately involved, would be a measure of his weakness. A weakness he could ill afford...not yet, anyway. Perhaps when Xethorn lay vanquished at his feet...

A sudden roar from the crowd reverberated around the hall.

"Looks like something's about to happen," said Carrie, sitting down on one of the steps.

From their raised vantage point, they watched as a short, fat man dressed in a dark suit surveyed the crowd. His hair was combed back and his plump face was gaudily made up, lipstick and all, giving him the appearance of a eunuch.

"Good people of Stranglewood." The compère's voice was shrill, almost girl-like. "Your attention, if you please."

Gradually, the clamour from the crowd died down.

"It is my great pleasure to present to you this evening an act of such quality, such...amusement and musical genius, that I, for one, am truly awe-struck." The man waddled to the centre of the stage, his gait that of a heavily pregnant walrus. "The entertainers of whom I speak have performed all over the empire, their shows playing to the greatest venues and to the largest audiences. Now in their fortieth year of playing to full houses, it is both a delight and an honour to welcome onto stage The..."

Before the compère could finish, a scrawny little man, dressed in a garish costume consisting of a pair of tight-fitting scarlet pantaloons, a green and white frilled shirt and a tricorne hat with a peacock feather in it, pranced out from behind the curtain. In one hand he carried a mandolin.

426

Unconvincingly flabbergasted, the compère stared, his reaction clearly rehearsed.

The interloper walked to the end of the stage. "Ladies and gentlemen. I'm afraid to have to tell you that, due to an unforeseen and somewhat embarrassing outbreak of the scabs, The Ullerby Slappers have been forced to cancel tonight's show."

The crowd voiced their discontent.

"However, I'm a troubadour of no little talent, and, if you'll permit, I would like to recite a poem or two that..."

The angry spectators were having none of it and let the stand-in bard know in no uncertain terms. They had come to see The Ullerby Slappers, not some skinny, surrogate songster.

Perhaps fearing a riot, the eunuch-lookalike ducked back behind the curtains.

"*Please!* Just hear me out." Plucking his mandolin, the bard started his melody, failing to drown out the disapproving roars from the crowd. Old boots, turnips and several eggs were flung at him. Then, all of a sudden, an almighty din nearly blasted him off the stage. For a moment, it seemed as though the storm from outside had somehow gatecrashed the performance. Sorcerous lights flashed all over the raised platform, dazzling the little man, who covered his ears and stared about, wide-eyed, before leaping off the stage.

The noise was a veritable cacophony of outrageous notes; a blatant, amplified assault on the ears that caused the very hall to tremble.

At the back of the makeshift auditorium, Everus and Carrie looked at each other and winced in a mutual show of distaste.

Out from one side of the stage there jumped a long-haired, fat, bare-bellied man, his sideways profile proudly accentuating his obesity. He was dressed in nothing but a pair of tight fitting britches that were cut off above the knee. In frog-like leaps, he bounded forward, a second, fatter man, similarly dressed and with hair down to his shoulders, behind him. In staggered hops, they sprang forward, another two, the last a truly gross individual of flabby flesh and wobbling fat, bringing up the rear.

In unison, they turned round to face the audience full on.

"*Come on!*" the biggest member roared. "*Make a noise!*"

The crowd went wild.

"*We can't hear you!*" the four human mammoths yelled, cupping their ears as though to prove the point.

The crowd screamed louder.

"*We still can't hear you!*"

"Maybe they're deaf," commented Everus, dryly, having to raise his voice so that Carrie, who sat within touching distance, could hear him.

"*Scream for me! Come on, scream for me!*" The largest of the quartet stuck his stomach out, his right hand poised to strike it. "*Scream if ye want it!*" He shook and wobbled in savage exuberance, his mane-like hair flailing wildly. The makeshift, reinforced stage shook as he jumped up and down.

Many in the audience seemed to go into hysterics. A wave of people pushed to the front. Others leapt into the air, eager to get a good sight of their blubbery idols.

Four meaty hands slapped against four flabby bellies, the sound produced more than just a fleshy thwack, for, whether due to the unusual acoustics within the hall or years of bodily conditioning, it made Everus think of the approaching drumbeats from a large marching army.

It was the kind of sound that heralded bloodshed...or, judging by the appearance of the creators of the sound; frenzied feasting on a gargantuan scale.

On stage, the four natural percussionists continued to beat their 'belly drums', their fat guts wobbling, brazenly – the sound anything but euphonious. They bounded about, their movements crudely synchronized. Sometimes two of them would clash together, the sound and the ungraceful motion of their stomachs colliding, elephantine. On several occasions, one of them would turn, showing that the backside of his britches had been cut out, thus presenting his fanatical onlookers with a pair of broad and hairy buttocks.

"Spare me," muttered Everus, having seen enough. When Carrie did not respond, either because she had not heard him or because she was too enthralled with the deafening, bizarre performance, he quietly made his way back upstairs, entered his room and went to bed. The roars and guffaws from below lasted till well past midnight but, even so, it did not take him long to fall asleep.

† † †

Creeps looked up from his now empty porridge bowl. "Ye missed a treat last night." He reached for a tankard of water. "The Ullerby

428

Slappers were on stage...an' what a performance. There must o' been o'er a hundred folk in 'ere." He drank like a cow at a trough.

"We watched some of it," replied Carrie, not wanting to look too closely. She had barely touched her breakfast. A full bowl of steaming gruel and a small plate filled with apple slices and unidentifiable meat chunks rested by her left elbow.

"I managed to get near the front, an' I can tell ye it were some show. Aye, it were no' bad at all. I don't ever seem to recall them playin' in Wyrm's Port." Belching, the thief leaned back in his chair, fresh porridge stains covering the front of his dirty shirt. "Did they ever appear in Wyrm's Port, Everus?"

Everus stared out of the window nearest to him, his mind on other things, such as the incredibly beautiful woman sitting next to him – a woman for whom many red-blooded men would willingly sacrifice all. And yet, there remained something about her; a niggling uncertainty that was proving hard to define. Paranoia – that unwanted, yet undeniably useful ally that had honed his personality – warned him to be careful, to keep his defences up. To think that she had practically offered herself to him last night and he had not taken up her offer. Was he mad?

"Ye all right?"

Everus turned and looked across the table. "What?"

"I said, are ye all right? Ye seemed to go all..."

"All what?"

Creeps sat back. "I were just askin' if them fat bastards..."

"What are you on about?" Everus interrupted, his words slow, measured and enunciated.

Averting his eyes, the thief looked down at his empty bowl and mumbled an incoherent response.

"Creeps was just asking about the performers we saw last night. He wants to know if they ever appeared in Wyrm's Port," said Carrie, realising that whatever fellowship there still remained between Everus and the thief was quickly disintegrating. In many ways she was an outsider, watching as a heavy chain was being wound in opposing directions. Links were already cracking, the inevitable snapping not that far away.

Everus sat back and laughed. "Ha! We're on a crusade to destroy Xethorn, the Lord of Murder, and all *he* can ask...is whether or not The Ullerby Slappers ever went to Wyrm's Port!" Tutting, he lifted a spoon and bounced it off the table edge. The metal utensil spun back over his right shoulder and tinkled off the stone floor.

For a time, no one spoke, allowing the uneasy tension to rise.

It was the sorceress who broke the hush. "Are you two going to come to some kind of agreement, or are we going to sit here all day like sulky children? For, as I'm sure you're both aware, we're here to get another piece of the hand."

"Do we know whereabouts it is?" inquired Creeps.

"Everus?" Carrie focused her eyes on him.

An unnecessarily long moment passed, as though Everus were reluctant to share his information with them. Either that, or he was intentionally letting the question hang, hoping that they would take his reticence as ignorance.

"You do know where it is, don't you?" Carrie prompted.

Everus sighed. "Yes. It's in the crypt of Klattermorch."

† † †

"The grip's too short." Everus handed the sword back to the hunchbacked weaponsmith. "What else?"

The hunchback looked at the sword. "What do ye mean, the grip's too short?" Holding it first in one hand and then in two, he made a few play attacks. "Feels perfectly good to me."

"Why don't ye go for a spear...or summat a bit different?" ventured Creeps, holding aloft a baazelgrig pike. "There's a lasso-thing on the wall there, although I don't know how good that'd be."

Everus strode over to a large rack that held dozens of blades. Some looked quite ornate, yet badly balanced – the playthings of youthful knights and show-offs – not the working tools of a professional murderer. Examining some of those on display, he silently cursed the loss of his own weapon – a viciously sharp bastard sword he had picked up in The City of the Glittering Spire on his first visit there. It had been a fearsome weapon, one that he had put to good use. Now it lay buried under a mountain of rubble in what little remained of Wathang-Hu.

"See anythin' ye like?"

"It's a wonder you can get away with selling this rubbish." Everus drew one of the swords from its support. "Look!" He patted the flat of the dull blade against a timber pillar and the weapon came apart. He turned to where the shop owner stood, nothing now but the hilt in his hand. "*Rubbish!* Absolute rubbish!"

"I've got some fine axes. Genuine grubban deathdealers, nothin' but the best. Blades retain their sharpness and they can cut through stone. Outstandin' craftsmanship. Go on, give one a whirl!"

"I told you. I want a sword." Everus scanned the small room, taking in the many and varied weapons and the odd pieces of armour that lay about, all stored in no particular order. "Is this *all* you've got?"

"Afraid so."

"Nothing magical? You see I had intended to spend a substantial amount if I saw the right thing. Such a waste. Looks like I'm going to have to leave empty-handed. Guess I was told wrong. You see, I was informed that you had some exceptional items for sale."

The weaponsmith looked about furtively and gulped. His bloodshot eyes darted like a hungry lizard's. "Well...could be that I've a little summat downstairs. Would...sir be interested in having a...perusal?" He rubbed his hands together as he spoke and looked up, questioningly.

"Now you're talking."

"If ye'd follow me." The hunchback led them into a smaller room that clearly served as an office of sorts. Although there were no weapons stored in here, the room was just as cluttered with furniture, piled papers, ledgers, dozens of stuffed cats and other pieces of junk. Removing a large key from a hook behind a mounted cat's head, he loped behind a small desk, crouched down, lifted a rug away and began to open a trapdoor. Once done, he grinned at Everus and descended into a torchlit cellar.

Everus followed, Creeps not far behind.

The basement was a veritable arsenal of outlawed weaponry.

Virtually everything looked sharp, gleaming and very dangerous.

There were Zethian hellspewers, giant Mzaahian khopeshes, Uttapian tridents and battle lances, several dozen Hyadean flanged maces, over twenty wall-mounted Yttorian composite bows, a score or more crates marked EXPLOSIVE and much, much more.

Everywhere Everus looked, his eyes beheld some other lethal creation.

"Welcome to ma bargain basement," said the hunchback, proudly displaying his wares.

"Where'd ye get all this shit?" asked the thief, his eyes roving.

"Oh, 'ere and there." The weaponsmith looked about, admiringly, for these were *his* children. The only family he had ever

431

known since being dumped in a bowl and put out for the dogs shortly after his birth. "Some...take those grubban arquebuses for example," he waved a hand towards a row of archaic firearms. "I obtained those a couple o' years ago from a dealer in Wyrm's Port. It's a bugger o' a job gettin' 'em to fire...but just look at the quality o' the craftsmanship. Ye don't get that kind o' thing nowadays." He shuffled, almost doubled-over, to the back of the room. "Come. Have a look at this." He dragged back a large tarpaulin to reveal a huge grubban cannon. "She's a beauty, ain't she? Ye wouldn't believe the trouble I had gettin' ma hands on her. Ye won't have any more troubles in the bedroom department after ye've blown the bitch's mutha away wi' this. Trust me."

"Quite a remarkable collection," Everus commented. He reached for a short, tapered javelin, its length covered with tiny symbols. "Where did you get this?"

"Ah...an A'bar-Donian javelin. That's part of an atl-atl set. The throwing stick'll be around somewhere. I got 'em from an old retired sea captain I used to know in Trade Peak. I used to have a fair number o' A'bar-Donian bastard-killers, soul-cutters and claymores as well, but I sold 'em on. Pity, ye'd o' liked 'em, especially the bastard-killers. Smashin' weapons they were, the real business. Could cut a man in two as though he were a cucumber, no trouble."

"I can't say I know many people who are like cucumbers. All the same, A'bar-Donian, I thought as much." Almost respectfully, Everus returned the javelin to its stand. "You know, while I'm here, I wonder if you'd be good enough to give me directions to Klattermorch's crypt."

The hunchback's eyes widened. "Ye don't want to be goin' there...that is, not least until ye've...bought a load o' weapons to...ye know, help ye out. It's a bad place, even if only half o' the rumours I've heard about it be true."

"Just tell me how to get there."

"Well, far be it for me to talk a man out o' suicide. If ye really want to go there, then ye'll be needin' to take the east road out o' town, past the turnip fields. Follow the road on fer a good league or so till ye come to a crossroads. Take the...left turn an' ye'll soon find yersel' in the woods. Be sure an' stick to the track lest ye wander into the middle o' Stranglewood Forest. I've heard weird stories about how folk have gone missin' in there, never to be found again. Not that long ago one o' the ol' gamekeepers found the remains o' some poor bugger impaled to a tree wi' one big spike. Aye, there be a lot o' strangeness goes on in there, so make sure ye don't stray off the path. Anyhow, as I was sayin', follow the track until ye come to another turnin' at which ye'll be wantin' to go...left. Or is it right? It's been yonks since I was last in there." The hunchback stopped and thought for a moment. "Left. Yeh, definitely left. That'll take ye to the cliffs on which the old ruins are standin'."

"I appreciate your help."

"Well, that's great, but it don't pay ma brothel bills. Look, ye're lookin' fer a sword, ain't ye? Well, I might have just the thing for ye." The deformed owner shambled over to a large trunk. He opened it and withdrew a weighty black scabbard from which protruded a finely-wrought hilt. Designs of intertwined dragons and horned skulls were stitched into the bound leather grip. "Now how's this fer a blade? Magic, I believe."

"Let's have a look." Everus' eyes lit up as he unsheathed the blade. It was exquisite and highly polished. "Yes. This feels much better." He cut the air one-handed in a series of masterful swings. "Very nice. There's a good, solid weight to it and I like its edge. Excellent balance. Any idea where it's from?"

"Not exactly sure...but as far as I remember, it used to belong to one o' the Black Ravers. They were a bunch o' ruthless brigands that used to plague the eastern road between 'ere and The Wreckins. Rumour tells that it's spilled enough blood to fill a small sea, but I couldn't tell ye any more than that."

"Hmm. It certainly is a fine weapon, and you say it's magical?"

"Aye. I mean, it's got to be. Just look at all these runes an' things along the blade. What else could they be for?"

"Decoration, perhaps?" replied Everus, mordantly. He tested the edge, easily drawing a line of blood on the palm of his left hand. It was certainly sharp. "How much are you asking for it?"

The owner shook his head and gave the question some thought. "It's a mighty weapon. One o' a kind. Magic too. Tell ye what, it's yers fer..." He ran a gnarled hand across his stubbled chin. "Oh, let's say, five and a half thousand gold."

Creeps stared wide-eyed and open-mouthed, unsure whether he had heard correctly. His hearing had certainly been impaired by the noise from the stage show he had attended the night before.

Everus took it all in his stride. His bargaining made easy by the fact that he knew he wanted this weapon and he knew he was going to have it. "Five and a half. Hmm. Tell you what...why don't you give it to me as a present, and I won't kill you?"

The owner backed away. "*What!?*"

"You heard."

"Well, aren't ye the big hero? Big tough man, eh? What a bloody hero! Bloody thievin' bastard! They should string the likes o' ye up. Ye unscrupulous swine."

"I'll take that as a yes. Many thanks." Sword in hand, Everus turned and followed Creeps up the ladder, leaving the disgruntled hunchback behind to lament his loss.

"Are ye no' worried he'll get the watch? Send that grubban nutter wi' 'Bertha' after us?" asked Creeps as they made their way across the main street, heading back to the tavern where Carrie waited.

"No. I think he'd much rather keep his treasures secret, don't you? You saw some of the stuff he had down there. I'm not so sure the local authorities would take too kindly to someone keeping that kind of an arsenal. He'd enough firepower down there to start another Cataclysm."

✝ ✝ ✝

No sooner had they left by the East Gate than the rain came down. Although it began as a steady, light drizzle, by the time they started to skirt the old and neglected turnip fields the hunchback had mentioned, it struck with a vengeance. The ancient cartwheel ruts on the track they were following filled with muddy pools, making the going soggy and difficult.

Irrigation dykes, filled with stagnant, smelly water, separated the fields from the levee on which the track had been laid. Those on either side looked particularly abandoned, only the occasional row of root vegetables visible amidst the mud and the tall, straggling weeds. Large black crows hopped about on the ground and some circled overhead, their caws adding to the miserable, depressing scene. Crude scarecrows, formed from rotted pumpkin heads and wooden cross-pieces, lay here and there; inanimate guardians of a largely dead and desolate land.

"We'll shelter under that tree up there." Hands in pockets, shoulders hunched, Everus stalked forwards, his boots squelching in the mud.

Distant thunder rumbled.

By the time they had all gathered under the leafless shelter of the large oak, it seemed as though the sky had become several shades darker. Despite the fact that it was not yet midday, a damp, oppressive gloom had fallen.

"So what're we doin'?" asked the thief. "I mean, are we goin' to go on...or, do ye think we should wait and maybe set out tomorrow? It might be a bit drier tomorrow."

Everus turned to Carrie. "What do you think?"

Wrapped in a heavy cloak, the sorceress looked about, taking in the sky and the lie of the land before them. Neither looked particularly appealing. "Well...I guess it depends on how long this rain's going to last. I can't say I'm looking forward to trudging into the woods soaked through."

Creeps sniffed and stuck out a hand, palm upright. "I think it might be easin'." He looked skywards. "Hard to tell." He wiped a drop of snot from his nose onto his sleeve. "I still reckon we'd have been better off had we taken the cart."

"We'd never have got it through the woods," replied Everus.

"What if, when we get there, we find that the relic's gone?" asked Carrie.

"I don't know."

"Rain's definitely easin'. Looks as though there might be a bit o' a clearin' in the clouds o'er there." Reaching into an inside jacket pocket, the thief took out his pipe and flint and steel. He lit up and puffed deeply.

"All right. Let's go for it." After ensuring that his newly acquired sword was well fastened onto his back, under his long coat, Everus set off.

Getting to Klattermorch's tomb proved harder than any of them had anticipated, for the directions they had been given turned out to be confusing and utterly misleading. Whether the hunchback had set out to intentionally misdirect them or not was hard to tell, however, with each step through the mud they seemed to be going further from the woods, which now lay a league to the north.

Everus looked about at the grim landscape, his eyes trying to follow the line of the track as it wound its way through the low foothills of the southern reaches of The Deadmoor Clumps, trying to detect a crossroads. He could see the grey-green mass of the uninviting Stranglewood Forest now almost directly behind him and the first of the high peaks of the distant Wreckins visible to the east. Further away, down the road, its foreboding silhouette framed against the dull, overcast sky, there stood a ruined castle, its broken towers and ravaged battlements an eerie reminder of the decades of conflict this land had seen.

Knowing some of that history, Everus found it easy to imagine the many wars that had been fought in this area. Everywhere he looked, his skilled eye could detect traces, invisible to most, of those old battles – whether it be in the frequent burial mounds or the extant earthworks; the ditches and the ramparts that were now largely trodden into the ground or lay, all but concealed, under the dense undergrowth.

Fierce and bloody had been those skirmishes. The earliest recorded battles had been fought between humans and grubbas, the former being the indigenous inhabitants of the whole region. However, with the advent of grubban territorialism and their desire for the rich mineral deposits known to exist in The Deadmoor Clumps, the meeting of the two races had been inevitable. After centuries of animosity and bitter feuding, fuelled by both religious and racial intolerances, the grubbas succeeded in driving the humans out. Their victory had been short-lived, however, for less than a decade after the final human expulsion, the grubbas found themselves facing a new enemy; the giants, who would later be referred to as the bagh'arulks and the Øggarbakken behemoths.

The grubban stand against the savage giants was legendary. For many, many long years, each side swung the war in their favour, only, in time, to meet with a reversal in fortunes. The dead from both sides were trampled into the earth and the streams and rivers ran red with blood. And still the carnage had gone on. The brutality, the strength and the animalistic frenzy of the giants, pitted against the doughty stubbornness, tenacity and much more advanced culture and weaponry of the grubbas. In the end, however, the sheer ferocity of the behemoths proved too much for the grubbas – destroying many and scattering the survivors out into the lowlands.

And yet, thought Everus, how hollow that triumph, when seen through the filter of the present, must be. For now, certainly from what he had heard, all the behemoths were gone; an entire species sacrificed in order to fuel Xethorn's diabolical machinations.

"What's that?"

Turning, Everus looked to where the thief pointed.

"Do ye think that's our turnin'?"

"Let's go and see." Everus set off, his companions close behind him. The weather had improved slightly and a glance at the sky told him that the worst of the rain that had struck earlier might now have blown over. The path became muddier however, the track degenerating into a short stretch of bog land.

Before them, leaning crookedly, was an old signpost. One arrow pointed back towards Stranglewood, and was so labelled. An unmarked arrow pointed in the direction of the forest, whilst two others indicated The Wreckins and South.

"I can't say I like the looks of that...the unmarked arrow," said Carrie. "It has an air of menace about it." Looking closely, she could see that there just was nothing on the sign. It was not as though it had been defaced, more that its creator knew that no title was required.

"Stranglewood Forest." Everus stared at the brooding woods, his mind dwelling uncomfortably on some of the stories he had heard about this place. Tales that would chill the blood and cause the bravest to cower – tales of the *dryadlich*; the bloodsucking leaves with faces of the dead on them or the *schrappingbäyer*; a child's ghost forever doomed to haunt the woods, the mere gaze from its eyes said to cause death.

"I'm not entirely convinced it's such a great idea going in there," commented Carrie.

"Nor I." Grimly, Everus headed forward.

Carrie turned to look at Creeps. The two of them then quickly fell in line behind their leader. After all, he was the one with the big sword.

✝ ✝ ✝

The woods were dark. It seemed as though wherever they went they ended up moving into greater darkness, almost as though the dense forest were alive with some kind of malevolence that was trying, and succeeding, to lure them in towards its deeper parts. And there were mysterious sounds as well; the abruptly silenced child's cry or the crashing of something large and unseen nearby.

Deeper into the forest they went, the identifiable species of trees; the oaks, the elms and the sycamores, now replaced with altogether more unusual growths. Towering trunks, dripping with moss, pressed close, as did smaller, thorny growths with dirty black leaves. Tentacled, sundew-like plants lived parasitically on some of the dying trunks, their grasping appendages squirming whenever neared.

"Everus. Tell me ye don't get any o' them bastard rat-things out 'ere." Creeps stared towards the upper branches of some of the trees.

"What? What are you on about?"

"Those bastard rat-things we were attacked by south o' Wyrm's Port that time. Remember?" Creeps took hold of his right ear lobe and gave it a waggle. The upper part of that ear had been bitten off during the encounter in question.

"You mean death squirrels?" Suddenly reminded of the dangerous, carnivorous vermin, Everus too looked towards the countless overhanging branches, which now formed a canopy across the track. "I don't know. However, this is a forest...and that is their natural habitat."

They kept walking, the track they were on now little more than a path. Clumps of bloated fungi clung to old bark and small things skittered along the forest floor and up tree trunks. Soon the growing darkness would necessitate the use of the lantern Creeps carried, but for the time being at least the aim was to cover as much ground as possible without attracting any undue attention.

More creaks and strange sounds brought them to a temporary stop.

After an uneasy time spent listening, they resumed their trek, the unexplained sounds and the sense of claustrophobia brought about by the looming trees all contributing to making the going uneasy. Soon they reached a clearing, a large, natural opening in the woods, its far side delineated by a high outcrop of jagged-peaked granite. At the top of which, standing dark and evil against the brooding greyness of the sky, was Klattermorch's crypt.

"This is it." Everus drew out his sword, the blade sliding silently from its sheath. "Looks like there's a trail of some sort going up those cliffs over there." Suddenly, there was a loud bang and a smoke-flash over to his left.

Carrie screamed and fell.

"*What the...?*" cried Creeps, looking from side to side.

"*Bloody thievin' bastards! Gun 'em down!*"

The air was filled with the acrid stink of gunpowder as two more blasts echoed through the clearing.

Fired shot whistled past Everus.

Out from the bracken stepped the aggrieved hunchback weaponsmith and two of his cronies. One was rapidly reloading his firearm, whilst the other now held a small crossbow. Dashing his weapon to the ground, the hunchback tore something from an ammo belt, lit it with the fat cigar in his mouth and lobbed it.

Unsure as to what it was, Everus watched as the smoking, ovate petard came closer. With a dull detonation, the bomb landed and exploded nearby, knocking him off his feet. Black smoke rose from the small blast crater. Clumps of turf and shrapnel blasted out, but fortunately it was not powerful enough to cause any serious damage. Although, had it been any closer...

"Steal from me, would ye?" Lumbering out of the smoke, clumsily swinging a large, double-bladed axe and having now discarded his cigar, came the hunchback.

Everus parried the hunchback's swing. He rolled to his right, sprang to his feet and parried a follow-up stroke. The hunchback may have been ungainly in his attacks but he was certainly strong. And now that Everus could see him better, he saw that, from the looks of it, the man had almost emptied his own arsenal in order to get his own back, for he must have had at least twenty knives sheathed at his belt. In addition, he had more bombs fastened to a large criss-crossing pair of bandoliers across his broad chest and there appeared to be four or five weapons of different types strapped awkwardly to his malformed back.

"Ye'll no' steal from me again!" Dashing the cumbersome axe to the ground, the hunchback whisked out two daggers, one in each hand. One was straight-edged, the other jagged.

Sidestepping a mis-timed attack, Everus sprang around his opponent and hacked down, his two-handed swing slicing down through cloth, flesh and bone.

Blood sprayed as a severed right arm fell to the ground.

"*Aaaagh!*" The unfortunate weaponsmith staggered back, blood now squirting from the gaping, ragged red hole at his shoulder, a knob of pale bone clearly visible. Reeling, his tongue lolling, he cursed and spat blood, his whole body juddering in pain and shock. Eyes glazed and wandering, he fell to his knees. With a final curse, he then slumped down in the mud, dead.

One of the 'cronies' was fidgeting with his crossbow, which had seemingly jammed.

Everus charged towards him, aware that, over to his left, Creeps was tussling with the other, both trying to get their hands on the long-barrelled firearm.

"*Sod this!*" The man Everus was going for threw down his crossbow, turned tail and fled.

Everus turned, relieved to see Carrie now on her feet. She clutched her left shoulder, where she had been winged by the opening shot. The wound looked blood-spattered and blackened. "Carrie! Are you all right?" he shouted.

"I...I think so. I think the..."

With a bang, the proto-rifle Creeps and the other man were fighting over went off. The shot whizzed skyward, blasting twigs and leaves.

"Give it 'ere, ye bastard!" shouted Creeps.

"Get off!" yelled the gunman.

Everus rushed to assist the thief.

Wide-eyed, the remaining ambusher stared as Everus approached. Obviously deciding that he could not handle two of them, he did as his friend had done, his morale clearly shaken. Dropping the weapon, he too turned to run. Unfortunately for him, however, Creeps stuck a foot out and tripped him up. With a scream, he landed, face-first, his chin smacking off a moss-covered rock.

Creeps winced at the bone-jarring crack.

"*Yeeeugh!*" The man rolled onto his back, blood streaming from his mashed lips. It took him a moment to open his jaws, both upper and lower sets of teeth clamped and splintered together, and when he did, he spat out a lump of glistening tongue.

Smiling, Everus was just about to chop down, bringing the unfortunate's life to a close, when, noting the gun in Creeps' hand, a notion struck him. Stabbing his sword into the ground, he gestured for the arquebus.

"*Gaaah.* Mishhhter, I..." Thick, dark red syrupy blood drooled from the man's mouth.

"Shut up!" Everus stood over the injured man and examined the long-barrelled musket. He turned to Creeps. "Do you know how this thing works?"

"Well sort o'. It's one o' 'em old 'hackbut' weapons. Ye need to load it up wi' smoke powder, stuff it wi' a bit o' paper an' then ye cram the shot-ball in. Once ye've got the barrel all ready, ye need to fill this 'ere pan wi' the powder and then ye..."

Everus passed the gun back to the thief. "Just load it up for me, would you? I dare say our friend here will have all the required pieces." He watched, mildly interested, as Creeps removed the necessary components of firing paraphernalia from the hapless man and began loading up.

Carrie staggered over, blood trickling from between the fingers clamped to where she had been shot. With a grimace, she nodded, assuring Everus that she would be all right, the wound, despite looking nasty, was obviously not serious.

"Well, my friend, I'm going to give you a chance." Everus hauled the would-be assassin to his feet.

"That's us loaded an' ready to fire." Pleased with himself, Creeps handed the gun back to Everus.

"Ye...ye ghhhaa canna khlishll...!" whimpered the hunchback's lackey, his words barely discernible through the gory mess that was his mouth. "I...I've gotsch lotsh o'...*Pleeeashh!*"

Menacingly, Everus looked down the line of the barrel, deaf to the man's pathetic pleas. "Now it could be that you're in luck...for I've never fired one of these things before. So, I dare say that my aim won't be too good."

"You're not going to just shoot him, are you?" Carrie asked. There was clearly quite a lot about Everus she had yet to learn.

Everus smiled. "I'm going to give him a chance. Which is more than I do for most who try and kill me." He turned to the man, addressing his would-be target practice. "You see that boulder over there? When you reach that point I'm going to fire. If I miss...you go free. You've my word I won't pursue you..." Offhandedly, he added, "However, if my aim is true...and by the way, I'll be aiming for your head...well...are you ready?"

"Buttsch...uuugh."

"I *said*, are you ready?"

Obviously failing to get any measure of sympathy, the man nodded.

"Just let him go, Everus, for I can't say I approve of this kind of cruelty," voiced the sorceress, her plea for clemency somehow lacking genuine conviction.

The challenge to Everus' conscience was a short one. "This isn't cruel, believe me. I know what cruelty...*real* cruelty is. This way, I'm giving him a sporting chance. I mean, let's not kid ourselves. Had we found ourselves in his situation, do you think we would get such a chance?" He shook his head. "I think not. I would be killed..."

"Ye did nick yer man o'er there's sword," interrupted Creeps.

"No, I didn't. I made a bargain – his life for the sword. He tried to get his sword back so he forfeited his life." Everus resumed his dialogue with Carrie. "As I was saying, I would be killed, you raped...and Creeps? The mind boggles. Perhaps 'Old Hunchy' had a thing for ugly gits. Maybe he'd have tied him to a tree and humped him senseless. I've heard of such perverts."

The thief chuckled dryly.

"Now then," said Everus, raising the gun. "If you're foolish enough to pray to any gods, you'd best hope that they're listening."

"Ye know that afore ye can fire it ye need to light this 'ere fuse?" commented Creeps. He struck sparks on his small tinderbox and set the fuse burning. "When this burns out, ye need..."

With a loud roar, a huge, dark grey bear broke through the undergrowth and came bounding towards them. Lumbering clumsily, its fur torn and mangy, its snout and fang-filled maw smattered and caked in dried gore, it looked more like a monster than a wild animal. From around its shaggy, maned neck dangled a thick length of snapped chain. Unlike Everus, his companions, the hunchback and his cronies, this animal had its own arsenal of killing tools; its teeth and claws both well suited for tearing limb from limb.

"*Shit!*" cried Creeps.

The small wick on the gun Everus held had now burnt out. Turning, he raised the weapon and fired, the power of the recoil jolting through his arms and kicking back against his braced shoulder.

With a bang, the fired shot whizzed through the air and struck the bear in the chest. Blood spurted and the great beast roared in pain. Now standing upright, its head skirting some of the low-hanging branches, it pawed the air before it, threateningly displaying its strength and anger. It was a truly fearsome sight.

The hunchback's pal was off, limping and loping. The prospect of either being shot in the back or ending up as bear shit fuelling his desperate escape.

Dashing the spent gun to the ground, Everus went for his sword.

Snarling aggressively, the grizzly bear staggered forward on its stumpy hind legs.

Suddenly a beam of rainbow colours shot from Carrie's outstretched hand and struck it full in the head. Blinded, confused and bleeding, it fell down again onto all fours.

Everus rushed forward and chopped into it, his sword cutting through fur and bone with equal ease.

The bear went berserk. Rearing up onto its squat haunches, it lashed out. First one paw, then the other, both catching nothing.

More blood sprayed as, again and again, Everus chopped into the savage carnivore – any suggestion that this monster may have had a mixed diet like others of its species, laughable. He drove the blade in, trying to reach the vital organs, aware that despite the severity of the wounds he was inflicting, this beast would fight till slain. It would never flee.

The enraged killing machine barged Everus aside, knocking him to the ground. Its head still engulfed within a chromatic cloud, it missed its follow-up bite, its jaws gnashing uncomfortably close. Its breath was disgusting – an old stink of digested forest creature and stripped bone.

Everus scrambled to his feet, well aware that if this thing were to pin him down then that would be it. He thrust with his sword.

The bear turned and the sword point struck one of the heavy chain links. Thrashing its head from side to side, it succeeded in disarming him. Despite its bulk, the beast was reasonably quick. Lashing out with a claw, it battered Everus to the ground once more. It reared up above him, froth drooling from its black-lipped jaws, before dropping in readiness to take a chomp.

"*Stick this in yer pipe!*" Creeps dashed forward, thrust the arquebus into the bear's mouth and fired at point-blank range.

With an ear-splitting bang, the back of the creature's head exploded, the multi-coloured haze now a foaming red. Bone, blood, fur and lumpy cranial tissue flew. Convulsing, one side of its head shattered from the impact, the savage beast stumbled to its rear feet, reeled spasmodically for a moment and then thumped to the ground.

"Got the bastard! Yer man's got away though."

Deafened by the blast, which had gone off less than a hand's width from his own head, Everus was stunned, his senses deadened. Then it hit him. His eyes streamed and his ears began ringing, the sound terrible. It felt as though his brain was leaking from his ears and nostrils. Unsteadily, he tried to get to his feet, accepting Creeps' offered helping hand. Snatching the smoking gun from the thief's grip, he then dashed it to the ground. "Watch what you're doing with that bastard thing!" he shouted.

CHAPTER TWENTY

Dead leaves swept by in the growing wind. Some whirled into small, seemingly living, tornadoes, the sound of their rustling uncanny, as though nature itself had been corrupted and found a fell voice in this dreadful place.

Everus raised his right hand, signalling his companions to a halt. He looked around at the grim ruins, his eyes taking in the collapsed stone walls, the three broken arches, the numerous leaning pillars and the breached tomb raised on higher ground. The slopes around the tomb were of deep-toned greys, growths of hawthorn and jutting headstones the darkest patches. He glimpsed the ancient statuary, the tortured shapes resembling surrealistic figures, misshapen heads and limbs twisted towards the crypt like a frozen tableau of anguished souls. A few steps away were several shallow, rock-cut graves, their man-shaped indents eroded and leaf-filled.

"What is it?" asked Carrie, nervously.

"Can't you feel it? I sense we're being watched."

"Bein' watched...who by?" Drawing his dagger, the arquebus slung over one shoulder, Creeps stared all around.

"Not sure." Everus, sword in hand, started towards the tomb.

Stepping around more hewn, hollow graves and several heaps of tumbled wall, they soon came to the first of thirty or so steps leading up to Klattermorch's crypt. The wind whirled, lifting a russet sheet of leaves, which, for a moment, seemed to rise above them like a patchwork phantom. Even as they were about to react, an abrupt change in the wind dissipated the insubstantial menace.

They climbed the age-worn steps, wary of the slightest movement.

Klattermorch's tomb now stood before them, silhouetted against the dark and angry sky. It was a forbidding sepulchre, the entrance they now faced flanked on either side by a tall, emaciated, bat-winged demon, which supported part of the arch. The double doors which provided access were almost destroyed – one lying, smashed, on the ground, the other leaning at an angle – allowing them to see that the interior appeared to be ruined as well. Carved along the cornice was a badly eroded frieze, its content dark and evil. Smaller stone, bat-like demons perched on the corners, their grins and sly looks unnerving.

"This is it." Everus turned full circle, his eyes searching, nerves tingling. He had never spoken of it, not wishing for others to know his fears, but the tale of Klattermorch had been one which, as a boy at least, had given him nightmares.

According to legend, Klattermorch had once been a noble, kind and compassionate king – a rarity of his age. Because of this, The Dark Gods had specifically sought him out, intentionally throwing at him all manner of upset and tragedy in the hope that his spirit would be broken and that he would renounce The High Three. Misery befell those he loved, his country and his people, yet still Klattermorch would not break; his belief – that salvation and deliverance from his tormentors would come with his death – resolute. And, as his loved ones fell and died horribly, The Dark Gods still could not break him…until the day when, having now been sent into exile by what family he still had, the good king was visited by one of his tormentors, who told the martyr that from now on all that he ate would be contaminated with corruption that would assuredly make him turn to their cause. Forced to starvation, Klattermorch began to feast on the only thing left available – his incorruptible self. And, so it was, that shortly before he left the mortal world, his arms and feet gnawed to the bone, his chest hollowed out and its contents devoured, his face defleshed and one eye peeled and sucked dry, that all of The Dark Gods re-appeared. Cruelly, they had laughed and taunted him, informing him that because he had taken his own life, he would be forever damned. Klattermorch had screamed to the heavens and The High Three, knowing that all his and his loved ones' suffering had been for nothing. With his dying breath, he had cursed them all for their retribution, vowing that he would return to wreak his vengeance on all who had damned him.

Or so the story went…

"Looks empty." Creeps stood by the wrecked entrance, his lantern out and already lit.

Everus approached.

Creeps shone the light inside. "Ye first."

Outside, the wind was picking up strength at an unnatural pace. The sky darkened, as ill-looking black clouds sped in from the north. It seemed, to Everus at least, that the atmosphere had become laden with menace. There was an almost tangible wickedness in the wail of the wind, as though each chill gust carried with it the laments of all those who had suffered because of Klattermorch's zealotry. He shivered as leaves rose and whipped at the stonework with the fervour of a flagellant.

"Let's get inside," said Creeps, looking skyward. "It's goin' to piss down any moment."

Distant lightning flashed and crackled.

Thunder rumbled.

A cold sweat trickled down Everus' spine as he crossed the tomb's threshold and stepped inside. The chamber was cold, his breath now visible and, despite the gale raging outside, it was eerily quiet, the howls of the wind strangely muffled as though they belonged to another world; another time. Detritus that had fallen from the ceiling now covered the floor. At one end, on the fringe of the lantern light, he could discern a slightly raised, dark and shadowy block.

Creeps crept in. Behind him came Carrie, removing leaves from her long hair.

"Carrie. You wait here," said Everus with some measure of concern. He gestured to the thief and the two of them headed over to the large stone coffin. As they neared it, he could see that it rested on a small, two-stepped dais. Fashioned from a solitary block of gneiss, the upper surface of the sarcophagus had been carved into the shape of one of the emaciated demon caryatid-like supports they had seen outside. Several large cracks zigzagged their way across the lid but none were deep enough to permit a view of the coffin's contents.

"So, there's a bit o' that hand in 'ere, is there?"

Ignoring the thief, Everus walked around the funerary container, unnerved at the uncanny way the carved demon's eyes seemed to follow him. Into his mind sprang images of some of the particularly gruesome pictures that had accompanied the tale of Klattermorch he had first read when but a boy. The remembered illustrations of the tormented king, forced to gnaw on his own bones and feed on his steaming, heaped and glistening innards, almost caused him to retch.

"It's goin' to be a bugger to open." Creeps wedged his dagger into the narrow gap between the slab-like lid and the main body of the sarcophagus, his arquebus propped against it. He yanked the dagger free. "If ye'd o' let me know I could o' made some o' ma..."

Carrie screamed.

The disturbing mental reminders disappeared instantly from Everus' mind. Leaping from the dais, he ran over to the entrance, aware that the sorceress was already backing further into the crypt, away from the opening.

"There's...there's..." Carrie mumbled, a hand raised and pointing outside.

"What is it?" Not waiting for an answer, Everus cautiously approached what remained of the doors. Outside, the wind and the rain raged like competing entities; each trying to out-do the other in terms of ferocity. It seemed that the brooding sky was filled with leaves and the rain bounced off the cemetery grounds relentlessly. A sudden movement among the sunken graves caught his eye. Even through the maelstrom, he could see that the thing was small, almost child-like in stature. It was draped in a ragged, dirty, grey hooded cloak, its movements fleeting and spectral. Blinking the rain from his eyes, he watched as the apparition began to glide effortlessly towards him. Up the headstone-covered slopes it floated, passing through physical barriers as though they were not there.

Quickly, he averted his gaze and backed into the tomb.

"What's goin' on?" asked Creeps.

"Whatever you do, don't look at its face. Keep your eyes shut." Everus followed his own orders.

"Eh?"

"Keep your eyes shut! It can't harm you if you..."

"Please...please help me," begged a little boy's voice from the entrance. "I...I'm lost and I don't know where..."

"*Don't look at it!*" Everus shouted, turning his back on the thing.

"Please..." The voice became a pathetic whimper. "I...beg you, kind people. Please...help me get home."

Everus could feel a deep evil in the unearthly voice. It gnawed at his mind, imploring him to open his eyes and turn around. In his mind's eye, he could see the wretched pale-faced urchin; arms extended, bedraggled hair lank and wind-swept, eye-sockets black and hollow.

"Please...turn around. I...I can't come in. Look, see how I'm bleeding."

"*Go away!*" Everus shivered uncontrollably. "We're not the ones responsible for abandoning you here!" In his mind, he could now see the blood pouring from the thing, streaming from its gaunt and wicked face, running in rivulets down its small body and massing about its dirty, bare feet. He could hear Carrie reciting the words to some spell or other – some magical phrase that would offer her protection.

"Look at me." The voice had changed. Although still that of a child, its pleas had now become far more menacing. "I won't ask again."

Everus could feel his will slipping. He tried to close his mind to the threat at the threshold. Historical facts and dates, names, genealogies, places – inexorably, his mind was drawn back to the deathly ghost, the *schrappingbäyer*. It felt as though his eyes were being pried open by grubby, grave-robber's fingers, the thing's blood now spreading out around his boots.

"Face me!"

"*No!*" Everus opened his eyes. It felt as though he were drowning in a frozen lake. Powerless to close his eyes, he noticed Creeps, eyes wide open and staring forward.

"Turn around!"

In a final act of desperation which shook his entire body, he cursed his rage and spun around to face the horror.

✝ ✝ ✝

Before him stretched the desert city of Umm-Dabba, its whitewashed, mud-brick buildings no longer gleaming in the bright sunlight. Instead, the air was filled with black smoke and the stench of burnt wood and the festering dead. Amidst the ruins loped gangly humanoids, their faces more lupine than human. Most wore dull suits of grey mail and all carried weapons.

As he watched, a group of cowering Umm-Dabbites were dragged from their hiding place and brutally slain, their throats cuts, their corpses piled high on a burning pyre. He then saw the leader of this group of marauders, these ghâr-ghârs, presented with a roll of papyrus that another had removed from the ransacked building that had once been Emir Ib-irem's palace. The leader read the document to himself, spat at it and tore it up. He then mounted an armoured hyenadon and rode east, leaving his forces to kill and plunder.

The desert disappeared.

He now saw a city in flames. Madly, citizens ran and tried to flee the inferno, their prospective mayor now a charred and unrecognisable skeleton in a burnt-out inn. The fire spread with a hunger; a seemingly driven and purposeful conflagration which consumed young and old, rich and poor, its flames mirrored in the thousands of reflective panels of a colossal tower.

The tower disappeared.

Cloaked and hooded, he gave a man a strange rock...the man, a hook for a hand, looked uncertain, but once paid, took it nonetheless. Later, he was on a ship...the man was there and they were talking around a table. Others were there but he could not make them out.

Then he was leaving, watching as the ship was scuttled and set ablaze, deliberately sent to the bottom of the sea by a crew of doomed lunatics.

And now...a great city; a bastion of civilization. Along its walls many men could be seen, their armour gleaming in the low sun of a cold dawn. A cry went up as an enemy was sighted. Giant skeletons charged, driven to murder by unholy magic. Fireballs and lightning bolts ruptured the smog and the smoke of war. Bodies fell. Bones exploded. The wall was breached. People screamed and fled. Hundreds perished.

The scenes of battle faded.

He screamed.

Another place. Another scene of destruction. A dusty town flattened...

He screamed again.

† † †

"Is he all right?"

"Aye...he'll be up in no..."

Everus opened his eyes. He found himself slumped on the hard stone floor of the tomb, his back against a wall.

"Ye all right?"

Dazed and confused, Everus held his head, his sight blurred. Stabs of white light lanced through his brain. "What...happened?"

Creeps looked him up and down. "Ye passed out."

"And the ghost?"

449

"The kid's gone. Ye don't need to be worryin' about him any more." Creeps removed the pipe from his mouth and turned towards the coffin.

Closing his eyes and then reopening them, Everus was relieved to discover that his sight had returned to normal. The sight that he now saw caused a quick intake of breath, for the interior of the tomb now looked as new as the day it had been finished.

The detritus from the floor had gone, as had the numerous cracks in the walls. Mosaics and crude paintings, most detailing bizarrely deformed creatures and scenes of famine, decorated the walls. The ruined doors they had passed in order to enter now stood sealed, their gilt inner surfaces covered in thousands of lines of tiny text. There was even a sickly sweet stench from the preservative salts used to embalm the recently dead in the air. In sconces around the wall flickered many small candles.

"Carrie, what's happened?" Everus asked.

"I'm not sure. It could be that..."

"Er...!" Creeps started. "I don't want to alarm anyone but there's a weird green mist comin' from this 'ere coffin."

Grabbing his sword, which lay nearby, Everus got to his feet. His grip tightening on the hilt, he stared as a bilious vapour seeped from the now highly polished sarcophagus.

The fog began to assume human form.

The three of them pulled back.

The vapour began to condense and then solidify into a tangible being – perhaps not a true flesh and blood one, but a being nonetheless. It was the ghost of Klattermorch. Much of the skin from his face had been peeled away with a knife and nails, leaving little more than a raw skull, from which one eyeball had been gouged free, his arms were naught but chewed bone and gristle from the elbows down. His chest was a mass of scraped rib and ripped muscle, the internal workings horribly exposed and glistening. Several gaping scars ran across the wrinkled and sallow flesh of his lower abdomen, revealing the points at which he had practiced his self-butchery; removing the intestines, liver, spleen, gall bladder and kidneys – all for his own consumption. His right leg, like both arms, was skeletal from the knee-joint down, whereas his left leg had been completely devoured, bone and all.

Carrie fainted and slumped to the floor.

"Not a pleasing sight, am I?" the thing groaned, its voice slow

450

and croaky, due in part to the lack of any vocal body parts. "Yet still I hunger."

"*Klattermorch!*" cried Everus.

"Aaaagh," the spectre wailed. It raised its mutilated arms, small strips of uneaten cartilage snapping like over-stretched rubber. "You know of me?"

"*Everus!* The bloody doors won't open! Come on, we need to get out o' 'ere!" shouted Creeps, from where he frantically pulled and pushed at the crypt doors.

"You will not escape! How dare you invoke the power of The High Three here!" cried Klattermorch.

Trembling uncontrollably, Everus retreated a step or two, recoiled by the sheer repulsiveness of the ghost's appearance and the almost overpowering stench of carrion which exuded from it. "The High...?" He turned to the thief. "Creeps!?"

"Get o'er 'ere an' help us wi' the doors!"

"*You!*" Klattermorch moaned, his ravaged face turning towards the thief. "Must my suffering continue so?"

"Perhaps...we can help?" Everus suggested, his voice uncertain. "Tell us how we can...alleviate your torment...in exchange for our release." He knew that this was an entity against which his sword – whether magical or not – would prove largely ineffectual.

An unearthly, spine-tingling wail escaped the ghost's mouth – or rather what was left of it. "There is nothing *you* can do or give me that will quell my hunger, my appetite for vengeance. I'm as trapped as you. Doomed to exist in this form, my only crime...the strength of my own belief. I tore the flesh from my body as others tore the humanity from my soul. Like you, I was, and still remain, nothing more than a pawn of the gods, a morsel to be toyed with and spat out. I can see that you and I are not unalike. How the gods plague us. I would damn them all, had I the power." More strings of tendon snapped. "*He* alone can destroy me. *He* possesses the means." Exposed bone pointed at Creeps. "Destroy me...I beg you."

Despite the terror of his situation, things Klattermorch had said had Everus interested. There were answers to questions he needed knowing. "Tell me more, foul spectre. I will see to your release, but first I must know more. In my dreams I've..."

Creeps dashed from the doors and made for the ghost.

"*Wait!*" Everus gripped the thief by the collar of his jacket. "I want to hear whatever Klattermorch has to say. For too long I've had

451

to listen to your lies." He nodded, signalling for the phantom to continue, to reveal whatever unworldly secrets it knew about him. "Tell me what you know."

"I tell...and you see to it that he destroys me?"

"On that you've my word."

"Very well," agreed Klattermorch. "You're becoming as I. Your soul blackens...and I can see something else; a dark shimmering, an aura of murder and evil. The High Three are manipulating you, controlling you, guiding your actions. All that you've done is preordained. They seek you to fulfil something."

Briefly, Everus considered the ghost's revelation. "You're mistaken. I alone control my destiny."

"*Hah!* Learn well the lesson of my story, mortal. Know of the inevitability of betrayal and evil. In this world there is no truth, only different degrees of deceitfulness." His gnawed body beginning to become gaseous once more, Klattermorch reached out with a partially devoured arm. "There is more I..." Before the spectre could complete whatever it was about to say, a dull purple haze engulfed it. Confused, it stared for a moment, more in bewilderment than fear.

Still gripping the thief, Everus drew back.

Klattermorch screamed, the sound hideous. He screamed for a moment longer, then he screamed no more. Disrupted, the revenant was lit in a haze of sparking violet energy. Portions of flayed bone seemed to implode, the bulk of the ghost's incorporeal self simply disintegrating, the composite particles suspended in air and then gone. The obliteration was rapid, all happening within two blinks of an eye.

Slightly stunned by the sudden nature of the ghost's disappearance, it took Everus a few moments to accept that Klattermorch was gone. Releasing his grip on the thief's jacket, he went over and saw to Carrie, helping the sorceress to her feet. "Are you all right?"

Carrie moaned sleepily, but soon came to, the sparkle in her eyes returning. "Yes. *The ghost?*"

"It's gone." Everus smiled, though deep down he felt cheated. He was sure Klattermorch could have provided him with some of the information he sought. Just what had happened, he did not know. "We must get the bones and leave this place. Let's hope..." A loud crash, caused by Creeps pushing over the sarcophagus lid made him jump and turn round. He watched as the thief reached in and withdrew a casket.

A sudden dark flash went off like one of the hunchback's bombs. Electrical charges flashed and lit the tomb further as, wailing like a tortured cat, Klattermorch reached out with a skeletal hand from whatever hell had claimed him. A nebulous void, a swirling vortex of chaos, tried to draw him back. His already ruptured form blackening and dissolving, he reached out and grabbed Creeps.

On contact, a violent discharge of opposed energies shook the tomb, blasting one of the portals off its great hinge and shattering the other.

Everus and Carrie were knocked flat by the shockwave.

For a moment, Creeps lit up in negative, his colours drained to vivid hues of black and white. He was thrown halfway across the tomb, his feet well clear of the ground.

Still Klattermorch held on, his arm horribly extending. The stretched limb convulsed with the strain, the contact draining Creeps of his aura; his life-force. Then, his damage done, Klattermorch, the damned fifth king of Mzaah and the first of the anthropophagi, was drawn back, dragging a thread of ethereal gold snatched from the thief's being. The void was compressed to a single glowing point. Then it blinked out of existence.

This surpassed any of the strangeness Everus had seen in his thirty-three years of life – and he had seen quite a bit. Wide-eyed, he staggered towards Carrie, his mind drowning in a sea of surreal images. "I've seen enough. Let's get out of here." He made for the destroyed tomb entrance, not knowing and to a large extent no longer caring whether the thief would follow; whether he would collect the casket or not. Obviously there were limits to the level of weirdness his mind was prepared to accept.

✝ ✝ ✝

"Grim tidings from the south, ain't it?" The fat-faced, unshaven barkeeper took Everus' payment and tipped it into a slotted box. "Aye...it's a bad business. Makes ye wonder where next."

Everus took a hearty drink and rested his tankard on the bar. "Do you know whether the city's fallen?"

"Messenger only said that it was under attack. Big bloody skeletons, if ye can believe it. Hundreds o' 'em, each as tall as a house." Mournfully, the barkeeper shook his head. "I don't know what the bloody world's comin' to. It's no' even safe to fart in the bath these days."

Taking the three drinks, Everus walked over to the table at which Carrie sat across from a visibly shaken Creeps. Placing Carrie's wine and the thief's ale before them, he sat down. "Ghavin's Keep may have fallen."

Carrie gasped and Everus could not help but feel a heartfelt sympathy for her.

"Creeps." It was the first Everus had spoken directly to the thief since leaving the Stranglewood Forest and its haunted crypt.

The thief raised his gaze from his tankard, a lost look in his eyes. It seemed as though he had aged a couple of decades. There was a weariness about him and far more wrinkles. His hair had become the colour of pipe ash and even his short moustache was flecked with white. The bags under his eyes now drooped towards the corners of his mouth and his hands and fingers looked knobbly and scrawny. He looked frailer somehow, as though in the early stages of mummy rot or some other sort of wasting disease.

"Explain to me what the ghost was on about." Everus took a measured sip of ale, a cold fire in his eyes. "No crap, or so help me I'll finish you here and now."

Sullenly, Creeps put his half-empty drink down. "What do ye want to know?"

"Hmm. Let's see...where to begin?" Everus thumped his tankard down. Ale and foam flew. "Let's begin with an easy one, shall we?" He leant forward, elbows on the table. "Who exactly are you? Don't take too long, it's not a trick question."

"I'm Creeps. First name Adolf, but I prefer Creeps."

"Question two," said Everus harshly, relishing the interrogation. "Regarding all this High Three crap, tell me, do they want to see Xethorn destroyed? Or are they, once again, merely toying with us all?"

"He'll be..." The thief hesitated.

"What?" Everus interrupted.

"They plan on...seein' to it that He's no longer a problem. That He's..."

"So you *are* still in contact with them?"

"*Were*," Creeps corrected. "How else do ye think I saved ye from that lad's ghost? Ye'd o' been killed outright had I no' done summat.

I've been instructed to make sure that ye're protected...ye see, ye're their last hope against Xethorn."

Carrie, who had sat silent throughout their discussion, sat up.

"Can't say that I'm all that surprised." Everus rested his chin in one hand. "Ever since I was teleported from the palace that time we fought against Him back in Wyrm's Port, I've had a suspicion that I'd been saved for a purpose." His eyes narrowed as he stared fixedly at the thief. "Another question. Why you?"

"What do ye mean?"

"I'm trying to make this easy." Everus maintained his cold stare. "What I can't figure out is why The High Three chose you to act as my...*guardian*. Why can't they defeat Xethorn themselves? Why get me to do their dirty work?"

Following Everus' gaze, Carrie looked to the thief, hanging on a response.

Tiredly, Creeps rubbed his eyes. "I don't have all the answers. All I know is that even the gods have rules an' laws that they must stick to. They can't destroy Xethorn themselves...don't ask me why. I mean, if they could, don't ye think they would o' by now? No...they use mortals...like me, like you, like their worshippers. It's the way o' the game, I guess. Perhaps this way, they're somehow ensurin' that we're no' all destroyed in another cataclysm-thingy. As to why *me*...I wish I knew. I really do. I mean, let's face it, even I'd no' pick me."

Everus leant back. "What if I choose not to go along with their game? What if I just set up shop here in Stranglewood – set myself up as an arms dealer, take over Old Hunchy's emporium, settle down, raise a family?" Surreptitiously, he glanced at Carrie.

She noticed his look and smiled back.

"Who knows?" Creeps shrugged his shoulders, for once a look of genuine ignorance on his worn, thin face. "I guess if that's what ye want to do..." He gave a nonchalant wave, "I can't stop ye."

"Whatever happens, surely Xethorn must be destroyed?" said Carrie. "If He's sacked Ghavin's Keep then nowhere remains safe. Now I don't care much for all this divine stuff you're both on about, but what I do care about is my city and my people. We could be the empire's last hope. Xethorn must be defeated...and, if the only way to do so is by using the hand of Cyrvilus, then so be it."

"One piece remains," Everus mused. "The question is, do I go after it? Do I allow myself to comply with whatever ploy The High Three have planned?" Gently biting his bottom lip, he looked at the thief, noting the latter's worried frown. "What to do?" Idly, he toyed with the tankard before him, scraping his thumbnail down its tin surface. "The golden aura? What was that?"

"That was what connected me wi' The High Three. I've been drained, Everus. Ma powers, ma whatevers...all gone. An' I feel so weak...no doubt it'll pass, but I've no' felt like this afore. It's as though I'm dyin' on the inside."

Although Everus had been told as much before, this time, more so after all that he had seen, he believed it. "You're not looking too good on the outside either. You seem to have aged."

Creeps sighed. "What's ten or twenty years 'ere or there? I'm o'er three hundred years old anyway. I was born in the second year o' the rule o' old Emperor Saraq."

Everus stared for a moment, struggling to take in what he had just been told. "*You're pissed!?*" he finally said, the incredulity on his face, blatant.

Creeps shook his head; an old man, a thief and a grave-robber once more. Stripped of his divinely given abilities, he looked, to a large extent, even more pathetic than Weaselnest. He sighed, resignedly. "No, it's true."

Mouth agape, Everus shifted in his seat. Apparently the madness that he had witnessed in Klattermorch's crypt was infectious and had somehow followed them. Doubts and questions formed in his brain, yet he was unable to articulate them into spoken words. *What?* What had Creeps just said? He clung to the only piece of reality he could and that was his historical knowledge – Saraq became emperor three hundred and forty years ago! Everything else was insane. How could Creeps be...?

"Xethorn must be stopped," Carrie muttered, as she looked absently at the thief.

Creeps, studying Everus' stunned face, decided that more information was needed. He cleared his throat. "I was part o' a gang. We were all thieves, temple defilers, call us what ye like." He hesitated for a moment, caught in the memories of long ago. "We were captured an' taken for execution. I was saved...rescued by summat weird, presumably The High Three, even though there was only one o' 'em. Anyway, I was given orders, told to do things, like help ye out, an' make sure them nutters ye used to work for didn't succeed in bringin' The Daemon God back."

"Were you not given a choice?" asked Everus.

456

"I got to choose...kind o'."

"Tell me, Creeps. When this is over...and *if* we defeat Xethorn, will I get a choice? Will I be allowed to live free and untroubled? Or will I instead become like Klattermorch – doomed if I do, damned if I don't?"

"I don't know."

Everus thought things over. He smiled as a thought entered his head. If, as Creeps had just told him, he was being protected and kept alive by The High Three in order to vanquish Xethorn, then was that not tantamount to a certain level of invulnerability? If Creeps were to be believed, then had *he* not access to divine protection – after all, surely the gods now needed him? He was to be their unwilling tool, their extension, their weapon to dislodge Xethorn. The more he thought about it, the more the picture cleared. For, just as Creeps had been 'on hand', as it were, to ensure that the Uhu'giaggothian worshippers; Dae'dicus, Dae'morogin and their cohort, did not succeed, now The High Three were once again trying to prevent The Daemon God's return. With that realisation, Everus felt a surge of power course through his veins. Clarity returned, and the path of his destiny now shone through the murk of uncertainty. A part of him wanted to destroy Xethorn unaided, but the practical part of him realised that, when it came to such an enemy, he should take whatever assistance he could get. He reached for his tankard and took a sip, the ale reasonable. "Let's see what we've got so far."

Unquestioningly, Creeps reached into his sack and pulled out the one casket in which he kept all the pieces they had collected. He put it on the table and pushed it across.

The heat from the hinged box had died down, Everus coming to the conclusion that the searing heat was only generated during the process of actual fusion. He opened it and gazed down at the almost complete skeletal hand. It was slightly larger than an average human hand and in places small scorch marks could be seen, but apart from that, it appeared relatively unremarkable.

"Are you sure you know where the final piece is?" asked the sorceress.

Everus did not answer immediately, his mind still going through the ramifications of what Creeps had said. He nodded. "Yes. In the land of Gossothus, to the east."

Carrie sighed. "That's at least ten days' journey from here. We shouldn't delay, for if Ghavin's Keep is under siege then time is of the essence. Each day that we spend here...increases the chance of disaster for the city. We must get going." Almost as an afterthought, she added: "That's if you're planning on seeing this through, of course."

"If only Mhoon was here. He told me that he'd been out that way and that he knew the way to Bhubbaal's Stronghold, where the bones are. He mentioned how his wife was being held hostage, a slave or something, I think he said. According to what he said, this Bhubbaal is not a normal man. He's a demon of some sort."

"All the more reason to add him to our list of vanquished foes." There was a surprising hardness in the sorceress' voice.

"Aye," agreed Creeps. "We owe yer man that at least. He was a good enough sort, even if he seemed to be away wi' the faeries most o' the time."

"All right." Remembering the promise he had made to the exorcist atop the tell in Wathang-Hu, Everus drained his drink. "You've talked me into it. We set off at daybreak."

"Something that's been niggling at me..." Carrie hesitated, waiting for a passing patron with a young child in tow to get out of earshot. "Regarding the hand, I trust you know how to make use of it once completed. I mean...how will it...well, help us?"

Creeps looked at Everus.

"Going solely on what I was told by Ib-irem back in Umm-Dabba; once complete, the hand will grant the owner the spell-like capabilities of Cyrvilus himself. In addition, it will offer the bearer complete protection from magic cast against him...or her." Everus smiled at Carrie.

"One final question. Do you know why it was scattered? I mean, why is it that there are pieces all over the empire and beyond?" Carrie's eyes were fixed on the ornate casket, her question asked absently, as though she already knew the answer.

"It's a long story, but I'll try to be brief." Everus scratched his chin, feeling the few days' growth of stubble. "According to legend, at the final battle between The High Three and The Daemon God, Cyrvilus and Xethorn were locked in a fierce fight. Although all the accounts of that conflict differ, in all likelihood it took place somewhere in Zeth, and it was the demonologist who had the upper hand. Some tales relate how, at the moment Cyrvilus was about to slay Xethorn, The High Three intervened, saving the...current resident of Wyrm's Port. No match for the power of The High Three, who by this time one must assume had managed to repel Uhu'giaggoth, Cyrvilus, knowing he was defeated, turned to flee. In His anger, Xethorn went in pursuit, took advantage of His foe's weakened powers and severed one of His enemy's hands. What happened after that remains the stuff of legend and conjecture. But, going back to the hand...I read somewhere, in *Eggar's Account of the Days of Darkness*, I think, the tale of how the hand was discovered by a patrol of Watchful Eye paladins, who had been assigned the holy duty of tracking down and destroying all of the remaining relics from the time of The Hellspawn Cataclysm. They were unable to completely destroy the hand, so, by order of Pope Edburgah II, it was broken up and dispersed. It took me some time to find one of the few who knew where the scattered pieces were."

A sudden memory of the vision of Umm-Dabba in the hands of the savage ghâr-ghârs flashed through his mind.

"You said no one knows what became of this...Cyrvilus," said Carrie.

Everus nodded. "That's true. Personally, I reckon he was slain by Xethorn. In fact, it's alluded to in one of his tomes. I think it may even be in *The Cyrvilus* itself."

"The...*Cyrvilus*?" Carrie looked confused.

"The eponymously titled tome the demonologist worked on. Along with *The Blasphemous Gobbledegook and Erroneous Writings of Malk-um Waeller*, *Ibaal's Dark Bible* and *Daddienman's Demonorium*, it ranks as one of the seminal treatise on...well, demons; their conjuration, their true names, their powers – everything you may, or may not, want to know about them. Although I've only skimmed through a rather poor and bastardised version, I found it...unsettling." Even mentioning such terrible works made Everus shudder inside, memories of his old mentor, Dae'dicus, rising unbidden to further plague his troubled soul. Instinctively, he turned and looked out of the window over to his left, certain for a moment that a small, hooded figure had been staring in.

Outside, it was growing dark.

† † †

They stood at the town's East Gate and looked out. The badlands east of Stranglewood were unwelcoming and unpopulated. The low, flat hills that lay to either side of the road were dark and brooding, rich with deep stream-filled gullies and dead-end canyons. Thick stands of trees grew all around, occasionally thinning out to stretches of dreary-looking moorland.

Sunlight struggled to fight its way through the grey clouds as the three travellers drew a halt and checked their equipment one final time.

In a twist of fate, the wagon Creeps had 'acquired' in Wathang-Hu had itself been stolen from the grounds of the inn at which they had been staying. The barkeeper had been profusely apologetic, more so when he had seen the great sword on Everus' back, but, in the end, he had said there was little he could do, and so, despite his compensatory offer of a couple of free nights with breakfast thrown in, they had to cut their losses and live with it. Everus had laughed when he had first heard about it, appreciating the unknown wagon-thief's audacity. The idea of some Stranglewood lowlife stealing from a former agent of The High Three appealed to his irreverent sense of humour.

The two extra nights of free accommodation had proved beneficial, despite the growing sense of urgency overriding their mission, for it had given Creeps more time to recover from his touch with death and to acclimatise to his new found mortality.

"I think we should at least o' seen about bringin' a mule wi' us." The thief cursed as he hefted his heavy pack onto his shoulders. The arquebus he had claimed and polished now hung alongside, the strap he had bought for it slung over his right shoulder. "It's goin' to be a bloody ball-ache carryin' this for the next ten days or so. These straps are bitin' into me like a bitch at a bone an' we've no' gone a step yet."

"You'll manage." Everus smiled, emptily. "Well, if we're ready, let's see about putting some leagues behind us. I hardly know a thing about this land, but from the looks of it the going shouldn't be too hard, providing we stick to the road. We keep the setting sun to our backs, The Wreckins to our front and we keep our eyes open. Although this land may be free of behemoths, there are other things best avoided. When we camp, we take shifts on watch. The slightest disturbance, you make a shout."

† † †

On the fourth day out, the going became harder, the state of the road varying between poor and downright atrocious; blocked completely in places by fallen trees or else overgrown with dense growths of bramble and gorse.

By mid-afternoon, as they climbed a short rise towards a great stone bridge which spanned a noisy river, the weather turned on them. Up until that point they had been lucky. For, although it had been cold during the day and almost freezing at night, they had managed to avoid the rain. But, as they neared the bridge, which, at least to Everus' eyes, bore all the hallmarks of old grubban engineering and thus was probably quite safe, the clouds broke and a vicious sleet rained from the sky.

Carrie and Creeps followed Everus' lead and ran for the shelter of one of the three huge arches. Together, the three of them scrambled down the rocky, tree covered embankment and huddled under the bridge.

"We'll wait here until the sleet stops." Unstrapping his pack, Everus sat down, his back against the damp brickwork. His companions did likewise – the thief delving into a side pocket for his baccy and his pipe.

The sorceress sniffled and brushed her damp hair. "I hate rain."

Nodding absently, Everus gazed at the fast flowing river, wondering briefly where its source lay and where it went. Fish leapt and splashed and, not for the first time in all his travels, he wished he knew how to catch such creatures with a rod and line. Looking up, he noticed the coarse brickwork of the nearest of the huge supports. Although he knew little of grubban architectural design, he could see that this bridge had been built to endure, and endure it certainly had. It had probably stood here for nigh on a thousand years. A sudden movement at the river's edge drew his eyes in that direction. His eyes widened as he saw a large, yellow-brown mottled toad, about the size of a small pony, hop from the water and land on one of the beach-like islands on which the central support had been built.

"Did ye see the size o' that bugger?" Creeps asked, pipe in hand.

"What? Where?" Carrie turned her head from side to side.

"It was a toad." Everus pointed. "It's gone behind that pillar. A big toad."

Creeps moved to one side, hoping to catch sight of it again. He liked toads and frogs. "There it is!" Even before the others could join him, a second large toad, about the same size as the other, burst free of a thick stand of bulrush growing nearby. It sprang towards them, its hop taking it to the spot where Carrie had stood prior to the start of its leap.

The sorceress pulled back further, one hand raised to her mouth in shock.

Thlumph. The toad's glistening tongue shout out and wrapped around one of her legs.

Sword drawn, Everus moved in. With a single chop, he cleaved through the disgusting fat bulk. Squelching, snot-like blood gushed from it. He hacked again, the blade cutting through the wet, soggy amphibian with ease. The toad was now splayed before him, looking more repulsive now that it had been killed.

With a look of disgust on her face, Carrie reached down and uncoiled the tongue from her left calf.

"Come on! Get your packs and we'll get moving." Everus scanned the locality, making sure that nothing else fat and green was preparing to lunge at them.

"It's still pissin' down," noted Creeps. "I think we'd be better holed up 'ere for a while. It's no' as though they toads pose much o' a problem, now is it? We keep our eyes open an' we should be all right. Besides, once ye've tried ma toad stew ye'll want to stay 'ere an' catch some more. Ye used to be able to catch some real whoppers in the sewers, though they were no' as big as these."

"Can you see where the other one's gone?"

"Aye, it's still there." Creeps indicated to the middle of the river. "It's watchin'...but I'd doubt it'll come 'ere."

Carrie wiped the last of the slime from her boot. "I think we should be all right if we rest here for a time, Everus."

"Very well. I'm going to tip this unsightly bugger back in the river, so that Creeps doesn't stink the place up with his toad soup or whatever." He got his right boot under it and, with some effort, tipped the bleeding toad into the water. A stinking trail of blood and custard-like guts remained on the rocks. "Although, saying that, I think there's enough there for you to scrape together a sandwich." Striding to the back wall of the great overhang, he drew his coat tight, pulled his hood up and sat down. "I'm going to try and get some shut-eye. Wake me as soon as the sleet eases."

✝ ✝ ✝

After another day and a half of steady walking, and as the rations they had brought with them began to dwindle, they started to enter the foothills of The Wreckins. The air here was icy, and yet as they began to climb, the cold did much to keep them refreshed, returning the vigour to their bodies that had been drained by the effort of the past five days.

A light snow fell from the pale grey clouds, dusting the rocky ground and making it sparkle.

Hands dug deep in his coat pockets, Everus led them on, stopping every now and then to make sure that they were still on track. He had not prepared for the possibility of getting caught out in a severe snowstorm and the prospects of either getting lost and being forced to wander the cold mountains before freezing to death, or simply being crushed in an avalanche, did not appeal. For the time being, the snow was light and wispy, but he knew, largely through past conversations with his widely-travelled associate, Grigalo Shan'alan, how quickly, at this altitude, the weather could turn. He increased the pace and led them to the crest of the foremost hill, the view it afforded doing something to compensate for the tiring climb.

Carrie gasped, although whether it was from fatigue or from the sight of the view before her, was not clear.

Creeps rubbed his eyes and stared.

So this is the land called Gossothus – the old ancestral land of the grubbas – thought Everus, his eyes and his mind taking in the wild and stark beauty of the panorama. It was akin to scenes from some of the great paintings which had once graced the walls of his parents' villa. Awe-struck, he lapsed into momentary silence, reflecting for a time on the history of this almost legendary country, which had borne witness to countless battles. It was the same old story that had happened all over the imperial frontiers; for whilst there was plenty of land for everyone, some would come along who wanted more, whether it be in order to lay direct access to the mineral resources, the wood or the agricultural land. There had been good years, when the grubban highland cattle had fattened on the alpine meadows, and there had been bad years, when the glaciers had melted, bringing water, snow and ice thundering down the slopes, burying all in their passage.

Gossothus had been such a land; an ancient, almost forgotten land, one that endured its growing pains during its transition between savagery and the rise and subsequent decline of grubban civilization. It had been a time which had bred hard folk, and ruthless killers, individuals determined to get to the top of the pecking order and stay there, no matter how many died to make their avaricious dreams a reality.

Dark woods clung to rugged peaks, their treetops frosted. Meandering rivers flowed from high cave mouths, twisting like glacial snakes to the valley bottoms below, the visibility of their flows broken in places by vertiginous bridges which spanned deep gullies. Several leagues distant, there lay a settlement of some sort, its urban greyness an untidy and yet welcome smudge on the cold, white landscape.

"I'm freezin'." Creeps flapped his arms, his breath wispy.

"I think we're now on the westernmost fringe of Gossothus. The land between here and the beginning of the mountain range over there, used to be home to the grubbas. It's widely believed that this is where they first came into existence; made from the very rock, if one believes their creation myths."

"Ha! Them stumpy bastards?" The thief chuckled. "They're just a bloody waste o' space. All they ever do is drink an' fight...an' get hauled out o' their mobile kitchens. I ain't got time o' day for them buggers. Do ye remember that Ozgo?"

"*Ozgo?*" Everus queried, the name sounding faintly familiar.

"Aye. I think that was his name. That arse wi' the axes. Remember, he killed a fella that night we went to the theatre in Wyrm's Port."

"Oh, yes. That delightful, well-spoken individual."

Creeps turned to Carrie. "What about yersel' missus? Do ye like 'em?"

"I can't say I've ever really got to know one of them. They do smell a bit."

"Well, as far as I'm concerned, they're all a bunch o' useless nummies. That is, wi' one exception. Used to work wi' one o' 'em. Went by the name o' 'Choppa'. Best damn lock-picker I ever knew. Could open the emperor's coffers wi' nothin' but a bent spoon. Anyway, his old man was Mûk 'the lucky', so-called cause he was the only livin' person to ever cross the Kingsway Boot Babies an' get away wi' it. Heard tell that he half-inched a couple o' sackloads from right under 'em, an' managed to do the whorehouse girls on Splatter Row a..."

"*Shhh!*" Silently, Everus drew his sword, his eyes scanning the

464

tree-line less than a hundred paces to their right. "I thought I saw something."

"Where?" Creeps unslung his firearm.

"Over there. Those trees."

From out of the shadow of the trees, there crept a wolf. It was large, its fur of deepest white, like snow – the only blemish; fresh blood around its muzzle. Stealthily, it edged forwards, cunning and hunger in its pale, amber eyes, despite the fact that it had recently fed.

"Well, are you going to shoot it?" Everus asked, his eyes never leaving the approaching carnivore.

"It'll be on us afore I load this bugger." Creeps fumbled with the arquebus as the wolf crept closer, its hackles raised and bristling, a low growl coming from its throat.

"I'll get it myself." Everus moved forward, his sword held in both hands.

The wolf snarled. There was a malign, voracious intelligence in its eyes. For a moment, it bobbed its head from side to side, weighing up its opponents, gauging which of the three posed the greater threat. Then, with a throaty howl, it expelled a freezing mass of ice and vapour from its maw. Glacial motes sparkled within the cloud of rimy breath, Everus its target.

Everus was quick to react. He leapt to his right, the frosty blast numbing his left-hand side instead of catching him full on. The cold was perishing, almost burning in its ferocity. With a scream of pain, he fell to his knees, dropping his sword, his right hand gripping his frozen left arm.

The wolf rushed forward.

A flash of glowing light struck its head. It ceased its charge and came to an abrupt halt, trying to shake Carrie's spell from its eyes, its efforts futile.

"*Aaagh! Bastard!*" Grunting, Everus got to his feet, his left hand-side encased in a frozen cocoon. "*Bastard!*" Teeth chattering, he picked up his sword with his right hand.

The wolf's movements became manic. It snapped at air, bluish-white smoke swirling from its muzzle.

Realising that the wolf posed little immediate threat, thanks largely to Carrie's spell, Creeps proceeded to load up. He was just about to stuff the ball into the gun when, to his horror, he saw a second wolf come tearing out of the trees. "*Shit!* There's another!"

he cried. If anything, this second one looked bigger, its raised hackles almost level with his eyes.

Painfully, Everus turned on hearing the thief's warning. Gritting his teeth, he awaited the wolf's arrival, wishing for nothing more than to have the delight of running his blade through its luxurious white coat and watching it die. All things considered, he may even ask Creeps to skin it for him in order to get a scarf, a vest and a pair of socks as well.

The wolf, obviously, had other plans – ones that no doubt concerned the tearing to pieces of the three before it and sharing what was left over with its mate and cubs. It came at a rush, initially heading for Carrie, but Everus moved to intercept. It leapt at him, its muzzle and sharp fangs dripping blood.

Everus took the full weight of the wolf, his sword strike missing. With a cry, he fell, the sword knocked from his hand, the huge carnivore on top of him. Frantic, he battered at its snout with his unfrozen hand, careful not to get his fingers in its jaws. The idea of getting blasted by its frozen breath at close range and dying with a head reduced to no more than slush, making his blows desperate.

Now in a frenzy, the wolf was about to bite down.

Everus tried to grip its neck.

The sudden bang of Creeps' gun going off startled the wolf, causing it to miss what would have undoubtedly have been its killing bite. It looked about, its amber eyes very much alive with a cold burning. It was then that Carrie chopped into its hindquarters. The beast shrieked, the sound almost human. The sorceress hacked into it a second time, her hits lacking the strength to inflict serious damage, but causing the wolf to leap off its prey. Turning to face her, bluish wisps rising like smoky tendrils from its muzzle, it began to growl, indicating that it was about to exhale its cloud of freezing death.

Carrie extended her right arm, muttered something and fired a bolt of orange-red fire from her palm. Her spell struck the wolf in the mouth, the magical fire extinguishing the icy breath and making the wolf howl in pain. It tried to expel the fire from its throat.

"Carrie!"

The sorceress turned and, understanding what Everus wanted, slung him his sword.

He caught it one-handed and, with a cry of rage, swung down and all but severed the wolf's head. Blood squirted as the carnivore crumpled to the ground. It was still alive, so he chopped down again and again, his third hit completing the decapitation. With a wry grin, he turned to see where the other had gone. It was nowhere to be seen – either it had fled, or its natural camouflage was making it hard to detect. It was then he noticed that the thief had fallen.

"Creeps!?" Carrie rushed over to where the thief lay, black fumes hovering over his head.

"Did the wolf get him?" asked Everus, rushing over to join her.

The thief lay sprawled before them, his face and hands and much of his jacket covered in black powder from where the arquebus had backfired. What remained of the gun – the wooden stock and the ruptured barrel, lay nearby.

Carrie knelt down.

"Is he alive?" Everus asked.

Creeps groaned as though in answer.

Everus crouched and helped the thief to his feet, the acrid reek of the black powder causing his eyes to weep.

Mumbling, Creeps held his head. Some of his face was black and burnt, but the damage seemed to be mostly superficial. It had been the proximity of the blast which had rendered him unconscious; the gun practically exploding and showering him in powder and shrapnel as he had taken aim and fired at the big wolf.

"I can't see the other one. I think it must have fled," said Carrie, staring into the frozen wilderness. "But all the same, I think it best if we get moving."

"What about my arm?" Everus pointed at his ice-compressed limb, anger in his voice. "If I were to strike it against a rock the bloody thing would probably snap off!" He looked about, confirming to himself that their immediate threat had passed. "We'll wait here for a while, if it's all right with you."

"I'm sorry. I didn't mean to..." started Carrie, her tone apologetic.

"Don't worry about it." With a pained expression, Everus chipped some of the ice coating free. "I don't think it's frozen solid, but it bloody hurts...almost burns in fact."

"I think we should try and get to that town or whatever it is," said Carrie, her eyes on the twinkling lights in the valley a league or less away. "It would be a better place to patch up your wounds than out here. It's getting colder and it wouldn't surprise me to find these hills teeming with wolves come nightfall."

Supporting the thief, Everus nodded. "Then lead on."

CHAPTER TWENTY-ONE

As Everus and his companions wearily entered the tavern, twenty or so wary faces turned to the door. They were a miserable and unfriendly-looking lot – their clothes, hands and faces covered in what looked like a month's amount of grime and dirt from working the fields. Most were short and stunted, undoubtedly the bastard offshoots of successive generations of breeding between humans and grubbas and, as Everus cast his judgemental and disapproving sight over the throng, he noticed a few true grubbas, their bearded, dour faces set in permanent scowls.

They made their way over to the bar, uneasy under the unwelcoming stares.

"I see ye've been had by a snowfang," a bearded half-grubba on a bar stool said, gruffly. "They're vicious bastards, ain't they?" He raised his buttocks in order to squeeze out a fart, which he then wafted towards his open mouth. He inhaled deeply, his eyes glazing as he filled his lungs with his own bodily fumes. The stench was as though a long-closed sewer covering had just been opened.

Everus stared for a moment in astonished disgust at the flatulent individual.

"What's the matter wi' yer face? This is better fer ye than smokin'. Cheaper too." The half-grubba grinned, his face contorting as he brewed another fart. Wincing, he let loose another. "Go on, have a sniff."

Shaking his head in disbelief, Everus turned away, searching for the owner.

A man noticed him looking and strode over. "Anythin' I can do for ye?" He smiled in a tight, wintry way, with the smile never reaching his eyes. He was tall and broad, with a thick, high-bridged nose and eyes set a little too close to it, giving him a mean, crafty look. His grey eyes fastened in a cold, inhospitable glare at Everus, drifting down to the frost-covered arm, then back up to the sword hilt visible over his left shoulder, then back to his unsmiling face, meeting his sharp, uncompromising gaze.

"We're looking for somewhere to rest. Some men at the gate told us that you may have a few spare rooms."

The innkeeper broke from Everus' stare and gave Carrie a lecherous once over. "How many rooms are ye wantin'? I mean, I see three of ye, but maybe ye an' the good lady...?" He gave a knowing wink to someone further up the bar.

"Three'll be fine." With his good hand, Everus reached into a pouch, removed a gold coin and placed it on the bar.

"Very good." The innkeeper's shifty eyes lit up. "Why don't ye and yer friends take a seat and I'll bring o'er some food an' drink. I'll also see if I've got some bandages fer yer arm." His brow furrowed as he looked at the thief. "I'm no' goin' to even ask what happened to him. He's no' been fightin' dragons, has he?" With a squeaky-sounding laugh, he picked up the coin, turned his back on his guests and entered a small back room before anyone could answer.

Everus looked about, searching for a quiet corner, still very much aware of the disturbing scrutiny he and his companions were under. Spotting a table near the crackling fire, he gestured to Carrie to head for it.

Creeps looked about, giving a friendly thumbs-up to a couple of heavily whiskered individuals who looked barely human. After they had looked away, he shrugged and turned to Everus. "What kind o' place is this?" he asked.

"Who cares?" Stretching out his legs, Everus turned his chair so that his left side was less than an arm's reach from the fire. "It's warm and it's got beds for the night." Under normal conditions, the heat from the flames would by now have been roasting, but still he could not feel it, the numbing coldness the only sensation.

The shifty-eyed man came over carrying a large tray of drinks. "I've just had a word wi' ma mother, an' it seems that we're all out o' bandages. I've got some soup on the boil, however." Resting the drinks on the table, he took a step back, staring in bewilderment at how close Everus was to the fire. A call, that sounded more like a dry cackle from the kitchen, summoned him back.

"Is your arm getting any better?" asked Carrie.

"A little." Everus shifted position in order not to burn his legs. He stood up and turned side-on to the fire, his left arm extended, almost in the flames. Slowly, the ice began to melt, sloughing from his arm like a shed skin, leaving little but a soaking patch on his sleeve.

The thief was finding it hard not to stare at the unsavoury locals. One sozzled drinker giggled as he shared his supper with a large rat that had crept up to his plate. Creeps shuddered and shifted his chair around so that his back was against a wall.

The soup, when it arrived, was warm and nourishing, if far too peppery for Everus' liking. He took only a couple of spoonfuls, turning his attention more to the small loaf of bread it came with. After a time, the feeling in his arm returned, leaving him with but a slight ache.

Finishing the last of her soup, Carrie pushed her plate back. "Very nice."

"I thought it had a bit o' a shitty taste to it...an' there's lumps in the beer, but still...it's drinkable." Creeps licked his spoon then used it to stir his ale. Tilting his tankard to his mouth, he took a hearty swallow.

"Everus. I take it you know where we go from here," said Carrie.

"Naturally." Everus answered. "Bhubbaal's Stronghold. Although how we get there, I don't know. I think it'd be best to ask around. See if anyone in here has ever heard of the place." Gazing around, he could see that only the diehard boozers now remained in the tavern – those who would probably stay until chucking-out time, stagger homewards and keel over in the street; easy victims for the muggers and cutthroats. The giggler Creeps had noticed earlier had now passed out, leaving the rat to finish the meal at leisure. Everus beckoned the innkeeper over.

"Aye? More drinks is it?"

The inn door slammed shut as some folk left.

"No. Information." Everus withdrew a gold coin, flicked it into the air and caught it.

"Oh aye? An' what would that be?"

"Have you heard of someone named Bhubbaal?"

The innkeeper scratched his unshaven face. "Bhubbaal?" He thought about it for a moment, leading Everus to the suspicion that he was trying to come up with some lie in order to claim the coin. He shook his head. "No. Can't say as I have. Doesn't sound like anyone from around these parts."

"Are you sure?"

"Sure I'm sure." The innkeeper began collecting the bowls and heaping them onto a tray. "Sounds like a Hyadean name to me. Bhub-baal. Aye, that's a Hyadean name. You're in the wrong bloody country."

"I know it's a Hyadean name." Clearly irritated, Everus spun the coin.

"Could be that some o' the lads might know of...is it a him or a her?" Before Everus could answer, the owner turned towards the table of diehard drinkers. "*Oi!* Any o' ye scabrous lot ever heard o' someb'dy called Bhubbaal?"

Several faces, that could not have been described as handsome, turned around. They were a rough-looking lot, comprised of at least two grubbas and a half-grubba. The three remaining members of the party *looked* human.

"Aye. The name sounds familiar," called out a tall and gangly man with a long drooping moustache, which seemed to dominate his face, although it could not quite detract from the cross-eyed stare that, in its own, strange way, regarded Everus and his group suspiciously.

"Now then, Stroppy. I don't want ye tellin' these good folk one o' yer made-up yarns." The innkeeper wagged a finger. "Don't want to have to set mother on ye."

With a nod to his mates, the cross-eyed man sauntered over to Everus' table. He walked with a certain confident arrogance, almost a swagger, as though he was expecting Everus to get up and give him his seat. "Name's Stroppy Jenkins." He gave a short bow – not out of courtesy but rather to get a better look at Carrie's cleavage. "Missus." Behind him, the rest of his group finished their drinks, helped the snoring drunk to his feet and noisily left the tavern.

"So you know of Bhubbaal?" asked Everus, tersely.

Stroppy scratched at his ratty moustache. His front teeth were sharp and crooked and there was a bad stink coming from him. "Well, I might. But first I'd like to know who's askin' an' whether or no' there's any payment involved. An' I'm no' talkin' about a drink or two either...answers to questions like that warrant a bit more in the way o' reward, if ye know what I mean." He scratched at a cluster of sores on his long chin and stared again at Carrie, obviously considering her as adequate payment.

"Listen here, 'Squinty'," said Everus, noticing the ripple of contained anger spreading across the stranger's face. "You get one gold. No more. Now tell me what you know."

Stroppy stepped back, a cheek muscle twitching. "*Pah*." He spat on the floor. "A lousy gold! Ye can stick that up yer posh-talkin' arse!"

Everus was on his feet in an instant, his chair knocked aside.

Stroppy was quick. Laughing like a loon, he darted towards the door. "Yeh. Come on ye little shit!" Wildly, he waved with both hands, goading Everus to come and get him. Upon seeing Everus rushing towards him, sword drawn, he sped out the door and scampered up the street.

At the door, Everus glared out into the night. The streets were dark, moon-thrown shadows making the towering, tumbledown houses seem all the more sinister.

"I'm o'er 'ere!" yelled Stroppy. "Come an' get me, ye little shit!"

The cry came from far up the street to Everus' left. Looking in that direction, he could see the dim outline of the cowardly, but strangely suicidal, Stroppy. He was still waving his hands like an idiot.

"Can ye see him?" asked Creeps, now at the doorway.

"He's over there. I imagine he's hoping that I'll chase him so he can lure me into a dark alley where no doubt the rest of his gang are waiting."

"Do ye want to go after him?"

Everus nodded. "I do. But...seeing as we don't know just how many..."

"I'd love to have a bit o' that whore ye're with! How much does she charge a night?" came a cry from the dark. "I bet she goes like a..."

Pushing Creeps back into the tavern, Everus turned and shut the door, rendering Stroppy's latest bout of verbal provocation ineffectual. With an angry glare at the landlord, he pulled the heavy bolt across the door. "If he gets in...I'll kill you both."

✝ ✝ ✝

Everus came awake swiftly and sharply, that part of his mind which had learned never to fully sleep dragging him back to consciousness at the faintest flicker of sound. For a long moment, he lay there on the low wooden bed, searching around in the darkness of the room with eyes and ears; straining to pick out the sound that had woken him, to identify it and pinpoint its location.

Then it came again – the faint sound of someone moving just outside the door to his room. As always, before going to bed, he had pulled his sword from its scabbard and left it propped by the bedstead, where it could be reached readily. His right hand grasped the hilt. Wearing only an open night shirt and a pair of breeches, he jumped to his feet, his eyes staring fixedly, almost cat-like, at the door.

He had locked the door before settling down for the night; a precaution he now took each and every night when staying indoors, but from the sounds of it, someone else had a spare key. It turned in the lock and he heard the handle twist. A moment passed before the door slowly creaked open. Through narrowed eyes, Everus caught a glimpse of the faint light from the corridor outside, shining around the edge of the door. Stealthily, he sidestepped to his right, clinging to the shadows in the room, making for the space behind where the door would open.

The door opened wider and a man edged his way inside – instantly shattering the hope that Everus had briefly held; that it was Carrie, half-dressed and seeking intimate companionship. Cautiously, the man crept in, his footsteps barely audible, his shadow probably making the greater noise. A faint gleam of lamplight on the blade he carried announced his intention – leaving Everus in no doubt that this was something other than a social visit.

The man crept in another step or two, giving Everus just enough time to get behind the door and see through the crack, checking to make sure there were not another four or so waiting outside. Quickly, he then moved forward and crashed the pommel of his sword down on the skull of his early morning intruder.

Uttering a curse, the man staggered back, falling to his knees under the staggering force of the blow. He lunged forwards, arms flailing, head down, pummelling into Everus as he pushed himself upright, catching him before he could crack down a second time. Together they crashed back, colliding with a chair and falling to the floor, both Everus' sword and the attacker's dagger spiralling out of the melee.

Scrambling to his feet, Everus grabbed Stroppy – for it was now clear who his would-be assassin was – by his shirt collar, and was just about to smash his right fist into the moustachioed face, perhaps knocking the squint from his eyes, when Stroppy jabbed him in the stomach. There was a dull roaring in his ears and all the wind seemed to rush out of his lungs. An uppercut from Stroppy sent Everus staggering back, his head temporarily swimming.

"Come on ye bastard!" Stroppy smacked a punch, then another, into Everus' face, before stepping back into the doorway, searching for his dagger.

With the back of his hand, Everus wiped blood from his busted lower lip. Snarling, he rushed at his attacker.

Stroppy pulled back, now in the dingy corridor. Hate grew in his piggish eyes. He met Everus' charge with a swing from a bunched fist, all of his wiry muscle behind the punch. Everus had guessed that this would be coming and this instinct made him double-up swiftly, so that the jab crashed into his side and not into the pit of his already pummelled stomach. The blow still sent a stab of agony lancing through him and he fell back, narrowly avoiding Stroppy's next rapid swing.

The fight lurched back into Everus' room.

A self-trained pugilist, Stroppy jabbed and dodged, his punches landing often, causing Everus to bite back the pain whenever they did. Pulling back, he almost tripped over a stool, the back of his legs striking some piece of crude furniture. Catching hold of one of Stroppy's arms, he hauled him close, his other hand reaching out and grabbing a handful of unwashed hair. He pulled violently, ripping hair from his assailant's scalp, before bringing the head down to meet his rising knee.

Howling in agony, Stroppy tried to break free, smacking two quick-fire jabs into Everus' ribs. Still Everus held on, using his strength to overbear the fist-fighter, to break his limbs if need be, then throw his jellied remains out of the window and watch as the dogs either ate them or crapped on them – both would be best but he would be happy with either.

Stroppy had other ideas. With a flurry of lefts and rights, he savagely broke free from Everus' hold. Then, even as Everus was about to launch his own attack, Stroppy spotted the shadowy outline of the sword and, clambering over the bed, he whisked it up. Everus was on him before he could take a swing, barging him into the wall, crushing the air from him and knocking the sword from his hands.

"Time to die!" Viciously, Everus hauled his attacker to his feet and spun him around, driving his head into the wall. Grabbing his stunned foe by the back of the collar, he repeated the act twice more before throwing the badly battered man to the floor. For a moment, he considered standing on Stroppy's throat, but he changed his mind and bent down to retrieve his sword. It was that moment's indecision that allowed Stroppy to act. With a twist of his boot, he tripped Everus up, sending him falling against the bed.

Before Everus could get to his feet, Stroppy was on him, punching and scratching. Fighting like crazed alley cats, the two tore at each other, each seeking to get in the one blow that would assure victory – whether it was a kick to the groin or a gouge in the eye. Blood from Stroppy's gashed forehead dripped onto Everus' face, threatening to drip into his eyes and temporarily blind him.

Still on top, the mad-eyed attacker went for a strangle-hold. His hands clasped around Everus' throat, his nails digging in and puncturing the flesh. His grip tightened and Everus now began to panic. Desperately, he reached out with his right hand, searching like a blind man for anything that might be of use. His hand gripped leather and, bringing up one of his boots, he whacked it hard against Stroppy's face. Dazed and still mildly concussed from having had his head used as a hammer, Stroppy released his hold. Everus brought the boot up a second time, then a third, each whack more savage than the one before. He pushed his attacker off and scrambled to his feet, aware that Stroppy was doing likewise.

Everus was the faster to react. With a cry that was aimed more at waking his companions, if indeed they were still alive, he sprang at the would-be murderer. Grabbing him in a headlock, he applied all of his strength, hoping to squeeze the life from him or break his neck.

Like a slimy eel, Stroppy wriggled free, nipped behind Everus and drove two quick kidney punches into him. Groaning his hurt, Everus half fell and reeled back into the corridor. Warped and bleary images dashed through his vision. He shook his head and tried to focus. Suddenly a chair came flying. He braced himself and it cracked off his right shoulder. A flash of pain exploded in his head. The force of the smash caused him to crash against the door across from his and, losing his footing, he stumbled through into Carrie's room. The room was lit and, with hardly a moment to spare, his mind registered the scattered blankets and the empty bed.

"Yeh, we took yer tart." Dagger in hand, the cross-eyed man advanced, a mad, almost feral grin on his sharp face. "The boys're probably seein' to her right now."

A deep rage flared in Everus, far deeper than the mere hatred which had so far consumed him. His eyes narrowed as he felt a fresh flow of anger rush through him. It surged into his muscles, making them tighten, empowering them and banishing the aches and the weariness.

Stroppy seemed to notice the transformation. He hesitated, his confidence and apparent madness now giving way to some semblance of sanity, almost as though he now realised the extent of the danger *he* was in. That thought did not last long however, after all, he was the one with the dagger. With a hiss, he came at a rush, his thrust caught by Everus' grip.

Everus forced the hand that held the dagger down, rapping it twice against the corner of a small dressing table on which Carrie had left some of her possessions, causing Stroppy to drop it. Noticing a small pair of nail scissors among the other toiletries, he lifted them and stabbed down, the sound of their jabbing particularly pleasing.

Stroppy cried out, the small wound smoking like an acid burn. He raised his hands, failing to ward Everus off as he brought the scissors down again and again. One stab pierced his right palm and it was only with a tug that Everus managed to stop Stroppy from involuntarily disarming him. Another stab ruptured the side of Stroppy's face, narrowly missing an eye. Blood now ran down his face in crimson rivulets, his moustache acting as a sponge. Small wisps of smoke rose from his cheek, causing Everus to wonder just what Carrie's scissors had been dipped in.

Stroppy screamed for Everus to stop.

Deaf to his victim's pleas, Everus rained down the attacks, the stabs from the scissors certainly damaging but not as deep as he would like. He would show this snivelling freak the real nature of murder; the joy of butchering, the bliss of slaying.

Smoke continued to rise from the wounded man.

The scissors came down again and now Stroppy was no longer screaming. His leather coat and dirty trousers were tattered and bloody. By the time Everus had finished, not a part of him was unscathed. Blood ran from the wounds in his ankles, his hands and his thighs. It leaked from his stomach as though it was a ruptured wine-flask. It oozed, viscously from his mouth and chest and a pool of it now seeped from under him, covering the floor and the rumpled bed sheets. His face had been sliced so badly it was now beyond recognition – resembling a plate of raw liver or something a fishmonger would scrape off his chopping board. Where he had been struck, the wounds were bubbling.

His right hand covered in blood, Everus stepped back and looked down upon his handiwork; a strange, pleasing emotion, akin to the satisfaction and pride in a job well done, filling his mind. That his gory and disfigured victim was still somehow alive, he had no doubt, for he could see the frequent twitch of fingers and the slow raising and lowering of his chest.

Content that the immediate threat was over, Everus rushed out to the corridor and booted the door to Creeps' room open. Not surprisingly, he found the room empty, the strewn blankets and overturned furniture clear enough signs that a struggle had taken place. It was with some relief that he noticed Creeps' pack lying in a corner. He rushed over to it, opened it and saw that the casket was still inside. He considered opening it just to make sure that the bones were still there when a groan from Stroppy made him dart back.

The mutilated man had rolled over on to his back. His eyes had rolled back in his head and were now little more than pools of blood.

"*Where are they?*" Everus snarled, bloody scissors in hand. Without waiting for an answer, he crouched down, grabbed Stroppy by the hair, turned his head and snipped a sliver of flesh from his right ear.

"*Aaaaaagh!*"

"It'll be your nose next! *Where are they?*"

"Eugh." Coughing, Stroppy spat blood. "Hah...we've got 'em."

"*Where?*" Everus opened the scissors and ran a blade into one of Stroppy's twitching nostrils.

Stroppy moaned, blood trickling from between his lips and out of his nose.

"*Tell me!*"

A half-smile flickered across Stroppy's scissor-ravaged face. He tried to spit but, lacking the strength, only managed a bloody drool. With a final act of defiance, he convulsed violently and died, his sudden death catching Everus unawares, for he had hoped to extract more information from him – as it was, he was left with no idea as to where his companions had been taken, what motive there was behind their abduction or whether they were still alive. He stood up, gave Stroppy a vicious kick and headed back to his room to get geared up.

✝ ✝ ✝

Everus was halfway down the stairs when he heard footsteps approaching the front door. Sword in hand, he sprang down the remaining steps just as the door was flung wide and an out of breath Creeps, dressed only in his dirty long johns, burst in. "Creeps!"

"*Everus! Quick!* They're comin'!" The thief rushed in and turned to face the door, obviously fearful of something close on his heels.

A heartbeat later, three ruffians, armed with clubs and pitchforks, emerged from the dark, their wild eyes staring. Everus was on them before they even knew what was happening. With a slash from his sword, one of them, the lout with the pitchfork, went down. He advanced, smoothly parried a heavy club swing and then drove his blade through his attacker's chest.

Gargling, a second thug fell.

Staring with measured surprise at Everus, and more particularly the sword he was using, the remaining brute stepped back. A thoroughly ugly individual, his sloping brow and jutting, bearded chin marked him as being at least half-grubban. His shoulders were almost as broad as he was tall and there was a murderous glint in his eyes. A throat-catching stink of dung seemed to hang over him, almost as though it was a protective aura – either that or he had recently shat his pants. The awkwardness of his bow-legged stance supported the latter supposition.

Everus was in no mood for talking with such a wretch. He leapt out, his two-handed swing slicing a gash across the half-grubba's chest, tearing through the rough leather of his heavy coat and scoring the mail vest he wore underneath. Blood and sparks flew.

"Oh, ye bastard! Ye'll pay fer that!" The angry brute shrugged off the injury and threw his weight into an attack. It was slow and clumsy, however, and easily avoided.

Everus hacked out. He raised his swing, aiming for the unarmoured head. The edge of the blade chopped through hair and bone, cutting the ugly face in two. Blood sprayed and after a moment's reeling, the stocky attacker fell to the ground. Everus took a couple of deep breaths – to think he had gone to bed hoping for a good night's sleep. At least the reek of blood and death did something to mask the stench of dung. After checking to make sure there were not any more crazies charging down the street, he turned to see Creeps standing several paces away, a bar stool gripped firmly in his hand.

"Ye get 'em?"

"Yes. Where's Carrie?"

"They've took her. There are about twenty o' 'em. All bloody crazy bastards. The innkeeper, he's one o' 'em. They were headin' for that mill buildin' I pointed out as we came into town, when I gave 'em the slip." The thief's words were rattled out, as though, now that he had regained his breath, he was eager to lose it again.

"Is she alive?" It was one of the worst questions Everus had ever asked.

"Aye. Was when I did a runner at any rate."

"Go and get your stuff...and don't forget the bones. I'll wait here and make sure that none get in. Then we'll go and get her." Everus turned and gazed out at the dark and chilly pre-dawn scene. It was eerily quiet and strangely tranquil, with the almost serene sparkling of a few stars in the heavens...and, of course, the three dead lying at his feet.

† † †

On the track leading to the old mill, they spotted a small group of folk out searching, probably wondering what had become of the three that had gone in pursuit of their escapee. After evading them, they sneaked across the small bridge that gave access to the mill yard proper. Outside the entrance to the dark, almost tower-like building a sentry had been stationed and, to give him credit, he was obviously alert enough to take down his lantern from its hook nearby before Everus grabbed him from behind, tilted his head and silently slit his throat.

Quietly, he let the body slide in his arms, dragged it round a corner and dumped it out of sight.

Following Everus' signal, Creeps crept up.

"Let's see what these bastards are up to," whispered Everus. "Our first concern is to rescue Carrie...if she's still alive."

"An' our second?"

Everus managed a wry grin. "To kill each and every one of them." He turned towards the wooden door before him. After finding it unlocked, he gave a gentle push and peeked beyond. A urinous stink came from inside. He could see a darkened room, the only light coming from the lantern, which rested close by. In one corner, he could make out several large barrels. There was another door facing him.

"What we got...anythin'?"

Everus crept to the facing door, aware that his movements were being watched by several large rats that were perched atop the barrels, their red eyes almost aglow in the dark. He turned the handle and the door opened. Beyond the door was a much larger room. Dim light from a few old lanterns suspended from several wooden roof supports revealed the state of its shadowy dereliction.

The interior was dominated by three large heaps of rubble and contorted timber that had collapsed from the floor above. Near to where Everus stood, lay a sprawl of thick and rusty metal chains, along with some huge, old cogs and dented buckets; components of some form of long-abandoned mining machinery that now lay broken and twisted, resembling a rust-covered, multi-legged, upturned giant insect. As his eyes adjusted to the gloom, he saw more battered skeletal frameworks; half-buried remnants of grubban engineering. To his right, clear of the rubble, a tunnel-like ramp descended into the depths, and there were buckled rail tracks and an overturned mine car on the ground.

"Got a bad feelin' about this. Feels as though we're bein' watched every step o' the way," said Creeps, nervously peering about.

"Stay close." Everus knew exactly what the thief meant, for he could sense it too. It was like an unreachable prickling between the shoulder blades; a cold heat that raised the sweat to his forehead. Senses strained, he could now detect sounds, barely audible sounds, like the burrowing of worms as heard by someone buried alive, or the fluttering of wings overhead as heard by someone drowning in a pool. The sounds grew louder. And now he was sure of both the source and the cause. *Rats*...scampering up the ramp, streaming from the deeps – a whole pattering, verminous horde, hungry for blood and eager for flesh. His eyes travelled slowly from side to side, watchful and alert.

A sudden and unexpected golden flash lit up the tunnel opening.

A moment later Carrie, dressed only in her ragged undergarments, staggered clear.

Everus' sense of relief was short-lived, for, as he rushed towards her, he stopped in mid-stride, completely unprepared for the sight of the hideous mob that came in her wake.

Out of the darkness they came, hissing their wrath; a horde of misshapen grotesques, their faces twisted and rat-like, their sackcloth cloaks torn and filthy. Some brandished weapons but most of the thirty or so were unarmed, their teeth and claws more than compensating. Wererats; the bane of civilised life, their existence a travesty, their goal – to feed on the living and the dead, to spread disorder and disease wherever and however they could. To a great extent, they were cowards, their force only manifest in numbers, much like their normal rodent-kin.

Carrie screamed and rushed to Everus.

"Retreat! Outside!" Everus felled the first to draw near with a deadly two-handed swing. He struck down another that came leaping at him from out of the shadows.

As a group, the three of them raced back to the entrance, the pack of loping monsters on their tails. Normal-sized rats swarmed around them, their actions undoubtedly controlled by their human-sized masters.

In the lead, Creeps kicked the outer door open. It was flung wide and fortuitously cracked into an approaching wererat, causing it stagger back with a flattened and bloody snout.

"Everybody out!" shouted Everus. He turned at the sounds behind him, his eyes taking in the three hunched, scabrous horrors before him – the fastest members of the pursuing pack. One came at him with a serrated saw-like weapon, its face and whiskers matted with dried blood and dirt, no doubt gathered from a lifetime of looting graveyards and gnawing on corpses. Parrying its blade, Everus chopped down with another two-handed swing and severed its left arm. Shaking madly and squirting blood, it fell backwards, the other two taking its place.

They were wary adversaries and not the bravest of creatures, preferring to attack sleeping opponents or else rush forth from ambush. Nonetheless, this was their domain and, as the first of the two prepared to attack, bolstered by the sounds of the approaching many, a red hunger flashed in its eyes. Snout twitching, fleas biting, it stepped up to meet Everus.

Everus could see the shadows and hear the squeals of the oncoming horde. Leaping outside, he slammed the door shut and held it. After beheading the stunned rat-man outside with a rather nonchalant slash of his sword, he turned to his companions. "Let's get out of here."

"My belongings are back at the inn," protested the sorceress.

"It's too dangerous." From inside, Everus could hear a multitude of obscene cries and curses. The door rattled but did not open. "We should be able to outrun them."

"Aye, if we don't run into any o' their patrols," cautioned Creeps.

Carrie gave a deep breath. "All right. We run."

✝ ✝ ✝

The wererats soon gave up the chase, but it had been a ghastly pursuit, for Everus had known that the possibility of tripping or running down a blind alley and encountering another group of them would almost certainly have proven fatal. As it was, the therianthropic horde had quickly fragmented, hoping that their prey would do likewise and thus be easier to pick off. And yet, despite the fact that the wererats had a much better knowledge of the layout of the town, Everus and his companions had given them the slip. By staying true to their course and never wavering or allowing themselves to rest, they had just kept up their run, not stopping until the town was but a darkened blur in the valley below them.

Eventually, Carrie could go no further. Her bare feet bleeding, her nightdress bloody and in tatters, her face marked with exertion, she fell to the grass.

As though that was an invitation to join her, Creeps did likewise.

Standing upright, Everus looked about, scanning the surrounding countryside as though half-expecting a rampaging mob of whiskered-faced freaks to crash through the nearby bushes. "All right. We'll stop here for a while." He took off his long coat and gave it to Carrie. "Take this."

"Thanks." The sorceress wrapped the coat over her shoulders.

"I'm gettin' way too old for this kind o' malarkey," muttered Creeps.

"The sun'll be up shortly," commented Everus, his stare fixed on the town below them. In the growing daylight it looked far more of a dump than they had first taken it for. "I'd doubt that those things will come out here to chase us...nonetheless, I'd feel much happier if we put some more leagues between us and them."

"I'm dead on ma feet," Creeps moaned. "I reckon they must've put some shit in our soup. Sleepin' draught or summat."

"Probably," replied Everus, remembering the peppery taste. "Still...unless you wish to end up as rat-shit come nightfall, I suggest we leave this place as soon and as quickly as possible." He gazed down at Carrie. From the looks of it she had managed to battle free from her captors with only the slightest of injuries, a feat that more than surprised him. His heart lurched as a sudden, dark suspicion flashed into his mind. "How...are you feeling?" he asked, apprehensively.

Carrie stared skyward. "I'll live...I guess."

"What happened?"

The sorceress sat up, her movement graceful. "What do you mean? Do you want to know how I was abducted...or, how I managed to escape?"

Everus stared into the sapphire pools of her eyes, wondering for a moment if she knew what he was thinking. "Tell me everything."

"Well, the first I knew I was being roughly gagged and bound. Then a sack, which smelled of mouldy potatoes or something like that, was thrown over my head. Next, I was being bundled by about four of them down the stairs of the inn. I heard Creeps cursing and then I remember being carried up to that terrible mill." Carrie shook her head at the distressing memory. "I was taken into a big chamber, a cavern almost, in which, after they'd removed my hood, I could see a score or more of the ugly things. They were gruesome – all whiskers and lice, their fur patchy and...eugh! It was horrible. They...they were going to sacrifice me to one of their gods, I think."

"How did you escape?"

"With the aid of this." Carrie reached for the necklace she wore and raised it. The lunarite amulet that Everus had first seen her wearing back in Stranglewood shone and sparkled, much like the gleam of joy in his otherwise black heart. "I...I always wear it when I go to bed. Lucky for me that I do, for when they went for me in that cavern, they suddenly found that in their rat forms they couldn't touch me."

All of Everus' doubt melted. He smiled at her. For a moment, the desire to just reach out and draw her close, to feel the touch of her lips on his, almost made him dizzy. He had all but convinced himself that she had been infected with the wererat's vileness and that she was now doomed to become one herself. The relief on hearing her explanation filled him with a rare sense of elation. Unable to contain his euphoria, he bent over and kissed her forehead.

Carrie was as surprised as he. After the moment had passed, she managed a confused smile, part of her seemingly wanting nothing more than to be kissed again.

Creeps tutted his disapproval.

It seemed as though a shockwave had travelled through Everus' emotions. Briefly, he wondered whether an apology was needed. Seeing the growing smile on Carrie's face, he decided not. He stood up, backing away slightly.

"Are you all right?" Carrie asked.

"Yes. I...I'm just wondering if we should go back and see what we can rescue of your belongings."

"Too dangerous," reasoned the thief. "Way too risky. They'll be crawlin' like ticks on a tramp's mattress lookin' for us."

"There wasn't much anyway," said Carrie. "Nothing of real value."

"What about your spellbook?" asked Everus. "You'll need that, surely?"

"*Oh shit!* Yes. My spellbook!" Carrie leapt to her feet. "*Damn!* I just have to get that back. Without it...I won't be able to perform any magic."

"Then I guess we go back." With a wry grin, Everus started back towards town. "Let's do this before they've time to organise themselves further."

† † †

With the rising sun still low in the sky, they made their way back into the town they had recently fled, their eyes darting to and fro at the slightest movement. Still some distance from the town gates, they came to a halt.

Everus happened to look down, noting only their cast shadows and the mud on the road. It was then that he was suddenly reminded of the peculiarities of Creeps' shadow for, whereas before it had appeared slightly darker than that of his own – an observation he had first made on their first journey to Ghavin's Keep – now, if anything, it appeared somewhat lighter.

"It's obvious that your sword can harm them," commented Carrie, distracting Everus from his thoughts.

Everus turned. "Say again."

"I said, your sword is capable of damaging them, the wererats. Like most shapeshifters, they're immune to most normal weapons. Some, it is said, are even immune to fire and lesser spellcraft."

Raising the blade, Everus looked at his sword, tracing the lines of runes along its fire-hardened steel. "Perhaps Old Hunchy was right. Maybe it is magical."

"You know, if they attack us, you're the only one who can put up much resistance. Without access to my spellbook, I'm pretty useless in a fight. However..." Carrie took hold of the lunarite amulet that dangled around her neck.

Creeps noticed her action. "If ye say that thing'll protect ye from 'em, then why no' give it to Everus? Then he can go in an' get yer book." He puffed on his pipe. "That way, I can't see it bein' much o' a risk?" He turned to Everus. "What say ye?"

"We could do it that way, I guess." The prospect of having to go back in there on his own did not particularly appeal, but it sounded a convincing argument, and, as the thief had said, there would be less of a risk. Everus' eyes narrowed as he took in the grim collection of dingy, towering buildings before him, each no doubt teeming with rats and their bipedal masters.

"But...remember, this will only work against them providing they're in their altered state," advised Carrie. "If they haven't transformed, then the invulnerability given by the talisman will be ineffectual, as I found out. Additionally, it will offer no protection against their traps, or normal rats for that matter." She blew a strand of hair from her eyes. "You know, I think we should all go. Perhaps that way they'll stay clear. Safety in numbers and all that."

"An' what do we do if they come at *us*?" asked Creeps, his concern aimed at the sorceress.

"We...hide behind Everus?" Carrie grinned at her suggestion.

"Just stay close," Everus warned. "If there are any out on the streets then I'll take them. It could be that now, with sunrise, they'll retreat to their lairs, bury themselves in their underground warrens. If not, then we may have a fight on our hands. Remember, only this..." He made a series of swings with his sword, "can harm them." He was about to set off when he was reminded of the fight with Stroppy. He looked to Carrie. "I fought with one of them in the tavern after you two had been taken. I'm sure I killed him...your scissors?"

Carrie smiled, knowingly. "Pure silver."

"Thought as much." Everus turned. Surveying the empty streets and the decrepit hovels, ready for anything, he entered the threatening town. The fact that there were no longer any gate guards on duty and the overall level of desolation led him to the belief that perhaps the rat-folk were whorish in their predation – in the sense that they only came out at night and they seemed only interested in easy flesh.

"It's so quiet," whispered Carrie.

"Yes. But they're still here somewhere." Everus turned full circle. "Creeps, you watch the rear."

The thief nodded dutifully.

They were now passing the dreadful mill-like structure. Daylight did nothing to mask the fact that this place was evil – it was almost as tangible as the ground beneath their feet or the chillness in the air. Whatever wickedness had been perpetrated there in homage to the wererats' foul deity had left an unholy residue; a lingering trace of corruption that, alongside the memories of what each had seen within, was enough to make the skin crawl.

"We should never have come here," voiced Carrie, shivering. Barefoot, she wrapped Everus' coat tighter around her. "As soon as we retrieve my book we should leave."

"My intentions exactly."

"An' what if yer book's no' there? What if they've nabbed it, eaten it...or burnt it?"

Carrie was about to reply to Creeps' disturbing possibility when, with a sweeping gesture of his right hand, Everus signalled for silence. He stopped and pointed to an upstairs window of one of the half-ruined houses, from which a dirty grey curtain flapped forlornly.

"Ye see summat?" inquired Creeps.

"Let's just keep walking, but keep an eye out. I don't fancy providing target practice for some long-tailed bastard with a crossbow."

Warily, they all passed by. They were now less than a hundred paces from the inn, the smell of the diseased growing stronger with every step.

When Everus had arrived here the previous evening he had been attracted to voices of what he had assumed were fellow human beings and the glow of a welcoming fire. Now, however, he could see that the whole building was one complete eyesore. In many ways it reminded him of one of the decayed structures he had seen on the pier in Ullerby; some of the windows were boarded up, others smashed. Parts of the roof were missing, as though several of the upper storeys had been blown-up by a bolt of lightning or an irate wizard, exposing a largely wrecked staircase and several destroyed rooms.

The corpses of the three he had killed earlier were gone.

"I'll go in. You stay out here." Everus made for the tavern door, the grip on his sword tightening.

"Aren't you forgetting something?" Carrie removed her pendant.

"No. You keep it."

"Everus. Take it."

"No." Everus shook his head. "Now's the time for me to see if The High Three really do want to keep me alive. Wait here. Shout if you need me." With no further talk, he dashed to the inn door and kicked it open. The room was as he and Creeps had left it earlier that morning, the tables still set as though in readiness for another evening's ale consumption – in addition to the odd little bit of food-poisoning, abduction, attempted murder and shape-shifting skulduggery. Apart from that, it was dark and empty.

He made his way in. In the gloom, he could just about make out the bar and the door beyond. To his right, around a corner, was where the stairs up to the first floor began. After a brief pause, during which he wrestled the mental images of the rat-faced horde from his mind, he made his way over to the foot of the stairs. Treading carefully, his eyes aware of the many shadowy shapes, he edged forward, his body pressed tightly against the wooden wall.

Before him the stairs ascended into darkness.

Not one to scare easily, Everus still found it hard to look up, to push his vision into the darkness. In his mind, he could see the many sets of red eyes that peered out from the shadows – eyes set at ankle-level and those much higher, each viewing him with a hungry malevolence.

There came a creak from overhead.

That same cold prickling that he had felt at the old mill crept unwelcomingly up his spine. Slowly, he started up the stairs, afraid now that each step would fall on a rotten tread and that he would crash through into a dark cellar where he would soon find himself surrounded by thousands of flesh-hungry rats.

The sound came again; the unnerving creak of tortured wood. It sounded like either a clumsy step on a loose board or the slow rocking of an old-fashioned chair.

Enough of this, thought Everus. Foolhardiness spurred him up the remaining steps. In the dark, he made his way along the corridor, his mind no longer dwelling on bogeymen lurking under the floorboards or grotesques pouring out of the shadows. He had known and seen death. There was nothing here to frighten him. He would kill all who got in his path...

487

He stopped.

The creaking was coming from Carrie's room.

Everus was now certain it *was* the back and forth motion of a rocking chair. He took a step closer, considering whether to open the door quietly or to kick it in. He decided to kick it in.

Shadows shifted, drawn back towards one corner, as though to conceal further the ragged form that sat huddled in its chair, reading by candlelight. It was a horrid thing, an ancient wererat, wrapped in a blanket, its furry arms wiry, its face more shrivelled and rat-like than any of the others – apart from the brass-rimmed pince-nez it had resting on its whiskered snout. Its pink-red eyes were rheumy, and yet as they turned to focus on Everus, he could see something almost akin to intelligence in them. What kind of intelligence, he had no intention of finding out.

The thing mewled, the sound horrible as, arthritically, it rose from its chair. Dried droppings fell from between its scrawny legs. Its dirty tail hung limply. This was the rat-mother, the wererat matriarch, the hive queen, as well as the proprietor of the inn. She was also the cook and that in itself was perhaps the worst thing about her. Granny Jenkins was not renowned for her culinary skills.

Fortunately, Everus was unaware of that fact, even though he had his suspicions. He felt that he was about to retch, and undoubtedly would have had he known just how she had prepared supper for them, squatting bow-legged over their soup bowls. Fighting back his disgust, he ran in and chopped down the flea-infested bundle of fur and filth. Without looking at the damage he had inflicted, he snatched up the spellbook the aged horror had been reading, turned and sprinted out. Down the corridor he ran. He leapt down the stairs and rushed out, eager to get into the daylight. Heart pounding, he handed the book over.

"You've got it!" cried Carrie.

Everus took some deep breaths and nodded. Resting his hands on his hips, he stared at the inn, wondering just what other horrors lay inside. He was half-expecting Creepy Geezer himself to come striding out, demanding an admittance fee. This was a true House of Horrors.

"Was there anything...inside?" asked Carrie, after she had made a cursory check of her spellbook. "I only ask because if not, I really could do with getting my boots and some clothes."

CHAPTER TWENTY-TWO

Everus sank down onto his haunches by the fire, stretching his hands out to the blaze as a cool wind began to sweep down from the direction of the mountain, now that the day was virtually gone. His companions set about sorting out their bedrolls whilst, at their backs, the sun dropped abruptly into a vast cauldron of exploding scarlet and gold, and twilight began to hurry down from the hills, drawing a veil over the sky. He threw a quick glance upwards towards the brooding tree line of the ridge they were on, then down towards the western horizon, where a faint yellow glow portended the appearance of one of the world's three moons.

"Ye any idea where we're goin'?" asked Creeps, adding another branch to the campfire. He rummaged about in his pack, removed a pouch loaded with baccy and filled his pipe. He lit up, the flare from the match momentarily illuminating his face in the growing darkness. "Ye've mentioned this Bhubbaal character, but it seems as though ye've no idea where he lives."

Everus gazed into the flames, lost in his own thoughts. After a while, he looked across at the thief. "You know something? You're quite right. I don't know where he lives, or for that matter, whether he lives at all. That's why I talked Mhoon into coming with us. He'd been here before. He knew where Bhubbaal's Stronghold was. Gossothus is not a large country. However, that's not to say that I plan on walking the length and breadth of it searching." He tore off a bit of beef jerky, which they had taken from amongst the more edible looking foodstuffs in the wererat's larder. It had an unusual taste, but his hunger convinced him it *was* cured beef.

"So just what are our plans?" asked Carrie.

"Well...despite our recent experience, I think we should try and find another settlement. We can then start to make some enquiries."

489

"*Oh aye!* An' run into another bunch o' them buggers again?"

"Does anyone have a better idea?" Everus switched his gaze between them. After a moment's silence, during which no other suggestions were voiced, he spat out a bit of hard gristle. He looked at it, somewhat relieved to notice there were not any toenails or tooth bits visible in it. "I'm hoping that those wererats were a one-off. I've heard nothing to make me believe that they're representative of this land's inhabitants."

"All right, let's assume ye're right," agreed Creeps. "But we're still in the back o' beyond. It could take ages to find another town or village."

"Creeps is right, Everus. Remember, time works against us. Each day that passes brings the fall of Ghavin's Keep closer...that's if it hasn't already happened. Not to mention Xethorn's summoning of Uhu'giaggoth."

"Which, as far as I'm aware, He can't do without the complete hand," added Everus.

"All the same..."

"Don't you think I know!?" Everus flung a rock into the fire. "I'm going about this as fast as I can. I'm open to suggestions as how best to tackle this, but neither of you have any." His eyes wandered from them back to the blaze. "I still think our best, if not only, available course of action is to stay on this road. After all, it must go somewhere. Thanks to our 'rat friends' we've got a fresh supply of provisions. Even Creeps has got his baccy, so that should keep him content for several days."

"*Several days?*" cried Creeps. "Ye're kiddin' me, right? This lot'll be gone come noon the 'morrow." He gave a dry laugh and returned the pipe to his mouth. "They didn't call me 'Puffin' Adolf' for nothin'."

"Anyway, if we haven't found any signs of habitation come two, no, let's say three days from now, then obviously we'll review matters. But I remain convinced that there must be a town or a village somewhere." Everus stretched his arms and gave a yawn. Reaching into a pouch, he took out a gold coin, flipped it into the air and caught it, slapping it down, still covered, on the back of his other hand. He looked at the thief. "Emperor or Gate?"

"Gate."

Removing his hand, Everus looked down at the image on the coin's verso – the fortified portcullis of Wyrm's Port. "Tough luck.

You're on first watch." He pocketed the coin and stretched out, wrapping himself in his long coat. Soon he was fast asleep.

✝ ✝ ✝

Some time before noon the following day, with the snow crunching underfoot and the skies promising to deliver more, they started climbing up into the higher ground. The road they had been following meandered up the wooded slopes, which clung to the mountainside like green stubble on its craggy, granite face. They stopped to get their breath at a place where the tree cover was thinnest, granting them a spectacular view of the land which they had spent the past few days crossing. Many leagues off, they could see the dark patch of the Stranglewood Forest and the nestling hills of The Deadmoor Clumps.

After their breather, they pressed on, the woods now losing much of their alpine pleasantness, becoming darker and deeper. In places, they could see large, moss-covered rocks and outcroppings where parts of the mountain had become dislodged due to earth tremors and glacial activity. They soon came to a place where a small stone bridge spanned a vertiginous ravine. That the bridge had been built by grubban hands, Everus had little doubt, for he could see a preponderance of runic lettering chiselled into the stonework. Unfortunately, it was far too archaic a script for him to make much sense of.

The road before them wound up and over the mountain.

The last rays of sunlight were just cresting the western skyline, drenching the snow-covered summits before them in a bloody glow, when they reached a place where the road started its descent. It had taken them the best part of the day to climb as far as the road had taken them and now, with legs aching, they set about looking for somewhere to camp.

With the last of the daylight dispersing through the pines and the firs, they discovered a relatively sheltered spot which afforded good views of the road winding below them. Here they decided to rest up and, as Creeps set about collecting firewood, Everus and Carrie sorted out their respective bedrolls and blankets.

With a yawn, Carrie stretched out and lay back.

Everus gazed skywards, taking in the high tree tops that were now flooded in the pale yellow light that came spilling over the mountain, from where the full round face of a moon had finally lifted clear of the dark ridges, sailing up into a clear velvet sky, dotted with countless thousands of stars. A chill went through him as the strange night glow came crowding in from the far horizons, bringing with it a strange and not particularly welcome sense of loneliness.

"How are you feeling?"

"I'll live." Everus strolled over to sit by Carrie. "You?"

"Fine. A little tired, but otherwise all right."

"You know, you were really lucky to escape those wererats. I thought the worst." Deep down, Everus just yearned to put an arm around her, to share in her warmth.

"Tell me about it." Carrie rolled onto her side so that she could see him better. "I...really appreciate you coming for me and returning to get my spellbook." She looked frankly at him, the gratitude clear. "Others would've just left me behind."

"Think nothing of it." Everus found he was taking pleasure in just looking at her, at tracing the lines of her figure as far as he could discern it through her clothes, enjoying the sweep of her remarkable hair. Realising he was staring, he moved his gaze and tried to wrench his thoughts back to safer ground. He could ill afford to become vulnerable again, no matter how much the desire in his heart compelled him to do otherwise. "I'd like to think that you'd do the same."

With a reassuring smile, Carrie was about to reply when, bearing a heap of fallen branches, Creeps noisily stumbled into view.

"There's summat movin' in the woods." Nervously, the thief stared back in the direction he had just come from. "I'm sure there's summat."

"What like? What did you hear?" Following Creeps' line of sight, Everus peered into the dark.

"It was like...pantin'. Ye know, like a wolf on the prowl or someb'dy out o' breath breathin' down the back o' yer neck."

"Well hurry up and get the fire lit. If it's a wolf, a normal wolf, it's unlikely to approach. Besides, I'm starving."

Soon the fire was going. Then the slices of cured beef were put in the pan, filling the air with the rich aroma of cooking. If there had been anything threatening out there it would surely have come to inspect – but nothing did.

Despite his hunger, Everus ate slowly, chasing his mouthfuls with glugs from one of the several small bottles of ale they had also raided from Granny Jenkins' larder. Close to midnight, with his lids drooping, he got out one of his 'lucky' coins and asked for Creeps to call the toss for first watch duty.

"Emperor," said Creeps, tiredly.

"Wrong again." Everus raised the frowning image of J'hann to his eye, silently cursing the thief for calling correctly once more. He pocketed the coin, rolled on his side and tried to sleep. After a while, the sounds of the burning wood crackling and popping faded from his ears and he drifted off. He dreamt of Carrie.

† † †

They were up before dawn and after a frugal breakfast of dried mushrooms and oatcakes, they started the downhill stretch of the mountain. The tree cover thinned with each step, depriving them of shelter from the snow that now began to fall. It came down lightly at first, building in strength until it fell as one continuous icy-white blanket, the speed of which took them unawares.

"Surely we're not going to keep going through this?" asked Carrie.

"It's either that or we get trapped up here. We have to get clear of this mountain before the road gets blocked. So yes, we've got to keep going." Everus tired to peer through the curtain of frozen water. "I don't think we've got much further to go. Perhaps less than a league."

They trudged on, a fierce wind now whipping up the snowstorm.

Fortunately, the snow had no time to form deep drifts, so its main hindrance was to partially blind them. The wind piped eerily through the rocks on either side and soon Everus was imaging all sorts of glacial beasts shambling out of the whiteness, the surreal sounds only adding to his fears.

Their going was slow, but by late morning they eventually cleared the mountain, relieved to be back on the level once more. The snow lessened considerably, allowing them to make out the surrounding land in better detail. From where they now stood, they could see the road curving its way to the right, for even though large areas were snow-covered it was relatively easy to trace its line amidst the overall ruggedness of the terrain before them.

The road stretched a further league or so before disappearing into the mouth of a great ravine; a yawning glacial rift in the mountains. In front of them and to their left, the bleak icy plain, broken here and there by several huge tors, seemed to run forever, delineated only by the faint trace of a further, higher mountain range, barely visible on the grey horizon.

"It looks like we're heading for that canyon," said Everus, staring fixedly like a hawk at the rocky divide. Mhoon had informed him that Bhubbaal was a warlord of sorts, thus it followed that he was in charge of some kind of army. Consequently, it was highly likely that he would have scouts and border patrols garrisoned at a strategic place such as this. "From here on in, everyone stay alert."

Nearing the rift mouth, they started to see signs of ruined fortifications, their sharp granite angles thrusting through the snow-covered ground like angry teeth. Most of the ruins were cone-shaped, their points jutting upright so that a passing aerial attacker looking down would have discerned them as a cluster of spikes, but some were squat and brick-shaped. All bore signs of damage, some lying completely shattered as though they had imploded.

Everus could see more defences running like a high spiked railing along the upper ledges of the cliff wall. Towers and crenellated walls protruded from the rock, their openings and archways dark and unwelcoming. There was little doubt in his mind that the grubbas of old had gone to great lengths to fortify this entrance, this pass through the mountains.

"What is this place?" Carrie asked, her voice carrying further than she had intended, the noise alerting them to the stillness all around.

"It reminds me o' that grubban place we went to wi' that Cu fella," replied Creeps, looking to Everus. "What was it called... Dourbelly's...summat or other?"

"Durgan's Rock," Everus corrected. "I'm not sure about this place. Grubban history was something that never really appealed to me." He looked about, his eyes trying to resurrect in his mind the scenes this ancient site must have witnessed and endured; the untold battles and the unrecorded acts of valour, as well as the grim routine of garrison duty on the frontier. "I'd say that this is either all that remains of Ungûd Khor...or, possibly, Ungûd Baad. Either way, it's lain like this for the best part of two thousand years. It wouldn't surprise me to learn that this was an outpost established to protect whatever quarries are in the vicinity. It looks like we've got to pass through, whatever the case."

Cautiously, they crept through the pass, leaving the towering bastions and guardhouses behind. It was dark, the sun never quite managing to cast its light into the high-walled canyon. Venturing further, they soon passed huge columns that had at one time supported light fixtures of some sort, but now these large defunct beacons served no purpose whatsoever. On either side branched cave-like openings, out of which came the very mountain's breath, cold and dank; a subterranean exhalation which stank of that which was long-buried.

"Have you noticed that parts of this rift have been hewn?" asked Everus, turning to Carrie, who walked close behind him. "If you look closely, you can see where they shored up the cliff walls."

"It's pretty amazing. Where do all these caves and things lead?"

"Barracks and temples. Living quarters, mess halls, armouries. You name it, the grubbas would have built it." Everus peered into the darkness of one particular vaulted opening they were now passing. Carved caryatid columns of squat burly grubban warriors in armour stood sentinel, daring anyone to enter. "Do you want to take a look?"

"I can't say that I do." Carrie shivered. "It's so dark and gloomy."

"Well it is now, but once this place would have been brightly lit. Its walls would have echoed to the sound of a thousand voices. Grubban soldiers, traders, engineers, miners…all would have dwelt herein. This would've been a thriving city, in addition to a military garrison; a place where generations of the little buggers would have lived and died. Count yourself lucky; not many of our kind have lived to see such a place."

"Unlucky, more likely," quipped Creeps. "The place's a bloody eyesore."

They journeyed on through the ancient grubban city, keeping to the floor of the gorge, knowing that the moment they left it they risked becoming hopelessly lost within the sunless depths. At one point, they saw a large, grey tentacled monstrosity slink across their path, but apart from that the ancient city was desolate.

Carrie breathed a sigh of relief when the gorge they were in began to widen, the daylight that now welcomed them seeming a long and forgotten dream. "It looks like we're heading out."

"Aye," agreed Creeps. Like the sorceress, he too seemed pleased to be leaving. "I don't fancy goin' through there again. Place gave me the willies. Too bloody confined for ma likin'. I mean, it's one thing crawlin' about in crypts...but livin' in one? No thanks!"

If Everus had heard either of them he did not respond. He led them out, his gaze fixed on the sight becoming clearer before him. Through the rocky division that was the other end of the canyon, he could see, still several leagues distant, more snow-capped mountains. Thrusting up from the nearest was a large, claw-shaped landmark, several dark talons stretching skywards, others curled, beckoning him onwards.

✝ ✝ ✝

"Borgrim's End," announced Everus, reading aloud the sign which pointed to the dreary-looking hamlet which nestled at the wooded base of the mountain. His gaze went upward in order to take in the dark, five-towered fortress that loomed high up on the mountainside. In the fading daylight, it seemed to have assumed an evil, purplish glow. Far off, he heard the baleful howl of a wolf, its cry sending a ripple of unease up his spine.

"Do ye think that's the place?" asked Creeps, eyes focused on the strange tower.

"Possibly. Although I'd have thought it would've been better guarded. So far we've encountered no guards, no soldiers...nor does there appear to be any sign of life up there. No lights, no smoke. So it could just be deserted."

"Everus. What if this...Borgrim's End, is inhabited by more wererats?" Carrie asked.

"Then I guess we'll have to kill them. But seriously, keep your wits about you and be wary of the food and the drink. Let's not fall into the same trap we did last time. Also, be mindful of what you say, this Bhubbaal could have spies and agents all over the place."

"Do you think that's what the wererats were? Spies, working for him?" asked Carrie.

"No, I think that's unlikely." The sun sank beneath the shadow-thrown western peaks, heralding the fall of night, its unnaturally fast disappearance sending a shiver through Everus as though he would never see it rise again. "It's cold. Come on, let's see about getting indoors."

It *was* cold, the chill from the loss of sunlight and the mountain air gnawing through their clothes as though in a concerted effort to drive them away. Onwards they walked, until the three of them soon reached the dark wooded trail that led to Borgrim's End. It was not particularly far, but it seemed to take them much longer than it should have, for it was dark and shadowy and the path was riddled with sudden dips and rises. To their right lay a thicket-covered ditch, perhaps as wide as two men and as deep as one, in which odd, little nocturnal things rustled and hissed.

Occasionally, a set of small luminous green or blue eyes would stare out at them from the wiry undergrowth with the intensity of a flame.

After climbing another short rise, they saw before them a small cluster of barrow-like earth, turf and stone dwellings, as well as several warped houses hollowed from tall and bloated tree trunks. Many of them looked reasonably habitable, with only one or two displaying signs of disrepair. Slightly off centre, built on a small knoll of rock, stood a stone building, on top of which was a small beacon – the green fire burning within bathing some of the strange hamlet in a lurid glow.

"What do you think the fire's for?" asked Carrie.

"To warn Bhubbaal that strangers are in town?" Ever the pessimist, Everus gave a wry grin.

"Do ye think we've been spied on already?" asked Creeps, staring all around.

"Who knows? But we're not going to discover anything stood here. You two wait for me, I'll just scout about a bit." Turning his back on his companions, Everus set off in the direction of the nearest house.

The building he was approaching was single-storeyed, squat and circular with a front door made from dark sycamore. Wooden blinds covered two, small, semi-circular windows. Smoke drifted lazily into the dark skies from a chimney in the flat, turf-thatched ceiling, carrying with it the unpleasant scent of poor cooking.

Suddenly the door opened and a man stepped out. He was slim-shouldered and of Creeps' height, his old and wrinkled, hatchet-face resembling gnarled wood that had seen more than its share of inclement weather. A small, grizzled, six-legged dog-like creature strained at the lead held in his right hand and it sniffed at the air before breaking into a series of loud barks and yaps.

Everus raised a hand in a show of friendship. "Relax, friend. I mean you no harm." He looked down at the barking animal, not particularly liking what he saw.

"Oh! I...I never saw ye there." Apprehension showed in the

stranger's pale blue eyes. Whatever uncertainty the old man felt was not shared by his pet however. Yapping, it stretched the length of rope, eager to defend its master.

Everus eyed the dog-thing warily, ready to reach for his sword if it was needed. It had a fairly nasty-looking set of jaws on it and it had a head like a farmer's bull. "I was wondering if you could be of assistance."

With some effort, the old man pulled the animal back. "How?"

"Bugger me!" cried Creeps, rushing forwards. "A snaggle-toothed ratter! I thought I recognised the bark." Obviously unconcerned about losing his fingers or his hand for that matter, he crouched down and stroked the little beast. The dog-thing ceased its growling, rolled onto its back and put its little legs in the air as Creeps tickled its underside. "I haven't seen one o' these in years. Where'd ye get it?"

The old man still looked wary. "Eh...I can't remember. I've had him for so long now."

"Ye're a cute little bugger, aren't ye?" The thief stroked the 'ratter' some more, its legs now paddling. He turned to look up at Everus. "I used to have one o' these. Bloody great little diggers!"

"What happened? Did you eat it?"

Creeps gave Everus a cold frown, as did the thing's owner, wondering for a moment if he had heard right. He tried, with some success, to pull it back. "Just how can I help ye folk?" There was a deliberateness to his question, as though he now wanted them away, unsure as to their true intentions.

"Is there an inn nearby?" asked Everus.

"Well...I wouldn't go so far as to call it an inn but ye could try Billy Jubbly's place. He might still have a few spare rooms left. May even provide ye wi' somethin' to eat."

"Where is it?"

"Just up 'ere a bit." The old man pointed, the leash now hanging limp, the little animal basking in Creeps' continued petting. "But mind, he's a bit, ye know..." He tapped his head with a knowing look. "And make sure ye're away before sunrise. He's minglin' wi' bad company, so just make sure ye're away before they return."

"Hmm. Interesting." Everus gave a curt nod, the extent of his appreciation. He was on the verge of asking the old man more questions, when he changed his mind, aware that he had to maintain a level of subterfuge and that asking too much so early was bound to draw attention. "Creeps. Leave your new friend alone. It doesn't know where you've been." Following the directions given, he led his companions towards a larger, three-storey dwelling. It was lodge-like, made from cut timbers and coarse stone. Lamplight shone from several of its ground floor windows and from inside could be heard the sounds of talking. Stable-like outbuildings could be seen annexed to the rear.

Before they got to the main entrance, the door opened and a grossly fat and ugly woman with huge breasts wobbled her bulk through the doorway. She was unsightly; a throwback to a time when humans had reproduced with whatever shared their world – their misbegotten offspring often forced into a life of seclusion and revilement. She was at least half bagh'arulk and part grubba; her face brutish and flabby, her eyebrows and moustache, bristling and hairy. One eye was severely bloodshot. The other wandered lazily, seemingly unable to focus.

Despite having encountered more monsters than would have comfortably fit in a lay wizard's bestiary, this questionably female's appearance turned Everus' stomach. "You...you have some spare rooms?" There was a quavering in his voice, a reflection of the state of unease he felt at the prospect of bunking down under the same roof as this...woman.

She gave a confused look, her face becoming markedly uglier. Clearly unable to understand what Everus was asking, she gave an apologetic grunt, gripped her bucket of slops tighter, and waddled outside, her backside barging into Creeps and almost knocking him flat.

"I hope this ain't the whorehouse," commented the thief sarcastically, once she had passed.

Now that she had left, Everus was given a better view of the lodge's interior. It was smoky, but light from numerous small lamps shone on two figures seated at a table. Stuffed heads – some of them human – antlers, and other trophies hung on one wall.

"Hello!" cried out one of the figures upon seeing Everus enter. "Hello!" he repeated, coming to greet them. "The name's Jubbly."

Everus walked forwards. "We're looking for some rooms. We were told you may have some spare." Now within hitting distance – his preferred distance for conversation – he could see that the seated figure at the table was a very fat woman, possibly the man's wife.

Jubbly himself was of average height and build. He was dressed in a grey-green vest and a pair of tight, dark brown leggings which, apart from covering his legs, assisted only in emphasising their skinniness. His dirty, bespectacled face was as round and ruddy as a freshly dug beetroot, which, along with his scruffy peasant attire, contributed to making him look like a scarecrow which had escaped from its support. His wife was just as shabby looking.

"Some rooms, ye cry? Aye, we've got rooms. How many are ye after?" Jubbly's voice was good-natured, if slightly mad. His breath carried with it the tang of strong apple cider.

"An' what about summat to eat?" inquired Creeps, edging forward.

"Rooms *an'* food? My, I think we can stretch to that." Jubbly clapped his hands together. "Woman! Get up off yer arse an' get into that kitchen an' rattle up some grub for our new guests." He pushed his thick-rimmed spectacles further up his nose, magnifying his eyes and making them look weird. "May I ask where ye're from, for ye're no' locals, are ye?" A rare friendliness sparkled in his enlarged eyes. His wife hauled herself up and headed for the kitchen.

"We're from...Wyrm's Port." Everus indicated himself and Creeps. He had thought of lying but decided otherwise.

"And I'm from Ghavin's Keep," Carrie added.

"Travellers, eh?" Jubbly grinned before baaing like a sheep, drawing a confused look from his guests. It was clear that he was more than a little idiotic. He continued as though nothing had happened. "Well, that's enough pryin' fer the time bein'. Please, come on in, sit yerselves down an' make yerselves comfortable. Now, I don't have much in the way o' drink but I can always nip to the store an' get ye somethin', that's if it's still open. Someb'dy told me it's been shut fer years. Anyway..." He froze for a moment as though suddenly completely paralysed, prompting his guests to stare at him anew. Grinning, he returned to some semblance of normality. "Aye...ye can't beat the smell o' the corn on the thatch." He cleared his throat. "It was rainin', I remember...no, it were drinks, wasn't it? Yes, that's it...I was going to go to the store an' get some. Only problem is Old Thom's been tendin' to shut earlier and earlier this past year or so. Think he's still mournin' the loss o' his Barty. Knew that stupid..."

"*Will you shut up!?* I haven't a clue what you're talking about," snapped Everus.

"All right mister, keep yer hair on." Jubbly scratched some more.

"Right. So it's three rooms, aye? I take it ye'll want a meal o' some sort. How's about a nice bit o' pumpkin pie, straight out o' the oven? Drinks'll arrive shortly, says he hopefully. An' what about a bath? Does anybody need a..." He baaed once more. "A bath? Ye can't beat...did I say bleat? No! What ye need's a good steamin' bath at the end o' the day. Sayin' that, there's no hot water so it'll have to be a cold bath. It's all the same...except..."

"Without the steam?" guessed Everus. His lips curled in an unbidden smile as an image of Carrie stripping off in order to climb into a suds-filled bath flashed through his mind. What he would give to share one with her. "Couldn't you heat up some water...and then put it in the bath?"

Jubbly stood transfixed, his face reddening further as though his head were about to explode and shower them in jam-like brain bits. It looked as though he was choking to death. Eventually, he exhaled. "*Why!* That's it! You truly are a..."

"A what?"

Scratching at a troublesome louse within his vest, Jubbly stared at the raftered ceiling before turning to his guests and giving a fruity laugh. "I was goin' to say a...but I've forgotten the word. Never mind, it'll come to me. Anyway, I'd better go an' see how that woman o' mine's comin' on. So, if ye'll just talk amongst yerselves fer a while." He bowed before waddling off towards the kitchen, scratching his bum all the way.

"Uneducated piece of retarded rubbish," commented Everus, disapprovingly.

"Seems friendly enough. Though could be he's been hit around the head wi' a shovel too many times." Creeps took out his pipe and began lighting up.

"You're not going to smoke that shit in here, are you?"

"Well...I, thought I..." With a disgruntled curse, Creeps returned the pipe to his jacket pocket. "So what's happenin' 'ere? Are we gettin' any drinks or what?" Deprived of his smoke, his questions came out acerbically.

Jubbly suddenly reappeared, a cleaver in one hand and a dead rabbit in the other. "Ye two gents mentioned ye were from Wyrm's Port, did ye not?"

"That's correct," replied Everus. "Why?"

"Oh, it's just that we've got some other guests stayin' wi' us at the moment. I'm sure they said they were from Wyrm's Port. Said somethin' about how the city's in a bad way or somethin' like that. Behemoths, them big hairy buggers, have attacked it, I think they said."

"Really?"

Jubbly rocked back on his heels. "Mind ye, if ye've come from that way ye probably already know. So why am I tellin' ye?" Puzzled by his own questioning, he frowned and puckered his lips.

"Who are these guests of yours?"

"Fine gentlemen, they are. The very pillars of our community, now." He put the rabbit and the cleaver down.

"Where are they?"

"Why, they'll be up at old Bhub...baa...baal's Stronghold. Pickin' it clean they are."

"*Bhubbaal's Stronghold!?*"

Hands on hips, Jubbly stared disbelievingly at Everus. "The castle-thing up on the mountain. The one that overlooks the village. Surely ye must've seen it enterin' town?"

"So that's Bhubbaal's Stronghold. I figured it was just another grubban ruin."

"Nah! That ain't grubban. I could tell ye a tale or two about that place. Stories that'd make yer balls run fer cover." The ruddy-faced man shook his head. Trembling, he bleated like a lamb caught in a fence before calming down once more. "Oh, aye. The things that used to go on up there. Just ain't normal." He froze once more, his thick glasses sliding on a sheen of sweat from his nose, a mad, open-mouthed smile on his face.

Like his companions, Everus stared, confused.

Just as the spectacles were about to slide from Jubbly's face he came to, fastening them back in place. He turned his head to the ceiling and bleated again.

Everus leant forward. "You said that your guests were up there right now?"

"That's right." Jubbly puffed his chest out, filling himself with self-importance. "Ye see, they're adventurin' types. They've brought out a fair old haul, treasure an' stuff. Still, they must have some balls on 'em. Ye wouldn't get me goin' up there, gold or no gold." He looked at them pointedly. "*Sod that!*" he rasped, spittle flying everywhere. Fortunately for him, none of it struck Everus, although Creeps got an eyeful.

"So...are you saying that Bhubbaal's no more?" Everus was finding this hard to take. All the time he had been under the impression, especially after all he had been told by Mhoon, that the Hyadean warlord was still alive – or at least, considering his semi-demonic nature, still in control.

"Aye. Old Bhub...baa...baal's been dead fer a couple o' years. He were...how would ye say it? No' very popular. His laws may've been a touch on the harsh side, an' I've heard that some folk lost their daughters to him, but by an' large he wasn't that bad. Not to us at any rate. Providin' we paid our taxes, he let us get on wi' things. Though I can't say as I would've liked to get on his wrong side. Heard tell that he could get quite ruthless...torturin' folk, the odd execution, ye know the score. Anyhow, there's been some mighty weird things happenin' up there o' late. Bangs an' flashes, ye name it. One night..."

"How long have these guests of yours been up there?" interrupted Carrie.

Their mad informant removed something unpleasant from a nostril, examined it to make sure it was not living and flicked it away. "Since this mornin'. Why?"

"No. Let me rephrase my question. How long have they been *here*, in town?"

"Oh, hard to say. Quite some time." Jubbly looked as though he was about to play 'statues' once more, but overcame the urge. "Kooper, he's the leader, I think. He's the one that does the most talkin' an' eatin' an' drinkin'. Nice enough bloke but not someone I'd want to cross, if ye get ma meanin'. Ex-army man I believe he said." That far off gaze returned to his eyes. "Her name was Eunice an' she wore these big, bright orange knickers..." He shook his head fiercely, shaking away his fleeting madness. "Kooper, aye. He's built like one o' those old ox-wrestlers we used to get out this way when the fair came to town. When he an' his men first arrived, I'd say there were about forty o' 'em. All good lads. But traps an' things have whittled their numbers down a bit. Still, I guess they know the risks they're takin'." He was about to divulge some more when the fat-arsed maid came back in, whatever chores she had been assigned now either done or abandoned. He excused himself, retrieved his dead rabbit and cleaver and went back into the kitchen, signalling for her to follow.

"I bloody hope she's no' the cook." Creeps was still tetchily missing his smoke. Obviously, he could have gone outside, but it was far too cold an evening, besides he was famished and supper was hopefully imminent.

"So now what do we do?" Everus looked at the two seated nearby, noting the disgruntled look of the thief and the somewhat pensive gaze of Carrie. She seemed to have drawn in on herself, no doubt as uncertain as he about how to proceed. He had been geared up for a confrontation with Bhubbaal, determined at least in some way to avenge Mhoon, so that now, after learning that Bhubbaal was no more, he had to think through things anew. Whatever happened, there remained the final piece of the hand. He had to hope that it was still obtainable. Everything now rested on finding several lumps of very old bone. "Any suggestions?"

"Well, it could be that these buggers have 'em," reasoned Creeps. "In which case all we have to do is find out what they've done wi' 'em. I mean, they've either sold 'em on...or, they've got 'em stashed somewhere. In which case all we have to do is nick 'em off 'em. For all we know, they might be lyin' in a box in one o' their rooms upstairs."

"It's not upstairs," muttered Carrie, that far away look still in her eyes. "The pieces of the hand we've collected so far carry a characteristic magical imprint. They leave a faint trace detectable by anyone attuned to magic."

Everus was giving this some thought when Jubbly and his wife came out of the kitchen carrying plates and cutlery, bowls of food and wooden mugs. When supper had been set before him, he tackled it eagerly, wolfing down the very undercooked rabbit, the stew and the bread. Such was his hunger, that it was only as he devoured the last of the bread that he remembered the possibility of being drugged, by which time it was obviously far too late. The table at which he sat with his equally famished companions was next to one of the windows that looked out onto the street and as he pushed his plate back he saw and heard the sounds of a commotion outside. He gazed out as some riders came to a halt just outside, dismounted and headed for the entrance.

"Aye, aye," muttered Creeps, turning in his seat as the door opened.

Everus scrutinised the dozen or so men who entered, noticing the swords that hung at their hips, the arrogant assurance in the way they moved and the harsh, coarse laughter that followed them. He had seen their kind many times before, too many not to recognise them immediately – mercenaries and sell-swords; young, brash, violent men who would kill and pillage unquestioningly so long as they were paid. There were probably wanted posters for every man there, now burnt or peeling in whatever remained of the old imperial capital.

Creeps gawped at them, not liking the look of any of them, or the situation for that matter, for it would be a squeeze to get out of the nearby window and they currently blocked the escape route to the door. Things could get nasty very quickly, and knowing Everus' temperament and unique brand of diplomacy, they probably would.

One of them walked over and drew up a chair next to Carrie. He was lean and unshaven, thin faced and sallow with a wolfish look to his grey eyes. A scar ran down one cheek, terminating beneath his jaw line. A dull chain mail shirt could be seen under the frayed and ripped leather jerkin he wore.

Everus watched the man coldly. "I don't remember inviting you to join us."

"A sarky one, eh? Well listen 'ere, cocker. Ye're sittin' in ma chair." 'Scarface' looked at Everus, trying to stare him down. He obviously saw something in those piercing green eyes that he did not like, for he could not hold Everus' stare for long.

"Well, what've we got here?" Another man strode forward, cracking his knuckles. He was tall and well built, grim-faced, bull-necked and toned. He was bearded and his hair was cropped short in the military style. Like some of the others, on brazen display, he wore a chain mail shirt and a weather-beaten surcoat bearing the livery of the Wyrm's Port cavalry, clearly no longer considering it a risk to be caught away from his post now that the city was in ruins. He reeked of menace.

Jubbly tried to intervene. "No trouble, Kooper. They only arrived..."

"Shut up, you old fart." With a snarl, Kooper pushed the tavern owner away by the face. "All right, sweetheart?" In a sudden move, he gripped Carrie by the hair, tilted her head and fiercely kissed her full on the lips.

"*Bastard!*" snarled Everus, wishing for a moment that he was once again imbued with Xethorn's powers, so that he could butcher the man before him and his cohort.

Roughly, Kooper pushed the sorceress back and glared at Everus, a madness in his eyes. "*What did you call me?*"

Everus' eyes narrowed, taking in the measure of them all, reckoning how many he could cut down before he himself fell to their blows.

"I asked you a question, 'Tit-Face'."

"He called ye a bastard, sarge. That's what he said," piped up one of the others. He was no more than a teenager, no doubt an expendable recruit, his face bespotted, his hair lank. "Ye're no' goin' to stand for that, are ye, sarge?"

"I'm sure I've seen these two before," remarked another, picking his nose.

"Now I don't know what kind o' people you're used to dealin' with, pal, but you've just gone an' made a big mistake," Kooper sneered. "You see, I was all set to be nice an' friendly...then you have to go an' say somethin' that pisses me off. You see I *am* a bastard. The meanest son o' a whore you'll ever clap eyes on...an', I *mean* the meanest. Now why'd you have to go an' tell everyone?" He turned to his men. "Anybody got any ideas?"

"Maybe he's nuts, sarge? Looks a bit, I don't know...a bit weird. An' just look at the scruff wi' him." The man who was talking, a fat-faced youth with a black eye, and whose extent of battlefield experience had probably been solely spectatorial, cuffed Creeps. "I mean, who in their right mind would hang about wi' a freak like this? I mean, he looks an' smells as though he's just crawled out o' a grave."

"A latrine, more likely," called out a voice from the crowd; a concealed face within the undisciplined ranks, his courage bolstered by the security ensured by superior numbers – his bravery the stuff of legend. Little did he know that he would be lying outside headless in the not too distant future.

Creeps muttered darkly through clenched teeth.

"Be sure an' wash yer hands, Rychie," said another.

"Aye, you're a braver man than me, touchin' him," said Kooper, winning a round of cruel laughter.

"I called you a bastard."

A hush fell; Everus' five words silencing the throng.

The tension in the room grew, as though in preparation for a thunderstorm.

"He *is* mad," a voice muttered.

"You're goin' to regret that!" said Kooper. "*Nobody* calls *me* a bastard!" With a snarl, he drew his sword and lunged with it across the table.

Everus had anticipated such a reaction. He sprang from his chair. Leaping to his right, his sword flashed from its scabbard. Darting forwards, he cut down two of Kooper's men before they could even draw their weapons, let alone move to avoid his blade. Kicking a chair over, he managed to fend off one of the faster ones from getting an attack in.

A chorus of angry shouts went up and chaos erupted. Swords leapt from sheaths as more chairs were overturned. A window smashed and Everus caught a glimpse of someone, probably Creeps, crashing through it – whether he had been assisted in his defenestration, he could not tell. Somewhere in the thick of the melee he caught a glimpse of Carrie. It seemed as though she was being restrained. Then Everus was rushing to the back of the room, pushing Jubbly out of the way, a trio of screaming swordsmen after his blood.

Foul-mouthed voices cried out, pursuing Everus up a flight of rickety steps to the floor above. He smashed a door open and ran along a corridor, from which over a dozen other doors led to the guest rooms. Kicking the third door on his left open, he rushed into a small room. It was poorly furnished and clearly belonged to one of his pursuers, for he saw a suit of badly cared for chain mail draped over a chair, in addition to a few weapons scattered here and there. A shield bearing the Wyrm's Port herald – the black rampant wyrm on a pale blue background – and a large unloaded crossbow rested on the unmade bed, beneath which, he could see a couple of bulging sacks, no doubt containing a share of the plunder from the ransacked Bhubbaal's Stronghold.

Everus slammed the door shut.

"Come on out, ye chicken-livered piece o' shit!" Outside, someone kicked the door.

Blood racing, Everus held the door firm.

"He's in 'ere, sarge!"

The door was kicked again.

Everus could hear movement outside. It sounded as though at least five of them had gathered there.

Someone rapped the door. "Are you in there, girlie?" It was Kooper.

Everus kept quiet, his back to the door, his eyes searching for anything of use. Trapped, his options were limited. He could either fight it out in the doorway, hoping to chop them down one by one; he could take his chances with the window, or he could try and negotiate. The fact that most of these men were trained soldiers, and not the usual rabble he could slaughter with comparative ease, rendered his first option all the more difficult, and even if he were to survive the drop from the window – which he was sure he would – odds were that more of the gang would be waiting outside. About the only point in his favour was that he was pretty sure these men *were* men, not wererats or rakshasas.

The door was battered again.

"I think he's crappin' his pants, sarge," said a voice from outside.

"Better not be! That's ma bloody room he's in," replied another.

Kooper thumped the door. "Oi, chicken-shit! Listen up! I'm goin' to count to ten, then I'm goin' to have this bloody door hacked down. You're outnumbered twenty to one and your little pal's done a runner. I'm givin' you this chance to sheath your weapon, after all, I'm sure we don't want anyone else to get hurt. So, you've got a ten count to disarm and put your hands on your head where I can see 'em. One...Two...Three..."

Everus' eyes darted about the room.

"Four...Five...Six..." It was like the build-up to an execution without the obligatory drum roll. "Seven...Eight..."

"All right. You win." Everus stepped away from the door, returning his sword to its scabbard.

"Nine. Ten." Kooper kicked the door open. Grinning triumphantly and, noting that Everus had sheathed his sword and now had both hands on his head, he stepped forward. "All right lads, time for me to show this piece o' shit how we..."

Everus lashed out with a kick which caught Kooper just below the right knee. He followed up with a punch that caught the now no longer grinning sergeant on the chest, forcing him back against a wall and causing him to drop his sword.

"Fancy a bit o' the old knuckle-fightin' do you!?" shouted Kooper. "Come on then! Let's have it!" He uttered a loud growl, almost like that of a cornered bear. Everus punched again but this time Kooper was ready for him and rode the blow, reducing its power even as he swung to one side, then feinted to the other and brought up his knee. Had Everus not been turning at that moment, the vicious blow might have finished the fight there and then. As it was, the bullish sergeant's knee caught him on the right thigh, sending a stab of agony lancing along his leg. Sucking in a deep breath, he forced the sensation of pain away. For a moment, his leg gave under his weight, pitching him forward as he was thrown off balance.

"Go on sarge! Kick him in the bollocks!" cried one of the soldiers in the doorway, obviously content to watch the fight unfold, although Everus was certain that if he started to gain the upper hand then a whole horde of them would pile in and he would find himself battling half a dozen.

Kooper's mad grin had returned. Everus saw his arm go back as he made to bring over a haymaker. He ducked and blocked the attack, biting back the agony in his body. Kooper's rock-hard fist caught him a glancing blow on the side of his head. Thunder roared through his brain. Lights flashed in front of his eyes as he fell back, stumbling over a chair. Somehow he shook his attacker loose, but by that time the blows were coming at him thick and fast, hammer-fisted smacks driving in, one after another.

There was pain in Everus' chest and it felt as if all of his ribs had been badly bruised, every breath he now took painful. Confident of the ultimate outcome of the brawl, Kooper moved in, for he could hear the rasping breath as it gushed in and out of his opponent's lungs, knew from the laboured breathing that some of his earlier blows had hurt.

"Go on sarge! *Hit him! Kick shit outta him! That's it! Kick his head in!*" screamed an over-excited nutter from the doorway, as at least four clamoured to see in; their one-time military training now devoted to violence and thuggery – hooligans to a man, and damn proud of it.

Kooper tried to hang on to Everus' right arm, for that was still dishing out the punches. Bringing his weight to bear, striving to pull down on it with all his strength, to throw Everus off balance again so that he might thrust him back against the wall, he grasped and cursed. Chopping down with the flat of his right hand against the man's neck, Everus felt him reel away. With any normal man, that blow would have snapped the neck bones like a rotten twig, but Kooper merely grunted, hung on for a moment to clear the fog from his mind, then lowered his head with a sudden motion and brought it up with a crack against Everus' chin.

Everus tried to pull back, but the wall was in the way. Dazed, he fell to one side, his left shoulder catching the edge of a table, bringing it down with him, a chair falling on top of him. Egged on by the cries of bloodlust from his men, Kooper attacked, this time stirruped boots first, jumping out of the air. Savagely, Everus twisted his body, getting himself out of the way of those booted heels with the sharp-edged spur rowels that came streaking for his throat. There was no mistaking his attacker's intentions now – he meant to kill. That killing fever Everus knew so well could be seen in Kooper's narrowed, deep-set eyes as he sprang feet first. But Everus' head was not there when Kooper landed, and the jar of the impact shuddered through his legs and up into his body. He let out a bellow, a huge shout compounded of pain and anger.

By the time Kooper had regained his balance, Everus was on his feet. His head had cleared during that brief respite and he now saw his attacker without the vague red mist that had danced in front of his eyes a few moments before. Kooper snarled something Everus failed to catch, although the meaning was fairly clear. Still, so far he had made no attempt to reach for his weapon or call for help, wanting to beat Everus with his bare hands, well aware that the eyes of his 'lads' were on him, weighing him and judging him on his performance. His reputation was built on felled enemies, the allegiance of his men, based on raw strength and bullying. For those reasons, he had to finish Everus now, knowing that if he failed, it could mean the end of his authority in the eyes of his underlings.

The charge came as Everus had expected, arms outstretched, curling a little, fingers stiff, as if he already had his foe in the circle of his arms, crushing him in a bear hug. But Everus had no intention of being caught in that unloving embrace. He leapt to one side and sent in two solid punches, both landing hard and firm on a bearded chin, Kooper's forward momentum adding weight and force to them. The sergeant's head danced loosely on his shoulders and his knees began to buckle, took a surge of strength, then buckled again as a third jab from Everus burst his nose, causing it to blossom like a red flower.

With a groan, Kooper slumped and fell on his backside.

Despite his aches, Everus was quick. Before any of the men in the doorway could react, he snatched up the crossbow that had been disturbed and now lay nearby, and violently forced the bow part of it over the bleeding sergeant's head, pulling back the string and locking it all in one motion.

Kooper twisted, trying to escape, but his actions were feeble, half-hearted, the punches he had received making him unfocused and weak.

One of the men in the doorway, a lanky youth with a cheeky face and more spots than could be picked in a day, moved in, his sword held back.

"Drop the sword or you'll be picking your friend's head up off the carpet." Everus cranked the crossbow, increasing the firing string's tension. Now, with just a squeeze of the trigger, he could severely wound the still stunned man he held hostage. Although he doubted whether his improvised guillotine would sever the head, it would be fun to try, and if the threat alone got him out, what was the difference?

"The bastard's got sarge!" someone shouted.

"*Back off!*" Everus hauled Kooper to his feet by his hair as though he were nothing more than a bleeding sack of potatoes. He swung him around, now content that by firing the crossbow he would at the very least slice the man's throat; it would certainly be a messy and ignominious way to die.

"Let's get him!" cried a soldier, tentatively making his way in.

"*Do you think I'm kidding?*" threatened Everus. Only the dumbest would think that he was. Staggering forward, the sergeant held before him, he gave the approaching man an icy stare.

Kooper mumbled something, his fingers reaching for the string that now bit into the flesh just above where his chain mail collar ended.

"Tell your men to retreat," Everus ordered, savagely pulling his hostage upright once more. "And put your hands by your side or I'll kill you here and now. Even if I don't take your head off, from this distance the blood from your cut throat will spray those in the doorway."

Waving a hand, Kooper signalled for his men to back away. Everus then half-dragged, half-pushed him forward, guiding him out into the corridor. Carefully, he forced him down the stairs and into the main eating hall, constantly on the look-out for any movement from his men. They kept their distance. Now that Kooper was emerging from his daze, he was also alert to any sudden movements, once having to pull the crossbow taut to prevent his prisoner from wriggling free.

"Keep your distance!" shouted Everus, forcing the men who waited downstairs clear. As soon as they saw their sergeant held hostage, they did just that, for, as Everus had already gathered, most of them were young and relatively inexperienced, unused to dealing with difficult circumstances; ripe for taking orders but useless at making any of their own. He looked about, failing to see any of his companions. "Where's the woman?" he shouted.

No one answered.

"Tell me or I'll finish him here!"

It was at that moment that Kooper twisted and struck out with an elbow, his actions taking Everus by surprise. Lunging to one side, the blood-crazed sergeant managed to pull free from Everus' hold even as he pulled back the trigger. The twanging string cut deep into Kooper's face, catching him just below the nose, slicing through his cheeks like a cheese-cutter. Blood squirted as he screamed and fell.

"Get him!" shouted one of the many.

Everus darted for the door. Dodging one sword swing, he leapt outside, the chill night air a welcome reprieve from the uncomfortable heat of indoors. Three, then five, then ten men came clamouring out behind him, pushing their way through the narrow bottleneck. The first out did not have long to regret his actions for, no sooner had he fought his way to the front of the pack, than Everus, upon hearing the closing footsteps, drew his sword, spun around and beheaded him. It all happened in an instant. Like a headless chicken, the man's momentum carried him on, the legs still operating despite the loss of the brain. With blood spraying from the neck, the decapitated form reeled drunkenly before stumbling back towards the crowd of screaming men. Horrified, they pulled back as the body collapsed amongst them.

Everus did not wait to assess their reaction. Into the dark he ran, knowing that, with their sergeant wounded, the group was now by and large leaderless – acephalous – like the man he had just killed. In some ways that made them worse, for they were now unpredictable, their actions no longer controlled. Just what that would mean for Carrie, if she was still alive, he dreaded to think. He rushed behind one of the smaller log cabins, watching from the darkness as the gang massed outside, no doubt wondering what they should do. It was then, however, that he saw Kooper come out, a hand clamped to his bleeding face.

A hurled pebble bounced off the log wall close to his head.

Turning, Everus saw Creeps beckoning him from a doorway some distance behind him. It was the man with the dog-thing's house, the one they had seen earlier that evening. Silently sprinting over, Everus rushed inside, the thief shutting the door quietly behind him.

"Quick! Down 'ere." The old man with the weathered face held the lid of a trapdoor open.

Suspicion immediately flashed through Everus' mind. He turned to Creeps. "Where is she?" he asked.

"I think they took her. She didn't escape wi' me, that's for sure."

Angry shouts could be heard outside. Seeing as Kooper was back in charge, it was only a matter of time before the mob would regroup, remobilise and set about a systematic search of the hamlet. From the sounds of it, the crazy sergeant was already organising his men into search parties.

"Ye'd better be quick!" cried the old man. "They're bound to scour every house till they find ye. An' when they do, they'll kill ye."

"If this is a trick..." began Everus, his eyes flicking between the stranger's face and the cellar opening.

"No trick. I hate those bastards as..."

"Hurry it up," hissed Creeps, peering through the blinds. "They're gettin' nearer."

Everus gave the thief a nod and indicated for him to descend first. The steps were old and dust-covered and the boards creaked as they went down. They had just reached the dry cellar floor, when the trapdoor closed, plunging them into semi-darkness. A faint light filtered through the narrow gaps in the trapdoor lid. Then a rug, or something similar was thrown over it, making the darkness complete.

For a moment, neither said a word.

The air in the cellar was stale, reminding Everus of the time spent under the ziggurat of Möthcra'aba. He was about to speak, when he heard the front door above his head being forcibly opened. Angry, questioning voices called out, demanding to know if the owner had seen anything suspicious, or whether he knew the whereabouts of two fugitives. From up above, he heard the old man's proclamation of ignorance, following which there came the noisy tramping of feet as three soldiers, maybe more, had a look around, the sounds of their destructive searching accompanied by the frenetic barking of the snaggle-toothed ratter.

"Craiglin, I told ye. If that thing ever barked at me again..."

"He...he didn't mean..."

Chop.

The yapping ceased.

"Heartless bastards!" muttered Creeps, his sentiments on this occasion shared by Everus.

The door slammed shut as the soldiers left. For a moment there was silence. Then the covering was pulled clear and the old man, his eyes watering, raised the trapdoor.

Everus climbed out.

"They...!" mumbled Craiglin. With a shaking hand, he pointed to where his pet lay, blood streaming from a fatal sword wound. Arthritically, he stumbled over to the corpse and crouched down, sobbing.

"Well, that's reason enough to kill 'em if nothin' else is," said Creeps, venomously. "*Bastards!*"

Everus moved over to the window and peered through the slatted blinds. Torch and lantern carrying figures moved about, going from door to door, determined to avenge their fallen. The pursuers had divided into groups of three and, as Everus tried to ascertain how many were out there, one such group walked straight past and entered a building opposite.

"What're ye goin' to do?" asked Craiglin.

"Why don't you get back to mourning your dog!?" snapped Everus, his thoughts clouded by the hatred that was welling within him. The thought of Carrie being abused and maltreated by Kooper and his men, and knowing that, certainly as things stood, he was powerless to intervene, filled him with rage. He would slay them. He would slay them all.

"But what *are* we goin' to do?" pressed Creeps.

"Well, first off, we have to find Carrie. Find out where she's being held." History was repeating itself. This was beginning to be like their wererat encounter all over again.

"*Carrie?*" Craiglin rose to his feet. His hands were bloody, his face tear-streaked. "*Carrie Orlandis?*"

Everus turned away from the window and stared at the old man.

"Carrie Orlandis?" Craiglin repeated.

"Yes...you know her?"

"I don't know *her*...but I know the name. Kooper's been waiting here for her arrival."

"*What?* What do you mean?" Everus stood rigid, mouth agape, uncertain as to what he was hearing, and its significance. Woodenly, he stumbled over to the old man and gripped him by the shoulders. "What? What are you telling me?"

Craiglin looked at Creeps for support, trying to gauge the risk involved in answering; clearly wondering whether this seemingly dangerous and volatile man standing before him would react violently to an answer he did not want to hear. "Look, all I know is that Kooper, the leader of those men that're after ye, has been waiting for this woman. He an' his men have been doing some pretty strange things up at Bhubbaal's Stronghold of late. There've been weird lights in the sky an' all manner of sounds comin' from up there. It's as though old Bhubbaal himself has returned."

Everus kept his grip, for a moment it tightened, forcing a grimace from Craiglin. Then, confused, he let go, stumbled to one side and sank in a dirty chair that was covered in dog hairs.

Angry voices shouted outside.

"*Carrie?* Are you sure?" Everus sat forward, an intensity back in his eyes.

Craiglin nodded. "When they first arrived, I was appointed by the elder o' the village to find out what I could...a spy, if ye like. Anyway, he soon disappeared, murdered no doubt, along wi' several other villagers. Shortly after that, Kooper sets himself up as the new mayor an' he and his men practically take over. They've been runnin' the place since. Killin' any who oppose them. I've kept ma head down and ma ear to the ground, an' I can tell ye that Kooper's been waitin' on this woman for some time now."

Everus turned to Creeps.

"Well, summat stinks 'ere, doesn't it?" The thief gave his head a quick scratch, removing the last pieces of glass from the window he had escaped through from his scalp. "There's summat I can't quite put ma finger on. Part o' me's wonderin' if, well, whether we've been set up."

"*By Carrie?* Why would she...?" Everus leapt to his feet. "*The casket!* Have you still got the casket?"

Reaching into his pack, Creeps pulled out the small brass box. "Aye, here we..." He opened it and found it empty.

CHAPTER TWENTY-THREE

By lamplight, in the dry cellar of Craiglin's house, Everus and Creeps hid and plotted. The table they sat at was old and musty and neither had managed to eat much of the rather unappetising food their host had provided, far too occupied with their current concerns.

Creeps lit up, Everus no longer caring. "So, now what do we do?"

Everus shook his head, still struggling to come to terms with all that he had been told and what he had discovered. "I don't know." He reached for his mug of water and took a sip. He still ached from the punch-up with Kooper, but fortunately he had not sustained any serious injury.

"Well, the way I see it, we've got to get those bones back. That dirty tart must've nicked 'em straight out o' ma pack when I was sleepin'. The question is...how do we do it?"

"How many men do you think Kooper's got? A dozen? Fifteen?"

"More than that, I'd o' thought. I think at least a dozen o' 'em were still outside, seein' to their horses when the fight broke out. Thirty or more, all in."

"Hardly an even fight, is it?" mused Everus.

"Is it ever?"

"Guess not." Morosely, Everus stared into his tankard, lost in his own thoughts. He was still trying to come to terms with Carrie's apparent treachery. No matter how hard he tried, it was proving nigh on impossible to work out just *why* she had done what she had, and for that fact alone he was still desperately seeking an alternative explanation. Could it be that Craiglin had been confused and that it was just unlucky and highly coincidental that the sorceress had been abducted? What did she seek to gain by switching her allegiance? Could it be that he and Creeps had not been fast enough and she was now hoping that by joining Kooper and his men she could get the bones and ride back to Ghavin's Keep in time to save it from Xethorn's wrath? There was of course a darker speculation, and that was that she was acting for Xethorn. But even that failed to make much sense for, as far as he was aware, Xethorn had never had any female worshippers. Not human ones anyway.

"We might be able to rally some o' the locals. That old boy upstairs..."

"Oh yes, that's the answer. Me, you and a dozen old men with sticks take on thirty or so highly trained, well-armed, ex-members of the Wyrm's Port cavalry." Everus tutted his disapproval at the thief's suggestion. "These folk are cowed. They'll never stand up to that crazy sergeant and his men...and even if they did, how long do you think they'd last? No, we've got to find out what they're up to. I've a feeling that this trap has been well planned, that Carrie sought to rendezvous with these men from the beginning. This has all been arranged."

"What, in order to get the last bit o' the hand?"

"Exactly. You know, the more I'm thinking about this, the more I'm beginning to believe that she *has* been working for Xethorn. All that bullshit about being an agent for the archmage in Ghavin's Keep was probably no more than a front. She does what you did back in Wyrm's Port when I went after the three Xethornite wards. She follows me around, maintains a veneer of camaraderie, then guess what? She lands us in the shit at the most opportune moment. Not only that, but now she is only one step away from gaining the complete hand. Guess I should've just shagged her and kicked her out the door when we first met. *Bitch!*" Everus' face hardened in anger. "I bet Xethorn must be laughing His arse off right now."

Creeps took his pipe from his mouth. "That's if she's workin' for Him."

"Who else is there? Uhu'giaggoth?"

"Maybe," replied Creeps with a nod of the head.

"No. Why would one of The Daemon God's worshippers seek the hand...?" Everus' expression changed as a sudden, worrying thought entered his troubled mind. "Unless...unless, of course, to provide Xethorn with the *means* of completing His summoning. Perhaps that's how it's been all along. The bitch has set out to return the hand to Xethorn, presenting Him with the..." He thumped a clenched fist against the wall. "*Shit!* The crazy sow is going to start another cataclysm! We've got to stop her."

"Well if it's all right wi' ye, I think I'll wait 'ere if ye want to have a look around. No point in both o' us sneakin' about. Besides, I'm aching all over."

An uncomfortable silence passed until, glaring angrily at the thief, Everus rose from his chair. "All right. I'll do it myself. I'll do it *all* myself." Without looking back, he climbed up the stairs and slipped out of Craiglin's house, quietly disappearing into the shadows. His mind was confused, filled with countless disturbing possibilities that became increasingly darker the more he thought about them. What was up with Creeps? Was he now part of the problem? Was Carrie to blame or was there something even stranger going on? Was the old man lying? He turned his paranoid thoughts to staying alive, now aware that every step was fraught with danger. The enemies in his head could wait till he had dealt with those outside.

Voices called out in the dark.

Far off, a door slammed loudly.

Stealthily, Everus crossed the street, caught a glimpse of one of Kooper's units heading in his direction, and pressed himself tightly against the front of a house, holding himself perfectly still, blending with the shadows. He drew his sword as three men walked past him, their own swords hanging from their belts, one of their number munching on an apple. Sucking air down into his lungs, he could feel the thudding of his heart against his ribs. He thrust the sword back, deep into leather. He waited until they had gone before skulking around the back of the house and making his way towards Billy Jubbly's inn.

The snorting of horses was the first thing that he detected. Everus dashed to the rear of the nearest lodge and crouched down, eyes peering like a panther on the hunt. From around the side of Jubbly's place a handful of riders emerged, others saddling up, preparing to ride out. Whilst he was watching, assessing their numbers, his heart jumped as he saw Carrie leave the inn, Kooper in tow. His eyes narrowed and for a moment, he considered throwing all caution to the wind and just dashing out, seeing if he could catch them unawares and get to within striking distance of either before the mob reacted. On seeing the loaded crossbows held by some of the riders, he had to accept the futility of such a plan; no longer having any faith in The High Three's protection. No longer having any faith in anything.

Everus watched as Kooper waved frantically to his men,

signalling for them to hurry up and get his horse. Moments later, a large black stallion was brought forth and the vicious sergeant was helped up. Then Kooper led the group of twenty or so riders, Carrie included, out of Borgrim's End.

✝ ✝ ✝

Following the directions given to them by Craiglin, Everus and Creeps sneaked out of Borgrim's End. Evading what patrols Kooper had left behind, they headed for the wooded trail that the old man had spoken of, the one that led towards Bhubbaal's Stronghold. It was still dark, but a gradual lightening in the sky – a change from black to deep grey – signalled the beginning of dawn, its light barely enough for the two to make out where they were going, neither wishing to draw attention to themselves by lighting a lantern.

The overgrown path was easy to find but hard to navigate, for it was blocked by tangled brambles, making the going both difficult and painful. It was also proving to be a noisy business and that, more than the fact that it was slow going, caused Everus the greater concern, for he was well aware that stealth was going to be crucial if he wanted to take out Kooper and his men.

Neither of them spoke as they struggled on, shaking away their silent cursing as the thorns tore and snagged.

Eventually they fought their way free of the dense thicket, emerging at a part of the trail that was bisected by a rocky slope – a scar left by an ancient landslide. One slip here and one would risk tumbling to the bottom of the valley, dislodging rocks all the way – thus if the fall did not kill, getting buried in an avalanche of earth and boulders probably would.

Creeps took a look, shuddered briefly, then squared his thin shoulders and turned to Everus. "I'll go first."

"As you wish."

Gingerly, the thief crouched down and reached for the nearest protruding rock. Content that it would bear his weight, he shifted position and edged out, feet searching for a hold. He found one, dug his toes deep in a nest of knotted tree roots and started his climb. For a three hundred and something year old, he was amazingly sprightly, his scrawny body utilised to full effect, making the difficult climb look easy. Without dislodging a single rock from the craggy surface, he made it up and across to the other side.

519

"How is it?" asked Everus, trying to form a mental map of the route the thief had taken in his mind, working on the assumption that if the handholds used by Creeps were safe then that would be the way he would go.

"Piece o' piss. Just make sure o' yer grips afore ye put any weight on 'em. An' watch that big root stickin' out there. It gave a little."

Everus nodded, acknowledging the warning. He started out, reaching for a cluster of rocks, then shuffling forward with his feet, seeking purchase. Slowly, he shifted his weight, earth crumbling and drizzling away under him. Edging out further, he was now halfway across, and from here he had to climb, his progress so far being limited to going sideways. With his right hand, he reached for a rock, inadvertently pulled it free, pressed his body tight against the slope and searched for another hand-hold. Up he clambered, dislodging a few more rocks. It was then that his right foot slipped from its hold and he had to make a lunge for the root that he been warned about. The ropy length slithered out like a snake in his grip, causing him to slide, his body scraping on the steep, rocky surface.

The root became taut, threatened to snap and then slid out further.

Everus held on and gritted his teeth, his heart racing, aware that if he let go or if the root were to snap then he would slide to his death. With a grunt, he started to pull himself up, hoping that the root would hold his weight. Pushing himself forward with his knees, he scrambled to another overhang, managed to make his way around it and then up another part of the slope. By the time he got to the other side, his legs and hands were chafed and covered in dirt. The knuckles on his right hand were bleeding where he had scraped them.

"Ye made a meal o' that," commented Creeps, lending a helping hand.

Grasping the offered hand, Everus pulled himself to his feet. Ignoring the comment, he brushed the dirt from his coat and trousers and looked to where the path seemed to continue. "Right. Where's this lead?"

"Trail goes on through 'ere. There's more scrub an' brambles an' then it appears to head straight for that cliff face. There's part o' a ruined wall or summat at the top, probably a part o' that castle-thing. I'm hopin' that the path makes its way around, otherwise we might have to climb again."

"Let's go." Everus set off.

They pushed their way through the last stretch of bramble and soon found themselves in a clearing. Before them, the path went up at an angle, ran parallel to the treacherous slope, then turned to the left, weaving its way through a patch of large boulders. Pulling themselves up this second slope was far easier, the protruding root hand-holds sturdier, the incline less acute. Soon they were at the top. Without resting, well aware that Carrie and her new-found 'friends' were probably already at the stronghold, they trekked on.

The path soon joined an ancient road.

It was wooded and dark, the nascent daylight feebly starting to slice its way through the clouds, bringing with it little more than a grey gloom to the mountainside. It was now virtually impossible to tell if the trail they had followed had once cut across the road or not. The side opposite to where they stood, where logically the path would have been, was blocked by a cruel-looking barrier of hawthorn-like bush. To their immediate left, the overhanging canopy of the forest gave the road the appearance of a tunnel opening, the entrance verdant and brooding. To their right, the road curved around an up-thrust of rock and vanished from sight. Despite the fact that neither of them had much experience in tracking, it was plain to see that the road had been churned up by the passage of heavy horses.

Creeps took a couple of deep breaths, the exertion of the last little climb taking its toll.

"Ready?" Everus turned, not waiting on an answer, and set off, the thief jogging along behind. As he entered the wooded tunnel, the atmosphere became close and threatening. An unwelcome tingle ran down his spine like melting ice, as the memory of the schrappingbäyer – the orphan's spectre – flashed in his mind. Swallowing dryly, he spun round, that uneasy feeling of being watched, creeping uncomfortably through him. He was sure he would glance back and catch sight of something fleeting dart behind a tree, or that he would look straight up at some grinning evil perched high up on a branch, its smile a mass of fanged teeth.

With each step, things seemed to blur into existence all around him and whether it was due to the constricting darkness or the dark presence of these woods, he found it hard to shake off the terrifying images. Terrifying visions struck at him without remorse; his mother being torn to pieces by a gaggle of evil-eyed children; Klattermorch, chewing at his own grisly innards; Uncle Tarby, the hideous dummy from a Wyrm's Port cabaret act staggering out of the dark, a coffin on its back, and finally a pseudo-memory of himself hacking his way through a temple filled with screaming cultists – only now they were not demonic worshippers but students at the Wyrm's Port Academy.

Had this happened?

Ethereal, black tentacled things seemed to swim and ooze before his eyes.

Tormented and oblivious to how Creeps was faring, Everus staggered on, the images now warping and melding in front of him as he stubbornly tried to escape the cursed wood. He tripped, the reality of the pain somehow enabling him to temporarily blot out the horrifying illusions, to force the images from his mind. He pushed himself to his feet and grabbed the thief, who seemed to be trapped within his own nightmare experiences.

An evil wind gusted through the trees, bringing with it the first wisps of a purple mist.

Together, the two of them staggered on.

Half-dragging Creeps, Everus forged on, his goal the faint light of day, barely visible at the end of the wooded tunnel. "Come on! We've got to get out of here!" He felt sick but could feel the dream-haunts and the nightmare-wraiths weakening with each step they took towards the light.

Creeps stumbled against a tree and threw up, strands running from his nose and mouth. He heaved and vomited a second time.

"We're nearly out." Everus waited for the thief to regain some form of composure before jogging towards the exit of the hoary grove. There he waited for the thief to catch up. "I think we're safe now. It seems as though the daylight's chased them away. Either that, or whatever they were are confined to in there." He pointed into the shadowy, gnarly maw they had just exited. "Whatever the case, we should get going. Come on. Let's go." He was becoming increasingly concerned that, by the time they reached the five towers, Carrie and her minions would be long gone, the complete Cyrvilian relic now in her possession.

The road before them continued its ascent, the woods now thinning away completely, this side of the mountain more open. From here on, they would have to rely on the hope that none of Kooper's men had been assigned lookout duties.

They continued for some time, the encroaching grey dawn

enabling them to discern more of the rugged landscape. The road they were following degenerated, becoming little more than a mountain path, which wound its way around the large, sharp boulders that lay in a deep ravine, the cliffs on either side riddled with dark, grilled openings which led to subterranean dungeons and places no sane person would ever consider exploring. Then, turning around a large mountainous crag, they saw the towering ruins of Bhubbaal's Stronghold rearing high above them.

As Everus had first seen when he had exited the grubban rift-city, the foul stronghold was constructed to resemble a giant hand. Whether such a design was purely coincidental, he did not know. But from the history of its owner, he surmised that the hand was, in all likelihood, an allegorical symbol signifying the power of undeath, hence its rupturing from the ground; rather than piety, representative of its reaching into the heavens. The five towers – the fingers – protruded at odd angles, for whereas the thumb and the forefinger stood almost vertical, the other three towers were curled, the little finger bent down, perpendicular to the core of the building, the palm. There was a crookedness to the whole thing that left a feeling of unease, as though the stronghold was an architectural abomination, an affront to engineering conventions – a disaster in waiting. It gave the impression that it was organic and that at any time those cracked towers would uncoil, forming a savage, clawed hand, and that the whole thing would rise into the air on a great arm attached to some larger, chthonic fiend; a titanic monster, something from the dead core of the planet that would unnerve the very gods.

"The path heads up that cliff," said Creeps, pointing. "Ye see? Up by that old drawbridge."

Everus looked to where the thief pointed, tracing the line of the track as it made its way up the cliff face, heading for the great bridge that spanned the ravine they were currently in. It looked like it would be another hard climb and he silently cursed Craiglin for urging them not to take the road up. The old man had said that it would have taken five times as long, for the main road, the one that Kooper and the others had undoubtedly taken, wound its way all around the mountain like a great snake.

Without warning, three horsemen thundered across the bridge, heading away from the stronghold.

"Riders," said Creeps.

"Hmm. I wonder what they're up to?" Everus watched as the

riders disappeared from view, the speed of their departure suggesting that they had left with some pressing purpose in mind. He had been unable to make out the identity of any of them, making it possible that one of them had been Carrie – perhaps making off with the retrieved relic. He had to find out, and knowing that time was of the essence, resolve provided him with speed and energy. Without waiting for Creeps, he sprinted up the path, weaving around the gorse bushes, stunted cacti and fallen rocks which littered the ravine floor.

The climb up to the stronghold was harder than first appearance had suggested, the difficulty compounded by the presence of numerous hollows in which nested many small, yet vicious, dark grey scorpions. It seemed that no matter where they reached or where they stood, either one of them would provoke the wrath of a handful of the stinging, nipping little arachnids. Fortunately, their venom was very weak, for both Everus and Creeps had received more than their share of stings by the time they got half-way up, but they were still painful, those nips which managed to hit exposed flesh quickly drawing blood.

The thief cursed as one of them latched on to his right hand. With his other hand, he plucked it free, dashed it to the ground and stomped on it.

"Shhh! We're near the top now." Everus gazed up, examining their route, not liking the look of the final climb, for the path they had been following came to an end at the base of a large sheet of coal-black, slab-like basalt. Like a natural glacis, it sloped up towards the higher level on which the ruins stood and, no matter how hard he looked, he could not see an easy means of ascent.

"We should o' brought some rope," commented Creeps, gauging the climb before them.

"Well we didn't," Everus snapped. He looked up at the five bizarre towers. In the early morning light, he could see that they appeared to be covered with a sickly, purplish moss or similar growth. As he was looking, a part of it fell free in a disgusting snot-like drip, as though it were some kind of phlegmatic membrane.

"*Gads!* What's that shit?" queried Creeps, he too having witnessed the dripping.

"No idea, but suffice it to say it doesn't look wholesome. Come on, we've got to get to the top." Everus began clambering up the slope, relieved to discover that the gradient was not as steep as he had first assumed. It was still hard going, the distinct lack of any proper hand-holds or anything else to grab hold of necessitating the rather undignified use of his knees. Once he almost lost it, nearly overbalancing and tumbling backwards, but luckily he managed to regain his equilibrium, his hands frantically grasping at the tiniest of ledges. Slowly, carefully, he edged his way up, aware of his vulnerability, knowing that if any of Kooper's men happened to be standing at the top on sentry duty with a crossbow, then he would be finished, for even if the shot missed he would assuredly slip and fall to his death. Even as his mind wrestled with such morbid thoughts, the angle became gentler, the going easier, indicating that the worst of the climb was over and that he was nearing the top.

As though it had been a race, Creeps scampered past him.

Now at the crest of the slope, Everus fell to the ground, aware that the thief had done likewise. Together, they crawled over to a stretch of ruined wall. They could see more of that weird, purplish gunge spattered here and there, covering the ground and tufts of grass and gorse, smothering it like a foul, alien parasite.

Everus' nose wrinkled in disgust. "Stinks, doesn't it?"

"It's bloody awful. What is it?" asked Creeps.

Everus shook his head in mystification, his face contorting upon catching a more pungent blast from the foul-smelling wind. The place was filled with the terrible reek, the stench strong enough to turn stomachs and water eyes. It was a chemical stink, acidic and strangely organic, like a drunkard's piss that had been stored and allowed to ferment, only far, far worse.

The thief blew out a lungful of polluted air from his lungs. "Bleugh! Someb'dy's farted a beauty. No wonder them riders cleared off." Pinching his nose, he began wafting the tainted air before him. "That stink'd kill a horse."

Everus peeked over the low wall. "Can't see anyone around. I guess the others are still inside."

"So ye think they're still 'ere?"

"Only one way to find out. Stay low and keep on the lookout."

Together they made their way towards the great entrance to the ruined, gunge-festooned castle. Through a wrecked maze, formed from destroyed out-buildings, shattered exterior towers and breached walls they sneaked, the ghastly stench growing with each step closer to their destination. All around, the slimy goo dripped and bubbled from the dank stonework. Like a living organism, it seemed to creep and fester, spreading like a voracious contagion.

Before them, across a spattered, rubble strewn courtyard, a once ornate stairway, flanked on either side by grotesquely fat, bat-like statues, reached up into the core of the immense 'palm'. It curved, serpent-like, to the top before vanishing into the dark opening in the centre of the upright hand.

At the base of the stairs, no more than thirty steps from where Everus and Creeps were, lay five bodies. They all looked as though they belonged to Kooper's platoon.

"A trap, do ye think?" asked Creeps.

Everus drew his sword, its weight and lethality a comfort in this unmistakably evil place. That there was evil here, he had no doubt, for one had only to look around or sniff the polluted air to be certain. Whatever had transpired here, whatever blight had poisoned the very earth and the mortar of this sinister building was still here, as though even in its scale of desecration and destruction it had not been satiated. It was then that he noticed that the purplish contamination was not confined to just the tangible surroundings – it was in the air as well. A noxious, wispy smog, like that he had seen in the cursed wood, swirled and danced like viperous wraiths.

"What is it?" asked the thief, not liking the concerned way in which Everus took in his surroundings.

"Something *really* bad has happened here. Can you not sense it?"

"Summat stinks, I'll grant ye."

"It has an evilness about it. A foulness...not of this world." With a shake of displeasure, Everus looked about once more, before stalking over to where the five bodies lay. They were, as he had first guessed, some of the cavalrymen he had encountered the night before. From the look of it they had not been dead long, the blood that now congealed around the various sword stab wounds still fresh.

"They died fightin'," reasoned Creeps.

"Amongst themselves, by the looks of it."

"No sign o' yer boss fella or missus woman."

With his boot, Everus turned one of the corpses over. There was nothing untoward – just a dead man, and he had seen more than his share of those. The individual's eyes were filled with blood and a nasty-looking cut to the throat gave some indication as to how he had met his end, the only other significant clue being a trail of spattered red circles leading up the stairs, indicating that at least someone had survived the fight. Either that or the man had staggered from that direction, but given the severity of his injuries that looked unlikely.

"Ye any idea what's goin' on?"

"Hmm. I think this may have been a mutiny. I guess it would also explain the rather hasty departure of those riders we saw...deserters doing what they do best."

"Ye think they've set about killin' each other?"

"Well, even if not, it's eight less for us to bother with."

"So what's that leave? Twelve? Thirteen?" Creeps gave his chin a quick scratch. His thief's mind turned to larcenous thoughts. "Don't suppose they've got anythin' worth nickin' have they?"

"No time for that. If we survive we can loot their rooms back at the inn." Cautiously, Everus started the climb up the winding stairway. It ran like a coiled python, constantly going up but not always in the right direction. It seemed that it had been constructed with the intention to perplex and frustrate, the length of the route at least six times longer than necessary.

Upon reaching the top, they were greeted by an immense, open-mouthed demonic face – the opening to Bhubbaal's Stronghold. The carved face was fat and lumpy, the mouth resembling that of some puckered sea horror. The sphincter-like, circular entrance gave the impression that, had the keep been operational, then the mouth could close, forming a tightened ring of fanged-edged stone. Around the obscene opening were five eye-like protuberances – magical, optical spy holes to permit the viewing of unwanted visitors.

Four more soldiers lay dead by the bizarre opening. One corpse was decapitated, the head nowhere to be seen.

Despite the unsettling location, Everus managed a rare show of glee. "Good. That's twelve taken care of." He was about to examine the bodies for any clues as to what had happened when suddenly a foul cry echoed from somewhere within, gusting out from the hideous aperture like a fart from a gaping arsehole.

"What was that?" asked Creeps as, with dagger drawn, he stared into the unwelcoming, smelly hole.

"It sounded human." For a moment, Everus waited, ears straining to pick up anything else. After a protracted spell of silence, he gestured to the thief and together they approached the entrance. He drew up short before it and gripped Creeps by a shoulder. "Do you want to see if it's trapped?"

Creeps turned and grinned. "I'm on it." He stepped forward, appraising the strange circular opening, its diameter wide enough to accommodate five men walking side by side. Beyond it was a large chamber. After he had completed his investigation, he gave Everus an assuring nod and slinked inside.

There was a cavernous chamber beyond.

Despite the scale of the destruction, no matter where he looked, Everus could see traces of Bhubbaal's Hyadean background. There was no love of aesthetic beauty here, no displays of high art, as would have undoubtedly graced the wealthy abodes of most rulers, its mere consideration a blasphemy. Only the cruel and the morbid, the dangerous and the degenerate, the wicked and the perverted had the right to call this place home and, whereas other rulers would have sought to conceal whatever dungeons and torture chambers they may have secretly owned, burying them deep out of sight, not wishing to give the casual visitor the wrong impression, Bhubbaal had blatantly opted for the opposite effect. To this end, the vast entrance chamber had been purposefully built as a bastion of pain.

In the centre of the chamber there was a great circular pit and, as the two tentatively approached it, its function became apparent. It was a sunken amphitheatre. Tiers of steps descended down towards a bare stone arena, its floor strewn with the festering remains of long dead combatants. Amidst the slain, partially eaten myrmidons and gladiators, glistened large afterbirth-like globs of monstrous mucus and several, now shrivelled, giant scorpions.

"*Gads!* What a reek! It's nearly as bad indoors as out," commented Creeps, looking down, his words echoing far too loudly for Everus' liking.

"Shhh." Grimly, Everus surveyed the huge battle-pit. Although gladiatorial contests were a source of great entertainment throughout the empire, the crowd baying for its share of blood, he had never actually been to one. He had of course heard tell of them, one of his trainers at the Xethornite temple in Wyrm's Port having been at one time a highly respected slayer himself, but his view had always been that combat, specifically the art of killing, was not something to be made light of, not something to be exercised in order to appease the bloodlust of others.

"Looks a bit like a bigger version o' that fightin' pit they used to have at the back o' The Scabby Rat," whispered Creeps.

"What?"

"This. This fightin' pit. It's a bit like the one they used to have at the back o' The Scabby Rat. It were a cheap alehouse on the East Side o' Wyrm's Port. They used to have cock fights..."

"Cocks?"

"Ye know...they look a bit like chickens."

Everus nodded his understanding.

"An' dog fights. On some nights they used to put on some good biff-biff fights." Creeps sniffed as he threw a couple of unthreatening jabs. "Saw many o' the best there. 'Arry Brash. Blackfoot Macaw. Stoneribs Murgotroyde. Ye were guaranteed at least one bust nose a night. Sometimes, if ye were really lucky, ye'd..."

"Shhh!" hissed Everus. From one of the many arches which led to other shadowy chambers, he could see the flashes of approaching lantern light as they danced over the tunnel walls. Along with the thief, he scampered over to one side, hoping that they would not be seen, yet at the same time, wanting to see who was coming.

The reflected light became stronger.

Carrie, Kooper and four others came into view. Whereas the sorceress carried herself with an assertive swagger, the five men looked drained and exhausted, their faces grey and expressionless – as though they were suffering from a fatigue born in the soul, rather than the body. Carrie held two large tomes tucked under one arm. Raising her free hand, she brought the group to a halt.

Everus felt his heart leap, certain that she had sensed them, certain that she would give the order and he would find himself pitted once more against the mad sergeant and his men. Holding his breath, not daring to move, he watched and waited. In those lingering moments, he considered rushing out and forsaking the relative safety of the shadows. The pull became stronger, almost as though it was Carrie's unspoken command for him to rush to his death. He began to get to his feet. It was the thief's grip on his shoulder, and the shake of his head, that broke either her spell or his self-defeating compulsion. He watched as the sorceress looked about, no doubt trying to throw her gaze into the darkness outside the radius of illumination which bathed her and her followers. Everus heard Kooper moan. The sergeant was then struck with a backhand slap from Carrie which almost knocked him off his feet. Sent reeling, he bumped into one of his men before wobbling forward like a bottom-heavy statue.

"No love lost there then," muttered Creeps.

Carrie looked in their direction, her piercing, cat-like eyes aglow in the dark.

Everus' knuckles whitened around the handle of his sword, needing the comfort of its grip, now no longer glad to be concealed by the shadow. The feeling that the dark was not his friend, that it no longer concealed him, filled him with the desire to rush screaming for the purplish-tainted daylight outside. Blood coursed through his veins, creating a dull throb in his head.

Still Carrie stood there. Silent. Motionless. Knowing. Eyes peering.

The waiting was agonising and Everus was just about to scream, to let his breath howl from his lungs, when the sorceress broke her stare and with a wave to her companions, set off for the exit.

"Now what?" whispered Creeps, as the six disappeared through the circular opening.

"We follow them."

✝ ✝ ✝

If the terrible purple ooze had spread from somewhere then Everus and Creeps had finally discovered where, for they now looked down at a reeking crater caked with the stuff, the outer walls of the Hyadean warlord's stronghold little more than an arrow's shot behind them. The slopes of the crater were covered with goo and, although not deep, the way in which the stuff had been vomited out gave Everus the impression that whatever had occurred here must have been almost volcanic in proportion.

They watched as Carrie and the five men made their way down towards the floor of the caldera.

"What do ye think they're goin' down there for?" asked Creeps.

"I don't know. I think we should try and get closer all the same. We may have to get to her before she does anything." The stink was horrendous, a sudden blast from a fumarole almost causing Everus to collapse. Shaking his head, he spat, ridding his mouth of the chemical taste. If evil was ever bottled and sold to the malevolent, then this was how it would taste. There was death also in the air, that much was certain, but from the smell alone he could tell more, such as how those deaths had been reached. He would catch a whiff that suddenly made him 'see', in his mind, the newly-married peasants viciously kebabed on one huge spike and turned on a spit for the delight of Bhubbaal and his men, or the peeled babies, salted and left out for the carrion birds. And there was more; brutal, depraved acts of murder which made the infantile excarnations look positively merciful.

"Guess we don't want any o' those buggers to see us," said Creeps. "It might be best if we try an' head for them boulders."

Grimly, Everus nodded in agreement and together they scurried around the outer rim of the crater, making for the large rocks Creeps had pointed out. The fact that they now had the advantage of higher ground, made him wonder how effective a barrage of hurled stones would be against their enemy. He was still considering that tactic when they reached the relative security of the boulders. He had just crouched down when he saw Carrie and the others reach the bottom.

They watched as the woman they had once trusted set about ordering Kooper and his remaining men; ritualistically preparing them, positioning them, readying them for sacrifice. To this end, she stood each man apart, in line, the five towers of Bhubbaal's Stronghold her model, her template.

"Ye any idea what she's up to?"

Everus did not like the look of this one bit. "We've got to get closer. Come on."

Using whatever rocky outcropping or irregularity there was, the two slid and scrambled deeper into the crater. At one stage, Everus inadvertently triggered a miniature avalanche of purple ooze-coated scree, and he froze for a moment, certain that the ritualist would detect him. With a nervous glance at Creeps, he sank low, willing his body to sink into the ground, even if it would mean becoming one with the corrupted earth.

Fortunately, Carrie never looked up, preoccupied with her preparations. The two tomes she had brought from the stronghold lay atop a rock nearby.

Nearing the bottom, Everus' heart sank, for he could see that the base of the crater was in actuality a great, circular stele; a massive slab which had undoubtedly taken an aeon to carve, many of its masons and perverted artisans no doubt driven mad by its creation. For it was not a mere piece of art or some elaborate pit-covering. It was a seal, designed explicitly for entombing a being of great power. As such, it had been made with the utmost precision, each angle and curve conforming to specific, sacred, geometrical measurements. In addition, the entire face of the slab sloped, almost imperceptibly, towards the centre, where there was a circular opening. This feature had seemingly been incorporated intentionally. It permitted whoever had commissioned it to pour the blood of their enemies onto points of the slab at the circumference. The blood would then cover the surface with its crimson embrace before being funnelled to the aperture in the middle, from which it would drain into the pit below.

It had to be the Great Stele beneath which Cyrvilus, himself, was supposedly entombed.

They could now hear the dark mutterings that came from the sorceress' lips and see for themselves the blank, almost dead look on the faces of the five men. From where they crouched, directly behind her, they could see that each man had been planted in accordance to the leaning of the five towers that were visible just above the opposite lip of the crater. Kooper had been positioned bolt upright, mimicking the 'thumb', the man on his right ever so slightly stooped. Each of the other three was likewise contorted, the last in line almost bent double into the shape of the fifth tower.

Carrie went from one to the other, moulding them and stepping back to appraise her slight alterations, looking up to check the angle of the towers.

"Now would be a good time to get her, afore she finishes whatever she plans on doin'," whispered Creeps. "They men looked stuffed or summat. Ye could charge her from behind. A stab in the back, that's all it would take."

Everus had to agree. To let her complete her ritual could well prove disastrous. He had to hope that Kooper and the other men were drugged or charmed and that they would not alert her to his approach. Stealthily, he started towards her. Under the zombie-like gaze of the five men, he crept nearer, his nerves afire. He stopped suddenly as he noticed her cock her head to one side.

"Everus. Just in time." Her back still to him, Carrie finished her bizarre sculpting and stepped back as though in order to appraise her handiwork. "What do you think, is the one in the middle about right? Position *is* everything." She turned to face him, hands on hips.

"Hand over the bones...and I *may* spare you."

"*You*...may spare me?" Carrie smiled. "Would that be in the same way that you spared my *sister?*"

Sister? Confused, Everus took a step back.

"Oh, I'm sorry. You didn't know, did you? My sister...you would have known her as Julia Camberra."

A tidal wave of despair and hatred battered Everus' mind as memories of the raven-haired, ruby-lipped, voluptuous succubus he had murdered crashed through him. Almost as if he had been struck in the face, he staggered back as that very act replayed itself in his mind. With the utmost vividness, he watched as, ruthlessly, he murdered her and her two abominable offspring, slaying them as they slept – at that time not knowing that they were all demonic but well aware that she was responsible for the ruination of his life. He had killed her for her part in instigating a witch-hunt against his father, initiated by concealing demonic statues in his study and promoting heretical lies about him. Unbeknownst to him at the time, their deaths had signified the beginning of a murderous spiral; a crusade which had been sinisterly orchestrated, initially by Dae'dicus, and later by his successor, Dae'morogin, both high priests of Uhu'giaggoth – with the sole aim of summoning The Daemon God once again.

"I believe she played a small part in..." Carrie thought for a moment, "encouraging you to leave your chosen career path. Forgive me if I sound a little callous but, in the end, her death was preordained. A necessary sacrifice to awaken the interest of the book that lies over there." She gestured to where the two tomes rested.

The shock of her revelation already dying, Everus strode forward. "So. Yet another demon-bitch I must add to my kills."

Carrie threw her head back and laughed. Seductively, she licked her lips, looking every bit the sexiest woman Everus had ever seen. "You still want me, don't you? I can sense your lust. Even after all you know." She raised the hem of her skirt high enough to reveal the long, beautiful curves of her legs. "I am desirable...am I not?" She pouted and threw him a kiss.

It was as though a poisoned crossbow bolt had pierced his heart. Howling his pain, Everus clutched his chest and fell to his knees. Moaning, he tried to get to his feet.

"Please. Let me give you a hand."

Through pained eyes, Everus saw Carrie remove a withered, grey hand from the confines of her robe. She muttered something and an instant later an invisible power sprang him to his feet and raised him off the ground. There was no grip, no squeezing. It was just as though the ground had tired of supporting his murder-drenched soul and had decided to repulse him.

"Behold the hand of my father. *The hand of Cyrvilus.*" Carrie raised the putrescent corpse-hand, glorying in its display. The dry bones they had collected were now fused together and had somehow gained a covering of desiccated skin, as if the hand were already in the process of regenerating itself. On returning her gaze to Everus and taking in his carefully unimpressed expression, the sorceress merely smiled and walked closer. "Since the time of The Hellspawn Cataclysm the pieces have been lost. Scattered. Hidden. Reviled. But now, the waiting of an age nears its end...the preparations for my father's return are all but complete. This time..."

"*Oi!* Missus!"

The demon spawn turned, just in time to witness Creeps draw his dagger across Kooper's throat. Blood spurted as the burly sergeant slid to the ground. The four others already lay sprawled, blood draining from similar wounds. Carrie screamed, knowing that the sacrifice had been corrupted. She raised the clawed hand.

Guessing correctly that the two books possessed some form of power, the thief had both of them now within easy reach. He raised the lighter of the two and for a dreadful moment the tome crackled with a dark violet energy as whatever destructive spell Carrie had launched at him clashed with the unholy words of power contained inside.

The book blazed with a dark fire.

Everus, released from his reversed gravity, fell to his feet.

Still Creeps held onto the book, *The Cyrvilus*, the demonic codex whose author had fathered the twin succubi. Fire and lightning flashed, wreathing him in its blaze. His whole body shook with the strain, his flesh and clothing becoming partially transparent, his skeleton dancing visibly. His straggly hair ignited. Flames shot from his eyes and mouth, his body smoking. Electrified by the arcane, the thief rose into the air, the book still clutched to him. Then, with a violent convulsion, he burst into flames, the book doing likewise.

Carrie screamed in anger.

"*Hellspawn!*" With a two-handed swing of his sword, Everus slashed across the sorceress' back. She staggered forward, a second hack sending her flying to the ground, the cursed hand spiralling from her grip. Face down, she tried to push herself up but again he struck her, the back of her cloak now drenched in a vile, black ichor. With the heat from Creeps' immolation burning his face, he continued to butcher – the bitch refusing to die. Repeatedly, his sword struck, the demoness' oleaginous essence spattering his blade, making it hiss with relish. *"Die! Die! Die!"* he cried.

But the thing would not.

Carrie, her face and body resembling a montage of the worst carnage gathered from a battlefield, shrugged off Everus' attacks and rose to her feet. With a roar of rage, she tore out of the sorceress' skin, the mask, the cocoon in which she had resided.

The horror that now slavered and growled before Everus caused his nerve to falter. What had once been a highly attractive woman of about his age was now a loathsome entity, its warty hide a saurian-green, veined and dripping. It stood on a pair of goat-like legs, their hooves cloven, and whilst the upper torso remained that of a curvaceous – if horribly skinned – woman, the face was a mass of writhing, slime-soaked tentacles.

Gargling, it sprang forward, clawed hands extended.

Everus met the charge with a forward thrust of his blade, sinking it deep between her pert breasts, the momentum of the fiend's leap making the blade puncture with ease. Straight through it went and with a savage twist, he pulled it free before leaping clear of a slashing swipe.

The succubus pulled back, hurt. The protection from its outer, corporeal armour now spent, saturated.

Bolstered by sensing its vulnerability, Everus grinned. "You felt that, didn't you?" With a cry of rage, he rushed towards it, his first swing slicing naught but air. Skilfully, he sidestepped and flashed the sword up a second time, cutting it across a raised arm, severing it at the elbow. Black goo jetted from the stump and the goat-legged thing screamed, from where he had no idea, for there was no mouth visible. An uncanny volume of demon ichor slurped and steamed from where it had been wounded. Then it launched a counterattack. With its remaining hand, it grabbed his sword arm and began to rend, causing him to drop his weapon. Bringing up his left fist, he jabbed with two rapid punches, both sinking into the jellied mass of wet feelers that served the horror for a face. It was like punching a bowl of cold porridge. Bits spattered and he almost threw up at the revolting stench that his action created. Still, it made it release its hold long enough for him to retrieve his sword and drive in a second thrust to its chest. Once more he twisted the blade as he freed it, enlarging the wound. He then barged the thing with a shoulder, knocking it to the ground. With a cry of triumph, he was just about to chop down, certain that this would be the killing blow, when...

The monstrosity disappeared, the image vanishing as though it had never been.

Sprawled before him, her face and clothes torn and bloody, lay Carrie, her eyes pleading, hands raised, begging him to stay his attack.

"Everus. Please...no. Don't!" she said, fear evident in her voice.

Rage still blazed in his eyes. He gritted his teeth as his eyes narrowed, wanting nothing more than to chop this shape-shifting, demonic bastard to pieces. Wavering, sword held aloft, he stood over her, ready at the slightest provocation to bring her life to a deserved end.

"Everus. Please. You must understand..."

"Speak...demon." Everus struggled with the words, that cogent part of his mind telling him to slay the succubus, and to do so quickly. But as he beheld her beauty, her helplessness, he began to struggle, the conflict that bubbled within sowing seeds of doubt. Had he seen what she had become or was it just another phantasm, some evil and beguiling illusion conjured by the powers of the hand? "No...no," he muttered to himself, stepping back even as she rose to her feet. She was as gorgeous as ever, her hair long and tousled, her eyes blue and bright. His mind was slipping, drowning in the sapphire pools that had captivated him from the first moment they had met.

"You've been tricked, Everus. We've all been tricked," said Carrie. "When I was abducted by Kooper and his men I was forced to read from that foul book. The power of Cyrvilus was too great for me. It broke my mind...instructing, ordering me to comply, forcing me to perform this ceremony in the hope that it would in some way restore the long-dead demonologist to life. I had to do it. There was no other choice."

"I..."

"Believe me. You've got to believe me. If you don't, we're all doomed." Carrie started to move towards him, arms outstretched.

Everus pulled back, unconvinced, mentally wrestling with a dark horde of possibilities. What if she spoke the truth? Could it be that the power within the book had warped his mind, creating hostile images in the hope that he would slay this woman whom, it had to be said, had assisted him and offered him friendship? Was that part of its chaos? He was momentarily broken from his thoughts when, over to his right, Creeps' charred and smoking form collapsed to the ground.

"I've found out more than I could've imagined." Carrie took her eyes from him, glanced briefly to where the thief's partially incinerated body lay and then took in the destruction all around. "The wreckage and the devastation that you can see was born from a prior attempt to resurrect Cyrvilus. The fool, Bhubbaal, tried to restore life to..." For a moment she glanced up at the five towers, a strange look in her radiant eyes. "He failed, but..."

Everus waited, noting the sudden evil look that came over her face as she hesitated.

"He...*Damn you Dragonbanner! May your soul burn in the fires of Uhu'giaggoth!*" With a dark flash, the demonic ungulate returned, no longer able or willing to maintain its charade. Screaming like an angry banshee, it leapt forward. With its remaining hand it delivered a powerful smack that caught Everus full in the face, knocking him off his feet and sending him to the carved stone of the Great Stele. It sprang high in the air, before coming down and savagely landing on his back.

With a roar of pain, Everus rolled to one side. Narrowly dodging the vile thing's second leap, he reached for his sword and rolled further, trying to keep well clear of the demoness' vicious, hoofed stomping. Groaning, he managed to get to his feet, just in time to fend off the horror's snatching claw. The ground seemed to shift under him as he darted to one side, ragged, dagger-like nails flashing before his face.

Everus brought his sword overhead. With a sickening squelch, he cleaved through the pulsating jungle of grimy feelers, his enchanted blade sinking deep into the thing's chest, cutting it to the navel. Almost cut in two, the Carrie-thing writhed spasmodically, its limbs flailing as though seeking in some way to undo the damage he had caused. Unwholesome organs squelched and farted, their oily, sausage-like appearance filling him with disgust. Tar-black fluids sprayed and oozed as he pulled free the enchanted, fire-hardened steel.

The foul thing reeled, thick ichor drooling from its now riven trunk. Jellied innards began to spray from it. Suddenly a dark glow appeared in its remaining hand and shot forwards, striking Everus on the right shoulder. The force of the infernal blast knocked him back off his feet and sent his sword spiralling from his hand. He had barely the time to realise he had been struck, when the demoness conjured two more bolts. Both struck home, the first going off with the sound of an arquebus blast as it hit him full in the chest, the second catching him as he was still reeling, lifting him up and throwing him into the air.

With a crash that sent jolts of pain through his entire body, Everus struck the hard stone. Smoking and barely conscious, he raised his bleeding face from the ground, the hellish, purple by-product of Bhubbaal's failed resurrection, caking his body. Stunned, he tried to push himself upright, the clomping of hoof-beats drawing slowly nearer as though the succubus now sensed his defeat and wanted to prolong his suffering. A fourth blast of demonic sorcery battered into him, driving him forward, lifting him up once more. He collapsed to the ground, his left hand falling onto the remaining tome.

Instantly, a searing heat shot up his left arm. His palm sizzled as though it were being forced down onto a hot stove. His initial reaction – to try and remove his hand – proved futile, the intense heat fusing skin and the strange, bound leather together. Roaring with the pain, his nostrils filling with the unsavoury stench of his own burnt flesh, he raised his hands to try and ward off the demon-bitch's attack, the smoking grimoire now welded to his hand.

Screaming like a hooligan, Creeps rushed into the fray. Burnt and blistering, his face blackened, his clothes smouldering, he brought the sword he had taken from the dead sergeant slashing across.

Accompanied by a thick jet of blood, Everus' left hand, book and all, flew into the air.

The cloven horror withdrew.

Creeps crumpled, his final act of desperate intervention over.

Everus went into a convulsion. Eyes wide, unfocused, numbed, he fell to his knees, blood continuing to squirt, his attempts to stem the crimson release feeble. He threw up.

Like a shark drawn to the scent of blood, the corpse-hand of the dead Cyrvilus scampered over from where it lay, temporarily forgotten. With uncanny speed, it darted past the succubus and latched on to the amputee's stump; bones, veins and arteries knitting together with incredible swiftness. Like wet leather, a sealing of putrescent flesh spread out from the dead hand, drawing itself tight, moulding itself like a bizarre glove.

A sudden surge of energy coursed through Everus in one violent pulse that sprang him to his feet. Almost as though time itself had been rewound, his blade came flying back to his right hand, following the reverse trajectory of his disarming.

The succubus clip-clopped further back, sweating its ichor like liver bubbling on a hot plate.

With the vile, potent blood of Cyrvilus now strengthening him, Everus leapt to the attack, his jump taking him effortlessly across a sizeable measure of the crater bottom. His first slash chopped the already mutilated thing in half. Part of a torso, one complete arm and its polyp-like head cart-wheeled. His second chop came whilst the upper half was still in mid-flight.

A pair of satyr-like legs, now no longer attached, kicked for a moment and then kicked no more.

Everus inhaled a lungful of air as he flexed his demonic transplant and stared at the carnage; the sticky remains of Cyrvilus' spawn, the blasted tomes and, off to one side, the scorched thief. He felt exhilarated and, as the pain from his numerous injuries seeped away, the power grew within him intoxicatingly. "I like," he whispered.

CHAPTER TWENTY-FOUR

Everus had found the outlying stockade where the riders had corralled their horses and had kept two, setting the remainder free. He now stood at the top of the ridge, looking down at the Great Stele.

The sliver of a crimson moon floated over the lip of the crater, bathing one side in a hellish glow. The moon rose higher, its reflected light transforming the caldera into a demon's demesne; the depression slowly filling, the red glow seeping like blood down the far ridge.

It was deathly quiet.

The moon rose higher.

Still Everus stood and stared, his mind seeking clarity. What had happened to him in that abominable pit had changed him forever. He was now tainted. Touched by the chaotic. The dead hand that had latched onto him was even now exerting its influence, filling his mind with the promise of darker deeds to come. Somewhere between delusion and reality, he now envisaged Cyrvilus' energies running like a dark network throughout his body, its tenebrous roots branching and crawling through him, its tendrils suffocating what soul remained within him.

With the crater below him now resembling a blood-filled tarn, Everus raised his sword – now certain its previous owner had spoken the truth when he had claimed that it had spilled enough blood to fill a small sea. A strange power began to flow from the enchanted, fire-hardened steel, as though the souls of those it had slain were in some way discharging through him. For a time, he felt like screaming, the sensation wracking. Mercifully, it did not last long and, shortly after, he began to return to some semblance of normality.

Everus paced over to a nearby rock, resting on which was the book that had cost him his left hand. He looked down at the weighty, scarred tome, which, now assisted by the thought-memories of Cyrvilus, he knew everything about. The book went by many names; *The Necronomicon*, *The Book of Dead Names*, *The Catalogue of the Daemondamned* – each adequately describing its true function. Countless dark and unholy rites had been performed in its creation, culminating in the incarceration of a demoness' essence. In this case, the demoness in question had been the succubus, Darguliassa – a demon-bitch that had assumed the identity Julia Camberra – wife of Otha Camberra, mother of his twin demon-hybrid daughters and, along with Carrie, or rather Jallathu, one of the bastard offspring of Cyrvilus. Her murder had initiated both the damnation of himself and countless others – for it was Darguliassa's sacrifice that had acted as the channel between the world of the living and the world of the demonic. It had been her essence which had destroyed the hundreds whose deaths had been predestined when the book was first ensorcelled. It was she who had harvested the souls of the dead in order to create the gate through which the book's creator, high priest Dae'dicus, had sought to usher forth The Daemon God.

With his non-living hand, Everus reached down and turned the cover, the mark where his palm had been burnt onto it sickening to behold. The last time he had seen this book it had been in the possession of Dae'morogin, whom he now knew it had later consumed. Somehow, Carrie must have retrieved it from the ruins of the old Xethornite temple in Wyrm's Port, or more likely, she had arranged for Kooper to do so.

Pentacles and other occult symbols decorated the frontispiece, but other than that whatever contents the book may have at one time possessed were now destroyed. At some time in the book's recent past, blood or some other fluid had drenched many of its pages, for all were still sticky and discoloured to the point where they were impossible to decipher.

However, Everus was not interested in reading from it, in gathering whatever dark and foul didactic it may have once contained. Instead, he set about tearing out the pages and piling them carefully nearby.

The tome screamed at this savage violation, its inhuman howls echoing around the crater.

In time, the screaming came to an end.

Everus reached down and gathered up the heaped pages, on

which were recorded the many names of those whom the demoness had claimed. He grinned upon noting that the last name recorded was that of his former mentor, Dae'morogin. With nothing more than a wave from his withered hand, a glittering, dark purple gem materialised before him. Suddenly the pages burst into flames and the smoke produced began to solidify, compressing around a single wraith-like form. He watched, with a mixture of alarm and intrigue, as the shape began to dissolve, smoky tendrils heading skywards as the essence fragmented into many. In no time at all, he found himself in the centre of a ghostly gathering, the pain and the suffering etched on their spectral visages clearly visible.

As one, the Daemondamned glared at Everus. Then the spirits started to revolve in a dizzying, frenzied dance of the damned, the gem he had conjured acting as their focal point. There was a perverse enchantment, an unholy grace in their widdershins orbit, that filled him with wonder, despite the horror of his plight. Familiar faces flashed past; people he half-remembered, people he had murdered. Many, he had never seen before. Slowly, the spinning picked up momentum, the circling now becoming a spiral as the gem drew them in. Like drowning sailors caught in a whirlpool, the Daemondamned were dragged towards the centre, the magic stone flaring with each one taken.

✝ ✝ ✝

The air in the tunnel was cold and damp and filled with a foul stink. It was dark and, even though Everus carried a torch, it seemed as though the very darkness conspired to smother its illumination – the shadows reaching to put out the flames rather than being driven back by them.

He passed many doors and dark openings, the path he was taking leading deeper and deeper into the core of the building. He saw more and more evidence of the destruction that had been wrought herein. Pillars lay shattered alongside tangled webs of metalwork; rubble-filled stairwells closed much access to the lower levels and, on the odd occasion when the light did flare up, he could see great gaping holes in the ceiling, which seemed to look down on him with their own sense of malevolence.

Arriving at a large stone door, he stood for a moment, his eyes briefly studying the central, fanged, demonic carving. There was no handle or hinge visible, giving the impression that it was never meant to be opened, at least not from this side. Reaching out to the hideously wrought protrusion, he spoke a word of command. The carving rotated. Then, with a click, the door slowly began to rise. The stench that rushed out to greet him was disgusting, almost on a par with the gut-wrenching stink he had come to tolerate.

With the door now having all but cleared, he could see a set of cracked steps descending further into the shadowy depths.

The stink grew more fearsome as he neared the bottom.

He stepped out into a large chamber dominated by a small pyramid-shaped tomb. Around this, there were many stone coffins, several of which lay shattered, their lids lying broken on the floor.

A ragged, repulsive group of figures cowered in one corner and, as his torchlight fell upon them, he could see that they were all horribly twisted and malformed. Some were little more than jellied masses of pulsating wet flesh covered in sackcloth, lacking limbs or other discernible features. Others were at least partially human, though either stunted or painfully gaunt as though they had been wracked almost to breaking point. One grotesque was pincered and scurried about like a bloated crab, its body leaving a trail of mucus. Another consisted of a female head, sewn onto which were five hairy, and in one case heavily tattooed, arms. This abomination clung to the wall like a spider.

So these were all that remained of the ul-garu's thralls; the ugly, sickening creations, prisoners and offspring of Bhubbaal. Left to fend for themselves after the Hyadean warlord's destruction, brought about by his failed summoning, they had fed on the corpses down here beneath his stronghold and the occasional unlucky cavalryman in order to survive. Many of them had once been good people – innocents who had had the misfortune of falling into Bhubbaal's clutches. In the course of his experiments, some had been destroyed, terminated for not meeting his ideals. Others had been painfully kept alive – fashioned and modified to do his bidding. Some fought and died in his arena. Others perished in the preparations for the failed summoning. The truly unfortunate, including many whom Everus could now see, had been singled out for the vivisectionist's harem.

Under different circumstances they would have come shambling and skittering towards him, eager to feed. Now, however, the presence of the Cyrvilian hand kept them at bay and, as Everus took a couple of steps towards them, they shied away from him and began to wail. He watched for a moment as the spider-like horror climbed up the wall, its movements disturbing to the eye. He gazed hard. Raising his corpse-hand, he shot forth a beam of colourless energy, visible only as a wave of ripples in the stale air, towards it, causing it to fall from where it clung.

A pale yellow mist began to seep from the ghastly mutant.

The mist soon cleared to reveal the naked body of a brown haired woman. She lay, seemingly unconscious, on the stone floor.

The remaining monstrosities went crazy, hope perhaps leaping to the forefront of those still in possession of some form of rational thought. Others scattered, scared witless by such a display. They huddled further away as Everus paced over to the prone female and, bending down, heaved her over his shoulder.

✝ ✝ ✝

"Kooper will bother you no more. Nor will any of his men."

Craiglin returned from the small cot in which the woman lay and pulled up a chair. He sat down and presented Everus with a tired smile. "Where's yer friend? Is he coming along later?"

"No, not this time," Everus replied. For it was certain that Creeps was dead, his body dreadfully burned as he clasped *The Cyrvilus*. Whether it had been an accident or not, he could not decide. There had been a single-mindedness about the thief's actions that disturbed him. Did Creeps die simply to stop Carrie from succeeding, or had a very old man decided that he did not want to be around for the final showdown – whatever that might be? He had examined Creeps' body for any signs of life before leaving the crater and had seen that the magic ring, which had been found in the old Xethornite temple and which the thief had once credited with regenerative powers, had melted in the intense heat. He had left the blackened corpse in the open, reasoning that the thief had robbed too many graves to want one of his own. Better to let the scavengers and the elements do their work.

Yet...despite the fact that he had been infuriated, manipulated and frequently disgusted by Adolf Creeps, he felt his loss.

"I am sorry."

Everus returned his attention to the present, in time to hear Craiglin's words of condolence. He brushed them aside. "I'm trusting you to make sure that the woman is well looked after."

544

"Ye've my word. Um...who is she?"

"The widow of a man I knew," Everus answered. He pointed to a small bag he had put by the side of her bed. "I've left an explanation of sorts. Only let her read it when she's well enough. If she can't read, then tell her...tell her that she's been spared from a life of torment and that her husband was a good man. Take whatever gold you find from Kooper's stash to look after her and rebuild your town. You may also think about getting yourself a new mayor."

"Will do." A confused look passed over Craiglin's face. "So I take it ye'll be leavin' soon?"

"Tomorrow. At first light."

"That's a pity. We owe ye so much. I was rather hopin' that ye'd stay another night or so. There's much talk about what ye've done...freein' us from those soldiers an' all. We wanted to celebrate yer heroics."

"*Heroics?*" Everus queried coldly. He smiled thinly to himself, not fully liking the old man's description. He had never considered himself heroic – far from it. The heroes he had read about as a child had acted out of goodness and fairness, noble warriors who helped those less able and performed charitable deeds – bastards like Otha Camberra, before Everus had murdered his 'wife'. It got him thinking all the same.

"Are ye sure ye won't stay a while longer?"

"No. Believe me. It would be better if I go." Everus looked down at his clawed left hand, which he had kept hidden under the table, not wanting Craiglin to see. Already he could feel the dead flesh beginning to spread. He stood up and walked out the door into the chill night. A light drizzle was falling and he paused for a moment, staring at the foul transplant and willing thoughts towards it.

A moment later, he heard the familiar, annoying yapping of the snaggle-toothed ratter and Craiglin's happy cry of surprise.

He owed Creeps and the old man that at least.

✝ ✝ ✝

The suit of chain mail chinked as Everus forced it over his head. It was surprisingly comfortable, fitting well over the inner garment of cloth that he already wore. With the aid of the cursed hand, he had enchanted the armour prior to putting it on, now confident that it would serve him well in the battles that were sure to come.

He looked about the upstairs bedroom of Billy Jubbly's inn, his eyes taking in the wealth of treasure that Kooper and his men had stashed. That this had been the sergeant's room was fairly obvious, for not only was it the largest but it also contained the greatest amount of loot. There were sacks and chests crammed with coins, gold and silver dishes, goblets, gruesome ivories and several expensive, yet unspeakably vile, portraits. In short, it was a veritable treasure hoard containing all the trappings befitting a Hyadean warlord's conspicuous consumption – the portable ones anyway.

Material wealth, however, held no more allure – only the sounds of Xethorn's death cries would satiate Everus' craving.

He was in the process of searching through a bag of loot, when he felt a searing pain in the hand's fingers as though something was attacking his very blood. "*Bastard!*" he exclaimed. Wood splintered as he thumped a table with the sorcerous hand. With a howl of rage, he scattered coins in every direction. He closed his eyes and took a deep breath, trying to restore order to his brain, to shake off the influence that the demonic hand exerted. It was a hard fought battle, but after a time he seemed to win, his own thoughts struggling to the surface. Inhaling deeply, he savoured the feeling of air filling his lungs and liberating his brain...for the time being at least.

Everus screwed his eyes shut and clasped his head with his own hand, his fingers massaging his troubled brow. Suddenly, his head jerked up, eyes wide. His whole body shook with a wracking paroxysm of terror even as the clawed hand shot up to his throat. The force of the attack tipped him backwards, his boots catching the underside of the table and tilting it over. Now on the floor, he continued to shudder, the grasp squeezing, choking the life from him, crushing his windpipe.

With his right hand, Everus tore free the berserk hand and pulled it back, grasping it at the wrist. With a mind of its own, it tried to go for him, its dirty cracked nails eager to tear flesh and gouge his eyes from their sockets so that they would run bloodily down his face in wet, lumpy tears. Still he held on, squeezing the wrist as though attempting to strangle it. He was sure he heard bones crack as he battered it repeatedly off the upturned table edge. Then, with a wet stretching noise, it pushed out in a desperate attempt to escape his hold.

Tightening his grip, the clawed hand became still, seemingly resigned to its failure. As the life drained from it, Everus began to recover. The fierce trembling subsided. He panted, his face streaked with sweat. Releasing his hold, he watched, unnerved, as the fingers that were not his own, flexed and curled independently of his control. A thought flashed through his brain as he got to his feet. It was a dark thought – a message; informing him that, although it had not taken kindly to his petty acts of benevolence thus far, the hand was content to permit him to act as its host. It had had the opportunity to attach itself to the demoness, Carrie, but had chosen him instead, making him wonder whether it had some presentiment about his future. He looked closer, scrutinising the scarred and blistered palm and the small dried flaps of almost mummified flesh that hung between the ragged, practically skeletal, talon-edged fingers. The nails were sharp and cracked. Worm-like tendons rippled under the skin and he watched as a rivulet of black fluid pulsed out of the hand along the arteries at the wrist almost as though *it* were the heart.

With that, Everus knew that his days were few.

The hand would possess him and there was no power on this planet that could save him. Like a parasite, it would feed from him, sharing some of its powers, perhaps even granting him the power to defeat Xethorn, but after that it would take him over completely. Like a dark vine it would engulf him; irrevocably alter his very being.

Cyrvilus *would* return.

He now knew that whilst the physical remains of the demonologist were indeed interred beneath the Great Stele, it was Everus' body that Cyrvilus wished to commandeer – for what good to him was an ancient, virtually disintegrated corpse when he could take the form of a living being?

But right now there was no immediate worry. No danger; the black fluid that now seeped through Everus' body, mingling with the biological, psychological and, to a lesser extent, spiritual ingredients which made him *him*, anaesthetic.

The insights Everus suddenly gained were tremendous; magnificent revelations that had hitherto gone unsuspected. Even in his darkest nightmares, he could not have hoped to have witnessed such horror as when Uhu'giaggoth, The Daemon God, was revealed to him. It was not just the entity's appearance, nor its size, which filled his heart with utter dread – *but what it was*. For he now knew that it was a massive conglomeration of the dead. It was a titanic, roiling, festering mass of all that had died; a dark ocean of non-life, that oozed and bubbled its chaos-ridden, life-expunging way through the multiverse. Whenever anything died – from the humblest tick to the largest planet, its essence was absorbed, consumed and eradicated. Like a fire that raged eternally through the cosmos, its sole purpose was to snuff out existence. It was not evil, for it did not conform to such a mortal concept, but it was the antithesis of life.

Everus had once been religious. There had been a time when he had believed in an afterlife – a hope that what came after would be better; that all the suffering of today would make for a better tomorrow. The Xethornite teachings had always stressed that murder and mayhem prepared the soul for the struggles of what would be...but that had implied that there would be something to struggle against, some *thing* which could be conquered in order to ensure a blissful post-death existence. Now, he knew there was nothing. Not even the contented bliss of the escape from the mortal world – just the everlasting process of a state of dissolution within Uhu'giaggoth's demonic innards. For there was no reprocessing. The dead were not recycled, reshaped and returned – a hope that some other beliefs fervently clung to.

His thoughts spiralling darkly, Everus began to wonder about other things, each thought acting like a key, unlocking more secrets. How was it possible, taking into consideration what he now knew – or rather what he had been shown – for certain individuals to raise the dead as he himself had been? And what of ghosts?

The answer came to him in a golden flash which seared his mind and made the foul hand temporarily shrivel in a little on itself. There was another power – a flaming, galaxy-sized orb of brilliance from which, even as he stood rigid, to a casual observer looking at nothing more interesting than Kooper's booty-heaped bed, suns and planets were generated. There was an equal. A counterpart. A balance, existing in non-concordant opposition. The font of all life. The instigator of evolution. *Was this The High Three?*

Each of these twin polarities sought dominance in an on-going and perpetual power struggle and, although his understanding of such a conflict was vague at best, the power from the hand only attuned to the darker, negative side, he began to understand some of the dynamics of it. The physical world he had always and indeed only dimly known, was but one in a countless, infinite expanse of space. This was the battlefield; the contested domain of these two super, nay supra-entities. Each vied with the other and yet, strangely, existed in a form of chaotic symbiosis, one in which there was no law nor order – no omnipotent adjudicator to intervene if one gained supremacy. Undoubtedly biasedly, the more he thought about it, the more he came to the view that such a state of cosmic flux was an impossibility. Phenomenologically, it could not be – for it stood to reason that, whereas the one which created life would inevitably feed that which consumed it, such a dynamic was not reciprocated. From one there came everything. From the other, nothing.

And existence – was it no more than an ugly in-between?

Pondering this thought, some form of an answer, a reason, began to form. Like a dark design, it coalesced in his thoughts. Aeons ago, the thing which he took to be The High Three, knowing perhaps that it was at an increasing disadvantage, set about seeding the planets it had created with beings who would support its cause. Good and evil were irrelevant – some it created were malign, others benevolent, most just neutral, indifferent and uncaring. What mattered was that they would strive to maintain the balance, to keep the advances and the worshippers of The Daemon God in check.

Xethorn and all the others were not gods, merely enhanced mortals, demigods selected from a myriad of planets, their powers controlled and regulated. Like cabbage growers working the imperial allotments, each had been allocated a domain by The High Three and allocated a portfolio of limited responsibility, a mandate. They were pawns in the great conflict, nothing more. Knowing this, Everus smiled at the effrontery of Xethorn, the naivety of His consideration to even contemplate destroying that which the inhabitants of this insignificant world called Uhu'giaggoth. Only once had a true god been born on this world and that god had been Cyrvilus.

Everus' mind rebelled against this thought.

He knew Cyrvilus was no god, knew the hand was trying to overcome his mind. He tried to shout his defiance but was unable to move a muscle. Sweat streaked down his face, the hand compelling him to *see* what it wanted him to *see*, to *think* as it wanted him to *think*.

The nightmare images continued.

Fashioned from the best and most depraved of human stock, Cyrvilus had been the greatest of demonologists. His dark deeds had singled him out for selection. He alone would become The Daemon God's representative on this pitiful ball of mud and all would perish before him. He alone possessed the strength to survive the infusion.

An agent of the demonic, Cyrvilus would spread the gospel of Uhu'giaggoth through the book he would write. For it had contained unholy word-crafted passages which warped the mind; testaments which drained the soul and chaos-corrupted catechetical canticles which sapped the brain of rational, human thought. In effect, it was the ultimate vehicle for disseminating the doctrines of damnation. A hellish damnation, the source of which originated from a sidereal, extra-dimensional realm.

And now the book was no more. The great covenant was gone.

The scene changed again.

The hand sprang open, clawed fingers stiffening, ready to rend. And there was the thief...only now he was bathed in that strange golden glow Everus had seen Klattermorch snatch from him. And then all was made clear. Creeps, despite the anachronism of his claimed existence, had been the other's champion, the one chosen to maintain balance and enforce its will.

New images swam in his mind.

Now Everus saw Cyrvilus as he had been at the time of The Hellspawn Cataclysm – the first great push by Uhu'giaggoth to usurp this planet. The demonologist was a tall and cruelly imposing figure, his face sharp and angular, almost wolf-like, his eyes bestial. Clad in a suit of hard ebonite armour which was assuredly magical, he stood on a great splinter of rock, high above the ravaged lands of Zeth, his pose striking, intentionally vainglorious. In one hand, he grasped a scythe-bladed halberd, its pole length adorned with runes of demonic power from which a black pennant fluttered. Fire and lightning flashed all around, the demonologist seemingly impervious to their effects – indeed, he was the one in control. The elements themselves shrank away from him, as though fearful of the retribution he could mete out upon them. Before him there stretched a vast army. From where he stood, to the rim of the world, they amassed – a host never before seen and never since exceeded – a multitudinous gathering of the infernal.

Part of Everus was well aware that what he was being shown was the edited version of events, that Cyrvilus could not have been so invincible. After all, something had stopped him from achieving his design – Uhu'giaggoth had not swallowed all life. Managing to shake his head, he tried to force the images to reveal the truth and slowly the scene began to alter.

There was Cyrvilus again, standing on the rock and there was his army, but now Everus could see an answering force appear. Leading an assorted army of men and grubbas was Xethorn and a host of other demigods and entities, including many of the semi-divine autochthones, such as Whaggustraag, the great earth kraken; Shaab-Utu, the desert fertility power and Mad o' Gadin, the grubban rock-lord. All of the latter were surrounded by a nimbus of great intensity. And, as he watched, Xethorn Himself cleaved His way through the demonic horde, seemingly unaware that His every move was almost impossibly augmented by another, more powerful, force. Across the corpse-strewn lava fields of the blistered land He hacked his way, ready to confront...

The door creaked open and Jubbly peered in, nervously. "I...I was just..." He hesitated, not liking one bit the look on Everus' cold face. "I thought I heard a baa...baa...bang...that's all. I'll let ye get back to yer..." Smiling tentatively, he waved a hand at the heaps of treasure looted from Bhubbaal's Stronghold, before backing out the door.

The door closed.

Everus grinned and paced over to the open window, the strange sights he had borne witness to evaporating from his eyes. A cool evening breeze gusted down from the harsh mountains, Bhubbaal's Stronghold barely visible in the dying light. The visions would come again, of that he was certain. There was more the hand would reveal. For the time being, however, he had more important things to take care of and he knew just how much time worked against him.

† † †

Dawn was still some way off as he climbed a steep incline of loosely-packed rock and dirt, the mountainside roughening around him. The drab, eerie-looking pines which covered the lower slopes of the mountain grew more stunted before disappearing completely, the ground now degenerating into an undulating course of hump-backed ridges and shallow ravines – the remains of fossil grooves scored in the rock by ancient lava flows. Holding to the crests as much as possible, he hiked on, the few lights twinkling far below him the only indication of Borgrim's End, which lay deep amidst the otherwise pitch-black of the moon-thrown shadows.

Everus came out of the shadows into the red moonlight to find that he was on a wide plateau, with the night wind sighing down at him from the lofty peaks of the mountains, soft but cold. The terrain

551

around him was now rock and baked ash, with only meagre, hardy types of vegetation clinging to it. For a moment, he felt a twinge of uncertainty, an inner shiver, warning him of the potential danger, even though something within his mind assured him there was nothing to fear.

A light drizzle began to fall, the coolness it brought refreshing.

On top of the plateau, he could see many rocks, as though a mountain core had shattered here. Most were scattered randomly; some no more than pebbles, others bigger than houses, but there was power here. An ancient, arcane power that pre-dated Cyrvilus.

Nearing the centre of the plateau, Everus suddenly knew what had happened here over two and a half thousand years ago. In his mind, he saw how the demonologist had sought out this place, an area where his power was magnified; where it was possible to bend the natural laws which governed this planet. He 'watched' as Cyrvilus blasted the top off the mountain in order to reach the optimum point of the power source. He had then marked the ground so that he alone could use it.

And it was here, at this place, that Cyrvilus had stood against Xethorn and The High Three. For although he had lost his hand in Zeth, it was here that, bolstered by the power from this sacred site, he had made a formidable last stand.

It was here that he had perished.

And it was from here that he would start his retaliation.

Everus walked over to the deliberately flattened surface, scuffing away the dirt and loose gravel in order to trace the design branded on the bare rock of the truncated mountain. It was unmistakably the hugely enlarged imprint of the hand which was now attached to his left wrist. The hand print covered much of the area of the plateau, its image somehow burned into and through the very rock. He could feel the Cyrvilian hand tingle in response to the ancient lines, and he could not help but smile as he looked over to his left and saw, less than a league away, the five towers of Bhubbaal's Stronghold. To think that the Hyadean warlord had travelled all the way from his native country to seek out this place, hoping to recreate Cyrvilus' power and resurrect him by using but one fragment of the hand.

The significance of the hand was not in the positioning of the fingers, nor the size of the towers – Bhubbaal's monument being no more than a physical elevation of the pattern here. The truth was that Cyrvilus had manipulated this power source so that it would only answer to him, or more specifically, to his hand. None of his followers had known this, not even his twin demon daughters, for he had trusted none with this knowledge, but now Everus, through the transfusion of thoughts from the hand and the vile juices it secreted, knew and could use it – indeed, was being willed and guided as to how to do so. What he was about to do surpassed all manner of hitherto performed magery.

In a moment of lucidity, Everus wondered whether Xethorn had known that the hand had been central to Cyrvilus' potency when He had chopped it free, or had He just been lucky?

The hand provided him with no answer.

The drizzle became a light rain as a cold glow on the jagged, eastern horizon precipitated the first rays of morning sunlight. Rotten fingers flexed in anticipation. Reverently, Everus paced into the centre of the large petroglyph and turned to stare, unblinking, at the horizon.

He waited.

And as the sun, that feeble star credited by the ignorant as the progenitor of life, rose above the distant peaks, Everus continued to stare. He raised his arms. "*Behold, Xethorn. You may shroud a city in darkness. But I...I will cover the whole world!*" His ostentatious boast echoed off the mountain sides as, slowly, the great ball of celestial fire began to darken. It was no eclipse. There was no piecemeal shadowing. Rather it was a disease-like darkening, as though its internal fire was dying.

By some unholy miracle, the hand had succeeded in turning day into night. What stars still shone shifted, some disappearing from view.

This was a feat which had cost the demonologist that dwelt within greatly, and yet it was one he had deemed necessary to perform.

For the first real time since the cursed transplantation, Everus could *see* as he wanted to see – not that there was much to behold in a world of rapidly dwindling light. How long it would take for the hand to recharge itself – for its energies to peak once more, he had no way of knowing, but for the time being at least he...

Suddenly all light vanished, yet still, somehow, he could see.

Like a disc of shimmering obsidian, the sun hung in the sky. And as he stared up at it, fascinated by its nebulous incandescence, a pinpoint of incredibly bright red light appeared on its surface. It danced for a moment and then sped towards Everus and engulfed him in a burning orb. The heat was intense and would surely have destroyed him, immolated him, had it lasted more than a moment.

✝ ✝ ✝

In an explosion of flashing lights, the nightmare ended and, like a gout of dragon's breath, Everus was expelled from the fiery portal. He staggered and fell to his knees. His nerves tingled uncomfortably as though he wore a skin of nettles, and as he landed on the damp grass, a jolt of agony lanced through his head, bringing tears to his eyes and causing him to grit his teeth. The pain was blinding, and with his eyes screwed shut, he could feel the alien motion continuing. It went on and on – spinning end over end, his limbs weightless, his brain revolving. Bile rose. His stomach jumped like a drunk jester. Up and down. Up and down. Up and...

"*Where'd he come from?*"

Everus opened his eyes, his sight unfocused. Striding towards him came a short man dressed in a suit of mud-spattered mail, his spear thrust out before him. Other, barely discernible figures could be seen behind him.

"No idea."

"Well, get him on his feet and let's get out of here. If he can walk, he walks. Otherwise throw him in the cart with the dead. Can't afford to leave any bodies around. Not after last time."

"I can walk," said Everus, getting to his feet. With his sight improving, he could now make out that the men before him appeared to be soldiers. All ten wore the armour and the livery of Ghavin's Keep, their faces bloody and haggard.

The short man advanced, his spear poised at the ready. "Then hurry it up and fall...hang on, you're..." Bemusedly, he turned to his commander. "Look at his armour! He's from Wyrm's Port!"

"*What!?*"

Everus rubbed the last of the fog from his eyes in order to better take in his surroundings. He stood on the fringe of a vast, dreary moor, desolate bar the men gathered before him and a few lone trees some distance away. It was cold and it was cloudy, but he was relieved to see that a watery, late afternoon sunlight filtered down from the clouds above. Obviously the magic wrought by the Cyrvilian hand had only been temporary. He had no idea where he was and, from the looks on the faces of the soldiers before him, danger could strike at any moment.

The commander stepped forward. Curious, he stared at Everus' armour and the frayed surcoat he wore. He was a tall, slender man, his hair greying at the temples, his face creased into a permanent frown of worry. "How'd you get here? I was told that you'd all been killed."

"I'm not sure. Where am I?"

"You're on the Southern Uplands, three leagues or so from Wyrm's Port." The commander turned to the rest of his men. "Now come on, hurry it up and let's get out of here. We've got to reach camp before nightfall."

✝ ✝ ✝

Rain drummed incessantly on the canvas ceiling of the large tent. Inside, ten makeshift bunks lay side by side, the snoring coming from many of their current inhabitants adding to the noise. It was dark, the only light provided by a lantern suspended from a pole outside, and the air was choked with the stink of sweaty farts and stale beer. Every so often a spear-carrying silhouette would pass by outside.

Distant thunder rumbled.

Everus lay at one end of the row of beds, eyes focused on the damp ceiling, relieved that the hand had still not awoken. He had slept little, his armour uncomfortable and stiff, and yet the orders were to wear it at all times.

After falling in line with the soldiers, he had joined them on a miserable trudge during which the first of the early evening rain had started to fall. As they marched, he had gleaned some useful information from one of the soldiers at the end of the file. Contrary to the report he had heard second-hand whilst staying at Stranglewood, Ghavin's Keep had not fallen. It had been attacked and the battle had been bloody, with the defenders losing far more than their giant skeletal attackers, but on the third day of the siege, if his informant was to be believed, the enemy had withdrawn. Why, no one was really sure – for it was clear that they were winning. The great wall had been breached in numerous places and most of the army, including many of the militant wizards, had been slain or severely wounded.

Whatever the reason, Ghavin's Keep had been spared.

Everus was giving this some thought when the sound of approaching voices made him sit up. He watched as two shadows appeared at the tent flap, his ears managing to pick up the end of their whispered conversation.

"You know the routine. Why was I not informed straight away?" demanded a stern female voice. "I'll be making a full report when we get back. Now where is he? Is he in here?"

The tent was opened and a woman entered. Behind her, his face lit by the lantern he had removed from its support, was the lean commander of the squadron he had met earlier. Several disapproving groans came from some of the men in the beds, the resting soldiers not taking too kindly to this early morning intrusion.

Everus could see that the woman was a tall and slim brunette, her long, braided hair falling from beneath her winged helmet. She noticed him looking and advanced towards him, her hazel eyes ablaze in the poor illumination provided by the lantern behind her.

"You. Come with us." She looked about. "The rest of you get back to sleep."

Everus got to his feet and picked up his sword. Sheathing the blade, he nodded towards her, silently accepting her authority. Along with the commander, who carried the lantern, they made their way outside, the cold and the rain a pleasant change from the close, malodorous air inside the tent. Without a word spoken, the three headed through the camp, passing several other large tents and their tired, bored sentries.

They soon came to a smaller tent.

Two guards stood on duty outside, their faces concealed under the large hooded coats they wore over their chain mail, their spears pointing up into the dark skies. Light from inside enabled Everus to discern the shadow of a table and several chairs, a low bed and some other pieces of furniture. The woman muttered something he failed to catch to the commander, who, with a shrug of his shoulders then headed off back the way they had come. She stepped inside and, with nothing more than a nod of her head, beckoned Everus to follow.

She sat down at a table and fiddled for a moment with a low-burning oil lamp, turning up the flame in order to provide greater light. She removed her ornate helmet and rested it on the table. "Take a seat."

Everus sat down, his clawed hand resting on his left thigh under the table. The flicker of a smile rose to his lips as he remembered the events of earlier that evening, when he had joined the other soldiers in the mess tent. He had sat at a table with three others and when one had commented on his hand, he had replied that he had been lucky to survive a fireball, his hand taking the brunt of the fiery blast. It had been when one of the others had suggested, jokingly, that he should go and consult a palmist in Ghavin's Keep that he had found it hard not to laugh. That *had* been funny, the kind of thing Creeps might have said. Whereas the uncouth remark from the other, who, after noticing the difficulty Everus had holding his knife and fork, commented that at least it had not been his 'pleasuring' hand, had done nothing but win a dark glare.

Thunder rumbled ominously.

After a moment of uncomfortable silence, the woman shifted in her seat, both elbows resting on the table. "I've some questions for you. Questions that I want answered. First, introductions. I'm field captain Gwennifer Jannson and, from what I've been told, you've forgotten your name. That said, I'm hoping that you can tell me exactly what happened to your detachment."

"They're all dead. I'm the only survivor," answered Everus flatly.

Gwennifer squinted at him, clearly unconvinced by his reply. "Let me get this right. From what you told commander Toth, you were part of a cavalry consignment sent into The Deadmoor *prior* to the fall of Wyrm's Port in order to reconnoitre Øggar movements."

Everus nodded.

"And...you've been wandering the wilderness ever since?" Her question was asked with measured disbelief. Her hands met, covering her mouth, her fingers locking as though in prayer just under her nose.

"I don't know how long it's been. I guess that's what happens when you lose contact with others and are forced to live..."

"You look rather healthy for someone who's been living on wild berries and the occasional rabbit," Gwennifer interrupted.

"It's better than the fare the army provides."

Gwennifer gave that whisper of a smile. "According to the commander, you were found near the road some three and a half leagues north of here." She reached for a map resting nearby and spun it around so that Everus could see it the right way up. "That would be about...here." She pointed to the position in question.

Everus leaned forward in order to get a better look. The map was smudged and dirty. Blood stained one corner. Lines, arrows and other military symbols he did not know the meaning of were scribbled over much of it but he could recognise enough to pick out their location.

"Slap bang in the middle of no-man's land." The field captain drummed the nails of her right hand on the table top. "Would you care to explain how you got there?"

"I can't remember."

Gwennifer sat back, maintaining eye contact. Her lips pursed. Nails still drumming, she took her eyes from him and looked to the ceiling, clearly thinking over her next line of inquiry. She looked back at him. "I see. So...I take it you don't have much of an idea as to what's happened in your absence?"

"I'd guess that Wyrm's Port's fallen. That much seems obvious. It would also explain why you lot are here."

Gwennifer waited for the latest bout of thunder to cease. "Then you know nothing about Xethorn...or His attack on Ghavin's Keep?"

"Just what I overheard in the mess tent," lied Everus. "Something about how the Lord of Murder has taken control of Wyrm's Port with the help of the Øggarbakken behemoths and..."

"The behemoths are gone. Dead." Gwennifer's unsmiling face fixed him with a cold frown. Outside, a flash of lightning lit the shadowy interior. "The bastard's turned them into huge skeletons. That's what we've been fighting for the past many days. Giant, bloody skeletons. Not only that, but by some kind of foul sorcery He's also been making our dead come back to life, turning them against us. We've got to cart our dead off the battlefield in order to prevent Him getting to them."

Everus shook his head in feigned concern. "That's terrible."

"Terrible? *Terrible!?*" Gwennifer glared at him as her voice hardened. "It's a bloody sight worse than that! Have you any idea what it's like having to cut down your own friends? To have to dismember, then cremate the pieces? To have to run for your life, pursued by nothing more than...*bits?* Heads. Arms. You name it." After a moment's pause, and realising that she was getting little more than a token display of sympathy, she continued, her tone calmer, as though the bile from her experiences had been spewed forth. She took a deep breath. "That aside, we're pushing Xethorn's forces back. His attack on Ghavin's Keep was mercifully short-lived."

"I was told that He may have ordered the withdrawal for tactical reasons."

"Yes, well, whatever the case, I think His forces got more than they bargained for when they tried to take the city. They managed to breach a part of the north wall and some even broke into the city proper, destroying much of the northern avenues, but they didn't hold it for long. For two days we battled them, myself and many of the men you've seen here tonight were part of the unit that eventually kicked them out. We've been given orders to set up a kind of buffer zone between Wyrm's Port and our city – to act as a deterrent in case the bastard gets any more crazy ideas."

"And what do *you* think? Did His forces retreat...or did you eject them?"

Lightning flashed.

A much louder crack of thunder broke.

Gwennifer's brow furrowed as she tried to take in the measure of the man seated before her. There was something unsettling about him that, from the look on her face, she was finding hard to grasp and that worried her. Most of her subordinates were brain-dead, 'give 'em a sword, point 'em in the right direction and tell 'em what to hit' types. "What...do you mean?"

"Well..." Everus sat back, enjoying the challenge his querying was posing to her attempts to pigeonhole him, "several things. Firstly, have you considered the possibility that such a foray may have been intentionally provocative...in the hope that you would, well, come out of the safety of the city and fight on the plains?" He smiled at the notion of unease in her eyes. "Or could it be that He views His armies as expendable, seeing as how the supply of skeletons from the various city graveyards is nigh on unlimited. Therefore, He can afford to fight on His terms, well aware that the only way you can defeat Him is to launch an all-out assault on Wyrm's Port itself? And...if, as I've been told, the city is shrouded in a strange darkness, then that is perhaps not achievable." His smile widened, almost cruelly. "Then again, what about the possibility that His forces' intentions were not to *take* the city...but rather to take something from it?"

"Take something from...?" Gwennifer's reply went unfinished for a loud series of trumpet blasts suddenly rent the stormy night.

The camp was under attack.

Everus felt his withered hand awaken, the nails digging into his thigh. In a blur, Gwennifer rushed past him, snatched up her helmet and sword and rushed outside. He followed, his senses now succumbing once more to Cyrvilus' murk, the energies exuded by the hand both strengthening and numbing. What he saw as the field captain flung the canvas flap to one side sent a dark, almost tangible, wave of fear through what remained of his uncontaminated mind.

Illuminated by a flash of lightning, Magmabreath, the great skeletal brimstone dragon he had last seen on display in The Grand Repository in Ghavin's Keep, reared before him, only this time the thing was no longer inanimate. With a sweep of one of its huge claws, three armoured soldiers were scattered, their bodies torn apart, their dying screams adding to the sounds of unfolding chaos. Bones grinding, the sulphurous remains fell to all fours, its great neck swinging round in order to allow the monstrous fanged skull to turn to Everus. A spear clattered off it. A spray of ineffectual arrows whistled through and off its cavernous ribcage, chipping bone but little else.

The rain was coming down in sheets.

Gwennifer ducked and rolled to avoid a claw which would have ripped a horse in two. A swing from a huge vertebrae-ridged tail flattened a tent and sent two of her soldiers flying.

The fleshless dragon shook its tail, batting a second tent to the ground, and screamed at the night. Its screech – the voice of the dark and its power over the light – sent a wave of fear through an approaching phalanx of spearmen, for it touched upon the primal fears buried in the marrow of all living creatures. Many of the men fell to the mud, their knees buckling under them, their shit flowing freely. Others turned tail and ran screaming into the night, their spears and shields falling from their trembling hands.

Even Everus, his will bolstered by the demonic and a life of ghastly experiences, pulled back.

"By all the gods!" cried the field commander, looking up. "*What manner of beast...!?*" A huge clawed foot came down upon her, squeezing her innards out of her armour and driving her remains into the soaked ground like a well-swung mallet would a tent peg.

Magmabreath ground the woman's corpse further. It drew itself up to its full height, Gwennifer's helmeted-head embedded like a thorn in the bones of its foot. The fossilised remains flinched as a flurry of shot arrows snapped off its skull, one lucky shot entering an empty eye-socket and rattling in its braincase until shaken free.

A sudden thought – no doubt generated from the Cyrvilian hand – flashed into Everus' mind. He would make the dragon a thing of flesh and blood, for only then could it be truly slain. Only if it bled could it be permanently killed. As things stood, the remains could no doubt be destroyed and shattered, obliterated as could any skeleton, but, as Everus knew only too well, bones could be rejoined – the hand testament to that. Lacking a brain, the bones were just animated remains – an extension of Xethorn no doubt dispatched to discover the surge of power the hand had emitted earlier when it had enabled him to teleport from Borgrim's End, which lay many normal days' travel to the east.

The withered hand flexed in readiness as the towering mass of bones crashed nearer.

Incensed at the death of their field commander, two brave souls, the cream of the Ghavin's Keep infantry corps, charged forward. One was plucked from the ground and crushed to a bloody pulp, his helmeted head popping like a cork from a well-shaken bottle. The other managed to get a few hefty hacks in with his heavy two-handed sword before he too was smacked aside, his plate mail clad body sent reeling. Their efforts, although foolhardy and short-lived, were not entirely futile, for they enabled a group of reinforcements to arrive on the scene. Dragging two huge loaded ballistae, these soldiers took one look at the dragon and fled, their morale broken at the sight of the thing and the carnage strewn about it.

The infantrymen's rather ineffectual intervention had given Everus the time needed to harness Cyrvilus' magic. Raising the hand, he shouted words of power which seemed to come from outside his body, if not from outside his very soul. These were alien words uttered in an arcane and demonic language that none had dared speak openly for a very long time. These were words that even Dae'dicus and Dae'morogin had never spoken.

Magmabreath turned, its movements stiff and slow. Momentarily affected by the spell, the fearsome skeleton seemed to solidify further, paralysed, temporarily returning to nothing more than an awe-inspiring museum-piece once more. Silence fell, Everus' incantation now ended. The words he had muttered, long-since forgotten, were carried by the aether on wings of evil, to disturb the living wherever they slept. The spell began to take a greater effect, and, with a crackle of energy, a deep green glow took hold of the dragon's clawed foot, Gwennifer's mashed skull its focal point. Like a macabre, sprouting thing, blobs of filthy grey-pink corpulence burst forth, covering the bones in wet flesh.

A volley of hurled javelins clattered against the rigid dragon.

More screams sounded from those who had only just awoken and now stared with bleary and unbelieving eyes at the living nightmare.

Everus grinned, his eyes fixed on the unfolding spectacle. He watched as, faster now, the strands of flesh spread from the bloody stain, the residual skin and gore from the dead field commander's pulverized head leaping and wrapping its way around the stained bones of the dragon. Like a parody of the damage wrought on his own hand, the skin engulfed the dragon's lower forelimb.

Suddenly Magmabreath stirred into action, the hold broken. It struggled, shaking its now flesh-covered foot vigorously in a doomed attempt to free itself from the bizarre coating that now spread to smother its bones. In response to the agitation, the flesh spread faster, bridging its ribs and leaping to its lower jaw with a disgusting squelch. Under the gelatinous membrane pulsed veins and arteries, the juices they carried vile and dark – toxic, oleaginous dragon blood that had not flowed for countless years. And as the blood pulsed, the dragon's movements became sluggish, its new casing hampering its mobility, its jellied musculature now a poor substitute for the dark necromancy that had maintained it.

Making the brimstone dragon a thing of flesh was not something Everus would have contemplated under normal circumstances. And as the massive thing assumed corporeality, the magical skin working to coat it in a layer of vulnerability, more soldiers turned and fled, the sight before them now even more monstrous. Half a dozen members of the garrison gathered for a moment, eyes fixed on the unsightly transformation, before taking to their heels.

With a fierce stretching, as though the horror had become mammalian and was now giving birth, a series of throbbing organs, each as big as a man, blossomed inside its great ribcage, to be quickly enveloped in a sheet of semi-liquid hide. Gone now were the basalt-hard scales that had encrusted over decades on the lava beds of Zeth and had snapped the sturdiest lances of the knights of old; scales that had once been impervious to fire and spell now gone. Its exoskeleton had never been breached – for Magmabreath had been poisoned, hence its excellent state of preservation. Now, with its throat filling with wet tissue and, as the scholars at The Grand Repository had correctly deduced, capable of speech, Magmabreath reared up onto its hind legs and gagged like a cat with a fur ball. Gobbets of unformed flesh leapt from its jaws only to snap back, vanishing into the dark pit of its gullet. Slitted, kite shield-sized eyes formed in once-empty eye-sockets. A ridge of bulbous horns burst forth, forming a crest which erupted down the length of its spine, creating a large, veined dorsal fin. Whether in part due to the fact that its chicken egg-sized brain had now coalesced inside its skull, or due to the fact that Everus stood smiling triumphantly before it, something almost akin to worry sent a ripple down the length of the dragon's spine, its nervous system now fully rewired.

Now enwrapped completely, it looked far worse; a loathsome, new-born gargantuan, glistening and pulsating. In places, the skin steamed and plopped, setting and dribbling like a plasterer's mixture.

Drawing upon the telekinetic powers of the hand, Everus moved the two wheeled ballistae into position. The twin giant crossbows trundled forward, their multiple firing spears ready to be unleashed. Around him, the camp resembled a slaughter yard. Recognisable body parts, and bits that were not, lay here and there. Light from a fiercely burning fire revealed the flattened tents, splintered weapon racks, crushed barrels and demolished watch tower, which lay uprooted alongside a destroyed section of palisade.

With a final stretching, the last remnants of skin dripping like hot candle wax, Magmabreath's pudgy incarnation was complete. Sagging slabs of flesh hung like cadavers in a cannibal's larder, gruesome folds of fat drooping like flowstone over ancient stalagmites. In places, the skin had not covered the dragon quite as thoroughly, its bones visible amongst the pseudo-meat's translucency.

Flesh had finally returned to that which had been fleshless.

The twin siege weapons were now in position. Through willpower alone, Everus readied them, drawing back the taut firing strings, which under normal conditions, required the might of three men. With an audible click, he knew they were set, ready to unleash their lethal load at the moment of his command.

Magmabreath seemed to realise the danger of the situation.

Now having been transformed into the semblance, if not the actuality, of a living entity, one capable of independent thought, the necromantic connection that attuned it to its master weakened. No longer a mere extension of Xethorn, the dragon's bestial instincts now took hold; the dominant one being the prolongation of its own survival, a consideration which even overruled its allegiance to the Lord of Murder. For too long its dragonic essence had festered, its fleshy carcass allowed to disintegrate in the cinder fields of Zeth, after having been trapped and gassed by The Watchful Eye paladins of Pope Edburgah II. And for what had seemed an equally long time, it had been forced to endure the probing and the inspection of the imbecilic buffoons at The Grand Repository as they had subjected its remains to a battery of scientific and magical tests, all aimed at understanding its being. Throughout such torment, its essence had been ever present; forced to witness the violation and the butchery, the dissection and the subsequent conjoining of its remains as well as the mistaken blunderings and the foolish conjectures that had been reached. Drawing upon that rage, which it had harboured over the centuries it had lain dormant, it mustered the will to make a sudden lunge.

The attack took Everus off guard. He leapt to one side, his boots sliding in the mud. Falling to one knee, he was forced to make a mad scramble to get back on his feet, even as a huge blubbery foot stomped down where only moments before he had stood. So, there was still life in the old bones was there? His abilities enhanced by the hand, he somersaulted backwards, dodging a clumsy gnash from the dragon's jaws. Unsteadily, he landed atop an overturned cart, rocked for a moment in order to maintain his balance and then, with a bunching of the Cyrvilian fist, he discharged both ballistae.

Six huge spears sped through the air, catching Magmabreath in a wicked crossfire. Three missiles sank deep into the dragon's left flank – two vanishing inside and a third striking bone, its shaft deeply embedding. One spear lodged in the monster's extended neck. Two missiles missed, whistling off into the darkness.

Magmabreath gave a throaty howl, a lumpy foot attempting to remove the spear from its skewered throat. The spear shaft snapped, the point still lodged deep inside. The fleshy bulk roared – physical pain a sensation it had never felt before. Staggering to one side, it crumpled, its bulk tottering. It crashed with a ground-shaking thump.

Smugly, Everus gazed at his handiwork. "So this is the best you can do?" His question was aimed at Xethorn, whom he was sure could both see and hear him. "Pathetic." Leaping down from the cart, he cast a quick look around, wondering what else he could throw at the quivering mountain before him...just how much more punishment should he inflict before deciding enough was enough and going for the jugular?

The dragon groaned noisily.

Oily blood streamed from its heaving chest where the spears had struck. With a pained roar, Magmabreath pushed itself upright. Drawing its neck high into the air, it then lunged down and belched forth a great cloud of acrid, black smoke.

Everus was caught in the thick of it. Eyes stinging, he coughed and fell to his knees. The smoke was burning, the reek of brimstone almost overpowering. What was more, he could no longer see where he was going, or, for that matter, in which direction the dragon hid. That it was near he knew, for the sound of its deep, laboured breathing seemed to come from all around.

The breathing was becoming louder, throatier.

And then...a torrent of lava engulfed the field of battle, its orange-red glow blasting through the choking smog. Vomited from the dragon's maw, the spray of thick, fiery death reduced much of the immediate vicinity into a blazing sea of magma; a raging storm of swirling, hungry fire. The corpse-strewn ground was incinerated, the once muddy earth now engulfed in a conflagration. Burning pools plopped and smoked. Geyser-like, globs of molten spume were spat into the air.

The moment the first of the liquid fire tore through the murk, the hand suddenly clenched, bringing a shimmering barrier around Everus. It was similar to the magical aura he had seen surrounding Creeps on several occasions and the Xethornite, Blackmorg, back in Whaggustraag's temple in Wathang-Hu. The temperature inside was freezing, icy, but its coldness was gone before it was even felt, for the sudden wash of the blazing regurgitation instantly negated it.

In a clash of powerful forces, dense white vapours condensed into the air.

Fortunately for Everus, Magmabreath's deadly exhalation had not targeted him directly. Whether because the dragon had also been partially blinded by the sulphurous smog or for some other reason, he did not know. What he was certain of, as he looked around at the burning desolation becoming clearer through the dissipating clouds of magic, was that nothing living could have survived the ferocity of a direct hit, protected or not.

Even the dragon, the initiator of the pyroclastic gout, seemed to have suffered. For although, surprisingly, it had been capable of unleashing such an attack, it had obviously not taken into account the fact that it was no longer invulnerable to its intensity. Devoid of its scales, the lower half of its head was now bone once more, the instant skin Cyrvilus had sheathed it in now burnt away. Similarly with the neck and body, where a long, still-smoking, black-red weal of exposed ribcage was now visible. Much of its body was likewise on fire, the splashes from its breath, which had reduced many a paladin of yesteryear to nothing more than a smouldering heap of metal, bone and ash, now melting *its* skin. Wreathed in flames from head to tail tip, Magmabreath thrashed insanely, spreading the blaze throughout the camp.

Aware that the spell that had saved him was already weakening, the barrier now popping and blistering like a heated balloon, Everus rushed from the scorched area. A flow of lava ran alongside him, carving its own fiery trench in an unstoppable, blazing seep. He ran for the edge of the burning camp – aware that the magical expenditures had once again cost the cursed hand dearly, the hold it had over him melting away like the timber outpost around him. Common sense told him that now was probably not the best time to go after the dragon. He would get as far from here as possible, rest up and then plan for an attack on Xethorn.

Soon it would be time to take the war to Wyrm's Port.

CHAPTER TWENTY-FIVE

"Aye...an' ye can kiss ma swingers an' a'. I'll no' be goin' back there. *Shit!* I'd rather walk intae Wyrm's Port an' take ma chances wi' the Øggars efter whit I've seen. Yon bloody dragon-thing was *enormous!* It swallowed a man whole afore ma eyes, b'gods! So it did!"

"Aye, that's right," confirmed another grubba. "I saw it an' a'."

Commander Toth turned from the two kilted, grubban soldiers and faced Everus. "What about you?"

For a moment, Everus ignored the implied order, his gaze focused on the rising black smoke less than a league away. "I think they're all dead...commander. It would be a waste of time. To go back is nonsensical."

"Non...*whit?*" cried one of the grubbas. "Whit's he on aboot?"

"Ye cannae go back there, b'gods. It'd be a slaughter...suicide," protested his sibling. "Look at it – it's been burnt tae the grun. Naeb'dy could be alive in there. Everyb'dy who was in ma tent was burnt tae buggery. Ye'd be needin' a dustpan an' brush to get 'em oot."

Toth's face hardened, disliking the reality of the situation. He looked to his boots, pondering the next course of action. Gwennifer had been the one in charge. She had been the one who had made all the decisions – telling him when to act and when to withdraw. She had been the military strategist, the tactician, the one who could work out when and how to launch an offensive and how to optimise a retreat. She had been the brains behind the expulsion of Xethorn's forces from Ghavin's Keep and the pursuit of His forces towards Wyrm's Port. But now...now she was gone and he was the next in the chain of command. There were others, higher up, in the imperial city, but how could he return to them and inform them that not only had Gwennifer been killed but that the entire northern front had now been reduced to but a handful of men and two grubbas?

"We could always...well...launch an attack on Wyrm's Port?" suggested Everus, understanding something of the commander's dilemma.

"Yeh, let's go fer it!" growled one of the grubbas, fiercely sinking his claymore into the ground at his feet. "Enuff o' this pussyfootin' aboot. Let's get the bastard an' grip Him b' the girtiest till He screams fer His mutha!"

"Or farts like a duck! *Hic!*" replied the other. The way he rocked unsteadily from side to side and the pissed look in his eyes suggested he was just that. His long brown beard was flung casually over his right shoulder like a shawl. "Mebee...mebee then He'll ken that He cannae mess wi' the Ghavin's Keep mil...militia. *Hic!* Bastard that He is."

"Sounds good," said Everus, approvingly. He looked about, taking in the Ironaxe brothers, Sledge and Slagg, as well as the nine human infantrymen and their commander. From the looks on *their* faces, not all of them shared the grubbas' blood-crazed and alcohol-induced enthusiasm.

"Now...let's not make any rash decisions, here," said Toth. "There are, what...thirteen of us? And hundreds of them?" He shook his head disapprovingly. "It'd be absolute madness. No one in their right mind would even consider..."

"I'd go," interrupted Slagg.

"Aye, an' so would I," seconded Sledge. His words were slurred, but something more than drunkenness now shone from behind his pale grey eyes – passion and a will to fight. "The bastard Øggars burnt doon oor fayther's pub! So methinks it's aboot time someb'dy kicked His arse fer Him! *Hic!*"

"But...there's no way in. The city's covered in a dark cloud," argued Toth. "You'd never..."

"There is a way in, commander," Everus interjected. "There's a system of tunnels that run into the city from along the coastline, near to where The Dark Sea reaches the beginning of the Wyrm's Port harbour. The tunnels of which I speak were built during the early days of the city, for sewage maintenance and tidal defence. An ambitious plan, but it never saw completion. The tunnels were largely forgotten about..."

"Then how do you know about them?" interrupted Toth.

"Your...field captain, Gwennifer, told me. She said that she'd received intelligence from someone back in Ghavin's Keep. She was in the process of telling me and asking if I would be able and willing to act as a guide, seeing as I'm from the city, when..." Everus' face set grimly as he nodded in the direction of the destroyed camp. Although much of what he was saying was utter fabrication, the tunnels did exist. He had actually been inside one, a long time ago. He and his old adventuring companion, Grigalo Shan'alan, had gone down in order to investigate rumours of a giant crocothrash and a long-lost treasure. From what little he remembered, it had been dank and smelly and at the end of it they had stunk for days and found nothing. Admittedly, they had not ventured too far, the echoing splashes and the flitting shadows enough to make them stay within easy reach of the exit.

"And, these tunnels...you say that they lead into the city?" asked Toth, reluctantly. He fixed Everus with a hard stare. Although certain the man was telling the truth, part of him was trying to find a way out, for the idea of skulking through the sewage outlets in search of the Lord of Murder did not rank highly on his enjoyment scale – not when a return to Ghavin's Keep and a nice whore-warmed bed offered a more comfortable alternative.

"Yes, according to what I was told. Apparently, there are several exits. I think I can lead us directly into the heart of the city. From there, it would be easy enough to get close to Xethorn."

"An' then what?" inquired a soldier, an arm in a sling. "I've heard that He's a god! How are *we* supposed to fight *Him?*"

Toth and many of the others added their voices in support.

Everus reached for the necklace he wore. "With this." The dark purple gem which contained the trapped essence of the Daemondamned sparkled, for a moment its inner light playing unnervingly over his face.

"What's that?" asked Toth, moving closer to get a better look. He was about to reach out and try to examine it when a strange, unsettling feeling – as though he were about to shake hands with a corpse – came over him, and he quickly drew his hand away.

"I've no idea," Everus lied. "But if what Gwennifer told me is true, then it can destroy Xethorn. All we have to...is get near enough."

For a time no one spoke, each lost in their own thoughts – thoughts about avenging fallen friends and loved ones; thoughts of fear and impending doom melding with those of glory and triumph. Could they conceivably return to Ghavin's Keep knowing that a chance to assassinate The Dark Slayer had slipped through their fingers?

"Well, whit're we waitin' fer?" cried Slagg, breaking the silence. "Come on!"

Whether due to the power lying dormant in the hand, or because of the semi-hypnotic influence of the soul gem, Everus knew that these men were now in effect his to command. They would not follow him blindly nor, as yet, would they do anything suicidal, but they would go where he led. For Toth at least, the lie that they would be continuing with Gwennifer's commands was something of a comfort. For the others, the horrors they had seen would drive them to seek a definite end to the nightmare. Everus looked about him at the surrounding bleakness of the land, its relative flatness and uniformity broken only by the low foothills which rose several leagues to the east. A few stunted, lightning blasted trees dotted the predominantly grey and brown-green landscape. There was no sign of the dragon however. Either it had crawled its way back to Xethorn or else it had gone somewhere to die. He hoped for the latter.

When all were ready; weapons checked, armour buckled and what rations they had remaining divided, they set out.

† † †

By mid-morning the sky overhead had turned an unhealthy slate-grey, the clouds gusting their way on a strong north wind, which brought with it the unsavoury tang of the sea. With each step north, the sky seemed to darken, the clouds now piling high on the far horizon, massing into ominous thunderheads. The mood amongst most of the men mirrored that of the weather conditions, for now that the initial relief at having survived the slaughter at the camp and having a fresh incentive had passed, each began to doubt the survival prospects of their new mission.

Some muttered darkly, but as soon as Everus turned to them they shut up and kept marching.

Rain began to fall from the menacing sky.

Despite the gloom, Everus could now see the dark cloud that cloaked his home city as it shimmered like a perverse heat haze on the western skyline. A league further along, they came to a junction, an old wooden sign pointing in the direction of the cursed city. It bore the simple legend:

WYRM'S PORT

A faint smile formed on Everus' grim and rain-streaked face. Off in the distance, just beyond and to the right of the dark smudge of shadow that was the city itself, he saw the cold, black-blue expanse of water that was the southern edge of The Dark Sea.

Once a thriving channel for trade, from which the produce of many lands and peoples had been funnelled into the city, via the well-protected sea routes and shipping lanes, it now lay desolate and gloomy, cold and unwelcoming, haunted and no doubt polluted by the activities from within the city itself. The tall ships and the extravagant merchant vessels were now a thing of the past. Even the pirate ships from the wicked ports of Uxu and Mo-chang on the isle of Tavocos had gone – their crews now dead and drained of blood by Xethorn, if what he had heard was true.

Everus fleetingly remembered his fight with 'Bloody' Magruder in the lighthouse at the end of Damp Street. Presumably all of the pirate's men – The Wild Breed, he recalled – had perished under Xethorn's unforgiving regime – despite the fact that Magruder himself had been a worshipper of Xethorn.

"I take it this is the trail we want." There was a tired look in Toth's eyes and the greyness which flecked his hair seemed to have increased noticeably since yesterday, when Everus had first encountered him.

"Yes. This is it." Everus could see that all the men were tired.

Suddenly a cry went up from one of the soldiers.

"What is it!?" cried Toth, drawing his sword.

"Skeletons!" came back the shout.

Everus rushed over to where three of the men were gathered. Pushing one aside, he looked to where one of the others pointed and saw, some distance away, a patrol of lumbering bonework. Lacking flesh and bodies as such, it was hard to discern numbers, but there must have been at least half a dozen of them. Like gaunt, bleached trees, the assortment of ragged, giant skeletons appeared to be in pursuit. Some looked as though they had been fused together; no longer resembling the bipedal behemoths from which they were derived but rather a twisted mass of limb bones and skulls, fashioned anew and augmented.

"Do you think they've seen us?" asked one of the men, a sharp-faced veteran called Turrell. Like some of the others, he gripped his iron-headed hammer, the mass-produced weapon that had been designed with the specific intention of breaking bones in mind. He was big, bearded and stocky and more than ready to wade in and give the skeletons what for.

"Well, I don't plan on waiting here to find out," Toth answered. "Come on. Let's get a move on."

Tired and aching, the eleven men and two grubbas ran for the westward trail that wound down a slight decline. There were tricky patches of ground to cross – long wrinkles in the earth formed from centuries of wagon tracks and coils of tripping briar – making the going difficult. Fear of what lay behind drove them on all the same.

The rain still fell, although a break in the clouds over to the east gave some hope for improvement.

Out of choice, Everus fell to the back, enabling those slower than himself – notably the two grubbas and the man with his arm in a sling – to get in front. He wanted to see if the skeletal behemoths were indeed after them and thus try and deduce whether they were specifically homing in on the hand. If such were the case, then any evasion was short-lived, for sooner or later either this lot would catch up or they would run into another group. The soldiers were mostly dead on their feet but still they kept going, their military training and no doubt the horrors they had seen befall their comrades at the hands of their undead enemy, spurring them on.

The trail they were on soon levelled out.

Before them, across a broad stretch of open heathland, the landscape dipped down on its path to the coast. A rough league or so of desolate land now lay before them, the track they were following, narrowing and becoming muddier.

Jogging along at the rear of the group, Everus was forever turning to look back, half-expecting to see one of the great scythe-wielding bone colossi come bearing down on him. A quick flash of their blade and that would be it – for as long as the evil hand lay dormant, he was as vulnerable as the next man. A blade to the neck...and all his suffering would be for naught. Heart pounding, he ran on.

Like driven slaves, they all kept going, knowing that to stop could well mean death.

The track became less rutted, yet soggier, the closer they got to the sea. A chill tidal wind blasted towards them, the stench it brought with it unwelcome, for it carried the strong reek of decay. It was a clogging stink, the kind that permeated the clothes and, if one imagined too hard, the skin as well.

In the lead, Toth skidded to a halt, signalling for his men to do likewise. They gathered around, the look of displeasure on their faces obvious. One or two of the younger ones started to retch, the smell was that bad, their faces turning a sickly grey.

"Why are we stopping?" asked Everus, harshly.

"I think we may've found one o' yer sewer tunnels," replied a man called Warburg. He was short, but strongly-built. His face was more or less flat, giving Everus the impression that either he had fallen face-first from quite a height or else someone had smacked him hard with a shovel. He had a bloody bandage around his bald head and carried what looked like half a garrison's amount of equipment on his broad back. "Look!" He pointed to a rectangular stone construction.

There was little doubt that this was where the awful smell was coming from and, as Everus pushed past a few of the soldiers and started to make his way towards it, he could see that the culvert-thing had been built atop an artificial mound of heaped rock. The structure resembled four sarcophagi slabs laid out end-to-end. In each, a shaft had been dug or drilled and the drain blocked with an equally heavy-looking metal grill. The pipes were perhaps wide enough for an unarmoured man to squeeze through – but it would be a tight fit. Around the edges and all over the slabs themselves, hung seaweed and flaps of indiscernible filth.

Triggered by the sight and the smell of this dismal outlet, an unwelcome reminder of the Ullerby hag flashed through Everus' mind. This was the kind of place he could envisage a monster of her sort inhabiting – lurking amongst the trapped sewage and the dripping effluent, her nights spent feeding on slugs and scum, whilst wallowing in a sea of turds.

Toth climbed up. "Tell me this isn't where you plan on going?"

Everus grinned. "This isn't where *we're* going." He moved closer in order to check one of the metal grills. It had been securely padlocked even though the metal had badly corroded. He stamped down on it with his right foot and shattered its rusty hinge. With a muffled clang, the metal struck stone and then the entire opening gave way and fell into the cylindrical, mess-clogged pipe, the sound echoing. He looked down into its horrible depths and waited for the splash.

A heartbeat or so later it came, the dull plop indicating it had struck liquid waste.

"Are these...part of this sewer network you're on about?" asked the commander, clambering closer to peek down. The stink emanating from below brought a flood of bile to his gullet. He turned to one side and threw up.

Everus waited for Toth's nausea to pass, taking the time to look back to the higher ground and make sure that Xethorn's minions were not on the advance. All was clear. "I reckon this must be part of it, but...this is not the one we want to take. Besides, it would be a hard job trying to fit down one of these pipes." He looked down another one, half-expecting to see some slimy, slithering thing come crawling up. "We should get moving. There's no telling if those dead behemoths will come after us. Nor do I know how far we've still got to go." From his slightly raised vantage point, he could see much of the land before him. The track cut across country more or less in a straight line before skirting the nearest fringe of the sea.

To either side, the land was bleak and empty, the tidal flats and salt-marshes riddled here and there with sunken pools and the washed-up remains of old boats. That this whole area was susceptible to tidal flooding was obvious, the traces of seaweed around the noisome drain entrance and the presence of the stranded fishing vessels clear indicators.

Surveying the strange coastal landscape, it was not difficult for Everus to imagine how it must look when fully submerged; the shallow gully in which most of the soldiers were waiting would be under a fathom of sea water, the land transformed into a vast watery grave. He could see many other gullies akin to the one they had traversed; trenches dug not by men for the sake of warfare but channels gouged out of the seabed by the process of erosion. The sight of some of them made him think of the impressions of primordial creatures he had seen in rocks; fossil imprints of organisms a few scholars at The Academy had claimed pre-dated the arrival of the very gods themselves.

"Are we going?" asked Toth, he, like the rest of his men, now keen to be moving.

"Yes." Everus peered into the thickening gloom. "This way."

The land proved deceptive. Distances stretched themselves out and, although it had initially looked as though they could easily reach the sea's edge before nightfall, it was soon apparent that it was further off than it appeared. They trekked on, their movements hushed in the deepening twilight. Every so often the track became un-navigable, the way blocked by a deep pool of rank water, and on such occasions they had to climb out of the shallow gully and make a detour, their boots squelching, the odd curse the only other sound.

Pausing to glance about him, Everus saw that they had reached a tiny island of raised ground. Glancing back, he could make out the trail they had followed and, in the distance, lying like a dense black fog over the flats, the place they were trying to reach.

In every direction, the land was unwelcoming. What had once been relatively pleasant countryside was now twisted and corrupted. The very soil, sand, silt and mud under their feet seemed infected with evil, as though it were possessed with a malign, mischievous force which seemed to trip, cling and sink with every boot which fell on it. Muddy water, laced with what looked like blood, bubbled, squelched and flowed in rivulets from the befouled ground.

Everus knew that it was imperative to at least reach the sewer entrance before nightfall and, even now, the darkening sky actively seemed to race against them. Throughout the weary, miserable trudge, the Cyrvilian hand had remained calm, leading him to wonder whether it was doing so intentionally. Was it aware that its energising attracted Xethorn's eye? Or was it like a crocothrash – its dormancy nothing more than a cunning deception? Or had the powers used truly drained it so much?

The never-ending sound of the tide and the chill its advance brought with it, broke him from his thoughts.

High above, the sky to his left was now a darkening cobalt, merging through various hues so that the sky to his right was a vibrant midnight-indigo – the span of the firmament as yet unsullied by either Uhu'giaggoth's or Xethorn's touch, although, admittedly, The Dark Slayer's previous attempts to breach the planar boundary had resulted in some impressive, if temporary, atmospheric damage.

Under different circumstances, the fall of this particular evening would have been breathtakingly beautiful, the kind of day's end artists and poets would die for, if they could but capture its essence in their works. However, Everus' view was short-lived. For no sooner had he turned his head in order to take in the shadowy sweep of the coastline, when a twinge from the hand let him know that Cyrvilus was once again stirring. With the returning powers, he began to feel more alive than ought to be possible for one who had been through what he had. The aches and the stiffness in his limbs seemed to disappear entirely – the heaviness of the chain mail shirt he wore fading to nothing. His eyesight became sharper, far away details now becoming clearer, even though the darkness sought to conceal all. On the horizon, he could discern the white-flecked rollers as they made their way landwards. And then, as he drew his gaze from the sea in order to scan the land to his left, he saw what had to be their goal.

† † †

Everus stared into the foul-smelling outlet. It was somewhat larger than he had at first anticipated, the diameter of the circular tunnel perhaps wide enough for two men to walk side by side. The grilled-gate now hung from rusty hinges, the two grubbas having displayed their strength by wrenching it open.

The other men sat about rummaging through their packs and finishing off the last of their meagre rations. Some sharpened their weapons, as others looked around nervously.

"*Can you believe it?* Not one sodding torch amongst the lot of them!" exclaimed Toth, walking up to join Everus.

For a time, Everus did not respond, his mind elsewhere. Cyrvilus was forcing his own demonic will into him, his grip harder than iron and far colder. With what free will he still clung to, he tried to order his thoughts; decide for himself what plan of action to take. It was blatantly obvious that most of the men were exhausted. The question was whether to let them rest and thus possibly forfeit the all important element of surprise – if such a thing still existed, or to keep going – risking whatever hidden and additional dangers haste and weariness could create.

"I tell you, since that damned dragon attack, they've lost all sense of discipline," Toth complained.

"I imagine seeing one's comrades burnt to cinders and torn to rags might have that effect," Everus commented wryly. "I'm sure we can improvise something. Who knows, perhaps that gem Gwennifer gave me might help us out?"

"Yes, and while we're on the subject, can you tell me any more about it?" There was interest in Toth's voice. "I mean, did she tell you where she got it? She certainly didn't mention it, or this mission, to me."

"Alas, no. All she said was that she'd been given secret and explicit orders to launch a surprise attack on Wyrm's Port." Grim-faced, Everus thumbed at the unwelcoming tunnel opening. "This is where she planned to go."

"You know where it leads?"

"Yes...I..." Everus hesitated. Currents of dark fire seemed to flow inside his left arm, its passage visible to his eyes alone. He felt like roaring his agony to the skies, the injection of chaos fluids no longer pain-numbing. Now it burned and froze, devoured and drained, the searing pain unlike anything he had ever felt before. He staggered forward, his other arm outstretched, his free hand saving him from a fall.

"Are you...?"

Everus took a deep breath, filling his lungs with air. The pain subsided. He steadied himself. "I'll be all right. It's just...an old wound." He looked down at the dead hand. In his mind, he imagined the skin breaking out in a web of dark veins.

Toth followed his gaze, wincing at the sight. "You know, that looks really nasty. What happened? It looks all..."

"Atrophied?"

"Eh...yeah, I guess so. Have you managed to get anyone to have a look at it?"

"It's not too..." Everus' face tightened and he ground his teeth as another wave of pain surged through him. It was how he imagined the final moments of being quartered would feel – something he had once seen happen to some unfortunate, deep within the old Xethornite temple in Wyrm's Port, where all the trouble had started. Hatred for Xethorn welled through him, alongside the pain. A rage and a bitterness that went way beyond the desire for revenge filled his brain. Whether such intense emotions were due to Cyrvilus' influence or his personal inclination towards hatred, he neither could tell nor cared.

In an instant, the pain vanished. Such was the relief that he felt like laughing, the sensation almost alien to him now. He contained himself, still unsure about how to proceed. For reasons as yet unknown, the long-dead demonologist had deemed it unwise to take full possession of him. Could it be that it sensed the men around him – that it was ashamed or perhaps fearful to display itself before others whilst still not at full strength? Had it made the conscious decision that now was not the time to do so – like a hibernating bear that had stirred too early? Or, could it be that his own will had proved greater, and that, against all probabilities and expectations,

577

he had shrugged of the Uhu'giaggothian-worshipper's attempted possession?

"You sure you're all right?" There was confusion written all over the commander's concerned face.

"Yes. I'm all right." Everus nodded and turned back to the gaping pipe. "We have to go in tonight. I know the men are tired, but the sooner we get through to the other side the easier things will be." He removed the dark gem with the withered hand, the crystalline stone like ice in his grip. It pulsed as though it were a heart. Its purple light shone feebly for a moment before bathing him and the commander in a bright aura.

"By all the gods!" cried Toth in amazement, blinking and shielding his eyes.

"Looks like we won't be needing torches after all." Everus smiled coldly and stepped into the dripping, ominous drain mouth.

† † †

Things other than flesh crawled down here. Things that dripped and slithered. Things that lacked name or identification. Things that no scholar, no matter how desperate for fame, would care to study...at least not too closely.

For the main, these horrors shied away from the light, their splashing and plopping heard as opposed to seen, their very invisibility enough to make the men nervous – the fear of the unknown ten times worse than that of the known. A sort of group vulnerability seemed to come over them now that the entrance was far behind them; a demoralising, fear-induced sickness brought about by the dreadful environment. It was as though they were no longer well-trained fighting men wading through a defunct sewer, but little boys lost in the dark woods. Fear gripped the hearts of all but Everus, making each step leaden, the shin-deep effluent assuming the viscosity of a mason's glue.

Toth called a halt. "Let's take a breather."

"I'm tryin' not to breath...this place stinks," voiced one of the soldiers.

"Have you any idea how much further?" Toth asked Everus, who was visibly displeased at having to stop.

"I think we must be half-way by now."

"Only half-way! You gotta be pissed!?" said the man with his arm in a sling. "I'm knackered...I don't think I could go another step."

"Fine, we'll leave you here," snarled Everus. From the look in his eyes it was clear that he would feel no remorse in doing just that.

"Come on lad!" said Slagg, wading through the liquid waste, which was up to his chest, and extending a helping hand. "Just do what I do when I cannae go on. Grip yersel' b'the bollocks an' pull."

That won a few tired chuckles from the surrounding men.

"We keep going." Everus turned his back on them and kept going, certain that, despite their complaints and their weariness, the others would follow. Yet, although they had shown great courage in venturing so far, how would they react when they emerged into the city? And, for that matter, how would he? Now that the hand's influence had waned somewhat, he felt his old persona reassert itself. Like a familiar scent, his own thoughts and opinions drifted into his mind, temporarily washing away the stain of the demonologist's infection. *Why am I doing this?* he wondered. In all likelihood he was doomed to be overrun by the hand's persistent evil, left to be nothing more than a shell into which Cyrvilus would be born anew. For the latter part of his thirty-three years of life, he had been a fighter, a killer, trained to slay and to do so well – so why was he not trying to combat it, to find some way to extricate himself from this hideous symbiosis? If Creeps was alive he could have tried to implore The High Three for help – they could surely not want Cyrvilus to walk the mortal world once more, could they? But Creeps was most definitely dead, and he suspected that the thief had willingly embraced death in an act he had thought would result in a triumph over chaos – whatever that meant. A deluded hero, he thought wryly. There was the possibility that, if he were to take his own life – if indeed that remained a viable option – or be killed by Xethorn, perhaps the cursed hand would die with him. And as for the damage and destruction his actions had wrought – well, perhaps, such things, like him, would be best buried and forgotten...and best buried deep, away from the inquiring eyes of those who delved with mischief in mind. To the last of his strength, he would resist Cyrvilus and if, at the last, there appeared no other option, no way in which the process could be reversed, he *would* try and take his own life, undoubtedly damning himself for all time, yet spitting his defiance into the demonologist's eye. After all, there was nothing left to tie him to this existence. He had lost everything he had ever loved or valued and many of the memories that had gone with them. As he thought of his parents, Katryna and his old life, and how they had been taken from him, he grew colder still, the pain he had endured and carried with him for so many years, a tangible knot in his chest. The ice of his doubts melted away as he let himself bathe in the unrelenting bitter anger he still felt to all who had hurt him. He would *never* forget. He would *never* forgive. Revenge against Xethorn – and Uhu'giaggoth – and everyone else was all that remained, all that motivated him, and, right now, as the corrupted stink of humanity wafted out from the sewer before him, it was all that he needed. *Slay them all!* came an echo from the past.

How long they had been going, none could guess. In this stinking, sunless world of dank stone and ooze it was all too easy for the imagination to run wild, each new shadow or darkened opening a nightmare in waiting. However, by the guiding glow from the Daemondamned gem, they finally reached the sewer exit, and now the terrible tunnels seemed almost pleasant as they contemplated what might await them in the dead city of Wyrm's Port.

† † †

A dirty grey smog hung over everything.

Even had he emerged from the sewers in total darkness, Everus would have instantly known that they were close to the sea, for a nauseous, fishy smell pervaded the air, catching at the back of his throat and stinging his eyes. He looked about, relieved to note that at least they were not shrouded in complete darkness, as he had at first thought they would be. Before him, he could see the spires of several old and now undoubtedly defunct and desecrated temples. All lay in states of advanced decrepitude, with slates missing from the steeples and gaping holes showing in their brickwork exteriors. Huge warehouses stood along the waterfront, which lay a little to his right, their contents lying rotten, ransacked and abandoned. Looking left, beyond a collapsed bridge, he could just make out a row of tall, dark, shadowy buildings and from his reasonably good memory of the city's layout, he reckoned that one of them was the Northern Palace. Whether Xethorn would be there was another issue, but it would be there where he would commence his search.

"*Hey!* What's happened to your light?"

Everus spun round.

Gathered together, like sheep in a pen, commander Toth and his men stood at the sewer mouth, gaping out with wide eyes.

Everus looked for a moment at the purple gem, its internal light still burning. "What do you...? It's here."

"We can't see a thing. Where are you?" cried Toth.

Everus stepped back into the sewer pipe, the suddenness of his re-appearance drawing gasps of surprise from some of the soldiers as they themselves retreated.

"Where did you go?" asked Toth.

Everus cottoned on to their dilemma quickly. Outside, it *was* pitch dark, a land of continuous midnight, a dark, that, at least for the soldiers' sake, the gem could not illuminate. "Well...this is going to be a problem. Outside this opening is the city, or what remains of it. But it would appear that you can't see through the darkness."

"What do you mean?" asked Toth, a spark of hope leaping to the forefront of his mind. If this was as far as they could go then all the better. "Are you saying that we should head back...abort the mission?"

"We cannae turn back now. We're practic'lly there, b'gods," argued Slagg. "We'd be cowards."

"Yes, but...if..." began Toth, trying to think along two tracks at once. On the one hand, he wanted nothing more than to call it a day and head back to Ghavin's Keep – after all there was no dishonour in retreating from a battle that could not be fought. And on the other hand, he was silently cursing his now dead field captain for having assigned the two grubbas to his command. Mad bastards.

"Maybe it'd be for the best if I go on alone." Everus surveyed the grime-covered, weary faces before him. Proud and valiant men, there was no doubt about that – men that were similar to and yet so unlike the undisciplined troopers that had followed the deserter, Kooper. But now they had reached the end of the tunnel. To go on with them in tow through the shattered city would do nothing but compound an already terrible situation a hundredfold.

For a time no one said a word, each lost in their own thoughts.

It was Toth who broke the silence. "So I take it you can see out there?"

"Yes."

"And...what is there? Is the city...occupied?"

"Looks deserted. Empty. From a brief glance, most of it's in ruins. There's no-one around." Everus' mind temporarily drifted back to the time when he, Creeps and countless thousands had been forced to flee the city. The streets had become clogged with screaming citizens, each rushing to escape the fires and the bloodthirsty behemoths. It had been chaos on a scale that he had never witnessed before in the waking world, and yet, from some dark corner of his mind – a shadowy alcove in which many of his darker memories were locked – a sudden flash of insight informed him that he *had* seen this before. The first ward – the magical device which had been one of three used to imprison Xethorn. The one he had retrieved from Vorga'la Thrangu's tomb. It had given him a glimpse of the future. It had shown him what his actions would do. "The wards...?" he mumbled to himself.

"Eh?" queried Toth, catching Everus' hushed words.

"Is it all predestined then?" Everus spoke to himself, looking out at the ravaged cityscape.

"What are you talking about?" Toth was now unsettled, a dark possibility creeping into his mind. "What do you think we should do now?"

Coming to his senses, Everus turned to face Toth and his men. If he went on and abandoned the men before him, he would, in all likelihood, be consigning them to their deaths, for without a light source they would never find their way back through the sewers. Yet, as the grubba had said, to turn back now could be construed as cowardly. If he were to let them follow him, their fate could be far worse. With a final salute to Toth, he stepped through the dark shimmering barrier, plunging the soldiers once more into darkness.

✝ ✝ ✝

In the half-light that now shrouded Wyrm's Port, Everus made his way through the dead streets, the magic gem held before him. His progress was slow, for many of the buildings had been partially or totally destroyed and rubble was everywhere. Among the fallen bricks and timbers were occasional reminders of the city's once vibrant and eclectic population; a well sculpted statuette, leaning at a drunken angle in the wreckage here, or a foreign water jug, somehow unbroken, there. Many of the buildings had lost their front walls and the once private rooms now lay exposed to scrutiny, although no-one had been left alive to see in. These houses reminded Everus of fatally wounded men, their organs exposed for the first and last time. In the absence of bodies, the despoiled homes seemed to stand for the savagery that the abandoned citizens of this urban wasteland had suffered. Xethorn must have let His minions run wild, killing and burning as they liked, before He drained them for His sacrifice. To a great extent, the Lord of Murder had forsaken His own tenets in the depraved attempt to summon forth Uhu'giaggoth for one last, glorious battle.

Deeper into the necropolis he went, the hand at his side becoming more active with each step taken. It was driving him on, propelling him forward, despite the cries of his common sense to escape this place. Death and decay hung in the very air, the stench of carrion and rotted bone enough to turn a vulture's stomach. The mass killings had obviously been neither merciful nor quick.

Even though Xethorn's undead armies had gathered up the countless corpses to squeeze like oranges for their blood, enough dead had lain in the streets to stain the cobbles with their fluids and the air with their fumes.

Continuing his slow journey through the city he had lived in for over thirty years, Everus made his way to the steps of the old monument to General Adakaar, one of the city's early heroes. The monolithic granite statue had been badly worn when he was last here and it did not look much different now. Too heavy to topple and too unimportant to bother with, the general had survived one more conflict. Hauling himself up the steps and onto the plinth, Everus looked out over the city.

The skyline was dreadfully altered; the temple of The High Three over in the north was still partially standing, but its gold and platinum dome had caved in like a broken eggshell; The Wizard School to the south had been blasted in the first offensive and nothing remained of its elegant, twisted spires and aerial walkways. Looking west, towards the area he had grown up in, he could see none of the familiar landmarks of home. Nothing but a pall of thick, black smoke hung there now.

Sickened, Everus let himself drop to the ground. He could now feel Cyrvilus gnawing at him like a parasite in his brain; could feel the demonologist's delight in the aftermath of so much death and destruction. It was almost as if he had a wizened, deformed child inside him, one that was eager to get out and devour its parent. The revulsion that came to him was sudden and crippling, his body trying to reject the interloper, but the strength of Cyrvilus' grip on him grew ever more constricting, picking him up and working his legs. Everus cursed and wrestled back control over his limbs, determined to defeat Xethorn himself. If it took everything he had, he would be the one to deliver the death blow – even if Xethorn's dying screams were the last thing he ever heard.

Stumbling and staggering, the two conjoined souls painfully made their way towards a ruined bridge; the thin span of stone jutting out from the bank all that now remained of one of Wyrm's Port's finest landmarks. Passing by a smashed window, Everus caught sight of his own reflection, his pain-wracked features overshadowed by an old, evil face, one which would soon replace his own. *"Damn you! Not yet!"* he cursed through gritted teeth, the madness that burned within him threatening to rend him asunder. *"No!"* he cried. This was not how it would end.

With a scream that smashed the treacherous, jagged, mirrored surface, Everus tore some control away from Cyrvilus; a small victory in a doomed struggle. Panting, he turned his attention to the broken bridge. It had always been notable for its twin statues, one at either bank. As he looked at the far figure, it seemed almost to mock him. He walked out to the edge, peering across to the other side, wondering how to get there. Wearily, he decided that the only way was to walk along the rubble-strewn embankment to see if any of the smaller bridges had survived. He turned and began to walk away.

Cyrvilus had other ideas.

Everus yelped in pain as he was forcefully spun around to face the far bank once more. He was then propelled forwards at full sprint along the bridge. When he reached the edge, he found himself leaping into the air, the awful hand stretching out, pulling him onwards across the water beneath him, impossibly covering the distance. His breath caught and his eyes wept and he was sure that his arm would be wrenched out of its socket at any moment. For the briefest of time, his legs pumped thin air, then gravity took hold and he fell. Arms outstretched, he tumbled forwards; somersaulting. He landed, clumsily, lost his footing, and tripped, falling forwards. His momentum propelled him further and, with a cry, he rolled. Feet striking a raised ledge, he cartwheeled head over heels over yet another drop. He got a brief glimpse of a bulbous, grey-white form, festooned in dark slime, rising up from below, arms outstretched as though to catch him.

A moment later, he crashed painfully off the statue.

Almost as though he had tackled it from on high, both he and it went down. The statue shattered, weird, web-bedecked limbs flying in different directions. Still spinning, he tumbled down a set of cracked steps, chunks of broken statuary cascading with him. Into a darkened, tunnel-like opening he went, his movements only coming to a sudden stop when he collided with a rusty, grill-covered archway. Growling his displeasure, he shook himself down and got to his feet. Things hurt, there was no denying it.

Battered and bruised, Everus limped back up the steps. The scenes of devastation on this bank were even worse. What little remained of the once fine houses, guild halls and imperial buildings were stained with a dark red soot that, from first appraisal, covered a vast area. Where it met the river, the tainted water looked like blood. He took a few moments to regain some semblance of composure, aided by the waning hold of Cyrvilus. For, although the demonologist had a firm hold of him, it appeared that any direct commandeering of his body diminished it for a time. Scanning his eyes over the area, he almost did not recognise the Northern Palace, of which Emperor J'hann had been so proud, for now the once grandiose outer columns had been replaced with massive metal pipes which twisted up, down and through the core of the palace. Protruding from the roof were many crude and lopsided chimneys, the red soot staining their rims an indicator of the barbarities that had transpired here. For the palace had been transformed into a factory – a processing plant, a butcher's paradise, a temple dedicated to the art of excarnation.

Living flesh, be it from the behemoths, humans, grubbas or any other unfortunate creatures, had been the raw material that had passed through its doors, and, like coal shovelled into a furnace, its sole purpose had been to provide fuel for Xethorn's abominable schemes.

Xethorn was inside, of that Everus now had no doubt. Even as he paced towards the great iron gates, their railings topped with misshapen skulls, he could detect the aura of the debased demigod. A cold rage flooded him, the twin vendettas nursed by himself and Cyrvilus focused on a single point.

The gates squealed on their hinges as they parted before his raised left hand.

✝ ✝ ✝

It was strangely still inside the former palace. The endless reception rooms and offices had once been busy with courtiers, servants and useless sycophants, but now the rooms were either stripped bare or filled with bones. Along the walls, where escutcheons of the previous emperors of Wyrm's Port used to take pride of place, there now hung shields and banners, foul trophies and grim totemic displays – heraldic and emblematic devices dedicated to Xethorn. Monstrous black dogs, sinuous octopi and great, red-eyed ravens were just some of the designs that Everus recognised.

Soot-encrusted vents and corroded gratings lay everywhere, and throughout all, twisting and turning like nasty, burrowing, rusty maggots, were the pipes, which squealed and rattled to themselves as they ferried their liquid and solid waste.

Walking through the perverted palace, sword drawn, he could feel the eagerness of Cyrvilus to overtake his body and soul and confront Xethorn once again, the presence behind his eyes almost gleeful.

Half-dragged by the demonologist's will, Everus stumbled the length of a dark corridor, a huge set of gold and ebony inlaid doors at its far end. He felt dizzy. With each step forward it seemed as though the distance between himself and the doors increased. An illusion. It had to be an illusion. Trying to fight off the debilitating fugue, he summoned his dwindling resolve and ploughed on, a rivulet of dark sweat leaking from his brow. Raising his normal hand, he wiped it away and was shocked to see the ink-like fluid on his palm. The secretions of Cyrvilus. Blurred images swam before his eyes, the corridor seeming to extend before him as though reflected in a carnival mirror.

And then...his outstretched palm, the cursed hand, hit wood. He had reached the doors. They swung open before his touch and, with a pained groan, he stumbled over the threshold, his legs giving way. His sword clattered off the tiled, marble floor.

Without warning, a darting shadow fell around him.

A powerful kick to his ribs lifted him into the air and sent him hurtling across the room. With a howl of agony, Everus smashed against a column. A sea of pain washed over him as pounding waves of agony battered inside his head. A scathing voice drifted to him out of the semi-darkness and he was vaguely aware of something else – a darker force trying to pull him to his feet. Feebly, he managed to force himself upright, the pain in his side crippling.

Then, with a metallic flash, a blade scythed out of the red fog that blurred his vision. A shower of burning sparks flew as it bounced off an invisible barrier before him. The force of the swing was still strong enough to send him careering, his right shoulder cracking off a wall. With barely a moment to register what was happening, he turned in time to dodge away from another vicious attack.

Before him, encased in a night-black suit of intricately carved and embossed, spiked plate mail, stood Xethorn. From under a great helm fashioned from steel and tusk shone a pair of luminous red eyes. Wisps of smoke curled about Him.

"My beloved disciple?" sneered Xethorn. "I see your allegiance has changed once more. Nevertheless, my faith in you is rewarded. I see you've brought me the hand." With a harsh laugh, the Lord of Murder leapt forward, His huge two-handed sword a flash of lightning in His hands.

This time the mighty blade cleaved through the magical barrier, the sound of its breaching like the caterwauling of a thousand tortured cats. It smote Everus at chest height, the ensorcelled chain mail armour he wore taking the brunt of the damage.

A neon green flash lit the throne room as the blade shattered.

"You...you've broken my sword." Xethorn stared for a moment in utter disbelief at what remained of His weapon, before throwing it aside.

Everus got to his feet, the deep gash in his armour the only sign of the damage inflicted. Suddenly a gauntleted hand lashed at his face. Acting more by instinct than anything else, he sidestepped and turned his head swiftly to one side so that the blow narrowly missed. He retreated further, for the moment self-preservation overruling both the will of Cyrvilus and his own desire for revenge. Getting himself killed here would fulfil the desires of neither.

Now, having lost both His sword and the element of surprise, Xethorn too pulled back, those twin crimson points of light dulling for a moment.

For an unsettling moment, both surveyed and weighed up the other.

Everus was battered and bleeding, his armour sliced and ragged. He ached visibly, his body driven to levels of endurance and pain no mere mortal could tolerate.

The hatred that existed between the two was a tangible presence. To Everus, Xethorn was the false hope, the god in whom he had once entrusted his very soul, only for everything to then turn against him. Betrayed and left for dead, his god had cast him aside, treated him as no more than a tool to bring about His own resurrection. Whilst to Xethorn, Everus was now the embodiment of the greatest mortal enemy He had ever known; His old nemesis – the vile, demonic agent, Cyrvilus.

It was Everus who broke the silence. "So tell me. Do you want me to kill you now or would you rather I let you beg for a moment?"

The fire returned to Xethorn's eyes. "Don't make me laugh, little one. I could kill you a hundred times over."

"I'd be impressed if you can manage it once," Everus replied dryly. He could feel power beginning to surge into him from the hand, bolstering his physical and mental strength. "Kick me on the floor, would you? Coward! Think that's the only way you'll beat me, eh?" He was deliberately taunting Xethorn, hoping to instil a rage into Him which could well make Him less cautious and thus easier to defeat.

"I wanted to make this clean. I wanted to kill you without recourse to sorcery. To make the sacrifice pure. I thought I owed my disciple that much. Call it a pang of conscience, if you like." The demigod's voice was as cold as a snowfang's breath.

"What sacrifice?"

"Why yours of course! And the entity you bear within. I think between the two of you there should be more than enough energy to breach the planar boundary. My previous offerings, my blood-gifts, have weakened it sufficiently. Uhu'giaggoth stirs as we speak. I can sense it, Everus. Can't you? When you're gone, know that it will be *I* who slays The Daemon God once and for all. *I'll* be the saviour this world has cried out for. A messiah of a new age. *I'll* be the one that The High Three honour. No longer will I be confined to the shadows."

"You stupid bastard!" Everus exclaimed. "You've no idea, have you? *You* can't kill Uhu'giaggoth. You couldn't even..."

"*I can do anything!*" Xethorn thundered. "I've slain thousands. The Daemon God will be but one more."

Suddenly Everus felt as though he had self combusted. The agony of being burnt alive made him scream as the dark force he had borne for the past few days now started to take full control, the intelligence it possessed deciding now was the time to act. He watched as the chain links covering his left arm ran and dripped free like melting butter. The tunic underneath disintegrated. His exposed flesh began to pop and blister as a network of black veins crawled to the surface.

A huge blade of dark fire materialised in Xethorn's hands – a sword forged from the darkest sorcery. Long, flickering tongues of red-edged flame licked and hissed along its razor-sharp edge.

"What's up...hands not good enough?" Everus spat, painfully, the scorn evident despite his agony.

"More than enough." Xethorn's sword vanished. "As you'll find out as I tear you apart with them." With a deafening roar which caused the walls to tremble, He sprang forward.

Everus stepped inside the wildly flailing arms, delivering two sharp, jolting punches to the demigod's face with the empowered hand. The blows were short but they carried authority. The fire dimmed once more from Xethorn's eyes as His helmet cracked down one side. He stumbled back, more surprised than hurt. Then, like a poorly designed mask, the visored helmet fell, in several pieces, from His face. The angular features behind it, marked by the scars of countless battles, knew all there was to know about combat. There was a savage, dangerous look now on His shockingly mortal face, a murderous hate in the sunken eyes that stared venomously at His adversary.

The anger at His unmasking propelled Xethorn's next attack. With a snarl, He rushed forward, hands held high, hoping to force Everus to the floor, where He could then use every dirty trick ever dreamt of in addition to some of His own making.

Another swift blow hammered Xethorn's now unprotected head, snapping it back on His shoulders, but it did not make Him lower his guard, and before Everus could strike again, a fist of studded metal caught him on the side of the head. Had he not been protected by Cyrvilus, the blow would have shattered his skull like a dropped crystal bowl. Shaking his head in an effort to clear it, he moved back in an attempt to avoid a follow-up swing. He was not quick enough and Xethorn, grabbing him fiercely by the right arm, swung him savagely off balance, hurling him towards a stone upright. His collision with it sent him crashing down and he hit the floor with the small of his back, the dual impacts squeezing much of what life he still had from him. Fear and the Cyrvilian power banished the ache from his limbs. There was the salty taste of blood in his mouth and, as he spat it out, another tide of anger seared through him, providing him with the strength to lift one knee as Xethorn went to kick him in the guts. The pointed iron boot stabbed into the side of his shin, causing him to cry out in pain. He was only vaguely aware of the imposing figure standing over him, readying to kick again when, suddenly, he found himself somersaulting backwards in a move that was physically impossible, the throne room and all within it transforming momentarily into an upside-down blur. Unsteadily, he landed on his feet.

Unfazed by Everus' acrobatics, Xethorn let out a bellow and charged forward.

This time it was Everus who grasped at an outstretched arm, pulled sharply and twisted.

Xethorn howled as the wrench on His captured arm tightened. He reared up awkwardly, His wicked face a seething cauldron of rage – each scar burning with the hatred which consumed Him.

Mustering the unholy strength that now flowed through him, Everus gave a cry and spun his foe towards a wall. With a deafening crash of stonework, the dark demigod smashed through it.

Shaking aside His hurt, Xethorn pushed His way back into the wrecked throne room. "You cannot kill me." Arms wide, He circled in, His gaze never once leaving Everus' eyes. He lunged forward, feinting with His right hand before bringing His left sweeping round for Everus' head. Everus ducked, barely managing to twist aside as a spiked knee-guard scraped along his thigh. Then Xethorn was on him once more, immensely powerful arms grasping at his throat. Taloned, iron hands crushed like a vice. Everus felt his senses begin to swim – knew that he would perish if he could not break the strangle hold.

Grinning fiercely, Xethorn continued to squeeze, pushing His enemy down, forcing him to his knees.

Reaching up, his face reddening, Everus managed to get the heel of Cyrvilus' hand under Xethorn's jaw, thrusting His head back. He felt the slackening of the gauntleted-grip at his neck as he pushed. As the pressure eased, he pushed himself back to his feet before bringing his right knee up sharply into an armour-plated groin. It was a nasty attack, but right now he did not care. This was never destined to be a storybook encounter in which the two arch rivals battled it out with flair and finesse – swinging from chandeliers and romantically slashing and dashing their way across a moonlit battlement.

Grunting, Xethorn released His hold and stumbled back a few steps, His body bent forward as He strove to ease the hurt in His mid-section. Even demigods had bollocks and getting kneed there was painful. He was on the point of forcing Himself to straighten up when the bunched Cyrvilian fist struck solidly against His exposed jaw. For a moment, He remained upright, swaying unsteadily, eyes glassy, a red-black ichor trailing from His split bottom lip. Then His legs buckled under Him and, with a crash, He tumbled. A miniature storm of electric-blue fire crackled down His head, sparks dancing off His breastplate.

In a flash, Everus summoned his sword to his hand and set the point against Xethorn's vulnerable throat. Both he and the demonic agent within exulted in this moment of perceived victory, the dark joy bubbling up at the sight of their enemy ripe for destruction. A sadistic smile curled his lips. "Now to finish..."

Xethorn just laughed and Everus' sword, the magical blade of the Black Ravers, turned to dust. With the agility of a panther, He sprang to His feet. "As I said. *You* cannot kill me. But I can kill you...and if by magic, then so be it!" Twin fiery scimitars appeared in each hand. With a crossing of the blades, a pillar of fire roared down from the ceiling and engulfed Everus where he stood.

Immediately, Cyrvilus surged to the forefront of Everus' being, countering this new threat, magically extinguishing the flames before they could inflict any damage to the physical shell. He began to speak rapidly, the demonologist's tongue sibilant and alien. In that next moment Xethorn was pitched upside-down, dropping His weapons in surprise. He countered with a spell of His own, righting Himself in a flash of sorcery.

Everus had become nothing more than a puppet. Within him, Cyrvilus spun and whirled, tracing an elaborate symbol that hung in the air in green, writhing lines. A dark, rolling stream of matter flowed from the sigil, twisting and expanding as it reached out to grasp Xethorn, entangling Him in a poisonous web. Instantly, the fallen scimitars leapt into air and began to slash at the strands and, as each one was severed, it let out a puff of noxious smoke.

"Your victory at our last meeting was solely due to the intervention of your gods. Do you not remember, or have the millennia robbed you of your memory as well as your sanity?" Cyrvilus taunted, his own long-unspoken accent overlaid on Everus' voice. "Even then, you couldn't complete my destruction, and now

I've returned. Let's see if you can survive me on your own." The dread hand tightened and a dark, billowing cloud formed between the two.

Xethorn took a few steps back, visibly unnerved at the flashes of crimson coming from within the swirling void. He knew this was true demoncraft – a magic born of Uhu'giaggoth. From out of the chaotic maelstrom there flew a ghastly mouth filled with row upon row of gnashing, shark-like teeth. Two, then three, then half a dozen of the hideous, snapping, disembodied jaws emerged before Him. He slashed out at them as they circled and harried like hyenas around a dying prey, forcing Him back. Three of them lunged in, biting deep, tearing into His armoured bulk and making Him scream with pain. Like a criminal being stoned, He tried feebly to ward off the attacks. He stumbled over a pile of bones, the ravenous demons now tearing lumps from Him. Strands of bloody iron and semi-divine flesh stretched like rubber. Somehow, He heaved off the entities, His frame now torn and ragged, unsightly slabs of flesh hanging in teeth-marked loops like stretched crimson putty. With a howl, He bolted for the archway at the rear of the chamber, the slavering, demonic conjurations weaving through the air in pursuit.

✝ ✝ ✝

Eyes searching, Everus stalked through the labyrinth that was the Northern Palace. Shadows seemed to rove and shift, the light cast by the unholy gem he held stirring them into lives of their own. When Xethorn had fled, so too, to a lesser extent, had Cyrvilus' hold, so that now, as he went in search of his quarry, it was his own desire for vengeance that drove him. His footsteps echoed down the hallway, as a dull sense of pride swelled within him, his embattled soul lifting at the defeat, albeit temporary, of the Lord of Murder.

Everus turned a corner. Before him, the doors flung wide, he saw a side exit from the palace. Intuition told him that Xethorn had fled in this direction and that the next phase of their ongoing conflict would take place outside. A soul-weary uneasiness prickled down his spine and ruffled the hairs on the back of his neck. He tensed, then forced himself to relax as the unwelcome shiver subsided. Like a shadow himself, he moved towards the outer door. Beyond, he could see a large courtyard, its far side delineated by a high raised wall of cyclopean stonework, spiked with cruel railings.

Standing, nonchalantly, as though in wait, was Xethorn.

Swordless, Everus drew the dagger from his boot. He stepped out of the palace and casually made his way down the short flight of steps to the courtyard. From somewhere, an icy wind picked up, sweeping up a cloud of the dead's dust which covered the ground. It blew towards him, stinging his eyes and filling his nostrils with a bitter stench. Rubbing away the foul grit, he was relieved to notice that his foe had not taken advantage of his temporary blindness. Holding the Daemondamned gem before him, he strode purposefully forward.

Xethorn had clearly managed to rid Himself of the teeth-demons but He had taken considerable damage in doing so. He was watching Everus warily, as though trying to gauge whether or not Cyrvilus was still in control.

"It's me this time. Just me, your last disciple," said Everus. "The only one of your old followers still alive, thanks to your unique way of repaying devotion. First you killed them and drained their blood. Then you let them loose as a skeletal army." He looked around at the deserted courtyard, taking in what he could see of the silent, obliterated cityscape beyond its perimeter. "What have you done with them now, all your mindless skeletons...ground them to dust? No wonder you're weakened, you've no living worshippers left. Why, even your mindless bones have deserted you."

"You think so?" Xethorn replied, the controlled expression on His face giving way to a look of evil satisfaction.

The courtyard darkened as though a thunderhead had drifted over it. Everus looked up to see a nightmare towering *over* the palace. At first, he thought it was the dragon, Magmabreath, made larger by some trick of perspective, then he saw that the apparition far surpassed the dragon in height and breadth. Eyes widening, he saw the reptilian skull and long neck bones of Magmabreath, but they were only part of the gargantuan golem. All kinds of creatures had been stripped of their flesh to construct this fused, mismatched horror. The massive bones of Øggarbakken behemoths intertwined with those of horses, elephants, humans and much smaller creatures. A set of knuckles formed from a ridge of human skulls here; a ribcage like the hull of a warship there. Tusks and spines jutted out everywhere, the identifiable bones indicating that this was the perverted culmination of Xethorn's exploitation of all the doomed creatures that had been left in Wyrm's Port when the darkness had descended.

Awestruck, Everus fell back as a gnarled claw reached over the exterior walls and into the open area, dislodging roof tiles, each talon twice his size. He retreated back up the steps, hoping to get inside but the bonework monstrosity tore through the roof of the palace as though it were made of straw. With a crash, roofing slabs and bone fragments collapsed around him. Staggering from a blow to the head, he fell to one knee, the grinding and the creaking from the skeletal construct painful to the ears.

Cyrvilus had been depleted in the recent magical attacks and was unable to assist and Everus knew there was no way he could fight it. It would take all of his skill and whatever luck he still had to simply dodge its massive claws and jaws and beaks. The only option left to him was to go for a direct attack against Xethorn in the hope that it would cause Him to call off the bone-fused creation.

Dodging falling masonry and grasping claws, he dashed across the exposed courtyard, hoping to reach the weakened demigod before the animated bone tower reached him. Leaping over fallen blocks of stone, he was but half-way there when an ossified avalanche crashed down upon him. Mindless, but directed by Xethorn, the skeletal entity had dashed its entire, impossible mass at him, destroying itself in the process but trapping him beneath a ragged ruin of interlocked bone and horn. Painfully smashed to the hard ground, he ached from a hundred places. Several large, needle-like slivers had pierced his legs and his good hand was horribly twisted, broken at the wrist. Blood, red and inky, streamed from his gashed left shoulder, leaking out from under his armour.

"What? No sorcerer left to help you? No irritating flunkey to save your pitiful life?" Xethorn laughed.

Everus was pinned, trapped under the cage of skulls, vertebrae and a mountain of other skeletal remains that Xethorn had harvested from the dead. Some bones were mouldy and yellow with age, while others gleamed white and raw. They all reeked and they all made it impossible for Everus to escape. Feebly, he tried to push himself free.

"Time to fulfil your destiny, Everus." Xethorn raised His hand and a swirling ball of red energy appeared in it. It hovered there for a moment before He flung it forward.

† † †

Groggily, Everus opened his eyes, trying to ignore the nausea and pain which threatened to overwhelm him. His sight was blurred, yet, with horror, he realised that he had been stripped naked, his limbs outstretched in an upright racking position, pulled taut by thick linked chains attached between two rune-covered stone and metal posts. He was bleeding profusely from countless small shallow wounds – nicks and slices which had been performed with almost surgical precision. The mingled blood – his and Cyrvilus' – dribbled from him, collecting and steaming in a ghastly, demon-mouthed, pipe-connected receptacle below him.

Xethorn was standing a little way off, next to a strange church organ-like contraption which consisted of numerous tubes and levers, pipes, metal funnels and siphons. Gases belched and hissed from it as He frantically pushed levers and turned flywheels.

As his sight sharpened, Everus could vaguely make out several other figures gathered around, all blurred and hazy, as though wreathed in smoke. They seemed to be conversing, pleading with Xethorn, and, as his senses grew, he began to hear more of what they were saying.

"Xethorn. You must stop. You'll obliterate this world if you do this!" spoke one voice in a manner unlike anything he had ever heard before.

"If you allow Uhu'giaggoth to breach the planar barrier and enter our world we'll all perish, demigods and mortals alike. You too will die," claimed another.

Xethorn turned from his diabolical machine. "You're all fools! Cowards! Have not your godhoods given you the ability to understand and grasp your own potential, your own strength? When The Daemon God arrives I will slay it! Such is the strength granted to me."

"We implore you," pleaded a female-sounding voice. "For the sake of us all, don't do this."

"We'll fight ye, if need be," threatened a croaky, grubban-like voice.

For a time there was an uncomfortable silence, as though the unimaginable, the unthinkable and the unmentionable had just been declared. It permitted Everus time for his sight to clear, and he was astonished to see that the figures Xethorn was arguing with were none other than the twelve soldiers he had left to die in the sewers. Some of the men looked to have been severely clawed and wounded. One of the grubbas, possibly Slagg, was missing an arm. Even Toth looked battered and bloody. And yet, an intensity illuminated each of their faces, as though a halo of bright light shone from within.

"*Fight me?*" Xethorn's chill voice cut through the silence like an executioner's blade. "You seem to have forgotten, that's against the rules. Luckily for you, we cannot fight one another. *They* will not allow it. Only through the actions of mortals can we settle our differences." With a gauntleted hand, He reached for a huge flywheel that protruded from a large column.

"We beg you," cried out the voices.

"Look at you – standing like frightened children, afraid to face the new age that my actions will unleash. Like me, you are gods. If you cannot embrace that then you're not worthy of the position. You're pathetic! You dare not, or cannot, even manifest properly...instead you hide behind these carcasses from the battlefield. When the final rites are performed over the blood that I've gathered, then you will witness my true power. No longer will I be forced to..." Xethorn stopped mid-sentence as His audience slumped and fell to the floor – ten dead men and two dead grubbas once more, their ragged corpses stinking of the sewers. "Flee then and cower!" He spat.

Flee they did, but not far.

The essences of Krüshe, Qabaal, Oola-Sha'lligh, Mad o' Gadin, Shaab-Utu and seven of the other demigods of his world flowed into Everus, honing him to be their weapon. And, even as Xethorn stared in confusion, Everus' body glowed, the chains snapping and falling to the floor as energy coursed through his limbs. Still hovering in mid-air, the combined voices of the demigods cried out, summoning the Daemondamned gem Xethorn had stolen and hidden into the hands of their mortal vessel and conveying unto him the knowledge of its use – the final word of power needed to activate it.

The pain of this mass inhabitation was agonising, far worse than the torture he had just undergone or the infection of Cyrvilus, but he knew he could bear it if it meant he could finally kill Xethorn. Determined to endure the agony for as long as it took, he raised the gem, cried out his defiance and dashed it to the ground.

With a dull explosion, the gem shattered.

For a moment, nothing happened, prompting a derisory laugh from Xethorn.

Then, from out of a haze of purple mist, screamed the Daemondamned; a sentient, malign whirlwind of retribution. They sped towards Xethorn. Like iron filings drawn to a lodestone, they latched on to Him, obscuring Him in a vortex of doomed souls.

Xethorn screamed.

Wreathed in the chaotic column of tortured spirits, He tried to beat them away, but to no avail. The Daemondamned began to tear at Him, spinning His already wrecked and damaged body around like a child's top. Fragments of plate mail armour, then gobbets of flesh-like matter, flew out from the demonic cyclone. Still He struggled. Hoisted into the air, the golden essence that was His divinity, His endowment from The High Three, was torn from Him. Still screaming, still twirling, He collided with a wall, stone splintering in zigzagging cracks as what remained kicked and struggled like a fly in a spider's web.

With a final cry, He disintegrated.

The dying shriek from the Lord of Murder echoed around the chamber. Then all was silent, the Daemondamned vanishing in a dark purple flash.

Everus felt the divine ones inside him rush out, felt their mingled satisfaction and sense of genuine regret at having lost one of their number, but most of all he felt his own joy. At last he had destroyed all those he held accountable for the misery of his own life. The list had been long, but he had reached the end of it, and now he craved nothing more than to embrace the long denied release of death, no longer caring what became of his tarnished soul.

The vacuum inside him suddenly swelled as Cyrvilus took over the space the dozen deities had just vacated and, to Everus' consternation, he felt his numerous wounds begin to close and his life force build, as the demonologist set about repairing the body he was about to inhabit.

His mind darkened.

† † †

He hung before a blazing sun, the only star in the void. There was no sensation – just awareness. Then, from nowhere, yet everywhere, a question formed in his head.

"Will you, Everus Dragonbanner, assume the mantle of the one you deposed? Will you slay for us as He did, denying The Engulfer of Life?"

"I don't understand," his mind replied.

"Xethorn, alone of all the demigods of your world, had a unique

597

purpose – to kill for us. The souls of His victims became our fuel. All that perish without His intervention are absorbed by the entity you know as Uhu'giaggoth. Xethorn did not truly understand His role but you will. We are the embodiment of life and creation yet we derive our power from denying Uhu'giaggoth souls. On your world you are to reap a harvest for our consumption."

"Why me?"

"Because you have been prepared. Everywhere you go, death follows. Behold."

And in his mind, Everus saw. He saw how he had been controlled, and that everywhere he had been he had caused death – the desert city of Umm-Dabba now lay in ruins, overrun by the desert tribes he had provoked into war by stealing the land rights for Emir Ib-irem. He witnessed Dram, the demented, grubban takeaway owner, vent his cold, paranoiac rage against the population of Ullerby by 'intentionally' poisoning his snacks, believing that the attack on him had been planned all along. Many had died before discovering the identity of the poisoner. The grubba had been burned alive in his new caravan by an angry, vengeful mob. In his sleep, Everus had been instructed to burn down The Dragon and Anchor tavern in The City of the Glittering Spire – after the suspicious death of its newly-elected mayor, hundreds had died in the fire and the riots that followed. He saw himself, cloaked and hooded, hand the Bubbling Gob he had mysteriously found amongst his belongings to Garoth – all hands had been lost when the cursed sailors had scuttled their ship and the loss of the ship's cargo had prompted violent clashes in both the sailors' port town and in Trade Peak. His vision altered, and now he saw the mass executions carried out on the orders of the maddened, grief-stricken King Braith of Torl, in retribution for his son's murder in the Triton's Bounty. Further images assaulted his mind. Vicious weaponry falling into the wrong hands...then, a massive explosion, Stranglewood in flames, the bodies of the hunchbacked weaponsmith's cronies blown to pieces – along with countless others – as they had tried to smuggle barrels and crates filled with explosive powder stolen from their dead accomplice's secret arsenal. Two of The Ullerby Slappers would never 'slap' again.

And as for the citizens of Wyrm's Port, Ghavin's Keep and Wathang-Hu...

Throughout his crusade, he had been the instigator of death and destruction.

In this context, it seemed as though the quest for the cursed hand had been nothing more than a *means* for him to bring about such carnage; a subtle scheme, no doubt orchestrated by The High Three's own representative – Creeps, his disguise as Emir Ib-irem now revealed. All of this deceit had been ingeniously designed, premeditated and intended to promote him, to elevate him to the apogee, of demigod. The position of The Dark Slayer had always been granted to the biggest murdering bastard on the planet and Everus had more than fulfilled the criteria, whether knowingly or otherwise.

Everus was repulsed by the visions and the offer, by the prospect of being manipulated yet again and of there being no possibility of respite. "All I want is to be left alone, to be myself for once...or to be allowed to die. Find some other stooge to feed you!" In his mind, he shouted his defiance. And yet, deep down, a part of him yearned for the power.

"If you do not accept our gift, then you must accept that of the other. Cyrvilus *will* claim you. Shortly after you return to your world, your existence will end and yet you will continue to suffer. Your damnation will last for all eternity and nothing will save you. Through you, chaos will devour your world and Uhu'giaggoth will spread his spawn further across the multiverse."

So this was the freedom of choice he was given and, yet again, he had to think just how much had been contrived in order to bring him to this moment; this choice. He would rather die than be used once more, but death it seemed was not an option. He could either embrace his apotheosis and become Xethorn's replacement or he could permit himself to become swallowed by chaos, sinking into the morass that was the reviled persona of Cyrvilus – to be nothing more than a conduit for The Daemon God. Demigod or agent of chaos? At least one would enable him to retain something of his own identity.

"Make your choice."

"My choice is made." There was no point any more in him raving about the injustices done to him. He had defeated Xethorn, killed those who had wronged him and been offered an elevation to the godhead. Many would fight for such a prize. Some, like Xethorn, had leaped at the chance, for He had craved the power, the kudos that Lord of Murder entailed, but for Everus, it was merely another level of manipulation. As he reflected on it, the entity known as

Klattermorch came to mind – doomed if you do, damned if you don't. Then he thought of Creeps and how he said he had been given a choice, perhaps his had been similarly meaningless. "You know the answer, as you've always known."

"So be it."

EPILOGUE

The reek of dung, blood and sheer terror struck the noses of the miserable prisoners as they were led out of the city jail and herded through the vengeful crowds. Boil-ridden hags and bedraggled, hungry children jeered and spat, their ugly faces and obscene curses and gestures all part of a long-standing tradition. Over to one side of the gallows square, a gathering of merchants added their voices to the clamour, their usually more refined behaviour now reduced to that of the angry rabble.

Clouds darkened as a light rain began to fall, but for the masses of Wyrm's Port the weather was no deterrent. They had gathered in their hundreds, eager to witness the public executions. Such was their appetite for death, many had stayed overnight in the dirty square, pitching camp wherever they could. Those fortunate enough to have dwellings around the square had made quite a profit by renting out the many seedy rooms that overlooked it.

"Well, ma lad. This don't be lookin' too good," an aged prisoner at the end of the manacled line muttered to the one in front of him.

"Shut up at the back!" barked one of the two dozen or so spear-armed guards.

Still chained together, the prisoners were dragged onto the wooden platform where the gallows stood. Once there, they were spread out and allocated their own hanging post. A black-hooded hangman went to each, fastening a noose and testing its sturdiness, his heavy feet creaking on the timber trapdoor lids.

Nine criminals were now only a heartbeat from death.

With a raise of a hand, a crimson-robed officiator silenced the spectators. "Today, we bring judgement on those who have chosen not to adhere to the laws of our exalted emperor, Saraq."

"*Sar-aq! Sar-aq! Sar-aq!*" chanted the crowd, those at the front with their granny tokens chanting the loudest.

"Enough!" With a cutting wave of his hand, the robed official again brought silence. He beckoned to a guard, who handed him a rolled scroll, from which he began to read. "By the will of his most exalted, Saraq, and in the interests of the citizens of Wyrm's Port, I now proclaim a sentence of death by hanging, on..." The clouds darkened ominously, prompting the officiator to look nervously skywards for a moment. "George Daggs, Sammy Daggs, Pat Daggs, 'Choppa'..."

"I love ye 'Choppa'! I'll always love ye!" yelled a large-breasted woman from an open window.

At hearing his name called, the grubban thief looked up.

"...Geezer Sneer, Jon Numbfingers, Derek Bettis, Adolf Creeps and 'Old Man' Creeps."

Then, with a crash and a scream, nine trapdoors opened and nine bodies fell. And while death and darkness engulfed eight of those, their bodies twitching, their piss running down their legs, one of their number was chosen and taken. Rescued from the retribution of a mortal world, Adolf Creeps found himself in a truly frightening place.

With unbelieving eyes and a mind that could not comprehend what he was seeing, he stared as, all around, galaxies and star systems, planets and suns whirled and danced in the endless carousel of the cosmos. He was un-anchored, a floating, helpless, lonely speck in a nebulous gulf that seemed to have no end. Weightless, he moved and found himself spinning. Out of control, he spun to one side, but there was no floor, no ground or earth to stop him and so he just kept spinning.

Dizzier than he had ever been and feeling a hundred times drunker than a human could be, he tried to shout for help, but his voice was instantly hushed, as though his cry had been inhaled. So this was death...that cold, empty void which ushered and housed all the departed souls. With that thought, he tried to halt his uncontrollable reeling and see if any of his 'associates' were about.

There was no one.

He was alone.

Loneliness was the worst of it.

From an early age, he had been surrounded by others – from his fourteen siblings to those shadowy figures within his father's network. He had accompanied his father on many criminal forays, especially on his grave-robbing missions. Although never rich, his father's ghoulish profession had provided, to some extent, for his large, illegitimate family. As the eldest, Creeps had picked up much from his dad, including when to run and when not to. He had been introduced to the thieving trade at an early age and for a time they had become a scourge of the city's temple district – breaking into tombs, mugging clerics, forging prayer books and stealing from shrines. It was on one such 'job' that the 'Old Man' and his gang had not run fast enough.

Captured, they had all been interrogated and subjected to a sanctimonious lecturing from the high priest. As the leader of the group, Creeps' dad had joked and laughed along, attempting to play on the apparently senile old cleric's good nature to let them go with but a sermon addressing their irreverence. But the smiles and the joviality had died when the group were rounded up by the temple guards and prodded at spear point into the dungeons. They had been there just a day before being transferred to the city gaols.

There, along with the rats, they had waited to die.

How long Creeps had been alone in the void he could not tell – it was as though he were in a kind of stasis, his body frozen yet strangely aware. He seemed not to age. His hair did not grow and his nails remained as dirt-encrusted as ever. Bits of rotten vegetable mulch which had been thrown in the lead up to his 'execution' by the angry mob, still clung to his hair – not that he needed food, nor water. Air itself did not exist.

Alone with his memories, he began to wonder; could this indeed be death? Nothing – absolute and unequivocal?

And so it had gone on, for a time beyond measure, until, out of seemingly nothingness, there came light. And as the light shot through the oceans of emptiness, Creeps could feel the searing heat of its revelation. His soul ached in its desire to become one with the light, to embrace it and be destroyed in its rapture. His mind swam with dreams and desires, with creations and epiphanies, with events that he had witnessed and those he had yet to see.

And still the burning went on.

And for what seemed like an aeon that was how it had been.

Until, from beyond the light there came darkness. It was a dark so deep that nothing could escape its encroachment. It swelled and crept, blotting out the stars and throwing some of the divine fire into shadow, as with its grasping tentacles it seemed to parasitically flow and slither around one edge of the dazzling light. A moon-sized, red eye glared from within its chaotic, bubbling mass...

His vision and mind swam...

A brief flash of tenebrous unreality – something other than the void. He struggled to remember. Was he mortal once? Had something happened? Faces twisted before him – a man with dark hair, a book, a hand. Had he seen these? He remembered a light, a blaze like no other and a futile hope of eternal rest, then a silence broken by familiar presences.

Once more he found himself somewhere else.

The air in the sepulchre was cold on his skin, its touch welcome. A warm trickle down his chest caught his attention and he was startled to see a rivulet of blood leak from under his leather jacket. He grimaced as he touched where the dart had struck, silently cursing his own stupidity for having failed to notice the trap. Luckily, the dart had not been poisoned.

Stealthily, he made his way down the tunnel. Passing the skeleton-filled niches, he raised his guttering torch higher, its light playing over the rows of mouldering bones. The scurrying of a large rat made him jump, but he reassured himself there was nothing dangerous here. At least, nothing he could not handle. He had explored countless tombs, crypts, ruins and deserted palaces, anywhere there might be a convenient and suitable hiding place. Very few places had proved inaccessible in the course of his career, and here would be no different.

Coming to a junction, he ferreted in a pocket and brought out a dirty scrap of parchment. He traced a finger along the marked route. The tunnels down here could be confusing and he had to find a very specific tomb. As usual, he had been given this task, and a deadline, but had been left to sort out the details for himself. Ghavin's Keep had changed considerably since his last visit, but the damp and musty resting places of the dead had a certain familiarity, which he had always found reassuring. He hurried on, following the tunnel deeper into the darkness.

Turning a corner, the light from the torch reflected off a marble sarcophagus, the quality of its decoration far superior to the others he had passed. Grinning, he moved his torch closer and read the inscription. "Utterance XIII. This is it," he muttered to himself. Slinging his pack to the floor, he knelt down, opened it and drew out a roll of thick cloth, which he carefully unwrapped. He paused briefly in order to examine the three gold amulets within, feeling the power they contained, an energy that would repulse most people and probably all grave-robbers. Sure, they would be found one day, for not only was that inevitable, it was preordained. The coffin before him would provide as good a place as any for one of them until it was needed.

Standing up, he rested an amulet on the lid. He ran his hands down one side, searching for a secret catch left by its stonemason. Exerting pressure with his thumbs, he pushed and managed to shift the lid. With a heave, he slid it back further to reveal a splendidly interred corpse, a beaten gold face mask covering its skull. Picking up the amulet, he eased it over the head of the late high priest. The bones shifted dryly, in protest at this desecration, but the partially desiccated body remained intact and was gradually entombed once more as he pushed the lid back into place.

Two more amulets to hide and then *maybe*, just maybe, he would earn a reprieve. He had been so sure that he had managed it last time, relinquishing his body to the searing flames of a demonic attack. He had desperately hoped to be accepted into The High Three's welcoming, fiery oblivion, but once again the light had hauled him back from the brink and dispassionately informed him that he had not yet finished.

Trudging wearily back through the catacomb, he remembered something of the conversation.

"We have need of you."

"But I'm dead! I've been burnt to buggery!" he protested.

"No matter. You will return and continue your task. He grows restless, intractable and dangerous, as they always do. For just as His predecessor targeted His vengeance at The Devourer of Life, He has decided to target us. His bitterness is undying. In His eyes, all remain unforgiven. His worshippers are now assassinating the priests of all other religions and He Himself has managed to murder three of His fellow demigods. Such deicide cannot be allowed to continue. If He were to successfully transfer His seat of power to the mortal world as did His predecessor then He would accelerate His campaign to rid the world of all religions, even His own, such is His madness. The resulting chaos would only serve to attract The Daemon God's attention. We will bind Him and you must scatter the wards."

"So, another Lord o' Murder goes nuts. This is gettin' ridiculous."

"It is an unfortunate effect of the position."

"How long did Everus last then?"

"Long enough, but the time has come to set the transfer in motion. We will return your body and you will do our bidding."

"All right. I mean, it's no' like I've a choice, is it?"

"You chose long ago and you chose to obey."

"Yeh, yeh! Ye rob one bloody temple an' yer soul's doomed for all time," he muttered. "Ye realise that Everus is a fair bit more intelligent than Xethorn was. He's bound to see the pattern."

"That is our problem, not yours."

"It'll be ma bloody problem if He recognises me! What should I do, shave the 'tache off?"

"His memory has faded. Over nine hundred years have elapsed since the city known as Wyrm's Port fell. That world, unlike Him, has moved on."

Then the light had banished him and he had awoken in an unfamiliar room, the wards of binding by his side. He had left shortly after, sidling out onto the busy night streets, his moon-cast shadow unnaturally dark.